Units

Symbol	Name	Measure of	Conversion Factors
Å	Angstrom	Length	10^{-10} m, 0.1 nm
Bq	becquerel	Radioactivity	1 disintegration/sec, 60 dpm
°C	centigrade degree	Temperature	°K − 273
Ci	curie	Radioactivity	3.7 x 10^{10} Bq
cm	centimeter	Length	10^{-2} m, 10^{7} nm
cpm	counts/min	Radioactivity	dpm x counting efficiency[a]
d	dalton	Molecular Mass	1.66 x 10^{-24} g (1⁄12 mass of carbon atom)
dpm	disintegrations/min	Radioactivity	0.016 Bq, cpm/counting efficiency[a]
g	gram	Mass	6.0 x 10^{23} d
°K	Kelvin	Temperature	°C + 273
kb	kilobase	Nucleotides	1000 bases or base pairs
kcal	kilocalorie	Energy	4.18 kilojoules
kd	kilodalton	Molecular Mass	1000 d
l	liter	Volume	1000 ml
m	meter	Length	100 cm, 10^{9} nm
M	molar	Concentration	moles solute per liter of solution
μg	microgram	Mass	10^{-6} g
min	minute	Time	60 sec
ml	milliliter	Volume	1 cm^3
mole	mole	Number	6.0 x 10^{23} molecules
mV	millivolt	Electrical Potential	10^{-3} volts
nm	nanometer	Length	10^{-9} m, 10 Å
sec	second	Time	3600 sec/hour, 86,400 sec/day
V	volt	Electrical Potential	1000 mV

[a] See table of radioactive isotopes (inside back cover) for efficiency of counting of specific isotopes.

Cover Problem

The cover photograph shows the chromosomes from an infant with multiple congenital abnormalities. The chromosomes were treated with an anti-kinetochore antibody (yellow fluorescence) and a DNA stain (orange fluorescence). What is peculiar about this child's chromosomes, and how might it account for the birth defects of the child? (See inside back cover for Answer.)

MOLECULAR BIOLOGY OF

THE CELL

THE PROBLEMS BOOK

MOLECULAR BIOLOGY OF

THE CELL

THE PROBLEMS BOOK

John Wilson · Tim Hunt

Garland Publishing, Inc.
New York & London

We dedicate this book to our students, who taught us everything we know.

John Wilson received his Ph.D. from the California Institute of Technology (in 1971) and is currently a Professor of Biochemistry and Molecular Genetics at Baylor College of Medicine in Houston, Texas. He is a coauthor of *Biochemistry: A Problems Approach* and *Immunology*. His laboratory studies genetic recombination and genome rearrangements in mammalian cells.

Tim Hunt received his Ph.D. from the University of Cambridge (in 1968) and is currently a Lecturer in the Biochemistry Department at the University of Cambridge in Cambridge, U.K. His laboratory studies protein synthesis and the control of the cell cycle.

Published by Garland Publishing, Inc.
136 Madison Avenue, New York, NY 10016

Printed in the United States of America

15 14 13 12 11 10 9 8 7 6 5 4 3 2

Preface

The Problems Book is designed as a companion volume to the second edition of *Molecular Biology of the Cell* by Bruce Alberts, Dennis Bray, Julian Lewis, Martin Raff, Keith Roberts, and James Watson. The intent of the book is to engage the reader actively in exploring the principles of cell biology. We firmly believe that principles must be examined, questioned, and played with in order to be fully understood. We hope to complement the elegant presentation in MBOC by encouraging a more questioning attitude toward cell biology. Textbooks make things as plain as possible and do not normally interrogate the reader. Yet, if the reader is not challenged, some of the richness and depth is lost. Accordingly, we present three different kinds of questions—simple review questions, more challenging thought questions, and problems based on experiments. These are integrated with the main text to provide a kind of running commentary that should help the reader learn and, above all, understand.

Our most important aim is to introduce readers to the experimental foundation of cell and molecular biology in order to increase their appreciation of the link between the behavior of molecules and the biology of cells. Experiments are the only way we have to find out how nature works, and our knowledge is only as sophisticated as our experiments permit. In the real world of research biology, half the battle is knowing what question to ask, the other half is finding a way to answer it. In biology, new knowledge rarely comes from simply sitting back and thinking. Unfortunately, no book can replace the actual doing of experiments, but we have tried to capture some of the flavor of the process, especially the thinking that leads from observation to interpretation. Most of our problems are based on real experiments. Some are from classic papers in cell biology, some are from studies that provide the crucial experimental support for our current concepts, and some are taken from papers at the frontiers—ones that were hot off the press when the problems were devised. All are meant to involve the reader actively in the thinking behind the experiments that form the basis of our knowledge of cell biology.

Our greatest difficulty was finding papers that could be turned into suitable problems. The authors of MBOC were always helpful in pointing out important papers, as were our friends and colleagues. But papers that make really good problems are rare. The majority—even many excellent ones that measurably advance our understanding—are difficult to cast in problem form. In general, the papers we selected were simplified considerably in abstracting data for the problems. We limited each problem to a few essential points, and we provided just the information necessary to reason through to the answer. Real life in the lab is not like this, of course: it rarely happens that one can look at a single Petri dish and know that the genetic code uses nonoverlapping triplets. In our efforts to simplify, we also handled data in a way that may occasionally require a word of apology to the authors. We tried carefully not to damage the sense or logic of the work, however, and hope that we will stimulate a closer reading of the many excellent papers we used.

Composing these problems took us a very long time and an enormous amount of work, but it was almost always stimulating and enjoyable. We very much hope that some of the fun we had is transmitted to our readers. Our object is to explore and explain, not to baffle and bamboozle.

Acknowledgments

We thank our many friends and colleagues who tolerated our questions and provided insights into fields outside our own. In particular, we thank Buzz Brown, Lutz Birnbaumer, Liz Davies, Colin Dingwall, Joe Gall, Gil Gilbert, Barry Gumbiner, Brij Gupta, Rod Hafner, Elliot Hertzberg, Andrew Huxley, Hugh Huxley, Malcolm Irving, Stuart Kornfeld, Paul Lazarow, Peter Moore, Andrew Murray, Greg Petsko, Jim Pipas, Jasper Rine, Jim Rothman, John Silva, Jeremy Thorner, Lewis Tilney, Nancy Lane, and Richard Treisman.

We are grateful for the excellent problems that were contributed by David Allis, Susan Berget, Xiu-Bao Chang, Ramon Diaz-Arrastia, Al Edwards, Susan Fullilove, Steve Halford, Ming-Derg Lai, Peter Lund, Kathryn Meier, Deborah Mowshowitz, Andrew Murray, Hamida Qavi, David Roth, Sharon Yoder Roth, Nancy Lane, and Anthony Weiss.

All of the problems were attempted by students. Their comments and criticisms were extremely useful and helped to eliminate many errors, ambiguities, and verbiage. In particular, we thank Mark Krieger, Emily Chan, and Peter Kaiser, who worked nearly all the problems, but we are very grateful to all the students who worked through early drafts of the chapters and provided us with constructive suggestions: Lucy A. Godley, Lisa Grumbach, Christine Kim, Roy S. Lackey, Mei Lin, Jennifer Luebke, Nancy Mayer, Jordan Raff, Rebecca Richardson, Evan Rosenfeld, Diana Scouras, Fei F. Shih, Henry Shin, Kathy Steine, Ivan J. Suner, and Jonathan Winograd.

We are especially indebted to Dr. Alastair Ewing. He worked the problems, collated comments from the student reviewers, and made many wise recommendations for style and content. His efforts improved the book enormously and saved us from several embarrassing mistakes.

We thank Dixie Brewer, Meredith Riddell, Lynda Thomas, and Carol Winter for assistance with the manuscript and with many organizational details. Our searches in the literature were greatly helped by friendly librarians at the Scientific Periodicals Library at the University of Cambridge, the Imperial Cancer Research Fund Library in London, the Library of the Marine Biological Laboratory at Woods Hole, Massachusetts, the libraries of the Departments of Life Sciences, Biochemistry, and Molecular Biology at the University of California, Berkeley (thanks to Bruce Ames and John Gerhart), and the Library of the Robert Woods Johnson Medical School of New Jersey (thanks to John Doonan). Robert Brooks and Richard Summers helped us with some of the photographs, and Carol Morita advised us on computer graphics. We thank Peter Walter for the autoradiograph of the sequencing gel in Figure 5–45. We owe special thanks to the Cambridge undergraduates who contributed the data in Figures 5-4 and 10-3 as part of laboratory exercises.

From the beginning, we worked very closely with Bruce Alberts, Dennis Bray, Julian Lewis, Martin Raff, and Keith Roberts. They were stimulating company, and their wisdom got us out of many a tight corner. The illustrations, in particular, were always improved by advice from Keith Roberts. In addition, we thank Miranda Robertson for her sage counsel and consistent good cheer and Jim Watson for his timely encouragement and generosity.

The work of writing was made much more enjoyable by the surroundings in which it was done. We are especially grateful to Sheila Archibald for providing a welcome home away from home in London and to Anne and Lucy, whose cooking was an education in itself. We could not have completed this project without the professional help of the staff at Garland Publishing, especially Perry Bessas, Shirley Cobert, Janet Koenig, and Alison Walker. Ruth Adams, in particular, was tireless: she found student reviewers, coordinated their efforts, worked out production schedules, and stimulated us with sticks or carrots as the need arose. We acknowledge a very special debt to Gavin Borden, who initiated this project and encouraged its progress at every stage of its long development. He eased the pressures of writing and inspired us to our best efforts. Finally, we are most grateful for the patience and support of our families, friends, colleagues, and students during these years of distraction from our other duties. To all of them—especially Helen Epstein, Chester Kalter, Susan Berget, and Lynda Thomas—our heartfelt thanks.

Contents

Cell Growth and Division 13

Cell Adhesion, Cell Junctions, and the Extracellular Matrix 14

A Note to the Reader

We designed *The Problems Book* as an integrated companion to *Molecular Biology of The Cell*, covering the central core of cell biology (Chapters 5 to 14). Each chapter of problems is divided into sections that correspond to the sections of the main textbook. You will find references to page numbers in the second edition of MBOC throughout this book; the problems all assume that you are somewhat familiar with the contents of the relevant section. Each chapter begins with two straightforward questions that are designed to help readers review what they have just read and to check their understanding of it. The fill-in-the-blanks questions—essentially a vocabulary test—include most of the terms in bold print in MBOC; the true-false questions cover many of the key concepts and critical facts. All of these questions are answered at the back of the book.

The principal focus of each section is a set of research-oriented problems derived from the scientific literature. They cover a broad range of difficulties and will require more attention from the reader. Some are very simple, requiring no more than translation of the genetic code, for example. A few questions are very challenging, to the extent that we would be surprised if even experienced cell biologists could do them without the hint or two we provide. The majority of problems, however, are intermediate in difficulty. In all cases we tried to design the questions to lead the reader through the problems in manageable steps. More than half of the problems are answered in the back of the book. The answered problems will allow readers to check their reasoning quickly and to verify their mastery of basic concepts. The unanswered questions allow readers to test their prowess on their own—in the absence of easily accessed answers. Unanswered problems are marked with an asterisk (*); they are answered in the Instructor's Manual. We selected the answers to omit with care, but the choices were not easy. We left in the answers to many of the more difficult problems and to problems that made interesting points that might be overlooked. We imagine that the reader will gain most who makes a serious attempt to solve a problem before consulting the answer. We hope that both the answered and unanswered problems will also prove useful to instructors, as a source of homework assignments, as a framework for class discussions, and perhaps as the basis for exam questions.

Many problems in the book involve calculations. Where the calculations are based on an equation, we provide the equation with a brief explanation of any foreign symbols. Many calculations, however, involve the straightforward conversion of information from one form into another. Both kinds of calculations use constants and conversion factors that may not be included in the problem. All are listed inside the book covers (along with the standard genetic code and the one-letter amino acid code). In answering problems involving calculations, we have included the units (dimensions) for each element in the calculation. This practice, which is termed unit analysis (or dimensional analysis), is a powerful general approach to calculations, and we recommend it strongly. If the units are arranged so that they cancel to give the correct units for the answer, the numbers will take care of themselves. We naturally welcome comments, criticisms, and corrections, which should be addressed c/o Gavin Borden, Garland Publishing, Inc., 136 Madison Avenue, New York, NY 10016.

Basic Genetic Mechanisms

RNA and Protein Synthesis (MBOC 201–220)

5–1 Fill in the blanks in the following statements.

A. ____________ copies a stretch of DNA into RNA in a process known as ____________.

B. RNA synthesis begins at a ________ in the DNA and ends at a ________.

C. The ____________ in a tRNA molecule is designed to base-pair with a complementary sequence of three nucleotides, the ____________, in an mRNA molecule.

D. Enzymes called ____________ couple each amino acid to its appropriate tRNA molecule to create an ____________ molecule.

E. The genetic code is said to be ____________ because most of the amino acids are represented by more than one codon.

F. A ____________ contains two binding sites for tRNA molecules: the ________, or P-site, holds the tRNA molecule that is linked to the growing end of the polypeptide chain, and the ____________, or A-site, holds the incoming tRNA molecule that is charged with an amino acid.

G. Peptide bond formation is catalyzed by ____________, a catalytic activity that is thought to be mediated by the major ____________ molecule in the large ribosomal subunit.

H. Proteins called ____________ bind to ____________ codons in the A-site on the ribosome, causing peptidyl transferase to hydrolyze the bond that links the nascent polypeptide to the tRNA molecule.

I. In all cells, a special __________ molecule, recognizing the __________ codon AUG and carrying the amino acid ____________, provides the amino acid that begins a protein chain.

5–2 Indicate whether the following statements are true or false. If a statement is false, explain why.

__A. Binding to the promoter orients RNA polymerase so that it transcribes the adjacent gene; however, the choice of template strand is dictated by additional protein factors.

__B. In any one region of the DNA double helix, only one DNA strand is usually used as a template.

__C. Bacterial cells use one type of RNA polymerase to transcribe all classes of RNA, whereas eucaryotic cells use three different types of RNA polymerase.

__D. Modified nucleotides, which are especially common in tRNA molecules, are produced by covalent modification of the standard nucleotides before incorporation into RNA transcripts.

___ E. If the anticodon of a $tRNA^{Tyr}$ were modified by a single-base change to recognize a Ser codon and then added to a cell-free system, the resulting protein would have Tyr at all positions normally occupied by Ser.

___ F. Each aminoacyl-tRNA linkage is activated for addition of the next amino acid to the growing polypeptide chain rather than for its own addition.

___ G. Wobble base-pairing occurs between the first position in the codon and the third position in the anticodon.

___ H. The primary function of the small ribosomal subunit is to bind mRNA and tRNAs, whereas the large ribosomal subunit catalyzes peptide bond formation.

___ I. Overall, the synthesis of proteins, which uses four high-energy phosphate bonds per added amino acid (4/codon), consumes less total energy than the transcription of DNA into RNA, which uses two high-energy phosphate bonds per added nucleotide (6/codon).

___ J. Because AUG serves as the start codon for protein synthesis, methionine is found only at the N terminus of proteins.

___ K. Inserting a delay between the binding of a charged tRNA to the ribosome and its utilization in synthesis increases fidelity by giving improperly base-paired tRNAs an opportunity to diffuse off the ribosome.

___ L. Many antibiotics used in modern medicine selectively inhibit bacterial protein synthesis by exploiting the structural and functional differences between procaryotic and eucaryotic ribosomes.

5–3 One strand of a section of DNA isolated from *E. coli* reads

$^{5'}$GTAGCCTACCCATAGG$^{3'}$

A. Suppose mRNA is transcribed from this DNA using the complementary strand as template. What will be the sequence of the mRNA?

B. What peptide would be made if translation started exactly at the 5′ end of this mRNA? (Assume no start codon is required, as is true under certain test tube conditions.) When $tRNA^{Ala}$ leaves the ribosome, what tRNA will be bound next? When the amino group of alanine forms a peptide bond, what bonds, if any, are broken, and what happens to $tRNA^{Ala}$?

C. How many different peptides are encoded in this mRNA? Would the same peptides be made if the other strand of the DNA served as the template for transcription?

D. Suppose this stretch of DNA is transcribed as indicated in part A, but you do not know which reading frame is used. Could this DNA be from the beginning of a gene? The middle? The end?

***5–4** A few amino acids are removed from the C-terminal end of the beta-lactamase enzyme from *B. lichenformis* after it is synthesized. The sequence of the C terminus of the enzyme can be deduced by comparing it to a mutant in which the reading frame is shifted by insertion or by deletion of a nucleotide. The amino acid sequence of the purified wild-type enzyme and that from the frameshift mutant are given below from amino acid residue 263 to the C-terminal end.

wild type: N M N G K
mutant: N M I W Q I C V M K D

A. What was the mutational event that gave rise to the frameshift mutant?

B. Deduce the number of amino acids in the synthesized form of the wild-type enzyme and, as far as possible, the actual sequence of the wild-type enzyme.

5–5 You are studying protein synthesis in *Tetrahymena*, which is a unicellular ciliate. You have good news and bad news. The good news is that you have the first bit of protein and nucleic acid sequence data for the C terminus of a *Tetrahymena* protein, which is shown as follows:

*Problems with an asterisk (*) are answered in the Instructor's Manual.

I M Y K Q V A Q T Q L *
AUU AUG UAU AAG UAG GUC GCA UAA ACA CAA UUA UGA GAC UUA

The bad news is that you have been unable to translate purified *Tetrahymena* mRNA in a reticulocyte lysate, which is a standard system for analyzing protein synthesis *in vitro*. The mRNA looks good by all criteria, but the translation products are mostly small polypeptides (Figure 5–1, lane 1).

To figure out what is wrong, you do a number of control experiments using a pure mRNA from tobacco mosaic virus (TMV) that encodes a 116 kd protein. TMV mRNA alone is translated just fine in the *in vitro* system, giving a major band at 116 kd—the expected product—and a very minor band about 50 kd larger (Figure 5–1, lane 2). When *Tetrahymena* RNA is added, there is a significant increase in a higher molecular weight product (Figure 5–1, lane 3). When some *Tetrahymena* cytoplasm (minus the ribosomes) is added, the TMV mRNA now gives almost exclusively the higher molecular weight product (Figure 5–1, lane 4); furthermore, much to your delight, the previously inactive *Tetrahymena* mRNA now appears to be translated (Figure 5–1, lane 4). You confirm this by leaving out the TMV mRNA (Figure 5–1, lane 5).

A. What is unusual about the sequence data for the *Tetrahymena* protein?
B. How do you think the minor higher molecular weight band is produced from pure TMV mRNA in the reticulocyte lysate?
C. Explain the basis for the shift in proportions of the major and minor TMV proteins upon addition of *Tetrahymena* RNA alone and in combination with *Tetrahymena* cytoplasm. What *Tetrahymena* components are likely to be required for efficient translation of *Tetrahymena* mRNA?
D. Comment on the evolutionary implications of your results.

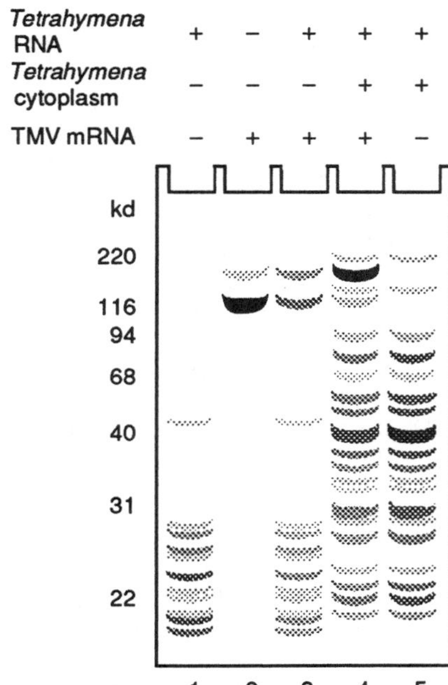

Figure 5–1 Translation of TMV mRNA in the presence and absence of various components from *Tetrahymena* (Problem 5–5).

5–6 Consider the following experiment on the coordinated synthesis of the α and β chains of hemoglobin. Rabbit reticulocytes were labeled with ^{3}H-lysine for 10 minutes, which is very long relative to the time required for synthesis of a single globin chain. The ribosomes, with attached nascent chains, were then isolated by centrifugation to give a preparation free of soluble (finished) globin chains. The nascent globin chains were digested with trypsin, which gives peptides ending in C-terminal lysine or arginine. The peptides were then separated by HPLC and their radioactivity was measured. A plot of the radioactivity in each peptide versus the position of the lysine residues in the chains is shown in Figure 5–2.

A. Do these data allow you to decide which end of the globin chains (N or C terminus) is synthesized first? How?
B. In what ratio are the two globin chains produced? Can you estimate the relative numbers of α- and β-globin mRNA molecules from these data?
C. How long does a protein chain stay attached to the ribosome once the termination codon has been reached?

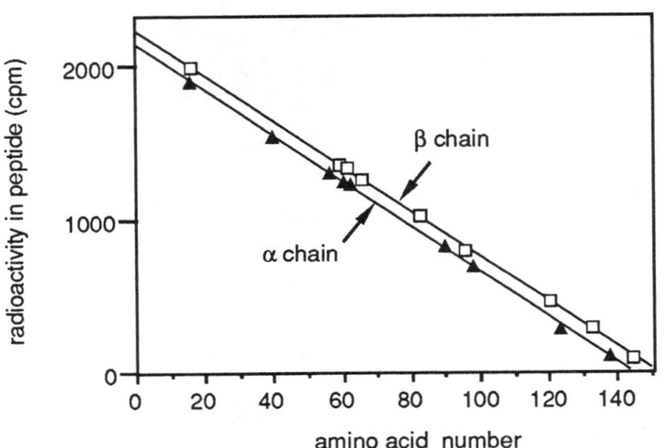

Figure 5–2 Synthesis of α- and β-globin (Problem 5–6).

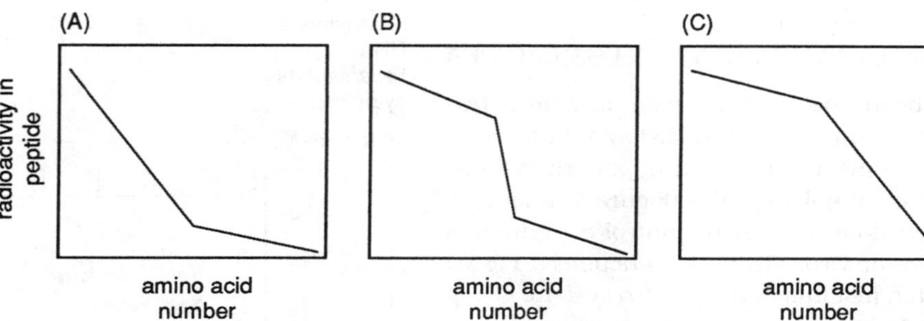

Figure 5–3 Hypothetical curves for globin synthesis with a roadblock to ribosome movement at the midpoint of the mRNA (Problem 5–6). These schematic diagrams are analogous to the graph in Figure 5–2.

D. It was once suggested that heme is added to nascent globin chains during their synthesis and, furthermore, that ribosomes must wait for insertion of heme before they can proceed. The straight lines in Figure 5–2 indicate that ribosomes do not pause significantly, and heme is now thought to be added after synthesis. From among the graphs shown in Figure 5–3, choose the one that would result if there were a significant roadblock to ribosome movement halfway down the mRNA.

***5–7** Rates of peptide chain growth can be estimated from data such as those shown in Figure 5–4. In this experiment, a single TMV mRNA species encoding a 116,000 dalton protein was translated in a rabbit-reticulocyte lysate in the presence of ^{35}S-methionine. Samples were removed at one-minute intervals, subjected to electrophoresis on polyacrylamide gels, and the translation products were visualized by autoradiography. As is apparent in the figure, the largest detectable proteins get larger with time.

A. Is the rate of synthesis linear with time? One simple way to evaluate linearity of synthesis in this experiment is to plot the molecular weights of the standards, which are shown on the left in Figure 5–4, against the time at which the largest peptide in a sample is equal to that molecular weight.

B. What is the rate of protein synthesis (in amino acids/minute) in this experiment? Assume the average molecular weight of an amino acid is 110.

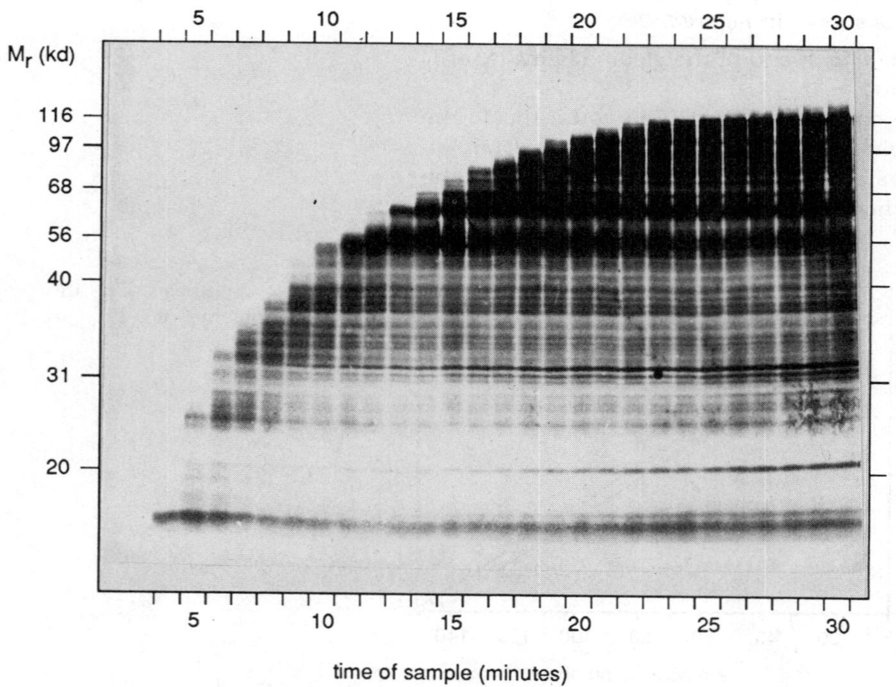

Figure 5–4 Time course of synthesis of a TMV protein in a rabbit-reticulocyte lysate (Problem 5–7). No radioactivity was detected during the first 3 minutes because the short chains ran off the bottom of the gel.

C. Why does the autoradiograph have so many bands in it rather than just a few bands that get larger as time passes; that is, why does the experiment produce the "actual" result rather than the "theoretical" result shown in Figure 5–5? Can you think of a way to manipulate the experimental conditions to produce the theoretical result?

5–8 Termination codons in bacteria are decoded by one of two proteins. Release factor 1 (RF1) recognizes UAG and UAA, whereas RF2 recognizes UGA and UAA. The molecular details of how these proteins recognize stop codons and catalyze chain termination are unknown. However, the genes for RF1 and RF2 recently have been cloned and sequenced. For RF2, a comparison of the nucleotide sequence of the gene with the amino acid sequence of the protein revealed a startling surprise, which is contained within the sequences shown below the map of the gene in Figure 5–6. Sequences of the gene and protein were checked carefully to rule out any artifacts.

A. What is the surprise?

B. What hypothesis concerning the regulation of expression of the RF2 gene is suggested by it?

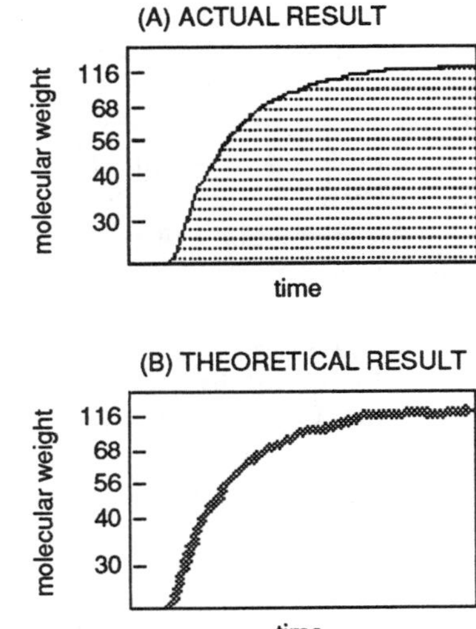

Figure 5–5 Actual (A) and theoretical (B) outcomes of protein synthesis experiment (Problem 5–7).

5–9 The overall accuracy of protein synthesis is very difficult to measure, partly because it is extremely accurate and mistakes, therefore, are very rare and partly because cells tend to destroy their mistakes very quickly. Technically there are problems, too. For example, how exactly do you identify a protein that, by definition, is not like the one you know how to purify and identify?

One ingenious approach to this problem used flagellin (molecular weight 40,000), which is the sole protein in bacterial flagella. Flagellin offers two advantages. First, flagella (hence flagellin) can be sheared off bacteria and purified by differential centrifugation. Second, flagellin contains no cysteine, thereby allowing a sensitive measure of the misincorporation of cysteine into the protein.

Bacteria were labeled with $^{35}SO_4$ (specific activity 5.0×10^3 cpm/pmol) for exactly one generation in the presence of excess unlabeled methionine. (No detectable radioactivity enters methionine under these conditions.) The resulting flagellin was purified and run on an SDS polyacrylamide gel. The 8 μg of flagellin recovered from the gel were found to contain 300 cpm of ^{35}S radioactivity.

A. Of the flagellin molecules that were synthesized during the labeling period, what fraction contain cysteine? Assume that the mass of flagellin doubles during the labeling period and that the specific activity of cysteine in flagellin is equal to the specific activity of the $^{35}SO_4$ used to label the cells.

B. In flagellin, cysteine is misincorporated at the arginine codons, CGU and CGC. In terms of anticodon-codon interaction, what mistake is made during misincorporation of cysteine for arginine?

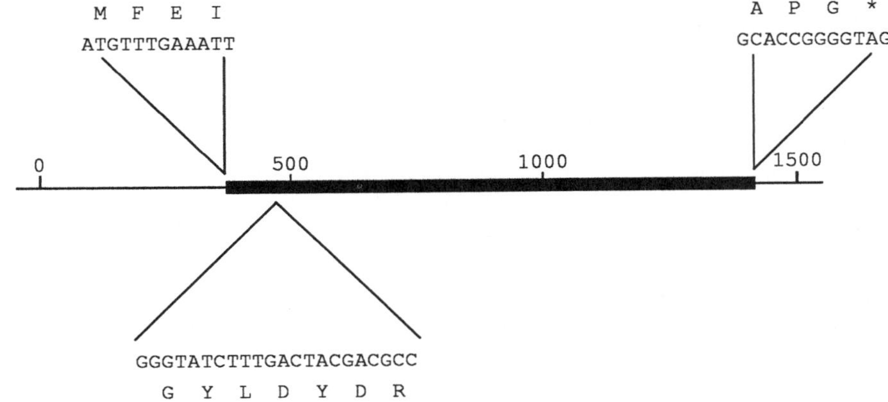

Figure 5–6 Schematic representation of the gene for RF2 (Problem 5–8). The coding sequence is shown as a thick line, with sequences at the start and finish shown for reference.

C. Given that there are 18 arginines in flagellin and that all arginine codons are equally represented, what is the frequency of misreading of each sensitive (CGU and CGC) arginine codon?

D. Assuming that the error frequency per codon calculated above applies to all amino acid codons equally, estimate the percentage of molecules that is correctly synthesized for proteins 100, 1000, and 10,000 amino acids in length. (The probability of not making a mistake is one minus the probability of making a mistake.)

***5–10** You have isolated an antibiotic, named edeine, from a bacterial culture. Edeine inhibits protein synthesis but has no effect on either DNA synthesis or RNA synthesis. When added to a reticulocyte lysate, edeine stops protein synthesis after a short lag, as shown in Figure 5–7 where it is contrasted with cycloheximide, which stops protein synthesis immediately. Analysis of the edeine-inhibited lysate by centrifugation in sucrose density gradients showed that no polyribosomes remained by the time protein synthesis had stopped. Instead, all the globin mRNA accumulated in an abnormal 40S peak, which contained equimolar amounts of the small ribosomal subunit and initiator tRNA.

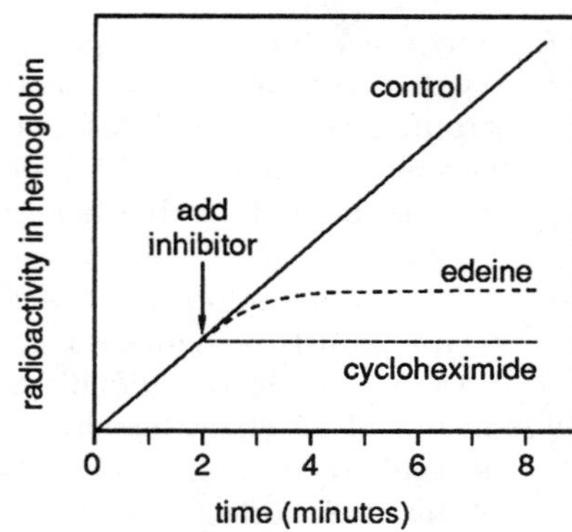

Figure 5–7 Effects of the inhibitors edeine and cycloheximide on protein synthesis in reticulocyte lysates (Problem 5–10).

A. What step in protein synthesis does edeine inhibit?

B. Why is there a lag between addition of edeine and cessation of protein synthesis? What determines the length of the lag?

C. Would you expect the polyribosomes to disappear if you added cycloheximide at the same time as edeine?

DNA Repair Mechanisms (MBOC 220–227)

5–11 Fill in the blanks in the following statements.

A. Most spontaneous changes in DNA are quickly erased by a correction process called ______________; only rarely do DNA maintenance procedures fail and allow a permanent sequence change, which is called a ______________.

B. The genes encoding the ______________, which are discarded during blood clotting, accumulate mutations without being selected against.

C. Two common spontaneous changes in DNA are ______________, which results from disruption of the *N*-glycosyl linkages of adenine and guanine to deoxyribose, and ______________, which converts cytosine to uracil.

D. DNA repair involves three steps: recognition and removal of the altered portion of the DNA strand by enzymes called ______________, resynthesis of the excised region by ______________, and sealing the remaining nick by the enzyme ______________.

E. In DNA a deoxyribose lacking an attached base is rapidly recognized by the enzyme ______________, which cuts the DNA phosphodiester backbone at the altered site.

F. A ______________ recognizes a single type of altered base in DNA and catalyzes its hydrolytic removal from the deoxyribose sugar.

G. Those types of DNA damage that create large distortions in the DNA helix are removed by a ______________ repair pathway.

H. In *E. coli* any block to DNA replication caused by DNA damage produces a signal that induces the ______________, which allows replication through the block, hence giving the cell a chance for survival.

5–12 Indicate whether the following statements are true or false. If a statement is false, explain why.

__ A. The fibrinopeptides, which are discarded from fibrinogen when it is activated to form fibrin during blood clotting, are especially useful for estimating mutation rates because they apparently have no direct function.

__ B. Estimates of mutation rate based on amino acid differences in the same protein in different species always will be underestimates of the actual mutation rate because some mutations will compromise the function of the protein and will vanish from the population under selective pressure.

__ C. Since histone H4 proteins are virtually identical in all species, one would expect histone H4 genes in different species to be virtually identical as well.

__ D. Observed mutation rates, although extremely low, nevertheless limit the number of essential genes in any organism to about 60,000.

__ E. There are a variety of repair mechanisms, but all of them depend on the existence of two copies of the genetic information, one in each chromosome of a diploid organism.

__ F. Spontaneous depurination and the removal of a deaminated C by uracil DNA glycosylase both leave an identical intermediate, which is the substrate recognized by AP endonuclease.

__ G. Only the first step in DNA repair is catalyzed by enzymes that are unique to the repair process; the later steps are catalyzed by enzymes that play more general roles in DNA metabolism.

__ H. The principal function of the SOS response in *E. coli* is to increase cell survival by introducing compensating mutations near the site of the original DNA damage.

__ I. All the spontaneous deamination products of the usual four DNA bases are recognizable as unnatural when they occur in DNA.

5–13 Several genes in *E. coli*, including *uvrA*, *uvrB*, *uvrC*, and *recA*, are involved in repair of UV damage. Strains of *E. coli* that are defective in any one of these genes are much more sensitive to killing by UV light than are nonmutant (wild-type) cells, as shown for *uvrA* and *recA* strains in Figure 5–8A. Individual mutations in different genes can be combined in pairs to make all the possible double mutants. The sensitivity of the double mutants varies much more than that of the single mutants. The combinations of *uvr* mutants with one another show little increase in sensitivity relative to the *uvr* single mutants. The combination of *recA* with any of the *uvr* mutations, however, gives a strain that is exquisitely sensitive to UV light, as shown for *uvrArecA* on an expanded scale in Figure 5–8B.

A. Why do combinations of a *recA* mutation with a *uvr* mutation give an extremely UV-sensitive strain of bacteria, whereas combinations of muta-

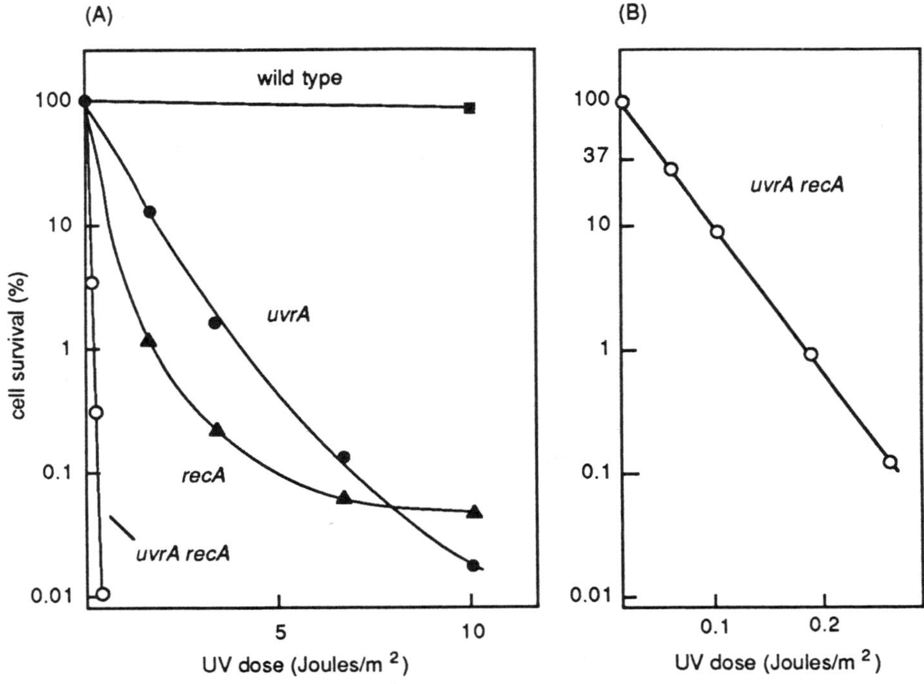

Figure 5–8 Cell survival as a function of UV dose (Problem 5–13). (A) Survival of wild-type cells, a *uvrA* mutant, a *recA* mutant, and a *uvrArecA* double mutant. (B) An expanded scale for *uvrArecA* survival.

Table 5–1 Frequency of UV-induced Mutations in Various Strains of *E. coli* (Problem 5–14)

Strain	Survival (%)	Mutations/10^{10} Survivors
Wild type	100	400
recA	10	1
uvrA	10	40000

tions in different *uvr* genes are no more UV sensitive than the individual mutations?

B. According to the Poisson distribution, when a population of bacteria receives an overall average of one lethal "hit," 37% (e^{-1}) will survive because they actually receive no hits. For the double mutant *uvrArecA*, a dose of 0.04 J/m^2 gives 37% survival (Figure 5–8B). Calculate how many pyrimidine dimers constitute a lethal hit for the *uvrArecA* strain, given that *E. coli* has 4×10^6 base pairs in its genome, which is 50% GC, and that exposure of DNA to UV light at 400 J/m^2 converts 1% of the total pyrimidine pairs (TT, TC, CT, plus CC) to pyrimidine dimers.

***5–14** In addition to killing bacteria, UV light causes mutations. You have measured the UV-induced mutation frequency in wild-type *E. coli* and in strains defective in either the *uvrA* gene or the *recA* gene. The results are shown in Table 5–1. Surprisingly, these strains differ markedly in their mutability by UV.

A. Assuming that the *recA* and *uvrA* gene products participate in different pathways for repair of UV damage, decide which pathway is more error prone. Which pathway predominates in wild-type cells?

B. The error-prone pathway is thought to result from misincorporation of nucleotides opposite a site of unrepaired damage. When forced to, DNA polymerases tend to incorporate an adenine nucleotide opposite a site with ambiguous coding properties, such as a pyrimidine dimer. Is this so-called "A rule" a good strategy for dealing with UV damage? Calculate the frequency of base changes (mutations) using the A rule versus random incorporation (each nucleotide with equal probability) for *E. coli* where pyrimidine dimers are approximately 60% TT, 30% TC and CT, and 10% CC.

***5–15** The SOS pathway in *E. coli* represents an emergency response to DNA damage. As illustrated in Figure 5–9, under normal conditions the SOS set of damage-inducible genes is turned off by the lexA repressor, which also partially represses its own synthesis and that of recA. In response to DNA damage, a signal (thought to be single-stranded DNA) activates recA, which then mediates the cleavage of lexA. In the absence of lexA, all genes are maximally expressed. The SOS response increases cell survival in the face of DNA damage and transiently increases the mutation rate, hence variability, in the bacterial population. Although indispensable during an emergency, the constant expression of the SOS genes would be very deleterious.

One aspect of the regulation of the SOS response appears paradoxical: the expression of lexA (the repressor of the SOS response) is substantially increased during an SOS response. If the object of the response is maximal expression of the damage-induced genes, why should the repressor be expressed at high levels? Put another way, why is lexA not expressed at a low rate all the time? Do you see any advantage that the induced expression of lexA offers for the regulation of the SOS response?

5–16 The patterns of UV-induced mutations occurring in the *E. coli lacI* gene have been extensively analyzed. Figure 5–10 shows the total number of

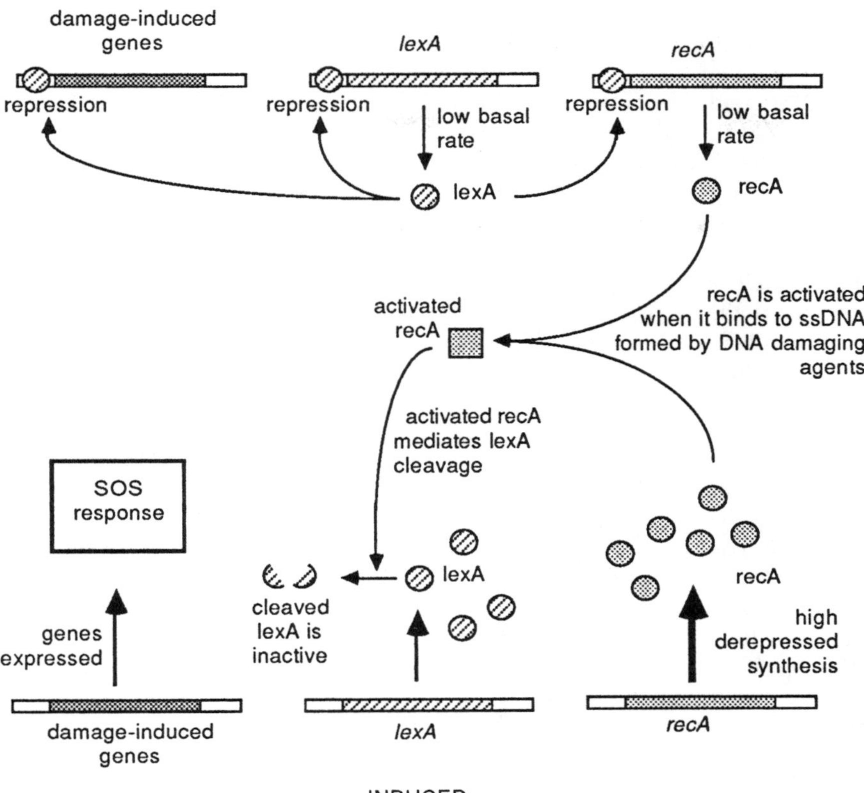

Figure 5–9 The SOS response in *E. coli* (Problem 5–15).

independently isolated missense (amino acid substitution) mutations (above the line) and frameshift (change in the reading frame) mutations (below the line). There are almost equal numbers of mutations in each category. Missense mutations were identified by scoring for loss of function of the protein specified by the *lacI* gene (the lac repressor); the frameshift mutations were scored by a gene-fusion assay, which is independent of the function of the lac repressor.

A. Why do you think that there are so many more missense mutations at the ends of the gene than in the middle? Why do you think that the frameshift

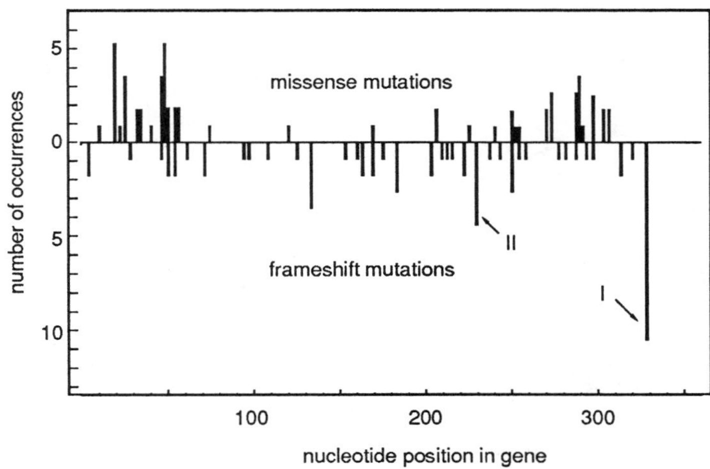

Figure 5–10 Pattern of UV-induced mutations in the *E. coli lacI* gene (Problem 5–16).

mutations are more or less evenly distributed across the gene (except for one or two "hotspots")?

B. DNA sequence analysis of the hotspot (labeled I in Figure 5–10) revealed that its wild-type sequence was TTTTTC and that the mutated sequence was TTTTC. The next most common mutation (labeled II in Figure 5–10) was the change from GTTTTC to GTTTC. Analysis of other frameshifts indicated that they resulted most commonly from the loss of one base; no insertions were found. Based on what you know of the nature of UV damage, can you suggest a molecular mechanism for the loss of a single base pair?

5–17 In addition to uvrABC endonuclease repair, recombinational repair, and SOS repair, bacteria have an even more potent repair system for dealing with pyrimidine dimers (one that is not discussed in the text). This phenomenon was discovered by careful observation to define an uncontrolled variable in an investigation of the effects of UV light on bacteria—not unlike the scenario described below.

You and your adviser are trying to isolate mutants in *E. coli* using UV light as the mutagenic agent. To get plenty of mutants, you find it necessary to use a dose of irradiation that kills 99.99% of the bacteria. You have been getting much more consistent results than your adviser, who also requires tenfold to a hundredfold higher doses of irradiation to achieve the same degree of killing. He wonders about the validity of your results since you always do your experiments at night after he has left. When he insists that you come in the morning to do the experiments in parallel, both of you are surprised when you get exactly the same results. You are a bit chagrined because the results are more like your adviser's, and you had confidently assumed you were better at doing lab work than your adviser, who is rarely seen in a lab coat these days. When you repeat the experiments in parallel at night, however, your adviser is surprised at the results, which are exactly as you had described them.

Now that you believe one another's observations, you make rapid progress. You find that you need a higher dose of UV light in the afternoon than in the morning to get the same degree of killing. Even higher doses are required on sunny days than on overcast days. Your laboratory faces west. What is the variable that has been plaguing your experiments?

***5–18** Mutagens such as N-methyl-N′-nitro-N-nitrosoguanidine (MNNG) and methyl nitrosourea (MNU) are potent DNA methylating agents and are extremely toxic to cells. Nitrosoguanidines are used in research as mutagens and clinically as drugs in cancer chemotherapy because they preferentially kill cells in the act of replication.

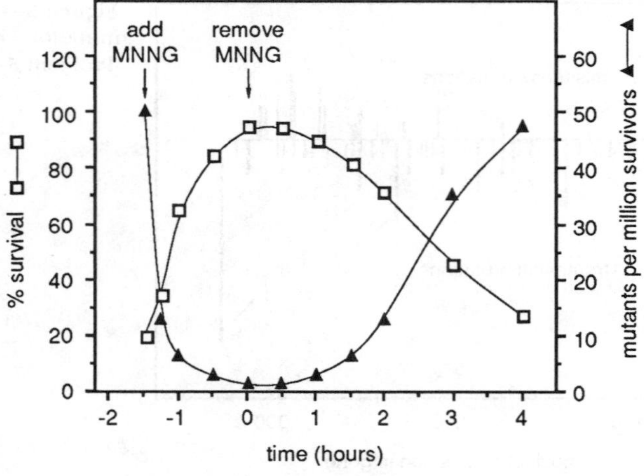

Figure 5–11 Adaptive response of *E. coli* to low doses of MNNG (Problem 5–18). MNNG at 1 μg/ml was present from −1.5 to 0 hours. Samples were removed at various times and treated briefly with 100 μg/ml MNNG to assess the number of survivors and the frequency of mutants.

The original experiment that led to the discovery of the alkylation repair system in bacteria was designed to assess the long-term effects of exposure to low doses of MNNG (as in chemotherapy), in contrast to brief exposure to large doses (as in mutagenesis). Bacteria were placed first in a low concentration of MNNG (1 μg/ml) for 1.5 hours and then in fresh medium lacking MNNG. At various times during and after exposure to the low dose of MNNG, samples of the culture were treated with a high concentration (100 μg/ml) of MNNG for 5 minutes and then tested for viability and the frequency of mutants. As shown in Figure 5–11, exposure to low doses of MNNG temporarily increased the number of survivors and decreased the frequency of mutants among the survivors. As shown in Figure 5–12, this adaptive response to low doses of MNNG was prevented if chloramphenicol (an inhibitor of protein synthesis) was included in the incubation.

A. Does the adaptive response of *E. coli* to low levels of MNNG require activation of preexisting protein or synthesis of new protein?

B. Why do you think the adaptive response of *E. coli* to a low dose of MNNG is so short-lived?

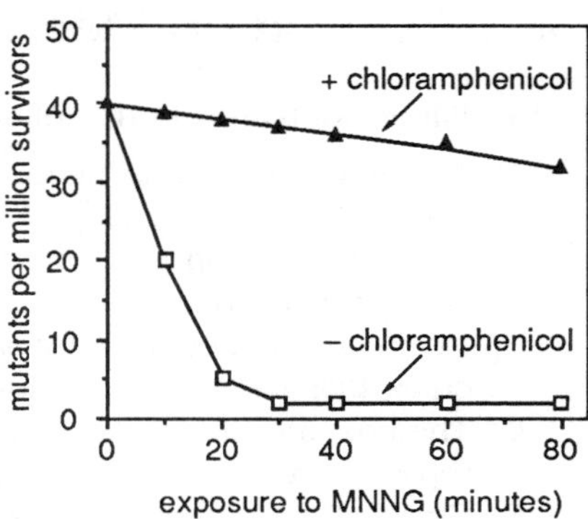

Figure 5–12 Effects of chloramphenicol on the adaptive response to low doses of MNNG (Problem 5–18). After different times of exposure of bacteria to 1 μg/ml MNNG, samples were removed and treated with 100 μg/ml MNNG to measure susceptibility to mutagenesis.

5–19 The nature of the mutagenic lesion introduced by MNNG and the mechanism of its removal from DNA were identified in the following experiments. To determine the nature of the mutagenic lesion, untreated bacteria and bacteria that had been exposed to low doses of MNNG were incubated with 50 μg/ml ^{3}H-MNNG for 10 minutes. Their DNA was isolated, hydrolyzed to nucleotides, and the radioactive purines were then analyzed by paper chromatography as shown in Figure 5–13.

To examine the mechanism of removal of the mutagenic lesion, the enzyme responsible for removal was first purified. The kinetics of removal were studied by incubating different amounts of the enzyme (molecular weight, 19,000) with DNA containing 0.26 pmol of the mutagenic base, which was radioactively labeled with ^{3}H. At various times samples were taken, and the DNA was analyzed to determine how much of the mutagenic base remained (Figure 5–14). When the experiment was repeated at 5°C instead of 37°C, the initial rates of removal were slower, but exactly the same endpoints were achieved.

A. Which methylated purine is responsible for the mutagenic action of MNNG?

B. What is peculiar about the kinetics of removal of the methyl group from the mutagenic base? Is this peculiarity due to an unstable enzyme?

C. Calculate the number of methyl groups that are removed by each enzyme molecule. Does this calculation help to explain the peculiar kinetics?

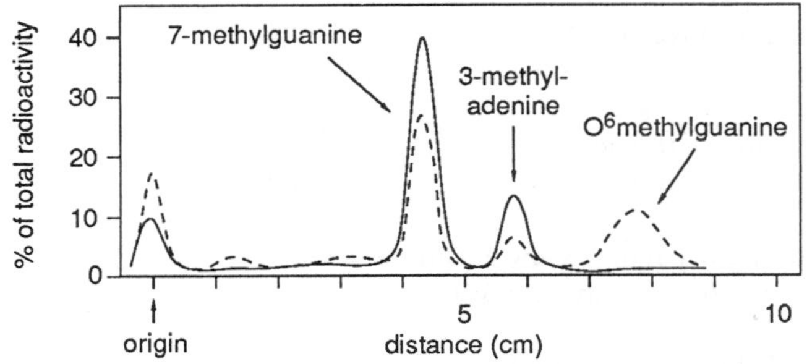

Figure 5–13 Chromatographic separation of labeled methylated purines in the DNA of untreated bacteria and bacteria treated with low doses of MNNG (Problem 5–19). The solid line indicates methylated purines from the DNA of untreated bacteria; the dashed line shows the results from MNNG-treated bacteria.

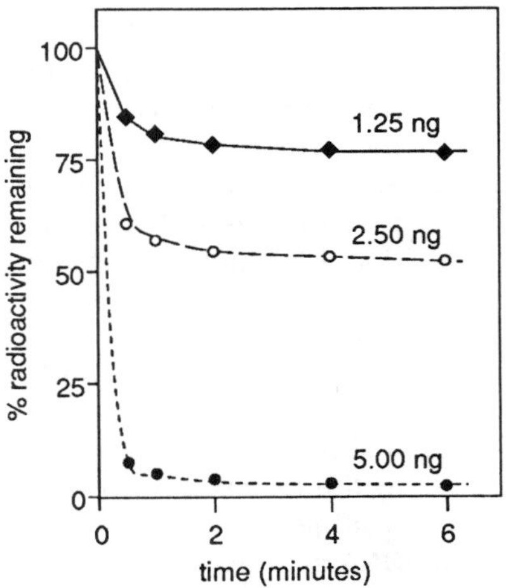

Figure 5–14 Removal of ^{3}H-labeled methyl groups from DNA by purified methyltransferase enzyme (Problem 5–19). The quantities of purified enzyme are indicated.

DNA Replication Mechanisms (MBOC 227–239)

5–20 Fill in the blanks in the following statements.

A. The enzyme responsible for DNA synthesis in both replication and repair is called ____________.

B. The active region of a chromosome involved in replication is a Y-shaped structure called a ____________.

C. In *E. coli* the most recently synthesized DNA is transiently found in molecules 1000 to 2000 nucleotides long, called ____________.

D. The enzyme that seals nicks in the DNA helix during DNA synthesis and repair is called ____________.

E. During DNA replication, the daughter strand that is synthesized continuously is called the ____________, and the strand that is synthesized discontinuously is known as the ____________.

F. Unlike RNA polymerase, DNA polymerase absolutely requires the 3′-OH end of a base-paired ____________ on which to add additional nucleotides.

G. If DNA polymerase adds an incorrect nucleotide to the 3′terminus, a separate catalytic domain containing a 3′-to-5′ ____________ activity removes the mismatched base.

H. Initiation of DNA synthesis on the lagging strand requires short primers made by an enzyme called ____________, which uses ribonucleotide triphosphates as substrates.

I. The unwinding of the DNA helix at the replication fork is catalyzed by a ____________, which uses the energy from ATP hydrolysis to move unidirectionally along DNA.

J. ____________, which aid DNA unwinding, bind to single-stranded DNA in such a way that the bases are still available for templating reactions.

K. If DNA polymerase makes a mistake, thus creating a pair of incorrectly hydrogen-bonded bases, the mistake is corrected by a special ____________ system that uses methylation to distinguish new strands from old.

L. For bacteria, as well as for several viruses that grow in eucaryotic cells, replication bubbles have been shown to form at special DNA sequences called ____________.

M. ____________ can be viewed as "reversible nucleases" that create either a transient single-strand break (type I) or a transient double-strand break (type II).

5–21 Indicate whether the following statements are true or false. If a statement is false, explain why.

__ A. In *E. coli* where the replication fork moves forward at 500 nucleotide pairs per second, the DNA ahead of the fork rotates at nearly 3000 revolutions per minute.

__ B. Semiconservative replication means that the parental DNA strands serve as templates for the synthesis of the new progeny DNA strands, so the new double-stranded DNA molecules are composed of one old and one new strand.

__ C. When read in the same direction (5′ to 3′), the sequence of nucleotides in the newly synthesized DNA strand is the same as in the parental template strand.

__ D. A 5′-to-3′ synthesis of DNA means that growth occurs by addition of dNTPs to the exposed 3′-OH group, with expulsion of inorganic pyrophosphate residues.

__ E. DNA synthesis occurs in the 5′-to-3′ direction on the leading strand and in the 3′-to-5′ direction on the lagging strand.

__ F. If DNA polymerization occurred in the 3′-to-5′ direction, it would require that the growing end of the chain terminate in a 5′-triphosphate or that 3′-deoxynucleoside triphosphates act as precursors.

__ G. Loss of the 3′-to-5′ exonuclease activity of DNA polymerase in *E. coli* should slow the rate of DNA synthesis but not affect its fidelity.

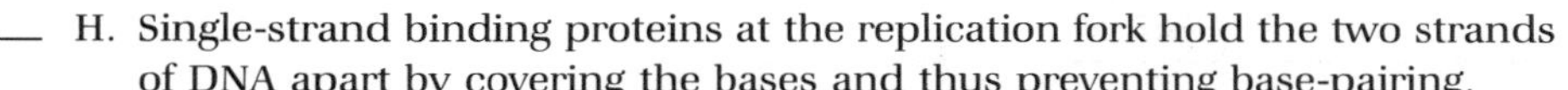

— H. Single-strand binding proteins at the replication fork hold the two strands of DNA apart by covering the bases and thus preventing base-pairing.

— I. The methylation-dependent mismatch-repair system in *E. coli* can distinguish the parental strand from the progeny strand as long as one or both are methylated, but not if both strands are unmethylated.

— J. In *E. coli* and eucaryotic viruses, new rounds of DNA replication are initiated at a specific site, which often contains several copies of a short sequence that binds a complex of initiator proteins.

— K. Topoisomerase I does not require ATP to break and to rejoin DNA strands because the energy of the phosphodiester bond is stored transiently in a phosphotyrosine linkage in the enzyme's active site.

— L. Topoisomerase II mutants in yeast can replicate their DNA but cannot separate their chromosomes at mitosis.

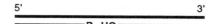

Figure 5–15 A DNA fragment with a single-stranded gap on the bottom strand (Problem 5–22).

5–22 The DNA fragment in Figure 5–15 is double stranded at each end but single stranded in the middle. The polarity of the top strand is indicated.

A. Is the indicated phosphate (P) on the bottom strand at the 5′ end or the 3′ end of the fragment to which it is attached?

B. How would you expect the gap to be filled in by DNA repair processes inside a cell?

C. How many pieces will the bottom strand contain if the gap is filled in a test-tube reaction containing only deoxyribonucleoside triphosphates and DNA polymerase?

***5–23** The electron microscope is an important tool for studying DNA replication because it is possible to observe the replication fork directly and, for small DNA molecules, to observe the entire replicating structure. In addition, by using appropriate techniques of sample preparation, one can distinguish double-stranded DNA from single-stranded DNA.

A series of hypothetical replicating molecules are illustrated schematically in Figure 5–16, with regions of single-stranded DNA shown as thin lines. In an important early electron microscope study of bacteriophage lambda replication, some of these structures were observed commonly and others were never observed.

A. Draw a diagram of a replication structure with two forks moving in opposite directions. Label the ends of all strands (5′ or 3′), and indicate the leading and lagging strands at each replication fork.

B. Based on your knowledge of DNA replication, pick out the four structures in Figure 5–16 that were most commonly observed.

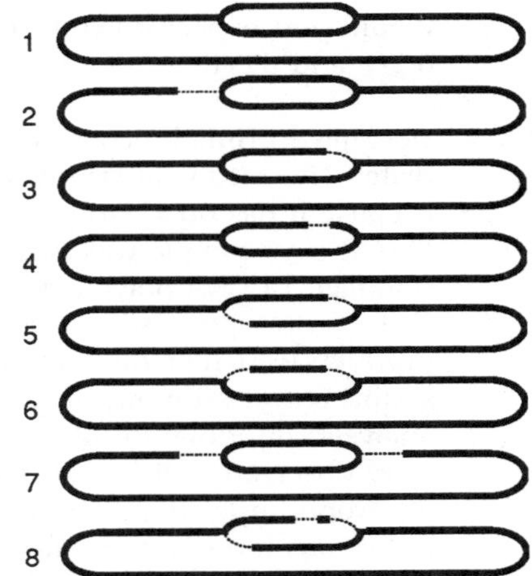

Figure 5–16 Hypothetical structures of replicating molecules (Problem 5–23).

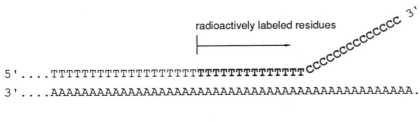

5–24 DNA polymerase I possesses a 3′-to-5′ exonuclease activity in addition to its polymerizing activity. This activity functions during proofreading to remove mismatched bases from the terminus of the newly polymerized DNA strand. To examine this activity, you prepare an artificial substrate with one poly(dA) strand and one poly(dT) strand that contains a few ^{32}P-labeled dT residues followed by a few ^{3}H-labeled dC residues at its 3′ end as shown in Figure 5–17. You measure the loss of the labeled dT and dC residues either without any dTTP present, so that no DNA synthesis is possible, or with dTTP present, so that DNA synthesis can occur. The results are shown in Figure 5–18.

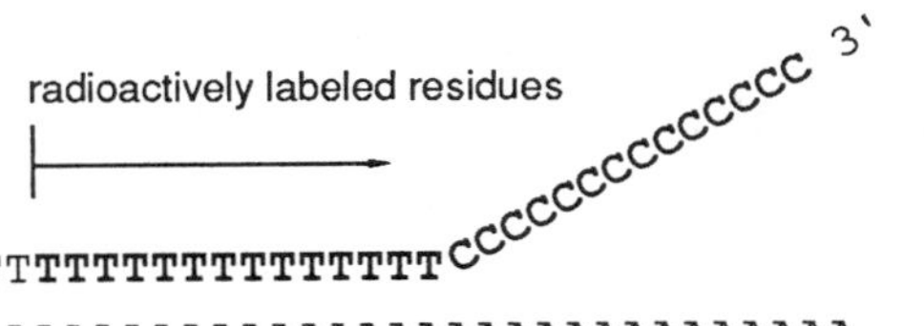

Figure 5–17 Artificial substrate for studying proofreading by DNA polymerase I of *E. coli* (Problem 5–24). Bold letters indicate nucleotides that are radioactively labeled.

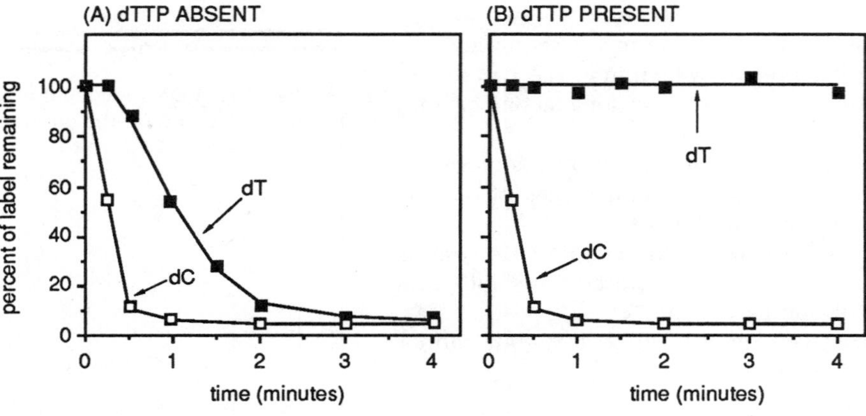

Figure 5–18 Proofreading by DNA polymerase I in the absence (A) and presence (B) of dTTP (Problem 5–24).

A. Why were the T and C residues labeled with different isotopes?
B. Why did it take longer for the T residues to be removed in the absence of dTTP than the C residues?
C. Why were none of the T residues removed in the presence of dTTP, whereas the C residues were lost regardless of whether or not dTTP was present?
D. Would you expect different results in Figure 5–18B if you had included dCTP and dTTP?

***5–25** Does RNA priming occur at specific sites or at random sites on the template? The M13 viral DNA is an ideal template for studying this question because it has no 3′-OH group to confuse the issue. To answer this question, the M13 circle was completely copied in the presence of the bacteriophage T4 DNA polymerase, the T4 primosome (a complex of a helicase and an RNA primase), rNTPs, and dNTPs. The double-stranded circular products were then digested with a restriction enzyme that makes a double-strand cut at a unique site. The digestion products were denatured and analyzed on a high-resolution DNA sequencing gel. Many discrete bands were observed. If the digestion products were treated with RNase before electrophoresis, they all became five nucleotides shorter as judged by their faster migration on the sequencing gels.

Knowing that each product ended at the unique restriction site, it was possible to deduce the template sequence near their 5′ ends from their length. (The complete sequence of M13 is known.) Some of these template sequences are shown on the left side of Figure 5–19. The DNA sequence at each of the corresponding 5′ ends of the product strands was determined after removal of the priming ribonucleotides. These sequences are shown on the right side of Figure 5–19, on the same line as the region of complementary sequence in the DNA template.

site	M13 template sequences (5' → 3')	DNA sequences linked to RNA primer (5' → 3')
1	A T C C T T G C G T T G A A A T	A G G A T
2	T C T T G T T T G C T C C A G A	C A A G A
3	A T T C T C T T G T T T G C T C	A G A A T
4	A C A T G C T A G T T T T A C G	C A T G T
5	A T T G A C A T G C T A G T T T	T C A A T
6	A T C T T C C T G T T T T T G G	A A G A T
7	A A A T A T T T G C T T A T A C	T A T T T
8	C T A G A A C G G T T A C C C T	T C T A G

Figure 5–19 M13 template sequences (*left*) and the corresponding DNA sequences produced at each site (*right*) during the priming reaction (Problem 5–25). The RNA primers were removed from these DNA chains prior to sequencing.

From these data, deduce the start site for the RNA primer on each template sequence. What is the likely signal for starting the RNA primase reaction?

5–26 The *dnaB* gene of *E. coli* encodes a helicase (dnaB) that unwinds DNA at the replication fork. Its properties have been studied using artificial substrates like those shown in Figure 5–20. The experimental approach is to incubate the substrates under a variety of conditions and then subject a sample to electrophoresis on agarose gels. The short single strand will move slowly if it is still annealed to the longer DNA strand, but it will move much faster if it has been unwound and detached. The migration of the short single strand can be followed selectively by making it radioactive and examining its position in the gel by autoradiography.

The results of several experiments are shown in Figure 5–21. Substrate 1, the hybrid without tails, was not unwound by dnaB (Figure 5–21, lanes 1 and 2). However, when either substrate with tails was incubated at 37°C with dnaB and ATP, a significant amount of small fragment was released by unwinding (lanes 6 and 10). For substrate 3 only the 3′ half-fragment was unwound (lane 10). All unwinding was absolutely dependent on ATP hydrolysis.

Unwinding was considerably enhanced by adding single-stranded DNA binding protein (SSB) (compare lanes 5 and 6 and lanes 9 and 10). Interestingly, SSB had to be added about 3 minutes after dnaB; otherwise it inhibited unwinding.

A. Why is ATP hydrolysis required for unwinding?
B. In what direction does dnaB move along the long single-stranded DNA? Is this direction more consistent with its movement on the leading strand or on the lagging strand at the replication fork?
C. Why might SSB inhibit unwinding if it is added before dnaB but stimulate unwinding if added after dnaB?

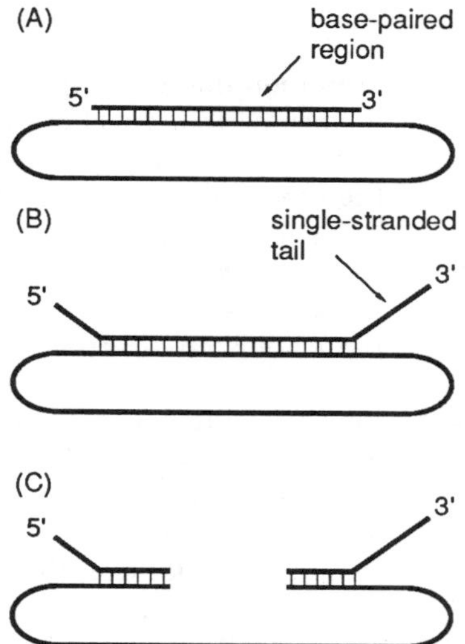

Figure 5–20 Substrates used to test the properties of dnaB (Problem 5–26). (A) Substrate 1. (B) Substrate 2. (C) Substrate 3.

5–27 The laboratory you joined is studying the life cycle of an animal virus that uses a circular, double-stranded DNA as its genome. Your project is to define the location of the origin(s) of replication and to determine whether replication proceeds in one or both directions away from an origin (unidirectional or bidirectional). To accomplish your goal, you isolated repli-

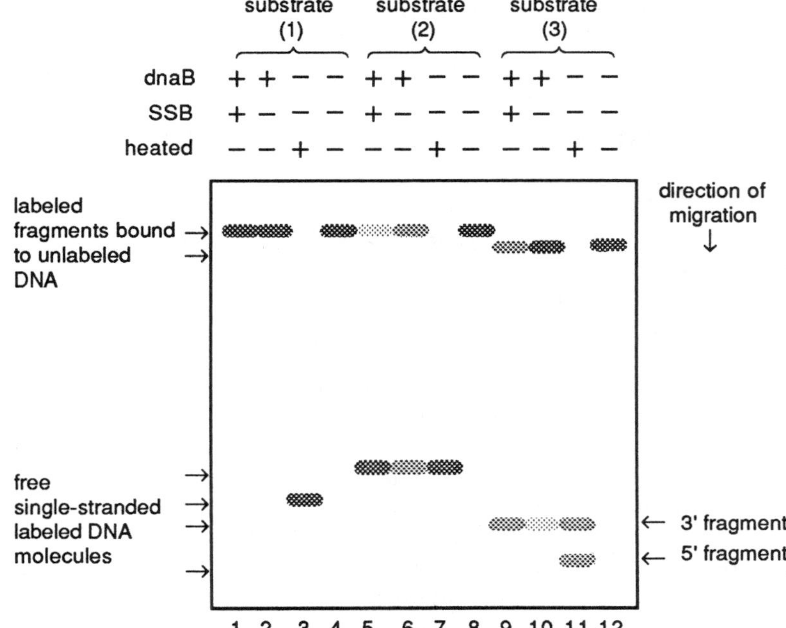

Figure 5–21 Results of several experiments to measure unwinding by dnaB (Problem 5–26). Only the single-stranded fragments were radioactively labeled. Their positions are shown by the bands in this schematic diagram.

cating molecules, cleaved them with a restriction enzyme that cuts the viral genome at one site to produce a linear molecule from the circle, and examined the resulting molecules in the electron microscope. Some of the molecules that you have observed are illustrated schematically in Figure 5–22. (Note that it is impossible to tell one end of a DNA molecule from the other in the electron microscope.)

You must present your conclusions to the rest of the lab tomorrow. How will you answer the questions that your adviser has posed for you? (1) Is there a single, unique origin of replication or several origins? (2) Is replication unidirectional or bidirectional?

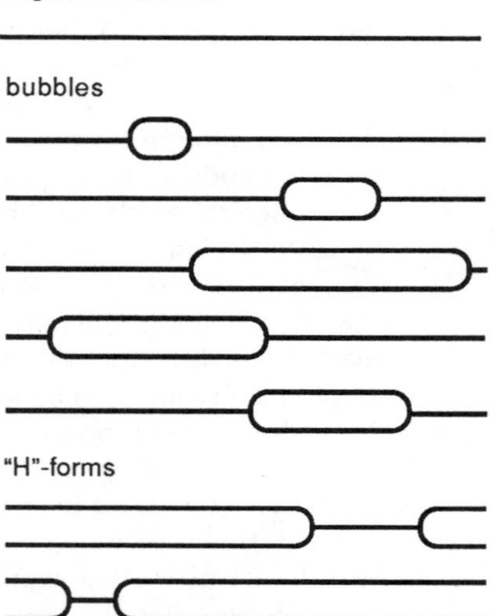

Figure 5–22 Parental and replicating forms of an animal virus (Problem 5–27).

***5–28** Conditionally lethal mutations are very useful in genetic and biochemical analyses of complex processes such as DNA replication. Temperature-sensitive (ts) mutations, which are one form of conditional lethal mutation, allow growth at one temperature (for example, 30°C) but not at a higher temperature (for example, 42°C).

A large number of temperature-sensitive mutants have been isolated in *E. coli*. These mutant bacteria are defective in DNA replication at 42°C but not at 30°C. If the temperature of the medium is raised from 30°C to 42°C, these mutants stop making DNA in one of two characteristic ways. The "quick-stop" mutants halt DNA synthesis immediately, whereas the "slow-stop" mutants stop DNA synthesis only after many minutes.

A. Predict which of the following proteins, if temperature sensitive, would display a quick-stop phenotype and which would display a slow-stop phenotype. In each case explain your prediction.

1. DNA topoisomerase I
2. A replication initiator protein
3. Helix-destabilizing protein
4. DNA helicase
5. RNA primase
6. DNA ligase

B. Cell-free extracts of the mutants show essentially the same patterns of replication as the intact cells. Extracts from quick-stop mutants halt DNA synthesis immediately at 42°C, whereas extracts from slow-stop mutants do not stop DNA synthesis for several minutes after a shift to 42°C. Suppose extracts from a temperature-sensitive DNA helicase mutant and a temperature-sensitive DNA ligase mutant were mixed together at 42°C. Would you expect the mixture to exhibit a quick-stop phenotype, a slow-stop phenotype, or a nonmutant phenotype?

Genetic Recombination Mechanisms (MBOC 239–247)

5–29 Fill in the blanks in the following statements.

A. In ____________, genetic exchange occurs between homologous DNA sequences, most commonly between two copies of the same chromosome.

B. At the site of exchange, a strand of one DNA molecule has become base-paired to a strand of the second DNA molecule to create a ____________ between the two double helices.

C. Two single-stranded, complementary DNA molecules come together to form a fully double-stranded helix by ____________, which is thought to start with a slow ____________ step.

D. The ____________ is required for chromosome pairing in *E. coli*; it binds to single-stranded DNA and promotes its pairing with homologous, double-stranded DNA.

E. Once synapsis has occurred, the short heteroduplex region where the strands from two different DNA molecules have begun to pair is enlarged through a reaction called ____________.

F. A central intermediate in general recombination is the ______, which is also called a ______, after its discoverer.
G. Occasionally during recombination between two slightly different copies of the same gene (alleles), one allele is replaced by the other in a process known as ______.
H. Mobile DNA sequences and some viruses enter and leave a target chromosome by ______ genetic recombination.

5–30 Indicate whether the following statements are true or false. If a statement is false, explain why.

__ A. General recombination requires long regions of homologous DNA on both partners in the exchange, whereas site-specific recombination requires only short, specific nucleotide sequences, which in some cases need be present on only one of the exchanging partners.

__ B. General recombination involves the physical exchange of DNA segments, which entails the breaking and rejoining of phosphodiester bonds in the DNA backbone.

__ C. The recA protein combines a site-specific, single-strand nicking activity with an ATP-dependent DNA helicase function that can unravel single-stranded "whiskers" off a duplex DNA molecule.

__ D. The SSB protein of *E. coli* melts out short hairpin helices in single strands by binding to the sugar-phosphate backbone and holding the bases in an exposed position.

__ E. The recA protein binds both single-stranded and double-stranded DNA so that it can catalyze synapsis between them.

__ F. The cross-strand exchange contains two distinct pairs of strands (crossing strands and noncrossing strands), which cannot be interconverted without breaking the phosphodiester backbone of at least one strand.

__ G. Gene conversion is the process whereby fungi occasionally change sex; normally, equal numbers of male and female spores are produced by a mating event, but occasionally the ratio is 1:3 or 3:1.

__ H. All known mechanisms of gene conversion require a limited amount of DNA synthesis.

__ I. The integration of the lambda genome into the *E. coli* genome is catalyzed by a site-specific topoisomerase (called lambda integrase), which recognizes short, specific DNA sequences on both chromosomes.

5–31 Using Figure 5–23A as a guide, draw the products of a crossover recombination event between the homologous regions of the molecules represented in Figure 5–23B. In the figure the DNA duplex is represented schematically by a single line and the targets for homologous recombination are represented by the arrows.

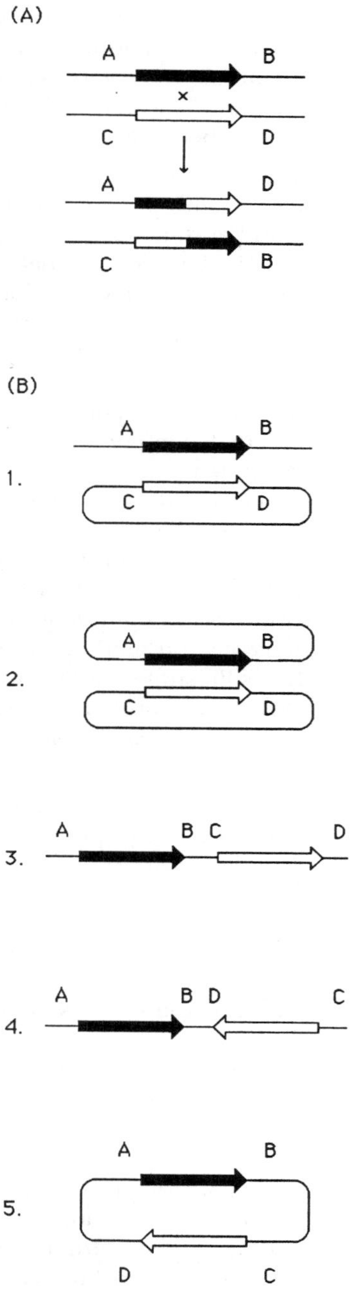

Figure 5–23 A variety of recombination substrates (Problem 5–31).

***5–32** Specific DNA sequences, known as Chi sites, locally stimulate recBCD-mediated homologous recombination in *E. coli*. Presumably, interaction between the recBCD protein and the Chi site stimulates a rate-limiting step in the recombination pathway. To study this interaction in detail, recBCD was purified and incubated with a linear, double-stranded DNA fragment containing a Chi site (Figure 5–24).

Different samples of the linear DNA were first labeled specifically at the 5′ end on the left (5′L), at the 5′ end on the right (5′R), at the 3′ end on the left (3′L), and at the 3′ end on the right (3′R). Each sample was then incubated in a reaction buffer containing recBCD. As a control, a separate aliquot of labeled DNA was incubated in the reaction buffer without recBCD.

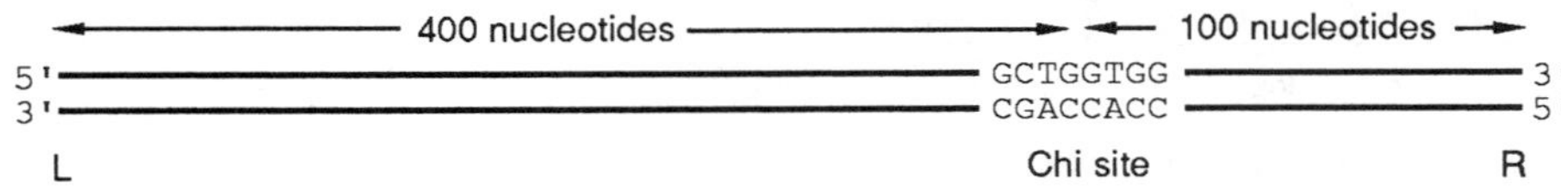

Figure 5–24 A linear DNA fragment containing a Chi site (Problem 5–32). The sequence of the Chi site is shown. L and R indicate the left and right ends of the fragment.

After 1 hour of reaction the DNA was denatured by boiling, and the resulting single strands were separated by electrophoresis through a polyacrylamide gel. The pattern of radioactively labeled DNA fragments is shown in Figure 5–25. As a further control, a sample of 3′R that had been incubated with recBCD was run on the gel without first denaturing it (Figure 5–25).

A. What is the evidence that recBCD cuts the DNA at the Chi site? Does it cut one or both strands? If you decide it cuts only one strand, specify the strand and indicate your reasoning.
B. What is the evidence that recBCD can act as a helicase; that is, that it can separate the strands of duplex DNA?
C. How might the action of recBCD stimulate homologous recombination in the neighborhood of a Chi site?

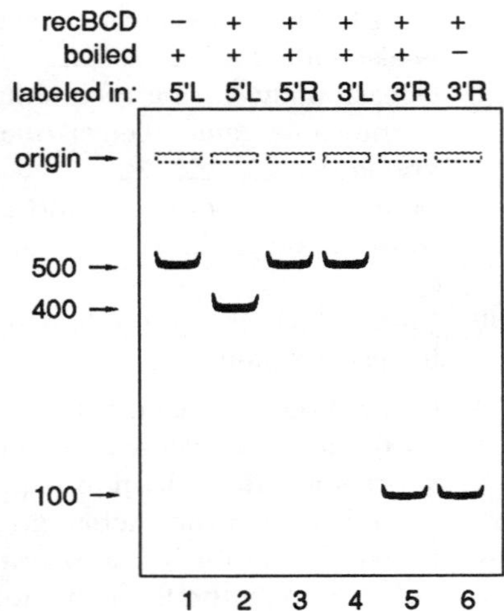

Figure 5–25 Results of incubating the recBCD protein with Chi-containing DNA fragments, which were labeled at the ends of defined strands (Problem 5–32). Numbers adjacent to bands indicate the length of the labeled fragment in nucleotides. All samples were denatured before electrophoresis, except the unboiled sample in lane 6.

5–33 Bacteriophage T4 encodes a single-stranded DNA binding protein (SSB protein) that is important for recombination and DNA replication. T4 mutants with a temperature-sensitive mutation in the gene that encodes the SSB protein rapidly cease recombination and DNA replication when the temperature is raised.

The T4 SSB protein is an elongated monomeric protein with a molecular weight of 35,000. It binds tightly to single-stranded, but not double-stranded, DNA. Binding saturates at a 1:12 weight ratio of DNA to protein. However, the binding of SSB protein to DNA shows a peculiar property that is illustrated in Figure 5–26. In the presence of excess single-stranded DNA (10 μg), virtually no binding is detectable at 0.5 μg SSB protein (Figure 5–26A), whereas almost quantitative binding is seen at 7.0 μg SSB protein (Figure 5–26B).

A. At saturation, what is the ratio of nucleotides of single-stranded DNA to molecules of SSB protein? (The average molecular weight of a single nucleotide is 330.)
B. At the point at which binding of SSB protein to DNA reaches saturation, are adjacent monomers of SSB protein likely to be in contact? Assume that a monomer of SSB protein extends for 12nm along the DNA upon binding and that the spacing of bases in single-stranded DNA after binding SSB protein is the same as in double-stranded DNA (that is, 10 nucleotides per 3.4 nm).
C. Why do you think that the binding of SSB protein to single-stranded DNA depends so strongly on the amount of SSB protein, as shown in Figure 5–26?

***5–34** The recA protein catalyzes both the initial pairing step of recombination and subsequent branch migration in *E. coli.* It promotes recombination by binding to single-stranded DNA and catalyzing the pairing of such coated single strands to homologous double-stranded DNA. One assay for the action of recA is the formation of double-stranded DNA circles from a

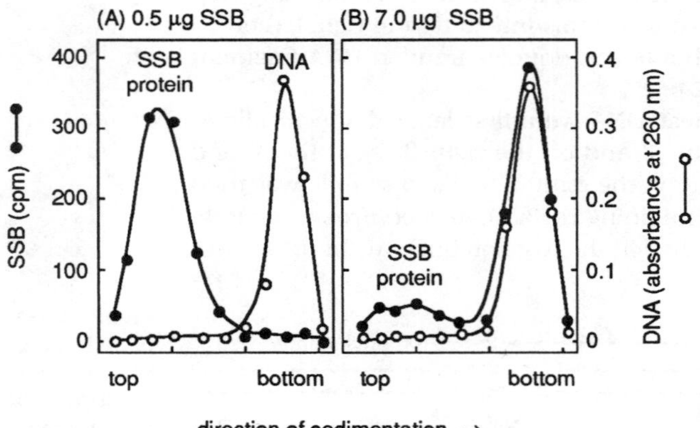

Figure 5–26 Binding of T4 SSB protein to single-stranded DNA (Problem 5–33). The binding of SSB protein to DNA was analyzed by centrifugation through sucrose gradients, on which the much more massive DNA sediments more rapidly than protein and is consequently found closer to the bottom of the gradient.

mixture of double-stranded linears and homologous single-stranded circles, as illustrated in Figure 5–27. This reaction proceeds in two steps: circles pair with linears at an end and then branch migrate until a single-stranded linear DNA is displaced.

One important question about the recA reaction is whether branch migration is directional. This question has been studied in the following way. Single-stranded circles, which were uniformly labeled with ^{32}P, were mixed with unlabeled double-stranded linears in the presence of recA. As the single-stranded DNA pairs with the linear DNA, it becomes sensitive to cutting by restriction enzymes, which do not cut single-stranded DNA. By sampling the reaction at various times, digesting the DNA with a restriction enzyme, and separating the labeled fragments by electrophoresis, you obtain the pattern shown in Figure 5–28.

A. By comparing the time of appearance of labeled fragments with the restriction map of the circular DNA in Figure 5–28, deduce which end (5′ or 3′) of the (−) strand of the linear DNA the circular (+) strand invades. Also deduce the direction of branch migration along the (−) strand. (The linear double-stranded DNA was cut at the boundary between fragments a and c on the restriction map.)

B. Calculate the rate of branch migration, given that the length of this DNA is 7 kb.

C. What would you expect to happen if the double-stranded linear DNA carried an insertion of 500 nonhomologous nucleotides between restriction fragments e and a?

5–35 Two homologous parental duplexes and two sets of potential recombination products are illustrated in Figure 5–29. Diagram a Holliday junction between the parental duplexes that could generate the indicated recombination products. Label the left end of each strand in the Holliday junction 5′ or 3′ so that the relationship to the parental and recombinant duplexes is clear. Indicate which strands need to be cut to generate each set of recombination products. Finally, draw the recombinants as they would look after one round of replication.

***5–36** When plasmid DNA is extracted from *E. coli* and examined under the electron microscope, the majority of the plasmids are monomeric circles, but there are a variety of other forms, including dimeric and trimeric circles. In addition, about 1% of the molecules appear as figure-8 forms, in which the two loops are equal (Figure 5–30A).

You suspect that the figure 8s are recombination intermediates in the formation of a dimer from two monomers (or two monomers from a dimer).

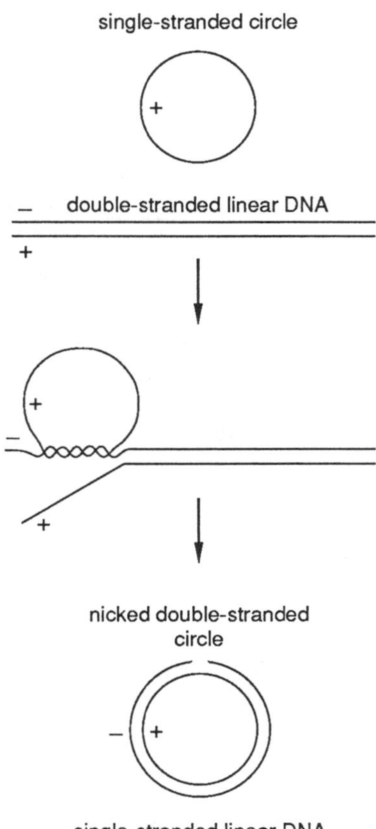

Figure 5–27 Strand assimilation assay for the recA protein (Problem 5–34). The single-stranded circle (+) is complementary to the (−) strand of the linear duplex and identical to the (+) strand of the duplex.

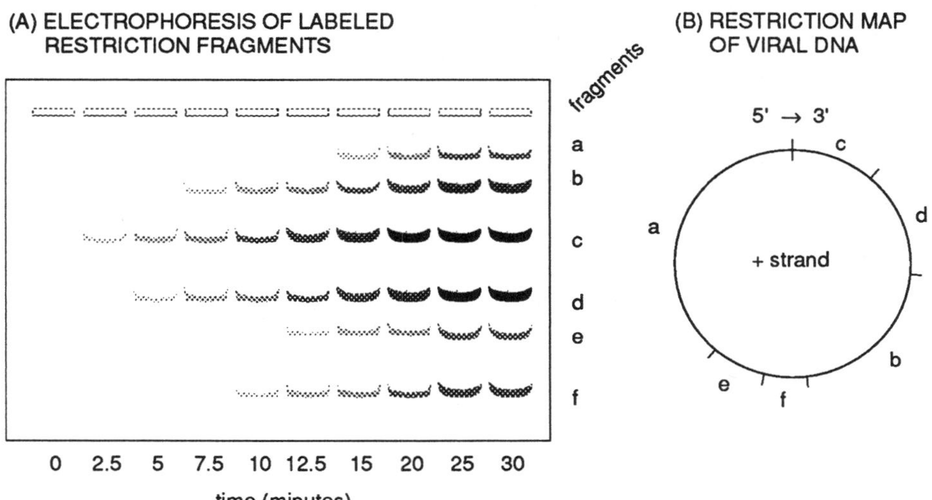

Figure 5–28 Electrophoretic separation (A) of labeled restriction fragments as a function of time of incubation with recA (Problem 5–34). The restriction map (B) is shown for reference on the circle; clockwise around the circle is the 5′-to-3′ direction.

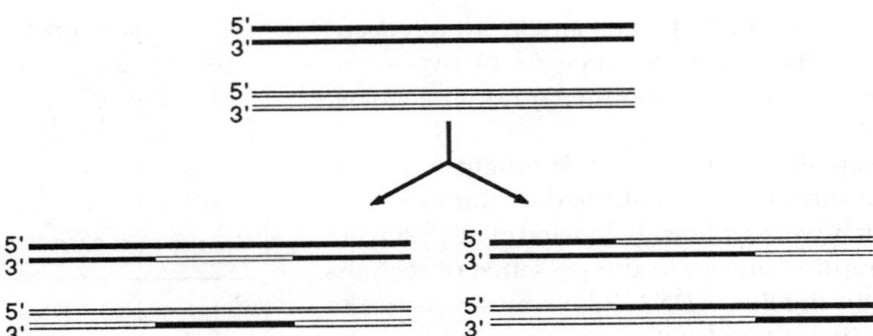

Figure 5–29 Parental and recombinant duplexes (Problem 5–35).

However, to rule out the possibility that they represent twisted dimers or touching monomers, you cut the DNA sample with a restriction enzyme, which cuts at a single site in the monomer, and then examine the molecules. After cutting, only two forms are seen: 99% of the DNA molecules are linear monomers, and 1% are χ forms (Figure 5–30B). You note that the χ forms have an interesting property: the two longer arms are the same length, as are the two shorter arms. In addition, the sum of the lengths of a long arm and a short arm is equal to the length of the monomer plasmid. However, the position of the crossover point is completely random.

Unsure of yourself and feeling you are probably missing some hidden artifact, you show your pictures to a friend. She points out that your observations prove you are looking at recombination intermediates, which arose by random pairing at homologous sites.

A. Is your friend correct? What is her thinking?
B. How would your observations differ if you repeated your experiments in a strain of *E. coli* that carried a nonfunctional *recA* gene?
C. What would the χ forms have looked like if the figure 8s were intermediates in a site-specific recombination between the monomers?
D. What would the χ forms have looked like if the figure 8s were intermediates in a totally random, nonhomologous recombination between the monomers?

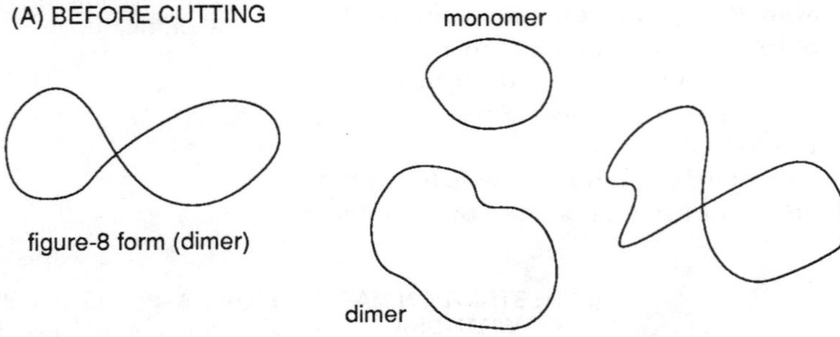

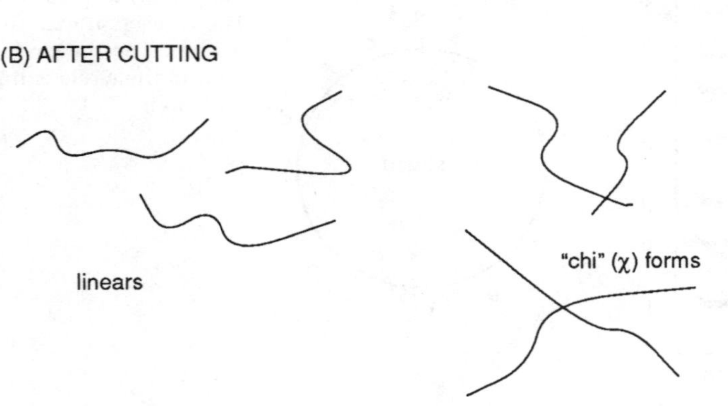

Figure 5–30 Plasmid molecules observed (A) before digestion with a single-cut restriction enzyme and (B) after digestion (Problem 5–36).

Viruses, Plasmids, and Transposable Genetic Elements (MBOC 248–258)

5–37 Fill in the blanks in the following statements.

A. The viruses that infect bacteria are called ____________.

B. Virus multiplication is lethal, if the host cell must break open (________) to allow the progeny virus to escape.

C. The protein shell that surrounds a viral genome is called the ________.

D. The outermost shell of ____________ viruses is a typical membrane that is usually acquired in the process of budding from the plasma membrane.

E. Since normal cells do not have enzymes that copy RNA into RNA, viruses with RNA genomes must encode an ____________ or ____________ to replicate.

F. If the viral RNA serves directly as mRNA, the virus is called a ________ virus; if the complement of the viral RNA serves as mRNA, the virus is called a ____________ virus.

G. ____________ bacteria carry a dormant but potentially active viral genome in their chromosomes: The integrated viral genome is known as the ____________, a term that also is used to describe analogous viral genomes present in mammalian cells.

H. Viruses that can integrate their DNA into bacterial chromosomes are known as ____________.

I. Animal cells that do not support the lytic infection of DNA viruses are called ____________ cells.

J. Animal cells that have been converted from their normal state to a cancerous one by a viral infection are said to have undergone a virus-mediated ____________.

K. The enzyme ____________, which transcribes RNA chains into complementary DNA molecules, accounts for the permanent genetic changes caused by ____________.

L. ____________ move from place to place in the host genome using their own site-specific recombination enzymes, known as ____________.

M. The yeast Ty1 element is an example of a ____________, whose transposition requires the synthesis of a complete RNA transcript, which is then copied into a DNA double helix and subsequently is integrated into a new chromosomal location.

N. Independently replicating elements, called ____________, can replicate indefinitely outside the host chromosome.

O. ____________, which are disease agents in plants, are small, single-stranded, circular RNA molecules that do not code for any protein.

P. Viruses occasionally pick up DNA sequences from one host cell and transfer them to another in a process called DNA ____________. (This process should not be confused with DNA transfection, in which naked DNA is introduced into a cell.)

5–38 Indicate whether the following statements are true or false. If a statement is false, explain why.

__ A. Since bacteriophage T4 encodes at least 30 different enzymes involved in genome replication and transcription, it is completely independent of the host DNA and RNA polymerases, though it must, of course, rely on the host protein synthesis machinery.

__ B. Small DNA viruses such as SV40 and ϕX174 rely entirely on the host replicative machinery to replicate their DNA.

__ C. Negative-strand viruses do not contain genes that code for proteins.

__ D. Adenovirus has proteins covalently attached to the 5′ ends of its genome that act as primers for initiation of replication, thereby allowing the ends of the linear genome to be fully replicated.

___ E. When bacteriophage lambda infects a suitable *E. coli* host cell, it usually carries out a lytic infection, releasing several hundred progeny viruses; more rarely, it integrates into the host chromosome, producing a lysogenic bacterium carrying the proviral lambda chromosome.

___ F. Infection by retroviruses often leads simultaneously to the nonlethal release of progeny virus and a permanent genetic change in the infected cell that makes it cancerous.

___ G. Viruses that reproduce by budding through their host cell membranes cause cancer by the changes that budding makes to the cell surface.

___ H. One simple way to classify a new virus as an RNA or DNA virus is to see whether its growth is inhibited by actinomycin D, which blocks DNA-dependent RNA synthesis but not RNA-dependent replicases: if viral growth is inhibited by actinomycin D, it must be a DNA virus.

___ I. Transposases recognize sufficiently extensive sequences surrounding the integration sites so that the transposon does not become integrated into the middle of a gene, for gene disruption could be lethal to the cell.

___ J. The capacity of plasmids to replicate indefinitely without being part of a host chromosome distinguishes them from transposable elements.

___ K. Large viruses are more likely than small viruses to have overlapping genes because they have so many more genes.

___ L. Viroids are unusual because they encode no proteins and yet are able to replicate and to cause severe diseases in plants.

5–39 The one-step growth curve, which measures the increase in virus number during a single cycle of infection, was extremely important for defining the basic parameters of the interactions of phages with bacteria. Consider the following one-step growth curve with bacteriophage T4.

A small sample (0.1 ml) of a T4 phage suspension (10^{10} phage/ml) was mixed with a 100-ml culture of *E. coli* (10^7 bacteria/ml) and incubated at 37°C. At 5-minute intervals after mixing, duplicate samples of the infected bacteria were shaken with chloroform to kill the bacteria. One sample was treated with the enzyme lysozyme to break open the bacteria; the other was not treated. Neither chloroform nor lysozyme kills T4. The concentration (titer) of phages in all samples was measured, with the results shown in Figure 5–31.

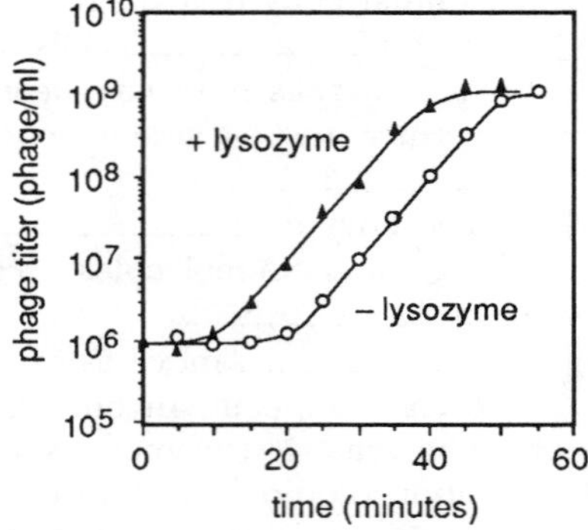

Figure 5–31 One-step growth curve of bacteriophage T4 (Problem 5–39).

A. What was the initial titer of T4 immediately after it was mixed with the bacterial culture?

B. Why is the phage titer at 5 minutes less than it was initially?

C. Explain why the phage titer rises more slowly in the samples that were not treated with lysozyme but ultimately reaches the same level as the lysozyme-treated samples.

D. Calculate how many phages were produced on average per infected bacterium.

***5–40** Bacterial and viral infections are fundamentally different and demand different strategies for treatment. Antibacterial drugs kill bacterial cells selectively without harming the host. However, a virus subverts the host cell's metabolic machinery to its own needs. As a consequence, agents directed at cellular components would harm infected and uninfected cells alike. Successful treatment of viral infections requires drugs that selectively block virus-specific processes but do not damage normal host cells.

Acyclovir (acycloguanosine) is one example of a clinically useful antiviral drug; it is a potent inhibitor of the replication of herpesvirus. Acyclovir is phosphorylated to acyclo-GTP by the thymidine kinase encoded in the herpesvirus genome but not by the normal cellular thymidine kinase. Acyclo-GTP is then incorporated into the replicating viral DNA by the DNA polymerase encoded in the herpesvirus genome. Incorporation of acyclo-GTP blocks replication because it lacks the requisite 3′-OH needed for addition of the next nucleotide to the growing chain.

Acyclovir-resistant mutants of herpesvirus have been isolated from patients treated with acyclovir. Replication of these herpesvirus mutants is not affected by acyclovir. Propose two different explanations for how herpesvirus might mutate so as to become resistant to acyclovir.

5–41 When a small number of T4 phages is mixed with a large excess of *E. coli* strain B and spread in a thin layer of soft agar over the surface of a Petri dish containing a deep layer of nutrient agar, the bacteria grow up to form a continuous "lawn." However, in the places where a phage-infected bacterium happens to land, the phages multiply and kill the surrounding bacteria, causing the formation of a clear, round "plaque" in the cloudy lawn. One readily observable kind of virus mutation alters the plaque morphology. The "*r*" mutants of bacteriophage T4 were first noticed because they formed much larger plaques on lawns of *E. coli* B (*r* stands for rapid lysis). One class of *r* mutants, the r_{II} mutants, do not form plaques on *E. coli* strain K. Although they initiate an infection in *E. coli* K, the infection is abortive and progeny viruses do not form. Their distinctive plaque morphology on *E. coli* B and their inability to grow on *E. coli* K were elegantly exploited early on to define the general nature of genetic mutation and to elucidate the triplet structure of the genetic code.

As a practical introduction to these classical studies, you have been given 8 r_{II} mutants to characterize. First, you perform a set of spot tests. You infect one plate of *E. coli* K with a high concentration of mutant 1 and a second plate with a high concentration of mutant 2, so that many of the bacteria on each plate are infected. You then put a drop of each mutant and wild-type T4 in a ring around the plate. As a control, you spot the mutants and wild-type T4 on uninfected *E. coli* K. After overnight incubation you observe the results shown in Figure 5–32.

These results certainly appear meaningful, but you are still puzzled. To determine what kind of phage is present in the clear spots, you collect some of the phages from the wild-type spot and the clear spot formed by mutant 5 and test their growth. The phages from the wild-type spot form normal plaques on both *E. coli* B and *E. coli* K, as you expected. The majority of phages from the mutant-5 spot still behave as mutants: they form *r* plaques on *E. coli* B but do not grow on *E. coli* K. However, some of the phages from the mutant-5 spot appear to be wild type: they form normal plaques on both strains. The frequency of wild-type phages is too high to arise from back mutation (reversion), which does occur, but only at a frequency of 10^{-5} to 10^{-6}.

A. Why do some mixtures of mutant phages grow in the spot test and others do not?
B. What pattern of growth would you expect if you repeated the spot test using *E. coli* K infected with mutant 3?
C. How did the small fraction of wild-type T4 arise in the clear spot formed by mutant 5?

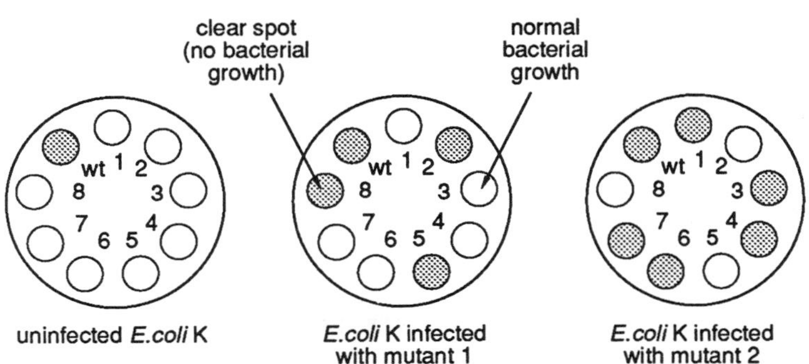

Figure 5–32 Spot tests with various r_{II} mutants (Problem 5–41).

Table 5–2 Characteristics of Three RNA Viruses (Problem 5–42)

	Protein Synthesis	Endogenous Polymerase	
		RNA	DNA
Virus 1	–	+	–
Virus 2	+	–	–
Virus 3	+	–	+

*5–42 You have isolated three different viruses from animal cells. Each one contains a single-stranded RNA as its genome. To characterize them, you test them in two ways. First, you purify their RNA genomes and measure their abilities to serve as mRNA for cell-free protein synthesis. Second, you measure their endogenous polymerase activities by gently disrupting the intact viruses and then incubating them either with radioactive ribonucleoside triphosphates (NTPs) to check for RNA synthesis or radioactive deoxyribonucleoside triphosphates (dNTPs) to check for DNA synthesis. The results are shown in Table 5–2. From these results, briefly outline a life cycle for each virus, and give an example of a known virus with the same life cycle.

5–43 When retroviruses infect cells, their linear RNA genome is copied into a linear, double-stranded DNA by the viral enzyme reverse transcriptase. This linear DNA contains the viral genes "sandwiched" between two direct repeats, known as long terminal repeats or LTRs (Figure 5–33). The linear DNA can circularize by homologous recombination between the LTRs, forming a circle containing one LTR, or, alternatively, it can circularize by ligation of the ends, forming a circle that contains two LTRs. Some form of the extrachromosomal DNA integrates into the chromosome. This leads to the typical integrated form of the virus, which always contains two LTRs, one on either side of the viral genes.

Although the precise mechanism of integration is not known, deletion of the sequences at the ends of the LTRs prevents integration, indicating that at least part of the LTR structure is essential. Since there are three forms of unintegrated DNA, any or all of them could be the precursor to the integrated form. To define the precursor, three different retroviral genomes were used to infect cells. These genomes are shown as linear DNA in Figure 5–34: A is the normal genome, B is a genome with one internal LTR, and C is a genome with two internal LTRs that are ligated end-to-end.

After infection with each genome, the populations of cells containing integrated viral genomes were analyzed. Chromosomal DNA was prepared from the three cell populations and digested with diagnostic restriction enzymes, which cleave the viral DNA as indicated in Figure 5–34. The resulting DNA fragments were separated by gel electrophoresis, and fragments containing retroviral DNA were visualized by hybridization to a la-

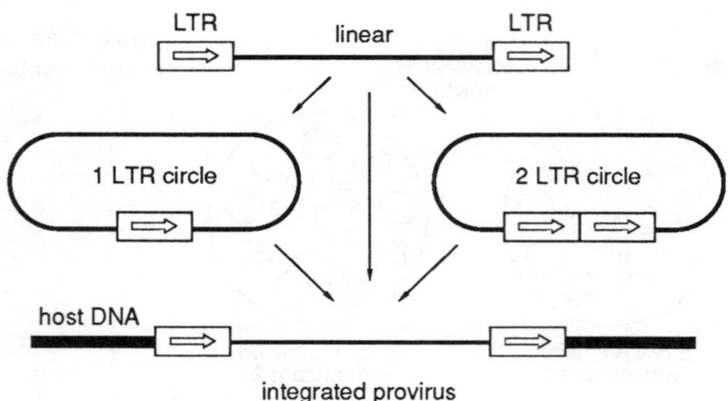

Figure 5–33 Various forms of retroviral DNA in infected cells (Problem 5–43).

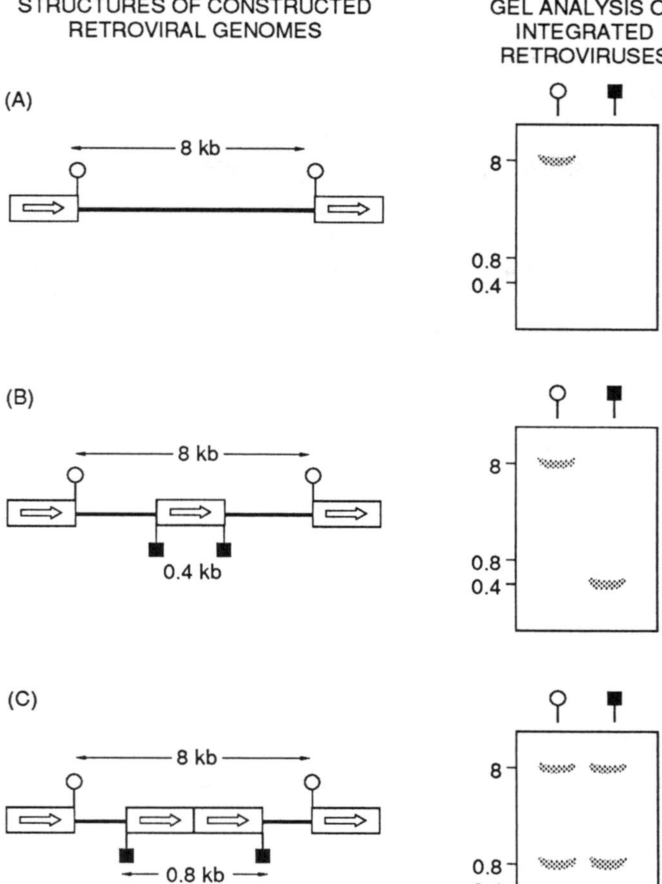

Figure 5–34 Structures of constructed retroviral genomes and analysis of the integrated forms of the genome after infection (Problem 5–43). Diagnostic restriction sites are indicated by circles and squares. Numbers refer to the lengths of DNA segments (in kb).

beled probe specific for retroviral sequences. The results are shown at the right in Figure 5–34. For clarity, fragments that contain cellular DNA in addition to retroviral sequences are not shown.

From these results, deduce the structure of the precursor to the integrated form of the virus, and state your reasoning.

5–44 You are studying the procaryotic transposon Tn10 and have just figured out an elegant way to determine whether Tn10 replicates during transposition or moves directly without intervening DNA replication. Your idea is based on the key difference between these two mechanisms: both parental strands of the Tn10 will move if transposition is nonreplicative, whereas only one parental strand will move if transposition is replicative (Figure 5–35). You plan to mark the individual strands by annealing strands from

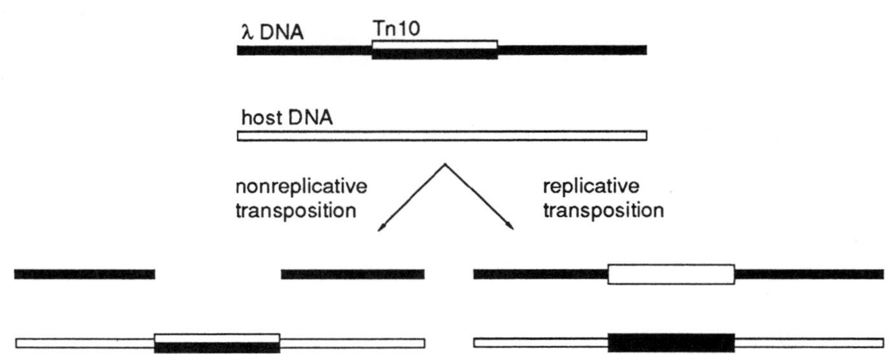

Figure 5–35 Replicative and nonreplicative transposition of a transposable element (Problem 5–44). The transposable element is shown as a heteroduplex, which is composed of two genetically different strands—one black and one white. During replicative transposition, one strand stays with the donor DNA and one strand is transferred to the recipient DNA. In nonreplicative transposition, the transposable element is cut out of the donor DNA and transferred entirely to the recipient DNA.

two different Tn10s. To deliver these heteroduplex Tn10s efficiently into bacteria, you use Tn10-containing bacteriophage lambda DNA, which can be manipulated *in vitro* and then packaged into capsids to make infectious phage. You make sure to use a phage genome that is inactive due to other mutations, so that it cannot replicate or integrate and is ultimately destroyed; thus, the contribution of the phage genome can be ignored.

Your phage DNA carries slightly different versions of Tn10 inserted at the same site. Both Tn10s contain a gene for tetracycline resistance and a gene for lactose metabolism (*lacZ*), but in one, the *lacZ* gene is inactivated by a mutation. This difference provides a convenient way to follow the two Tn10s since *lacZ*$^+$ bacterial colonies (when incubated with an appropriate substrate) turn blue, but *lacZ*$^-$ colonies remain white. You denature and reanneal a mixture of the two bacteriophage DNAs, which produces an equal mixture of heteroduplexes and homoduplexes (Figure 5–36). You then package the mixture into phage capsids, infect *lacZ*$^-$ bacteria, and spread the infected bacteria onto Petri dishes that contain tetracycline and the color-generating substrate.

Once the phage DNA is inside a bacterium, the transposon will move (at very low frequency) into the bacterial genome, where it confers tetracycline resistance on the bacterium. The rare bacterium that gains a Tn10 survives the selective conditions and forms a colony. When you score a large number of such colonies, you find that roughly 25% are white, 25% are blue, and 50% are mixed with one blue sector and one white sector.

A. Explain the source of each kind of bacterial colony and decide whether the results support a replicative or a nonreplicative mechanism of Tn10 transposition.
B. You performed these experiments using a recipient strain of bacteria that was incapable of repairing mismatches in DNA. How would the results differ if you used a bacterial strain that could repair mismatches?
C. Integration of bacteriophage lambda DNA into a bacterial genome by site-specific recombination occurs much more frequently than does transposition. How would the results differ if you used a mutant of bacteriophage lambda that could not replicate but could integrate?

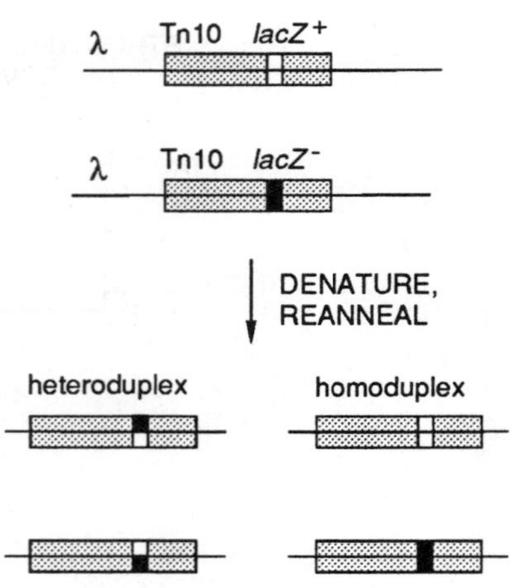

Figure 5–36 Formation of a mixture of heteroduplexes and homoduplexes by denaturing and reannealing two different Tn10-containing bacteriophage lambda genomes (Problem 5–44). The phage DNA is shown as a thin line, and Tn10 is shown as a box. The mutational difference between the two Tn10s is indicated by the black and white segments.

***5–45** Bacteriophage ϕX174 shows an astonishing economy in the use of its limited coding capacity. It makes only a single mRNA. Yet one particular stretch of DNA encodes four completely different proteins that overlap as illustrated in Figure 5–37.

A. Which, if any, of the overlapping genes are translated left to right in Figure 5–37?
B. Which, if any, of the genes are translated in the same reading frame?
C. A mutation at a particular tyrosine codon (TAC) in the gene for protein K gives rise to a stop codon (TAG). This mutation is accompanied by a glutamine (CAA) to glutamic acid (GAA) change in protein B. What is the mutational change in protein A? In protein C?

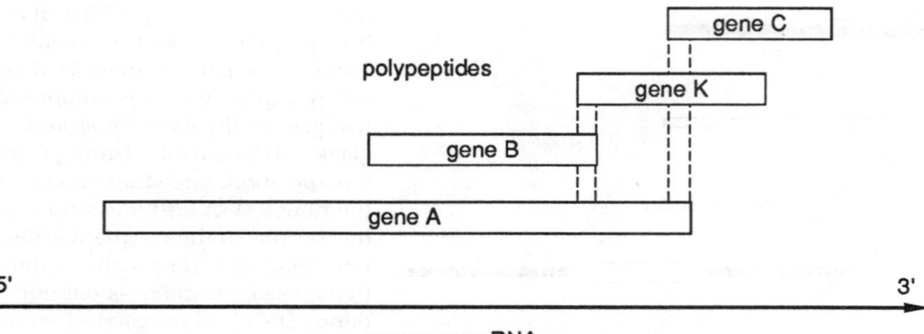

Figure 5–37 Four overlapping genes in ϕX174 along with the associated mRNA (Problem 5–45). Dashed lines indicate the two regions where three genes overlap.

DNA Cloning and Genetic Engineering (MBOC 258–271)

5–46 Fill in the blanks in the following statements.

A. ___________, which cut double-helical DNA helix at specific sequences of four to eight nucleotides, produce DNA fragments of strictly defined sizes that are known as ___________.

B. Eucaryotic DNA fragments can be inserted into specially adapted bacterial viruses or plasmids, known as ___________, in order to amplify and thus purify particular genes of interest.

C. A colony of cells derived from a single ancestor is called a ___________ of cells.

D. A single colony of bacteria that harbors a plasmid containing a fragment of human DNA is referred to as a ___________; the entire collection of such bacteria would constitute a ___________.

E. Eucaryotic mRNA, after being copied into double-stranded DNA using reverse transcriptase, can be inserted into cloning vectors to generate a ___________, which can be probed to find individual clones corresponding to particular mRNAs.

F. If two closely related cell types are available from an organism, only one of which produces the protein or proteins of interest, ___________ can be used to enrich for particular nucleotide sequences prior to cDNA cloning.

G. The use of overlapping clones to move from a known gene to a nearby gene is a technique known as ___________.

H. To determine whether a particular clone contains DNA that encodes a previously characterized protein, one often employs ___________, in which the cloned DNA is used to capture the corresponding mRNA, whose translation product can then be compared to the known protein.

I. Plasmids or viruses with strong regulatable promoters positioned so that the product of a cloned gene can be made in large amounts are called ___________ vectors.

J. A novel hybrid gene that encodes a ___________ can be produced by joining portions of the coding sequences of two different genes.

K. ___________ mice have chromosomes in their germ line cells that have been permanently altered by integration of cloned DNA.

L. Purified DNA polymerases and synthetic DNA oligonucleotides can be used to amplify selected regions of the genome in a technique known as ___________.

5–47 Indicate whether the following statements are true or false. If a statement is false, explain why.

___ A. Not all restriction nucleases produce staggered cuts in DNA.

___ B. Plasmid cloning vectors should be small, contain unique restriction sites to accept foreign DNA, have their own DNA replication origin, and have a gene that confers resistance to some antibiotic.

___ C. cDNA libraries contain only those sequences that were expressed in the tissue from which the original mRNA was prepared, whereas genomic DNA libraries contain a random sample of all the sequences present in the whole organism.

___ D. One can deduce the amino acid sequence of a eucaryotic protein equally well from a cDNA clone or a genomic clone.

___ E. Particular types of rare mRNA can be purified by immunoprecipitation of polysomes, using a specific antibody against ribosomes.

___ F. Subtractive hybridization is a way of enriching for mRNAs that are present in one cell type but absent in another cell type in the same species.

___ G. To produce large amounts of a eucaryotic protein in bacteria, a genomic clone that contains the entire gene is placed in an expression vector with a strong regulatable promoter.

___ H. Transgenic animals can be produced by microinjecting DNA into a somatic cell nucleus where it can integrate into a chromosome and thus be retained and expressed in subsequent cell generations.

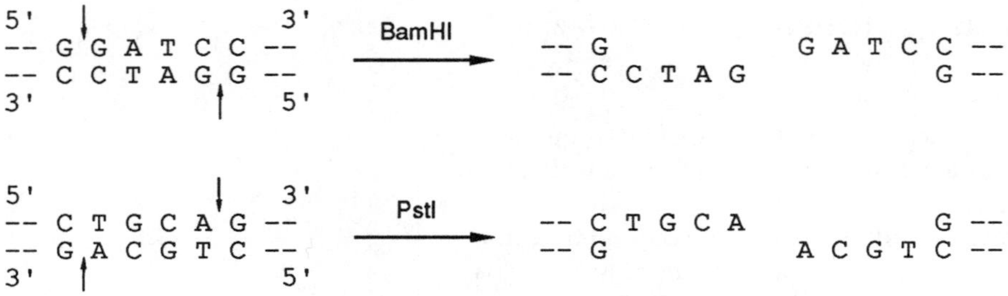

```
5'  |         3'      BamHI
-- G'G A T C C --   --------->   -- G                 G A T C C --
-- C C T A G,G --                -- C C T A G                 G --
3'          |  5'

5'          |  3'     PstI
-- C T G C A'G --   --------->   -- C T G C A                 G --
-- G,A C G T C --                -- G                 A C G T C --
3'  |          5'
```

Figure 5–38 Cleavage at BamHI and PstI recognition sequences (Problem 5–48). Only the nucleotides that form the recognition sites are shown.

5–48 The restriction enzymes BamHI and PstI cut their recognition sequences as shown in Figure 5–38.

A. Indicate the 5′ and 3′ ends of the cut DNA molecules.

B. How would the ends be modified if you incubated the cut molecules with DNA polymerase in the presence of all four dNTPs?

C. After the reaction in part B, could you still join the BamHI ends together by incubation with T4 DNA ligase? Could you still join the PstI ends together? (T4 DNA ligase will join blunt ends together as well as cohesive ends.)

D. Will joining of the ends in part C regenerate the BamHI site? Will it regenerate the PstI site?

***5–49** The restriction enzyme Sau3A recognizes the sequence -GATC- and cleaves on the 5′ side (to the left) of the G. (Since the top and bottom strands of most restriction sites read the same in the 5′ to 3′ direction, only one strand of the site needs to be shown.) The single-stranded ends produced by Sau3A cleavage are identical to those produced by BamHI cleavage (see Figure 5–38), allowing the two types of ends to be joined together by incubation with DNA ligase. (You may find it helpful to draw out the product of this ligation to convince yourself that it is true.)

A. What fraction of BamHI sites can be cut with Sau3A? What fraction of Sau3A sites can be cut with BamHI?

B. If two BamHI ends are ligated together, the resulting site can be cleaved again by BamHI. The same is true for two Sau3A ends. However, suppose you ligate a Sau3A end to a BamHI end. Can the hybrid site be cut with Sau3A? With BamHI?

C. What will be the average size of DNA fragments produced by digestion of chomosomal DNA with Sau3A? With BamHI?

5–50 You have purified two DNA fragments, which were generated by BamHI digestion of recombinant DNA plasmids. One fragment is 400 nucleotide pairs, and the other is 900 nucleotide pairs. You want to join them together as shown in Figure 5–39 to create a hybrid gene, which, if your speculations are right, will have amazing new properties.

You mix the two fragments together in the presence of DNA ligase and incubate them. After 30 minutes and again after 8 hours, you remove samples and analyze them by gel electrophoresis. You are surprised to find a complex pattern of fragments instead of the 1.3-kb recombinant molecule of interest (Figure 5–40A). You notice that with longer incubation the smaller fragments diminish in intensity and the larger ones increase in intensity. If you cut the ligated mixture wih BamHI, you regenerate the starting fragments (Figure 5–40A).

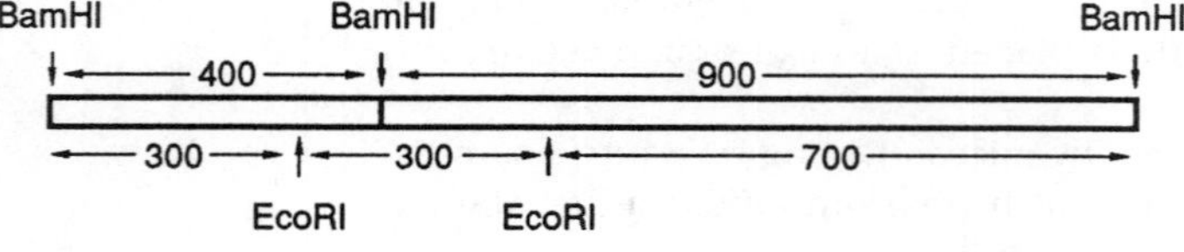

Figure 5–39 Final structure of hybrid gene (Problem 5–50).

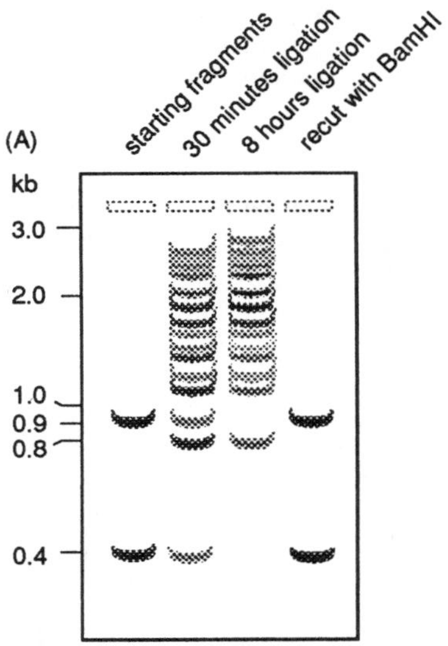

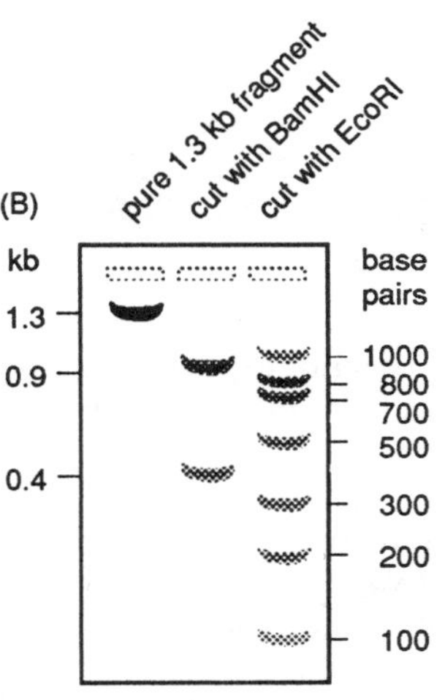

Figure 5–40 Ligation of pure DNA fragments (A) and diagnostic digestion of the purified 1.3-kb fragment (B) (Problem 5–50).

Puzzled, but undaunted, you purify the 1.3-kb fragment from the gel and check its structure by digesting a sample of it with BamHI. As expected, the original two bands are regenerated (Figure 5–40B). Just to be sure it is the structure you want, however, you digest another sample with EcoRI. You expected this digestion to generate two fragments 300 nucleotides in length and one fragment 700 nucleotides in length. Once again you are surprised by the complexity of the gel pattern (Figure 5–40B).

A. Why are there so many bands in the original ligation mixture?

B. Why are so many fragments produced by EcoRI digestion of the pure 1.3-kb fragment?

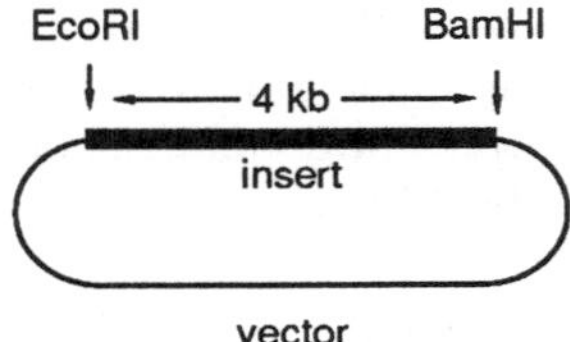

Figure 5–41 Recombinant plasmid containing a cloned DNA segment (Problem 5–51).

***5–51** You have cloned a 4-kb segment of an important gene into a plasmid vector (Figure 5–41) and now wish to prepare a restriction map of the gene in preparation for other DNA manipulations. Your adviser left instructions on how to do it, but she is now on vacation so you are on your own. You follow her instructions as outlined below.

1. Cut the plasmid with EcoRI.
2. Add a radioactive label to the EcoRI ends.
3. Cut the labeled DNA with BamHI.
4. Purify the insert away from the plasmid.
5. Digest the labeled insert briefly with a restriction enzyme so that on average each labeled molecule has been cut about one time.
6. Repeat step 5 for several different restriction enzymes.
7. Run the partially digested samples side-by-side on an agarose gel.
8. Place the gel against x-ray film so that fragments with a radioactive end can expose the film to produce an autoradiogram.
9. Draw the restriction map.

Your biggest problem thus far has been step 5; however, by decreasing the amounts of enzyme and lowering the temperature, you were able to find conditions for partial digestion. You have now completed step 8, and your autoradiogram is shown in Figure 5–42.

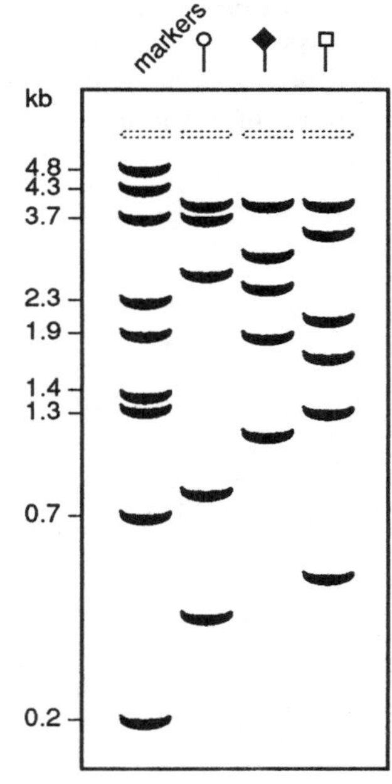

Figure 5–42 Autoradiogram showing the electrophoretic separation of the labeled fragments after partial digestion with the three restriction enzymes represented by the symbols (Problem 5–51). Numbers at the left indicate the sizes of a set of marker fragments (in kb).

```
        10         20         30
MFYWMIGRST EDWMPLYMKD FWAKHSLICE
```

Figure 5–43 The first 30 amino acids in your friend's protein-sequenator run. (Problem 5–52).

```
      L  R  D  P  Q  G  G  V  I
5' - CTTAGAGACCCGCAGGGCGGCGTCATC - 3'
```

Figure 5–44 Sequence of DNA and encoded protein (Problem 5–53).

Unfortunately, your adviser was not explicit about how to construct a map from the data in the autoradiogram. She is due back tomorrow. Will you figure it out in time?

***5–52** It's midnight. Your friend has awakened you with yet another grandiose scheme. He has spent the last two years purifying a potent modulator of the immune response. Tonight he got the first 30 amino acids from a protein-sequenator run (Figure 5–43). He wants your help in cloning the gene so it can be expressed at high levels in bacteria. He argues that this protein, by stimulating the immune system, could be the ultimate cure for the common cold. He's already picked out a trade name—Immustim.

Even though he gets carried away at times, he is your friend, and you are intrigued by this idea. You promise to call him back in 15 minutes as soon as you have checked out the protein sequence. What two sets of 20-nucleotide-long oligonucleotides will you recommend to your friend as the best hybridization probes for screening a genomic DNA library?

5–53 From previous work, you suspect that the glutamine (Q) in the protein segment in Figure 5–44 plays an important role at the active site. Your adviser wants you to alter the protein in three ways: change the glutamine to lysine (K), change the glutamine to glycine (G), and delete the glutamine from the protein. You plan to accomplish these mutational alterations by hybridizing an appropriate oligonucleotide to the M13 viral DNA, such that when the oligonucleotide is extended around the M13 circle by DNA polymerase, it will complete a strand that encodes the complement of the desired mutant protein. Design three 20-nucleotide-long oligonucleotides that could be hybridized to the cloned gene on single-stranded M13 viral DNA as the first step in effecting the mutational changes.

5–54 A particularly clear example of a dideoxy sequencing gel is shown in Figure 5–45. Try reading it. As read from the bottom of the gel to the top, the sequence corresponds to the mRNA for a protein. Can you find the open reading frame in this sequence?

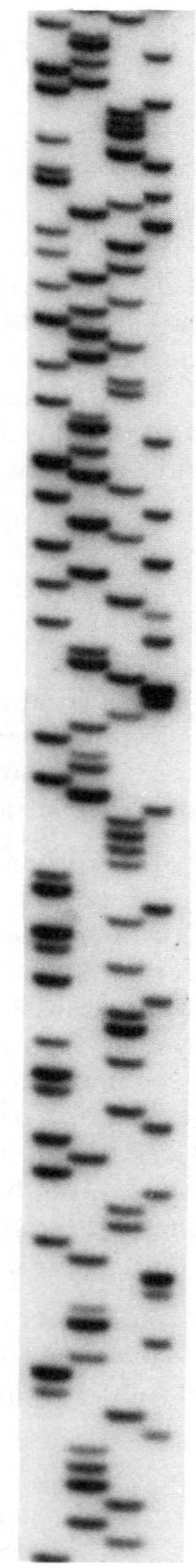

Figure 5–45 A dideoxy sequencing gel of a cloned DNA (Problem 5–54).

The Plasma Membrane

The Lipid Bilayer (MBOC 276–284)

6–1 Fill in the blanks in the following statements.

A. Lipid molecules in biological membranes are arranged as a continuous double layer called the ____________, which is about 5 nm thick.

B. The three major types of lipids found in cell membranes are called ____________, ____________, and ____________.

C. All the lipids found in membranes are said to be ____________ because they have one hydrophilic end and one hydrophobic end.

D. The hydrophilic end of a phospholipid consists of a ____________ head group, and the hydrophobic end contains two ____________ tails.

E. When amphipathic molecules are placed in an aqueous environment, they tend to aggregate so as to bury their hydrophobic ends and expose their hydrophilic ends to water, giving rise to two different kinds of structures, either spherical ____________ or planar ____________, with the hydrophobic tails sandwiched between the hydrophilic head groups.

F. Synthetic bilayers containing defined lipids or mixtures of lipids can be made either as spherical vesicles, called ____________, or as planar bilayers, called ____________ membranes.

G. The technique of electron spin-resonance spectroscopy, which is very useful for studying the movement of lipid molecules in biological membranes, requires that lipids be labeled with a ____________ such as a nitroxide radical.

H. Artificial lipid bilayers made from a single type of phospholipid change from a liquid state to a rigid crystalline state or vice versa at a characteristic temperature; this change of state is called a ____________.

I. Oligosaccharide-containing lipids called ____________ are found only in the outer half of the bilayer and their sugar groups are exposed at the cell surface.

J. The glycolipid ____________, which is the main neutral glycolipid in the multilayered membrane surrounding nerve axons (the ____________ sheath), may play an important role in the interaction between the axon and the cell that wraps the membrane around the axon.

K. Glycolipids that contain sialic acid are called ____________. One example is ____________, to which cholera toxin binds.

6–2 Indicate whether the following statements are true or false. If a statement is false, explain why.

__A. A lipid bilayer is the fundamental structural component of all cell membranes.

__B. Maintenance of the lipid bilayer in the plasma membrane requires special enzymes and the hydrolysis of ATP.

__C. Although lipid molecules are free to diffuse in the plane of the bilayer, they cannot flip-flop across the bilayer unless enzyme catalysts called phospholipid translocators are present in the membrane.

__D. The temperature at which a eucaryotic membrane "freezes" is determined solely by how much cholesterol it contains.

__E. Changes in membrane shape that require extreme compression or expansion of the two sides of the lipid bilayer are facilitated by a high cholesterol content because, unlike phospholipids, cholesterol can readily flip-flop between the two monolayers in response to such forces.

__F. Mutant eucaryotic cells that cannot synthesize cholesterol lyse when cholesterol is added to their culture medium.

__G. The phospholipid head groups on the outside of the cell carry a net positive charge because the choline head groups of phosphatidylcholine—$(CH_3)_3N^+CH_2CH_2OH$—are located predominantly in the outer monolayer.

__H. The cytoplasmic face of the red cell membrane carries a net negative charge because of the relative excess of phosphatidylserine present on this side of the bilayer.

__I. Glycolipids are never found on the cytoplasmic face of membranes in living cells.

6–3 A principal function of the plasma membrane is to control the entry of nutrients into the cell. This function is especially important for the epithelial cells that line the gut because they are responsible for absorbing virtually all the nutrients that enter the body. As befits this important role, their plasma membranes are specialized so that the surface facing the gut is folded into numerous fingerlike projections, termed microvilli. Microvilli increase the surface area of the intestinal cells, providing for more efficient absorption of nutrients. Microvilli are shown in profile and cross-section in Figure 6–1. From the dimensions given in the figure, estimate the increase in surface area that microvilli provide (for the portion of the plasma membrane in contact with the lumen of the gut) relative to the corresponding surface of a cell with a "flat" plasma membrane.

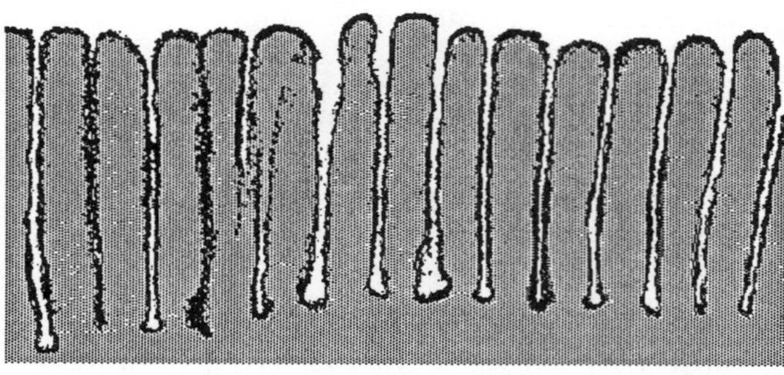

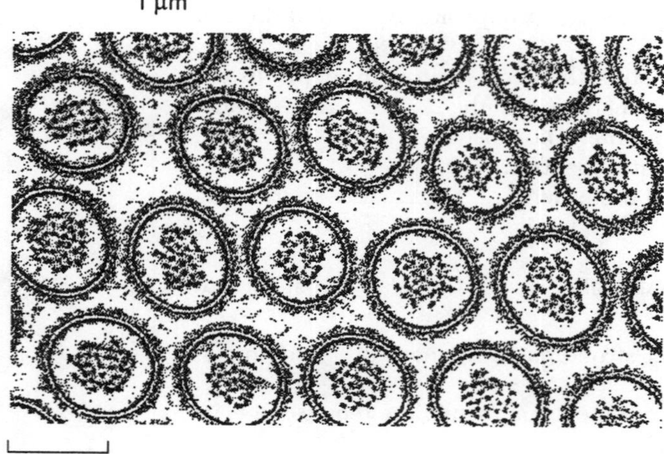

Figure 6–1 Microvilli of intestinal epithelial cells in profile and cross-section (Problem 6–3). (Courtesy of Dr. Ito and Dr. Ichikawa.)

***6–4** A friend of yours has just returned from a nearly disastrous African safari. While crossing the Limpopo River, he was bitten by a poisonous water snake and nearly died from extensive hemolysis. A true biologist at heart, your friend captured the snake before he passed out; he has asked you to analyze the venom to discover the basis of its hemolytic activity. You find that the venom contains a protease (which breaks peptide bonds in proteins), a neuraminidase (which removes sialic acid residues from gangliosides), and a phospholipase (which cleaves bonds in phospholipids). Treatment of isolated red blood cells with these purified activities gave the results shown in Table 6–1. Analysis of the products of hemolysis produced by phospholipase treatment showed an enormous increase in free phosphorylcholine (choline with a phosphate group attached) and diacylglycerol (glycerol with two fatty acid chains attached).

A. What is the substrate for the phospholipase, and where is it cleaved?
B. In light of what you know of the structure of the plasma membrane, explain why the phospholipase causes lysis of the red blood cells, but the protease and neuraminidase do not.

Table 6–1 Results of Treatment of Red Blood Cells with Enzymes Isolated from Snake Venom (Problem 6–4)

Purified Enzyme	Hemolysis
Protease	no
Neuraminidase	no
Phospholipase	yes

6–5 You wish to determine the distribution of the phospholipids in the plasma membrane of the human red blood cell. Phospholipids make up 60% of the lipids in the red cell bilayer, with cholesterol (30%) and glycolipids (10%) accounting for the rest. The phospholipids comprise phosphatidylcholine (28%), phosphatidylethanolamine (27%), sphingomyelin (26%), phosphatidylserine (13%), with the remaining few percent distributed among a variety of phospholipids. To measure the distribution of the individual phospholipids, you react intact red cells and red cell ghosts (1) with two different phospholipases and (2) with a membrane-impermeant fluorescent reagent, abbreviated SITS, which specifically labels primary amine groups.

Treatment with sphingomyelinase degrades up to 85% of the sphingomyelin in intact red cells (without causing lysis) and slightly more in red cell ghosts. The phospholipases in sea snake venom release only phosphatidylcholine breakdown products from intact cells (without causing lysis) but in red cell ghosts they degrade phosphatidylserine and phosphatidylethanoamine as well. SITS labels phosphatidylethanolamine and phosphatidylserine almost to completion in red cell ghosts but reacts less than 1% as well with intact red blood cells.

A. From these results, which are summarized in Table 6–2, deduce the distribution of the four principal phospholipids in red cell membranes. Which of the phospholipids, if any, are located in both monolayers of the membrane?
B. Why did you use red blood cells for these experiments?

***6–6** The behavior of lipids in the two monolayers of a membrane can be studied conveniently by labeling individual molecules with nitroxide groups, which are stable organic free radicals (Figure 6–2). Such spin-labeled lipids can be detected by electron spin-resonance (ESR) spectroscopy, a technique that does not disturb living cells. To introduce spin-labeled lipids into cell membranes, one first sonicates a mixture of labeled and unlabeled phospholipids

Table 6–2 Sensitivity of Phospholipids in Human Red Cells and Red Cell Ghosts to Phospholipases and a Membrane-impermeant Label (Problem 6–5)

	Sphingomyelinase		Sea Snake Venom		SITS Fluorescence	
Phospholipid	**Red Cells**	**Ghosts**	**Red Cells**	**Ghosts**	**Red Cells**	**Ghosts**
Phosphatidylcholine	–	–	+	+	–	–
Phosphatidylethanolamine	–	–	–	+	–	+
Sphingomyelin	+	+	–	–	–	–
Phosphatidylserine	–	–	–	+	–	+

*Problems with an asterisk (*) are answered in the Instructor's Manual.

to prepare small lipid vesicles. When these vesicles are added to intact cells under appropriate conditions, they fuse with the cell, thereby transferring the labeled lipids into the plasma membrane.

The two spin-labeled phospholipids shown in Figure 6–2 were incorporated into intact human red cell membranes in this way. To determine whether they were introduced equally into the two monolayers of the bilayer, ascorbic acid (vitamin C), which is a water-soluble reducing agent that does not cross membranes, was added to the medium to destroy any nitroxide radicals exposed on the outside of the cell. The ESR signal was followed as a function of time in the presence and absence of ascorbic acid as indicated in Figure 6–3.

A. Ignoring for the moment the difference in extent of loss of ESR signal, offer an explanation for why phospholipid 1 (Figure 6–3A) reacts faster with ascorbate than does phospholipid 2 (Figure 6–3B). Note that phospholipid 1 reaches a plateau in about 15 minutes, whereas phospholipid 2 takes almost an hour.

B. To investigate the difference in extent of loss of ESR signal with the two phospholipids, the experiments were repeated using red cell ghosts that had been resealed to make them impermeable to ascorbate. In these experiments the loss of ESR signal for both phospholipids was negligible in the absence of ascorbate and reached a plateau at 50% in the presence of ascorbate. Offer an explanation for the difference in extent of loss of ESR signal in these experiments with red cell ghosts and the experiments shown in Figure 6–3, which used intact red cells.

C. Were the spin-labeled phospholipids introduced equally into the two monolayers of the red cell membrane?

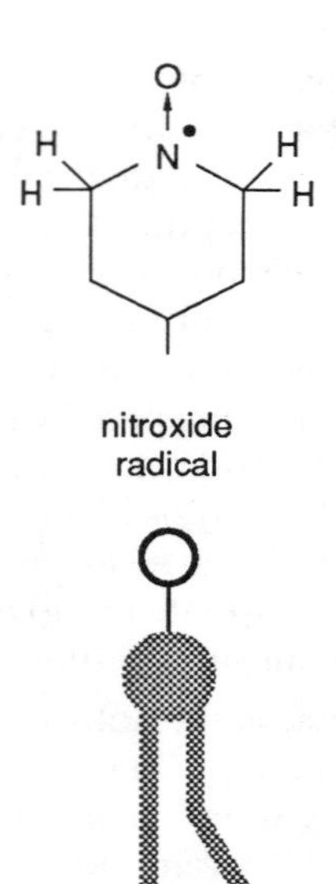

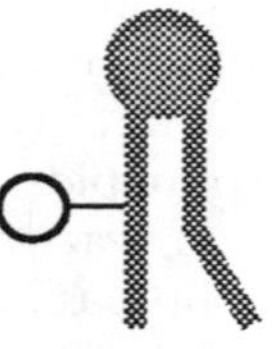

Figure 6–2 Structures of two nitroxide-labeled lipids (Problem 6–6). The nitroxide radical is shown at the top and its position of attachment to the phospholipids is illustrated schematically below.

6–7 The asymmetric distribution of phospholipids in the two monolayers of the plasma membrane implies that very little spontaneous flip-flop occurs or, alternatively, that any spontaneous flip-flop is rapidly corrected by appropriate phospholipid translocators that return phospholipids to their appropriate monolayer. The rate of phospholipid flip-flop in the plasma membrane of intact red blood cells has been measured to decide between these alternatives.

One experimental measurement used the same two spin-labeled phospholipids described in Problem 6–6 (Figure 6–2). To measure the rate of flip-flop from the inner to the outer monolayer, red cells with spin-labeled phospholipids exclusively in the inner monolayer were incubated for various times in the presence of ascorbate and the loss of ESR signal was followed. To measure the rate of flip-flop from the outer to the inner monolayer, red cells with spin-labeled phospholipids exclusively in the outer monolayer were incubated for various times in the absence of ascorbate and the loss of ESR signal was followed. The results of these experiments are illustrated in Figure 6–4.

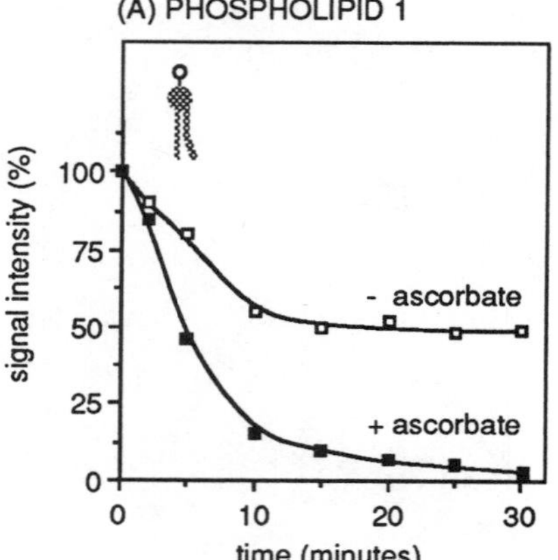

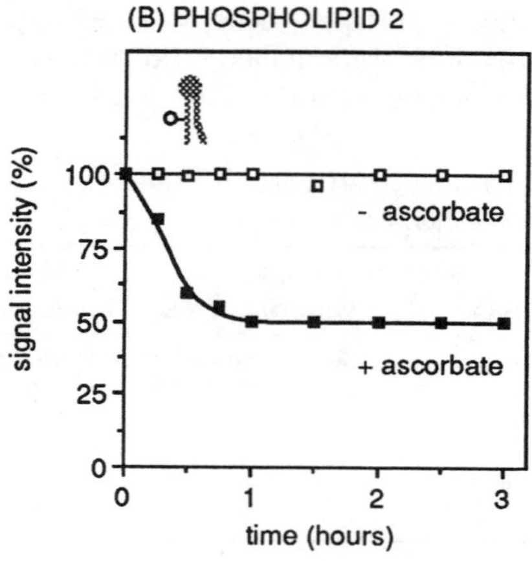

Figure 6–3 Decrease in ESR signal intensity as a function of time in intact red cells in the presence and absence of ascorbate (Problem 6–6). (A) Phospholipid 1. (B) Phospholipid 2.

A. From the results in Figure 6–4, estimate the rate of flip-flop from the inner to outer monolayer and from the outer to the inner monolayer. A convenient way to express such rates is as the half-time of flip-flop—that is, the time it takes for half the phospholipids to flip-flop from one monolayer to the other.

B. From what you learned about the behavior of the two spin-labeled phospholipids in Problem 6–6, deduce which one was used to label the inner monolayer of the intact red blood cells, and which one was used to label the outer monolayer.

C. Propose a method to generate intact red cells that contain spin-labeled phospholipids exclusively in the inner monolayer, and a method to generate cells spin-labeled exclusively in the outer monolayer.

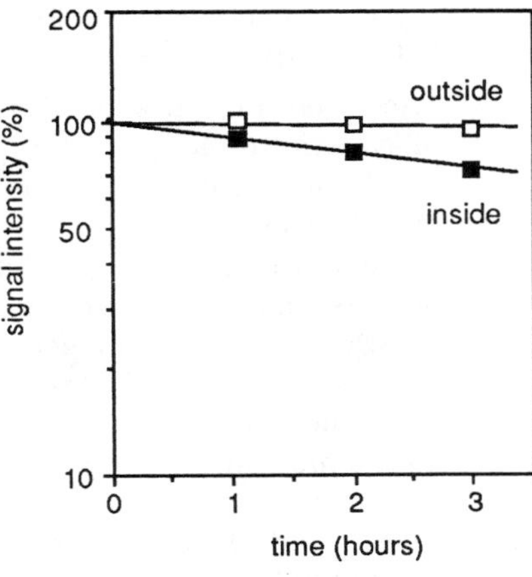

Figure 6–4 Decrease in ESR signal intensity of red cells containing spin-labeled phospholipids in the outer monolayer (outside) and inner monolayer (inside) of the plasma membrane (Problem 6–7).

Membrane Proteins (MBOC 284–298)

6–8 Fill in the blanks in the following statements.

A. Proteins that extend across the bilayer and are exposed to an aqueous environment on both sides of the membrane are called ____________ proteins.

B. ____________ proteins can be released from membranes by gentle procedures, such as extraction by a salt solution, whereas ____________ proteins can be removed only by totally disrupting the bilayer with detergents or organic solvents.

C. The most useful agents for disrupting hydrophobic associations and destroying the bilayer are ____________, which are small amphipathic molecules that tend to form micelles in water.

D. Membrane proteins solubilized by the ionic detergent SDS often are of no use for functional studies because they are ____________ and, having lost their normal three-dimensional conformation, are inactive.

E. The technique of using a membrane-impermeant radioactive or fluorescent labeling reagent to determine the sidedness of membrane proteins is termed ____________.

F. ____________ is a long fibrous molecule composed of a complex of two very large polypeptide chains, arranged in a filamentous meshwork on the cytoplasmic surface of the red blood cell membrane.

G. ____________ is the anion channel in red cells that is responsible for the exchange of HCO_3^- for Cl^- when CO_2 from the tissues is delivered to the lungs.

H. In ____________ electron microscopy, a lipid bilayer is split into its two monolayers; the face representing the hydrophobic interior of the cytoplasmic (or protoplasmic) monolayer is called the ____________, and the face representing the hydrophobic interior of the external half of the bilayer is called the ____________.

I. The purple membrane of the bacterium *Halobacterium halobium* is a specialized patch in the plasma membrane containing a single species of protein molecule, ____________, which converts light energy into a proton and a voltage gradient that in turn drives production of ATP.

J. The bacterial ____________ was the first membrane protein to be crystallized and studied by x-ray diffraction.

K. Like membrane lipids, membrane proteins are able to rotate about an axis perpendicular to the plane of the bilayer (____________ diffusion), many are able to move laterally in the membrane (____________ diffusion), and they do not tumble (____________) across the bilayer.

L. Direct evidence that some plasma membrane proteins are mobile in the plane of the membrane was provided in 1970 by an elegant experiment using hybrid cells called ____________, which were produced artificially by fusing mouse and human cells.

M. The lateral diffusion rates of membrane proteins that contain a chromophore or bind a fluorescent ligand can be quantitated using a technique called ____________.

6–9 Indicate whether the following statements are true or false. If a statement is false, explain why.

___ A. The basic structure of biological membranes is determined by the lipid bilayer, but their specific functions are carried out largely by proteins.

___ B. Membrane proteins form an extended monolayer on both surfaces of the lipid bilayer.

___ C. Proteins that span a lipid bilayer twice are likely to have their transmembrane segments arranged as β sheets.

___ D. In SDS polyacrylamide-gel electrophoresis, individual proteins migrate in the electrical field at rates determined by their molecular weight: the larger the protein, the more it is retarded by the complex meshwork of polyacrylamide molecules that constitutes the gel and, therefore, the more slowly it migrates.

___ E. Human red blood cells contain no internal membranes other than the nuclear membrane.

___ F. One can determine if a membrane protein is exposed on the external side of the plasma membrane by covalent attachment of a labeling reagent or by protease digestion only if the membrane is intact.

___ G. Spectrin, ankyrin, band 3, band 4.1, and actin are linked together noncovalently on the cytoplasmic surface of the red cell membrane to form a filamentous network, which is thought to be involved in maintaining the biconcave shape of the red cell.

___ H. Each molecule of bacteriorhodopsin contains a single chromophore called retinal, which, when activated by a photon of light, causes a conformational change in the protein that results in the transfer of protons from the inside to the outside of the cell.

___ I. The mobility of membrane proteins can be restricted by interactions with structures outside the cell or inside the cell.

___ J. Although membrane domains with different protein compositions are well known, there are at present no examples of membrane domains that differ in lipid composition.

6–10 Which of the arrangements of membrane-associated proteins indicated in Figure 6–5 have been found in biological membranes?

***6–11** Proteins that span a membrane have a characteristic structure in the region of the bilayer. Which, if any, of the three 20-amino acid sequences listed below is the most likely candidate for such a transmembrane segment? Explain the reasons for your choice.

A. I T L I Y F G V M A G V I G T I L L I S

B. I T P I Y F G P M A G V I G T P L L I S

C. I T E I Y F G R M A G V I G T D L L I S

6–12 Enzymatic digestion of sealed right-side-out red cell ghosts was originally used to determine the sidedness of the major membrane-associated proteins: spectrin, band 3, and glycophorin. These experiments made use of

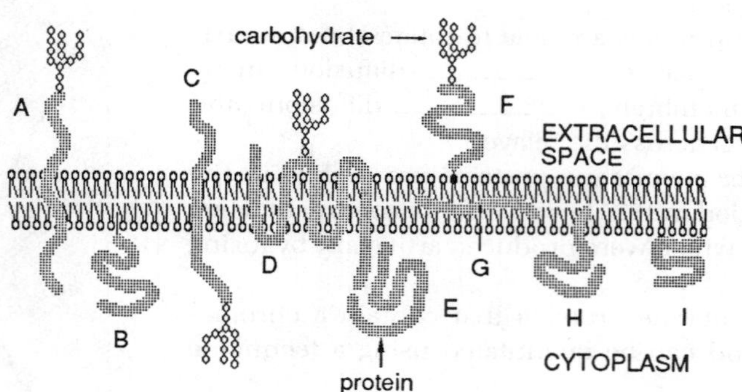

Figure 6–5 A variety of possible associations of proteins with a membrane (Problem 6–10).

Table 6–3 Proportion of Stain Associated with Three Membrane-associated Proteins (Problem 6–13)

Protein	Molecular Weight	Percent of Stain
Spectrin	250,000	25
Band 3	100,000	30
Glycophorin	30,000	2.3

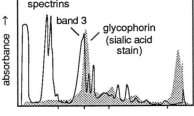

sialidase, which removes sialic acid residues from protein, and pronase, which cleaves peptide bonds. The proteins from normal ghosts and enzyme-treated ghosts were separated by SDS polyacrylamide-gel electrophoresis and then stained for protein and carbohydrate (Figure 6–6).

A. How does the information in Figure 6–6 allow you to decide whether the carbohydrate of glycophorin is on the cytoplasmic or external surface, and how does it allow you to decide which of the red cell proteins are exposed on the external side of the cell?

B. When you show your deductions to a colleague, she challenges your conclusion that some proteins are not exposed on the external surface and suggests instead that these proteins may be resistant to pronase digestion. What control experiment can you propose to test this possibility?

C. How would you modify this enzymatic approach in order to determine which red cell proteins span the plasma membrane?

***6–13** Estimates of the number of membrane-associated proteins per cell and the fraction of the plasma membrane occupied by such proteins provide a useful quantitative basis for understanding the structure of the plasma membrane. These calculations are straightforward for proteins in the plasma membrane of a red blood cell because red cells are readily prepared from blood and they contain no internal membranes to confuse the issue. Plasma membranes are prepared, the membrane-associated proteins are separated by SDS polyacrylamide-gel electrophoresis, and then they are stained with a dye (Coomassie blue). Because the intensity of color is roughly proportional to the mass of protein present in a band, quantitative estimates can be made as shown in Table 6–3.

A. From the information in Table 6–3, calculate the number of molecules of spectrin, band 3, and glycophorin in an individual red blood cell. Assume that 1 ml of red cell ghosts contains 10^{10} cells and 5 mg of total membrane protein.

B. Calculate the fraction of the plasma membrane that is occupied by band 3. Assume that band 3 is a cylinder 3 nm in radius and 10 nm in height and is oriented in the membrane as shown in Figure 6–7. The total surface area of a red cell is 10^8 nm^2.

6–14 One difficult problem in membrane biology is to define the associations between different membrane proteins. The associations involving spectrin, ankyrin, band 3, and actin, which generate the filamentous meshwork on the cytoplasmic surface of the red cell plasma membrane, have been investigated in several ways. One general method is to use antibodies that

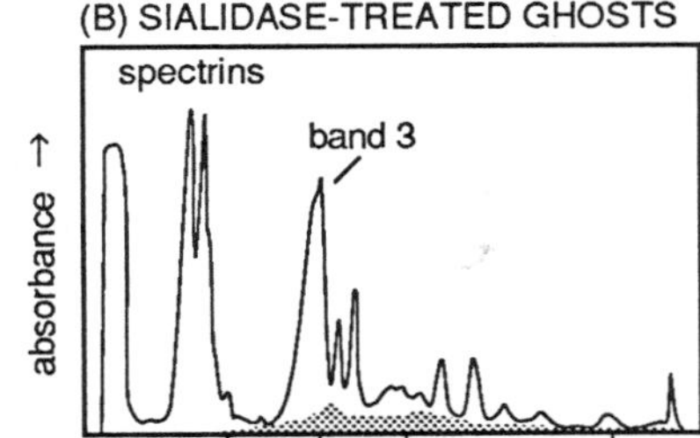

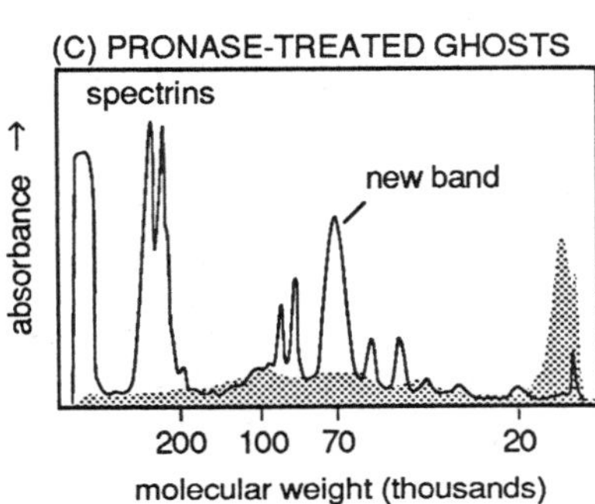

Figure 6–6 Analysis of proteins associated with red cell ghosts before and after digestion with sialidase and pronase (Problem 6–12). Membrane-associated proteins were separated by SDS polyacrylamide-gel electrophoresis and then stained for protein and for carbohydrate. Lines indicate the distribution of proteins, and shaded regions indicate the distribution of carbohydrate.

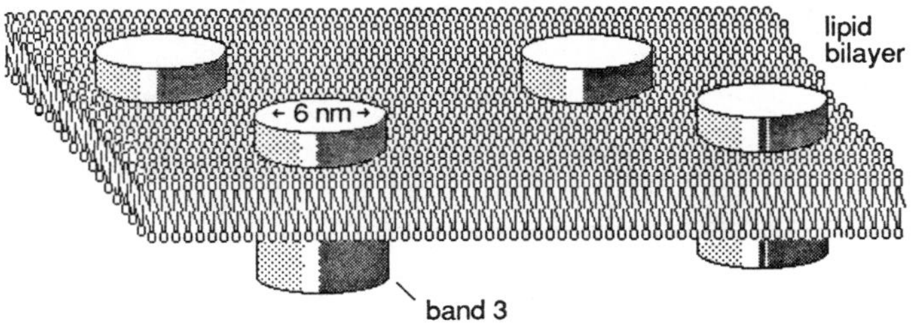

Figure 6–7 Schematic diagram of band 3, represented as a cylinder, in the plasma membrane (Problem 6–13).

Table 6–4 Precipitation of Red Cell Plasma Membrane Proteins by Antibodies Specific for Individual Proteins (Problem 6–14)

Protein Mixture	Antibody Specificity	Proteins in Pellet
1. Band 3 + actin	actin	actin
2. Band 3 + spectrin	spectrin	spectrin
3. Band 3 + ankyrin	ankyrin	band 3 + ankyrin
4. Actin + spectrin	spectrin	actin + spectrin
5. Actin + ankyrin	ankyrin	ankyrin
6. Spectrin + ankyrin	spectrin	spectrin + ankyrin

are specific for individual proteins. A mixture of two proteins is incubated together, and then an antibody specific for one of them is added. The resulting antibody-protein complexes are then precipitated and analyzed. This technique, when applied to pairwise mixtures of spectrin, ankyrin, band 3, and actin, yields the results summarized in Table 6–4. From the information in the table, deduce the associations between these proteins.

***6–15** The plasma membranes of cells are not static structures. In a motile cell, such as a fibroblast in culture, new lipid bilayer typically is added by exocytosis at the leading edge of the cell, while old lipid bilayer is taken up by endocytosis over most of the cell surface (Figure 6–8). This process creates a directional flow of lipid away from the leading edge at a rate of about 1 μm per minute. Membrane proteins that maintain a random distribution in the membrane must diffuse rapidly enough to counteract the directional flow of lipids or they will be swept to the back end of the cell. Estimates of the diffusion rates of proteins in the plasma membrane vary from about 10^{-8} cm²/sec to 10^{-10} cm²/sec at 37°C. Are these estimated diffusion rates sufficient to ensure a random distribution?

A protein is randomly distributed if the ratio of its concentrations at two well separated points on the cell surface is near 1; if the ratio of concentrations is much less than 1, the protein is not randomly distributed. An expression that relates membrane-flow rate and protein-diffusion rate to the concentrations of a protein at two points on the cell's surface is

$$\frac{C_A}{C_B} = e^{-(FL/D)}$$

where C_A and C_B are the concentrations of a protein at points A and B on the cell surface (see Figure 6–8), F is the membrane flow rate, L is the distance between points A and B located along the direction of the membrane flow, and D is the diffusion rate of membrane proteins.

A. Using this expression, decide which, if any, of the measured diffusion rates for membrane proteins (10^{-8}, 10^{-9}, or 10^{-10} cm²/sec) is sufficient to maintain a random distribution.

B. Predict the consequences of decreasing the diffusion rate of a membrane protein by cross-linking it into large aggregates using an antibody specific for that protein.

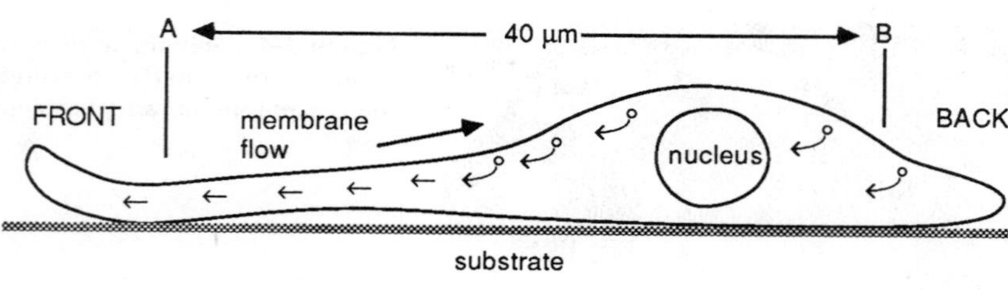

Figure 6–8 Schematic diagram of a cross-section through a motile fibroblast moving toward the left (Problem 6–15). Arrows inside the cell represent endocytosis of lipid by coated pits (small circles) and movement through the cell on the way to the front of the cell for reinsertion at the leading edge. Continuous insertion of new membrane at the leading edge creates a flow in the plasma membrane toward the back of the cell.

Membrane Carbohydrate (MBOC 298–300)

6–16 Fill in the blanks in the following statements.

A. Three kinds of molecule on the surface of eucaryotic cells contain carbohydrate: ____________, ____________, and ____________.

B. Oligosaccharides attached to membrane proteins are linked either to asparagine residues (____________ oligosaccharides) or to residues of serine or threonine (____________ oligosaccharides).

C. Proteins that recognize specific sugar residues are called ____________.

D. The carbohydrate-rich zone at the surface of most eucaryotic cells is known as the ____________ or ____________.

6–17 Indicate whether the following statements are true or false. If a statement is false, explain why.

__ A. The majority of cell-surface proteins carry sugars, whereas fewer than 10% of the lipids in the external bilayer of most plasma membranes are glycolipids.

__ B. Glycolipid molecules have only one oligosaccharide side chain, whereas glycoproteins often have many.

__ C. Proteoglycans contain more protein than carbohydrate, whereas glycoproteins contain more carbohydrate than protein.

__ D. Although most proteoglycans are extracellular matrix molecules, integral membrane proteoglycans also exist.

__ E. Whereas all the carbohydrate in the plasma membrane faces outward on the external surface of the cell, all the carbohydrate on internal membranes faces inward toward the cytoplasm.

__ F. The carbohydrate that makes up the glycocalyx is always attached to glycoproteins and proteoglycans that are integral membrane proteins.

***6–18** You are studying the binding of proteins to the cytoplasmic face of cultured neuroblastoma cells and have found a method that gives a good yield of inside-out vesicles from the plasma membrane. Unfortunately, your preparations of inside-out vesicles are contaminated with variable amounts of right-side-out vesicles. Nothing you have tried avoids this variable contamination. A friend suggests that you pass your vesicles over an affinity column made of lectin coupled to solid beads. What is the point of your friend's suggestion?

6–19 Cytochalasin B, which is often used as an inhibitor of actin-based motility systems, is also a very potent competitive inhibitor of D-glucose uptake into mammalian cells. When red blood cell ghosts are incubated with ^{3}H-cytochalasin B and then irradiated with ultraviolet light, the cytochalasin becomes cross-linked to the glucose transporter. Cytochalasin is not cross-linked to the transporter if an excess of D-glucose is present during the labeling reaction; however, an excess of L-glucose (which is not transported) does not interfere with labeling. If membrane proteins from labeled ghosts are separated by SDS polyacrylamide-gel electrophoresis, the transporter appears as a fuzzy radioactive band extending from 45,000 to 70,000 daltons. If labeled ghosts are treated with an enzyme that removes attached sugars before electrophoresis, the fuzzy band disappears and a much sharper band at 46,000 daltons takes its place.

A. Why does D-glucose, but not L-glucose, prevent cross-linking of cytochalasin to the glucose transporter?

B. Why does the glucose transporter appears as a fuzzy band on SDS polyacrylamide gels?

Membrane Transport of Small Molecules (MBOC 300–323)

6–20 Fill in the blanks in the following statements.

A. Specific proteins called ____________ proteins must be present in order for cell membranes to be permeable to small polar molecules such as ions, sugars, and amino acids.

B. There are two major classes of membrane transport proteins: ____________ proteins, which bind specific solutes and change conformation to transfer the solute across the membrane; and ____________ proteins, which form water-filled pores that allow specific solutes to cross the membrane down their electrochemical gradients.

C. Two general transport processes control the entry of solutes into cells: ____________ transport requires no energy input by the cell, whereas ____________ transport pumps specific solutes across a membrane against a concentration gradient.

D. The concentration gradient for a charged solute and the membrane potential constitute the ____________ gradient for that solute.

E. The transport of sugars into intestinal cells occurs by inward ____________ of Na^+ ions along with the sugar molecules.

F. The band 3 protein of the human red blood cell, which is an ____________ carrier, couples transport of Cl^- in one direction with HCO_3^- transport in the other and is thus a good example of an ____________ transporter.

G. The ____________ is inhibited by ouabain.

H. The network of tubular sacs in muscle cells that stores Ca^{2+} by means of an ATP-driven Ca^{2+} pump is called the ____________.

I. Most vertebrate cells contain a ____________ exchange carrier in their plasma membrane that plays an important part in regulating intracellular pH; it is the target for the inhibitory drug ____________.

J. Thin fingerlike projections called ____________ on the apical surfaces of kidney and intestinal epithelial cells increase their absorptive area by as much as 25 times.

K. The transport of some sugars across the plasma membrane of bacteria involves phosphorylation of the sugars during transport, using the high-energy-phosphate donor phosphoenolpyruvate rather than ATP; this type of transport is called ____________.

L. Bacteria with double membranes (such as *E. coli*) contain a variety of channel-forming proteins called ____________ in the outer membrane. The space between the inner and outer membranes contains water-soluble ____________ proteins, which bind solutes as the first step in transport and also act as receptors in chemotaxis.

M. ____________ proteins form water-filled pores across membranes; almost all such proteins in eucaryotic plasma membranes are concerned with selective ion transport and are therefore referred to as ____________.

N. Four kinds of perturbation that can cause gated ion channels to open or close are ____________, ____________, ____________, and ____________.

O. The uneven distribution of ions on either side of the plasma membrane gives rise to a voltage across the membrane known as the ____________. This voltage depends crucially on the existence of ____________ channels, which make most animal cells about 100 times more permeable to K^+ than to Na^+.

P. Voltage-gated ion channels in the plasma membrane of nerve and muscle cells enable these cells to conduct an ____________, which is a transient self-propagating depolarization of the membrane.

Q. A very important technique that has made it possible to study the behavior of single channels in cell membranes is called ____________ recording.

R. The toxic agent in the delicious—but dangerous—Japanese puffer fish, ____________ (TTX), and the poison found in shellfish exposed to the dinoflagellates responsible for red tide, ____________, both specifically block the ____________ Na^+ channel.

S. The transmission of signals between nerve cells and target cells occurs at specialized regions known as ____________, where transmitter-gated ion channels in the target cell respond to the presence of a signaling molecule, called a ____________, by opening or closing channels and producing a voltage change across the membrane.

T. During signal transmission between nerve cells and skeletal muscle cells, the nerve cells release ____________, which binds to ____________ embedded in the muscle cell membranes at the neuromuscular junction.

U. Small hydrophobic molecules that make membranes more permeable to certain ions are called ____________. There are two kinds, known as ____________ carriers and ____________ formers. Valinomycin and A23187 are examples of the first kind, with specificity for ____________ and ____________, respectively; gramicidin A is the classic example of the second kind.

6–21 Indicate whether the following statements are true or false. If a statement is false, explain why.

__ A. The plasma membrane is highly impermeable to all charged molecules.

__ B. All membrane transport proteins so far known traverse the lipid bilayer, and their polypeptide backbones generally extend back and forth across the membrane a number of times.

__ C. Carrier proteins transport their ligands like a revolving door, thereby maintaining a sealed lipid bilayer.

__ D. The Na^+-K^+ pump consumes a third of the cell's total ATP supply and is responsible for maintaining the high concentration of K^+ inside cells, for controlling cell volume, and for driving the uptake of sugars and amino acids in the intestine and kidney.

__ E. ATP supplies the energy for the Na^+-K^+ pump by phosphorylating an aspartate residue if, and only if, Na^+ is bound; this aspartylphosphate becomes dephosphorylated if, and only if, K^+ is bound. The conformational changes associated with this phosphorylation-dephosphorylation cycle drive the pump.

__ F. In resting muscle the sarcoplasmic reticulum Ca^{2+} pump is phosphorylated, activating the pump and keeping the intracellular Ca^{2+} concentration low; in stimulated muscle the pump is dephosphorylated, thereby inactivating it and allowing Ca^{2+} to flow out of the sarcoplasmic reticulum to initiate muscle contraction.

__ G. The light-activated proton pump of *Halobacterium* synthesizes ATP from ADP and P_i when H^+ ions are pumped across the membrane out of the cell.

__ H. The rise in intracellular pH that accompanies fertilization of sea urchin eggs requires Na^+ outside the eggs and is inhibited by the drug amiloride, suggesting that a Na^+-H^+ exchange carrier is responsible.

__ I. Channel proteins (such as the voltage-gated Na^+ channel) transport ions much faster than carrier proteins (such as the Na^+-K^+ pump), but they cannot be coupled to an energy source; therefore, transport mediated by channels is always passive.

__ J. The resting membrane potential of a typical animal cell arises predominantly through the action of the Na^+-K^+ pump, which in each cycle transfers 3 Na^+ ions out of the cell and 2 K^+ into the cell, leaving an excess of negative charges inside the cell.

__ K. Upon stimulation of a nerve cell, two processes limit the entry of Na^+ ions: (1) the membrane potential reaches the Na^+ equilibrium potential, which stops further net entry of Na^+, and (2) the Na^+ channels are inactivated and cannot reopen until the original resting potential has been restored.

__ L. The voltage gradient across the lipid bilayer changes dramatically during the passage of a nerve impulse, causing conformational changes in voltage-gated channel proteins.

— M. Ligand-gated ion channels open in response to specific neurotransmitters in their environment but are insensitive to the membrane potential; therefore, they cannot by themselves generate an action potential.

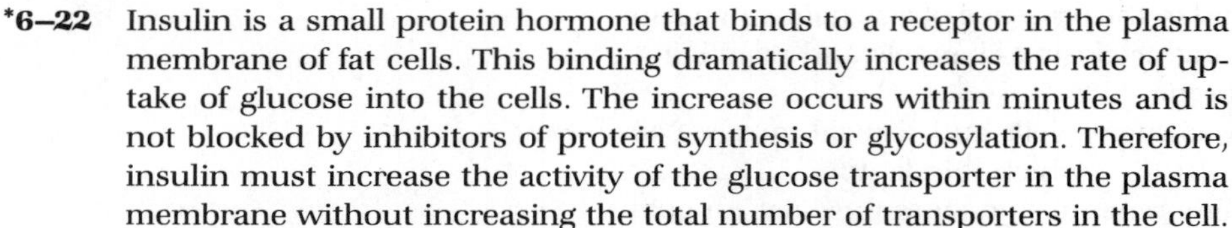

***6–22** Insulin is a small protein hormone that binds to a receptor in the plasma membrane of fat cells. This binding dramatically increases the rate of uptake of glucose into the cells. The increase occurs within minutes and is not blocked by inhibitors of protein synthesis or glycosylation. Therefore, insulin must increase the activity of the glucose transporter in the plasma membrane without increasing the total number of transporters in the cell.

The two experiments described below suggest a possible mechanism for the insulin effect. In the first experiment, the initial rate of glucose uptake in control and insulin-treated cells was measured, with the results shown in Figure 6–9. In the second experiment, the concentration of glucose transporter in fractionated membranes from control and insulin cells was measured, using the binding of radioactive cytochalasin B as the assay (see Problem 6–19), as shown in Table 6–5.

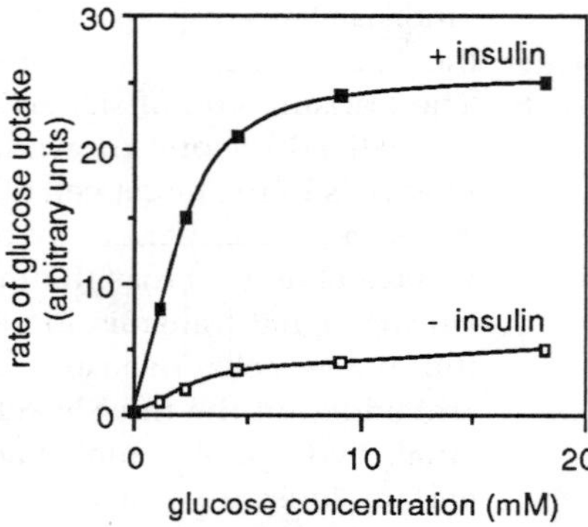

Figure 6–9 Rate of glucose uptake into cells in the presence and absence of insulin (Problem 6–22).

A. Deduce the mechanism by which glucose transport is increased in insulin-treated cells.
B. Transport proteins, like enzymes, can be characterized by the kinetic parameters K_M (the concentration of substrate at which the rate of transport is half-maximal) and V_{max} (the rate of transport achieved at saturating substrate concentration). Does insulin stimulation alter either of these kinetic properties of the glucose transporter? How can you tell from these data?

6–23 How much energy does it take to pump substances across membranes? Or, to put it another way, since active transport is usually driven directly or indirectly by ATP, how steep a gradient can ATP hydrolysis maintain for a particular solute? For transport into the cell the free-energy change (ΔG_{in}) per mole of solute moved across the plasma membrane is

$$\Delta G_{in} = -2.3\ RT \log_{10} \frac{C_o}{C_i} + zFV$$

Where
R = the gas constant, 1.98×10^{-3} kcal/°K mole
T = the absolute temperature in °K (37°C = 310°K)
C_o = solute concentration outside the cell
C_i = solute concentration inside the cell
z = the valence (charge) on the solute
F = Faraday's constant, 23 kcal/V mole
V = the membrane potential in volts (V)

Since $\Delta G_{in} = -\Delta G_{out}$, the free-energy change for transport out of the cell is

$$\Delta G_{out} = 2.3\ RT \log_{10} \frac{C_o}{C_i} - zFV$$

At equilibrium, where $\Delta G = 0$, the equations can be rearranged to the more familiar form known as the Nernst equation.

$$V = 2.3 \frac{RT}{zF} \log_{10} \frac{C_o}{C_i}$$

Table 6–5 Amount of Glucose Transporter Associated with the Plasma Membrane and Internal Membranes in the Presence and Absence of Insulin (Problem 6–22)

	Bound ^{3}H-Cytochalasin B (cpm/mg vesicle protein)	
Membrane Fraction	**Untreated Cells (– Insulin)**	**Treated Cells (+ Insulin)**
Plasma membrane	890	4480
Internal membranes	4070	480

For the questions below, assume that hydrolysis of ATP to ADP and P_i proceeds with a ΔG of -12 kcal/mole; that is, ATP hydrolysis can drive active transport with a ΔG of +12 kcal/mole. Assume that V is −60 mV.

A. What is the maximum concentration gradient that can be achieved by the ATP-driven active transport into the cell of an uncharged molecule such as glucose, assuming that 1 ATP is hydrolyzed for each solute molecule that is transported?

B. What is the maximum concentration gradient that can be achieved by active transport of Ca^{2+} from the inside to the outside of the cell? How does this maximum compare with the actual concentration gradient observed in mammalian cells (see MBOC Table 6–3)?

C. Calculate how much energy it takes to drive the Na^+-K^+ pump. This remarkable molecular device transports five ions for every molecule of ATP that is hydrolyzed: 3 Na^+ out of the cell and 2 K^+ into the cell. The pump typically maintains internal Na^+ at 10 mM, external Na^+ at 145 mM, internal K^+ at 140 mM, and external K^+ at 5 mM. As shown in Figure 6–10, Na^+ is transported against the membrane potential, whereas K^+ is transported with it. (The ΔG for the overall reaction is equal to the sum of the ΔG values for transport of the individual ions.)

D. How efficient is the Na^+-K^+ pump? That is, what fraction of the energy available from ATP hydrolysis is used to drive transport?

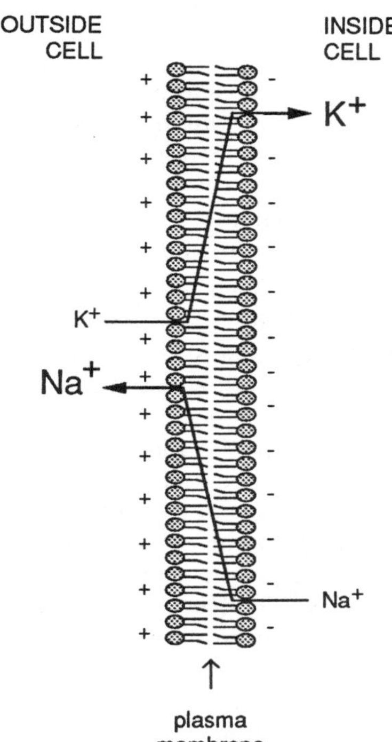

Figure 6–10 Na^+ and K^+ gradients and direction of pumping across the plasma membrane (Problem 6–23). Large letters symbolize high concentrations and small letters symbolize low concentrations. Both Na^+ and K^+ are pumped against chemical concentration gradients; but Na^+ is pumped up the electrical gradient, whereas K^+ runs down the electrical gradient.

6–24 The squid giant axon occupies a unique position in the history of our understanding of cell membrane potentials and action potentials because its large size (0.2–1.0 mm in diameter and 5–10 cm in length) allowed electrodes, large by modern standards, to be inserted so that intracellular voltages could be measured. When an electrode is stuck into an intact giant axon, a membrane potential of -70 mV is registered. When the axon, suspended in a bath of seawater, is stimulated to conduct a nerve impulse, the membrane potential rises transiently from -70 mV to +40 mV.

The Nernst equation relates equilibrium ionic concentrations to the membrane potential.

$$V = 2.3 \frac{RT}{zF} \log_{10} \frac{C_o}{C_i}$$

For univalent ions at 20°C (293 °K),

$$V = 58 \text{ mV} \times \log_{10} \frac{C_o}{C_i}$$

A. Using this equation, calculate the potential across the resting membrane (1) assuming that it is due solely to K^+ and (2) assuming that it is due solely to Na^+. (The Na^+ and K^+ concentrations in axon cytoplasm and in seawater are given in Table 6–6.) Which calculation is closer to the measured resting potential? Which calculation is closer to the measured action potential? Explain why these assumptions approximate the measured resting and action potentials.

B. If the solution bathing the squid giant axon is changed from seawater to an artificial seawater in which NaCl is replaced with choline chloride, there is no effect on the resting potential, but the nerve no longer generates an action potential upon stimulation. What would you predict would happen to the magnitude of the action potential if the concentration of Na^+ in the external medium were reduced to a half or a quarter of its normal value, using choline chloride to maintain osmotic balance?

Table 6–6 Ionic Composition of Seawater and of Cytoplasm from the Squid Giant Axon (Problem 10-24)

Ion	Cytoplasm	Seawater
Na^+	65 mM	430 mM
K^+	344 mM	9 mM

***6–25** The number of Na^+ ions entering the squid giant axon during an action potential can be calculated from theory. Because the cell membrane separates positive and negative charges, it behaves like a capacitor. From the known capacitance of biological membranes, the number of ions that enter during an action potential can be calculated. Starting from a resting potential of -70 mV, it can be shown that 1.1×10^{-12} moles of Na^+ must enter the cell per cm^2 of membranes during an action potential.

To determine experimentally the number of entering Na^+ during an action potential, a squid giant axon (1 mm in diameter and 5 cm in length) was suspended in a solution containing radioactive Na^+ (specific activity $= 2 \times 10^{14}$ cpm/mole) and a single action potential was propagated down its length. When the cytoplasm was analyzed for radioactivity, a total of 340 cpm were found to have entered the axon.

A. How well does the experimental measurement match the theoretical calculation?

B. How many moles of K^+ must cross the membrane of the axon, and in which direction, to reestablish the resting potential after the action potential is over?

C. Given that the concentration of Na^+ inside the axon is 65 mM, calculate the fractional increase in internal Na^+ concentration that results from the passage of a single action potential down the axon.

D. At the other end of the spectrum of nerve sizes are small dendrites about 0.1 μm in diameter. Assuming the same length (5 cm), the same internal Na^+ concentration (65 mM), and the same resting and action potentials as for the squid giant axon, calculate the fractional increase in internal Na^+ concentration that results from the passage of a single action potential down a dendrite.

E. Is the Na^+-K^+ pump more important for the continuing performance of a giant axon or a dendrite?

6–26 Intracellular changes in ion concentration often trigger dramatic cellular events. For example, when a clam sperm contacts a clam egg, it triggers ionic changes that result in the breakdown of the egg nuclear envelope, condensation of chromosomes, and initiation of meiosis. Two observations confirm that ionic changes initiate these cellular events: (1) suspending clam eggs in seawater containing 60 mM KCl triggers the same intracellular changes as do sperm; (2) suspending eggs in artificial seawater lacking calcium prevents activation by 60 mM KCl.

A. How does 60 mM KCl affect the resting potential of eggs? The intracellular K^+ concentration is 344 mM and that of normal seawater is 9 mM. Remember from Problem 6–24 that

$$V = 58 \text{ mV} \times \log_{10} \frac{C_o}{C_i}$$

B. What does the lack of activation by 60 mM KCl in calcium-free seawater suggest about the mechanism of KCl activation?

C. What would you expect to happen if the calcium ionophore, A23187, was added to a suspension of eggs (in the absence of sperm) in (1) regular seawater and (2) calcium-free seawater?

***6–27** One important parameter for understanding any particular membrane transport process is to know the number of copies of the specific transport protein present in the cell membrane. You wish to measure the number of voltage-gated Na^+ channels in the rabbit vagus nerve. You have found a potent toxin in spider venom that specifically inactivates voltage-gated Na^+ channels in these nerve cells; moreover, you have shown that the toxin can be labeled with ^{125}I without affecting its toxic properties. Assuming that one toxin molecule binds per channel, the number of Na^+ channels in a segment of vagus nerve will be equal to the maximum number of bound toxin molecules.

To make this measurement, you incubate identical segments of nerve for 8 hours with increasing amounts of labeled toxin. You then wash the segments to remove unbound toxin and measure the radioactivity associated with the nerve segments to establish a titration curve for binding, which is shown in the upper curve in Figure 6–11. You are puzzled because you expected to see binding reach a maximum (saturate) at high concentrations of toxin; however, no distinct endpoint was reached. Indeed, binding continued to increase with the same slope at even higher concentrations of toxin than those shown in the upper curve in the figure. After careful thought, you design a control experiment in which the binding of labeled toxin is measured in the presence of a large molar excess of unlabeled toxin. The results of this experiment, which are shown in the lower curve in Figure 6–11, make everything clear and allow you to calculate the number of Na^+ channels in the membrane of the vagus nerve axon.

A. Why does binding of the labeled toxin not saturate? What is the point of the control experiment, and how does it work?

B. Given that 1 g of vagus nerve has an axonal membrane area of 6000 cm^2 and assuming that the Na^+ channel is a cylinder with a diameter of 6 nm, calculate the number of Na^+ channels per square micrometer of axonal membrane and the fraction of the cell surface occupied by the channel. (Use 100 pmol as the amount of toxin specifically bound to the receptor.)

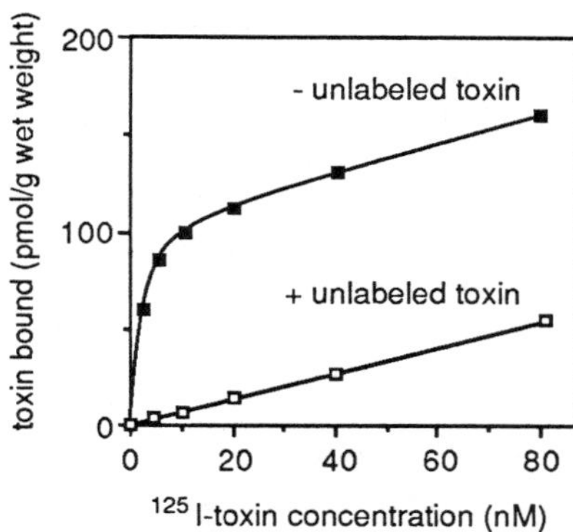

Figure 6–11 Toxin-binding curves in the presence and absence of tetrodotoxin (Problem 6–27).

Membrane Transport of Macromolecules and Particles: Exocytosis and Endocytosis (MBOC 323–337)

6–28 Fill in the blanks in the following statements.

A. Intracellular vesicles fuse with the plasma membrane by a process known as ____________.

B. Cells ingest macromolecules and particles by enclosing them in segments of plasma membrane that pinch off to form intracellular vesicles: a process known as ____________.

C. Many of the unpleasant symptoms associated with allergic reactions are due to ____________, which is secreted by ____________ cells.

D. Small vesicles containing extracellular fluids and solutes are ingested by ____________, whereas large particles such as bacteria are ingested by ____________.

E. Most of the non-membrane-bound contents of endocytic vesicles end up in ____________, which are the specialized sites of intracellular digestion; however, selected membrane components can be retrieved from ____________ and recycled to the plasma membrane.

F. The endocytic cycle begins at specialized regions of the plasma membrane called ____________, which occupy about 2% of the surface of various cultured cells.

G. The best-characterized protein found in coated vesicles is ____________, which is composed of three large and three small polypeptide chains arranged as a three-legged structure known as a ____________.

H. Macromolecules that bind to specific cell-surface receptors are taken into the cell by a process called ____________; substances dissolved in the extracellular fluid are also internalized, but much more slowly, by a process called ____________.

I. Most of the cholesterol in the blood is present in large (22-nm) spherical particles called ____________, or LDL for short.

J. Endocytosed macromolecules enter the ____________ compartment, appearing in ____________ within a minute or so and in ____________ after 5 to 15 minutes.

K. Iron is carried in the blood by a specialized transport protein called ____________.

L. Epithelial cells are stimulated to divide upon the binding of a small protein, called ____________ (EGF), to specific receptors in the plasma membrane.

M. The binding of EGF causes its receptors to be internalized and degraded in lysosomes; the resulting decrease in the concentration of EGF receptors on the cell surface is known as receptor ____________.

N. In newborn mammals, antibodies from the mother's milk are carried across the gut epithelium by ____________.

O. In motile cells, lipids and receptors in the plasma membrane move backward from the leading edge in a process called ____________, which may explain why plasma membrane molecules that are cross-linked by antibodies or lectins are swept to the back of the cell in a process known as ____________.

P. The two kinds of "professional phagocytes" in mammals are ____________, which are found in many tissues besides blood, and ____________, which are confined to the bloodstream.

Q. During ____________, cell debris and microorganisms are ingested via large endocytic vesicles called ____________; these vesicles fuse with lysosomes to form ____________.

R. ____________, which comprises the adherence and joining of lipid bilayers, is probably catalyzed by specialized ____________ proteins.

6–29 Indicate whether the following statements are true or false. If a statement is false, explain why.

__ A. Exocytosis and endocytosis both involve membrane fusion but occur in opposite directions relative to the plasma membrane.

__ B. Substances that are secreted in response to an extracellular signal are stored in secretory vesicles; substances that are secreted via the constitutive pathway do not pass through vesicles.

__ C. Secretion of materials into the medium from secretory vesicles and addition of new plasma membrane components from the Golgi apparatus both involve exocytosis.

__ D. Cells take up macromolecules by two different molecular mechanisms: individual macromolecules are taken up by receptor-mediated endocytosis, whereas particles are taken up by phagocytosis.

__ E. The endocytic cycle begins at specialized regions of the plasma membrane known as coated pits, at which clathrin and associated proteins drive the invagination of the membrane.

__ F. Perinuclear endosomes fuse with lysosomes to form secondary lysosomes.

__ G. The acidic environment of lysosomes plays a crucial role in sorting: some receptors change their conformation, dissociate from their ligand, and return to the plasma membrane; other receptors are unaffected by the low pH, retain their ligand, and are destroyed in the lysosome.

__ H. The pH inside an endosome is reduced to about pH 5 by the operation of the Na^+-H^+ exchange protein. The Na^+ ions that enter the cytoplasm are subsequently expelled from the cell by the Na^+-K^+ pump, so the acidification is driven indirectly by ATP hydrolysis.

__ I. Transferrin is the protein responsible for transporting ferritin into cells.

__ J. Transferrin receptors escape destruction by lysosomal hydrolysis because the receptors are resistant to proteolysis at low pH.

__ K. Cell-surface receptors for EGF concentrate in coated pits only after they have bound EGF, whereas LDL receptors enter coated pits even in the absence of bound ligand.

__ L. Coated pits act as molecular filters that concentrate certain plasma membrane proteins but exclude others.

__ M. An important difference between receptor-mediated endocytosis and phagocytosis is that the former occurs continuously, whether or not ligands are present, whereas the latter occurs only when a cell encounters something to eat.

__ N. Since phagocytosis is inhibited by cytochalasin whereas receptor-mediated endocytosis is not, actin is probably involved in phagocytosis but not in receptor-mediated endocytosis.

— O. Influenza viruses, which are enveloped viruses that get into cells by receptor-mediated endocytosis, exploit the low pH of the endosome to initiate membrane fusion by activating a fusogenic glycoprotein.

6–30 You are interested in exocytosis and endocytosis in a line of cultured liver cells that secrete albumin and take up transferrin. To distinguish these events, you add transferrin tagged with colloidal gold to the medium, and then after a few minutes you fix the cells, prepare thin sections, and react them with ferritin-labeled antibodies against albumin. Colloidal gold and ferritin are both electron dense and therefore readily visible when viewed by electron microscopy; moreover, they can be easily distinguished from one another on the basis of size and density.

A. Will this experiment allow you to identify vesicles in the exocytic and endocytic pathways? How?

B. Not all the gold-labeled vesicles are clathrin coated. Why?

6–31 The recycling of the membrane receptors for transferrin has been studied by labeling transferrin receptors on the cell surface and following their fate at 0°C and 37°C. Intact cells at 0°C were reacted with radioactive iodine under conditions that label cell-surface proteins. If the cells were kept on ice and treated with trypsin, which destroys the receptors without damaging the integrity of the cell, the radioactive transferrin receptors were completely degraded. (The transferrin receptors were detected as a spot after separation of cell proteins by two-dimensional polyacrylamide-gel electrophoresis.) If the cells were first warmed to 37°C for 1 hour and then treated with trypsin on ice, about 70% of the initial radioactivity was present in the spot. At both temperatures, however, most of the receptors, as visualized by a protein stain, remained intact.

A second sample of cells that had been surface labeled at 0°C and incubated at 37°C for 1 hour was analyzed with transferrin-specific antibodies. If intact cells were reacted with antibody, 0.54% of the labeled proteins were bound by antibody. If the cells were first dissolved in detergent, 1.76% of the labeled proteins were bound by antibody.

A. Why does trypsin treatment destroy the labeled transferrin receptors, but not the majority of the receptors, when the cells are kept on ice? Why do the labeled receptors become resistant to trypsin when the cells are incubated at 37°C?

B. What fraction of the total transferrin receptor is on the cell surface after a 1-hour incubation at 37°C? Do the two experimental approaches agree?

***6–32** The average time for transferrin receptors to cycle from the cell surface through the endosomal compartment and back again to the cell surface has been determined by labeling cell-surface receptors with radioactive iodine at 0°C and then following their fate at 37°C. At various times after shifting labeled cells to 37°C, samples were diluted into ice-cold medium that contained trypsin. The amount of radioactivity in trypsin-resistant transferrin receptors was measured after separation from other membrane components by two-dimensional polyacrylamide-gel electrophoresis. The results are shown in Figure 6–12.

A. The initial rate of internalization of labeled transferrin receptors is indicated by the dashed line. Why does the rate of internalization of labeled receptors decline with time?

B. Using the initial rate of internalization, estimate the fraction of surface receptors that are internalized each minute.

C. What fraction of the *total* receptor population is internalized each minute?

D. At the rate determined in part C, how many minutes would it take for the equivalent of the entire population of receptors to be internalized? Explain why this time equals the average time for a receptor to cycle from the cell

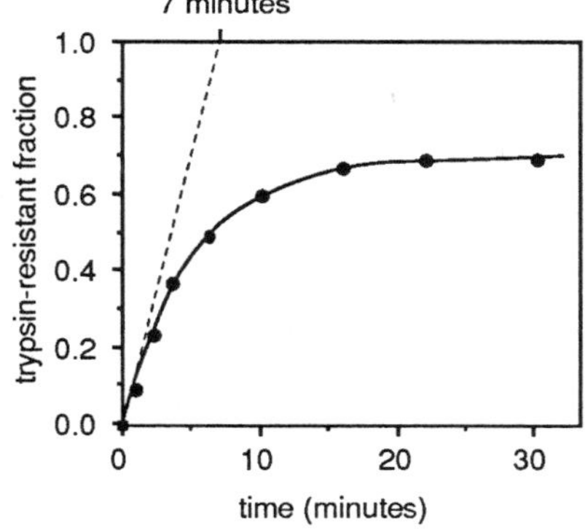

Figure 6–12 Fraction of labeled transferrin receptor that is trypsin resistant as a function of time after labeling (Problem 6–32). The dashed line indicates the initial rate of internalization.

surface through the endosomal compartment and back to the cell surface.

E. On average, how long does each transferrin receptor spend on the cell surface?

6–33 Cholesterol is an essential component of the plasma membrane, but people who have very high levels of cholesterol in their blood tend to have heart attacks. Cholesterol in the blood is carried in the form of cholesterol esters in low-density lipoprotein (LDL) particles. LDL binds to a high-affinity receptor on the cell surface, enters the cell via a coated pit, and ends up in lysosomes. There its protein coat is degraded and cholesterol esters are released and hydrolyzed to cholesterol. The released cholesterol enters the cytoplasm and inhibits the enzyme HMG CoA reductase, which controls the committed step in cholesterol biosynthesis. Patients with severe hypercholesterolemia cannot remove LDL from the blood. As a result, their cells do not turn off normal cholesterol synthesis, which makes the problem worse.

LDL metabolism can be conveniently divided into three stages experimentally: binding of LDL to the cell surface, internalization of LDL, and regulation of cellular cholesterol synthesis by LDL. Skin cells from a normal person and two patients suffering from severe familial hypercholesterolemia were grown in culture and tested for LDL binding, LDL internalization, and LDL regulation of cholesterol synthesis. The results are shown in Figure 6–13.

A. In Figure 6–13A the surface binding of LDL by normal cells is compared with LDL binding by cells from patients FH and JD. Why does binding by normal cells and by JD's cells reach a plateau? What explanation can you suggest for the lack of LDL binding by FH's cells?

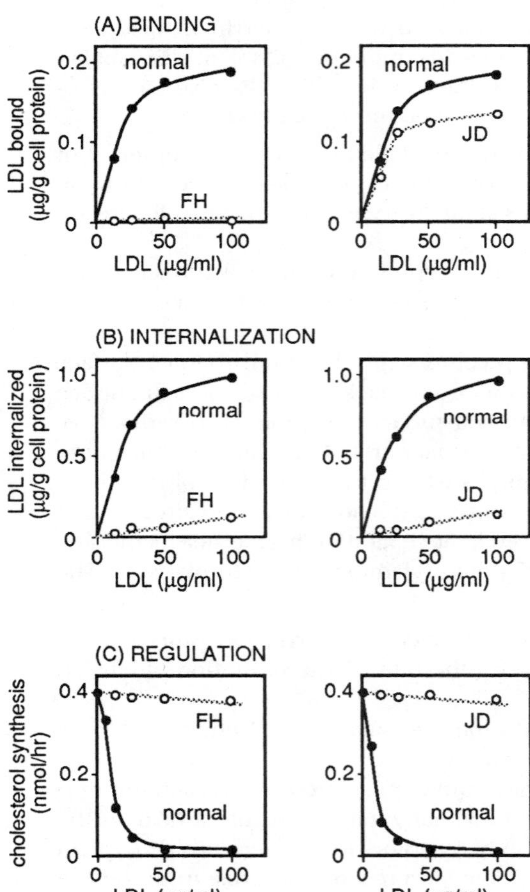

Figure 6–13 LDL metabolism in normal cells and in cells from patients with severe familial hypercholesterolemia (Problem 6–33). (A) High-affinity surface binding of LDL. (B) Internalization of LDL. (C) Regulation of cholesterol synthesis by LDL. Binding and uptake of LDL can be followed by labeling LDL either with ferritin particles, which can be visualized by electron microscopy, or with radioactive iodine, which can be measured in a gamma counter. Surface binding can be reversed by washing with negatively charged polymers, but internalized label cannot be washed away.

B. In Figure 6–13B internalization of LDL by normal cells increases as the external LDL concentration is increased, reaching a plateau fivefold higher than the amount of externally bound LDL. Why does LDL not enter cells from patients FH or JD?

C. In Figure 6–13C the regulation of cholesterol synthesis by LDL in normal cells is compared with cells from FH and JD. Why does increasing the external LDL concentration inhibit cholesterol synthesis in normal cells but not affect it in cells from FH or JD?

D. How would you expect the rate of cholesterol synthesis to be affected if normal cells and cells from FH or JD were incubated with cholesterol itself? (Free cholesterol crosses the plasma membrane by diffusion.)

Table 6–7 Distribution of LDL Receptors on the Surface of Cells from JD and His Parents as Compared with Normal Individuals (Problem 6–34)

	Number of LDL Receptors	
	In Pits	**Outside Pits**
Normal male	186	195
Normal female	186	165
JD	10	342
JD's father	112	444
JD's mother	91	87

***6–34** Referring to the data in Problem 6–33 what is the matter with JD's metabolism of LDL? JD's cells bind LDL with the same affinity as normal and in almost the same amounts as normal, but the binding does not lead to internalization of LDL. Two classes of explanation could account for JD's problem:

1. JD's LDL receptors are defective in some internal portion so that the receptors cannot enter the cell, even though the LDL binding domains on the cell surface are perfectly normal.
2. JD's LDL receptors are normal, but there is a mutation in the cellular internalization machinery such that the loaded LDL receptor cannot be brought in.

To distinguish between these explanations, JD's parents were studied. Since the gene encoding the LDL receptor is autosomal, each parent must have donated one of their two genes to JD. JD's mother suffered from mildly elevated blood cholesterol. At 4°C her cells bound only half as much LDL as normal, but when her cells were warmed to 37°C, the bound LDL was internalized at the same rate as normal. JD's father also had mild hypercholesterolemia, but his cells bound 50% more LDL than normal at 4°C. When his cells were warmed to 37°C, about half of the label was internalized normally, but the other half was not internalized at all.

The association of this family's LDL receptors with coated pits was studied by electron microscopy, using LDL that was labeled with ferritin. The results are shown in Table 6–7.

A. Why does JD's mother have mild hypercholesterolemia? What kind of LDL-receptor gene might she have passed on to JD?

B. Why does JD's father have mild hypercholesterolemia? Can you make an argument to distinguish between explanations 1 and 2 (above), based on the inability of cells from JD's father to internalize all the LDL they bind?

C. Can you account for JD's hypercholesterolemia from the behavior of the LDL receptors in his parents?

D. What do the electron microscopic studies suggest is wrong with JD's LDL uptake?

6–35 Cells take up extracellular molecules by receptor-mediated endocytosis and by fluid-phase endocytosis. The efficiencies of these two pathways were compared by incubating human epithelial carcinoma cells with epidermal growth factor (EGF), to measure receptor-mediated endocytosis, and with horseradish peroxidase (HRP), to measure fluid-phase endocytosis. A quantitative comparison of uptake was made by incubating cells with 40 nM ferritin-labeled EGF and 20 μM HRP (500-fold higher concentration than EGF) for various times, after which the cells were fixed and stained for HRP activity and examined for the presence of ferritin in vesicles. Both EGF and HRP were present in small vesicles with an internal radius of 20 nm, but EGF was very common whereas HRP was rare.

The rates of uptake of EGF and HRP were compared as shown in Figure 6–14. Uptake of HRP was linear with respect to both time and concen-

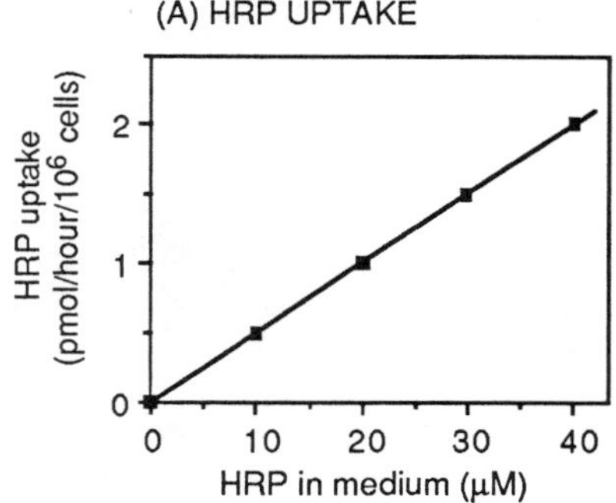

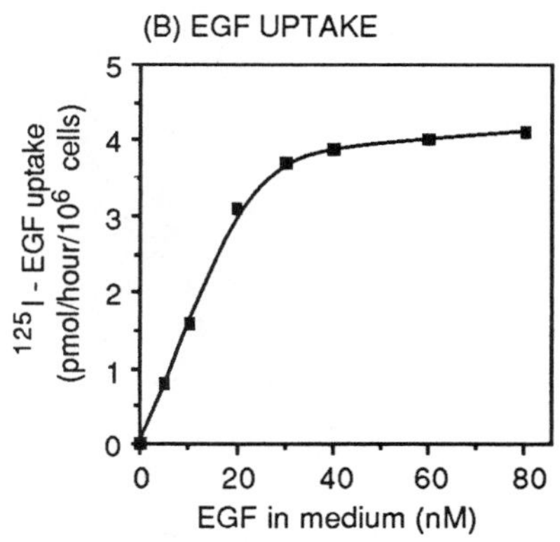

Figure 6–14 Uptake of HRP and EGF as a function of their concentration in the medium (Problem 6–35).

tration: cells took up HRP at a rate of 1 pmol/hour at 20 μM HRP (Figure 6–14A). EGF uptake showed an initial linear phase but reached a plateau at higher concentrations of EGF in the medium (Figure 6–14B).

A. Explain why the shapes of the curves in Figure 6–14 are different for HRP and EGF.

B. Calculate the number of EGF receptors on the surface of each cell.

C. Calculate how many HRP molecules get taken up by each endocytic vesicle (radius 20 nm) when the medium contains 1 mg/ml HRP (molecular weight 40,000). (The volume of a sphere is $\frac{4}{3}\pi r^3$.)

D. The scientists who did these experiments said at the time, "These calculations clearly illustrate how cells can internalize EGF by endocytosis while excluding all but insignificant quantities of extracellular fluid." Explain what they meant.

Energy Conversion: Mitochondria and Chloroplasts

7

The Mitochondrion (MBOC 342–356)

7–1 Fill in the blanks in the following statements.

A. The mitochondrial inner and outer membranes create two separate mitochondrial compartments: the internal ____________ and a much narrower ____________.

B. The mitochondrial ____________ membrane resembles a sieve that is permeable to all molecules, including small proteins of 10,000 daltons or less.

C. The enzymes of the ____________ are embedded in the ____________ mitochondrial membrane; they are essential to the process of oxidative phosphorylation, which generates most of the animal cell's ATP.

D. The inner membrane is usually highly convoluted, forming a series of infoldings, known as ____________, which greatly increase the area of the inner membrane.

E. ____________, which are composed of three molecules of fatty acid held in ester linkage to glycerol, have no charge and are virtually insoluble in water, coalescing into droplets in the cytosol.

F. The large, branched polymer of glucose that is contained in granules in the cell cytoplasm is known as ____________.

G. The ____________ accounts for about two-thirds of the total oxidation of carbon compounds in most cells, and its major end products are CO_2 and NADH.

H. The transfer of electrons from NADH and $FADH_2$ to oxygen releases a large amount of energy that is harnessed to drive the conversion of ADP + P_i to ATP in a process known as ____________.

I. The energy released by the passage of electrons along the respiratory chain is stored as an ____________ across the inner mitochondrial membrane.

J. The flow of electrons across the inner membrane generates a pH gradient and a membrane potential, which together exert a ____________ force.

K. ____________ synthesizes ATP from ADP and P_i in the mitochondrial matrix in a reaction that is coupled to the inward flow of protons.

7–2 Indicate whether the following statements are true or false. If a statement is false, explain why.

__ A. Due to the many specialized transport proteins in the inner and outer membranes, the intermembrane space and the matrix space are chemically equivalent to the cytosol with respect to small molecules.

__ B. The number of cristae is threefold greater in the mitochondria of a cardiac muscle cell than in the mitochondria of a liver cell, presumably reflecting the greater demand for ATP in heart cells.

___C. To ensure a continuous supply of energy from oxidative metabolism, animal cells store fuel in the form of fatty acids and glucose.

___D. The most important contribution of the citric acid cycle to metabolism is the extraction of high-energy electrons during the oxidation of the two acetyl carbon atoms to CO_2.

___E. The energy released during transport down the respiratory chain in the mitochondrial inner membrane is used to pump protons across the inner membrane from the intermembrane space into the matrix.

___F. Each respiratory enzyme complex in the electron-transport chain has a greater affinity for electrons than its predecessor, so that electrons pass sequentially from one complex to another until they are finally transferred to oxygen, which has the greatest affinity of all for electrons.

___G. In a typical cell the membrane potential accounts for nearly three-quarters of the total proton-motive force across the inner membrane of a respiring mitochondrion.

___H. The orientation of ATP synthetase in the inner mitochondrial membrane is such that ATP is generated in the intermembrane space, allowing it to diffuse into the cytosol through the pores in the outer membrane.

___I. The net change of disorder in the universe due to a reaction is reflected in the change in free energy associated with the reaction: the larger the increase in free energy (so that ΔG is very positive), the more favored the reaction.

___J. The remarkable efficiency of cellular respiration is due primarily to the many intermediates in the oxidation pathways, which allow the huge amount of free energy released by oxidation to be parceled out into small packages.

***7–3** In 1904 Franz Knoop performed what was probably the first successful use of a labeling experiment to study metabolic pathways. He fed fatty acids labeled with a terminal benzene ring to dogs and analyzed their urine for excreted benzene derivatives. Whenever the fatty acid had an even number of carbon atoms, phenylacetic acid was excreted (Figure 7–1A). However, whenever the fatty acid had an odd number of carbon atoms, benzoic acid was excreted (Figure 7–1B). (Actually in both experiments the excreted compounds were found esterified to a sugar, which helped solubilize them; these modifications are irrelevant to the metabolism of the fatty acids.)

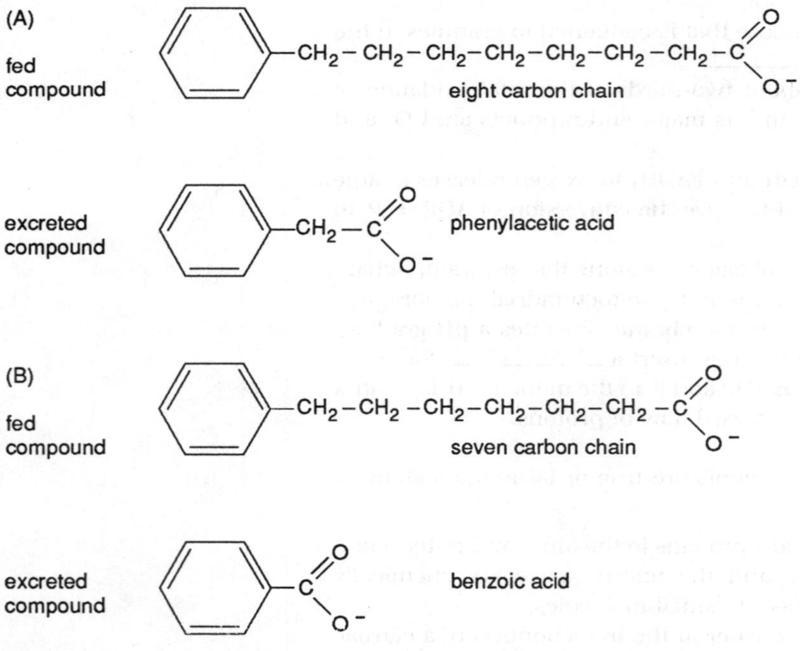

Figure 7–1 Fed and excreted derivatives of examples of an even-chain (A) and an odd-chain (B) fatty acid (Problem 7–3).

*Problems with an asterisk (*) are answered in the Instructor's Manual.

From these experiments Knoop deduced that oxidation of fatty acids to CO_2 and H_2O involved removal of two-carbon fragments from the carboxylic acid end of the chain. Can you explain the reasoning that led him to conclude that two-carbon fragments, as opposed to any other number, were removed, and that degradation was from the carboxylic acid end, as opposed to the other end?

7–4 In 1937 Hans Krebs deduced the operation of the citric acid cycle from careful observations on the oxidation of carbon compounds in minced preparations of pigeon flight muscle. (Pigeon breast is a rich source of mitochondria, but the function of mitochondria was unknown at the time.) The consumption of O_2 and the production of CO_2 were monitored with a manometer, which measures changes in volume of a closed system at constant pressure and temperature. Standard chemical methods were used to determine the concentrations of key metabolites. (Remember, radioactive isotopes were not available then.)

In one set of experiments Krebs measured the rate of consumption of O_2 during the oxidation of endogenous carbohydrates in the presence or absence of citrate. As shown in Table 7–1, addition of a small amount of citrate resulted in a large increase in the consumption of oxygen. Szent-Gyorgyi (1925) and Stare and Baumann (1936) had previously shown that fumarate, oxaloacetate, and succinate also stimulated respiration in extracts of pigeon breast muscle.

When metabolic poisons, such as arsenite or malonate (whose modes of action were undefined), were added to the minced muscles, the results were much different. In the presence of arsenite, 5.5 mmol of citrate were converted into about 5 mmol of α-ketoglutarate. In the presence of malonate an equivalent conversion of citrate into succinate occurred. Furthermore, in the presence of malonate roughly 5 mmol of oxygen were consumed (above background levels in the absence of citrate), which was twice as much as in the presence of arsenite.

Finally, Krebs showed that the minced muscles were actually capable of synthesizing citrate if oxaloacetate was added and all traces of oxygen were excluded. None of the other intermediates in the cycle led to a net synthesis of citrate in the absence of oxygen.

A. If citrate ($C_6H_8O_7$) were completely oxidized to CO_2 and H_2O, how many molecules of O_2 would be consumed per molecule of citrate? What is it about the results in Table 7–1 that caught Krebs's attention?

B. Why is the consumption of oxygen so low in the presence of arsenite and malonate? If citrate were oxidized to α-ketoglutarate ($C_5H_6O_5$), how much oxygen would be consumed per molecule of citrate? If citrate were oxidized to succinate ($C_4H_6O_4$), how much oxygen would be consumed per molecule of citrate? Does the observed stoichiometry agree with the expectations based on these calculations?

C. Why in the absence of oxygen does oxaloacetate alone cause an accumulation of citrate? Would any of the other intermediates in the cycle cause an accumulation of citrate in the presence of oxygen?

D. Toward the end of the paper Krebs states, "While the citric acid cycle thus seems to occur generally in animal tissues, it does not exist in yeast or in

Table 7–1 Respiration in Minced Pigeon Breast in the Presence and Absence of Citrate (Problem 7–4)

	Oxygen Consumption (mmol)		
Time (minutes)	**No Citrate**	**3 mmol Citrate**	**Difference**
30	29	31	2
60	47	68	21
90	51	87	36
150	53	93	40

E. coli, for yeast and *E. coli* do not oxidize citric acid at an appreciable rate." Why do you suppose Krebs got this point wrong?

7–5 The relationship of free-energy change (ΔG) to the concentrations of reactants and products is important because it predicts the direction of spontaneous chemical reactions. Familiarity with this relationship is essential for understanding energy conversions in cells. Consider, for example, the hydrolysis of ATP to ADP and inorganic phosphate (P_i).

$$ATP + H_2O \rightarrow ADP + P_i$$

The free-energy change due to ATP hydrolysis is

$$\Delta G = \Delta G^o + RT \ln \frac{[ADP][P_i]}{[ATP]}$$

$$= \Delta G^o + 2.3\ RT \log_{10} \frac{[ADP][P_i]}{[ATP]}$$

where the concentrations are expressed as molarities (by convention, the concentration of water is not included in the expression). R is the gas constant (1.98×10^{-3} kcal/°K mole), T is temperature (assume 37°C, which is 310°K), and ΔG^o is the standard free-energy change (-7.3 kcal/mole for ATP hydrolysis to ADP and P_i).

A. Calculate the ΔG for ATP hydrolysis when the concentrations of ATP, ADP, and P_i are all equal to 1 M. What is the ΔG when the concentrations of ATP, ADP, and P_i are all equal to 1 mM?
B. In a resting muscle, the concentrations of ATP, ADP, and P_i are approximately 5 mM, 1 mM, and 10 mM, respectively. What is ΔG for ATP hydrolysis in resting muscle?
C. What will ΔG equal when the hydrolysis reaction reaches equilibrium? At $[P_i]$ = 10 mM, what will be the ratio of [ATP] to [ADP] at equilibrium?
D. Show that, at constant $[P_i]$, ΔG decreases by 1.4 kcal/mole for every tenfold increase in the ratio of [ATP] to [ADP], regardless of the value of ΔG^o. (For example, ΔG decreases by 2.8 kcal/mole for a 100-fold change, by 4.2 kcal/mole for a 1000-fold change, etc.)

***7–6** One of the two ATP generating steps in glycolysis is outlined in Figure 7–2. This sequence of reactions yields ATP and produces pyruvate, which is subsequently converted to acetyl CoA and oxidized to CO_2 in the citric acid cycle. Under anaerobic conditions ATP production from phosphoenolpyruvate accounts for half of a cell's ATP supply. These "substrate-level" phosphorylation events (so named to distinguish them from oxidative phosphorylation in the mitochondrion) were the first to be understood. Consider the conversion of 3-phosphoglycerate to phosphoenolpyruvate, which constitutes the first two reactions in Figure 7–2.

The equation relating ΔG^o to the equilibrium constant is

$$\Delta G^o = -RT \ln K = -2.3\ RT \log_{10} K$$

where K_{eq} is the equilibrium ratio of the products over the reactants.

Figure 7–2 Conversion of 3-phosphoglycerate to pyruvate during glycolysis (Problem 7–6).

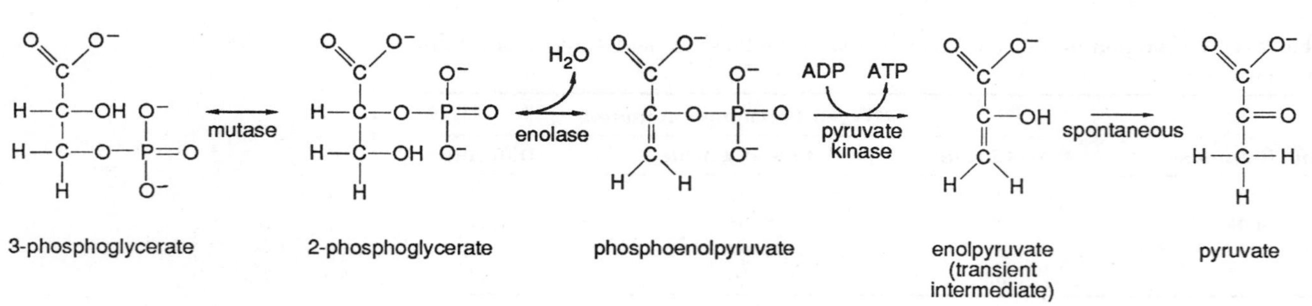

A. If 10 mM 3-phosphoglycerate is mixed with phosphoglycerate mutase, which catalyzes its conversion to 2-phosphoglycerate (Figure 7–2), the equilibrium concentrations at 37°C are 8.3 mM 3-phosphoglycerate and 1.7 mM 2-phosphoglycerate. How would the ratio of equilibrium concentrations change if 1 M 3-phosphoglycerate had been added initially? What is the equilibrium constant (K) for the conversion of 3-phosphoglycerate into 2-phosphoglycerate, and what is the $\Delta G°$ for the reaction?

B. If 10 mM phosphoenolpyruvate is mixed with enolase, which catalyzes its conversion to 2-phosphoglycerate, the equilibrium concentrations at 37°C are 2.9 mM 2-phosphoglycerate and 7.1 mM phosphoenolpyruvate. What is the $\Delta G°$ for conversion of phosphoenolpyruvate to 2-phosphoglycerate? What is the $\Delta G°$ for the reverse reaction?

C. What is the $\Delta G°$ for the conversion of 3-phosphoglycerate to phosphoenolpyruvate? ($\Delta G°$ for the overall reaction is the sum of the $\Delta G°$ values for the linked reactions.)

7–7 The study of substrate-level phosphorylation events such as that in Figure 7–2 led to the concept of the "high-energy" phosphate bond. The term "high-energy" bond is somewhat misleading since it refers not to the strength of the bond but, rather, to the free-energy change (ΔG) upon hydrolysis. In the conversion of 3-phosphoglycerate to phosphoenolpyruvate (the first two reactions in Figure 7–2) a low-energy phosphate bond is turned into a high-energy phosphate bond. The standard free-energy change ($\Delta G°$) of hydrolysis of the phosphate group in 3-phosphoglycerate is about −3.3 kcal/mole, whereas hydrolysis of the phosphate group in phosphoenolpyruvate (converting it to pyruvate) has a $\Delta G°$ of −14.8 kcal/mole. How is it that moving the phosphate to the 2 position of glycerate and removing water, which has an overall $\Delta G°$ of 0.4 kcal/mole, can have such an enormous effect on the free energy for the subsequent hydrolysis of the phosphate bond?

Consider the set of reactions shown in Figure 7–3.

A. What is $\Delta G°$ for conversion of 3-phosphoglycerate to pyruvate by way of phosphoenolpyruvate (PEP)? (Remember that $\Delta G°$ for the overall reaction is the sum of the $\Delta G°$ values of the individual steps.)

B. What is $\Delta G°$ for conversion of 3-phosphoglycerate to pyruvate by way of glycerate? What is $\Delta G°$ for conversion of glycerate to pyruvate? (It will help to remember that thermodynamic quantities are state functions; that is, they

Figure 7–3 Conversion of 3-phosphoglycerate to pyruvate and phosphate by two routes (Problem 7–7). For clarity the phosphate group is represented as a P in a circle. The bracketed compound, enolpyruvate, is a transient intermediate.

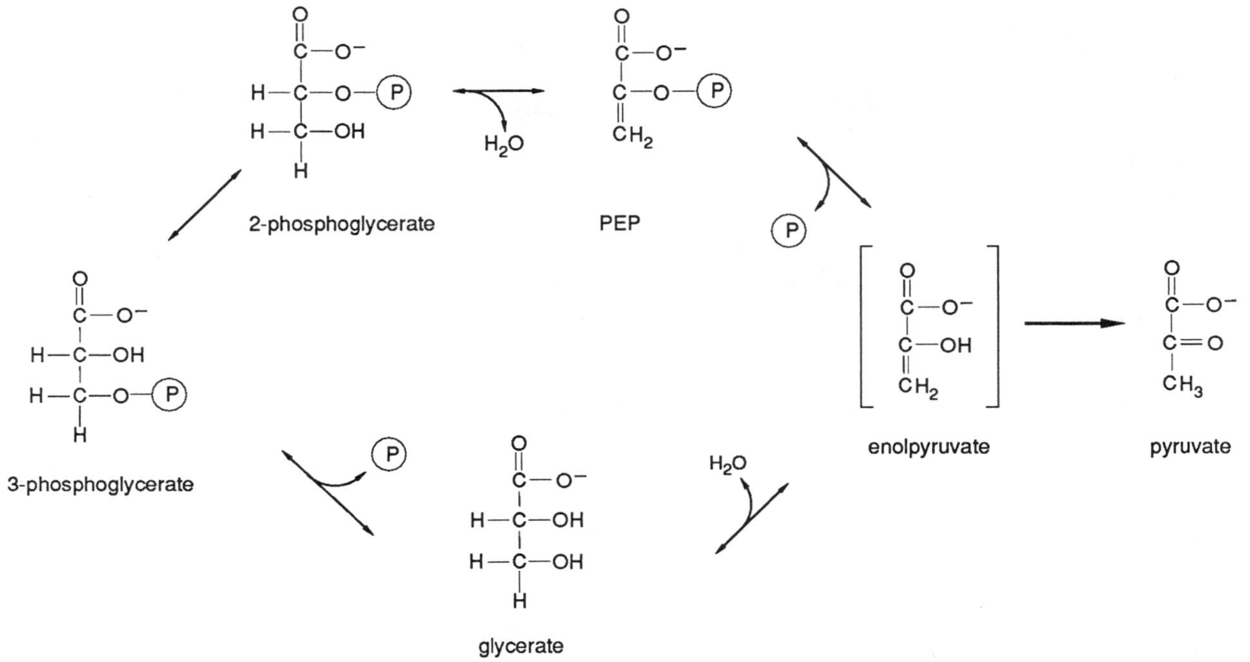

Table 7–2 Entry of ADP and ATP into Isolated Mitochondria (Problem 7–8)

Experiment	Substrate	Inhibitor	Relative Rates of Entry
1	absent	none	ADP = ATP
2	present	none	ADP > ATP
3	present	dinitrophenol	ADP = ATP
4	present	oligomycin	ADP > ATP

Note: In all cases the initial rates of entry of ATP and ADP were measured.

describe differences between the initial and final states—they are independent of the pathway between the states.)

C. Propose an explanation for why the phosphate bond in phosphoenolpyruvate is a high-energy bond, whereas that in 3-phosphoglycerate is a low-energy bond. (Assume that removal of water from glycerate has a $\Delta G°$ of -0.5 kcal/mole.)

D. In cells the conversion of phosphoenolpyruvate to pyruvate is linked to the synthesis of ATP as shown in Figure 7–2. What is $\Delta G°$ for the linked reactions?

***7–8** The ADP-ATP antiporter in the mitochondrial inner membrane can exchange ATP for ATP, ADP for ADP, and ATP for ADP. Even though mitochondria can transport both ADP and ATP, there is a strong bias in favor of exchange of external ADP for internal ATP under phosphorylating conditions. You suspect that this bias is due to the conversion of ADP into ATP inside the mitochondrion. ATP synthesis would continually reduce the internal concentration of ADP and thereby create a favorable concentration gradient for import of ADP. The same process would increase the internal concentration of ATP, thereby creating favorable conditions for export of ATP.

To test your hypothesis, you conduct experiments on isolated mitochondria. In the absence of substrate (when the mitochondria are not respiring and the membrane is uncharged), you find that ADP and ATP are taken up at the same rate. When you add substrate, the mitochondria begin to respire, and ADP enters mitochondria at a much faster rate than ATP. As you expected, when you add an uncoupler (dinitrophenol, which collapses the pH gradient) along with the substrate, ADP and ATP enter at the same rate. However, when you add an inhibitor of ATP synthetase (oligomycin) along with the substrate, ADP is taken up much faster than ATP. Your results are summarized in Table 7–2. You are puzzled by the results with oligomycin, since your hypothesis predicted that the rates of uptake would be equal.

When you show the results to your adviser, she compliments you on your fine experiments and agrees that they disprove the hypothesis. She suggests that you examine the structures of ATP and ADP (Figure 7–4) if you wish to understand the behavior of the antiporter. What is the correct explanation for the biased exchange by the ADP-ATP antiporter under some of the experimental conditions and an unbiased exchange under others?

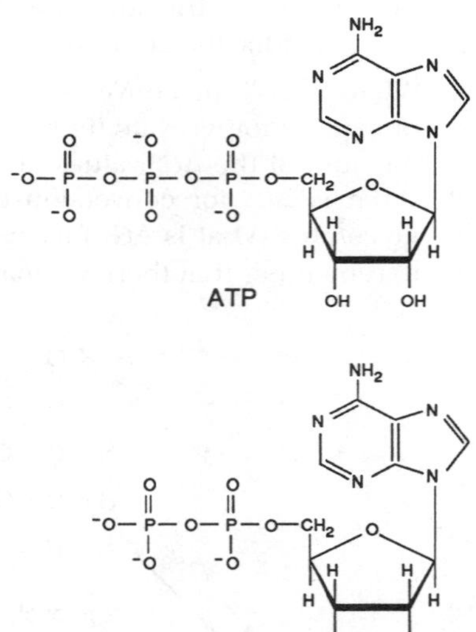

Figure 7–4 Structures of ATP and ADP (Problem 7–8).

The Respiratory Chain and ATP Synthetase

(MBOC 356–366)

7–9 Fill in the blanks in the following statements.

A. The F_1 ATPase is part of a larger transmembrane complex containing at least nine different polypeptide chains, which is now known as __________.

B. The __________ constitute a family of colored proteins that are related by the presence of a bound heme group, whose iron atom changes from the ferric to the ferrous state whenever it accepts an electron.

C. Proteins from a second major family of electron carriers have either two or four iron atoms bound to an equal number of sulfur atoms and to an equal number of cysteine side chains, forming an ____________ on the protein.
D. The simplest of the electron carriers is a small hydrophobic molecule known as ubiquinone, which, because it is a ____________, can pick up or donate either one or two electrons at a time.
E. Mild ionic detergents, which solubilize selected components of the mitochondrial inner membrane in their native form, permitted identification and purification of the three major membrane-bound ____________ in the pathway from NADH to oxygen.
F. The ____________ accepts electrons from NADH and passes them through a flavin and at least five iron-sulfur proteins to ubiquinone.
G. The ____________ accepts electrons from ubiquinone and passes them on to cytochrome *c*.
H. The ____________ accepts electrons from cytochrome *c* and passes them to oxygen.
I. Pairs of compounds such as NADH and NAD^+ are called ____________, since one compound is converted to the other by the addition of one or more electrons plus one or more protons.
J. A 50:50 mixture of NADH and NAD^+ maintains a defined "electron pressure," or ____________, that is a measure of the electron carrier's affinity for electrons.
K. The direct inhibitory influence of the electrochemical proton gradient on the rate of electron transport is known as ____________.

7–10 Indicate whether the following statements are true or false. If a statement is false, explain why.

__ A. The inside-out nature of submitochondrial particles was important for purification of the proteins responsible for oxidative phosphorylation because the particles can readily be provided with the membrane-impermeant metabolites that would normally be present in the matrix space.
__ B. If ATP synthetase and bacteriorhodopsin, which is a light-driven proton pump, are incorporated into lipid vesicles, exposure of the vesicles to light will cause ATP to be made.
__ C. Although purified ATP synthetase will hydrolyze ATP to ADP and P_i, the normal membrane-bound form in the mitochondrion is tightly regulated so that it will only synthesize ATP.
__ D. If the flow of protons through ATP synthetase is blocked, the injection of a small amount of oxygen into an anaerobic preparation of submitochondrial particles will result in a burst of respiration that will cause the medium to become more basic.
__ E. The proteins that constitute the respiratory chain all use iron atoms as electron carriers.
__ F. The toxicity of the poisons cyanide and azide is due to their ability to bind tightly to the cytochrome oxidase complex and thereby block all electron transport.
__ G. The three respiratory enzyme complexes exist in structurally ordered arrays in the plane of the inner membrane to facillitate the correct transfer of electrons between appropriate complexes.
__ H. Since most cytochromes have a higher redox potential than iron-sulfur centers, the cytochromes tend to serve as electron carriers near the O_2 end of the respiratory chain.
__ I. The molecular mechanism by which electron transport is coupled to proton pumping is likely to be different for different respiratory enzyme complexes.
__ J. Lipophilic weak acids short-circuit the normal flow of protons across the inner membrane, thereby dissipating the proton-motive force, stopping ATP synthesis, and blocking the flow of electrons.
__ K. If a very large electrochemical gradient is imposed across the inner membrane, a reverse electron flow can be detected in some sections of the respiratory chain.

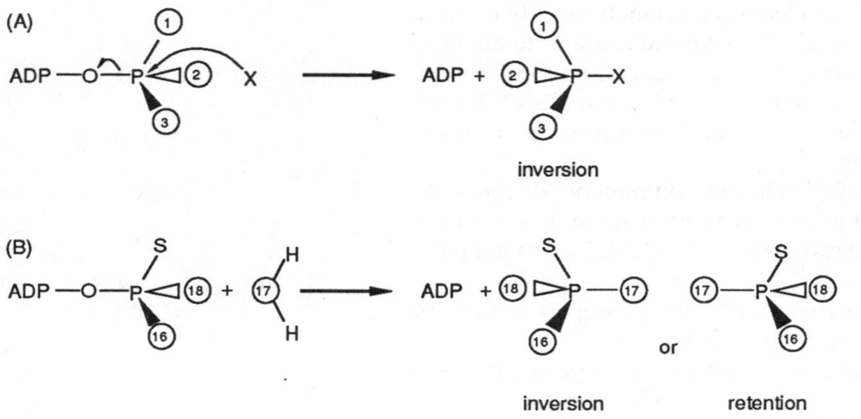

Figure 7–5 Stereochemistry of phosphate transfer reactions (Problem 7–11). (A) Inversion of configuration by a one-step phosphate transfer reaction. (B) Experimental setup for assaying stereochemistry of ATP synthesis by ATP synthetase. Thin bonds are in the plane of the page; thick white bonds point behind the page; and thick black bonds project out of the page. Oxygen atoms are indicated by their atomic number.

___ L. In brown fat cells mitochondrial respiration is normally uncoupled from ATP synthesis and the energy of oxidation is dissipated as heat.

___ M. Most bacteria, including strict anaerobes, maintain a proton-motive force across their plasma membrane, which is used to drive the flagellar motor and a variety of active transport processes.

7–11 The electrochemical proton gradient is undoubtedly the energy source for ATP synthesis during oxidative phosphorylation; however, the molecular mechanism by which the gradient is coupled to ATP synthesis remains to be determined. Is ATP synthesized directly from ADP and inorganic phosphate or is the phosphate transferred from an intermediate source, such as a phosphoenzyme or some other phosphorylated compound?

One elegant approach analyzed the stereochemistry of the reaction mechanism. As is often done, the investigators studied the reverse reaction (ATP hydrolysis into ADP and phosphate) to gain an understanding of the forward reaction. (A fundamental principle of enzyme catalysis is that the forward and reverse reactions are precisely the reverse of one another.) All enzyme-catalyzed phosphate transfers occur with inversion of configuration about the phosphate atom; thus one-step mechanisms, in which the residue is transferred directly between substrates, result in inversion of the final product (Figure 7–5A).

To analyze the stereochemistry of ATP hydrolysis, the investigators first generated a version of ATP with three distinct atoms (S, ^{16}O, and ^{18}O) attached stereospecifically to the terminal phosphorus atom (Figure 7–5B). This compound was then hydrolyzed to ADP and inorganic phosphate by purified ATP synthetase in the presence of H_2O that was enriched for ^{17}O. The resulting inorganic phosphate was analyzed by NMR to determine whether the configuration about the phosphorus atom had been inverted or retained (Figure 7–5B).

A. How does this experiment distinguish between synthesis of ATP directly from ADP and inorganic phosphate and synthesis of ATP through an intermediate phosphorylated substance?

B. Their analysis showed that the configuration had been inverted. Does this result support direct synthesis of ATP or synthesis of ATP through a phosphorylated intermediate?

7–12 In 1925 David Keilin used a simple spectroscope to observe the characteristic absorption bands of the cytochromes that make up the electron-trans-

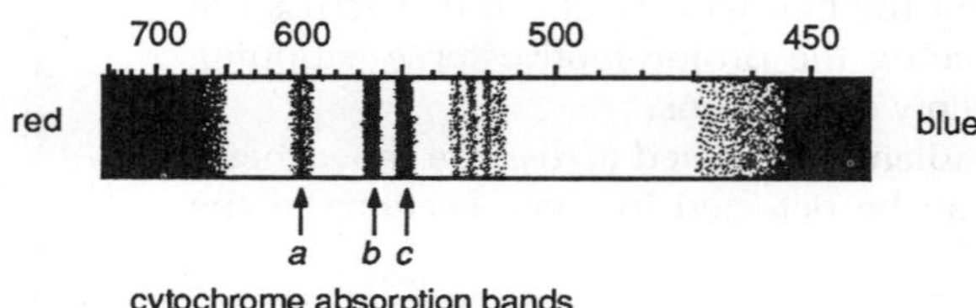

Figure 7–6 Cytochrome absorption bands (Problem 7–12). Numbers are the wavelengths of light in nanometers.

port chain in mitochondria. A spectroscope passes a very bright light through the sample of interest and then through a prism to display the spectrum from red to blue. If there are molecules in the sample that absorb light of particular wavelengths, dark bands interrupt the colors of the rainbow. Keilin found that tissues from a wide variety of animals all showed the pattern in Figure 7–6. (This pattern had actually been observed several decades before by an Irish physician named MacMunn, but he thought all the bands were due to a single pigment. His work was all but forgotten by the 1920s.)

The different heat stabilities of the individual absorption bands and their different intensities in different tissues led Keilin to conclude that the absorption pattern was due to three components, which he labeled cytochromes *a*, *b*, and *c* (Figure 7–6). His key discovery was that the absorption bands disappeared when oxygen was introduced (Figure 7–7A) and then reappeared when the samples became anoxic (Figure 7–7B). He later confessed, "This visual perception of an intracellular respiratory process was one of the most impressive spectacles I have witnessed in the course of my work."

Keilin subsequently discovered that cyanide prevented the bands from disappearing when oxygen was introduced (Figure 7–7C). When urethane (a no longer used inhibitor of electron transport) was added, bands a and c disappeared in the presence of oxygen, but band b remained (Figure 7–7D). Finally, using cytochrome *c* extracted from dried yeast with water, he showed that the band due to cytochrome *c* remained when oxygen was present (Figure 7–7E).

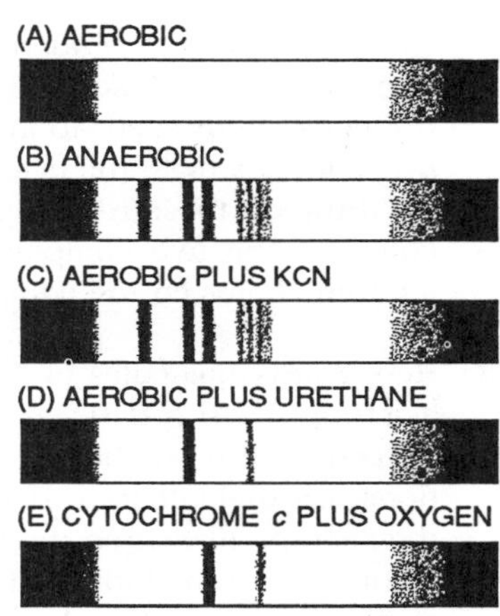

Figure 7–7 Cytochrome absorption bands under a variety of experimental conditions (Problem 7–12).

A. Is it the reduced (electron-rich) or the oxidized (electron-poor) forms of the cytochromes that give rise to the bands Keilin observed?

B. From Keilin's observations, deduce the order in which the three cytochromes carry electrons from intracellular substrates to oxygen.

C. One of Keilin's early observations was that the presence of excess glucose prevented the disappearance of the absorption bands when oxygen was added. How do you think that rapid glucose oxidation to CO_2 might explain this observation?

***7–13** During operation of the respiratory chain, cytochrome *c* accepts electrons from the *b*-c_1 complex and transfers them to the cytochrome oxidase complex. What is the relationship of cytochrome *c* to the two complexes it connects? Is cytochrome *c* linked simultaneously to both complexes like a wire, allowing electrons to flow through it from one complex to the other, or does cytochrome *c* move between the complexes like a ferry, picking up electrons from one and handing them over to the next? One source of information about this question is provided by the experiments described below.

Individual lysines on cytochrome *c* were modified to replace the positively charged amino group with a neutral group or with a negatively charged group. The effects of these modifications on electron transfer from the *b*-c_1 complex to cytochrome *c* and from cytochrome *c* to the cytochrome oxidase complex were then measured. Some modifications had no effect (Figure 7–8, open circles), whereas others inhibited electron transfer from the *b*-c_1 complex to cytochrome *c* (Figure 7–8A, shaded circles) or from cytochrome *c* to the cytochrome oxidase complex (Figure 7–8B, shaded

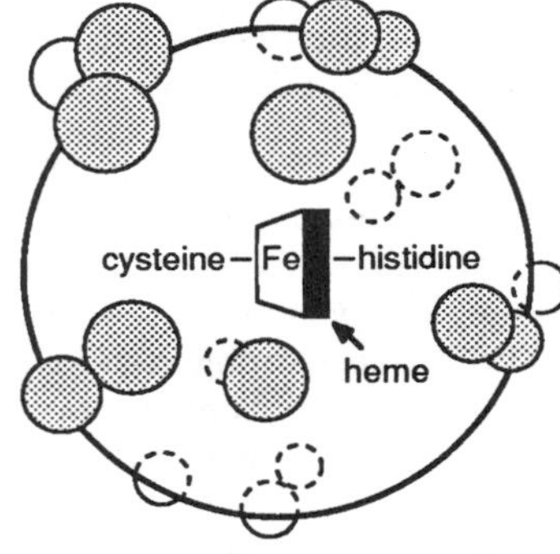

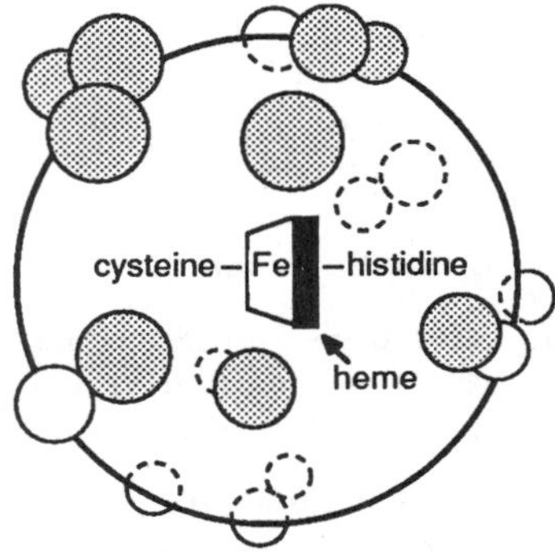

Figure 7–8 Positions of lysines that inhibit the transfer of electrons from (A) the *b*-c_1 complex to cytochrome *c* and (B) from cytochrome *c* to the cytochrome oxidase complex (Problem 7–13). One edge of the heme group protrudes from the front surface of cytochrome *c* toward the reader. Circles show the positions of lysines. Solid circles are on the front surface of the molecule; dashed circles are on the back surface. The larger the circle, the closer it is to the reader. Shaded circles indicate lysines that inhibit electron transfer; open circles indicate lysines that do not inhibit electron transfer.

circles). In an independent series of experiments, several lysines that inhibited transfer of electrons to and from cytochrome *c* were shown to be protected from acetylation when cytochrome *c* was bound either to the *b*-c_1 complex or to the cytochrome oxidase complex.

How do these results distinguish the possibilities that cytochrome *c* connects the two complexes by binding to them simultaneously or by shuttling between the complexes?

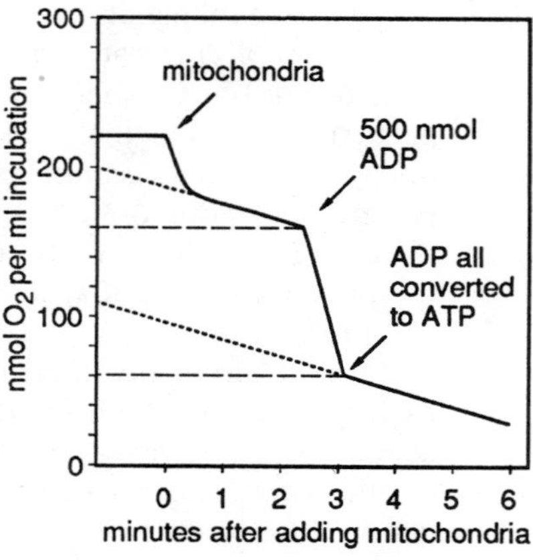

Figure 7–9 Consumption of oxygen by mitochondria under various experimental conditions (Problem 7–14).

7–14 How many molecules of ATP are formed from ADP + P_i when a pair of electrons from NADH are passed down the electron-transport chain to oxygen? Is the number an integer or not? These deceptively simple questions are difficult to answer from purely theoretical considerations, but they can be measured directly with an oxygen electrode, as illustrated in Figure 7–9. At the indicated time, a suspension of mitochondria was added to a phosphate-buffered solution containing β-hydroxybutyrate, which can be oxidized by mitochondria to generate NADH + H^+. After an initial rapid burst, oxygen consumption slowed to a background rate. When the rate of oxygen consumption stabilized, 500 nmol of ADP were added, causing a rapid increase in the rate of consumption until all the ADP had been converted into ATP, at which point the rate of oxygen consumption again slowed to the background rate.

A. Why did the rate of oxygen consumption increase dramatically over the background rate when ADP was added; why did it return to the background rate when all the ADP had been converted to ATP?

B. Why do you think it is that mitochondria consume oxygen at a slow background rate in the absence of added ADP?

C. How many ATP molecules were synthesized per pair of electrons transferred down the electron-transport chain to oxygen (P/2e^- ratio)? How many ATP molecules were synthesized per oxygen atom consumed (P/O ratio)? (Remember that 1/2 O_2 + $2H^+$ + $2e^-$ → H_2O.)

D. In experiments like this one, what processes in addition to ATP production are driven by the electrochemical proton gradient?

***7–15** Inhibitors of mitochondrial function have provided extremely useful tools for analyzing how mitochondria work. Figure 7–10 shows three distinct patterns of oxygen electrode traces obtained using a variety of inhibitors. In all experiments mitochondria were added to a phosphate-buffered solution containing succinate as the sole source of electrons for the respiratory chain. After a short interval ADP and then an inhibitor were added, as indicated in Figure 7–10. The rates of oxygen consumption at various times during the experiment are shown by downward sloping lines, with faster rates shown by steeper lines.

A. From the description of the inhibitors in the list that follows, assign each inhibitor to one of the oxygen traces in Figure 7–10. All these inhibitors stop ATP synthesis.

Inhibitor	Function
1. FCCP	Makes membranes permeable to protons
2. Malonate	Prevents oxidation of succinate
3. Cyanide	Inhibits cytochrome oxidase
4. Atractylate	Inhibits the ADP-ATP antiporter
5. Oligomycin	Inhibits ATP synthetase
6. Butylmalonate	Blocks mitochondrial uptake of succinate

B. Using the same experimental protocol indicated in Figure 7–10, sketch the oxygen traces that you would expect for the sequential addition of the pairs of inhibitors in the list below:

1. FCCP followed by cyanide
2. FCCP followed by oligomycin
3. Oligomycin followed by FCCP

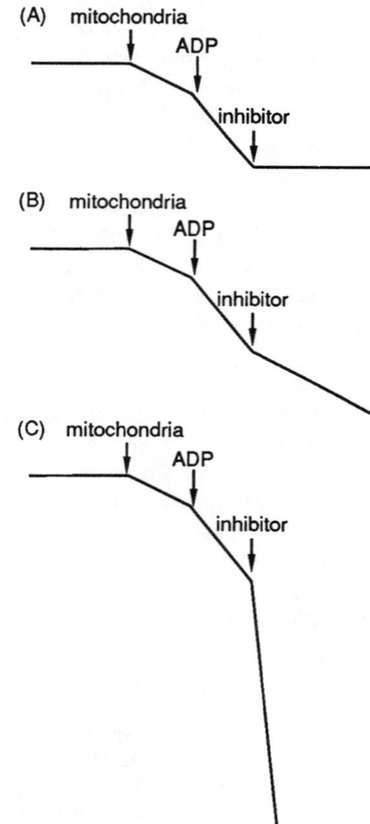

Figure 7–10 Oxygen traces showing three patterns of inhibitor effects on oxygen consumption by mitochondria (Problem 7–15).

***7–16** Methanogenic bacteria produce methane as the end product of electron transport. For example, *Methanosarcina barkeri,* when grown under hydrogen in the presence of methanol, transfers electrons from hydrogen to methanol, producing methane and water:

$$CH_3OH + H_2 \rightarrow CH_4 + H_2O$$

This reaction is analogous to those used by aerobic bacteria and mitochondria, which transfer electrons from carbon compounds to oxygen, producing water and carbon dioxide. However, given the peculiar biochemistry involved in methanogenesis, it was initially unclear whether methanogenic bacteria synthesized ATP by electron-transport phosphorylation or by substrate-level phosphorylation.

In the experiments depicted in Figure 7–11 methanol is added to a culture of methanogenic bacteria grown under hydrogen, and the production of CH_4, the size of the electrochemical proton gradient (ΔG_{H^+}), and the intracellular concentration of ATP are assayed. The effects of the addition of two types of inhibitor are measured: TCS, which dissipates the electrochemical proton gradient, and DCCD, which directly inhibits ATP synthetase. In all the experiments, addition of methanol produces an increase in the electrochemical proton gradient and an increase in intracellular ATP. Addition of TCS (Figure 7–11A) dissipates the electrochemical proton gradient and stops ATP synthesis; however, it does not stop CH_4 production. Addition of DCCD (Figure 7–11B) stops ATP synthesis and inhibits CH_4 production, but it does not significantly affect the electrochemical proton gradient. Addition of TCS after ATP synthesis and CH_4 production have been stopped by DCCD (Figure 7–11C) dissipates the electrochemical proton gradient but stimulates production of CH_4.

A. Would you expect 2,4-dinitrophenol, which dissipates the electrochemical proton gradient in mitochondria, to have an effect on mitochondria analogous to the effect of TCS on methanogens, that is, stopping ATP production but not blocking production of CO_2? Why?

B. Would you expect oligomycin, which inhibits ATP synthetase in mitochondria, to have an effect on mitochondria analogous to the effect of DCCD on methanogens, that is, blocking production of CO_2 without affecting the electrochemical proton gradient? Why?

C. Would you expect addition of 2,4-dinitrophenol to oligomycin-inhibited mitochondria to stimulate production of CO_2 in a manner analogous to the stimulation of CH_4 production by addition of TCS to DCCD-inhibited methanogens? Why?

D. Do methanogenic bacteria generate ATP by electron-transport phosphorylation or by substrate-level phosphorylation?

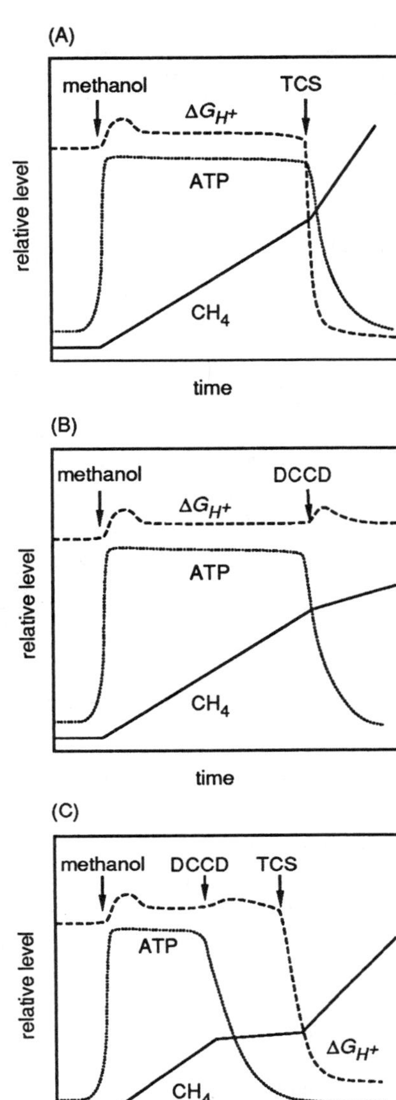

Figure 7–11 Time course of CH_4 production after addition of methanol to a culture of methanogenic bacteria growing under H_2 (Problem 7–16). The magnitude of the electrochemical proton gradient (ΔG_{H^+}), the intracellular ATP concentration, and the production of CH_4 are expressed in arbitrary units.

7–17 The electrochemical proton gradient is responsible not only for ATP production in bacteria, mitochondria, and chloroplasts, but also for powering bacterial flagella. The flagellar motor is thought to be driven directly by the flux of protons through it. To test this idea, you analyze a motile strain of *Streptococcus*. These bacteria swim when glucose is available for oxidation, but they do not swim when glucose is absent (and no other substrate is available for oxidation). Using a series of ionophores that alter the pH gradient or the membrane potential (the two components of the electrochemical proton gradient), you make several observations.

1. Bacteria that are swimming in the presence of glucose stop swimming upon addition of the proton ionophore, FCCP.
2. Bacteria that are swimming in the presence of glucose in a medium containing K^+ are unaffected by addition of the K^+ ionophore, valinomycin.
3. Bacteria that are motionless in the absence of glucose in a medium containing K^+ remain motionless upon addition of valinomycin.
4. Bacteria that are motionless in the absence of glucose in a medium

Table 7–3 Effects of Ionophores on the Swimming of Normal Bacteria (Problem 7–17)

Observation	Glucose	Ionophore	Ion in Medium	Effect on Bacteria
1	present	FCCP (H^+)	—	stop swimming
2	present	valinomycin (K^+)	K^+	keep swimming
3	absent	valinomycin (K^+)	K^+	remain motionless
4	absent	valinomycin (K^+)	Na^+	swim briefly

Note: The specificity of each ionophore is shown in parenthesis.

containing Na^+ swim briefly upon addition of valinomycin and then stop.

These observations are summarized in Table 7–3.

A. Explain how each of these observations is consistent with the idea that the flagellar motor is driven by a flux of protons. (The concentration of K^+ inside these bacteria is lower than the concentration of K^+ used in the medium.)

B. Wild-type bacteria can swim in the presence or absence of oxygen. However, mutant bacteria that are missing ATP synthetase, which couples proton flow to ATP production, can swim only in the presence of oxygen. How are normal bacteria able to swim in the absence of oxygen when there is no electron flow? How do you think the loss of the ATP synthetase prevents swimming in mutant bacteria?

Chloroplasts and Photosynthesis (MBOC 366–381)

7–18 Fill in the blanks in the following statements.

A. The inner chloroplast membrane surrounds a large central space called the ____________, which is analogous to the mitochondrial matrix.

B. The photosynthetic light-absorbing system, the electron-transport chain, and an ATP synthetase are all contained in a set of flattened disclike sacs, called ____________.

C. The many reactions that occur in photosynthesis can be grouped into two broad categories: the ____________ reactions and the ____________ reactions.

D. Carbon fixation is catalyzed by the enzyme ____________, which is widely claimed to be the most abundant protein on earth.

E. The conversion of CO_2 into carbohydrate occurs by a cycle of reactions, which is called the ____________ cycle.

F. The disaccharide ____________ is the major form in which sugar is transported between plant cells, acting in plant cells as glucose acts in animal cells.

G. Like glycogen in animal cells, ____________ is a large polymer of glucose that serves as a carbohydrate reserve.

H. Plants that pump CO_2 are called ____________ plants; all others are called ____________ plants.

I. The energy required to drive photosynthetic electron transport is derived from sunlight that is absorbed by ____________ molecules.

J. A photosystem consists of two closely linked components: an ____________, which is important for light harvesting, and a ____________, which transfers excited electrons to a chain of electron acceptors.

K. Photosynthesis in plants and cyanobacteria produces both ATP and NADPH directly by a two-step process called ____________.

L. The two electron-energizing steps catalyzed by photosystems I and II are linked together to form the ____________ of photosynthesis.

M. During ____________ chloroplasts switch photosystem I into a cyclic mode of operation in which its energy is directed into the synthesis of ATP instead of NADPH.

7–19 Indicate whether the following statements are true or false. If a statement is false, explain why.

__ A. In a general way, one might view the chloroplast as a greatly enlarged mitochondrion in which the cristae are condensed into a series of interconnected submitochondrial particles in the matrix space.

__ B. The conversion of CO_2 to carbohydrate requires light energy directly, whereas the formation of O_2 requires light energy only indirectly.

__ C. In the central reaction of carbon fixation, CO_2 from the atmosphere combines with the five-carbon compound ribulose 1,5-bisphosphate to give two molecules of the three-carbon compound 3-phosphoglycerate.

__ D. Both phosphate-bond energy (ATP) and reducing power (NADPH) are required for formation of organic molecules from CO_2 and H_2O.

__ E. To avoid the waste of photorespiration, many plants in hot, dry climates "pump" CO_2 into bundle-sheath cells to provide ribulose bisphosphate carboxylase with a high concentration of CO_2.

__ F. The process of energy conversion begins when a chlorophyll molecule is excited by a quantum of light and an electron is moved from one molecular orbital to another of higher energy.

__ G. When a molecule of chlorophyll in an antenna complex absorbs a photon, the excited electron is rapidly transferred from one molecule to another until it reaches the photochemical reaction center.

__ H. A photosystem enables light to activate a net electron transfer from a molecule such as a cytochrome, which is a weak electron donor, to a molecule such as a quinone, which is a strong electron donor in its reduced form.

__ I. The purple bacterium uses its photochemical reaction center to generate an electrochemical proton gradient across the plasma membrane, which is used to drive ATP synthesis and to drive a reverse electron flow to produce NADH.

__ J. The linking of two photosystems into the Z scheme of photosynthesis allows two electrons from H_2O to be energized sufficiently by two photons to reduce $NADP^+$ to NADPH.

__ K. The balance between noncyclic photophosphorylation, which generates ATP and NADPH, and cyclic photophosphorylation, which generates only NADPH, is regulated according to the need for ATP.

__ L. Intact thylakoid discs resemble submitochondrial particles in having a membrane whose electron-transport chain has its $NADP^+$-, ADP-, and phosphate-utilizing sites all freely accessible to the outside.

__ M. The export of glyceraldehyde 3-phosphate from the chloroplast provides not only the main source of fixed carbon to the rest of the cell, but also reducing power and ATP needed for other biosynthetic reactions in the cytosol.

7–20 Recalling Joseph Priestley's famous experiment in which a sprig of mint saved the life of a mouse in a sealed chamber, you decide to do an analogous experiment to see how a C_3 and a C_4 plant do when confined together in a sealed environment. You place a corn plant (C_4) and a geranium (C_3) in a sealed plastic chamber with normal air (300 parts per million CO_2) on a windowsill in your laboratory. What happens to the two plants? Do they compete or collaborate? If they compete, which one wins and why?

***7–21** How much energy is available in visible light? How much energy does sunlight deliver to the earth? How efficient are plants at converting light energy into chemical energy? The answers to these questions provide an important backdrop to the subject of photosynthesis.

Each quantum or photon of light has an energy of $h\nu$, where h is Planck's constant (1.58×10^{-37} kcal sec/photon) and ν is the frequency in sec^{-1}. The frequency of light is equal to c/λ, where c is the speed of light (3.0×10^{17} nm/sec) and λ is the wavelength in nm. Thus, the energy ($\mathscr{E}$) of a photon is

$$\mathscr{E} = h\nu = hc/\lambda$$

A. Calculate the energy of a mole of photons (6×10^{23} photons/mole) at 400 nm (violet light), at 680 nm (red light), and at 800 nm (near infrared light).
B. Bright sunlight strikes the earth at the rate of about 0.3 kcal/sec per square meter. Assuming for the sake of calculation that sunlight consists of monochromatic light of wavelength 680 nm, how many seconds does it take for a mole of photons to strike a square meter?
C. Assuming that it takes 8 photons to fix 1 molecule of CO_2 as carbohydrate under optimal conditions (8 to 10 photons is the currently accepted value), calculate how long it would take a tomato plant with a leaf area of 1 square meter to make a mole of glucose from CO_2. Assume that photons strike the leaf at the rate calculated above and, furthermore, that all the photons are absorbed and used to fix CO_2.
D. If it takes 112 kcal/mole to fix a mole of CO_2 into carbohydrate, what is the efficiency of conversion of light energy into chemical energy after photon capture? Assume again that 8 photons of red light (680 nm) are required to fix 1 molecule of CO_2.

7–22 Recently, your boss has expanded the lab's interest in photosynthesis from algae to higher plants. You have been assigned to study photosynthetic carbon fixation in the cactus, but so far you have had no success: cactus plants do not seem to fix $^{14}CO_2$, even in direct sunlight. Under the same conditions your colleagues studying dandelions get excellent incorporation of $^{14}CO_2$ within seconds of adding it and are busily charting new biochemical pathways.

Depressed, you leave the lab one day without dismantling the labeling chamber. The following morning you remove the cactus and, much to your surprise, find it has incorporated a great deal of $^{14}CO_2$. Evidently, the cactus fixed carbon during the night. When you repeat your experiments at night in complete darkness, you find that cactus plants incorporate label splendidly.

Although you are forced to shift your work habits (and your spouse is suspicious), at least now you can make some progress. A brief exposure to $^{14}CO_2$ labels one compound—malate—almost exclusively. During the night labeled malate builds up to very high levels in specialized vacuoles inside chloroplast-containing cells. In addition, the starch in these same cells disappears. During the day the malate disappears, and labeled starch is formed in a process that requires light. Furthermore, you find that $^{14}CO_2$ reappears in these cells during the day.

These results remind you in some ways of CO_2 pumping in C_4 plants, but they are quite distinct in other ways.

A. Why is light required for starch formation in the cactus? Is it required for starch formation in C_4 plants?
B. Using the reactions of the CO_2 pump in C_4 plants as a starting point, sketch a brief outline of CO_2 fixation in the cactus. Which reactions occur during the day and which at night?
C. A cactus depleted of starch could not fix CO_2, but a C_4 plant could. Why is starch required for CO_2 fixation in the cactus but not in C_4 plants?
D. Can you offer an explanation for why this method of CO_2 fixation is advantageous for cactus plants?

***7–23** Careful experiments comparing absorption and action spectra of plants ultimately led to the notion of two cooperating photosystems in chloroplasts. The absorption spectrum is the amount of light captured by photosynthetic pigments at different wavelengths. The action spectrum is the rate of photosynthesis (for example, O_2 evolution or CO_2 fixation) resulting from the capture of photons.

The first measurement of an action spectrum was probably made in 1882 by T.W. Englemann, who used simple equipment and an ingenious experimental design. He placed a filamentous green alga into a test tube along with a suspension of oxygen-seeking bacteria. He allowed the bac-

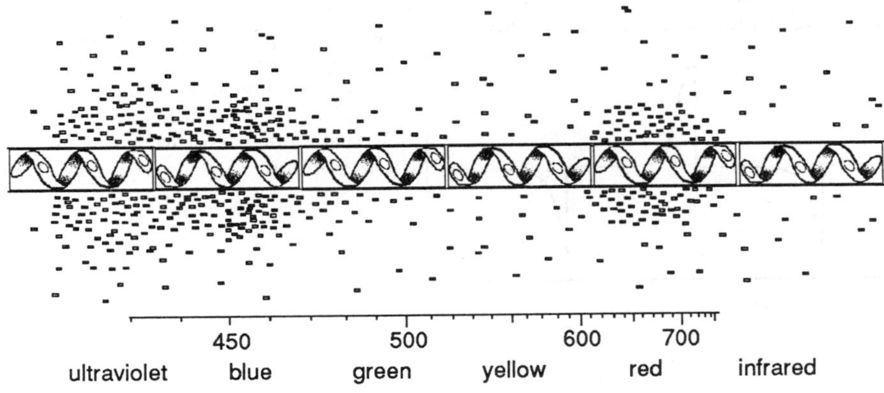

Figure 7–12 Experiment to measure the action spectrum of a filamentous green alga (Problem 7–23). Bacteria, which are indicated by the tiny rectangles, were distributed evenly throughout the test tube at the beginning of the experiment.

teria to use up the available oxygen and then illuminated the alga with light that had been passed through a prism to form a spectrum. After a short time he observed the results shown in Figure 7–12. Sketch the action spectrum for this alga and explain how this experiment works.

7–24 If all pigments captured energy and delivered it to the photosystem with equal efficiency, then the absorption spectrum and the action spectrum would have the same shape; however, the two spectra differ slightly (Figure 7–13A). When a ratio of the two spectra is displayed (Figure 7–13B), the most dramatic difference is the so-called "red drop" at long wavelengths. In 1957 Emerson found that if shorter wavelength light (650 nm) was mixed with the less effective longer wavelength light (700 nm), the rate of O_2 evolution was much enhanced over either wavelength given alone. This result, along with others, suggested that two photosystems (now called photosystem I and photosystem II) were cooperating with one another and led to the familiar Z scheme for photosynthesis.

One clue to the order in which the two photosystems are linked came from experiments in which illumination was switched between 650 nm and 700 nm. As shown in Figure 7–14, a shift from 700 nm to 650 nm was accompanied by a transient burst of O_2 evolution, whereas a shift from 650 nm to 700 nm was accompanied by a transient depression in O_2 evolution.

Using your knowledge of the Z scheme of photosynthesis, explain why these so-called chromatic transients occur, and deduce whether photosystem II, which accepts electrons from H_2O, is more sensitive to 650-nm light or to 700-nm light.

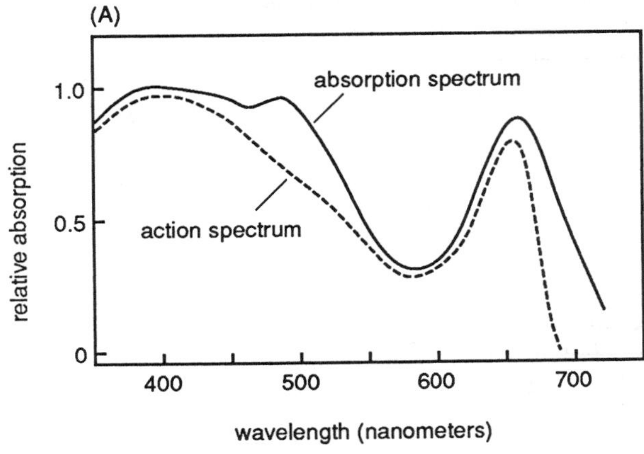

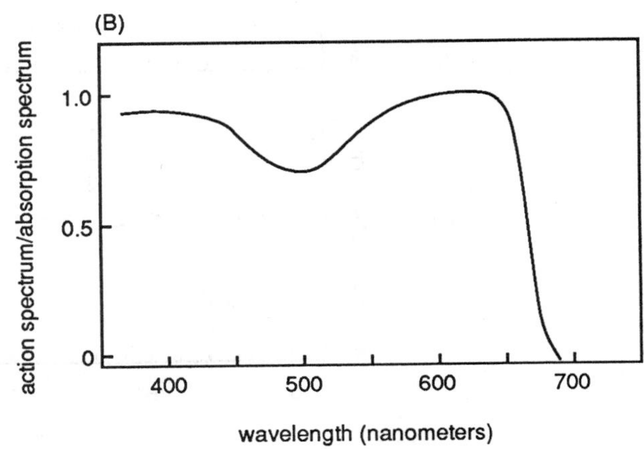

Figure 7–13 Absorption and action spectra (A) and the ratio of action spectrum to absorption spectrum (B) for the alga *Chlorella* (Problem 7–24). The action spectrum shows the evolution of O_2 at different wavelengths. The ratio of the action spectrum to the absorption spectrum is shown on an arbitrary scale.

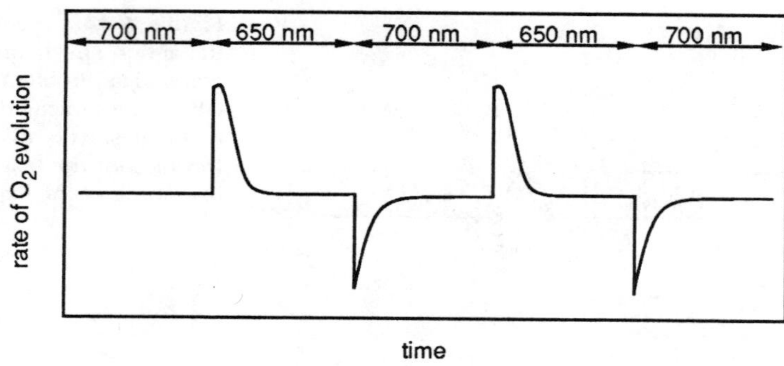

Figure 7–14 Chromatic transients observed upon switching between 650-nm light and 700-nm light (Problem 7–24). The intensities of light at the two wavelengths were adjusted beforehand so that alone each gave the same rate of O_2 evolution.

***7–25** The most compelling early evidence for the Z scheme of photosynthesis came from measuring the oxidation state of the cytochromes in algae under different regimes of illumination (Figure 7–15). Illumination with light at 680 nm caused oxidation of cytochromes (indicated by the upward trace); additional illumination with light at 562 nm caused reduction of the cytochromes (indicated by the downward trace); and both effects could be reversed by turning the lights off (Figure 7–15A). In the presence of the herbicide, DCMU, which blocks electron transport through the cytochromes and stops O_2 evolution, the reduction with 562-nm light disappeared and was replaced by a small additional oxidation (Figure 7–15B).

A. In these algae, which wavelength stimulates photosystem I and which stimulates photosystem II?

B. How do these results support the Z scheme for photosynthesis; that is, how do they support the idea that there are two photosystems that are linked by cytochromes?

C. On which side of the cytochromes does DCMU block electron transport—on the side nearer photosystem I or the side nearer photosystem II?

7–26 Photosystem II accepts electrons from water, generating O_2, and donates them via the electron-transport chain to photosystem I. Each photon absorbed by photosystem II can effect the transfer of only a single electron, and yet four electrons must be removed from water to generate a molecule of O_2. Thus, four photons are required to evolve a molecule of O_2.

$$2H_2O + 4h\nu \rightarrow 4e^- + 4H^+ + O_2$$

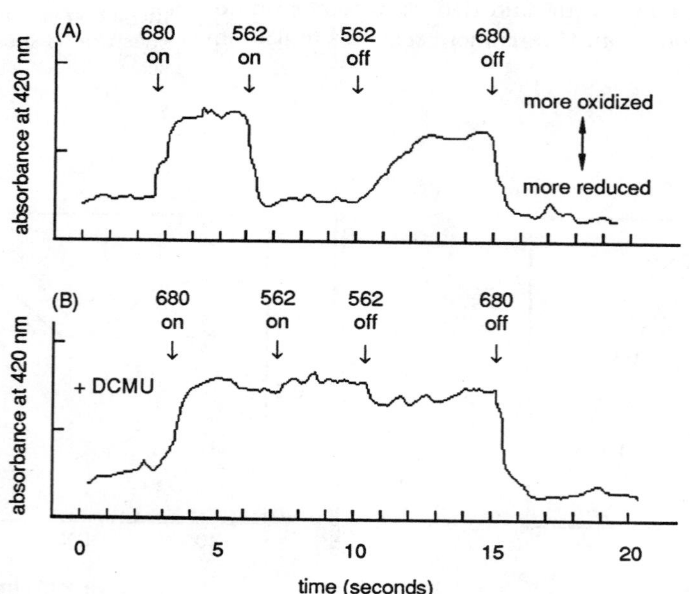

Figure 7–15 Oxidation state of cytochromes after illumination of algae with different wavelength light in the absence (A) and presence (B) of DCMU (Problem 7–25). An upward trace indicates oxidation of the cytochromes; a downward trace indicates reduction of the cytochromes.

How do four photons cooperate in the production of O_2? Is it necessary that four photons arrive at a single reaction center simultaneously? Can four activated reaction centers cooperate to evolve a molecule of O_2? Or is there some sort of "gear wheel" that collects the four electrons from H_2O and transfers them one at a time to a reaction center?

To investigate this problem, you expose dark-adapted spinach chloroplasts to a series of brief saturating flashes of light (2 μsec) separated by short periods of darkness (0.3 second) and measure the evolution of O_2 that results from each flash. Under this lighting regime most photosystems capture a photon during each flash. As shown in Figure 7–16, O_2 is evolved with a distinct periodicity: the first burst of O_2 occurs on the third flash, and subsequent peaks occur every fourth flash thereafter. If you first inhibit 97% of the photosystem II reaction centers with DCMU and then repeat the experiment, you observe the same periodicity of O_2 production, but the peaks are only 3% of the uninhibited values.

A. How do these results distinguish among the three possibilities posed at the outset (simultaneous action, cooperation among reaction centers, and a gear wheel)?

B. Why do you think it is that the first burst of O_2 occurs after the third flash, whereas additional peaks occur at four-flash intervals? (Consider what this observation implies about the dark-adapted state of the chloroplasts.)

C. Can you suggest a reason why the periodicity in O_2 evolution becomes less pronounced with increasing flash number?

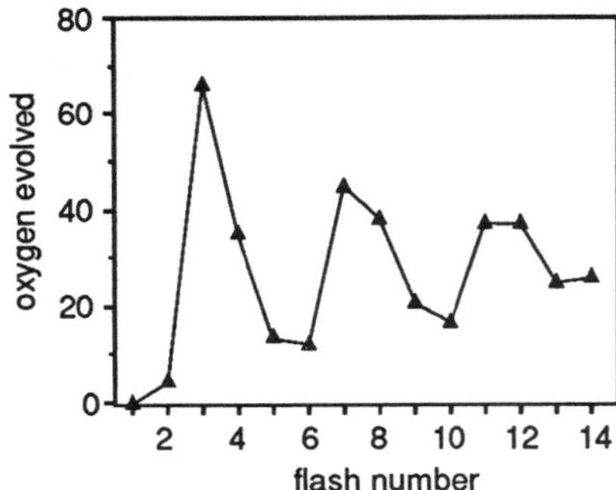

Figure 7–16 Oxygen evolution by spinach chloroplasts in response to saturating flashes of light (Problem 7–26). The chloroplasts were placed in the dark for 40 minutes prior to the experiment to allow them to come to the same "ground" state.

***7–27** Chloroplasts synthesize ATP much like mitochondria; they couple electron transport to the pumping of protons and then harvest the energy in the resulting electrochemical proton gradient by directing the protons through an ATP synthetase to make ATP. One of the earliest and most convincing tests of the chemiosmotic coupling of electron transport and ATP synthesis used thylakoid vesicles obtained from spinach chloroplasts.

In these experiments formation of ATP was assayed in a suspension of thylakoid vesicles (stromal surface facing outward, that is, right-side-out). These vesicles were first acidified to pH 4 and then made alkaline in the presence of ADP and $^{32}PO_4$. As shown in Figure 7–17, the yield of ATP was greater when the vesicles were acidified with succinic acid than it was when they were acidified with HCl. Furthermore, the yield of ATP increased with increasing concentration of succinic acid (even though pH 4 solutions were used in all experiments). As shown in Figure 7–18, the yield of ATP also depended on the pH of the alkaline stage of the experiment, with the yield of ATP increasing up to pH 8.5.

A. Why does acidification with succinic acid yield more ATP than acidification with HCl? And why does the yield of ATP increase with increasing concentrations of succinic acid? (Succinic acid has two carboxylic acid groups with pKs of 4.2 and 5.5.)

B. Why is the yield of ATP so critically dependent on the pH of the alkaline stage of the experiment?

C. Predict the effect of the following treatments during the alkaline incubation, and rationalize your prediction.

1. Addition of FCCP, which is an uncoupler of electron transport and ATP synthesis
2. Addition of DCMU, which blocks electron transport through the cytochromes
3. Illumination with bright light
4. Incubation in total darkness

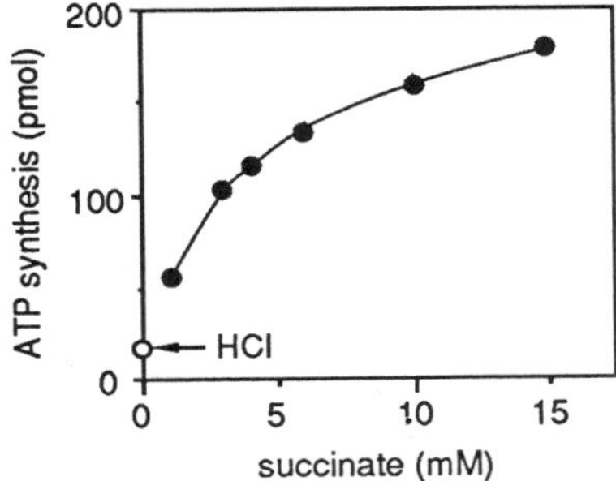

Figure 7–17 Yield of ATP with HCl and with increasing concentrations of succinic acid (Problem 7–27). The yield of ATP with HCl is shown on the Y axis, where the concentration of succinic acid is zero. In all cases the thylakoid suspension was treated with acid for 60 seconds, then treated with alkali for 15 seconds in the presence of ADP and $^{32}PO_4$, at which point the reaction was stopped and the yield of radioactive ATP was measured.

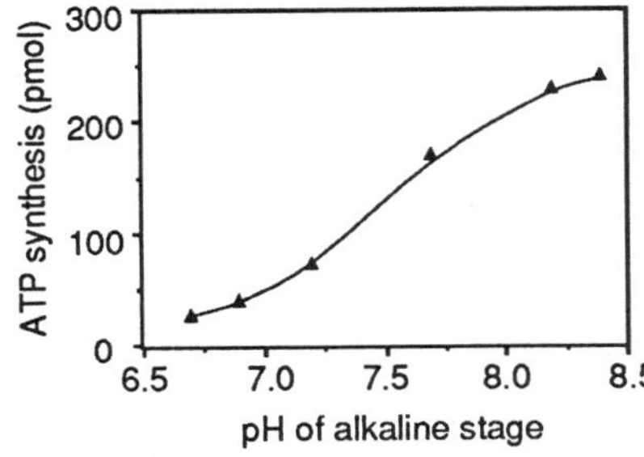

Figure 7–18 Yield of ATP at different pHs during the alkaline stage of the experiment (Problem 7–27).

7–28 *Thiobacillus ferrooxidans* is a bacterium that lives on slag heaps at pH 2. In the mining industry it is used to recover copper and uranium from low-grade ore by an acid leaching process. The bacteria oxidize Fe^{2+} to produce Fe^{3+}, which in turn oxidizes (and solubilizes) these minor components of the ore. It is remarkable that the bacterium can live in such an environment. It does so by exploiting the pH difference between the environment and its cytoplasm (pH 6.5) to drive synthesis of ATP and NADPH, which it can then use to fix CO_2 and nitrogen. In order to keep its cytoplasmic pH constant, *T. ferrooxidans* uses electrons from Fe^{2+} to reduce O_2 to water, thereby removing the protons.

$$4Fe^{2+} + O_2 + 4H^+ \rightarrow 4Fe^{3+} + 2H_2O$$

What are the energetics of these various processes? Is the flow of electrons from Fe^{2+} to O_2 energetically favorable? Is the electrochemical proton gradient across the membrane sufficient to permit the synthesis of ATP? How difficult is it to reduce $NADP^+$ using electrons from Fe^{2+}? These are key questions for understanding how *T. ferrooxidans* manages to thrive in such an unlikely niche. Addressing them requires an introduction to the energetics of redox chemistry.

In a redox reaction

$$aA_{ox} + bB_{red} \rightarrow cA_{red} + dB_{ox}$$

the tendency to donate electrons is given by ΔE_o, which is computed by subtracting E_o (the standard half-cell potential) for the half-cell that donates electrons (is oxidized) from the E_o for the half-cell that accepts electrons (is reduced).

$$\Delta E_o = E_o^{A} - E_o^{B}$$

When a redox reaction takes place under nonstandard conditions (standard conditions are 25°C or 298°K and all concentrations at 1 M), the tendency to donate electrons is

$$\Delta E = \Delta E_o - 2.3\frac{RT}{nF}\log_{10}\frac{[A_{red}]^c[B_{ox}]^d}{[A_{ox}]^a[B_{red}]^b}$$

where

R = 1.98 x 10^{-3} kcal/°K mole
T = temperature in °K
n = the number of electrons transferred
F = 23 kcal/V mole

ΔG is related to ΔE by the equation

$$\Delta G = -nF\,\Delta E$$

Note that the signs of ΔG and ΔE are opposite; thus, a favorable redox reaction has a positive ΔE and a negative ΔG.

A. What is ΔE for the reduction of O_2 by Fe^{2+}, assuming that the reaction occurs under standard conditions? The half-cell potentials are

$$Fe^{3+}/Fe^{2+},\ E_o = 0.77\ V$$
$$4H^+ + O_2/2H_2O,\ E_o = 0.82\ V$$

What is ΔG for this reaction?

B. Write a balanced equation for the reduction of $NADP^+ + H^+$ by Fe^{2+}. What is ΔE for this reaction under standard conditions?

$$NADP^+ + 2H^+/NADPH + H^+,\ E_o = -0.32\ V$$

What is ΔE if the concentrations of Fe^{3+} and Fe^{2+} are equal, the concentration of NADPH is tenfold greater than that of $NADP^+$ (ignore the protons), and the temperature is 310°K? What is ΔG under these two conditions?

C. The ΔG available from the transport of protons from the outside (pH 2) to the inside (pH 6.5) of *T. ferrooxidans* is given by the Nernst equation

$$\Delta G = 2.3\,RT\log_{10}\frac{[H^+]_{in}}{[H^+]_{out}} + nFV$$

where V is the membrane potential. In *T. ferrooxidans* grown at pH 2, the membrane potential is zero. Assuming that T = 310°K and that ΔG = 11 kcal/mole for ATP synthesis under the prevailing intracellular conditions in *T. ferrooxidans*, how many protons (to the nearest integer) would have to enter the cell through the ATP synthetase to drive ATP synthesis? In order for proton transport to be coupled to ATP synthesis, could the protons pass through the synthetase one at a time, or would they all have to pass through at once?

D. How many protons (to the nearest integer) would have to enter the cell to drive the reduction of $NADP^+$ by Fe^{2+} under standard conditions? Comment on the coupling of proton transport to $NADP^+$ reduction.

E. How many moles of Fe^{2+} does *T. ferrooxidans* have to oxidize to Fe^{3+} to fix 1 mole of CO_2 into carbohydrate via the Calvin cycle?

The Evolution of Electron-Transport Chains

(MBOC 381–387)

7–29 Fill in the blank in the following statement.

A. In the process of ____________, ATP is made by a substrate-level phosphorylation event that harnesses the energy released from the partial oxidation of a hydrogen-rich organic molecule.

7–30 Indicate whether the following statements are true or false. If a statement is false, explain why.

A. The excreted end-products of fermentation differ in different organisms, but they tend to be organic acids, thereby accomplishing the excretion of protons.

B. A lowering of the pH of the local environment would favor survival of bacteria with transmembrane proton pumps to pump H^+ out of the cell to prevent death from intracellular acidification.

C. The major evolutionary breakthrough in energy metabolism was the development of photochemical reaction centers that could produce molecules such as NADH from environmental molecules such as H_2S.

D. The evolution of organisms capable of using water to reduce CO_2 involved the cooperation of a photosystem I derived from green bacteria and a photosystem II derived from purple bacteria.

E. Although cyanobacteria arose about 3×10^9 years ago, the oxygen content of the atmosphere did not increase significantly until about 2×10^9 years ago due to the precipitation of large amounts of ferric oxides.

F. It is believed that mitochondria arose by the endocytosis of a bacterium that had lost the ability to survive on light energy alone and came to rely entirely on respiration.

The Genomes of Mitochondria and Chloroplasts

(MBOC 387–401)

7–31 Fill in the blanks in the following statements.

A. Mutations that are not inherited according to the Mendelian rules that govern the inheritance of nuclear genes are said to display ____________ and are likely to be located in organelle genes.

B. In budding yeast where a limited number of mitochondria enter the bud during mitosis, a cell with a mixture of mutant and wild-type mitochondria can give rise to daughter cells with a single type of mitochondria in a process known as ____________.

C. In higher animals, where mitochondria enter the zygote primarily through the egg cytoplasm, mitochondria are said to display ____________ inheritance.

D. Yeast mutants with large deletions in their mitochondrial DNA form unusually small colonies when grown on low glucose; all mutants with such defective mitochondria are called ____________ mutants.

E. The ____________ is the central metabolic pathway in mammals for the disposal of cellular breakdown products that contain nitrogen.

F. According to the ____________, eucaryotic cells started out in evolution as anaerobic organisms without mitochondria or chloroplasts and then established a stable symbiotic relationship with a bacterium.

7–32 Indicate whether the following statements are true or false. If a statement is false, explain why.

__ A. Individual energy-converting organelles replicate their DNA in synchrony with the nuclear DNA and divide when the cell divides, thereby maintaining a constant amount of organelle DNA.

__ B. Although it is not known how organelle DNA is packaged, it is more likely to resemble the structure of bacterial genomes rather than eucaryotic chromatin because there are no histones in organelles.

__ C. Although the protein synthetic machinery of chloroplasts is very similar to that in bacteria, it is much less similar to the machinery in mitochondria, which synthesize proteins more like the cytoplasm.

__ D. In higher plants, many of the chloroplast ribosomal proteins are actually encoded in the cell nucleus, but these nuclear genes have a clear bacterial ancestry.

__ E. The mitochondrial genetic code differs slightly from the nuclear code, but it is identical in mitochondria from all species that have been examined.

__ F. The simplicity of the mitochondrial genetic system, and its reduced fidelity, may contribute to the increased rate of nucleotide substitutions observed in mitochondrial genomes.

__ G. Plant mitochondrial genomes vary greatly in DNA content yet seem to encode only a few more proteins than the much smaller mitochondrial genomes from animal cells.

__ H. The presence of introns in organelle genes is not surprising since similar introns have been found in related genes from bacteria whose ancestors are thought to have given rise to mitochondria and chloroplasts.

__ I. Mutations that are inherited according to Mendelian rules affect nuclear genes; mutations whose inheritance violates Mendelian rules are likely to affect organelle genes.

__ J. The green and white patches in variegated leaves are caused by the mitotic segregation of normal and defective mitochondria.

__ K. Mitochondria, which divide by fission, can replicate indefinitely in the cytoplasm of proliferating eucaryotic cells even in the complete absence of a mitochondrial genome.

__ L. Mitochondrial and chloroplast function and gene expression are largely controlled by the cell nucleus.

__ M. Mitochondria from different tissues of the same organism contain the same complement of nuclear and mitochondrial proteins.

__ N. The transport of proteins through the mitochondrial and chloroplast membranes seems to occur at special adhesion sites where the inner and outer membranes are joined.

__ O. Chloroplasts tend to make most of the lipids they require, whereas mitochondria import most of their lipids.

__ P. Both animal and plant mitochondria probably descended from a purple photosynthetic bacterium, which had previously lost its ability to carry out photosynthesis and was left with only a respiratory chain.

7–33 Mouse cells contain roughly 1000 mitochondrial DNA molecules. The replication of an individual mitochondrial genome takes only about an hour, which is about 5% of the cell-generation time (20 hours). Since the average number of mitochondrial genomes per cell is constant, they must replicate, on average, once per cell cycle. How is the replication of mitochondrial

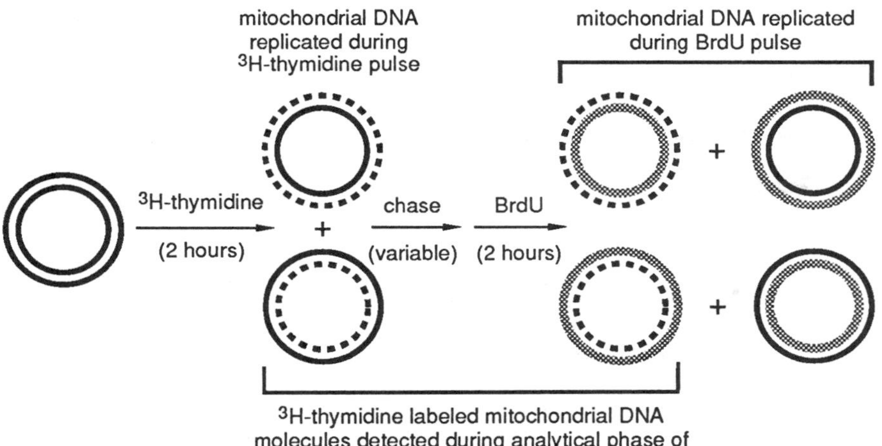

Figure 7–19 Experimental design to assess the timing of mitochondrial DNA replication (Problem 7–33). Unlabeled mitochondrial DNA is indicated with solid lines; DNA labeled with ^{3}H-thymidine is indicated with dashed lines; DNA labeled with BrdU is indicated with gray lines.

genomes coordinated? Does mitochondrial DNA replicate at random times throughout the cell cycle or is their replication, like nuclear DNA replication, confined to one particular stage, for example, S phase?

You have devised an elegant way to answer this question. In outline, your basic approach is to label mouse cell mitochondrial DNA with a short exposure (2 hours) to ^{3}H-thymidine, then to chase with nonradioactive thymidine for various times, and finally to label with 5-bromodeoxyuridine (BrdU) for 2 hours (Figure 7–19). Any DNA that was replicated during both exposures will be radioactive (due to the ^{3}H-thymidine) and have a higher density than normal mitochondrial DNA (due to the BrdU). Since mitochondrial DNA is circular, you can separate it cleanly from nuclear DNA and examine the two DNAs independently. Using density-gradient analysis, you separate heavy DNA (BrdU-labeled) from light DNA (non-BrdU-labeled) and measure the amount of radioactivity associated with each. You have just completed your analysis of the mitochondrial DNA and the results are shown in Figure 7–20. Your results show that a relatively constant fraction of ^{3}H-labeled mitochondrial DNA was shifted to a higher density, regardless of the separation of the labeling periods (the chase times).

A. Do these results fit better with your expectations for replication during a specific part of the cell cycle or with replication at random times? Why?

B. One of your colleagues criticizes the design of these experiments. He suggests that you cannot distinguish between random or timed replication because the cells were growing asynchronously (that is, within the cell population all different stages of the cell cycle were represented). How does this concern affect your interpretation?

C. Sketch your expectations (on Figure 7–20) for the results of your impending analysis of the nuclear DNA (assume that the DNA synthesis phase—S phase—of the cell cycle is 5 hours long).

D. Another of your colleagues wants to know what your results would look like if mitochondrial DNA was replicated at all times during the cell cycle, but once an individual molecule was replicated, it had to wait exactly one cell cycle before it was replicated again.

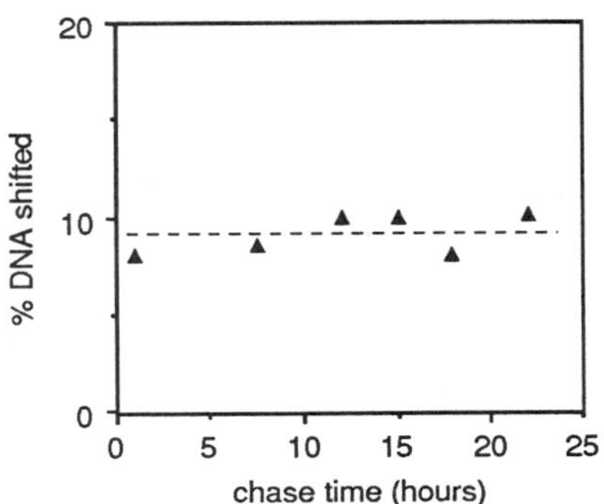

Figure 7–20 The fraction of mitochondrial DNA labeled with ^{3}H-thymidine that is shifted to heavy density after various lengths of chase (Problem 7–33). The fraction of DNA that is density shifted is the radioactivity at the heavy density divided by the total radioactivity. The length of chase is the time from the end of the ^{3}H-thymidine labeling to the beginning of the BrdU labeling.

***7–34** The majority of mRNAs, tRNAs, and rRNAs in human mitochondria are transcribed from one strand of the genome. These RNAs are all present initially on one very long transcript, which is 93% the length of the DNA strand. However, during mitochondrial protein synthesis these RNAs function as separate, independent species of RNA. The relationship of the individual RNAs to the primary transcript and many of the special features of the mitochondrial genetic system have been revealed by comparing the sequences of the RNAs with the nucleotide sequence of the genome. An overview of the map is shown in Figure 7–21.

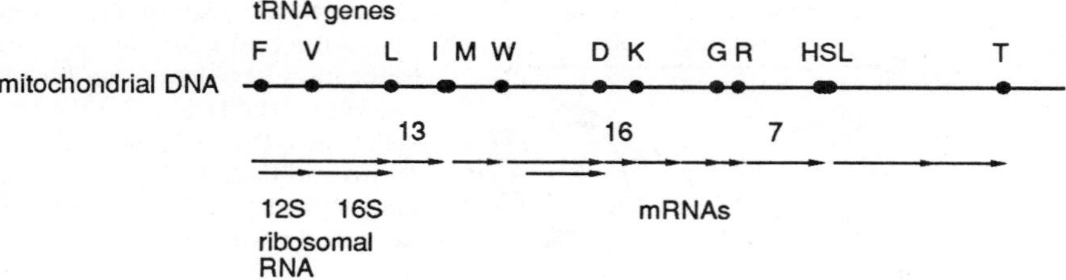

Figure 7–21 Transcription map of human mitochondrial DNA (Problem 7–34). Individual tRNA genes are indicated by black circles; the amino acids they carry are shown in the one-letter code. The three mRNAs whose detailed sequences are shown in Figure 7–22 are indicated by number.

Three segments of the nucleotide sequence of the human mitochondrial genome are shown in Figure 7–22 along with the three mRNAs that are generated from those regions. The nucleotides that encode tRNA species are underlined; the amino acids encoded by the mRNAs are indicated below the center base of the codon.

A. In terms of codon usage and mRNA structure, in what two ways does initiation of protein synthesis in mitochondria differ from intiation in the cytoplasm?

B. In what two ways are the termination codons for protein synthesis in mitochondria unusual? (The termination codons are shown in Figure 7–22 as asterisks.)

C. Does the arrangement of tRNA and mRNA sequences in the genome suggest a possible mechanism for processing the primary transcript into individual RNA species?

***7–35** Chloroplast DNA from higher plants is remarkably constant in size (120–180 kb) and in sequence arrangement. By contrast, the corresponding plant mitochondrial DNAs are quite variable in sequence arrangement and in size, ranging from 218 kb for turnip to 2400 kb for muskmelon. Some portion of this variability may result from the transfer of DNA from chloroplasts to mitochondria.

One experiment to search for genetic transfers between organellar genomes used a defined restriction fragment from spinach chloroplasts, which carried information for the gene for the large subunit of ribulosebisphosphate carboxylase. This gene has no known mitochondrial counterpart. Mitochondrial and chloroplast DNAs were prepared from zucchini, corn, spinach, and pea. All these DNAs were digested with the same restriction enzyme, and the resulting fragments were separated by electrophoresis.

```
tRNAleu                                   tRNAile
TTCTTAACAACATACCCAT.........CTCAAACCTAAGAAATATG     DNA
         ACAUACCCAU.........CUCAAACCUAAAAAAAAAA     mRNA 13
            M  P                 E  T  *           protein

tRNAasp                                  tRNAlys
TATATCTTAATGGCACATG.........CTCTAGAGCCCACTGTAAA     DNA
         AUGGCACAUG.........CUCUAGAGCCAAAAAAAAA     mRNA 16
          M  A  H              S  *                protein

tRNAarg                                   tRNAhis
ATTTACCAAATGCCCCTCA.........TTTTCCTCTTGTAAATATA     DNA
         AUGCCCCUCA.........UUUUCCUCUUAAAAAAAAA     mRNA 7
          M  P  L              F  S  S  *          protein
```

Figure 7–22 Arrangements of tRNA and mRNA sequences at three places on the human mitochondrial genome (Problem 7–34). Underlined sequences indicate tRNA genes. The sequences of the mRNAs are shown below the corresponding genes. The middle portions of the mRNAs and their genes are indicated by dots. The 5′ ends of the sequences are shown at the left. The 5′ ends of the mRNAs are unmodified and the 3′ ends have poly-A tails. The encoded protein sequences are indicated below the mRNAs, with the letter for the amino acid immediately under the center nucleotide of the codon. An * indicates a termination codon.

The fragments were then transferred to a filter and hybridized to a radioactive preparation of the spinach probe fragment. A schematic representation of the autoradiograph is shown in Figure 7–23.

A. It is very difficult to prepare mitochondrial DNA that is not contaminated to some extent with chloroplast DNA. How do these experiments control for contamination of the mitochondrial DNA preparation by chloroplast DNA?
B. Which of these plant mitochondrial DNAs appear to have acquired chloroplast DNA?

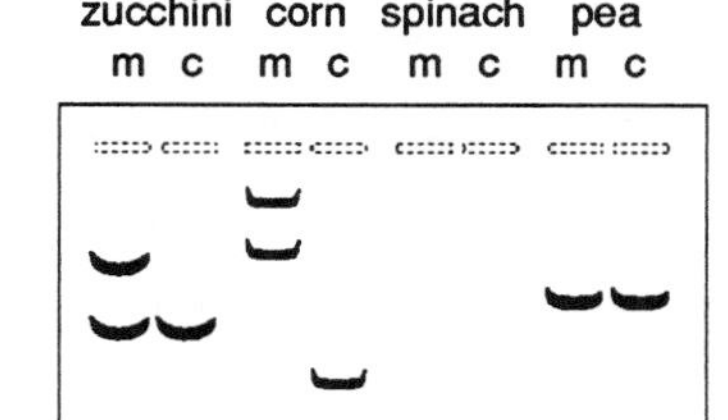

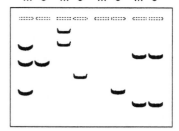

Figure 7–23 Patterns of hybridization of a probe from spinach chloroplast DNA to mitochondrial and chloroplast DNAs from zucchini, corn, spinach, and pea (Problem 7–35). Lanes labeled *m* contain mitochondrial DNA; lanes labeled *c* contain chloroplast DNA. Restriction fragments to which the probe hybridized are shown as dark bands.

7–36 A friend of yours has been studying a pair of mutants in the fungus, *Neurospora,* which she has whimsically named *poky* and *puny.* Both mutants grow at about the same rate, but much more slowly than wild type. Your friend has been unable to find any supplement that improves their growth rates. Her biochemical analysis shows that each mutant displays a different abnormal pattern of cytochrome absorption. To characterize the mutants genetically, she crossed them to wild type and to each other and tested the growth rates of the progeny. She has come to you because she is puzzled by the results.

She explains that haploid nuclei from the two parents fuse during a *Neurospora* mating and then divide meiotically to produce four haploid spores, which can be readily tested for their growth rates. The parents contribute unequally to the diploid: one parent (the protoperithecial parent) donates a nucleus and the cytoplasm; the other (the fertilizing parent) contributes little more than a nucleus—much like egg and sperm in higher organisms. As shown in Table 7–4, the "order" of the crosses sometimes makes a difference: a result she has not seen before.

Can you help your friend understand these results?

7–37 Mutants of yeast that are defective in mitochondrial function grow on fermentable substrates such as glucose, but they fail to grow on nonfermentable substrates such as glycerol. Nuclear and mitochondrial mutations can be distinguished by genetic crosses. Nearly 200 different nuclear genes have been defined by complementation analysis of nuclear petite (*pet*) mutants. Surprisingly, mutations in about a quarter of these genes affect the expression of single, or restricted sets of, mitochondrial gene products without blocking overall gene expression.

For example, *pet494* mutants contain normal levels of all the known mitochondrial gene products except subunit III of cytochrome oxidase (coxIII). However, *pet494* mutants contain normal levels of coxIII mRNA, which appears normal in size. Thus, some posttranscriptional step in expression of the gene for coxIII appears to be regulated by the normal *PET494* gene product. It could be required to promote translation of coxIII mRNA or to stabilize coxIII during assembly of the cytochrome oxidase complex. To distinguish between these possibilities, mitochondrial muta-

Table 7–4 Genetic Analysis of *Neurospora* Mutants (Problem 7–36)

Cross	Protoperithecial Parent		Fertilizing Parent	Spore Counts: Fast Growth	Spore Counts: Slow Growth
1	*poky*	×	wild	0	1749
2	wild	×	*poky*	1334	0
3	*puny*	×	wild	850	799
4	wild	×	*puny*	793	801
5	*poky*	×	*puny*	0	1831
6	*puny*	×	*poky*	754	710
7	wild	×	wild	1515	0
8	*poky*	×	*poky*	0	1389
9	*puny*	×	*puny*	0	1588

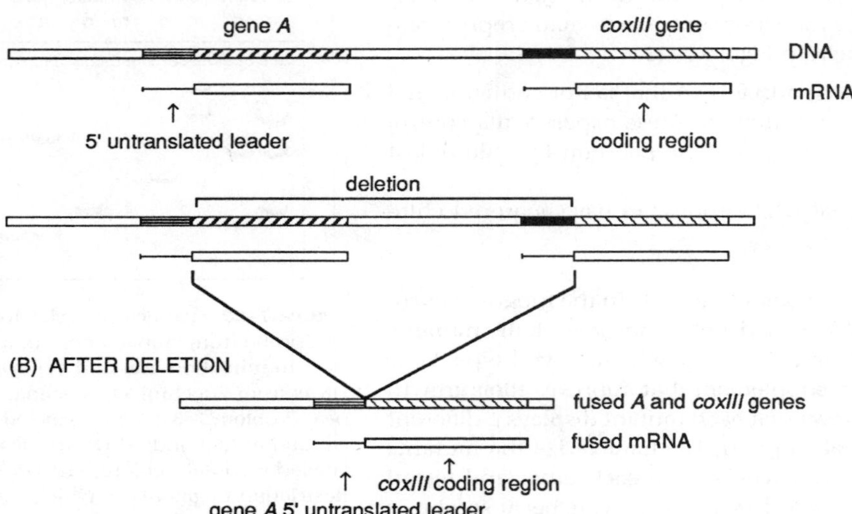

Figure 7–24 Schematic representation of the mitochondrial deletion mutations that suppress the nuclear mutation *pet494* (Problem 7–37).

tions that suppress the respiratory defect of *pet494* mutations were selected and analyzed. All these mutations were deletions that fused the coxIII coding region to the 5′ untranslated region of another gene, as illustrated in Figure 7–24.

A. How do these results distinguish between a requirement for translation of coxIII mRNA and a requirement for stabilization of the coxIII protein?
B. Each of the mitochondrial deletions eliminates one or more genes that are essential for mitochondrial function, yet these yeast strains contain all the normal mitochondrial mRNAs and make normal colonies when grown on nonfermentable substrates. How can this be?

***7–38** At the cellular level evolutionary theories are particularly difficult to test since fossil evidence is lacking. The possible evolutionary origins of mitochondria and chloroplasts must be sought in living organisms. Fortunately, living forms resembling the ancestral types required by the endosymbiotic theory for the origin of mitochondria and chloroplasts can be found today. For example, the plasma membrane of the free-living aerobic bacterium, *Paracoccus denitrificans,* contains a respiratory chain that is nearly identical to the respiratory chain of mammalian mitochondria—both in the types of respiratory components present and in its sensitivity to respiratory inhibitors such as antimycin and rotenone. Indeed, no significant feature of the mammalian respiratory chain is absent from *Paracoccus. Paracoccus* effectively assembles in a single organism all those features of the mitochondrial inner membrane that are otherwise distributed at random among other aerobic bacteria.

Imagine that you are a protoeucaryotic cell, looking out for your evolutionary future. You have been observing *proto-Paracoccus* and are amazed at its incredibly efficient use of oxygen in generating ATP. With such a source of energy your horizons would be unlimited. You plot to hijack a *proto-Paracoccus* and make it work for you and your descendants. You plan to take it into your cytoplasm, feed it any nutrients it needs, and harvest the ATP. Accordingly, one dark night you trap a lone *proto-Paracoccus,* surround it with your plasma membrane, and imprison it in a new cytoplasmic compartment. To your relief, the *proto-Paracoccus* seems to enjoy its new environment. After a day of waiting, however, you feel as sluggish as ever. What has gone wrong with your scheme?

Intracellular Sorting and the Maintenance of Cellular Compartments

8

The Compartmentalization of Higher Cells

(MBOC 405–416)

8–1 Fill in the blanks in the following statements.

A. The interior of each intracellular compartment, called its ____________, is like a separate subcellular reaction vessel endowed with specialized functions.

B. Secretory cells, such as the exocrine cells of the pancreas, store large amounts of their secreted products in ____________, which rapidly release their contents to the cell exterior in response to an external signal.

C. __________ secretion is triggered by an external signal, whereas __________ secretion occurs continuously in the absence of a stimulatory signal.

D. For some steps the sorting signal resides in a continuous stretch of amino acids called the ____________; this signal is often removed from the finished protein once the sorting decision has been executed.

E. For some steps the sorting signal consists of a particular three-dimensional arrangement of amino acids on the protein's surface; these ____________ generally remain in the finished protein.

8–2 Indicate whether the following statements are true or false. If a statement is false, explain why.

__A. The plasma membrane in a eucaryotic cell cannot provide enough surface area or house enough membrane-bound enzyme molecules to support all the vital functions that membranes must sustain in such a large cell.

__B. Internal membranes partition the cell into functionally distinct compartments, each with boundaries established by sealed, impermeable membranes.

__C. In terms of both area and mass, the plasma membrane is only a minor membrane in most eucaryotic cells.

__D. The interior of the nucleus and the lumen of the ER are both topologically equivalent to the outside of the cell.

__E. All proteins destined for internal membrane-bounded compartments are transferred into the ER as they are being synthesized and then are sorted to their final destination.

__F. All secreted proteins follow a similar pathway from ribosomes to the ER to the Golgi apparatus to secretory vesicles to the cell exterior.

__G. To function effectively, each transport vesicle must selectively take up only the appropriate proteins and must fuse only with the correct target membrane.

__H. The lumenal spaces of each of the organelles that communicate by means of transport vesicles are topologically equivalent to one another and to the outside of the cell.

__I. Depending on the individual protein, a signal peptide or a signal patch may direct the protein to the ER, mitochondria, chloroplasts, or nucleus.

__J. The signal peptides attached to proteins that share the same destination are functionally interchangeable, even though their amino acid sequences can vary greatly.

__K. If a membrane-bounded organelle, such as the ER or Golgi, were removed from a eucaryotic cell, the cell could regenerate the organelle from the information present in the DNA.

8–3 The rough endoplasmic reticulum (ER) is the site of synthesis of many different classes of membrane proteins. Some of these proteins remain in the endoplasmic reticulum, whereas others are sorted to compartments, such as the Golgi apparatus, lysosomes, and the plasma membrane. One measure of the difficulty of the sorting problem is the degree of "purification" that must be achieved during transport from the ER to the other compartments. For example, if membrane proteins bound for the plasma membrane represented 90% of all the proteins in the ER, then only a small degree of purification would be needed (and the sorting problem would appear relatively easy). On the other hand, if plasma membrane proteins represented only 0.01% of the proteins in the ER, a very large degree of purification would be required (and the sorting problem would appear correspondingly more difficult).

What is the magnitude of the sorting problem? What fraction of the membrane proteins in the ER are destined for other compartments? A few simple considerations allow one to estimate the answers to these questions. Assume that all proteins on their way to other compartments remain in the ER 30 minutes on average before exiting, and that the ratio of proteins to lipids in the membranes of all compartments is the same.

A. In a typical growing cell that is dividing once every 24 hours the equivalent of one new plasma membrane must transit the ER every day. If the ER membrane is 20 times the area of a plasma membrane, what is the ratio of plasma membrane proteins to other membrane proteins in the ER?

B. If in the same cell the Golgi membrane is three times the area of the plasma membrane, what is the ratio of Golgi membrane proteins to other membrane proteins in the ER?

C. If the membranes of all other compartments (lysosomes, endosomes, inner nuclear membrane, and secretory vesicles) that receive membrane proteins from the ER are equal in total area to the area of the plasma membrane, what fraction of the membrane proteins in the ER of this cell are permanent residents of the ER membrane?

The Cytosolic Compartment (MBOC 416–421)

8–4 Fill in the blanks in the following statements.

A. The ____________ imparts shape to the cell, mediates coherent cytoplasmic movements, and provides a general framework that may help organize enzymatic reactions in the cytosol.

B. In the ____________ pathway for protein degradation in eucaryotic cells, numerous copies of a small protein called ____________ are covalently linked to the target protein to be degraded.

C. If cells are exposed to elevated temperatures or other harmful treatments, they begin to express a special set of ____________ proteins.

8–5 Indicate whether the following statements are true or false. If a statement is false, explain why.

__A. Individual cytoskeletal filaments act as "highways" to direct each type of transport vesicle to its appropriate target membrane for fusion.

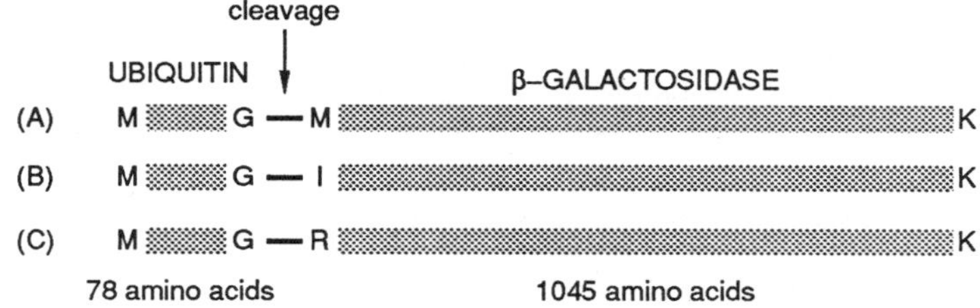

Figure 8–1 Fusion proteins encoded by three yeast plasmids (Problem 8–6). Upon expression in yeast, the fusion proteins are cleaved at the peptide bonds indicated by the arrow. The β-galactosidases liberated by cleavage differ only at their N termini.

__ B. All posttranslational modifications of proteins modify the covalent structure of the protein.

__ C. Proteins that are attached to the membrane by myristic acid are anchored by their N terminus; proteins attached to the membrane by palmitic acid are anchored near their C terminus.

__ D. Key regulatory proteins, such as those that catalyze rate-limiting steps in metabolism, generally are long-lived as befits their critical importance to the cell.

__ E. Ubiquitin is an ATP-dependent protease that rapidly cleaves proteins that are marked for degradation.

__ F. The most reliable way to determine the complete amino acid sequence of the functional form of a cytosolic protein is to sequence the gene.

8–6 The life spans of proteins are usually appropriate to their *in vivo* tasks; for example, structural proteins are usually long-lived, whereas regulatory proteins are often short-lived. The life span of a protein in a eucaryotic cell can be strongly affected by its N-terminal amino acid. The experiments that revealed the effects of N-terminal amino acids on protein stability used a hybrid protein consisting of ubiquitin fused to β-galactosidase. The original investigators examined a variety of plasmids encoding different versions of the fusion protein, such as the three shown in Figure 8–1. When these plasmids were introduced into yeast, the hybrid protein was synthesized, but the ubiquitin was cleaved off (by an undefined enzyme) exactly at the junction with β-galactosidase. This cleavage generated β-galactosidases with different N termini (Figure 8–1).

To measure the half-lives of these β-galactosidases, yeast were grown for several generations in the presence of a radioactive amino acid. Protein synthesis was then blocked with an inhibitor. The rate of degradation of β-galactosidase was determined by removing samples from the cultures at various times, purifying β-galactosidase using specific antibodies, and measuring the amount of radioactive β-galactosidase after SDS-gel electrophoresis. A sample gel showing the results at the five-minute time point is shown in Figure 8–2A. A graph depicting results for all time points is shown in Figure 8–2B.

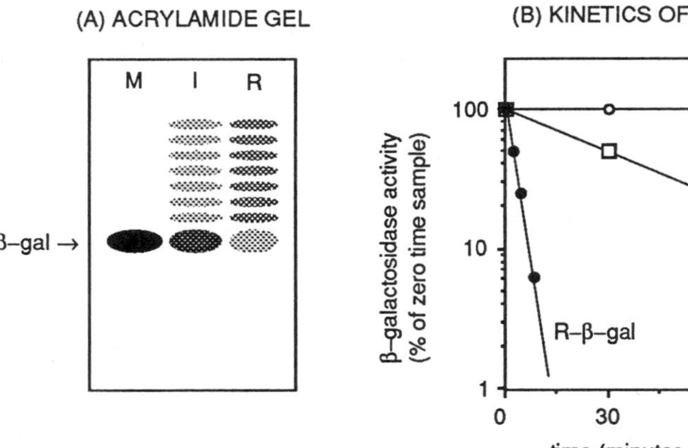

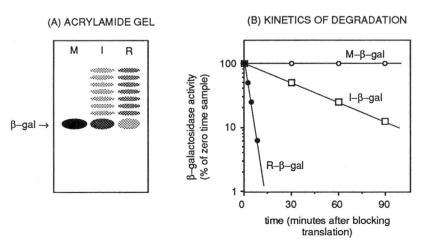

Figure 8–2 Results of experiments with three different fusion proteins (Problem 8–6). (A) Electrophoretic separation of radioactive β-galactosidase prepared by precipitation with antibodies directed against β-galactosidase. The N-terminal amino acids are indicated above the lanes. (B) Disappearance of β-galactosidases with time after termination of protein synthesis. The level of β-galactosidase is expressed as a percentage of that present immediately after protein synthesis was blocked.

A. By using recombinant DNA techniques, it would have been straightforward to generate a series of plasmids in which the first codon in the β-galactosidase gene was changed. Why do you think that this more direct approach was not tried?

B. Estimate the half-lives (time at which half the material has been degraded) of the three different species of β-galactosidase.

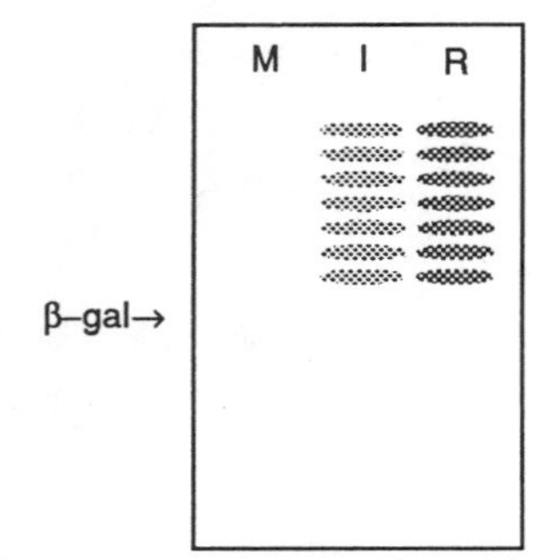

Figure 8–3 Electrophoresis of unlabeled β-galactosidase followed by reaction with labeled antibodies directed against ubiquitin (Problem 8–7). The N-terminal amino acids are indicated above the lanes. The position at which intact β-galactosidase runs is marked by an arrow.

***8–7** When you heard about the work described in the previous problem, you wondered about two aspects of the data. First, was ubiquitin actually removed from the N terminus? Second, what are the bands above the position of β-galactosidase in Figure 8–2A? Any fragments of β-galactosidase due to degradation should run below β-galactosidase.

To check that ubiquitin is cleaved from the hybrid protein to release β-galactosidase, you use antibodies to isolate nonradioactive β-galactosidase from cells containing the same three plasmids. You subject these samples to SDS-gel electrophoresis, transfer them to a filter paper, and then react them with radioactive antibodies specific for ubiquitin. As shown in Figure 8–3, antibodies against ubiquitin did not react with material at the position of β-galactosidase. However, the ubiquitin-specific antibodies did react with a ladder of bands above the position of β-galactosidase. These bands seem to be at the same positions as those in Figure 8–2A.

A. Do these experiments demonstrate that the ubiquitin at the N terminus of the hybrid protein is removed?

B. Offer an explanation for the presence of ubiquitin above the position of β-galactosidase in the experiments with isoleucine (I) or arginine (R) at the N terminus, but not in the experiment with methionine (M) at the N terminus.

8–8 Ornithine decarboxylase (ODCase) catalyzes the first step in the pathway leading to synthesis of polyamines, which bind to the sugar-phosphate backbones of DNA and RNA and are essential for cell growth. The activity of ODCase is normally regulated according to the physiological status of the cell.

You have isolated a line of mutant liver cells with a much higher than normal level of ODCase activity. Your preliminary experiments suggest that normal and mutant cells have the same number of ODCase genes, that the ODCase genes are transcribed at the same rate, and that there are no obvious differences in the structural and enzymatic properties of ODCase from the normal and mutant cells. However, when you add the protein synthesis inhibitor, cycloheximide, and assay enzyme activity at various times thereafter, you find that ODCase in the mutant cells has a half-life of 12 hours instead of the usual half-life of 14 minutes. The half-lives of other proteins in the mutant line are unchanged.

A. If ODCase is being made at the same rate as in normal cells, why do the mutant cells have so much more ODCase activity?

B. How might you determine whether ODCase instability in normal cells is due to destruction of protein or inactivation of ODCase activity by a reversible modification (such as phosphorylation, methylation, or acetylation)?

C. Assuming that ODCase instability in normal cells is due to destruction of the protein, offer an explanation for the stability of ODCase in the mutant cell line.

The Transport of Proteins and RNA Molecules into and out of the Nucleus (MBOC 421–426)

8–9 Fill in the blanks in the following statements.

A. The ______________ encloses the DNA and defines the nuclear compartment.

B. The nucleus is bounded by two concentric membranes: the ______________ membrane, which contains specific proteins that act as binding sites for the

*Problems with an asterisk (*) are answered in the Instructor's Manual.

nuclear lamina, and the ___________ membrane, which is continuous with the ER membrane.

C. The nucleus is perforated by ___________, each of which is embedded in a large disclike structure known as the ___________.

D. The selectivity of nuclear transport resides in ___________ signals, which are present only in nuclear proteins.

8–10 Indicate whether the following statements are true or false. If a statement is false, explain why.

__ A. The perinuclear space is continuous with the lumen of the ER.

__ B. At a nuclear pore, as elsewhere, the lipid bilayers of the inner and outer nuclear membranes are distinct from one another.

__ C. Because nuclear protein molecules need to be imported repeatedly, their signals are not cleaved off after transport into the nucleus.

__ D. Although import of proteins into the nucleus requires specific signals and uses the energy of ATP hydrolysis, export of RNA and ribosomal subunits from the nucleus is unlikely to require either signals or energy.

__ E. Because the nuclear envelope is continuous with the ER membrane, the contraction and expansion of the nucleus can be readily explained by membrane flow to and from the ER.

8–11 In principle, proteins might accumulate in the nucleus in two ways. (1) Proteins might diffuse into the nucleus passively and accumulate there by binding to a resident of the nucleus, such as a chromosome. (2) Proteins might be actively transported into the nucleus and accumulate there regardless of their affinity for nuclear components. Passive diffusion and active transport are particularly difficult to distinguish between since most, if not all, proteins in the nucleus are linked directly or indirectly to nuclear residents. Although the physical size of the nuclear pore (apparent diameter 9 nm) often is cited in favor of active transport, the arguments are not satisfying because the shapes of most nuclear proteins are unknown.

One straightforward experiment to address this problem used several forms of radioactive nucleoplasmin, which is a large pentameric protein involved in chromatin assembly. In addition to the intact protein, nucleoplasmin heads, tails, and heads with a single tail were injected into the cytoplasm or into the nucleus of frog oocytes (Figure 8–4). All forms of nucleoplasmin, except heads, accumulated in the nucleus when injected in the cytoplasm, and all forms were retained in the nucleus when injected there.

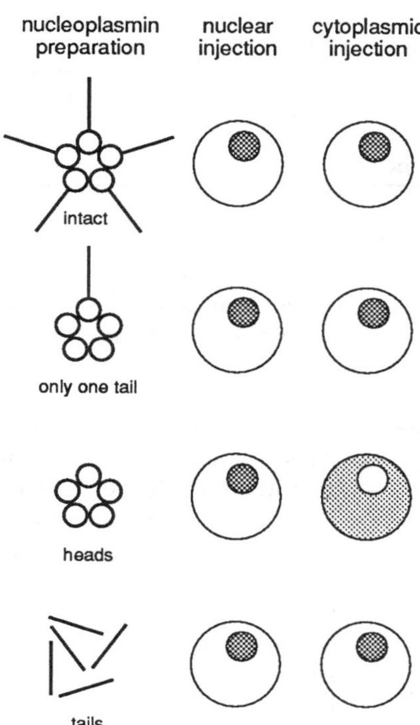

Figure 8–4 Cellular location of injected nucleoplasmin and nucleoplasmin components (Problem 8–11). Schematic diagrams of autoradiographs of cells show the cytoplasm and nucleus with the location of the nucleoplasmin indicated by the shaded areas.

A. What portion of the nucleoplasmin molecule is responsible for localization in the nucleus?

B. How do these experiments distinguish between active transport, in which a nuclear import signal triggers transport by the nuclear pore complex, and passive diffusion, in which a binding site for a nuclear component allows accumulation in the nucleus?

***8–12** You have just joined a laboratory that is engaged in defining the nuclear transport machinery in yeast. Your advisor, who is known for her extraordinarily clever ideas, has given you a project with enormous potential. In principle, it would allow a genetic selection for conditional-lethal mutants in the nuclear transport apparatus.

She gave you the two plasmids shown in Figure 8–5. Each plasmid consists of a hybrid gene under the control of a regulatable promoter. The hybrid gene is a fusion between a gene whose product is normally imported into the nucleus and the gene for the restriction enzyme, EcoRI. The plasmid pNL$^+$ contains a functional nuclear import signal; the plasmid pNL$^-$ contains a nonfunctional signal. The promoter, which is from the yeast *GAL1* gene, allows transcription of the hybrid gene only when the sugar galactose is present in the growth medium.

Following her instructions, you introduce the plasmids into yeast (in the absence of galactose) and then assay the transformed yeast in medium

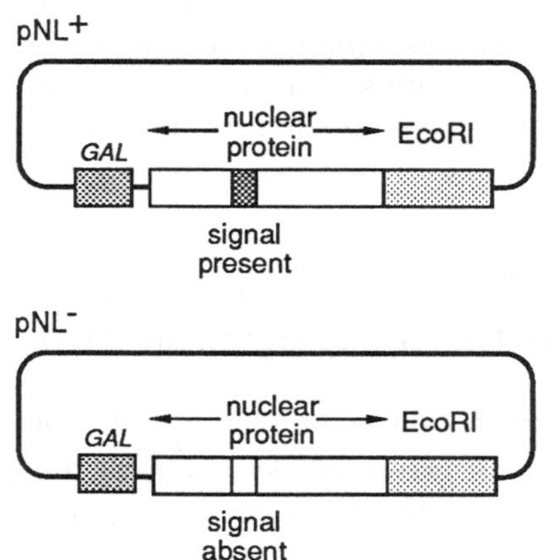

Figure 8–5 Two plasmids for investigating nuclear localization in yeast (Problem 8–12).

Table 8–1 Results of Growth Experiments with Yeast Carrying the Plasmids, pNL^+ or pNL^- (Problem 8–12)

Plasmid	Glucose Medium	Galactose Medium
pNL^+	growth	death
pNL^-	growth	growth

containing glucose and in medium containing galactose. Your results are shown in Table 8–1. You don't remember what your advisor told you to expect, but you know you will be expected to explain these results at the weekly lab meeting. Why do yeasts with the pNL^+ plasmid grow in the presence of glucose but die in the presence of galactose?

8–13 Now that you understand why plasmid pNL^+ (Figure 8–5) kills cells in galactose-containing medium, you begin to understand how your advisor intends to exploit its properties to select mutants in the nuclear transport machinery. You also understand why she emphasized that the desired mutants would have to be *conditionally* lethal. Since nuclear import is essential to the cell, a fully defective mutant could never be grown and thus would not be available for study. By contrast, conditionally lethal mutants can be grown perfectly well under one set of conditions (permissive conditions); under a different set of conditions (restrictive conditions), however, the cells exhibit the defect, which can then be studied.

With this overall strategy in mind, you design a selection scheme for temperature-sensitive (ts) mutants in the nuclear translocation machinery. You want to find mutants that grow well at low temperature (the permissive condition) but are defective at high temperature (the restrictive condition). You plan to mutaganize cells containing the pNL^+ plasmid at low temperature and then shift them to high temperature in the presence of galactose. You reason that at the restrictive temperature the nuclear transport mutants will not take up the killer protein encoded by pNL^+ and, therefore, will not be killed. Normal cells, however, will transport the killer protein into the nucleus and die. After one or two hours at the high temperature to allow selection against normal cells, you intend to lower the temperature and put the surviving cells on nutrient agar plates containing glucose. You anticipate that the nuclear translocation mutants will recover at the low temperature and form colonies.

When you show your advisor your scheme, she is very pleased at your initiative. However, she sees a critical flaw in your experimental design that would prevent isolation of nuclear translocation mutants, but she won't tell you what it is—she believes students learn more when they figure things out on their own.

A. What is the critical flaw in your original experimental protocol?
B. How might you modify your protocol to correct this flaw?
C. Assuming for the moment that your original protocol would work, can you think of any other types of mutants (not involved in nuclear transport) that would survive your selection scheme?

The Transport of Proteins into Mitochondria and Chloroplasts (MBOC 426–431)

8–14 Fill in the blanks in the following statements.

A. From inside to outside the four subcompartments of a mitochondrion are the ____________, the ____________, the ____________, and the ____________.

B. The two additional subcompartments of chloroplasts are the __________ and the ____________.

C. Cytosolic proteins that are destined for import into mitochondria are called ____________ proteins.

D. The ____________ at which the inner and outer mitochondrial membranes appear to be joined are thought to be the sites at which import into the matrix occurs.

E. Chloroplasts have an extra membrane-bounded compartment, which is called the ____________.

8–15 Indicate whether the following statements are true or false. If a statement is false, explain why.

__ A. The relatively small number of proteins encoded in the genomes of mitochondria and chloroplasts are located mostly in the inner membranes of both organelles.

__ B. Mitochondrial signal peptides are amphipathic α-helical structures with positively charged amino acids on one side and negatively charged amino acids on the other side.

__ C. The electrochemical proton gradient apparently drives insertion of the mitochondrial signal peptide into the outer mitochondrial membrane during the initial penetration of the precursor protein into the mitochondria.

__ D. Since a matrix protease can remove the N terminus of an imported protein while the C terminus is accessible to external proteases, precursor proteins must penetrate both the inner and outer membranes at the same time.

__ E. Since the folded state of a protein is of lower free energy than the unfolded state, unfolding a protein during import into the mitochondria requires an input of energy.

__ F. Proteins destined for the inner mitochondrial membrane apparently pass through the outer and inner membranes into the matrix and are then subsequently reinserted into the inner membrane.

__ G. Since the outer mitochondrial membrane contains very large pores, it does not present a permeability barrier to proteins.

__ H. Both chloroplasts and mitochondria exploit the electrochemical proton gradient to help drive the transport of precursor proteins across their outer and inner membranes.

8–16 To aid your studies of protein import into mitochondria, you treat yeast cells with cycloheximide, which blocks ribosome movement along mRNA. When you examine these cells in the electron microscope, you are surprised to find cytosolic ribosomes attached to the outside of the mitochondria. You have never seen attached ribosomes in the absence of cycloheximide. To investigate this phenomenon further, you prepare mitochondria from cycloheximide-treated cells and extract the mRNA that is bound to the mitochondria-associated ribosomes. You translate this mRNA *in vitro* and compare the protein products with similarly translated mRNA from the cytosol. The results are clear-cut: the mitochondria-associated ribosomes are translating mRNAs that encode mitochondrial proteins.

You are astounded! Here, clearly visible in the electron micrographs, seems to be proof that protein import into mitochondria occurs during translation. How can you rationalize this result with the prevailing view that mitochondrial proteins are imported after they have been synthesized and released from ribosomes?

***8–17** Amphipathic helices are a key feature of signal peptides used for protein import into mitochondria. A helix is amphipathic if one side is hydrophilic and the other side is hydrophobic. A simple way to decide whether a sequence of amino acids might form an amphipathic helix is to arrange the amino acids around what is known as a "helix-wheel projection" (Figure 8–6A). This representation shows the positions of the amino acids around an α-helix as viewed from the top of the helix. If hydrophobic and hydrophilic amino acids are intermixed in such a diagram, the helix is not amphipathic; however, if the hydrophobic and hydrophilic amino acids are segregated on opposite sides, the helix is amphipathic.

Figure 8–6 Potential signal peptides for mitochondrial import (Problem 8–17). (A) Helix-wheel projection of an α-helix. Numbers show the positions of the first 18 amino acids of an α-helix; amino acid 19 would occupy the same position as amino acid 1. (B) Amino acid sequences of three peptides. The N termini are shown at the left; hydrophobic amino acids are shaded; the charge on charged amino acids is indicated in a circle; and uncharged hydrophilic amino acids are unmarked.

Using the helix-wheel projection, decide which of the three peptides in Figure 8–6B can form an amphipathic helix that could serve as a mitochondrial import signal.

8–18 Chloroplasts contain six compartments—outer membrane, intermembrane space, inner membrane, stroma, thylakoid membrane, and thylakoid lumen (Figure 8–7)—each of which is populated by specific sets of proteins. Many of these proteins are encoded by nuclear genes, translated in the cytoplasm, and then posttranslationally directed to the appropriate chloroplast compartment. To investigate the import of proteins into chloroplasts, you have cloned the cDNAs for ferredoxin (FD), which is located in the stroma, and plastocyanin (PC), which is located in the thylakoid lumen. Furthermore, using recombinant DNA techniques, you have constructed two hybrid genes: ferredoxin with the plastocyanin signal peptide (PCFD) and plastocyanin with the ferredoxin signal peptide (FDPC). You translate mRNAs from these four genes *in vitro*, mix the translation products with isolated chloroplasts for a few minutes, reisolate the chloroplasts after protease treatment, and fractionate them to find which compartments the proteins have entered. The proteins that are present at each stage in the experiment and in each subchloroplast fraction are shown in Figure 8–8.

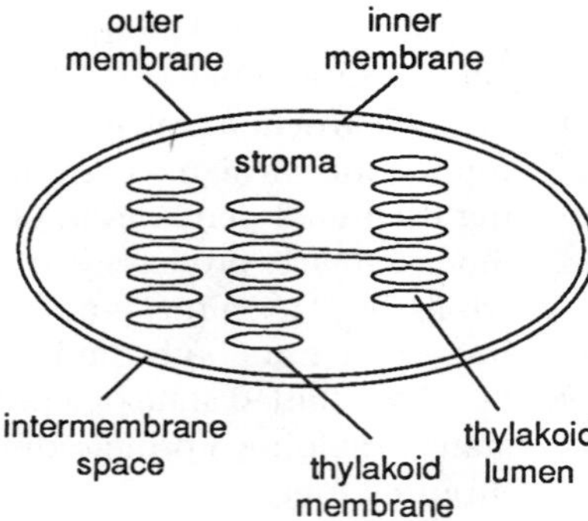

Figure 8–7 The six compartments of chloroplasts (Problem 8–18).

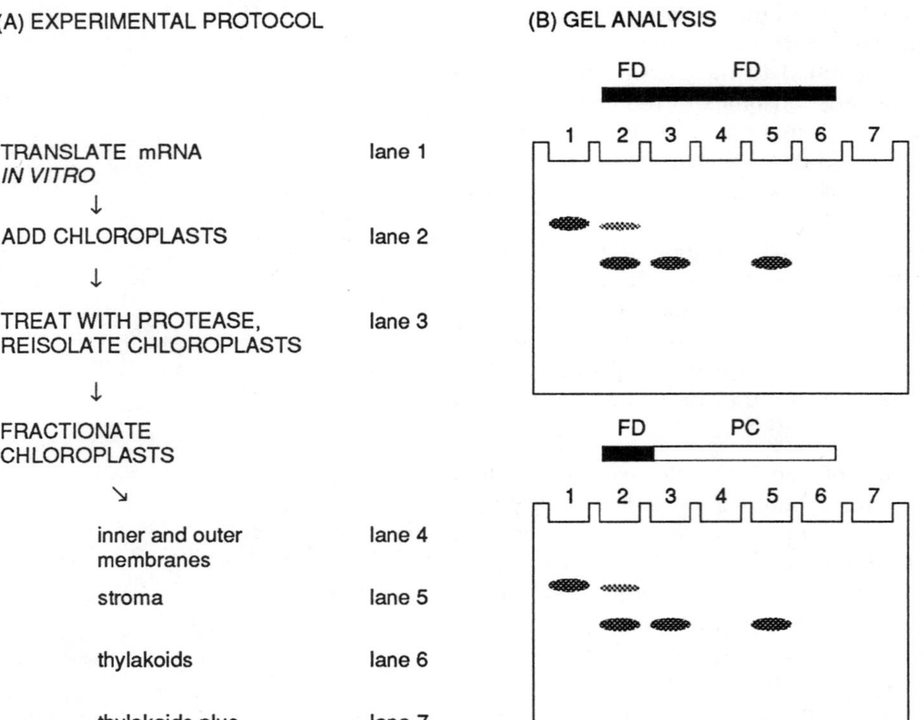

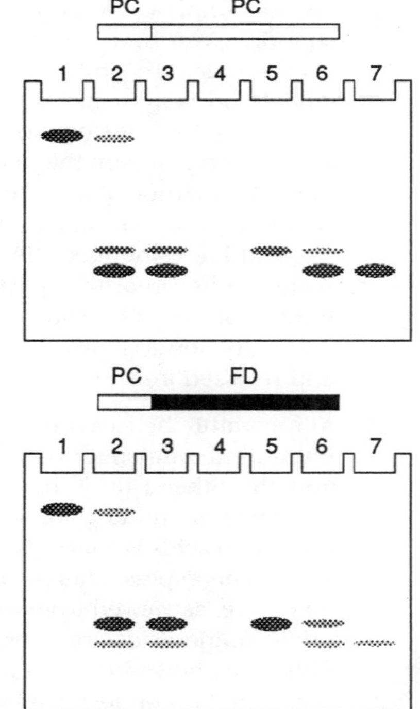

Figure 8–8 Import of ferredoxin and plastocyanin into chloroplast compartments (Problem 8–18). Samples were treated as indicated in (A) and then analyzed on gels as shown in (B). Each lane in (B) corresponds to a particular experimental treatment in (A).

A. How efficient is chloroplast uptake of ferredoxin and plastocyanin in your *in vitro* system? How can you tell?
B. Are ferredoxin and plastocyanin localized to their appropriate chloroplast compartments in these experiments? How can you tell?
C. Are the hybrid proteins imported as you would expect if the N-terminal signal peptides determined their final location? Comment on any significant differences.
D. Why are there three bands in experiments with plastocyanin and PCFD but only two bands in experiments with ferredoxin and FDPC? To the extent you can, identify the bands and their relationship to each other.
E. Based on your experiments, propose a model for the import of proteins into the stroma and thylakoid lumen.

Peroxisomes (MBOC 431–433)

8–19 Fill in the blanks in the following statements.

A. ____________, which are also called microbodies, resemble the ER in being a self-replicating membrane-bounded organelle that exists without a genome of its own.
B. Plants, but not animals, can convert fatty acids to sugars by a series of reactions known as the ____________, which is why the peroxisomes that carry out these reactions are also called ____________.

8–20 Indicate whether the following statements are true or false. If a statement is false, explain why.

__ A. In mammals peroxisomes are confined to a few cell types.
__ B. Peroxisomal oxidation reactions are particularly important in liver and kidney cells, whose peroxisomes detoxify various toxic molecules that enter the bloodstream.
__ C. The membrane "shell" of the peroxisome forms by budding from the ER, whereas the "content" is imported from the cytosol.

8–21 Trypanosomes are single-celled parasites that cause sleeping sickness when they infect humans. Trypanosomes from humans carry the enzymes for a portion of the glycolytic pathway in a peroxisomelike organelle, termed the glycosome. By contrast, trypanosomes from the tsetse fly—the intermediate host—carry out glycolysis entirely in the cytosol. This intriguing difference has alerted the interest of the pharmaceutical company that employs you. Your company wishes to exploit this difference to control the disease.

You decide to study the enzyme phosphoglycerate kinase (PGK) because it is in the affected portion of the glycolytic pathway. Trypanosomes from the tsetse fly express PGK entirely in the cytosol, whereas trypanosomes from humans express 90% of the total PGK activity in glycosomes and only 10% in the cytosol. When you clone PGK genes from trypanosomes, you find three forms that differ slightly from one another. Exploiting these small differences, you design three oligonucleotides that hybridize specifically to the mRNAs from each gene. Using these oligonucleotides as probes, you determine which genes are expressed by trypanosomes from humans and from tsetse flies. The results are shown in Figure 8–9.

A. Which PGK genes are expressed in trypanosomes from humans? Which are expressed in trypanosomes from tsetse flies?
B. Which PGK gene probably encodes the glycosomal form of PGK?
C. Do you think that the minor cytosolic PGK activity in trypanosomes from humans is due to inaccurate sorting into glycosomes? Explain your answer.

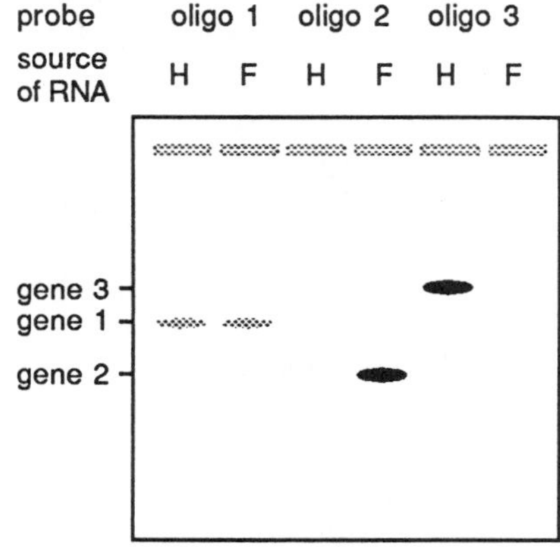

Figure 8–9 Hybridization of specific oligonucleotide probes to mRNA isolated from trypanosomes from humans (H) and from tsetse flies (F) (Problem 8–21). The intensity of the bands on the autoradiograph reflects the concentrations of the mRNAs.

***8–22** The origin of peroxisomes has been a point of scientific controversy. Some investigators think peroxisomes bud from the ER, but there is no direct evidence. Others argue persuasively that peroxisomes are self-replicating organelles. They cite three observations in support of this hypothesis: (1) all known peroxisomal proteins are imported from the cytosol, (2) no peroxisomal proteins have carbohydrate, and (3) peroxisomal membranes have no detectable proteins in common with ER membranes.

Is there an experiment that would unambiguously determine the origin of peroxisomal membranes? One possible test is based on the observation that peroxisomes are completely absent in the lethal human hereditary disease known as Zellweger syndrome. If cells collected from different patients were defective in different genes, how would fusing two such cells together distinguish between the two hypotheses? What result would you predict if peroxisomes arise from the ER? What result would you predict if peroxisomes come from preexisting peroxisomes?

The Endoplasmic Reticulum (MBOC 433–451)

8–23 Fill in the blanks in the following statements.

A. The membrane of the ____________ typically constitutes more than half of the total membrane of the cell, and the internal space, called the ____________, often occupies more than 10% of the total cell volume.

B. ____________, which are synthesizing proteins that are being concurrently translocated into the ER, coat the surface of the ER, and create regions termed ____________.

C. Transport vesicles carrying newly synthesized proteins and lipids bud off the ____________ for transport to the Golgi apparatus.

D. Muscle cells have a specialized and elaborate smooth-ER-like organelle called the ____________, which sequesters Ca^{2+} from the cytosol.

E. When cells are disrupted by homogenization, the ER is fragmented into many small closed vesicles called ____________.

F. The ____________ postulated that the amino-terminal leader serves as a signal peptide that directs the secreted protein to the ER membrane.

G. The signal peptide is guided to the membrane of the ER by at least two components: a ____________, which binds to the signal peptide in the cytosol, and the ____________, which is located in the ER membrane.

H. Most amino-terminal signal peptides are removed by a specific ____________ bound to the ER membrane.

I. In multipass transmembrane proteins, the fundamental unit translocated is a loop of polypeptide between a ____________ and a ____________, with both peptides serving as membrane-spanning domains in the mature protein.

J. The ER lumen contains a high concentration of a ____________ that seems to recognize incorrectly folded proteins, possibly by binding to their exposed hydrophobic surfaces.

K. The enzyme ____________ acts repetitively to cleave S-S bonds, allowing proteins to search rapidly through many different arrangements until the one with the lowest overall free energy is found.

L. Most proteins sequestered in the lumen of the ER are ____________, which carry covalently attached sugars.

M. During protein ____________, a preformed precursor oligosaccharide is transferred *en bloc* from a special lipid molecule, ____________, to an asparagine residue on the target protein.

8–24 Indicate whether the following statements are true or false. If a statement is false, explain why.

__ A. In mammalian cells the import of proteins into the ER begins before the polypeptide chain is completely synthesized—that is, it occurs co-translationally.

— B. Free ribosomes and membrane-bound ribosomes are identical.

— C. Detoxification by the cytochrome P450 family of enzymes involves cleavage of harmful drugs or metabolites into units small enough so that they can be excreted in the urine.

— D. Rough microsomes can be separated readily from smooth microsomes because their higher concentration of proteins makes them more dense.

— E. Although the smooth ER and the rough ER are continuous with one another, the rough ER contains several proteins that are not present in the smooth ER.

— F. If a protein that is normally secreted by the cell is synthesized *in vitro* in the presence of microsomes, it will be protected from degradation by added protease.

— G. The signal peptide, when it emerges from the ribosome, binds to a hydrophobic site on the ribosome causing translational arrest, which is lifted when the signal recognition particle binds to the signal peptide.

— H. Ribosomes of the rough ER use the energy released during protein synthesis to drive their growing polypeptide chains through the ER membrane.

— I. Regardless of the topology of the membrane protein, the amino terminus of a cleaved signal sequence is never exposed to the lumen of the ER.

— J. In a protein with multiple hydrophobic membrane-spanning segments, the odd-numbered segments (counting from the N terminus) act as start-transfer peptides and the even-numbered segments act as stop-transfer peptides.

— K. It seems likely that, by binding to an unfolded chain, BiP helps to keep improperly folded proteins in the ER and thus out of the Golgi.

— L. The ER lumen contains a mixture of thiol-containing reducing agents that prevent the formation of S-S linkages (disulfide bonds) by maintaining the cysteine residues of lumenal proteins in reduced (-SH) form.

— M. *N*-linked oligosaccharides are much more common on glycoproteins than are *O*-linked oligosaccharides.

— N. Some membrane proteins are attached to the cytoplasmic surface of the plasma membrane through a C-terminal linkage to a glycosylated phosphatidylinositol molecule.

— O. The initial formation of phosphatidic acid and its subsequent modifications to form other phospholipid molecules all take place in the cytosolic half of the ER lipid bilayer.

— P. Phospholipids are added to the ER and subsequently transported to the other membrane-bounded compartments of the cell by transport vesicles.

8–25 Translocation of proteins across the membrane of the ER is usually studied using microsomes, which are vesicles derived from the ER membrane during isolation. Microsomes from the rough ER carry ribosomes attached to their outer surface. Translocation of proteins across microsomal membranes can be assessed by several experimental criteria: (1) protection of the newly synthesized protein from exogenously added proteases, and lack of protection from proteases when detergents are present to solubilize the protecting lipid bilayer; (2) glycosylation of newly synthesized proteins by oligosaccharide transferases, which are localized exclusively to the lumen of the ER; (3) cleavage of signal peptides by signal peptidase, which is also active only on the luminal side of the ER membrane.

You want to use these criteria to decide whether the protein synthesized from a purified mRNA is translocated across microsomal membranes. Therefore, you translate the mRNA into protein in a cell-free system in the absence or presence of microsomes. You then prepare samples from these translation reactions in four different ways: (1) no treatment, (2) add a protease, (3) add a protease and detergent, and (4) disrupt microsomes and add endoglycosidase H (endo H), which removes *N*-linked sugars that are added in the ER. An electrophoretic analysis of these samples is shown in Figure 8–10.

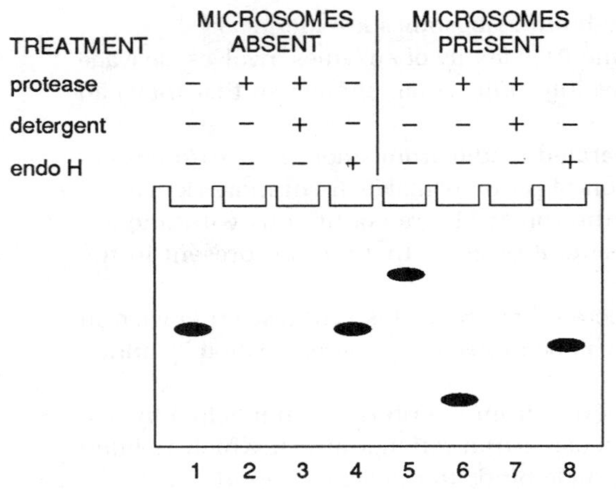

Figure 8–10 Results of translation of a pure mRNA in the presence and absence of microsomal membranes (Problem 8–25). Treatments of the products of translation before electrophoresis are indicated at the top of each lane. Electrophoresis was on an SDS polyacrylamide gel, which separates proteins on the basis of size with lower molecular weight proteins migrating farther down the gel.

A. Explain the experimental results that are seen in the absence of microsomes (Figure 8–10, lanes 1 to 4).
B. Using the three criteria outlined in the problem, decide whether the experimental results in the presence of microsomes (lanes 5 to 8) indicate that the protein is translocated across microsomal membranes. Explain the migration of the proteins in lanes 5, 6, and 8.
C. Is the protein anchored in the membrane, or is it translocated all the way through the membrane?

***8–26** The segregation of secretory proteins and membrane proteins into the lumen of the ER is normally coupled tightly to protein synthesis. The co-translational nature of translocation in eucaryotes provides a sensitive and specific assay for the early steps in the biosynthesis of these proteins. However, it also poses a serious obstacle to elucidating the mechanism of translocation. For example, in such a coupled system it is difficult to determine whether the ribosome "pushes" the protein across the membrane or the translocation machinery "pulls" the protein across.

In an attempt to uncouple translation from translocation you have cloned a gene onto a plasmid adjacent to a promoter for a bacteriophage RNA polymerase (Figure 8–11). This arrangement allows you to transcribe the gene *in vitro* by adding the phage RNA polymerase. In addition, by cutting the plasmid at different positions within the gene, you can create shorter mRNAs than normal (Figure 8–11). You prepare the three mRNAs indicated in Figure 8–11 and translate them *in vitro*. In one experiment you add microsomes before translation begins. In a second experiment you add microsomes after translation is completed (along with cycloheximide to inhibit any additional protein synthesis). To assess translocation, you treat some samples with protease or disrupt the microsomes and treat with endoglycosidase H (endo H), and then display the products by SDS-gel electrophoresis (Figure 8–12).

A. Are the proteins from each of the mRNAs translocated into microsomes when the microsomes are present during translation? How can you tell?
B. Have you managed to uncouple translocation from translation in any of the experiments? Explain your answer.
C. Do your experiments support the idea that ribosomes push proteins across the membrane of the ER, or the idea that the translocation machinery pulls proteins across the membrane? How so?
D. Why do you think that translocation of the shorter proteins can be uncoupled from translation, whereas translocation of the longer proteins cannot?

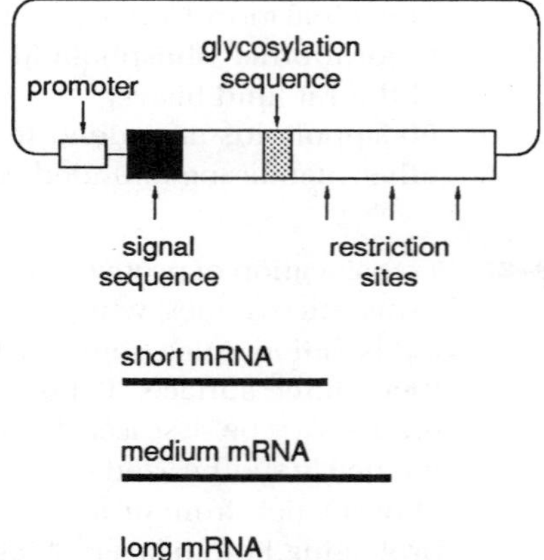

Figure 8–11 A cloned gene for testing the coupling of translation and translocation (Problem 8–26). Protein coding sequences start and stop at the ends of the large rectangle; promoter sequences are located in the small rectangle. Cleavage sites for restriction enzymes used to truncate the transcription template are indicated with arrows. The three different mRNA products of transcription from the truncated templates are indicated below the map of the gene.

8–27 Although the exact mechanism for co-translational insertion of proteins into membranes is undefined, it is possible to predict the final arrangement of a protein across the membrane if its membrane-spanning segments are known. If one numbers the membrane-spanning segments beginning at

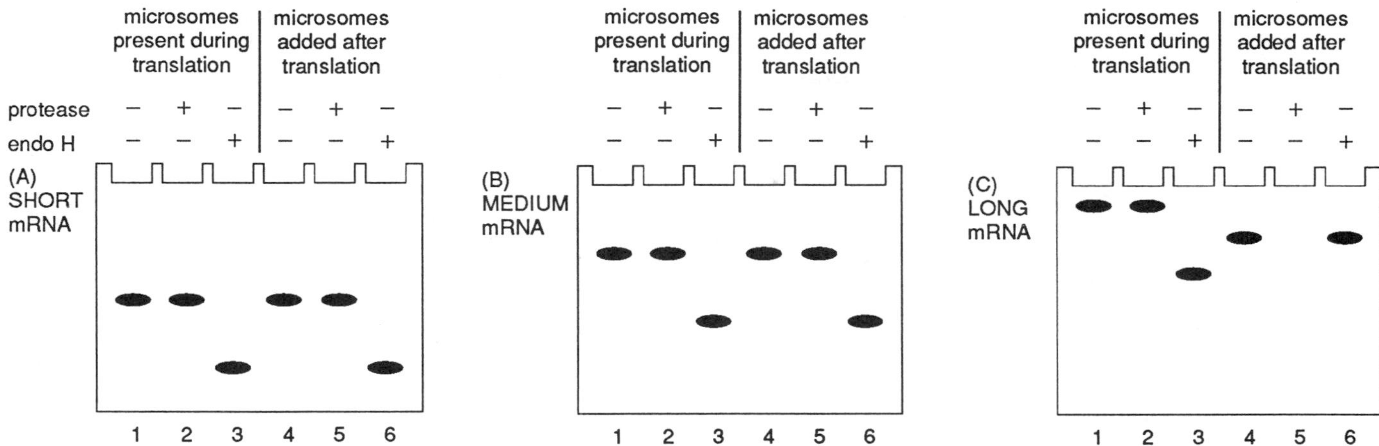

the N terminus, the odd-numbered segments initiate translocation (act as start-transfer peptides) and the even-numbered segments terminate translocation (act as stop-transfer peptides). Furthermore, because peptides are inserted into membranes as hairpins, start-transfer peptides are oriented with their N-terminal end pointing toward the cytoplasm and their C-terminal end pointing toward the lumen of the ER. This orientation of start-transfer segments fixes the stop-transfer segments to the opposite orientation; that is, with their N-terminal end pointing toward the lumen of the ER and their C-terminal end pointing toward the cytoplasm.

Four membrane proteins are represented schematically in Figure 8–13. The boxes represent membrane-spanning segments and the arrows represent sites for cleavage of the leader peptides. Using the above rules for co-translational insertion, predict how each of the mature proteins will be arranged across the membrane of the ER. Indicate clearly the N and C termini relative to the cytoplasm and the lumen of the ER.

Figure 8–12 Results of experiments to test the coupling of translation and translocation (Problem 8–26). The results with short (A), medium (B), and long (C) mRNAs are shown. Treatments of samples before electrophoresis are indicated above the gels. Endo H removes sugars of the type added in the ER.

***8–28** You are intrigued that the organization of a protein in a membrane can, in principle, be derived from the amino acid sequence itself. A hydropathy plot of the protein can be used to identify hydrophobic regions, which are likely to correspond to membrane-spanning segments. By applying the simple set of rules for co-translational insertion, you should be able to predict which parts of a protein will be exposed to the cytoplasm and which parts will be exposed on the outside of the cell. You wish to test this notion in *E. coli*, where you can bring powerful genetic tools to bear on the problem.

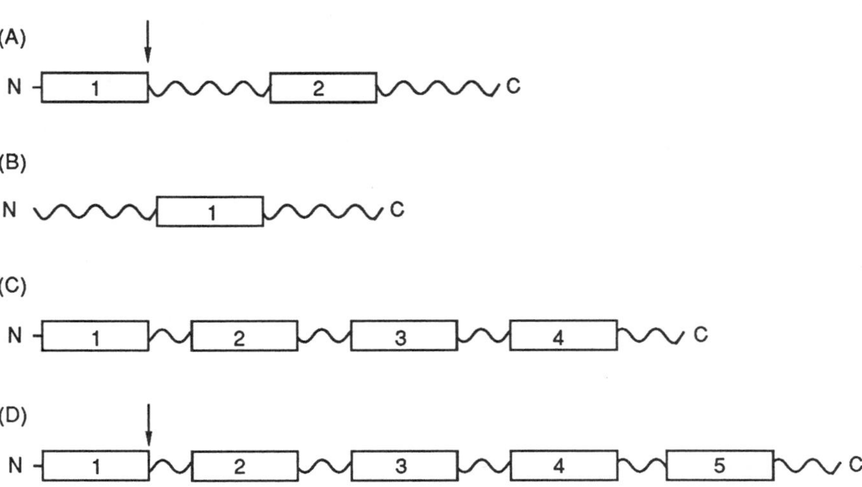

Figure 8–13 The distribution of membrane-spanning segments in proteins to be inserted into the membrane of the ER (Problem 8–27). Boxes represent membrane-spanning segments and arrows indicate sites at which signal peptides are cleaved.

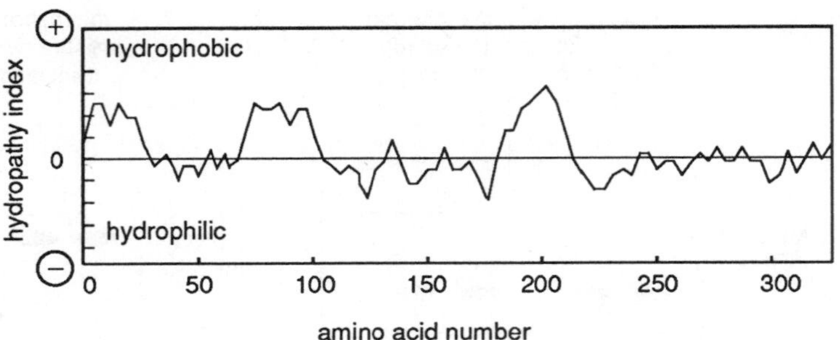

Figure 8–14 Hydropathy plot of a membrane protein (Problem 8–28).

You select as a test protein a membrane protein that has been cloned onto a plasmid and whose sequence is known. The hydropathy plot of this protein is shown in Figure 8–14. You plan to test your predictions by making hybrid fusion proteins with the membrane protein at the N terminus and alkaline phosphatase at the C terminus. Alkaline phosphatase is easy to assay in whole cells and has no significant hydrophobic stretches. Moreover, when it is on the cytoplasmic side of the membrane, its activity is low, and when it is on the external side of the membrane (in the periplasmic space), its activity is high.

You isolate six in-frame fusions of the membrane protein with alkaline phosphatase. The structures of the hybrid proteins (with the C-terminal amino acid of the membrane protein numbered) and the assayed levels of alkaline phosphatase activity (HIGH or LOW) are indicated in Figure 8–15. As an additional test of your predictive abilities, you use two conveniently located restriction sites in the gene for the membrane protein to create in-frame deletions that remove codons for amino acids 68 to 103. The results from these modified plasmids are also shown in Figure 8–15.

A. What organization of the protein in the membrane is predicted by the hydropathy plot in Figure 8–14? Are the results with the fusion proteins consistent with the predicted arrangement?

B. How is the organization of the membrane protein altered by the in-frame deletion? Are your measurements of alkaline phosphatase activity in the modified plasmids consistent with the altered arrangement?

C. Are the N terminus and the C terminus of the mature membrane protein (the normal, nonhybrid protein) on the same side of the membrane?

8–29 Mitochondria and peroxisomes, as opposed to most other cellular membranes, acquire new phospholipids in soluble form from phospholipid

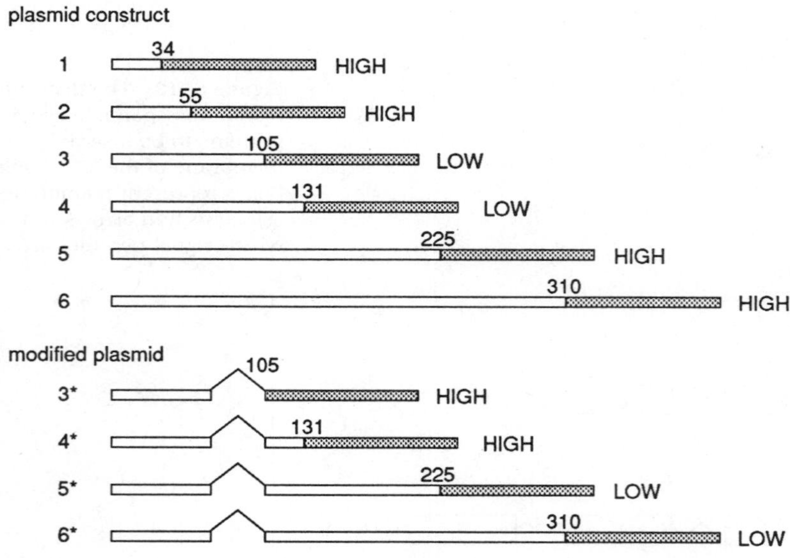

Figure 8–15 Structures of hybrid proteins used to test the usefulness of hydropathy plots in predicting the organization of proteins in membranes (Problem 8–28). The membrane protein (unshaded segment) is at the N terminus and alkaline phosphatase (shaded segment) is at the C terminus of the hybrid protein. The amino acids deleted from the modified hybrid proteins are indicated by the inverted V-shaped segment. The most C-terminal amino acid of the membrane protein is numbered in each hybrid protein. The activity of alkaline phosphatase in each hybrid protein is shown on the right.

transfer proteins. One such protein, PC transfer protein, specifically transfers phosphatidylcholine (PC) between membranes. Its activity is measured by mixing red blood cell ghosts (intact plasma membranes with cytoplasm removed) with synthetic phospholipid vesicles containing radioactively labeled PC in both monolayers of the vesicle bilayer. After incubation at 37°C, the mixture is centrifuged briefly so that ghosts form a pellet, whereas the vesicles stay in the supernatant. The amount of exchange is determined by measuring the radioactivity in the pellet.

Figure 8–16 shows the result of such an experiment along these lines, using labeled (donor) vesicles with an outer radius of 10.5 nm and a bilayer 4.0 nm in thickness. No exchange occurred in the absence of the transfer protein, but in its presence up to 70% of the labeled PC in the vesicles could be transferred to the red cell membranes.

Several control experiments were performed to explore the reason why only 70% of the label in donor vesicles was transferred.

1. Five times as many membranes from red cell ghosts were included in the incubation: the exchange still stopped at the same point.
2. Fresh transfer protein was added after 1 hour: it caused no further exchange.
3. The labeled lipids remaining in donor vesicles at the end of the reaction were extracted and made into fresh vesicles: 70% of the label in these vesicles was exchangeable.

When the red cell ghosts that were labeled in this experiment were used as donor membranes in the reverse experiment (that is, transfer of PC from red cell membranes to synthetic vesicles), 96% of the label could be transferred to the acceptor vesicles.

A. What possible explanations for the 70% limit do each of the three control experiments eliminate?
B. What do you think is the explanation for the 70% limit?
C. Why do you think that almost 100% of the label in the red cell membrane can be transferred back to the vesicle?

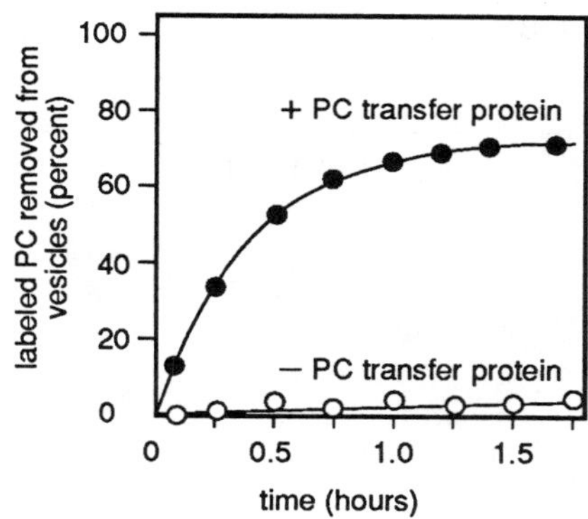

Figure 8–16 Transfer of labeled PC from donor vesicles to red cell membranes by PC transfer protein (Problem 8–29).

The Golgi Apparatus (MBOC 451–458)

8–30 Fill in the blanks in the following statements.

A. The ____________, which is usually located near the cell nucleus, contains a collection of flattened, membrane-bounded cisternae.
B. The Golgi stack has two distinct faces: a ____________, which is closely associated with the transitional ER, and a ____________, which is associated with a tubular reticulum called the *trans* Golgi network.
C. Carbohydrate chains that are attached to asparagine residues in proteins are termed ____________.
D. ____________ oligosaccharides have no new sugars added to them in the Golgi apparatus, whereas ____________ oligosaccharides contain a variable number of additional sugars.
E. The addition of sugars to selected serine or threonine side chains is termed ____________.
F. Proteins exported from the ER enter the ____________ compartment of the Golgi, then move on to the ____________ compartment, and finally to the ____________ compartment.
G. From the last compartment of the Golgi, proteins move to the ________, which is a tubular reticulum where proteins are segregated and dispatched to their final destinations.
H. Although the mechanism of protein and lipid transfer through the Golgi is not known with certainty, ____________ are thought to bud from the cisternal rims to carry this traffic from cisterna to cisterna through the stack.

8–31 Indicate whether the following statements are true or false. If a statement is false, explain why.

__ A. All of the sugars in the terminal region of complex oligosaccharides are added in the *trans* Golgi by a series of glycosyl transferases that act in a rigidly determined sequence.

__ B. All the glycoproteins and glycolipids in intracellular membranes have their oligosaccharides facing the luminal side, whereas those in the plasma membrane have their oligosaccharides facing outside the cell.

__ C. *N*-linked oligosaccharides aid in the transport of proteins through the ER and Golgi.

__ D. Proteoglycan core proteins are converted in the Golgi apparatus into proteoglycans by the addition of *O*-linked glycosaminoglycan chains.

__ E. The initial cleavages of many polypeptide hormones and neuropeptides are made by membrane-bound proteases that cut next to pairs of basic amino acid residues.

__ F. Exported proteins move unidirectionally through the three compartments of the Golgi and never skip an intervening compartment.

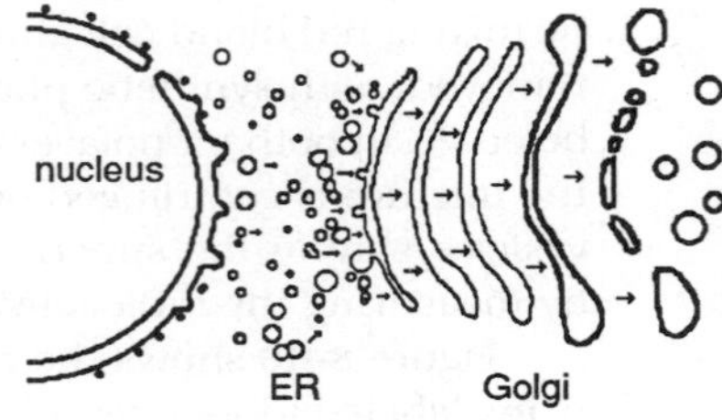

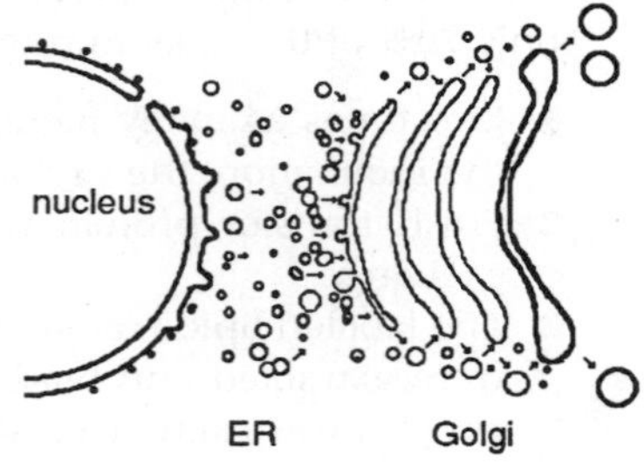

Figure 8–17 The cisternal progression model (A) and the vesicle transport model (B) for movement of material through the Golgi apparatus (Problem 8–32).

8–32 Until recently, there were two competing models for how material progresses through the Golgi apparatus (Figure 8–17). In the cisternal-progression model, new cisternae form continuously as vesicles from the ER coalesce at the *cis* face of the Golgi apparatus. Each newly formed cisterna moves through the stack (with appropriate modifications occurring to their contents) and finally breaks up into transport vesicles at the *trans* face. In the vesicle transport model, the cisternae remain fixed and the maturing glycoproteins move from the *cis* to the *trans* cisternae inside transport vesicles.

One test of these two models made use of mutant cells that are defective in the addition of galactose, which occurs in the *trans* compartment of the Golgi. The mutant cells were infected with vesicular stomatitis virus (VSV) to provide a convenient marker protein, the viral G protein. At an appropriate point in the infection an inhibitor of protein synthesis was added to stop further synthesis of G protein. The infected cells were then incubated briefly with a radioactive precursor of GlcNAc, which in the absence of protein synthesis is added only in the medial compartment of the Golgi. Next, the infected mutant cells were fused with uninfected wild-type cells to form a common cytoplasm containing both wild-type and mutant Golgi stacks. After a few minutes, the cells were dissolved with detergent and all the G protein was precipitated using G-specific antibodies. After separation from the antibodies, the G proteins carrying galactose were precipitated with a lectin that binds galactose. The radioactivity in the precipitate and in the supernatant was measured. The results of this experiment along with control experiments (which used mutant cells only or wild-type cells only) are shown in Table 8–2.

A. The movement of proteins between which two compartments of the Golgi apparatus is being tested in this experiment? Explain your answer.

Table 8–2 Addition of Galactose to G Protein after Fusion of VSV-infected Cells to Uninfected Cells (Problem 8–32)

	Precipitate	Supernatant
1. Infected mutant cells fused with uninfected wild-type cells	45%	55%
2. Infected mutant cells fused with uninfected mutant cells	5%	95%
3. Infected wild-type cells fused with uninfected wild-type cells	85%	15%

Radioactive G protein was purified and then reacted with a lectin that precipitates galactose-containing proteins. The percentage of total radioactivity in the precipitate (G protein with galactose) and the supernatant (G protein without galactose) is shown.

Table 8–3 Analysis of the Sugars Present in the *N*-linked Oligosaccharides from Wild-Type Cells and from Mutant Cell Lines Defective in Oligosaccharide Processing (Problem 8–33)

Cell Line	Man	GlcNAc	Gal	NANA	Glc
Wild type	3	4	2	2	0
Mutant A	3	4	0	0	0
Mutant B	5	3	0	0	0
Mutant C	9	2	0	0	3
Mutant D	9	2	0	0	0
Mutant E	5	2	0	0	0
Mutant F	3	3	0	0	0
Mutant G	8	2	0	0	0
Mutant H	9	2	0	0	2
Mutant I	3	4	2	0	0

Abbreviations: Man (mannose), GlcNAc (*N*-acetylglucosamine), Gal (galactose), NANA (*N*-acetylneuraminic acid or sialic acid), Glc (glucose).

Numbers indicate the number of sugar monomers in the oligosaccharide.

B. If proteins moved through the Golgi apparatus by cisternal progression, what would you predict for the results of this experiment? If proteins moved through the Golgi via transport vesicles, what would you predict for the results of this experiment?

C. Which model is supported by the results in Table 8–2?

***8–33** You have isolated several mutant cell lines that are defective in their ability to add carbohydrate to exported proteins. Using an easily purified protein that carries only *N*-linked complex oligosaccharides, you have analyzed the sugars in the *N*-linked oligosaccharides that are added in the different mutant cells. Each mutant is unique in the kinds and numbers of different sugars contained in its oligosaccharides (Table 8–3).

A. Arrange the mutants in the order that corresponds to the steps in the pathway for processing *N*-linked oligosaccharides.

B. Which of these mutants are defective in processing events that occur in the ER? Which mutants are defective in processing steps that occur in the Golgi?

C. Which of the mutants are likely to be defective in a processing enzyme that is directly responsible for modifying *N*-linked oligosaccharides? Which mutants might not be defective in a processing enzyme but, rather, in another enzyme that affects oligosaccharide processing indirectly?

8–34 The vesicular stomatitis virus (VSV) G protein is a typical membrane glycoprotein. In addition to its signal peptide, which is removed after import into the ER, the G protein contains a single membrane-spanning segment that anchors the protein in the plasma membrane so that a small C-terminal domain is exposed to the cytoplasm and a much larger N-terminal domain is outside the cell. The membrane-spanning segment consists of 20 uncharged and mostly hydrophobic amino acids that are flanked by basic amino acids (Figure 8–18). Twenty amino acids arranged in an α-helix is just sufficient to span the 3-nm thickness of the lipid bilayer of the membrane.

To test the length requirements for membrane-spanning segments, you modify a cloned version of the G protein to generate a series of mutants in which the membrane-spanning segment is shorter, as indicated in Figure 8–18. When you introduce the modified plasmids into cultured cells, roughly the same amount of G proteins is synthesized from each mutant as from wild type. You analyze the cellular distribution of the altered G proteins in several ways.

1. You examine the cellular location of the modified G proteins by immunofluorescence microscopy, using G-specific antibodies tagged with fluorescent markers.

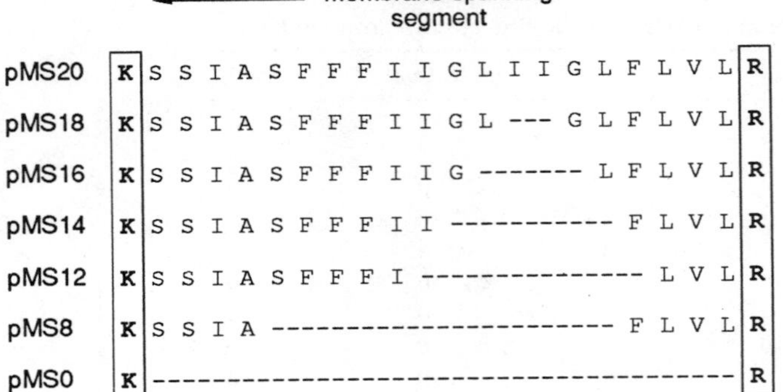

Figure 8–18 The membrane-spanning domains of normal and mutant VSV G proteins (Problem 8–34). Plasmid numbers indicate the number of amino acids in the membrane-spanning segment; for example, pMS20 contains the wild type, 20-amino-acid membrane-spanning segment. Dashed lines indicate amino acids that are missing in the other plasmids. Boxed letters indicate the basic amino acids that flank the membrane-spanning segment.

2. You characterize the attached oligosaccharide chains by digesting the G proteins with endoglycosidase H (endo H), which removes *N*-linked oligosaccharides up to a certain stage in their processing in the Golgi (see Figure 8–63 in MBOC).
3. You determine whether the altered G proteins retain the small C-terminal cytoplasmic domain (which characterizes the normal G protein) by treating isolated microsomes with a protease. In the normal G protein this domain is removed by (sensitive to) protease treatment.

The results of these experiments are summarized in Table 8–4.

A. To the extent these data allow, deduce the intracellular location of each altered G protein that fails to reach the plasma membrane.
B. For the VSV G protein, what is the minimum length of the membrane-spanning segment that is sufficient to anchor the protein in the membrane?
C. What is the minimum length of the membrane-spanning segment that is consistent with proper sorting of the G protein?

Transport of Proteins from the Golgi Apparatus to Lysosomes (MBOC 459–465)

8–35 Fill in the blanks in the following statements.

A. The ____________ is a membranous bag of hydrolytic enzymes used for the controlled intracellular digestion of macromolecules.
B. Hydrolytic enzymes that are active at low pH are termed ____________.
C. The compartment that receives newly synthesized lysosomal hydrolases and membrane proteins from the Golgi apparatus is called the ________.

Table 8–4 Results of Experiments Characterizing the Cellular Distribution of G Proteins from Normal and Mutant Cells (Problem 8–34)

Plasmid	Cellular Location	Endo H Treatment	Protease Treatment
pMS20	plasma membrane	resistant	sensitive
pMS18	plasma membrane	resistant	sensitive
pMS16	plasma membrane	resistant	sensitive
pMS14	plasma membrane	resistant	sensitive
pMS12	intracellular	+/− resistant	sensitive
pMS8	intracellular	sensitive	sensitive
pMS0	intracellular	sensitive	resistant

+/− in the endo H column indicates that only about 30% of the G protein was sensitive to endo H; other modified G proteins were either totally resistant or sensitive. In the protease column, "sensitive" indicates that the small C-terminal domain was removed by protease treatment; "resistant" indicates that the molecular weight of the G protein was unchanged by the protease treatment.

D. Obsolete parts of the cell can be destroyed in a process known as ____________, in which membranes derived from the ER enclose an organelle, creating an ____________, which then fuses with a lysosome.

E. Cells that are specialized for phagocytosis can engulf microorganisms to form a ____________, which is converted to a ____________ upon fusion with a lysosome.

F. The most dramatic form of lysosomal storage disease is a very rare disorder called ____________, in which almost all the hydrolases are missing from lysosomes.

8–36 Indicate whether the following statements are true or false. If a statement is false, explain why.

__ A. Lysosomal membranes contain a proton pump that utilizes the energy of ATP hydrolysis to pump protons out of the lysosome, thereby maintaining the lumen at a low pH.

__ B. Lysosomes are heterogeneous organelles that are found in all nucleated eucaryotic cells.

__ C. Endolysosomes are converted to mature lysosomes by loss of endosomal membrane components and further decrease in their internal pH.

__ D. Materials taken up by endocytosis fuse directly with lysosomes so that their contents can be digested to small molecules.

__ E. Lysosomal hydrolases are marked for delivery to lysosomes by having mannose 6-phosphate (M6P) groups added to their *N*-linked oligosaccharides in the lumen of the Golgi.

__ F. If cells are treated with a weak base such as ammonia or chloroquine, which raise the pH of organelles toward neutrality, M6P receptors accumulate in the Golgi because they cannot bind to the lysosomal enzymes.

__ G. Since all glycoproteins arrive in the Golgi with identical *N*-linked oligosaccharides, the signal for adding the M6P units to oligosaccharides must reside somewhere in the polypeptide chain of each hydrolase.

__ H. The recognition signal on lysosomal hydrolases is thought to be a conformation-dependent signal patch rather than a signal peptide, because recognition is virtually eliminated when a hydrolase is partially denatured.

__ I. In I-cell disease the lysosomes in some cell types contain a normal complement of lysosomal enzymes, implying that there is a second pathway for sorting hydrolases to lysosomes that is used in some cells but not in others.

8–37 Patients with Hunter's syndrome or Hurler's syndrome rarely live beyond their teens. Analysis indicates that patients accumulate glycosaminoglycans in lysosomes due to the lack of specific lysosomal enzymes necessary for their degradation. When cells from patients with the two syndromes are fused, glycosaminoglycans are degraded properly, indicating that the cells are missing different degradative enzymes. Even if the cells are just cultured together, they still correct each others defects. Most surprising of all, the medium from a culture of Hurler's cells corrects the defect in Hunter's cells (and vice versa). The corrective factors in the media are inactivated by treatment with proteases, by treatment with periodate, which destroys carbohydrate, and by treatment with alkaline phosphatase, which removes phosphates.

A. What do you think the corrective factors are, and how do you think they correct the lysosomal defects?

B. Why do you think the treatments with protease, periodate, and alkaline phosphatase inactivate the corrective factors?

C. Would you expect a similar sort of correction scheme to work for mutant or missing cytosolic enzymes?

***8–38** Children with I-cell disease synthesize perfectly good lysosomal enzymes but secrete them outside the cell instead of sorting them to lysosomes. The mistake occurs because the cells lack GlcNAc-P-transferase, which is required to create the mannose 6-phosphate marker that is essential for proper sorting. In principle, I-cell disease could also be caused by deficiencies in two other proteins: the phosphoglycosidase that removes GlcNAc to expose mannose 6-phosphate and the mannose 6-phosphate receptor itself.

These three potential kinds of I-cell disease could be distinguished by the ability of various culture supernatants to correct defects in mutant cells. Imagine that you have cell lines from three hypothetical I-cell patients (A, B, and C) that give the results below:

1. The supernatant from normal cells corrects the defects in B and C, but not the defect in A.
2. The supernatant from A corrects the defect in Hurler's cells, but the supernatants from B and C do not.
3. If the supernatants from the mutant cells are first treated with the phosphoglycosidase that removes GlcNAc, then the supernatants from A and C correct the defect in Hurler's cells, but the supernatant from B does not.

From these results deduce the nature of the defect in each of the mutant cell lines.

Transport from the Golgi Apparatus to Secretory Vesicles and to the Cell Surface (MBOC 465–471)

8–39 Fill in the blanks in the following statements.

A. Whereas all cells require the ____________ secretory pathway, specialized secretory cells also have a ____________ secretory pathway in which soluble proteins and other substances are stored in secretory vesicles for later release.

B. In cells in which secretion occurs in response to an extracellular signal, secreted proteins are concentrated and stored in ____________, from which they are released by exocytosis in response to the signal.

C. A typical epithelial cell has two physically continuous but compositionally distinct plasma membrane domains: the ____________ domain, which faces the lumen of a duct system, and the ____________ domain, which covers the rest of the cell.

D. Semliki forest virus is a typical enveloped virus that consists of an RNA genome surrounded by a protein shell, called a ____________, which in turn is surrounded by a lipid bilayer that contains three distinct ____________ proteins.

8–40 Indicate whether the following statements are true or false. If a statement is false, explain why.

__ A. Secretory vesicles bud from the *trans* compartment of the Golgi.

__ B. After a secretory vesicle fuses with the plasma membrane, the specialized proteins of the secretory vesicle membrane are rapidly retrieved from the plasma membrane by endocytosis and returned to the Golgi for reuse.

__ C. In a secretory cell, special sorting signals are required for each of the three types of proteins that leave the *trans* Golgi network: those destined for lysosomes, those destined for secretory vesicles, and those destined for immediate delivery to the cell surface.

__ D. Since polarized cells can secrete one set of proteins from the apical domain and a second set from the basolateral domain, apical and basolateral proteins must have different sorting signals to direct them to the appropriate domain.

__ E. Enveloped viruses that are taken up by endocytosis escape from the endosome by virtue of an envelope protein that causes the viral envelope to fuse with the endosome membrane, thereby releasing the nucleocapsid into the cytosol.

— F. Enveloped viruses that acquire their envelope by budding through internal membranes move outward from the ER and Golgi lumen toward the cell surface as if they were secreted proteins.

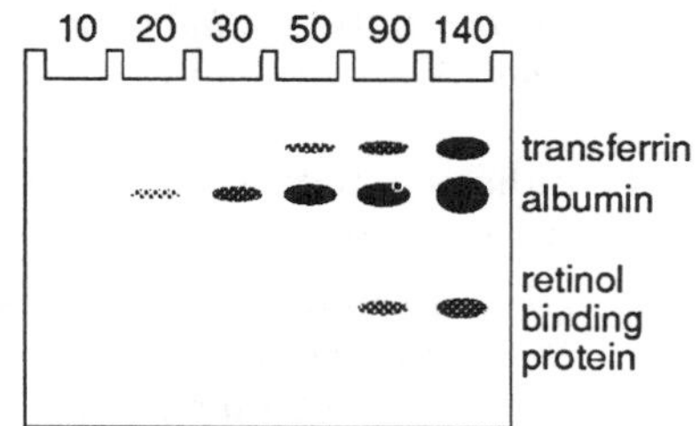

Figure 8–19 Time of appearance of secreted proteins in the medium (Problem 8–41). At various times after labeling, proteins were immunoprecipitated with specific antibodies, separated by gel electrophoresis, and subjected to autoradiography.

8–41 Liver cells secrete a broad spectrum of proteins into the blood via the constitutive pathway. You are interested in how long it takes for different proteins to be secreted. Accordingly, you add ^{35}S-methionine to cultured liver cells to label proteins as they are synthesized. You then sample the medium at various times to measure the appearance of individual labeled proteins. As shown in Figure 8–19, albumin appears after 20 minutes, transferrin appears after 50 minutes, and retinol binding protein appears after 90 minutes. You are surprised at the variability in secretion rates, which bear no obvious relationship to the size, function, or quantity of the individual proteins.

Why do transferrin and the retinol binding protein take so much longer than albumin to be secreted? You suspect that the slow step in constitutive secretion of these proteins occurs either in the ER or in the Golgi apparatus. To determine which, you label cells for 4 hours, which is a long enough labeling period so that the labeled proteins in the cells reach the normal steady-state distribution of unlabeled proteins. (At a steady state the influx into a pathway exactly equals efflux from the pathway.) You then homogenize the cells to break the ER and Golgi into vesicles and separate the vesicles by density on a sucrose gradient. You measure the amount of labeled albumin and transferrin that are associated with the two types of vesicles (Figure 8–20).

Does the slow step in the constitutive secretion of transferrin occur in the ER or in the Golgi? Where does the slow step in the constitutive secretion of albumin occur? How do these experiments allow you to decide?

***8–42** Polarized epithelial cells must make an extra sorting decision since their plasma membranes are divided into apical and basolateral domains, which are populated by distinctive sets of proteins. Proteins destined for the apical or basolateral domain of the plasma membrane seem to travel there directly from the Golgi. One way to sort proteins to these domains would be to use a specific sorting signal for one class of proteins, which would then be actively recognized and directed to one domain, and to allow the other class to travel via a default pathway to the other domain.

Consider the following experiment to identify the default pathway. The cloned genes for several foreign proteins were engineered by recombinant DNA techniques so that they could be expressed in the polarized cells. These proteins are secreted in other types of cells but are not normally expressed in the polarized cells. The cloned genes were introduced into polarized cells, and their sites of secretion were assayed. Although the cells remained polarized, the foreign proteins were released in roughly equal amounts from the apical and basolateral domains.

A. What is the expected result of this experiment, based on the hypothesis that targeting to one domain of the plasma membrane is actively signaled and targeting to the other domain is via a default pathway?

B. Do these results support the concept of a default pathway as outlined above?

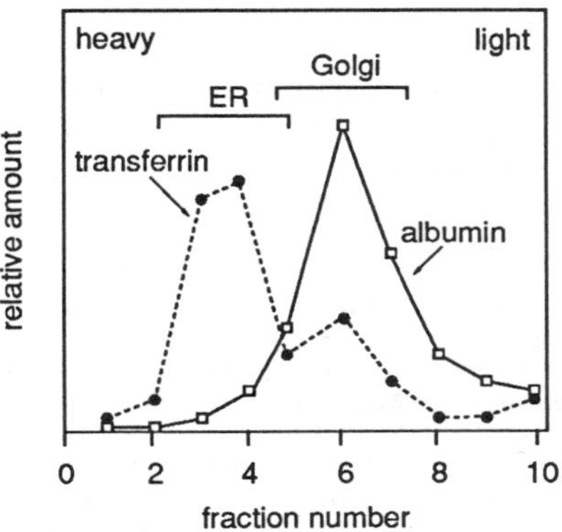

Figure 8–20 Distribution of albumin and transferrin in vesicles derived from the ER and Golgi (Problem 8–41). Labeled albumin and transferrin were assayed by immunoprecipitation, electrophoresis, and autoradiography.

Vesicular Transport and the Maintenance of Compartmental Identity (MBOC 471–475)

8–43 Fill in the blanks in the following statements.

A. ____________-coated vesicles carry receptor-mediated endocytic traffic from the plasma membrane to endosomes and receptor-mediated traffic from the *trans* Golgi network to endolysosomes.

B. ____________-coated vesicles carry material from the ER to the Golgi, from the *cis* to the *medial* compartment of the Golgi and from the *medial* to the *trans* compartment of the Golgi.

8–44 Indicate whether the following statements are true or false. If a statement is false, explain why.

__ A. For intracellular sorting to be specific, each transport vesicle must carry a "molecular address" label on its surface that allows it to deliver its contents to specific cell membranes.

__ B. If forward movement from the ER to the plasma membrane is automatic, then permanent residents of the ER and Golgi must carry signals that are responsible for their selective retention.

8–45 Vesicle transport between Golgi stacks and onward to the plasma membrane via the constitutive pathway apparently occurs in vesicles that do not have a clathrin coat. This transport is referred to as bulk transport, meaning that Golgi substituents do not become concentrated in the vesicles. Given that transport in clathrin-coated vesicles is so highly concentrating, you are skeptical that no concentration occurs during bulk constitutive secretion.

To determine whether vesicles in the constitutive pathway concentrate their contents, you infect cells with vesicular stomatitis virus (VSV) and follow the viral G protein. Your idea, an ambitious one, is to compare the concentration of G protein in the lumen of the Golgi stacks with that in the associated non-clathrin-coated transport vesicles. You intend to measure G-protein concentration by preparing thin sections of VSV-infected cells and incubating them with G-specific antibodies tagged with gold particles. Since the gold particles are visible in electron micrographs as small black dots, it is relatively straightforward to count dots in the lumena of transport vesicles (fully formed and just budding) and of the Golgi apparatus. You make two estimates of G-protein concentration: (1) the number of gold particles per cross-sectional area and (2) the number of gold particles per linear length of membrane. Your results are shown in Table 8–5.

Do the vesicles involved in bulk transport concentrate their contents or not?

Table 8–5 Relative Densities of G Protein in Golgi and Vesicle Lumena and Membranes (Problem 8–45)

Parameter Measured	Mean Density
Surface density over whole Golgi from *uninfected* cells	$5/\mu m^2$
Surface density over whole Golgi from *infected* cells	$271/\mu m^2$
Surface density over buds and vesicles of Golgi from *infected* cells	$233/\mu m^2$
Linear density over cisternal membranes of Golgi from *infected* cells	$6/\mu m$
Linear density over buds and vesicles of Golgi from *infected* cells	$4/\mu m$

The Cell Nucleus

Chromosomal DNA and Chromosomal Proteins

(MBOC 483–502)

9–1 Fill in the blanks in the following statements.

A. Each DNA molecule is packaged in a ____________, and the total genetic information stored in the chromosomes of an organism is said to constitute its ____________.

B. A functional chromosome requires three DNA sequence elements: at least one ____________ to permit the chromosome to be copied, one ____________ to facilitate proper segregation of its two copies at mitosis, and two ____________ to allow the chromosome to be maintained between cell generations.

C. Each region of the DNA helix that produces a functional RNA molecule constitutes a ____________.

D. In the genes of higher eucaryotes, short segments of coding DNA, called ____________, are usually separated by long stretches of noncoding DNA, called ____________.

E. Each type of cell in a multicellular organism contains a different mixture of ____________, which act in combinations to cause the expression of different genes.

F. Protein molecules bound to a DNA molecule will cause the DNA to move more slowly when subjected to electrophoretic analysis, which is the basis for a sensitive ____________ to detect sequence-specific DNA-binding proteins.

G. Several DNA-binding proteins contain one or more domains known as ____________, which comprise about 30 amino acids folded into a single structural unit around a Zn atom that links two cysteines and two histidines.

H. Several bacterial sequence-specific DNA-binding proteins have a stretch of about 20 amino acids arranged as two α helices separated by a short turn, forming what is known as a ____________ motif.

I. Two proteins that help each other hold onto the DNA more tightly when they bind are said to exhibit ____________.

J. The most stable structure for DNA is the so-called ____________ DNA; however, unusual nucleotide sequences can coil into other structures such as the right-handed ____________ DNA and the left-handed ____________ DNA.

K. The structure of eucaryotic chromosomes is dominated by a nucleoprotein particle, the ____________, which plays a major role in packing and organizing all of the DNA in the cell nucleus.

L. The complex of the abundant structural proteins, the ____________, and the ____________ proteins with the nuclear DNA of eucaryotic cells is known as ____________.

M. The five types of histones fall into two main groups: the ____________ histones and the ____________ histones.

N. Regions of DNA that lack nucleosomes are readily digested by trace amounts of deoxyribonuclease; these regions are known as ____________.

O. In the living cell, nucleosomes are packed upon one another to generate a ____________ fiber in which the DNA is more highly condensed than in the extended beads-on-a-string form.

9–2 Indicate whether the following statements are true or false. If a statement is false, explain why.

__A. Each chromosome contains a single long DNA molecule.

__B. A telomere allows a chromosome to be replicated precisely so that no nucleotides are lost from the end of the chromosome, thereby solving the end-replication problem.

__C. Population biologists estimate from the observed mutation rate that no more than a few percent of the mammalian genome can be involved in regulating or encoding essential proteins.

__D. In genes from higher eucaryotes, introns are usually larger and more numerous than exons.

__E. In a comparison between the DNAs of related organisms, such as human beings and mice, conserved sequences represent functionally important exons and regulatory regions and nonconserved sequences represent noncoding DNA.

__F. Each of the four possible nucleotide pairs (A-T, T-A, G-C, C-G) can be uniquely recognized by the specific arrangement of the atoms that protrude into the major groove of the DNA helix.

__G. Radiolabeled segments of DNA can be used to detect sequence-specific DNA-binding proteins by gel retardation assays, to purify the protein by DNA affinity chromatography, and to screen bacteria for expression of the protein.

__H. The zinc-finger structural motif is found only in eucaryotic sequence-specific DNA-binding proteins, and the helix-turn-helix structural motif is found only in bacterial proteins.

__I. If a DNA-binding protein forms a symmetric dimer, it is likely that the recognition site in the DNA is symmetric as well.

__J. If two sequence-specific DNA-binding proteins bind to partially overlapping DNA sequences, each will bind more tightly in the presence of the other; thus, their binding is said to be cooperative.

__K. In B-form DNA, both the exact tilt of the bases and the helical twist angle between base pairs depend on which nucleotides are adjacent to each other in the sequence.

__L. Special sequences, such as AAAAANNNNN repeated every 10 to 11 nucleotides, are required to allow DNA to bend into a tight coil inside the cell.

__M. Histones are relatively small proteins with a very high proportion of positively charged amino acids; the positive charge helps the histones bind tightly to DNA, regardless of its nucleotide sequence.

__N. A nucleosome consists of about 146 nucleotide pairs wrapped in two turns around a histone octamer, which is a complex of eight nucleosomal histones.

__O. While the majority of nucleosomes do not seem to be precisely positioned on DNA, striking examples of precise nucleosome positioning are known.

__P. Nuclease-hypersensitive sites in chromatin are located in the linker DNA between nucleosomes.

__Q. Disruption of the cooperative interactions between histone H1 molecules by gene regulatory proteins may be responsible for the local decondensation of chromatin that occurs around active genes.

__R. Electron micrographs of spread chromatin generally show different patterns of nucleosome beads in transcribed and untranscribed regions of DNA.

9–3 *Tetrahymena* is a ciliated protozoan with two nuclei. The smaller nucleus (the micronucleus) maintains a master copy of the cell's chromosomes; it participates in sexual conjugation, but not in day-to-day gene expression. The larger nucleus (the macronucleus) maintains a "working" copy of the cell's genome in the form of a large number of gene-sized double-stranded DNA fragments (minichromosomes), which are actively transcribed. The minichromosome that contains the ribosomal RNA genes is present in many copies; it can be separated from the other minichromosomes by gradient centrifugation and studied in detail.

When examined by electron microscopy, each ribosomal minichromosome is a linear structure 21 kb in length. Ribosomal minichromosomes also migrate at 21 kb when subjected to gel electrophoresis (Figure 9–1, lane 1). However, if the minichromosome is cut with the restriction enzyme, BglII, the two fragments that are generated (13.4 kb and 3.8 kb) do not sum to 21 kb (Figure 9–1, lane 2). When the DNA is cut with other restriction enzymes, the sizes of the fragments always sum to less than 21 kb; moreover, the fragments in each digest add up to different overall lengths.

If the uncut minichromosome is first denatured and reannealed before it is run on a gel, the 21-kb fragment is replaced by a double-stranded fragment exactly half its length, 10.5 kb (Figure 9–1, lane 3). Similarly, if the BglII-cut minichromosome is denatured and reannealed, the 13.4-kb fragment is replaced by a double-stranded fragment half its length, 6.7 kb (Figure 9–1, lane 4).

Explain why the restriction fragments do not appear to add up to 21 kb, and why the electrophoretic pattern changes when the DNA is denatured and reannealed. What do you think might be the overall organization of sequences in the ribosomal minichromosome?

	1	2	3	4
Bgl II digestion	–	+	–	+
denature and reanneal	–	–	+	+
Bands (kb)	21.0	13.4, 3.8	10.5	6.7, 3.8

Figure 9–1 Restriction analysis of the *Tetrahymena* ribosomal minichromosome (Problem 9–3). Numbers indicate the sizes of the bands in kilobases.

***9–4** You think you may have devised a clever strategy for generating minichromosomes in yeast. You know that the ribosomal genes of *Tetrahymena*, when cut with the restriction enzyme BamHI, yield a 1.5-kb fragment that contains the telomere. You plan to attach these fragments to each end of a linear form of a yeast plasmid; you hope that the plasmid will then persist as a linear molecule–a minichromosome.

As a source of plasmid DNA you use a circular yeast plasmid that contains a yeast origin of replication (ARS1), a selectable marker gene for growth in yeast (*LEU2*), and bacterial plasmid (pBR322) sequences (Figure 9–2). You linearize the 9-kb plasmid with BglII, which cuts the plasmid once. You then incubate the linear plasmid with the 1.5-kb fragments carrying the *Tetrahymena* telomere in the presence of DNA ligase and the two restriction enzymes, BglII and BamHI. When you analyze the ligation products, you find molecules of 10.5-kb and 12-kb in addition to the original components. You purify the 12-kb band, transform it into yeast, and select for yeasts that express the marker gene on the plasmid.

To test whether the plasmid is linear or circular, you prepare total DNA from one transformant, digest samples of it with the restriction enzymes HpaI, PvuII, and PvuI, separate the fragments by gel electrophoresis, and blot hybridize them to radioactively labeled pBR322 DNA. A diagram of the autoradiograph is shown in Figure 9–3.

A. How do the results of the analysis in Figure 9–3 distinguish between a linear and a circular form of the plasmid in the transformed yeast?

*Problems with an asterisk (*) are answered in the Instructor's Manual.

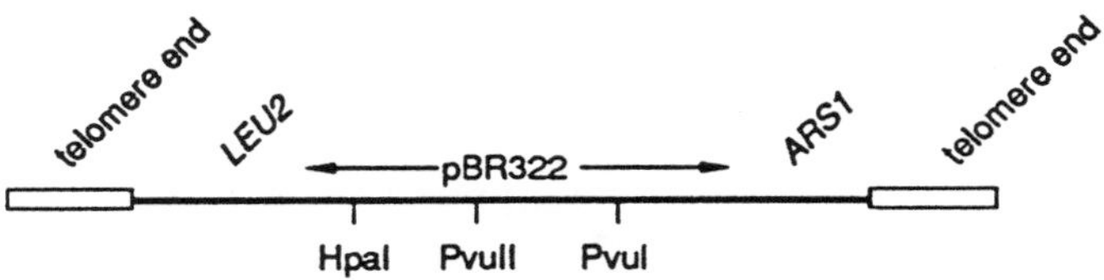

Figure 9–2 Structure of the intended linear chromosome with *Tetrahymena* telomeres flanking yeast and bacterial DNA (Problem 9–4). The sites of unique cutting by three restriction enzymes are indicated.

B. Explain how ligation of the DNA fragments in the presence of the restriction enzymes BamHI and BglII ensures that you get predominantly the construct you want. The recognition site for BglII is —A*GATCT—, where * is the site of cutting, and the recognition site for BamHI is —G*GATCC—.

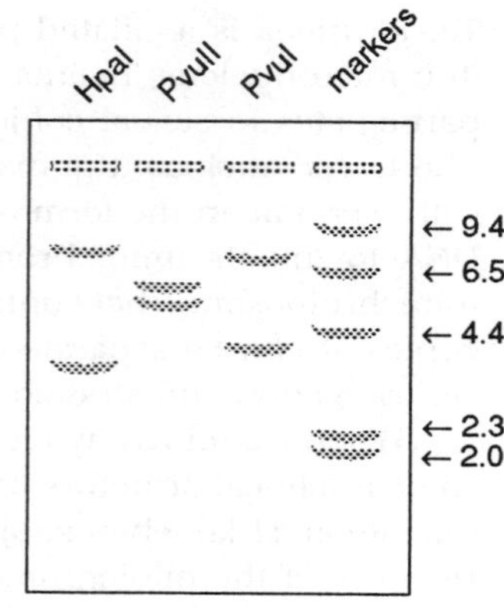

Figure 9–3 Autoradiograph of restriction analysis of plasmid structure (Problem 9–4). Marker DNAs of known fragment sizes (in kb) are shown at the right.

9–5 The precise structure of telomeres is not completely defined for any organism. The telomeres at the ends of the *Tetrahymena* ribosomal minichromosomes have been studied most extensively. The following observations give several important clues to their structure.

1. When ribosomal minichromosomes are incubated with DNA polymerase in the presence of ^{32}P-dCTP and the three other unlabeled dNTPs, the terminal 3.8-kb BamHI restriction fragments are much more extensively labeled than the central 13.4-kb fragment (Figure 9–4, lane 8). Incubations with single dNTPs give significant incorporation only with ^{32}P-dCTP (lane 1 versus lanes 2 to 4). Incorporation of dCTP in the presence of dATP is substantially greater than incorporation of dCTP alone (lane 5 versus lane 1). Incorporation of dCTP in the presence of dGTP or dTTP is no greater than dCTP alone (lanes 6 and 7).
2. Preincubation of the minichromosome with DNA ligase has little effect on incorporation into terminal fragments, but reduces incorporation into the central fragment by ten-fold (Figure 9–4, lane 9).
3. In the presence of the other three unlabeled dNTPs, ^{32}P-dCTP is incorporated into the tandemly repeated sequence 5′-CCCCAA-3′.
4. Minichromosomes labeled with ^{32}P-dCTP alone, when denatured, give rise to single-stranded fragments that are composed of 2, 3, or 4 CCCCAA tandem repeats.
5. If the free 5′ phosphates (free means not in a phosphodiester bond) in minichromosomes are replaced with labeled phosphates and then treated so that all bonds to purine nucleotides are broken, the predominant labeled fragment is CCC.
6. If the minichromosome is cleaved with the restriction enzyme AluI, which cuts very near the ends of the minichromosome, a very broad band containing the terminal fragment is generated. The leading edge of the band

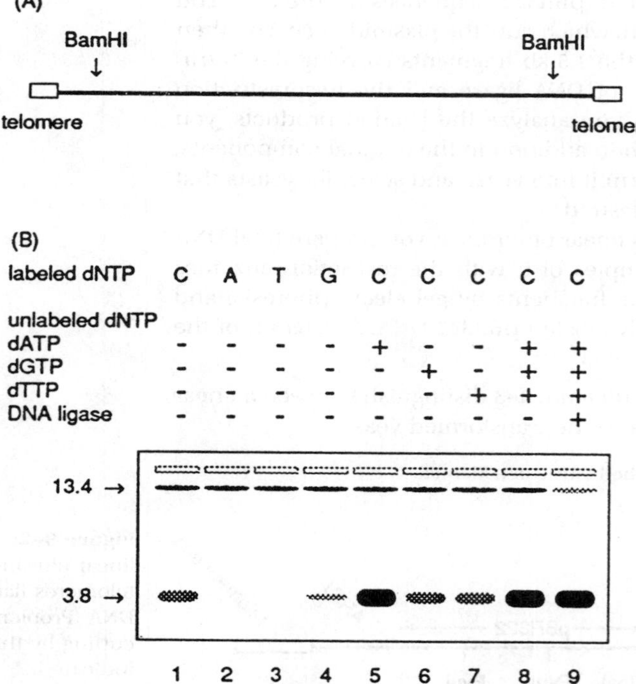

Figure 9–4 Structure of ribosomal minichromosome (A) and incorporation of radioactive nucleotides by DNA polymerase (B) (Problem 9–5). Ribosomal minichromosomes were incubated in the presence of various combinations of nucleotides, as indicated, and then cleaved with BamHI. The resulting fragments were separated by electrophoresis and visualized by autoradiography.

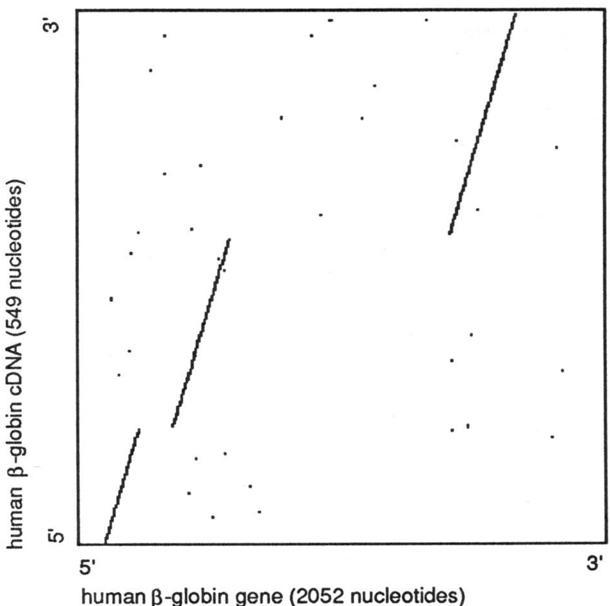

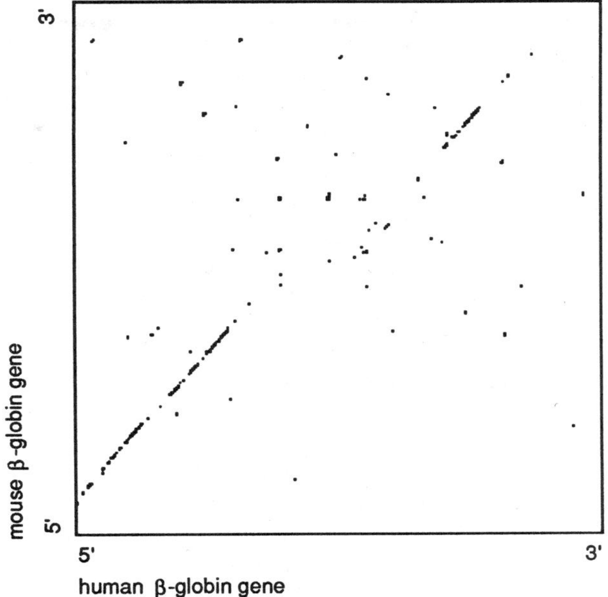

corresponds to about 360 nucleotide pairs and the trailing edge corresponds to about 520 nucleotide pairs.

7. DNA synthesis that begins within the tandem CCCCAA repeats moves progressively toward the center of the minichromosome.

A. Are the numbers of CCCCAA repeats in the telomere defined or variable? Give a minimum and maximum estimate of the number of repeats and explain your reasoning.

B. Are the CCCCAA repeats at the 5′ends of the individual strands of the minichromosome, or are they at the 3′ ends? Explain your reasoning.

C. Incorporation of label by DNA synthesis or by replacement of 5′ phosphates indicates that the nucleotides in the CCCCAA repeats are not all linked together by phosphodiester bonds. What do the various observations tell you about the nature of the single-strand interruptions in the CCCCAA repeats?

D. What is the spacing between the single-strand interruptions in the CCCCAA repeats?

E. Diagram as best you can from these data the structure of the telomeres on the *Tetrahymena* ribosomal minichromosome. (Note that these experiments do not define the structure of the very end of the chromosome, but only the structure of the CCCCAA repeats that make up the telomere.)

Figure 9–5 Diagon plots comparing the human β-globin gene (A) with the human β-globin cDNA and (B) with the mouse β-globin gene (Problem 9–6). The 5′ and 3′ ends of the sequences are indicated. The human gene sequence is identical in the two plots. The human cDNA (A) is shorter than the mouse gene (B), which is why the diagonal lines have different slopes in the two plots.

***9–6** A very useful graphic method for comparing nucleotide sequences is the so-called diagon plot. An example of this method is illustrated in Figure 9–5, where the human β-globin gene is compared to the human cDNA for β-globin (Figure 9–5A) and to the mouse β-globin gene (Figure 9–5B). These plots are generated by comparing blocks of sequence, in this case blocks of 11 nucleotides at a time. If 9 or more of the nucleotides match, a dot is placed on the diagram at the coordinates corresponding to the blocks being compared. A comparison of all possible blocks generates diagrams, such as the ones shown in Figure 9–5, in which sequence homologies show up as diagonal lines.

A. From the comparison of the human β-globin gene with the human β-globin cDNA (Figure 9–5A) deduce the positions of exons and introns in the β-globin gene.

B. Are the entire exons of the human β-globin gene homologous to the mouse β-globin gene (Figure 9–5B)? Identify and explain any discrepancies.
C. Is there any homology between the human and mouse β-globin genes that is outside the exons? If so, identify its location and offer an explanation for its preservation during evolution.
D. Have either of the genes undergone a change of intron length during their evolutionary divergence? How can you tell?

9–7 The binding of a protein to a DNA sequence can cause the DNA to bend in order to make appropriate contacts with chemical groups on the surface of the protein. Such protein-induced DNA bending can be readily detected by the electrophoretic migration of the protein-DNA complexes through polyacrylamide gels. The rate of migration of bent DNA through a gel depends on the average distance between the two ends: the more bent the DNA, the closer together the ends and the more slowly it migrates. If there are two sites of bending in the DNA, the end-to-end distance depends on whether the bends are in the same *(cis)* or opposite *(trans)* direction (Figure 9–6A).

You have demonstrated that the catabolite activator protein (CAP) causes DNA to bend by more than 90° when it binds to its regulatory site. You wish to know the details of the bent structure. Specifically, is the DNA at the center of the CAP-binding site bent so that the minor groove of the DNA helix is on the inside, or is the DNA bent so that the major groove is on the inside? To answer this question, you prepare two kinds of constructs, as illustrated in Figure 9–6B. In one, you place two CAP-binding sequences on either side of a central site into which you insert sequences that vary from 10 to 20 nucleotides in length. In the other, you flank the central insertion site with one CAP-binding sequence and one $(A_5N_5)_4$ sequence, which is known to bend with the major groove on the inside at its center. You now measure the migration of the two kinds of constructs and plot the migration versus the number of nucleotides between the centers of bending (Figure 9–6C and D).

A. Assuming that there are 10.6 nucleotides per turn of the DNA helix, estimate the number of turns that separate the centers of bending of the two CAP-binding sites at the point of minimum relative migration. How many helical turns separate the centers of bending at the point of maximum relative migration?
B. Is the relationship between the relative migration and the separation of the centers of bending of the CAP sites what you would expect if the *cis* configuration migrates slowest and the *trans* configuration migrates fastest? Explain why it is or is not.
C. How many helical turns separate the centers of bending at the point of minimum migration of the construct with one CAP site and one $(A_5N_5)_4$ site?
D. Which groove of the helix faces the inside of the bend at the center of bending of the CAP site?

***9–8** You are studying chromatin structure in rat liver DNA. When you digest rat liver nuclei briefly with micrococcal nuclease, extract the DNA, and run it on an agarose gel, it forms a ladder of broad bands spaced at about 200-nucleotide intervals. If you use the enzyme DNase I instead, there is a much more continuous smear of DNA on the gels with only the haziest suggestion of a 200 nucleotide repeat. If you denature the DNase-I-treated DNA before fractionating it by gel electrophoresis, however, you find a new ladder of bands with a regular spacing of about 10 nucleotides.

You are puzzled by the different results with these two enzymes. When you describe the experiments to the rest of your research group, one colleague suggests that the difference derives from the steric properties of the DNA-binding sites on the two enzymes: micrococcal nuclease can only bind and cleave DNA that is free; DNase I can bind and cut free DNA and DNA that is bound to the surface of a nucleosome. Your colleague predicts that

(A) DNA BENDING BY CAP

(B) TWO BENDY CONSTRUCTS

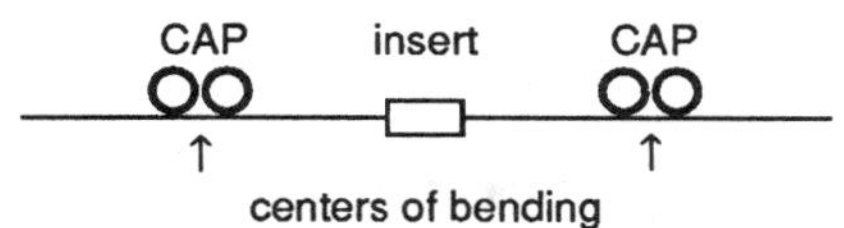

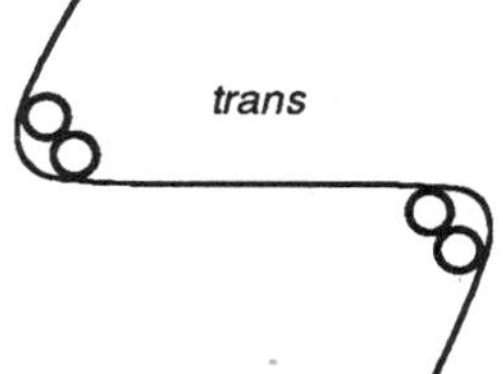

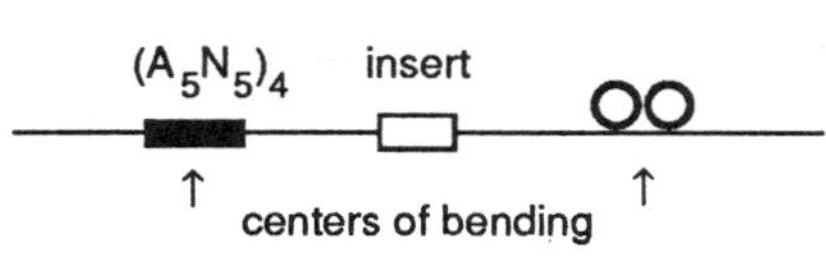

Figure 9–6 Bending of DNA by CAP binding (Problem 9–7). (A) *Cis* and *trans* configurations of a pair of bends. (B) Two constructs used to investigate DNA bending by CAP binding. Relationship between relative migration and number of nucleotides between the centers of bending in the CAP—CAP construct (C) and the $(A_5N_5)_4$—CAP construct (D).

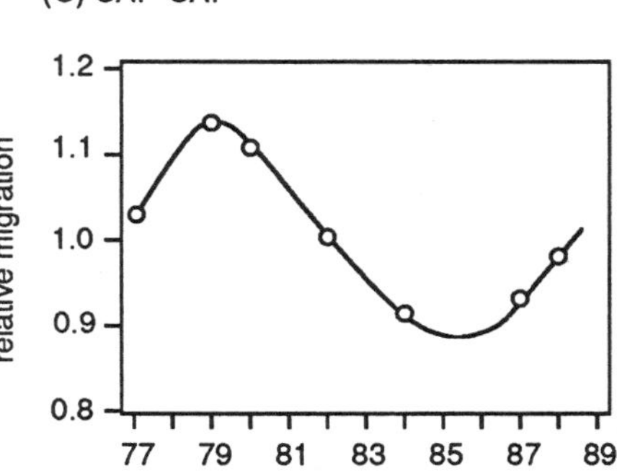

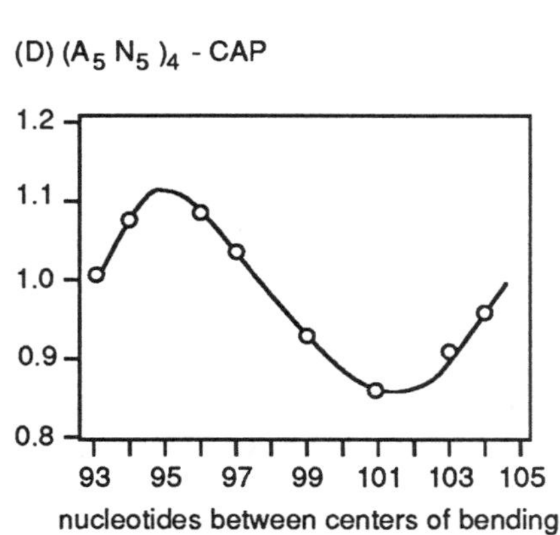

if DNA is bound to any surface and digested with DNase I, it will generate a 10-nucleotide ladder. You test this prediction by binding DNA to poly-lysine-coated plastic dishes and digesting with the two enzymes: micrococcal nuclease causes minimal digestion, but DNase I generates a 10-nucleotide ladder, verifying your friend's prediction.

A. Why does brief digestion of nuclei with micrococcal nuclease yield a ladder of bands spaced at intervals of about 200 nucleotides?

B. If you digested nuclei extensively with micrococcal nuclease, what pattern would you expect to see after fractionation of the DNA by gel electrophoresis?

C. Explain how your colleague's suggestion accounts for the generation of a 10-nucleotide ladder when nuclei are digested with DNase I.

***9–9** You have been sent the first samples of a newly discovered martian microorganism for analysis of its chromatin. The cells resemble earthly eucaryotes and are composed of similar molecules, including DNA, which is located within a nucleuslike structure in the cell. One member of your team has identified two basic histonelike proteins associated with the DNA in roughly an equal mass ratio with the DNA. You isolate nuclei from the cells and treat them with micrococcal nuclease for various times. You then extract the DNA and run it on an agarose gel alongside a similar digest of rat liver nuclei. As shown in Figure 9–7, the digest of rat-liver nuclei gives a standard ladder of nucleosomes, but the martian organism gives a smear of digestion products with a nuclease-resistant limit of about 300 nucleotides. As a control, you isolate the martian DNA free of all protein and digest it with micrococcal nuclease: it is completely susceptible, giving predominantly mono- and dinucleotides as the limit product.

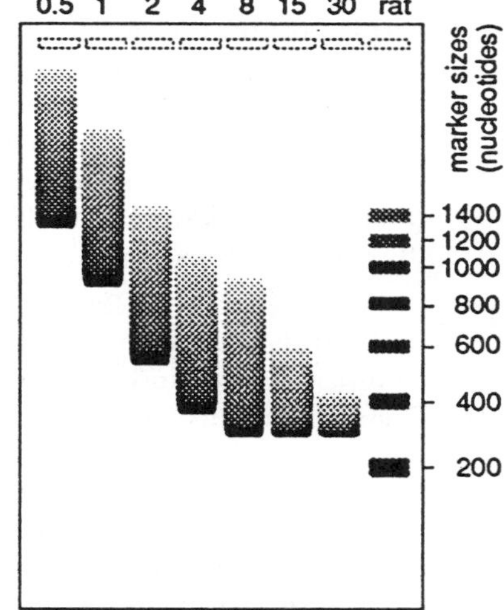

Figure 9–7 Micrococcal digest of chromatin from a martian organism (Problem 9–9). The results of digestion of rat-liver chromatin is shown on the right.

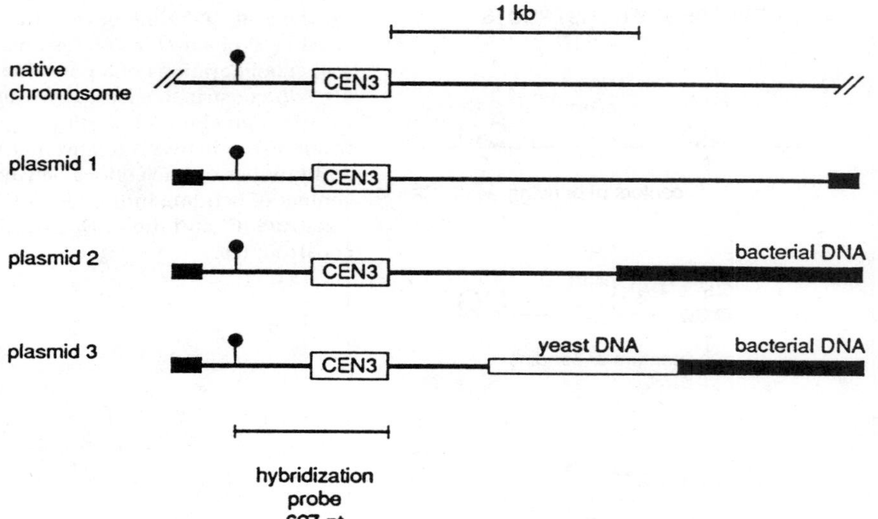

Figure 9–8 Diagram of the native chromosome and three plasmids around CEN3 (Problem 9–10). The native chromosome is linear; its true ends extend well beyond the position marked by the diagonal lines. The plasmids are circles, but they are shown here as linears for ease of comparison. The native yeast sequences around the centromere are shown as thin lines. Bacterial DNA sequences in the plasmids are shown as black rectangles. The yeast DNA in plasmid 3 that is shown as a white rectangle is a segment of yeast chromosomal DNA far removed from the centromere. The BamHI-cleavage site is shown as a closed circle to the left of the centromere. The location of the radioactive probe used in the hybridization is indicated at the bottom.

Do these results suggest that the martian organism has nucleosomelike structures in its chromatin? If so, how are they spaced along the DNA?

9–10 The arrangement of nucleosomes around the centromere is of special interest because the centromere is the chromosome attachment site for microtubules. Thus, the usual arrangement of nucleosomes in chromatin might have to be altered to accommodate microtubule attachment. You are set up to address this question because you have cloned and sequenced about two kilobases of DNA surrounding the centromere (CEN3) of yeast chromosome III. As a result, you can test the arrangement of nucleosomes not only on the native chromosome but also on the plasmids into which you cloned various lengths of the native chromosomal DNA around the centromere (Figure 9–8).

You prepare chromatin from native yeasts and from yeasts that carry individual plasmids. You treat these chromatin samples briefly with micrococcal nuclease and then deproteinize the DNA and digest it to completion with the restriction enzyme BamHI, which cuts the DNA only once in the region of the centromere (Figure 9–8). The digested DNA is fractionated by gel electrophoresis and then analyzed by blot hybridization using a segment of radiolabeled DNA from the centromere as a hybridization probe (Figure 9–8). This procedure (called indirect end labeling) allows you to visualize all DNA fragments that include the DNA immediately to the right of the BamHI-cleavage site. As a control, you deproteinize a sample of chromatin to produce naked DNA, treat it with micrococcal nuclease, and then subject it to the same analysis. An autoradiogram of your results is shown in Figure 9–9.

A. If the digestion with BamHI is omitted, regular though less distinct sets of dark bands are apparent. Why does digestion with BamHI make the pattern so much clearer and easier to interpret?

B. Draw a diagram showing the micrococcal-nuclease-sensitive sites on the chromosomal DNA and the arrangement of nucleosomes along the chromosome. What is special about the centromeric region?

C. What is the purpose of including a naked DNA control in the experiment?

D. The autoradiogram in Figure 9–9 shows that the native chromosomal DNA yields a regularly spaced pattern of bands beyond the centromere; that is, the bands at 600 nucleotides and above are spaced at 160-nucleotide intervals. Does this regularity result from the lining up of nucleosomes at the centromere, like cars at a stop light? Or, is the regularity an intrinsic property of the DNA sequence itself? Explain how your results with plasmids 1, 2, and 3 decide the issue.

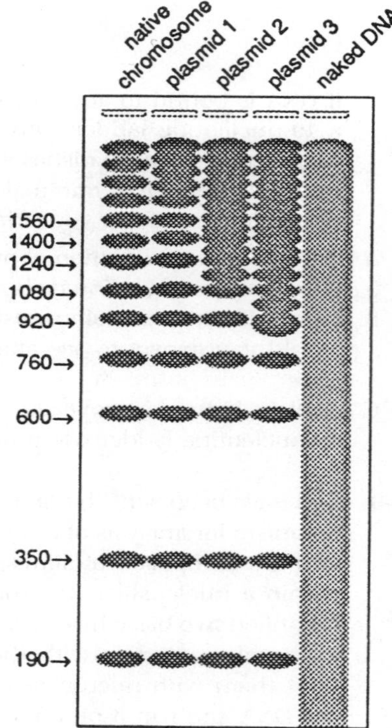

Figure 9–9 Results of micrococcal-nuclease digestion of DNA around CEN3 (Problem 9–10). Approximate lengths of DNA fragments in nucleotide pairs are indicated on the left of the autoradiogram.

The Complex Global Structure of Chromosomes

(MBOC 502–514)

9–11 Fill in the blanks in the following statements.

A. A general feature of chromosome structure seems to be the presence of ____________, which consist of loops of chromatin that extend at an angle from the main chromosome axis.

B. At the metaphase stage of mitosis the two daughter DNA molecules are separately folded to produce two sister ____________, which are held together at their centromeres.

C. The display of the 46 human chromosomes at mitosis is called the human ____________.

D. The meiotically paired chromosomes in growing oocytes are known as ____________ because they form unusually stiff and extended chromatin loops.

E. The precise side-to-side adherence of individual chromatin strands in ____________ greatly elongates the chromosome axis and prevents tangling.

F. The regions on a polytene chromosome that are being actively transcribed are decondensed, forming distinctive ____________.

G. ____________ chromatin is unusually sensitive to digestion with nucleases, and its nucleosomes are thought to be altered in a way that makes their packing less condensed.

H. A small fraction of the DNA from higher eucaryotic cells is in a specially condensed form, known as ____________, which remains unusually compact during interphase and is transcriptionally inactive.

9–12 Indicate whether the following statements are true or false. If a statement is false, explain why.

__ A. Organisms as different as flies and humans seem to have looped domains of similar average size, with a typical loop containing about 20,000 to 100,000 nucleotide pairs.

__ B. The coiling of chromosomes at mitosis, which reduces the length of DNA about 10,000-fold, is accompanied by the extensive phosphorylation of histone H1.

__ C. The staining of mitotic chromosomes with fluorescent dyes appears to distinguish mainly DNA rich in A-T nucleotide pairs (G bands) from DNA rich in G-C nucleotide pairs (R bands).

__ D. In lampbrush chromosomes most of the chromatin is in the loops, which are actively transcribed, but some of the chromatin remains highly condensed in the chromomeres, which are transcriptionally inactive.

__ E. In several types of secretory cells of fly larvae, all the homologous chromosome copies remain side by side through several rounds of replication, thereby generating a single, giant polyploid chromosome.

__ F. Studies of chromosome puffs suggest that a looped domain, which is thought to be folded to form a chromosome band, can decondense as a unit during transcription.

__ G. Classical genetic studies coupled with more recent molecular studies indicate that each band in a polytene chromosome probably corresponds to a single gene.

__ H. Treatment of the nuclei from different cells with an appropriate concentration of DNase I preferentially degrades DNA sequences that are actively transcribed in the particular cell type tested.

__ I. Nucleosomes in active chromatin selectively bind two closely related small chromosomal proteins, HMG 14 and HMG 17.

__ J. Transcriptionally inactive regions of chromosomes are condensed into a relatively nuclease-resistant form known as heterochromatin.

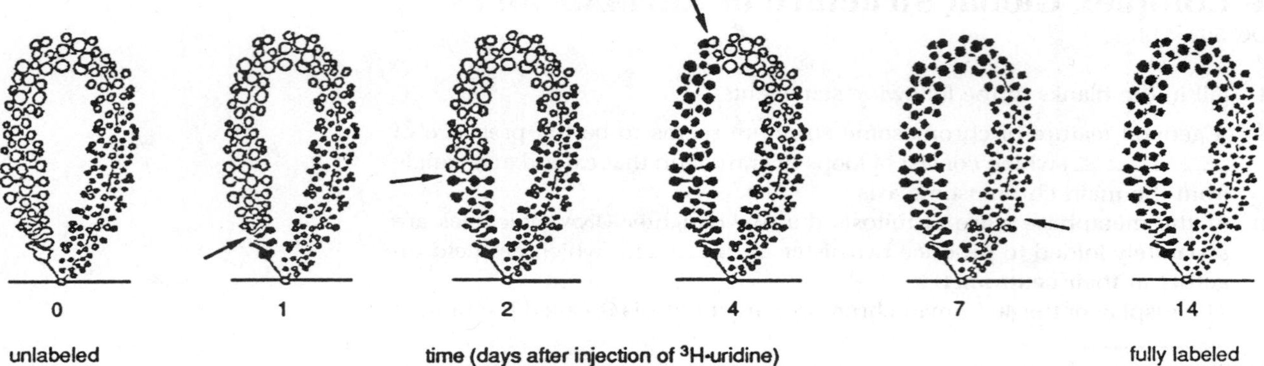

Figure 9–10 Autoradiography of a giant chromatin loop from a lampbrush chromosome of the newt (Problem 9–13). Arrows show forward progress of labeled regions around the loop at various times after injection of labeled uridine into the oocytes.

9–13 You are studying transcription in the lampbrush chromosomes of the newt *Triturus* by injecting ^{3}H-uridine into the oocytes, waiting for various times, and detecting the radioactive RNA by autoradiography. Initially, you focus on the largest loops; they incorporate label progressively around the loop as shown in Figure 9–10. It takes about 14 days before the entire loop becomes labeled. When you compare this labeling pattern with that of the smaller loops, which are much more common in lampbrush chromosomes, you are surprised: the smaller loops show uniform labeling even at the shortest times of sampling. With increasing time after injection of radioactive uridine, this uniform labeling intensifies all around each loop.

Many loops in lampbrush chromosomes represent single transcription units, in which RNA polymerase initiates and terminates synthesis at the base of the loop as shown in Figure 9–11. Assuming that the loops you have examined are single transcription units, which pattern of loop labeling would you expect: progressive, as in the large loops (Figure 9–10), or uniform, as in the smaller loops?

***9–14** The giant polytene chromosomes of *Drosophila melanogaster* have long been of interest to geneticists because their characteristic banding patterns provide a visible map of the genome. Bands apparently contain more DNA than interbands. Does this difference arise because DNA in bands is replicated more extensively than DNA in interbands? Or is all the DNA replicated to the same extent but folded in such a way that bands contain more DNA than interbands?

You are in a position to resolve this controversy because you have isolated a contiguous set of clones that span 315 kb of *Drosophila* DNA, including about 12 bands and interbands. You can use radiolabeled segments of these clones as hybridization probes to estimate the amount of corresponding DNA present in diploid tissues and polytene chromosomes. You isolate DNA from diploid tissues and polytene chromosomes, digest equal amounts of the DNA with combinations of restriction enzymes, separate the fragments by gel electrophoresis, and transfer them to nitrocellulose filters for hybridization analysis. In every case the restriction pattern is the same for the DNA from diploid tissues and polytene chromosomes, as illustrated for two examples in Figure 9–12. You measure the intensities of many specific restriction fragments and express the results as the ratio of the intensity of the fragment from polytene chromosomes to the intensity of the corresponding fragment from diploid tissues (Figure 9–13).

Do your results support differential replication or differential chromosome folding as the basis for the difference between bands and interbands?

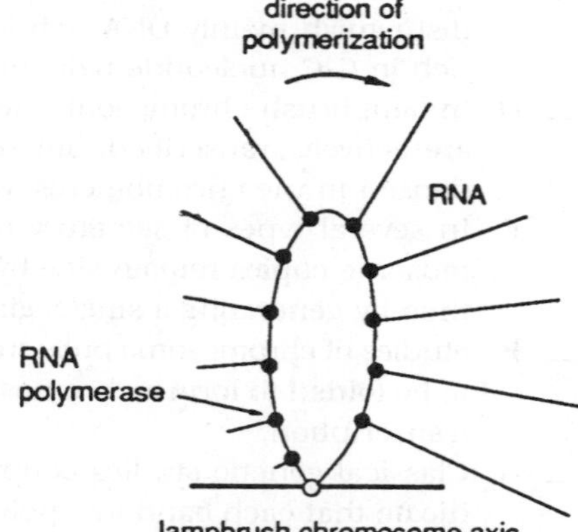

Figure 9–11 Diagramatic representation of a chromatin loop that is a single transcription unit (Problem 9–13). The progress of RNA polymerase molecules around the loop is illustrated along with the attendant growth of the nascent RNA chain associated with each polymerase.

9–15 To understand the relationship between chromatin structure and gene expression, you are studying two types of chicken cells. Chicken red blood cells express large amounts of globin mRNAs, but chicken fibroblasts do not express globin at all. You want to know whether the globin DNA sequences exist in the same or a different chromatin structure in these two cell types. As probes of chromatin structure you use two nucleases: micrococcal nuclease and pancreatic deoxyribonuclease I (DNase I).

You prepare a ^{3}H-thymidine-labeled complementary DNA (cDNA) copy of the globin mRNAs from red blood cells. This globin cDNA is completely digested by a single-strand specific nuclease (S1 nuclease). However, if the cDNA is first annealed with a vast excess of chicken DNA, more than 90% of it is protected from subsequent digestion with S1 nuclease.

You assay the effects of micrococcal nuclease and DNase I on the capacity of DNA from red cells and fibroblasts to protect the cDNA. To preserve the natural organization of the chromatin, you treat isolated nuclei with the nucleases before extracting the DNA and assaying it. Digestion of red cell nuclei or fibroblast nuclei with micrococcal nuclease (so that about 50% of the DNA is degraded) yields DNA samples that still protect greater than 90% of the cDNA from subsequent digestion with S1 nuclease. Similarly, digestion of fibroblast nuclei with DNase I (so that less than 20% is degraded) yields DNA that protects greater than 90% of the cDNA. An identical digestion of red cell nuclei with DNase I, however, yields DNA that protects only about 25% of the cDNA. These results are summarized in Table 9–1.

You repeat some of these measurements using ^{3}H-thymidine labeled total DNA from red blood cells in place of the globin cDNA. Annealing with total DNA or micrococcal-nuclease-digested DNA protects greater than 90% of the ^{3}H-labeled DNA, but annealing with DNase-I-digested DNA protects only 78% of the ^{3}H-labeled DNA (Table 9–1).

In a final set of experiments you first generate nucleosome monomers by digestion with micrococcal nuclease. DNA from the monomers protects more than 90% of globin cDNA. Treatment of the monomers with DNase I yields DNA that protects only 25% of globin cDNA. You then treat the monomers briefly with trypsin to remove 20 to 30 amino acids from the N-terminus of each histone molecule, redigest the modified nucleosomes with *micrococcal nuclease*, and isolate the DNA. This DNA protects 83% of total red cell DNA but only 25% of globin cDNA (Table 9–1).

A. Which nuclease—micrococcal nuclease or DNase I—digests chromatin that is being expressed (active chromatin)? How can you tell?
B. What fraction of red cell DNA is in active chromatin?
C. Does trypsin treatment of nucleosome monomers render a random population or a specific population of nucleosomes sensitive to micrococcal nuclease? How can you tell?
D. Is the alteration that distinguishes active chromatin from bulk chromatin a property of individual nucleosomes, or is it related to the way nucleosome monomers are packaged into higher order structures within the cell nucleus?

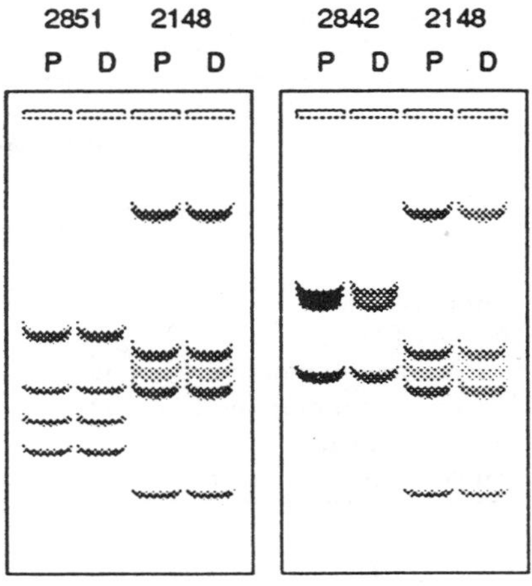

Figure 9–12 Autoradiographs of blot-hybridization analysis of polytene and diploid DNA (Problem 9–14). P and D refer to polytene and diploid, respectively. Numbers at the top refer to cloned DNA segments used as probes: 2851 and 2842 are from the 315-kb region under analysis (see Figure 9–13); 2148 is from elsewhere in the genome and was used in all hybridizations to calibrate the amount of DNA added to the gels.

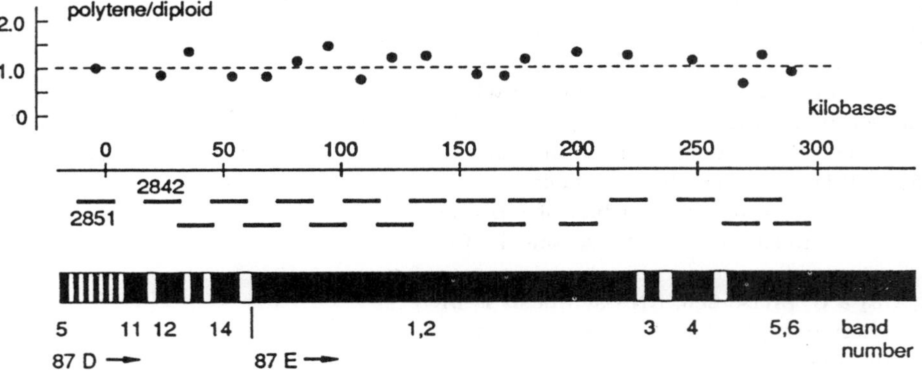

Figure 9–13 Relative amounts of DNA in diploid tissues and polytene chromosomes at different positions along the chromosome (Problem 9–14). The chromosomal segment covered by the cloned restriction fragments is shown at the bottom along with the cytological designations for the chromosome regions and bands. The cloned fragments are shown above the chromosomes, and the positions of 2851 and 2842 are indicated. The ratio of hybridization of each restriction fragment to DNA from polytene chromosomes and diploid tissues is given above each fragment.

Table 9–1 Protection of Globin cDNA and Total Red Cell DNA by Untreated and Nuclease-treated Chromatin Samples (Problem 9–15)

Excess DNA	Nuclease Treatment	Protected Globin cDNA	Protected Red Cell DNA
Total DNA	none	93%	95%
Red cell DNA	micrococcal nuclease	92%	94%
Red cell DNA	DNase I	25%	78%
Fibroblast DNA	micrococcal nuclease	91%	
Fibroblast DNA	DNase I	91%	
Nucleosome monomers	none	91%	94%
Nucleosome monomers	DNase I	25%	80%
Trypsin-treated nucleosome monomers	micrococcal nuclease	25%	83%

Chromosome Replication (MBOC 514–523)

9–16 Fill in the blanks in the following statements.

A. The DNA synthesis phase of the cell cycle is called the ____________.

B. DNA ____________ are initiated at special DNA sequences called ____________.

C. Replication origins tend to be activated in clusters of perhaps 20 to 80 origins, which are called ____________.

D. Multiple copies of SV40 ____________ bind specifically to the SV40 origin of replication and act both as an initiator protein and a DNA helicase to open the DNA helix at that site.

E. Since the whole genome must be replicated once and no more, eucaryotic cells must inactivate origins as they are used; this DNA ____________ is removed at or near the time of mitosis.

9–17 Indicate whether the following statements are true or false. If a statement is false, explain why.

__ A. Replication forks in bacteria and eucaryotic cells travel at the same rate, indicating that the packaging of DNA into chromatin does not hinder the replication process.

__ B. ARS elements in yeast appear to contain multiple copies of an A-T rich consensus sequence clustered within a region of about 100 nucleotides.

__ C. Two distinct types of DNA polymerase are needed in eucaryotes: DNA polymerase alpha on the lagging strand and DNA polymerase delta on the leading strand.

__ D. Like most proteins, histones are synthesized continuously throughout interphase, but they are deposited on DNA to make new chromatin only during S phase.

__ E. The G-rich strand of the telomere, which always forms the 3′ end of the DNA molecule, can fold back on itself making a special structure, involving G-G base pairing, that protects the chromosome end.

__ F. Chromosomal regions are replicated in large units, and different regions of each chromosome are replicated in a reproducible order.

__ G. The two X chromosomes in a female mammalian cell, only one of which is active, are replicated at the same time during the S phase.

__ H. Genes that are active in only a few cell types generally replicate early in the cells in which they are active and later in other types of cells.

__ I. Most G-C-rich bands (R bands) replicate during the first half of S phase, while most A-T-rich bands (G bands) replicate during the second half of S phase.

__ J. When an S-phase cell is fused with a G_2-phase cell, DNA synthesis is induced in the G_2-phase nucleus; when an S-phase cell is fused with a G_1-phase cell, however, the G_1 nucleus is not stimulated to synthesize DNA.

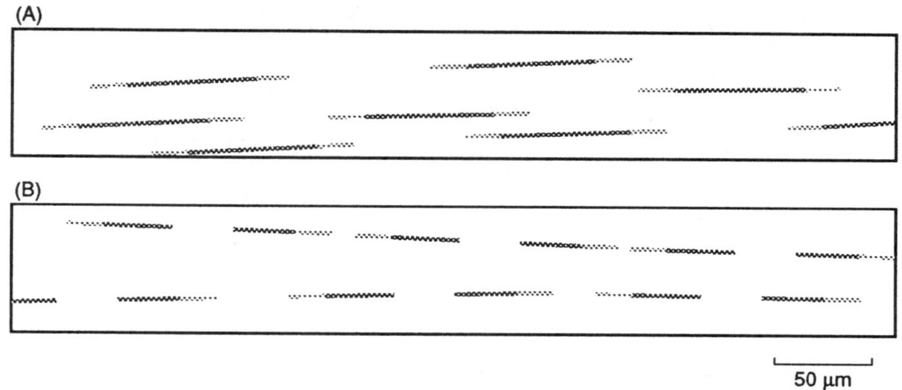

Figure 9–14 Autoradiographic results of experiments to investigate DNA replication in cultured cells (Problem 9–18). In (A) cells were labeled immediately after release from the synchronizing block. In (B) cells were labeled 30 minutes after release from the synchronizing block.

***9–18** You are investigating DNA synthesis in a line of tissue culture cells using a classic protocol. In this procedure ^{3}H-thymidine is added to the cells, which incorporate it at replication forks. Then the cells are gently lysed in a dialysis bag to release the DNA. When the bag is punctured and the solution slowly drained, some of the DNA strands adhere to the walls and are stretched in the general direction of drainage. This method allows very long DNA strands to be isolated intact and examined; however, the stretching collapses replication bubbles so that daughter duplexes lie side by side. The support with its adhered DNA is fixed to a glass slide, overlaid with a photographic emulsion, and exposed for 3 to 6 months. The labeled DNA shows up as tracks of silver grains.

You pretreat the cells to synchronize them at the beginning of S phase. In one experiment you release the synchronizing block and add ^{3}H-labeled thymidine immediately. After 30 minutes you wash the cells and change the medium so that the label is present at a third of its initial concentration. After an additional 15 minutes you prepare DNA for autoradiography. The results of this experiment are shown in Figure 9–14A. In the second experiment you release the synchronizing block and then wait 30 minutes before adding ^{3}H-thymidine. After 30 minutes in the presence of ^{3}H-thymidine, you once again change the medium to reduce the concentration of labeled thymidine and incubate the cells for an additional 15 minutes. The results of the second experiment are shown in Figure 9–14B.

A. Explain why in both experiments some regions of the tracks are dense with silver grains (dark), whereas others are less dense (light).
B. In the first experiment each track has a central dark section with light sections at each end. In the second experiment the dark section of each track has a light section at only one end. Explain the reason for the difference between the results in the two experiments.
C. Estimate the rate of fork movement (μm/min) in these experiments. Do the estimates from the two experiments agree? Can you use this information to estimate how long it would take to replicate the entire genome?

9–19 Autonomous replication sequences (ARS), which confer stability on plasmids in yeast, are thought to be origins of replication. Proving that an ARS is an origin of replication, however, is difficult, mainly because it is very hard to obtain enough well-defined replicating DNA molecules to analyze. This problem can be addressed using a two-dimensional gel-electrophoretic analysis that separates DNA molecules by mass in the first dimension and by shape in the second dimension. Because they have branches, replicating molecules migrate more slowly in the second dimension than linear molecules of equal mass. By cutting replicating molecules with restriction enzymes, it is possible to generate a continuum of different branched forms that together give characteristic patterns on two-dimensional gels (Figure 9–15).

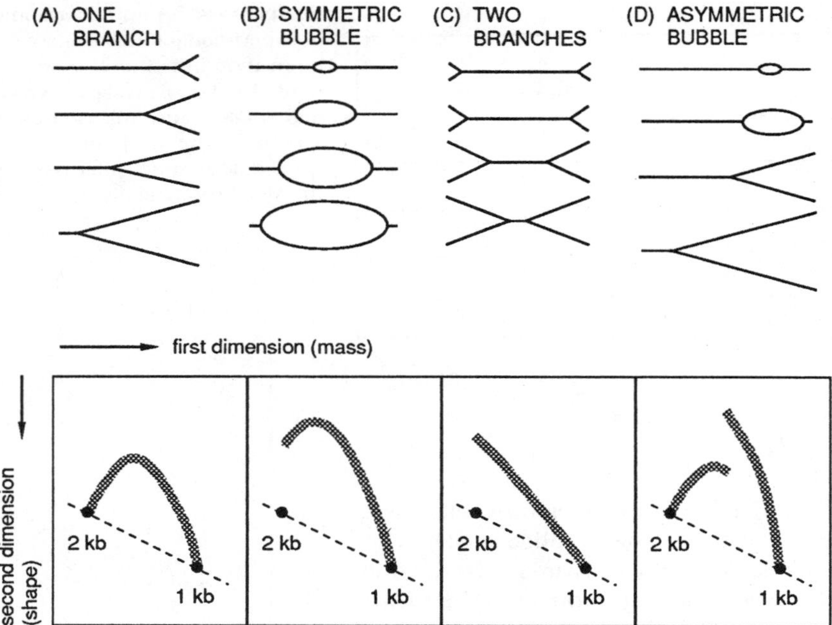

Figure 9–15 Two-dimensional gel patterns for molecules with (A) a single branch, (B) a symmetrically located replication bubble, (C) two branches, and (D) an asymmetrically located replication bubble (Problem 9–19). Intermediates in the replication of a hypothetical 1-kb fragment are shown at progressive states of replication at the top of the figure. The gel patterns that result from the continuum of such replication intermediates is shown below.

You apply this technique to the replication of a plasmid that contains ARS1. To maximize the fraction of plasmid molecules that are replicating, you synchronize a yeast culture and isolate DNA from cells in S phase. You then digest the DNA with BglII or PvuI, which cut the plasmid as indicated in Figure 9–16A. You separate the DNA fragments by two-dimensional electrophoresis and visualize the plasmid sequences by autoradiography after blot hybridization to radioactive plasmid DNA (Figure 9–16B).

A. What is the source of the intense spot of hybridization at the 4.5 kb position in both gels in Figure 9–16B?
B. Do the results of this experiment indicate that ARS1 is an origin of replication? Explain your answer.
C. There is a gap in the arc of hybridization in the PvuI gel pattern in Figure 9–16B. What is the basis for this discontinuity?

9–20 One important rule for eucaryotic DNA replication is that no chromosome or part of a chromosome should be replicated more than once per cell cycle. Eucaryotic viruses must evade or break this rule if they are to produce multiple copies of themselves during a single cell cycle. The animal virus SV40, for example, generates 100,000 copies of its genome during a single cycle of infection. In order to accomplish this feat, it synthesizes a special protein, termed T-antigen (because it was first detected immunologically). T-antigen binds to the SV40 origin of replication and in some way triggers initiation of DNA replication.

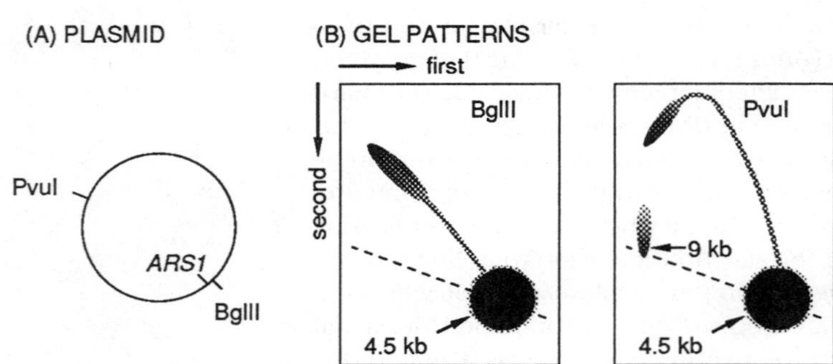

Figure 9–16 Structure of the ARS1 plasmid (A) and the two-dimensional gel patterns (B) resulting from cleavage with BglII and PvuI (Problem 9–19).

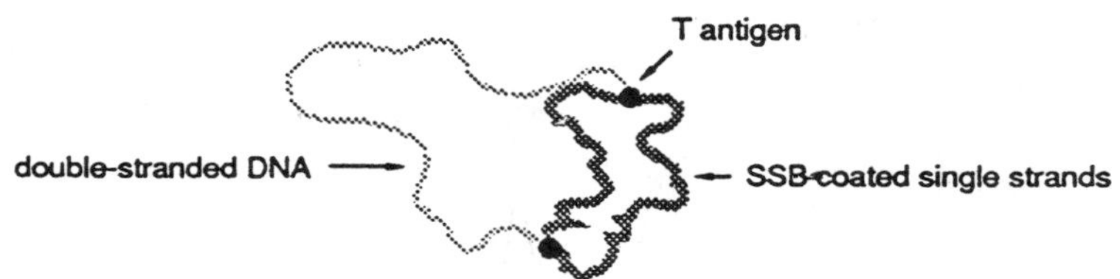

Figure 9–17 A typical example of a plasmid molecule carrying an SV40 origin of replication after incubation with T-antigen, single-strand binding (SSB) protein, and ATP (Problem 9–20).

The mechanism by which T-antigen initiates replication has been investigated *in vitro*. When purified T-antigen, ATP, and a single-strand binding (SSB) protein were incubated with a circular plasmid DNA carrying the SV40 origin of replication, partially unwound structures, such as the one shown in Figure 9–17, were observed in the electron microscope. In the absence of any one of these components, no unwound structures were seen. Furthermore, no unwinding occurred in an otherwise identical plasmid that carried a 6-nucleotide deletion at the origin of replication. If care was taken in the isolation of the plasmid so that it contained no nicks (that is, a covalently closed circular DNA), no unwound structures were observed unless topoisomerase I was also present in the mixture.

A. What activity in addition to site-specific DNA binding must T-antigen possess? How might this activity lead to initiation of DNA synthesis?
B. These experiments suggest that the structures observed in the electron microscope are unwound at the SV40 origin of replication. The location of the origin on the SV40 genome is precisely known. How might you use restriction enzymes to prove this point and to determine whether unwinding occurs in one or both directions away from the origin?
C. Why is there a requirement for topoisomerase I when the plasmid DNA is a covalently closed circle? (Topoisomerase I introduces single-strand breaks into duplex DNA and then rapidly recloses them, so that the breaks have only a transient existence.)
D. Draw an example of the kind of structure that would result if T-antigen repeatedly initiated replication at an SV40 origin that was integrated into a chromosome.

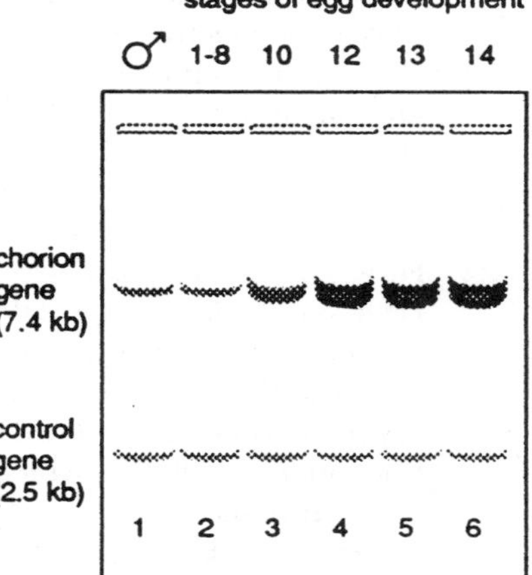

Figure 9–18 Blot hybridization of a chorion gene and a control gene at various stages of egg development (Problem 9–21).

***9–21** The shell of a *Drosophila's* egg is made from more than 15 different chorion proteins, which are synthesized at a late stage in egg development by follicle cells surrounding the egg. The chorion genes are grouped in two clusters, one on chromosome 3 and the other on the X chromosome. In each cluster the genes are closely spaced with only a few hundred nucleotides separating adjacent genes. During egg development the number of copies of the chorion genes increases by overreplication of a segment of the surrounding chromosome. This amplification can be detected by preparing DNA from eggs at different stages of development, digesting the DNA samples with a restriction enzyme, and analyzing them by blot hybridization using a chorion cDNA as a probe. As shown in Figure 9–18, the number of chorion genes increases substantially between stages 8 and 12, whereas the copy number of a control gene that is far removed from the chorion gene clusters stays constant. The level of amplification around a chorion gene cluster can be determined using cloned probes covering the entire region. Measurements of the relative intensities of bands on autoradiographs such as the one in Figure 9–18 show that amplification of the chorion cluster on chromosome 3 is maximal in the region of the chorion genes but extends for nearly 50-kb on either side (Figure 9–19).

The DNA sequence responsible for amplification of the chorion cluster on chromosome 3 has been narrowed to a 510-nucleotide segment immediately upstream of one of the chorion genes. When this segment is moved to different places in the genome (using transposons to carry the DNA segment), those new sites are also amplified in follicle cells. No RNA or protein product seems to be synthesized from this amplification-control element.

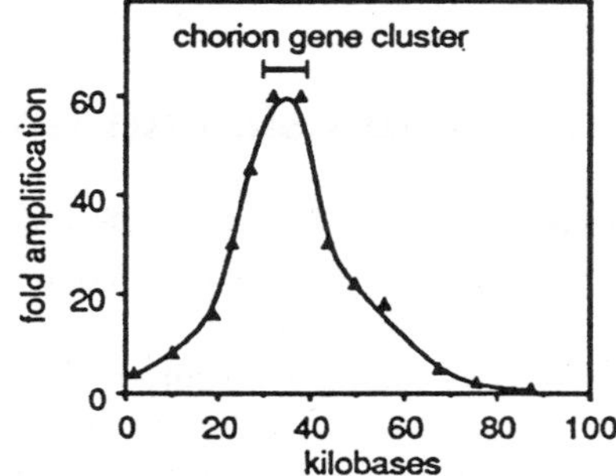

Figure 9–19 Levels of amplification in the region of the chromosome surrounding the chorion gene cluster (Problem 9–21).

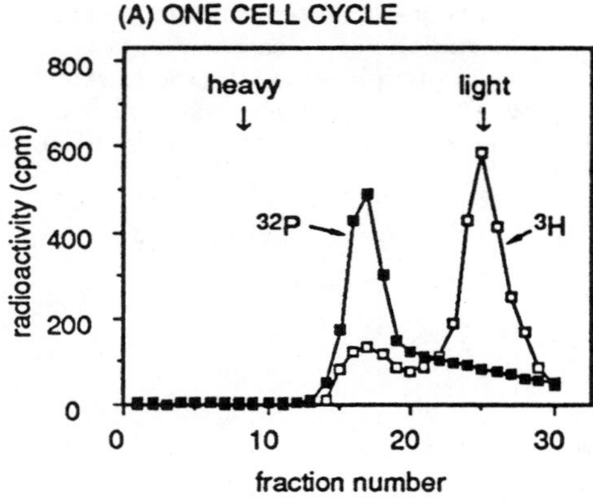

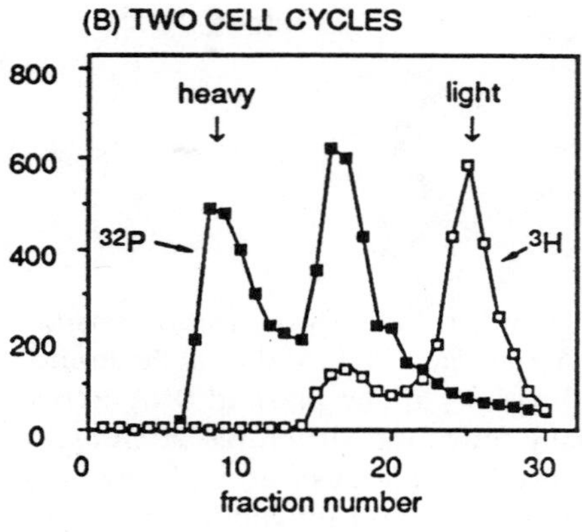

Figure 9–20 Density distribution of viral DNA after injection in fertilized frog eggs (Problem 9–22). (A) Results after one cell cycle. (B) Results after two cell cycles. The more dense end of the gradient is shown to the left *(marked heavy)*, and the less dense end of the gradient is shown to the right *(marked light)*. The ability to look specifically at the viral DNA depends on a technical trick: the eggs were heavily irradiated with UV light before the injection to block chromosomal replication.

A. Sketch what you think the DNA from an amplified cluster would look like under the electron microscope.
B. How many rounds of replication would be required to achieve a sixty-fold amplification?
C. How do you think the 510-nucleotide amplification-control element promotes the overreplication of a chorion gene cluster?

9–22 Fertilized frog eggs are very useful for studying the cell-cycle regulation of DNA synthesis. Foreign DNA can be injected into the eggs and followed independently of chromosomal DNA replication. For example, in one study ^{3}H-labeled viral DNA was injected. The eggs were then incubated in a medium supplemented with ^{32}P-dCTP and nonradioactive bromodeoxyuridine triphosphate (BrdUTP), which is a thymidine analogue that increases the buoyant density of DNA into which it is incorporated. Incubation was continued for long enough to allow one or two cell cycles to occur; then the viral DNA was extracted from the eggs and analyzed on CsCl density gradients, which separate DNA with 0, 1, or 2 BrdU-containing strands. Figure 9–20A and B show the density distribution of viral DNA after incubation for one and two cell cycles, respectively. If the eggs are bathed in cycloheximide (an inhibitor of protein synthesis) during the incubation, the results after incubation for one cycle or incubation for two cycles are both like those in Figure 9–20A.

A. Explain how the three density peaks in Figure 9–20 are related to replication of the injected DNA. Why is no ^{32}P radioactivity associated with the light peak, and why is no ^{3}H radioactivity associated with the heavy peak?
B. Does the injected DNA mimic the behavior that you would expect for the chromosomal DNA?
C. Why do you think that cycloheximide prevents the appearance of the most dense peak of DNA?

RNA Synthesis and RNA Processing (MBOC 523–546)

9–23 Fill in the blanks in the following statements.

A. Transcription begins when an ____________ molecule binds to a promoter DNA sequence.
B. The sigma subunit of the *E. coli* polymerase has a specific role as an ____________ for transcription: it enables the enzyme to find the *E. coli* consensus promoter sequence.
C. After about eight nucleotides of an RNA molecule have been synthesized, the sigma subunit dissociates and a number of ____________ become associated with the enzyme instead.
D. ____________ transcribes the genes whose RNAs will be translated into

proteins, __________ makes the large ribosomal RNAs, and __________ makes a variety of very small, stable RNAs.

E. One or more sequence-specific DNA-binding proteins, called __________, must be bound to the DNA to form a functional promoter.

F. TFIID, which is essential for many polymerase II promoters, is a large protein complex that is more commonly called the __________ because it can bind to a conserved A-T-rich sequence called the __________.

G. Eucaryotic RNA polymerase molecules begin and end transcription at specific chromosomal sites; the region between these sites is called a __________.

H. RNA polymerase II transcripts in the nucleus are known as __________ molecules because one of the first characteristics used to distinguish them from other RNAs in the nucleus was the heterogeneity of their sizes.

I. RNA polymerase II transcripts leave the nucleus as __________ molecules.

J. The addition of a methylated G nucleotide to the 5′ end of the initial transcript forms the __________, which seems to protect the growing RNA from degradation and plays an important part in the initiation of protein synthesis.

K. The 3′ end of most polymerase II transcripts is defined by a modification, in which the growing transcript is cleaved at a specific site and a __________ is added by a separate polymerase to the cut 3′ end.

L. Modifications at the 5′ and 3′ ends of an RNA chain complete the formation of the __________.

M. After the intron sequence has been cut out, the coding RNA sequences on either side of the intron are joined to each other in a reaction known as __________.

N. Newly made RNA in eucaryotes appears to become immediately condensed into a series of closely spaced protein-containing particles, called __________ particles.

O. The small U RNAs in the cell nucleus are complexed with proteins to form __________.

P. The conserved sequences at the boundaries of an intron are called the __________ (donor site) and the __________ (acceptor site).

Q. The large multicomponent ribonucleoprotein complex that carries out the splicing of the primary transcript is known as the __________.

R. Patients with __________ have an abnormally low level of hemoglobin—the oxygen-carrying protein in red blood cells.

S. The packaging of rRNAs with ribosomal proteins takes place in the nucleus in a large, distinct structure called the __________.

T. Each cluster of rRNA genes is known as a __________ region.

9–24 Indicate whether the following statements are true or false. If a statement is false, explain why.

__ A. In the RNA polymerase from *E. coli*, the initiation and elongation factors are permanent subunits of the enzyme, which allow it to recognize consensus promoter sequences and extend the RNA chain.

__ B. RNA polymerases I, II, and III are each composed of multiple subunits, but none of the subunits are shared by all three polymerases.

__ C. Whereas bacterial RNA polymerases can bind directly to the promoter, eucaryotic RNA polymerases can bind to their promoters only in the presence of additional protein factors already on the DNA.

__ D. Different RNA polymerase II start sites function with very different efficiencies, so that some genes are transcribed at much higher rates than others.

__ E. The 3′ end of most RNA polymerase II transcripts is defined by the termination of transcription, which releases a free 3′ end to which a poly-A tail is quickly added.

__ F. Only about 5% of the RNA synthesized by RNA polymerase II ever reaches the cytoplasm: the rest is degraded in the nucleus.

__ G. RNA splicing occurs in the cell nucleus, out of reach of the ribosomes, and RNA is exported to the cytoplasm only when processing is complete.

__ H. HnRNP particles and snRNPs resemble ribosomes in that each contains multiple polypeptide chains complexed to a stable RNA molecule.

__ I. Since introns are largely genetic "junk," they do not have to be removed precisely from the primary transcript during RNA splicing.

__ J. RNA splicing makes it possible to generate several different mRNAs, and thereby several different proteins, from the same primary RNA transcript.

__ K. The major difference between group I and group II self-splicing introns is that the attacking nucleotide is free in group I introns but a part of the intron sequence in group II introns.

__ L. In most vertebrate cells, the clusters of genes encoding 28S rRNA are transcribed independently of the clusters of genes that encode 18S rRNA and 5.8S rRNA.

__ M. Ribosomal RNAs are produced in the nucleolus, a specialized region of the nucleus, and are then transported into the cytoplasm, where they are packaged with ribosomal proteins to form ribosomes.

__ N. Unlike cytoplasmic organelles, the nucleolus is not bounded by a membrane.

__ O. There is no nucleolus in a metaphase cell.

__ P. The extended chromosomes in interphase cells are thought to be extensively intertwined.

9–25 The purification of specific transcription factors has caused you no end of trouble because the assays are slow and the factors tend to be unstable. By the time you identify the right fraction, the factor is often inactive. One day you have a brilliant idea for speeding up the assay. You realize that you can make a DNA sequence that contains no C nucleotides. If this sequence is placed next to a promoter and incubated in the appropriate reaction mix, the promoter should direct the synthesis of a transcript that contains no G nucleotides. Moreover, if GTP is omitted from the reaction mix, the only long RNA transcript should be made from the DNA sequence you synthesized. If you can show that your sequence encodes the only long transcript in the absence of G nucleotides, then you can rapidly assay specific transcription simply by measuring incorporation of a radioactive nucleotide!

To test your idea, you construct two plasmids carrying the test sequence: one with a promoter from adenovirus (pML1), the other without (pC1). You mix each of these two plasmids with pure RNA polymerase II, your best preparations of transcription factors, and ^{32}P-CTP. In addition, you add various combinations of GTP, RNase T1 (which cleaves RNA adjacent to each G nucleotide), and 3′O-methyl GTP (which terminates transcription whenever it is incorporated into a growing chain). You measure the products by gel electrophoresis with the results shown in Figure 9–21.

A. Why is the 400-nucleotide transcript absent in lane 4 but present in lanes 2, 6, and 8?

B. Can you guess the source of the synthesis in lane 3 when the promoterless plasmid is used?

C. Why is a 400-nucleotide transcript present in lane 5 but not in lane 7?

D. Your goal in developing this ingenious assay was to aid the purification of transcription factors. One of your colleagues points out that purification will begin with crude cell extracts, which will contain GTP. Can you assay specific transcription in crude extracts? How?

***9–26** Using your rapid assay for specific transcription (see Problem 9–25), you establish that transcripts accumulate linearly for about an hour and then reach a plateau. Your assay conditions use a 25 μl reaction volume containing 16 μg/ml of DNA template (the pML1 plasmid, which is 3.5 kb in length) with all other components in excess. From the specific activity of

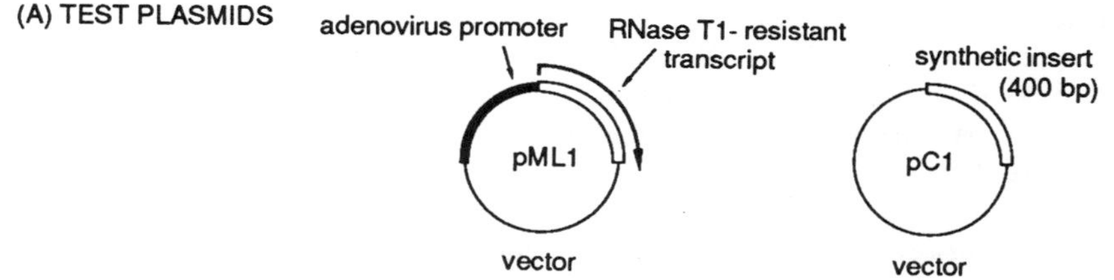

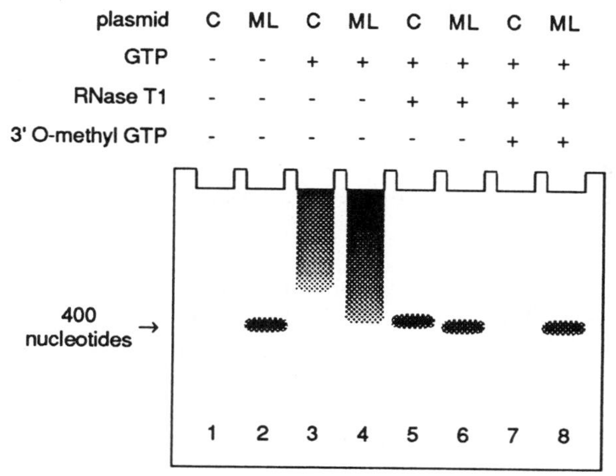

Figure 9–21 Structure of test plasmids (A) and results of transcription assays (B) under various conditions (Problem 9–25). All reactions contain RNA polymerase II, transcription factors, and ^{32}P-CTP. Other components are listed above each lane: (+) means the component is present in the reaction mixture; (−) means the component is absent.

the ^{32}P-CTP and the total radioactivity in transcripts, you calculate that at the plateau 2.4 pmol of CMP were incorporated. Each transcript is 400 nucleotides long and has an overall composition of C_2AU. (A nucleotide pair weighs 660 daltons.)

A. How many transcripts are produced per reaction?
B. How many templates are present in each reaction?
C. How many transcripts are made per template in the reaction?

***9–27** How does the packing of DNA into chromatin affect transcription in eucaryotes? You have decided to tackle this issue head-on using the C-minus transcription unit you developed in Problem 9–25. This template is transcribed very well in the presence of RNA polymerase II and four transcription factors—TFIIA, TFIIB, TFIID, and TFIIE.

To test the effect of chromatin on transcription, you first assemble the template into nucleosomes (using an extract from frog oocytes), purify the chromatin template, and then add the transcription components. There is no transcription (Figure 9–22, lane 2). You then try a different order of

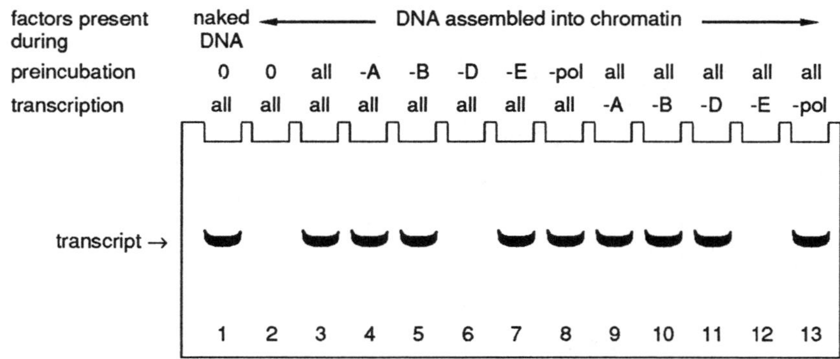

Figure 9–22 Effects of chromatin assembly on transcription (Problem 9–27). Transcription templates were preincubated with none, all, or all minus one of the transcription components (for example, −A means that TFIIA was left out and −II means that RNA polymerase II was left out). Assembly of the template into chromatin is indicated by +. The transcription assay was carried out in the presence of all or all minus one of the transcription components.

steps. You first incubate the template with the transcription components (in the absence of NTPs), then assemble the template into nucleosomes and purify the chromatin template. Now when you add the transcription components (in the presence of NTPs), transcription proceeds just as well as it does on the naked DNA template (lanes 1 and 3). You conclude that one or more of the transcription components must bind to the template and keep the promoter accessible.

To investigate this phenomenon in more detail, you carry out two additional kinds of experiments. In one you leave out individual transcription components during the preincubation (lanes 4 to 8). In the second you leave out individual transcription components during the transcription assay (lanes 9 to 13).

A. Which of the transcription components must be present during the preincubation to keep the template active during chromatin assembly?
B. Which of the transcription components form a complex with the template that is stable to chromatin formation and subsequent purification?
C. Which of the transcription components must be added during the assay in order to produce a transcript?

9–28 The trypanosome, which is the microorganism that causes sleeping sickness, can vary its surface glycoprotein coat and thus evade the immune defenses of its host. You are studying the synthesis of the variable surface glycoprotein (VSG) and have mapped the gene encoding this protein near the telomere of one of the chromosomes. However, you have been unable to locate the promoter, and your experiments suggest that it may be many thousands of nucleotides away from VSG gene.

An old friend has repeatedly suggested that you use UV irradiation to map the promoter—a technique he has used successfully to map adenovirus transcription units. Since RNA polymerases cannot transcribe through pyrimidine dimers (the damage produced by UV irradiation), the sensitivity of transcription to UV irradiation is a measure of the distance between the start of transcription and the point where transcription is assayed. Since you have had no luck with your other approaches, you decide to try his suggestion.

To calibrate your system, you test transcription through the ribosomal RNA genes. The 5S RNA transcription unit is just over 100 nucleotides long, whereas the 18S, 5.8S, and 28S RNAs are part of a single transcription unit

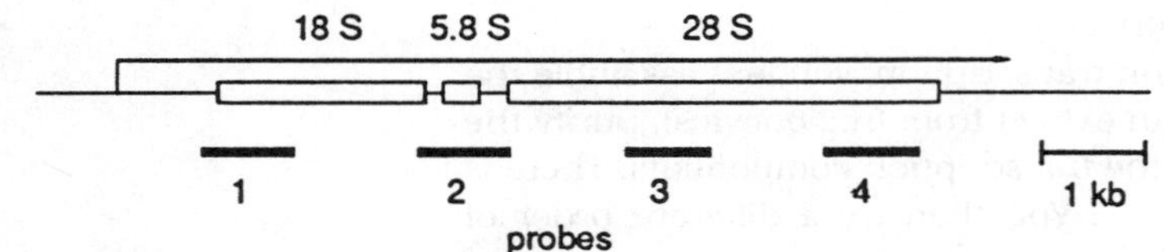

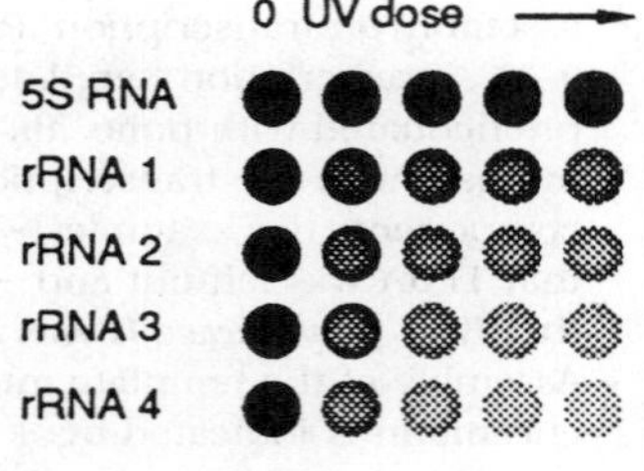

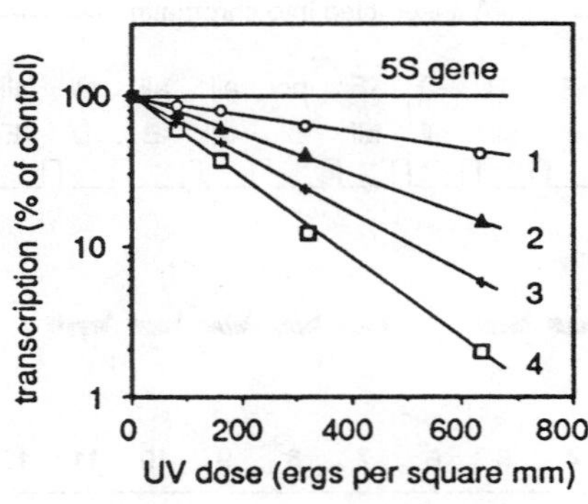

Figure 9–23 Structure of the ribosomal RNA transcription unit (A) and UV sensitivity (B) of 5S RNA and ribosomal RNA transcription units (Problem 9–28). The positions of the hybridization probes along with a scale marker are indicated in (A) relative to the promoter *(left end of thin arrow)* for the transcription unit. Transcription as a function of UV dose is indicated in (B) in the form of a "dot blot" *(left)* and graph *(right)*.

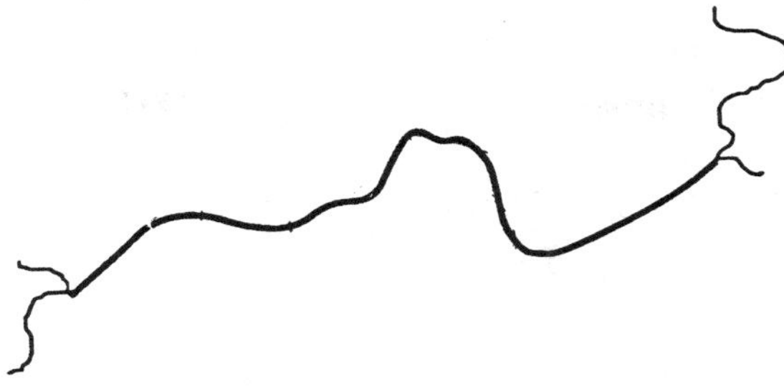

Figure 9–24 DNA-RNA hybrid between an mRNA and a restriction fragment from adenovirus (Problem 9–29).

that is about 8 kb long (Figure 9–23A). You expose trypanosomes to increasing doses of UV irradiation, isolate their nuclei, and incubate them with ^{32}P-dNTPs. You then isolate RNA from the nuclei and hybridize it to cloned DNA corresponding to the 5S RNA gene and various parts of the ribosomal RNA transcription unit (Figure 9–23B). When the logarithm of the counts in each spot is plotted against the UV dose, the data give straight lines (Figure 9–23B). The slopes of these lines are proportional to the distance from the hybridization probe to the promoter.

When you repeat the experiment with a probe from the beginning of the VSG gene, you find that transcription is inactivated about seven times faster for the VSG gene than for probe 4 from the ribosomal transcription unit.

A. Why does RNA transcription increase in sensitivity to UV irradiation with increasing distance from the promoter?
B. Roughly how far is the VSG gene from its promoter? What assumption do you have to make in order to estimate this distance?
C. You have found another gene about 10 kb upstream of the VSG gene. Transcription through this gene is 20% less sensitive to UV inactivation than is transcription through the VSG gene. Could these two genes be transcribed from the same promoter?

***9–29** You are studying a DNA virus that makes a set of abundant proteins late in its infectious cycle. An mRNA for one of these proteins maps to a restriction fragment from the middle of the linear genome. To determine the precise location of this mRNA, you anneal it with the purified restriction fragment under conditions where only DNA-RNA hybrid duplexes are stable and DNA strands do not reanneal. When you examine the reannealed duplexes by electron microscopy, you see structures such as that in Figure 9–24. Why are there single-stranded tails at the ends of the DNA-RNA duplex region?

9–30 The 3′ ends of most eucaryotic mRNAs are established by cleavage of a precursor RNA followed by addition of a poly-A tail 200 to 300 nucleotides long. The sequence AAUAAA just 5′ of the polyadenylation site is the dominant signal for polyadenylation. The importance of this signal has been verified in many ways. One elegant approach makes use of chemical modification to interfere with specific protein interactions. In this case an RNA containing the signal sequence is treated with diethylpyrocarbonate, which reacts with A and G to give carboxyethylated derivatives. This treatment renders the modified sites highly sensitive to breakage by aniline under appropriate conditions. If the starting RNA molecules are labeled at one end and treated to contain roughly one modification per molecule, then cleavage with aniline will yield a series of fragments whose lengths correspond to the positions of A's and G's in the RNA (Figure 9–25, lane 1). (This method is exactly analogous to the chemical sequencing of DNA.)

To define critical A and G residues, the modified (but still intact) RNA molecules are incubated with an extract capable of cleavage and polyadenylation. The RNA molecules are then separated into poly-A$^+$ RNA and poly-A$^-$ RNA, treated with aniline, and the fragments are analyzed by gel

Figure 9–25 Autoradiographic analysis of experiments to define the purines important in cleavage and polyadenylation (Problem 9–30). The sequence of the precursor RNA is shown at the left with the 5′ end at the bottom and the 3′ end at the top. All RNAs were modified by reaction with diethylpyrocarbonate. RNA that was not treated with extract (untreated) is shown in lane 1. RNA that was treated with extract but was not polyadenylated (poly A$^-$) is shown in lane 2. RNA that was polyadenylated (poly A$^+$) is shown in lane 3. RNA that was cleaved but not polyadenylated (cleaved) is shown in lane 4.

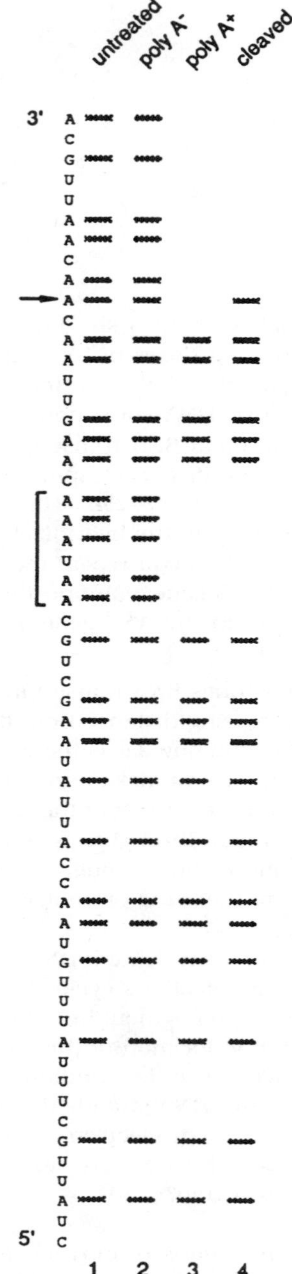

electrophoresis (lanes 2 and 3). In a second reaction EDTA is added to the extract to prevent addition of the poly-A tail (cleavage is unaffected), and the cleaved molecules are isolated, treated with aniline, and examined by electrophoresis (lane 4).

A. At which end were the starting RNA molecules labeled?
B. Explain why the bands corresponding to the AAUAAA signal (brackets in Figure 9–24) are missing from the poly-A$^+$ RNA and the cleaved RNA.
C. Explain why the band at the arrow (the normal nucleotide to which poly-A is added) is missing in the poly-A$^+$ RNA but is present in the cleaved RNA.
D. Which A and G nucleotides are important for cleavage, and which A and G nucleotides are important for addition of the the poly-A tail?
E. What information might be obtained by labeling the RNA molecules at the other end?

9–31 Unlike most mRNAs, histone messages do not have poly-A tails at the 3′ end. Instead, they are cleaved from a longer precursor a few nucleotides to the 3′ side of a stem-loop structure. Correct processing of the histone precursor depends, in addition, on a conserved sequence just beyond the cleavage site. From experiments with sea urchins it seems that this conserved sequence interacts with the RNA component of the U7 snRNP.

You are studying histone mRNA processing in mammalian cells and wonder if the same interactions define its 3′ end. As shown in Figure 9–26A, there is a striking similarity between the 3′ ends of histone mRNAs from sea urchin and human. You have shown that nuclear extracts from human cells correctly cleave a labeled synthetic histone mRNA precursor. Furthermore, if you pretreat extracts with a nuclease to digest RNA, the extract is no longer able to cleave histone precursor that is added subsequently. Activity can be restored to the treated extract by adding back a partially purified fraction containing snRNPs.

To define the processing reaction more thoroughly, you synthesize three DNA oligonucleotides corresponding to the region around the suspected site of snRNP interaction with histone precursors. One oligonucleotide matches the conserved sequence in human, one matches that in mouse, and one matches the consensus sequence derived from a comparison of all known conserved sequences in mammals (Figure 9–26B). When you preincubate these oligonucleotides with the extract in the presence of added RNase H (which cleaves RNA in a DNA-RNA hybrid) processing of the precursor was completely blocked by the mouse and consensus oligonucleotides, but the human oligonucleotide had no effect. The two inhibitory oligonucleotides also caused the disappearance of a 63-nucleotide snRNA from the extract. You manage to purify this snRNA and determine the sequence at its 5′ end (Figure 9–26C).

A. Explain the design of the oligonucleotide experiment. What were you trying to accomplish by incubating the extract with a DNA oligonucleotide in the presence of RNase H?
B. Since you were using a human extract, you were surprised that the human oligonucleotide did not inhibit processing, whereas the mouse and consensus oligonucleotides did. Can you offer an explanation for this result?

```
(A) HISTONE PRECURSOR RNA

human
5'                              ↓                              3'
ACCCAAAGGCUCUUUUCAGAGCCACCCAC UUAUUCCAACGAAAGUAGCUGUGAUAAUU
        ----->     <-----

sea urchin
5'                          ↓                             3'
AAACGGCUCUUUUCAGAGCCACC ACACCCCCAAGAAAGAUUCUCGUUAAA
    ----->     <-----

(B) DNA OLIGONUCLEOTIDES

human          5'  ACGAAAGTAGCTGTG 3'
mouse          5'  CGGAAAGAGCTGTT  3'
consensus      5' AAAGAAAGAGCTGGT  3'

(C) HUMAN U7 snRNA
5'  m3G-NNGUGUUACAGCUCUUUUAGAAUUUGUCUAGU.. 3'
```

Figure 9–26 Nucleotide sequences of histone precursor RNAs (A), DNA oligonucleotides (B), and snRNA (C) (Problem 9–31). In (A) the inverted repeat sequences capable of forming a stem-loop structure in the precursors are underlined with arrows. The site of cleavage is indicated by a vertical arrow. The conserved region is underlined in (A) and (B). In (C) m_3G is a trimethylated cap, which is characteristic of "U" RNAs. N refers to nucleotides whose identity is unknown.

***9–32** You have just got the computer to print out a whole set of DNA sequences for the β-globin gene family, and take the thick file to the country to study for the weekend. When you look at the printout, you discover to your annoyance that you forgot to indicate where in the gene you are. You know that the sequences in Figure 9–27 come from one of the exon/intron or intron/exon boundaries and that the boundary lies down the dotted line. You know that introns always begin with the dinucleotide sequence GT and end with AG, but you realize that these particular sequences would fit *either* as the start *or* the finish of an intron (Figure 9–27).

If you cannot decide which side is the intron, you will have to cut your weekend short and return to the city. In desperation, you consider the problem from an evolutionary perspective. You know that introns evolve faster (suffer more nucleotide changes) than exons because they are not constrained by function. Does this perspective allow you to identify the intron, or will you have to pack your bags?

***9–33** You are studying the transcriptional control of actin synthesis in nematode worms. Nematodes have four genes that encode actin mRNAs: three are clustered on chromosome 5 (genes 1 and 3 are identical in sequence) and one is located on the X chromosome (Figure 9–28). To identify the start site of transcription, you employ two techniques: S1 mapping and primer extension (outlined in Figure 9–29).

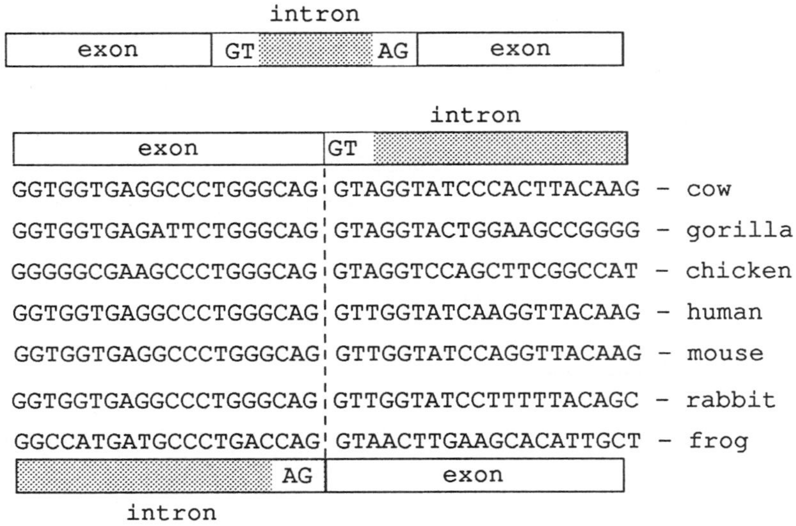

```
                     intron
| exon            | GT ░░░░░░░ AG | exon            |

                                  intron
| exon                 | GT ░░░░░░░░░░░░░░░░░░░░ |
GGTGGTGAGGCCCTGGGCAG ¦ GTAGGTATCCCACTTACAAG - cow
GGTGGTGAGATTCTGGGCAG ¦ GTAGGTACTGGAAGCCGGGG - gorilla
GGGGGCGAAGCCCTGGGCAG ¦ GTAGGTCCAGCTTCGGCCAT - chicken
GGTGGTGAGGCCCTGGGCAG ¦ GTTGGTATCAAGGTTACAAG - human
GGTGGTGAGGCCCTGGGCAG ¦ GTTGGTATCCAGGTTACAAG - mouse
GGTGGTGAGGCCCTGGGCAG ¦ GTTGGTATCCTTTTTACAGC - rabbit
GGCCATGATGCCCTGACCAG ¦ GTAACTTGAAGCACATTGCT - frog
| ░░░░░░░░░░░░░░░ AG | exon                 |
       intron
```

Figure 9–27 The relationship of DNA sequences from the β-globin genes in different species to exons and introns (Problem 9–32).

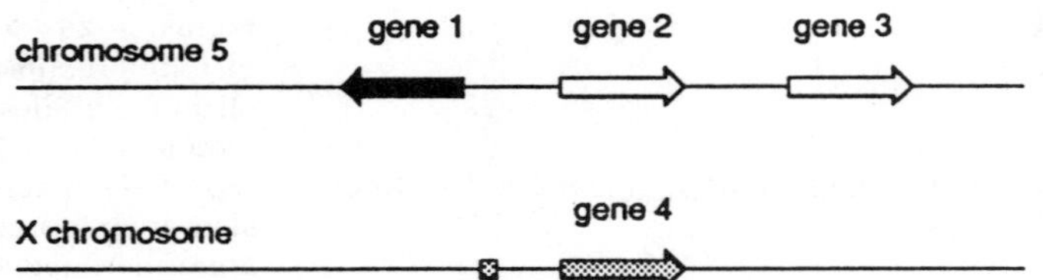

Figure 9–28 Location of the four actin genes in the nematode (Problem 9–33). Genes are indicated by arrows that show their direction of transcription.

To locate the 5′ end of the mRNAs by S1 mapping, you anneal a radioactive single-stranded segment from the 5′ end of the gene to the corresponding mRNA, digest the hybrid with S1 nuclease to remove all single strands, and analyze the protected fragment of radioactive DNA on a sequencing gel to determine its length (Figure 9–29A). For primer extension you hybridize specific oligonucleotides to each mRNA (gene 1 and 3 are identical), extend them to the 5′ end of the mRNA, and analyze the resulting DNA segments on sequencing gels (Figure 9–29B).

For gene 4 the two techniques agree, which is the usual case. However, for genes 1, 2, and 3, the mRNAs appear to be 20 nucleotides longer when assayed by primer extension. When you compare the mRNA sequences (which can be determined by primer extension) with the sequences for the gene, you find that each of these mRNAs has an identical 20-nucleotide segment at its 5′ end that does not match the sequence of the gene (Figure 9–30).

Using an oligonucleotide complementary to this leader RNA segment, you discover that the corresponding DNA is repeated about 100 times in a cluster on chromosome 5, but it is a long way from the actin genes on chromosome 5. This leader gene encodes an RNA about 100 nucleotides long. The 5′ end of the leader RNA is identical to the segment found at the 5′ ends of the actin mRNAs (Figure 9–30).

A. Assuming that the leader RNA and the actin RNAs are joined by splicing according to the usual rules, indicate on Figure 9–30 the most likely point at which the RNAs are joined.
B. Since the leader gene and actin genes 1, 2, and 3 are all on the same chromosome, why is it *not* possible that transcription begins at a leader gene and extends through the actin genes to give a precursor RNA that is subsequently spliced to form the actin mRNAs?
C. How would you explain the formation of the actin mRNAs with the common leader segment?

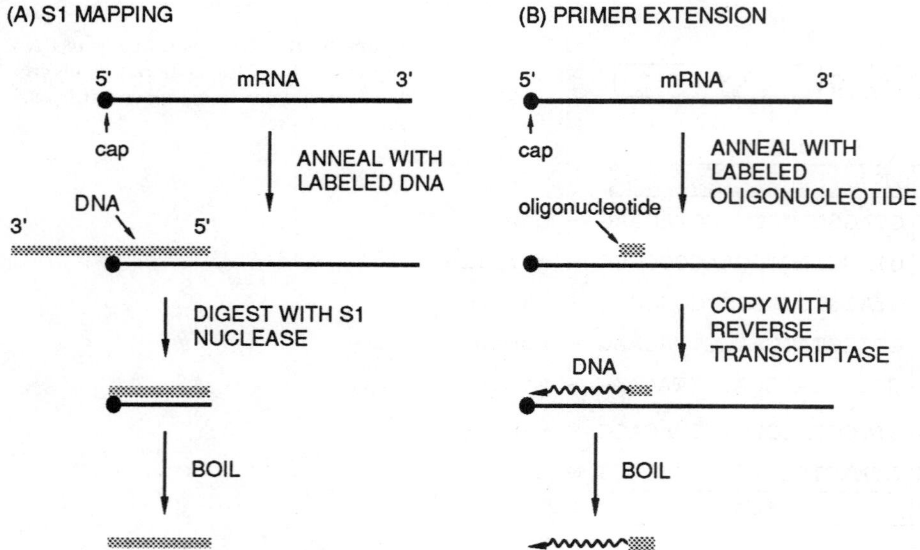

Figure 9–29 The use of (A) S1 mapping and (B) primer extension to locate the 5′ ends of the actin mRNAs (Problem 9–33).

ACTIN GENE 1

DNA: 5' TATTATCAATTTAATTTTTCAGGTACATTAAAAACTAATCAAAATG

RNA: 5' XGUUUAAUUACCCAAGUUUGAGGUACAUUAAAAACUAAUCAAAAUG

ACTIN GENE 2

DNA: 5' ATAATTCATAATTATTTTGTAGGCTAAGTTCCTCCTAATCTAATAAATCATG

RNA: 5' XGUUUAAUUACCCAAGUUUGAGGCUAAGUUCCUCCUAAUCUAAUAAAUCAUG

ACTIN GENE 3

DNA: 5' TATTATCAATTTAATTTTTCAGGTACATTAAAAACTAATCAAAATG

RNA: 5' XGUUUAAUUACCCAAGUUUGAGGUACAUUAAAAACUAAUCAAAAUG

LEADER RNA GENE

DNA: 5' GGTTTAATTACCCAAGTTTGAGGTAAACATTCAAACTGA

RNA: 5' XGUUUAAUUACCCAAGUUUGAGGUAAACAUUCAAACUGA

Figure 9–30 RNA and DNA sequences of actin genes and leader RNA genes (Problem 9–33). The start site for translation of the actin genes (ATG) is underlined in the DNA sequence. The leader RNA segment that is present at the 5′ ends of the actin genes and the leader RNA genes is underlined in the RNA sequences. The 5′ nucleotide on the RNAs (X) cannot be determined by primer extension.

9–34 Many higher eucaryotic genes contain a large number of exons. Correct splicing of such genes requires that neighboring exons be ligated to each other; if they are not, exons will be left out. Since all 5′ splice sites look alike, as do all 3′ splice sites, it is remarkable that skipping an exon occurs so rarely during splicing. Some mechanism must keep track of neighboring exons and ensure that they are brought together.

One proposal for maintaining exon order during splicing suggests that the splicing machinery binds to a splice site at one end of an intron and scans through the intron searching for a second splice site at the other end. Such a scanning mechanism would guarantee that an exon is never skipped. You are intrigued by this hypothesis and decide to test it. You construct two minigenes: one with a duplicated 5′ splice site and the other with a duplicated 3′ splice site (Figure 9–31). You transfect these minigenes into cells and analyze their RNA products to see which 5′ and 3′ splice sites are selected during splicing.

A. Draw a diagram of the products you expect from each minigene if the splicing machinery binds to a 5′ splice site and scans toward a 3′ splice site. Diagram the expected products if the splicing machinery scans in the opposite direction.

B. When you analyze the RNA produced from your transfected minigenes, you find that a mixture of products is generated from each minigene. Are neighboring exons brought together by intron scanning?

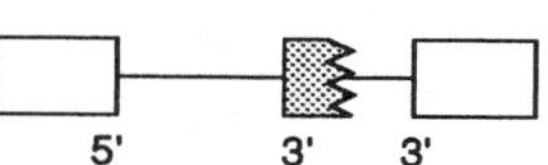

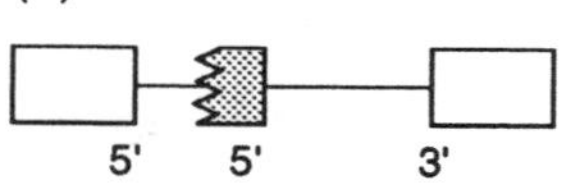

Figure 9–31 Minigene designed to test for intron scanning during RNA splicing (Problem 9–34). Minigene 1 (A) has two 3′ splice sites; minigene 2 (B) has two 5′ splice sites. Boxes represent complete *(open)* or partial *(hatched)* exons; 5′ and 3′ splice junctions are indicated.

THE SV40 ENHANCER

TGCACTTCAATTGCAGCAGCGGCCTCTCCAGCAGCAATTTCAGCTACTGAAAATCCAGTA

GCAGCAGCAGCTTCAGACACAGTAGCAATTAGGTCCCCCAACAGTGTTAAAGCAGCACCC

ATGGACCTGAAATAAAAGACAAAAAGACTAAACTTACCAGTTAACTTTCTGGTTTTTCAG

TTAACCTTTCTGGTTTTTTGCGTTTCCCGTCAACAGTATCTTCCCCTTCACAAAATTGCA

GCAAAAGCTCTAAAACAAACACAAAAAGGCGTTGAGCTGTTTTTTACTTTCAGTCCATG

ACCTACGAACCTTAACGGAGGCCTGGCGTGACAGCCGGCGCAGCACCATGGCCTGAAATA

ACCTCTGAAAGAGGAACTTGGTTAGGTACCTTCTGAGGCGGAAAGAACCAGCTGTGGAAT

GTGTGTCAGTTAGGGTGTGGAAAGTCCCCAGGCTCCCCAGCAGGCAGAAGTATGCAAAGC

ATGCATCTCAATTAGTCAGCAACCAGGTGTGGAAAGTCCCCAGGCTCCCCAGCAGGCAGA

AGTATGCAAAGCATGCATCTCAATTAGTCAGCAACCATAGTCCCGCCCCTAACTCCGCCC

ATCCCGCCCCTAACTCCGCCCAGTTCCGCCCATTCTCCGCCCCATGGCTGACTAATTTTT

->start of transcription
TTTATTTATGCAGAGGCCGAGGCCGCCTCGGCCTCTGAGCTATTCCAGAAGTAGTGAGGA

GGCTTTTTTGGAGGCCTAGGCTTTTGCAAAAAGCTTTGCAAAGATGGATAAAGTTTTAAA

CAGAGAGGAATCTTTGCAGCTAATGGACCTTCTAGGTCTTGAAAGGAGTGCCTGGGGGAA

TATTCCTCTGATGAGAAAGGCATATTTAAAAAAATGCAAGGAGTTTCATCCTGATAAAGG

AGGAGATGAAGAAAAAATGAAGA

This is the DNA sequence of the enhancer from SV40 virus, written so as to read left to right in the direction of early transcription. The start of the major transcript is indicated, and the ATG that starts T antigen (the product of this mRNA) is underlined. Can you find the 21 base-pair repeats and the 72 base-pair repeats? You should be able to locate the binding sites for SP1 in the 21 base pair repeats, but can you see binding sites for any of the other transcription factors listed in MBOC Table 10–1, page 566? The use of colored marker pens is strongly advised.

Control of Gene Expression

10

Strategies of Gene Control (MBOC 551–557)

10–1 Fill in the blanks in the following statements.

A. Regulation of gene expression by controlling when and how rapidly a given gene is transcribed is known as ____________ control.

B. Regulation of gene expression by controlling how the primary RNA transcript is spliced or otherwise processed is known as ____________ control.

C. Regulation of gene expression by selecting which completed mRNAs in the cell nucleus are exported to the cytoplasm is known as ____________ control.

D. Regulation of gene expression by selecting which mRNAs in the cytoplasm are translated by ribosomes is known as ____________ control.

E. Regulation of gene expression by selectively destabilizing certain mRNA molecules in the cytoplasm is known as ____________ control.

F. Regulation of gene expression by selectively activating, inactivating, or compartmentalizing specific protein molecules after they have been made is known as ____________ control.

G. Eucaryotic cells contain a large set of ____________, which are sequence-specific, DNA-binding proteins whose main function is to turn genes on or off.

H. Stimulation of transcription by the binding of a regulatory protein is known as ____________; inhibition of transcription by the binding of a regulatory protein is known as ____________.

I. A relatively few regulatory elements could generate a large number of cell types by ____________ gene regulation.

J. Branching networks of gene regulation, in which gene regulatory proteins control genes that produce other gene regulators, are coordinated by ____________ proteins.

K. A gene regulatory protein called ____________, which normally is expressed only in myoblasts and muscle cells, can subvert the normal gene controls of the fibroblast and convert it to a muscle cell when expressed at a high enough concentration.

10–2 Indicate whether the following statements are true or false. If a statement is false, explain why.

__ A. As a general rule, the changes in gene expression that underlie the development of multicellular organisms are not accompanied by changes in the DNA sequences of the corresponding genes.

__ B. A comparison of the most abundant proteins (2000 or so) in different cell types, such as liver and lung, shows that a large fraction are present in very different amounts.

— C. Although gene expression can be regulated at each step in the pathway from DNA to RNA to protein, transcriptional controls are the most common.

— D. Whenever a gene regulatory protein binds to its recognition sequence in the DNA, it stimulates transcription of the adjacent gene.

— E. The advantage of combinatorial gene regulation is that a very large number of different cell types can be specified by relatively few gene regulatory proteins.

— F. Most eucaryotic genes are regulated by the binding of only one or two gene regulatory proteins.

— G. Homeotic mutations in *Drosophila* convert one part of the fly's body into another.

— H. When myoblasts begin to fuse, the rates of synthesis of muscle-specific proteins increase by more than a factor of 500 and the rates of synthesis of many other proteins change as well—all apparently in response to a single gene regulatory protein called myoD1.

10–3 The gene for the κ-light chain of immunoglobulins contains a DNA sequence element (an enhancer) in one of its introns that regulates its expression. A protein called NF-κB binds to this enhancer and can be found in nuclear extracts of B cells, which actively synthesize immunoglobulins. By contrast, NF-κB activity is absent from precursor B cells (pre-B cells), which do not express immunoglobulins. You are interested in the strategy by which NF-κB regulates expression of κ-light-chain genes.

If pre-B cells are treated with phorbol ester (which activates protein kinase C, causing the phosphorylation of some cellular proteins), NF–κB activity appears within a few minutes in parallel with the transcriptional activation of the κ-light chain gene. This activation of NF-κB is not blocked by cycloheximide, which is an inhibitor of protein synthesis.

You discover by chance that cytoplasmic extracts of unstimulated pre-B cells contain an inactive form of NF–κB that can be activated by treatment with mild denaturants. (Denaturants disrupt noncovalent bonds but do not break covalent bonds.) To understand the relationship between NF–κB activation and transcriptional regulation of κ-light-chain genes, you isolate nuclear (N) and cytoplasmic (C) fractions from pre-B cells before and after stimulation by phorbol ester. You then measure NF-κB activity by a DNA gel retardation assay before and after treatment with the mild denaturants. The results are shown in Figure 10–1.

A. How does the subcellular localization of NF–κB change in pre-B cells in response to phorbol ester treatment?

B. Do you think that the activation of NF-κB in response to phorbol ester occurs because NF–κB is phosphorylated by protein kinase C?

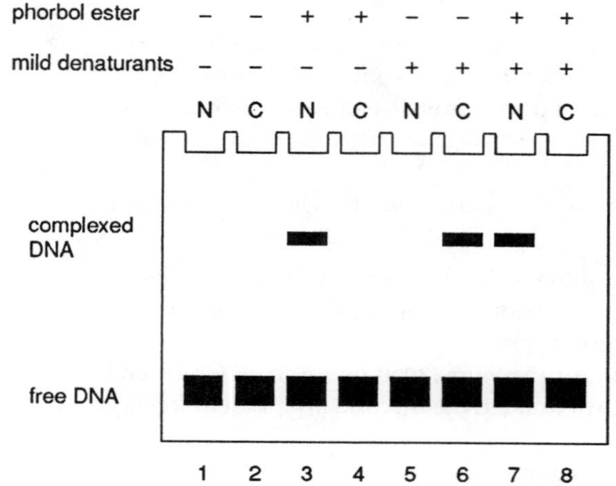

Figure 10–1 Gel retardation assay of NF-κB activity under various conditions (Problem 10–3). N and C refer to nuclear and cytoplasmic fractions, respectively. The mild denaturants are a combination of formamide (27%) and sodium deoxycholate (0.2%).

C. Outline a molecular mechanism to account for activation of NF-κB by treatment with phorbol ester.

*10–4 In the absence of glucose *E. coli* can metabolize and grow on arabinose, a pentose sugar, using an inducible set of genes that are arranged in three groups on the chromosome (Figure 10–2). In one of these the *araA*, *araB*, and *araD* genes encode enzymes for the metabolism of arabinose while the *araC* gene encodes a regulatory protein that binds adjacent to arabinose promoters and coordinates the expression of the genes in the arabinose operon. (The other two groups of genes encode proteins involved in arabinose transport.)

To understand the regulatory properties of the araC protein, you isolate a mutant bacterium with a deletion of the *araC* gene. As shown in Table 10–1, the mutant strain does not express the product of the *araA* gene when arabinose is added to the medium.

A. Do the results in Table 10–1 suggest that the araC protein is a positive regulator or a negative regulator of the arabinose operon?

B. What would the data in Table 10–1 have looked like if the araC protein were the opposite kind of gene regulatory protein?

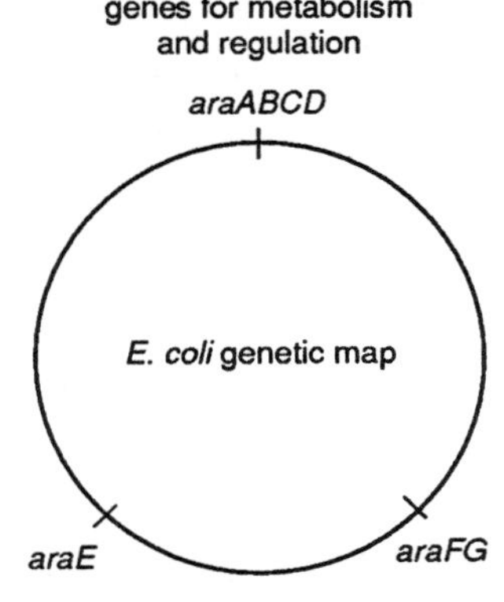

Figure 10–2 Chromosomal locations of the genes involved in arabinose metabolism (Problem 10–4).

10–5 The embryonic mouse fibroblast cell line, 10T1/2 (10 T and a half), is a very stable line with cells that look and behave like fibroblasts. If these cells are exposed to a medium containing 5-azacytidine (5-aza C) for 24 hours, however, they will then differentiate into cartilage, fat, or muscle cells when they grow to a high cell density. (Treatment with 5-aza C reduces the general level of DNA methylation, allowing some previously inactive genes to become active.) If the cells are grown at low cell density after the treatment, they retain their original fibroblastlike shape and behavior, but even after many generations of growth they still differentiate when they reach a high cell density. 10T1/2 cells that have not been exposed to 5-aza C do not differentiate no matter what the cell density.

When the treated cells differentiate, about 25% turn into muscle cells (myoblasts). The high frequency of myoblast formation leads your advisor to hypothesize that a single master regulatory gene, which is normally repressed by methylation, may trigger the entire transformation. Accordingly, he persuades you to undertake a high-risk, high-payoff project: clone the gene! You assume the gene is off before treatment with 5-aza C and on in the induced myoblasts. If this assumption is valid, you should be able to find sequences corresponding to the gene among the cDNA copies of mRNAs that are synthesized after 5-aza C treatment.

Your strategy is to screen an existing cDNA library from normal myoblasts (which according to your assumption will also express the gene) using a set of radioactive probes to identify likely cDNA clones. You prepare three radioactive probes.

Probe 1. You isolate RNA from 5-aza-C-induced myoblasts and prepare radioactive cDNA copies.

Probe 2. You hybridize the radioactive cDNA from the induced myoblasts with RNA from untreated 10T1/2 cells and discard all the RNA:DNA hybrids.

*Problems with an asterisk (*) are answered in the Instructor's Manual.

Table 10–1 Response of Normal and Mutant Bacteria to the Presence and Absence of Arabinose (Problem 10–4)

	araA Gene Product	
Genotype	**Minus Arabinose**	**Plus Arabinose**
araC$^+$	1	1000
araC$^-$	1	1

Table 10–2 Patterns of Myoblast cDNA Hybridization with Radioactive Probes (Problem 10–5)

Class	Probe 1	Probe 2	Probe 3
A	+	–	–
B	+	–	+
C	+	+	–
D	+	+	+

Probe 3. You isolate RNA from normal myoblasts and prepare radioactive cDNA copies, which you then hybridize to RNA from untreated 10T1/2 cells; you discard the RNA:DNA hybrids.

The first probe hybridizes to a large number of clones from the cDNA library, but only about 1% of those clones hybridize to probes 2 and 3. Overall, you find four distinct patterns of hybridization (Table 10–2).

A. What is the purpose of hybridizing the radioactive cDNA from the two kinds of myoblasts to the RNA from untreated 10T1/2 cells? In other words, why are probes 2 and 3 useful?

B. What general kinds of genes would you expect to find in each of the four classes of cDNA clone (A, B, C, and D in Table 10–2)? Which class of cDNA clone is most likely to contain sequences corresponding to the putative muscle regulatory gene you are seeking?

Controlling the Start of Transcription (MBOC 557–570)

10–6 Fill in the blanks in the following statements.

A. RNA polymerase binds to the ____________ to start transcription.

B. The ____________ protein inhibits transcription of the *lac* operon by binding to a specific DNA sequence called the operator that overlaps the promoter.

C. The binding of a ____________ protein to a specific DNA sequence turns a gene off; this type of gene control is called ____________.

D. In the type of gene control known as ____________, a ____________ protein binds to a specific DNA sequence and facilitates transcription of the adjacent gene.

E. The ____________ protein enables *E. coli* to use alternative carbon sources only if glucose, its preferred carbon source, is not available.

F. The ____________, which is one of the five major polypeptide chains of RNA polymerase, functions during initiation and is then ejected once the polymerase has successfully begun RNA synthesis.

G. The ____________, which binds to the consensus sequence TATAAA, tends to remain in a stable ____________ that can mediate multiple rounds of transcription by RNA polymerase II molecules.

H. DNA sequences that are required for gene transcription and extend for about 100 nucleotides pairs in front of the RNA start site are known as ____________.

I. An ____________ operates in both orientations, functions even when moved more than 1000 nucleotide pairs from the promoter, and stimulates transcription from either an upstream or a downstream position.

10–7 Indicate whether the following statements are true or false. If a statement is false, explain why.

__ A. Allolactose, which is formed by the cell in the presence of lactose, derepresses the *lac* operon by binding to the operator and stimulating transcription.

__ B. In bacteria an activator protein binds to specific DNA sequences that are positioned in such a way that the activator can touch the RNA polymerase and increase its likelihood of initiating transcription.

__ C. Gene activation in nitrogen metabolism involves the ntrC protein, a gene activator that turns on genes only in its phosphorylated form, and an enzyme, the ntrB protein, which can either phosphorylate or dephosphorylate the ntrC protein.

__ D. Although the ability of activator proteins to stimulate transcription from distant regulatory sites is prevalent in eucaryotes, it has not yet been observed in procaryotes.

__ E. Sigma factors bind to RNA polymerase but do not interact with specific DNA sequences; gene activator proteins bind to specific DNA sequences but do not interact with RNA polymerase.

__ F. Bacterial RNA polymerase recognizes a DNA sequence, but eucaryotic RNA polymerases normally recognize a protein-DNA complex formed by general transcription factors.

__ G. Recombinant DNA techniques combined with *in vitro* studies make it possible to identify the regulatory regions of eucaryotic genes even in the absence of any direct knowledge of the regulatory proteins that bind to them.

__ H. Enhancers generally function well in all cell types, but they usually function best in the specific cell types that express the gene with which they are normally associated.

__ I. If the DNA-binding domain of a glucocorticoid receptor protein is replaced with the DNA-binding domain of the estrogen receptor protein, the hybrid regulatory protein activates estrogen responsive genes in response to glucocorticoid.

__ J. Eucaryotic gene regulatory proteins are activated or inactivated almost exclusively by the binding of small signaling molecules.

__ K. Reasonable levels of gene activation are obtained in both yeast and mammalian cells if the transcription-activating domain of a gene regulatory protein is replaced by a region that is merely rich in acidic amino acids.

10–8 *E. coli* grows faster on the monosaccharide glucose than it does on the disaccharide lactose for two reasons: (1) lactose is taken up more slowly than glucose and (2) lactose must first be hydrolyzed to glucose and galactose (by β-galactosidase) before it can be further metabolized.

When *E. coli* is grown on a medium containing a mixture of glucose and lactose, it shows complex growth kinetics (Figure 10–3, squares). The bacteria grow faster at the beginning than at the end, and there is a lag between these two growth phases when they virtually stop growing. Assays of the concentrations of the two sugars in the medium show that glucose falls to very low levels after a few cell doublings (Figure 10–3, circles), but

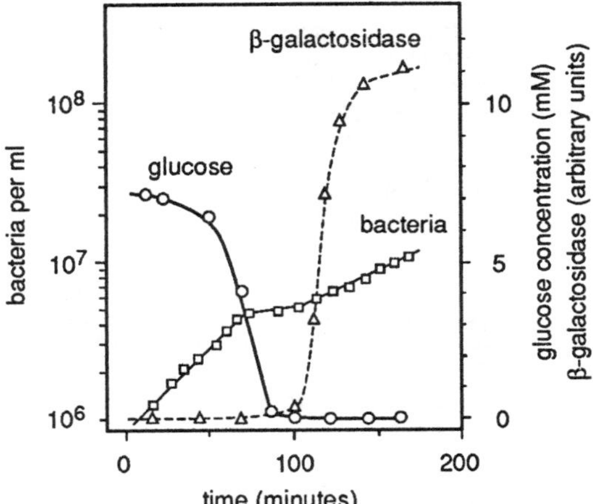

Figure 10–3 Growth of *E. coli* on a mixture of glucose and lactose (Problem 10–8).

lactose remains high until near the end of the experimental time course. Although the concentration of lactose is high throughout the experiment, β-galactosidase, which is regulated as part of the *lac* operon, is not induced until more than 100 minutes have passed (Figure 10–3, triangles).

A. Explain the kinetics of bacterial growth during the experiment. Account for the rapid rate of initial growth, the slower rate of final growth, and the delay in growth in the middle of the experiment.

B. Explain why the *lac* operon is not induced by lactose during the rapid initial phase of bacterial growth.

***10–9** Transcription of the bacterial gene encoding the enzyme glutamine synthetase is regulated by the availability of nitrogen in the cell. The key transcriptional regulator is the ntrC protein, which stimulates transcription only when it is phosphorylated. Phosphorylation of the ntrC protein is controlled by the ntrB protein, which is both a protein kinase and a protein phosphatase. The balance between its kinase and phosphatase activities—hence the level of phosphorylation of ntrC and transcription of glutamine synthetase—is determined by other proteins that respond to the ratio of α-ketoglutarate and glutamine. (This ratio is a sensitive indicator of nitrogen availability because two nitrogens—as ammonia—must be added to α-ketoglutarate to make glutamine.)

Transcription of the gene for glutamine synthetase can be achieved *in vitro* by adding RNA polymerase, a special sigma factor, and phosphorylated ntrC protein to a linear DNA template containing the gene and its upstream regulatory region. DNA footprinting assays show that the ntrC protein binds to five sites upstream of the promoter. Although binding of the ntrC protein is only slightly increased by phosphorylation, transcription is absolutely dependent on phosphorylation. However, RNA polymerase binds strongly to the promoter even in the absence of the ntrC protein.

The activation of transcription by ntrC was further explored using three different templates: the normal gene with intact regulatory sequences, a gene with the ntrC binding sites deleted, and a gene with three of the ntrC binding sites moved to the 3′ end of the gene (Figure 10–4A, B, and C, respectively). In the absence of phosphorylated ntrC protein, no transcription occurred from any of the templates. In the presence of 100 nM

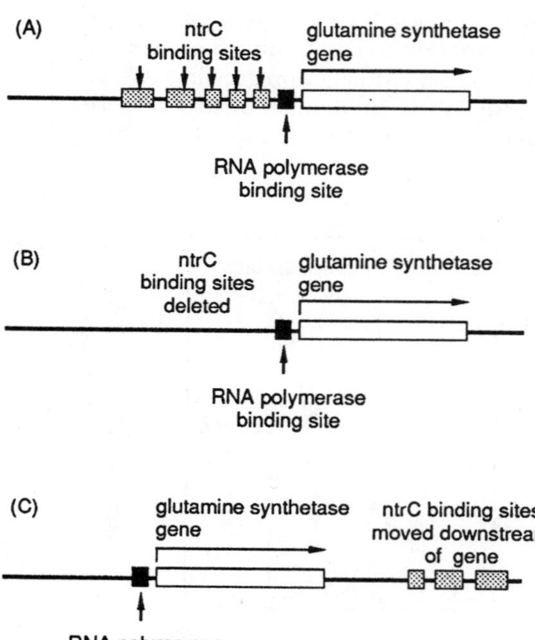

Figure 10–4 Three templates for studying the role of ntrC binding sites in transcription of the glutamine synthetase gene (Problem 10–9). (A) The normal gene with intact upstream regulatory sequences. (B) A gene with the ntrC binding sites deleted. (C) A gene with the ntrC binding sites moved to the 3′ end of the gene.

phosphorylated ntrC protein, all three templates supported maximal transcription. However, the three templates differed significantly in the concentration of ntrC protein required for half-maximal rates of transcription: the normal gene (A) required 5 nM ntrC protein, the gene with 3′ binding sites (C) required 10 nM ntrC protein, and the gene without ntrC binding sites (B) required 50 nM ntrC protein.

A. If RNA polymerase can bind to the promoter of the glutamine synthetase gene in the absence of the ntrC protein, why is the ntrC protein needed to activate transcription?
B. If the ntrC protein can bind to its binding sites regardless of its state of phosphorylation, why is phosphorylation necessary for transcription?
C. If the ntrC protein can activate transcription even when its binding sites are absent, what role do the binding sites play?

10–10 Regulation of the arabinose operon in *E. coli* is fairly complex. Not only are the genes scattered around the chromosome in three clusters, but the regulatory protein, araC, acts as both a positive and a negative regulator. For example, in the regulation of the *araBAD* cluster of genes (Figure 10–5A), araC binding at site 1 in the presence of arabinose (and the absence of glucose) increases transcription roughly 100-fold over the basal level measured in the absence of araC protein. Binding of araC at site 2 in the absence of arabinose represses transcription of the *araBAD* genes about 10-fold below the basal level measured in the absence of araC protein. The combined effects of negative regulation at site 2 (in the absence of arabinose) and positive regulation at site 1 (in the presence of arabinose) means that addition of arabinose causes a 1000-fold increase in transcription of the *araBAD* genes.

Positive regulation by binding at site 1 seems straightforward since that site lies adjacent to the promoter and presumably facilitates RNA polymerase binding or stimulates open complex formation. You are more puzzled, however, by the results of binding at site 2. Site 2 lies 270 nucleotides upstream from the start site of transcription. Regulatory effects over such distances seem more reminiscent of enhancers in eucaryotic cells. To study the mechanism of repression at site 2 more easily, you move the entire regulatory region in front of the *galK* gene, whose encoded

(A) *araBAD* REGULATORY REGION

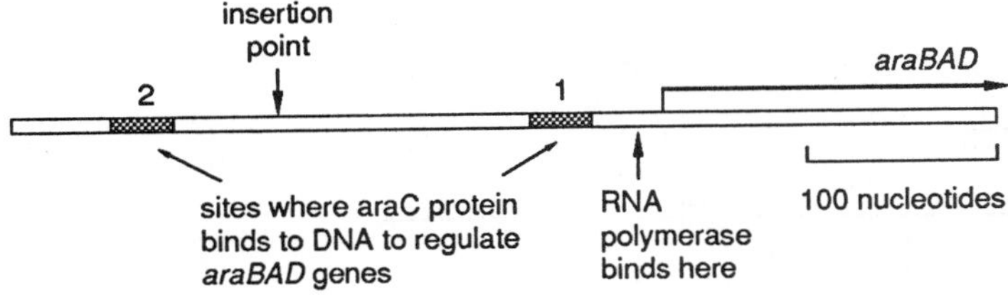

(B) GALACTOKINASE STREAK TEST

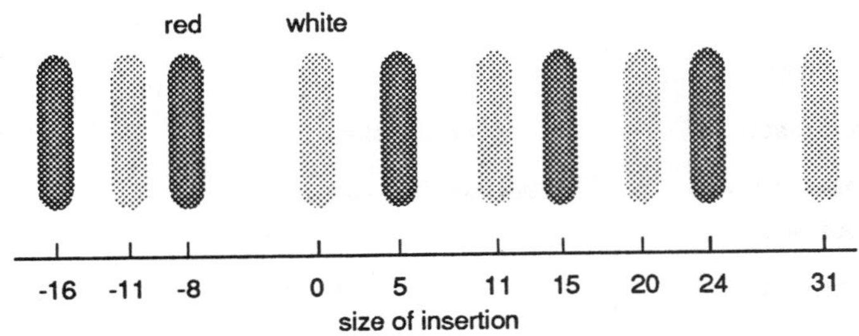

Figure 10–5 Arrangement (A) of araC binding sites in the *araBAD* operon and results (B) of altering the spacing between the araC binding sites (Problem 10–10). In (B) the *araBAD* genes have been replaced by the *galK* gene and various numbers of nucleotides have been inserted or deleted at the insertion point, as indicated on the scale at the bottom. Colonies that do not express galactokinase are white; those that do are red.

enzyme, galactokinase, is simpler to assay than are the enzymes encoded by the *araBAD* genes.

To determine the importance of the spacing between the two araC binding sites, you insert or delete nucleotides at the insertion point indicated in Figure 10–5A. The activity of the promoter in the absence of arabinose is then assayed by growing the bacteria on special indicator plates, on which the bacterial colonies are white if the promoter is fully repressed and red if galactokinase is produced. You streak out bacteria containing the altered spacings against a scale that shows how many nucleotides were deleted or inserted (Figure 10–5B). Much to your surprise, red and white streaks are interspersed.

When you show your results to your advisor, she is very pleased and tells you that these experiments distinguish among three potential mechanisms of repression from a distance. (1) An alteration in the structure of the DNA could propagate from the repression site to the transcription site, making the promoter an unfavorable site for RNA polymerase binding. (2) The protein could bind cooperatively (oligomerize) at the repression site in such a way that additional subunits continue to be added until the growing chain of subunits extends to and covers the promoter, blocking transcription. (3) The DNA could form a loop so that the protein bound at the distant repression site could interact with proteins (or DNA) at the transcription start site.

Which of these general mechanisms does your data support, and how do you account for the patterns of red and white streaks?

***10–11** You have developed an *in vitro* transcription system using a defined segment of DNA that is transcribed under the control of a viral promoter. Transcription of this DNA occurs when you add purified RNA polymerase II, TFIID (the TATA binding factor), and TFIIB and TFIIE (which bind to RNA polymerase). However, the low efficiency of the *in vitro* system suggests that there may be an additional regulatory sequence that binds a transcription factor that is not present among the purified components. To search for the DNA sequence to which this putative regulatory factor binds, you make a series of deletions upstream of the start site for transcription (Figure 10–6B) and compare their transcriptional activity in the purified system and in crude extracts. As an internal control, you mix

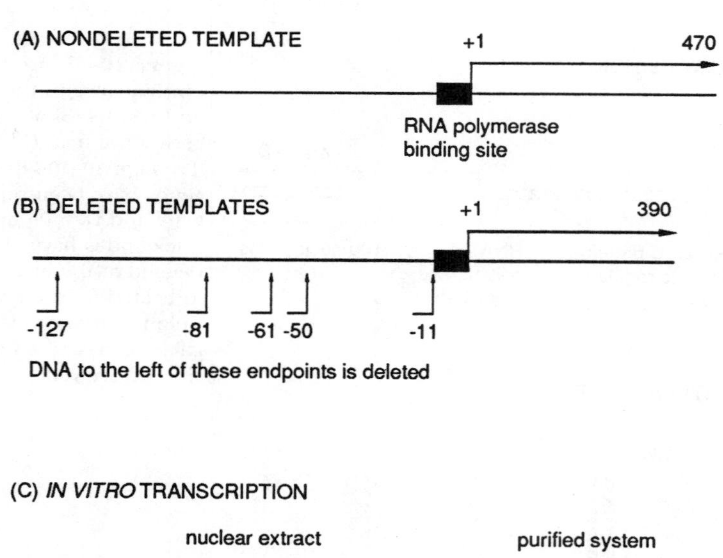

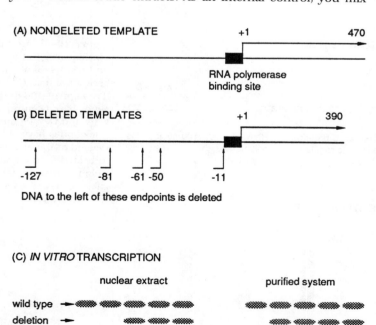

Figure 10–6 Transcription from a viral promoter (Problem 10–11). (A) Nondeleted template. (B) Deleted templates. The nondeleted template gives rise to a transcript that is 80 nucleotides longer than the transcript from the templates that carry deletions in the upstream regulatory region. The deletions remove DNA to the left of the indicated endpoints. Nucleotides are numbered from the start site of transcription (+1); negative numbers indicate nucleotides in front of the start site of transcription. (C) Results of transcription of a mixture of nondeleted and deleted templates in a crude extract (*left*) and using purified components (*right*). Negative numbers identify the particular deletion template that was included in each mixture.

each of the deletions with a nondeleted template that encodes a slightly longer transcript (Figure 10–6A). The results of these assays are shown in Figure 10–6C. Deletions up to −61 have no effect on transcription and the −11 deletion inactivates transcription in both the purified system and the crude extract. Surprisingly, the −50 deletion is transcribed as efficiently as the nondeleted template in the purified system, but not in the crude system.

You purify the protein that is responsible for this effect and show that it stimulates transcription approximately ten-fold from the nondeleted template and from the −61 deletion template, but does not stimulate transcription from the −50 deletion template. Footprinting analysis shows that the factor binds to a specific, short sequence upstream of the TATA site. Furthermore, although the factor binds very transiently to its site in the absence of TFIID (a 20-second half-life), in the presence of TFIID it binds stably (with a half-life greater than 5 hours).

A. Where is the binding site for the stimulatory factor located?
B. How is it that a *stimulatory* factor, when added to the other purified transcription components, causes transcripts from the −50 deletion template to be absent from the gel?
C. Why do you think there is such a marked difference in stability of binding of the stimulatory factor in the presence and absence of TFIID?

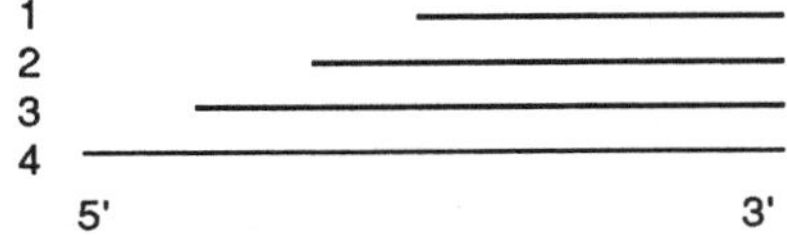

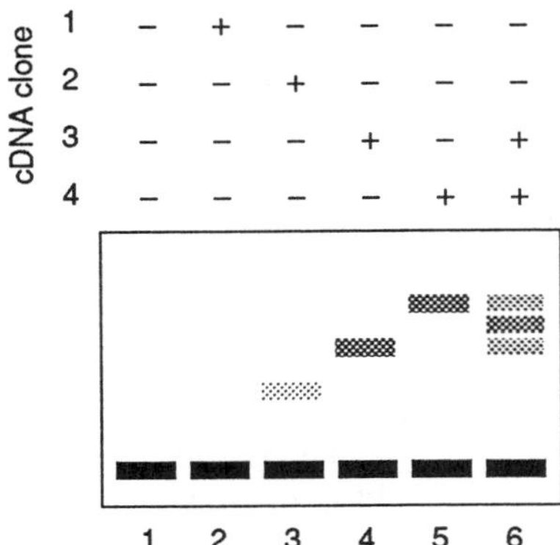

Figure 10–7 Structure of partial cDNAs encoding a transcription factor (A) and gel retardation assays (B) of the encoded proteins. Radioactivity of the bands is due to DNA (Problem 10–12).

10–12 You have cloned several partial cDNAs for a transcription factor into an expression vector to test whether the encoded portions of the factor will bind to the enhancer that the complete protein recognizes. The partial cDNA clones extend for different distances toward the 5′ end of the gene (Figure 10–7A). You transcribe and then translate these cDNA clones *in vitro* and then mix the translation products with highly radioactive DNA containing the enhancer. When the mixtures are analyzed by polyacrylamide gel electrophoresis, some of the proteins encoded by the cDNA clones bind to the DNA fragment causing a retardation in its migration (Figure 10–7B, lanes 3, 4, and 5). When cDNA clones 3 and 4 are mixed together before transcription and translation, three bands appear in the gel retardation assay (Figure 10–7B, lane 6).

A. Why are the retarded bands at different positions on the gel?
B. Where in the transcription factor is the binding domain for the enhancer located?
C. Why are there three retarded bands when cDNA clones 3 and 4 are mixed together? What does that tell you about the structure of the transcription factor?

***10–13** Hormone receptors for glucocorticoids alter their conformation upon hormone binding to become DNA-binding proteins that activate a specific set of responsive genes. Genetic and molecular studies indicate that the DNA and hormone binding sites occupy distinct regions of the C-terminal half of the glucocorticoid receptor. Hormone binding could generate a functional DNA-binding protein in either of two ways: by altering receptor conformation to create a DNA-binding domain or by altering the conformation to uncover a preexisting DNA-binding domain.

These possibilities have been investigated by comparing the activities of a nested set of carboxy-terminal deletions (Figure 10–8). Fragments of the cDNA, which correspond to the N-terminal portion of the receptor, were inserted into a vector so they would be expressed upon transfection into appropriate cells. The capacity of the receptor fragments to activate responsive genes was tested in transient co-transfections with a reporter plasmid carrying a glucocorticoid response element linked to the chloramphenicol acetyltransferase (*CAT*) gene. As shown in Figure 10–8, cells co-transfected with the intact receptor coding sequences responded as expected: in the absence of glucocorticoid no CAT activity was detected; in the presence of glucocorticoid (dexamethasone) CAT activity was readily

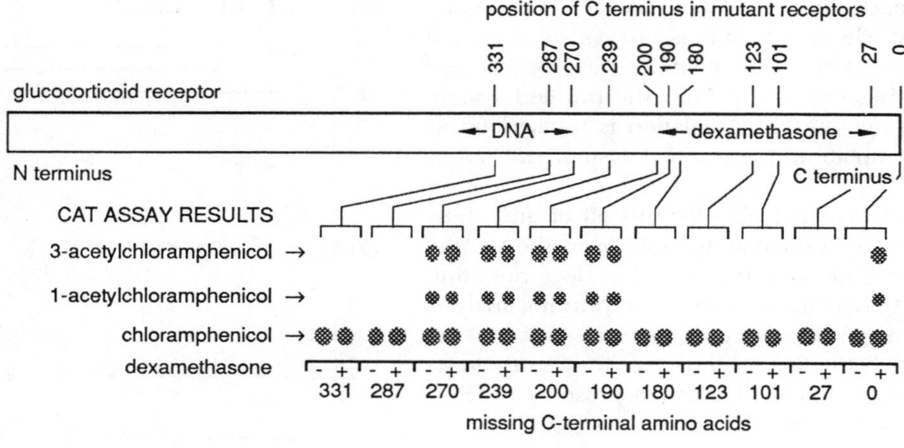

Figure 10–8 Effect of C-terminal deletions on the activity of the glucocorticoid receptor (Problem 10–13). The schematic diagram at the top illustrates the positions of the DNA binding site and the glucocorticoid binding site in the receptor, as well as the positions of the C-terminal deletions. The lower diagram shows the results of a standard CAT assay obtained by mixing cell extracts with ^{14}C-chloramphenicol: the lower spot is unreacted chloramphenicol; the upper spots show the attachment of one or two acetyl groups to chloramphenicol. The presence (+) or absence (−) of dexamethasone is indicated below appropriate lanes.

detected. Six mutant receptors, lacking 27, 101, 123, 180, 287, and 331 carboxy-terminal amino acids, failed to activate CAT expression in the presence or absence of dexamethasone. In contrast, four mutant receptors, lacking 190, 200, 239, and 270 carboxy-terminal amino acids, activated CAT expression in the presence and absence of dexamethasone. Separate experiments indicated that the mutant receptors were synthesized equally.

How do these experiments distinguish between the proposed models for hormone-dependent conversion of the normal receptor to a DNA binding form? Does hormone binding create a DNA binding site or does it uncover a preexisting DNA binding site?

The Molecular Genetic Mechanisms That Create Different Cell Types (MBOC 570–588)

10–14 Fill in the blanks in the following statements.

A. Site-specific inversion of a DNA segment in *Salmonella* with the attendant switch in the type of flagellin that is synthesized is known as ______________.

B. In yeasts, diploid cells are formed by a process known as ______________, in which two haploid cells fuse.

C. The three cell types in yeast—α, **a**, and diploid **a**/α—are controlled by the master gene regulatory proteins that are produced by the ______________ locus.

D. The switchlike mechanism that determines whether the lambda bacteriophage will multiply in the *E. coli* cytoplasm and kill its host or become integrated into the host cell DNA is controlled by two gene regulatory proteins: the lambda ______________ and the ______________.

E. Light microscopic studies in the 1930s revealed that regions of chromosomes called ______________ fail to decondense during interphase and maintain the highly condensed conformation of metaphase chromosomes.

F. In *Drosophila*, chromosomal rearrangements that place the middle of a region of heterochromatin next to a region of euchromatin tend to inactivate the nearby euchromatic gene in a process known as ______________.

G. A segment of DNA that is located 50,000 nucleotide pairs away from the globin gene cluster contains a group of six nuclease-hypersensitive sites that affects the entire cluster; it is referred to as a ______________ region.

H. In bacteria such as *E. coli* a special type II DNA topoisomerase, called ______________, uses the energy of ATP hydrolysis to pump supercoils continuously into the DNA to maintain the DNA under constant tension.

I. Vertebrate DNAs contain ____________, which has the same relation to cytosine that thymine has to uracil and likewise has no effect on base-pairing.

J. CG sequences are present at 10 to 20 times their average density in selected regions, called ____________, which surround the promoters of so-called ____________ genes.

K. ____________ genes encode proteins needed only in selected types of cells.

10–15 Indicate whether the following statements are true or false. If a statement is false, explain why.

__ A. Phase variation in *Salmonella* and *N. gonorrhoeae* occurs by gene inversion.

__ B. Mating-type switching in yeast is irreversible because the original mating-type gene at the MAT locus is discarded when it is replaced by the other mating-type gene.

__ C. The two silent mating-type genes are not transcribed at their storage locations because they lack appropriate promoter elements.

__ D. The lambda repressor protein and the cro protein can repress each other's synthesis, creating a two-state molecular switch that specifies a lysogenic state when the repressor dominates and a lytic state when the cro protein dominates.

__ E. Several of the master gene regulatory proteins of *Drosophila* stimulate their own transcription; at the same time they repress the transcription of a master gene that is expressed in a neighboring portion of the early embryo.

__ F. Facultative heterochromatin, which is localized around the centromere of each mitotic chromosome, is condensed in all cells; constitutive heterochromatin is unusually condensed during interphase in some cell types of an organism but not in others.

__ G. Because the condensed X chromosome is reactivated in the formation of germ cells in the female, no permanent change can have occurred in its DNA.

__ H. Gene control mechanisms that rely entirely on the action of diffusible regulatory proteins are sufficient to explain the heritability of heterochromatic forms of chromosome inactivation such as X inactivation.

__ I. Although the expression of transgenes is often restricted to the correct tissues, the level of transcription is generally five- to tenfold less than it should be in tissues where the gene is normally highly expressed.

__ J. The phenotypes of certain mutations suggest a two-step model of gene activation in higher eucaryotes: the first, to open up a large chromosomal domain; the second, to activate specific gene regulatory elements.

__ K. Unwinding the DNA at one specific site can produce topological effects that can be felt throughout the entire chromosome.

__ L. The maintenance methylase perpetuates the preexisting pattern of CG methylation; the establishment methylase initially sets up the pattern of CG methylation in the egg.

__ M. When 5-aza C is added briefly to cells, it is incorporated into DNA where it acts as an inhibitor of the maintenance methylase, thereby reducing the general level of methylation and activating previously unexpressed genes.

__ N. The CG islands in the promoters of housekeeping genes have been preserved during evolution because sequence-specific DNA-binding proteins protect the 5-methyl C nucleotides in the islands from accidental deamination and conversion to T nucleotides.

***10–16** It is relatively common for pathogenic organisms to change their coats periodically in order to evade the immune surveillance of their host. *Salmonella* (a bacterium that can cause food poisoning) can exist in two antigenically distinguishable forms, or phases as they were called by their discoverer in 1922. Bacteria in the two different phases synthesize different kinds of flagellin, which is the protein that makes up the flagellum. Phase 1 bacteria switch to phase 2 and vice versa about once per thousand cell divisions. Two kinds of explanation were originally considered for the switch mechanism: a DNA rearrangement, such as insertion or inversion, and a DNA modification, such as methylation.

The two flagellins responsible for phase variation are encoded by the unlinked genes, *H1* and *H2*, each of which encodes a completely functional flagellin. The genetic element that enables the bacteria to switch phases is very closely linked to the the *H2* gene. To distinguish between the mechanisms of switching, a segment of DNA containing the *H2* gene was cloned. When introduced into *E. coli* with no flagella, most bacteria that picked up the plasmid could swim, indicating that they were synthesizing the flagellin encoded by the *H2* gene. A few colonies of *E. coli*, however, were nonmotile even though they carried the plasmid. When DNA was prepared from cultures grown from these nonmotile colonies and introduced into a fresh culture of *E. coli*, some of the transformed bacteria were able to swim, indicating that H2 flagellin synthesis had been switched on.

Figure 10–9 Reannealed DNA fragments from cultures of switching *E. coli* (Problem 10–16). Arrows indicate single-stranded bubbles.

Plasmid DNA was prepared from these switching cultures, digested with a restriction enzyme, heated to separate the DNA strands, and then slowly cooled to allow DNA strands to reanneal. The DNA molecules were then examined by electron microscopy. About 5% of the molecules contained a bubble, formed by two equal-length single-stranded DNA segments, at a unique position near one end. Two examples are shown in Figure 10–9.

A. When *Salmonella* switch from synthesis of one type of flagellin to synthesis of the other, all the bacteria are able to swim. Why do *E. coli* switch between a form that is able to swim and a form that is immotile?
B. Explain how these results distinguish between a mechanism of switching that involves a DNA rearrangement and one that involves a DNA modification.
C. How do these results distinguish among site-specific DNA rearrangements that involve deletion of DNA, addition of DNA, or inversion of DNA?

10–17 One of the key regulatory proteins produced by the yeast mating-type locus is a repressor protein known as α_2 (see MBOC, Figure 10–29). In haploid cells of the α mating type, α_2 is essential for turning off a set of genes that are specific for the **a** mating type. In **a**/α diploid cells the α_2 repressor collaborates with the product of the $\mathbf{a}_1$ gene to turn off a set of haploid-specific genes in addition to the **a**-specific genes. Two distinct but related types of conserved DNA sequences are found upstream of these two sets of regulated genes: one in front of the **a**-specific genes and the other in front of the haploid-specific genes. Given the relatedness of these upstream sequences, it is most likely that α_2 binds to both; however, its binding properties must be modified in some way by the $\mathbf{a}_1$ protein before it can recognize haploid-specific sequence. You wish to understand the nature of this modification. Does $\mathbf{a}_1$ catalyze covalent modification of α_2, or does it modify α_2 by binding to it stoichiometrically?

To study these question, you perform three types of experiments. In the first, you measure the binding of $\mathbf{a}_1$ and α_2, alone and together, to the two kinds of upstream regulatory DNA sites. As shown in Figure 10–10, $\mathbf{a}_1$ alone does not bind DNA fragments that contain either regulatory site (lane 2), whereas α_2 binds to **a**-specific fragments but not to haploid-specific fragments (lane 3). The mixture of $\mathbf{a}_1$ and α_2 binds both **a**-specific and haploid-specific fragments (lane 4).

In the second series of experiments you add a vast excess of unlabeled DNA containing the **a**-specific sequence to the reaction along with the mixture of $\mathbf{a}_1$ and α_2 proteins. Under these conditions the haploid-

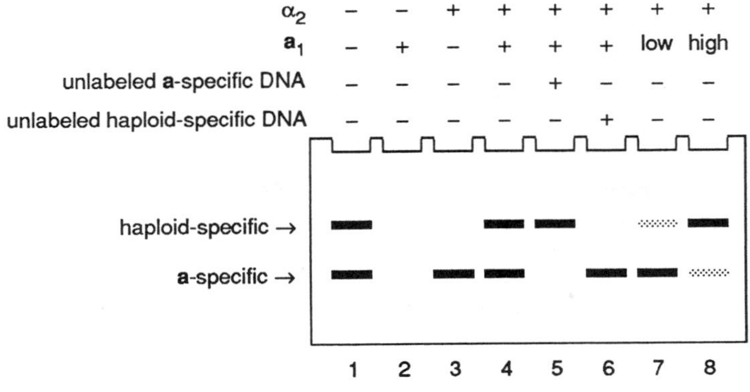

Figure 10–10 Binding of regulatory proteins to fragments of DNA containing the **a**-specific or haploid-specific regulatory sequences (Problem 10–17). Various combinations of regulatory proteins were incubated with a mixture of **a**-specific and haploid-specific radioactive DNA fragments (shown in lane 1). At the end of the incubation the samples were precipitated with antibody against the proteins and the DNA fragments in the precipitate were run on the gel. The gel was then placed against x-ray film to visualize the positions of the radioactive DNA fragments.

specific fragment is still bound (Figure 10–10, lane 5). Similarly, if you add an excess of unlabeled haploid-specific DNA to the reaction mixture, the **a**-specific fragment is still bound (lane 6).

In the third set of experiments you vary the ratio of $\mathbf{a}_1$ relative to α_2. When α_2 is in excess, binding to the haploid-specific fragment is decreased (Figure 10–10, lane 7); when $\mathbf{a}_1$ is in excess, binding to the **a**-specific fragment is decreased (lane 8).

A. In the presence of $\mathbf{a}_1$, is α_2 present in two forms with different binding specificities or in one form that can bind to both regulatory sequences? How do your experiments distinguish between these alternatives?

B. An α_2 repressor with a small deletion in its DNA-binding domain does not bind to DNA fragments containing the haploid-specific sequence. If this mutant protein is expressed in a diploid cell along with normal α_2 and $\mathbf{a}_1$ proteins, however, the haploid specific genes are turned on. (These genes are normally off in a diploid—see MBOC, Figure 10–29.) In the light of this result and your other experiments, do you consider it more likely that $\mathbf{a}_1$ catalyzes a covalent modification of α_2, or that $\mathbf{a}_1$ modifies α_2 by binding to it stoichiometrically to form an $\mathbf{a}_1\ \alpha_2$ complex?

10–18 You have discovered a new strain of yeast with a novel mating system. There are two haploid mating types, called M and F. Cells of opposite mating type can mate to form M/F diploid cells. These diploids can undergo meiosis and sporulate, but they cannot mate with each other or with either haploid mating type.

Your genetic analysis of the strains shows there are four genes that control mating type. When the genes *M1* and *M2* are at the mating-type locus, the cells are mating-type M; when the genes *F1* and *F2* are at the mating-type locus, the cells are mating-type F. You have also identified a set of genes that are expressed specifically in M-type haploids (Msg), a set of F-specific genes (Fsg), and a set of sporulation-specific genes (Ssg). You obtain mutants that are defective in each of the mating-type genes (all the mutants are viable) and study their effects on the mating phenotype and on expression of the different sets of specific genes they express. Your results with haploid and diploid cells containing different combinations of mutants are shown in Table 10–3.

Suggest a regulatory scheme to explain how the *M1*, *M2*, *F1*, and *F2* gene products control the expression of the M-specific, F-specific, and sporulation-specific sets of genes. Indicate which gene products are activators and which are repressors of transcription, and decide whether the gene products act alone and/or in combination.

10–19 You are interested to know whether a transcriptional complex can remain bound to the DNA during DNA replication. If it could, it might serve as a sort of biological memory that would allow daughter cells to inherit the parental pattern of gene expression. You have just the system to test this idea. You can assemble an active transcription complex on the *Xenopus*

Table 10–3 Phenotypes of Mutants That Affect Mating in a New Strain of Yeast (Problem 10–18)

	Mutant	Mating Phenotype	Genes Expressed
Haploid cells	wild type M	M	Msg
	$M1^-$	nonmating	Msg, Fsg
	$M2^-$	M	Msg
	$M1^-$, $M2^-$	nonmating	Msg, Fsg
	wild type F	F	Fsg
	$F1^-$	F	Fsg
	$F2^-$	nonmating	Fsg, Msg
	$F1^-$, $F2^-$	nonmating	Fsg, Msg
Diploid cells	wild type M,F	nonmating	Ssg
	$M1^-/F1^-$	F	Fsg
	$M1^-/F2^-$	nonmating	Msg, Fsg, Ssg
	$M2^-/F1^-$	nonmating	none
	$M2^-/F2^-$	M	Msg

Msg, M-specific genes; Fsg, F-specific genes; Ssg, sporulation-specific genes

5S RNA gene carried on a plasmid, induce its replication, and then test for transcription from the replicated genes. You are able to carry out all these steps *in vitro*.

To distinguish between replicated and unreplicated templates, you take advantage of restriction enzymes (DpnI, MboI, and Sau3A) that are sensitive to the methylation state of their recognition sequence GATC (Figure 10–11A). This sequence is present once at the beginning of the 5S RNA gene and, if the DNA is cleaved at this site, no transcription occurs. If the template is grown in wild-type *E. coli*, GATC will be methylated at the A on both strands by the bacterial *dam* methylase. Replication of fully methylated DNA *in vitro* generates daughter duplexes that are methylated only on one strand (hemimethylated) in the first round and unmethylated DNA in subsequent rounds. Your idea is to start with fully methylated DNA and induce its replication *in vitro*. You can then assay transcription from the replicated DNA by treating the DNA with DpnI, which cuts unreplicated DNA (which is fully methylated) thus preventing its transcription, but does not cut replicated DNA (which is hemimethylated or unmethylated).

To test whether the analytical part of your scheme will work, you construct a slightly longer than normal 5S RNA gene (maxigene), whose RNA transcript can be distinguished from that of the normal 5S RNA gene (Figure 10–11A). You then prepare mixtures of the fully methylated maxigene with either the hemimethylated or unmethylated normal gene and test their transcription before and after digestion with DpnI, MboI, and Sau3A. The specificity of the restriction enzymes is shown in Figure 10–11A and the results of the transcription experiments are shown in Figure 10–11B.

To test the effect of replication on transcription, you assemble transcription complexes on the fully methylated maxigene, induce replication, and assay transcriptional activity before and after cleavage with restriction enzymes. The results are shown in Figure 10–11B.

A. Does the methylation status of the 5S RNA gene affect its transcription? Explain your answer.
B. Does the pattern of transcription after cleavage with the various restriction enzymes match your expectations? Explain your answer.
C. In your experiment about half of the DNA molecules were replicated. Does the pattern of transcription after replication and cleavage indicate that

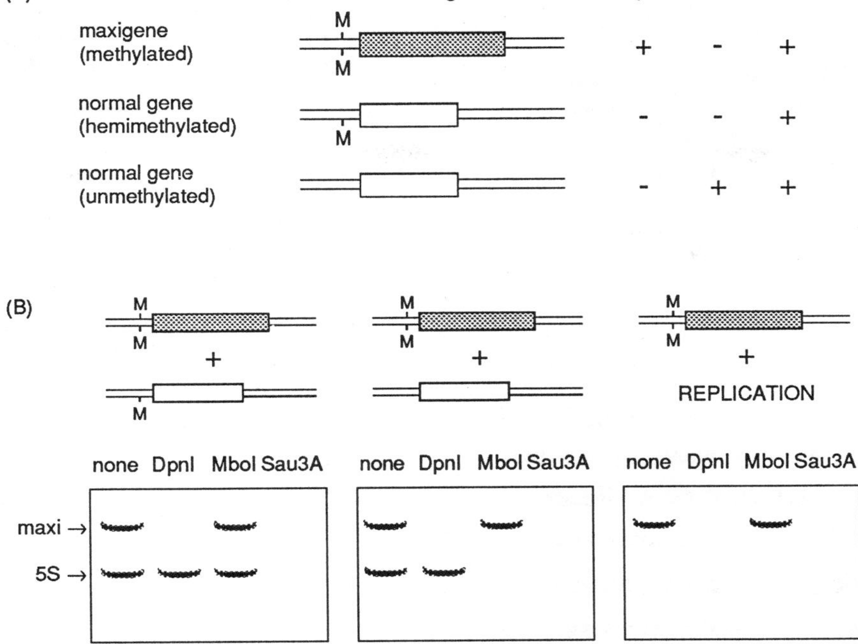

Figure 10–11 Sensitivity of 5S RNA genes in different methylation states (A) and transcriptional activity with and without replication (B) (Problem 10–19). The 5S RNA maxigene is shaded and the normal gene is white. M indicates that a strand is methylated. Sensitivity to cleavage by a restriction enzyme is indicated by (+), insensitivity is indicated by (−). In (B) the positions of the RNA transcripts from the normal 5S RNA gene and the maxigene are indicated by arrows.

the transcription complex remains bound to the 5S RNA gene during replication?

D. In these experiments you were careful to show that greater than 90% of the molecules were assembled into active transcription complexes and that 50% of the molecules were replicated. How would the pattern have changed if only 50% of the molecules were assembled into active transcription complexes? Would your conclusions have changed?

***10–20** You are studying the role of DNA methylation in the control of gene expression using the human γ-globin gene as a test system. Globin mRNA can be detected when this gene is incorporated into the genome of mouse fibroblasts, although at much lower levels than in red cells. If the gene is first methylated at all 27 CG sites, however, its expression is blocked completely. You are using this system to decide whether a single critical methylation site is sufficient to determine globin expression.

You use a combination of site-directed mutagenesis and primed synthesis in the presence of 5-methyl dCTP to create several different γ-globin constructs that are unmethylated in various regions of the gene. These constructs are illustrated in Figure 10–12, with the methylated regions shown in black. The arrangement of six methylation sites around the promoter is shown below the constructs. Sites 11, 12, and 13 are unmethylated in construct E, sites 14, 15, and 16 are unmethylated in construct D, and all six sites are unmethylated in construct F. You incorporate these constructs into mouse fibroblasts, grow cell lines containing individual constructs, and measure γ-globin RNA synthesis relative to cell lines containing the fully unmethylated construct (Figure 10–12B).

To check whether the methylation patterns were correctly inherited, you isolate DNA samples from cell lines containing constructs B, C, and F and digest them with HindIII plus CfoI or HpaII. CfoI and HpaII do not cleave if their recognition sites are methylated. The cleavage sites for these enzymes are shown in Figure 10–12A along with the sizes of relevant restriction fragments larger than 1 kb. You separate the cleaved DNA samples on a gel and visualize them by hybridization to the radiolabeled HindIII fragment (Figure 10–13).

A. To create some of the methylated DNA substrates you used a single-

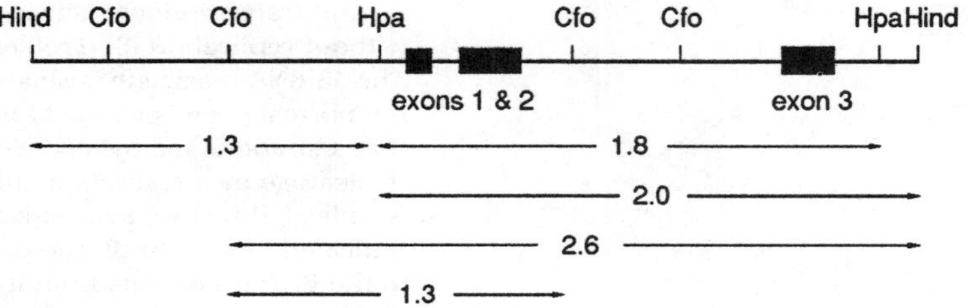

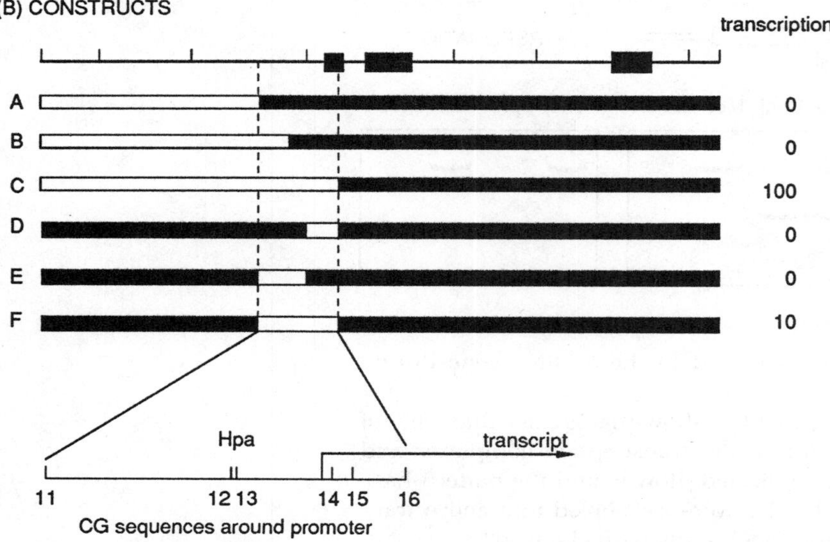

Figure 10–12 Effects of methylation on transcription of the γ-globin gene (Problem 10–20). (A) HindIII fragment containing the γ-globin gene. Sites of cleavage of the methylation-sensitive restriction enzymes, CfoI and HpaII, are indicated along with the sizes of the larger fragments that are observed on the gel in Figure 10–13. (B) Methylated constructs of the γ-globin gene. The methylated segments of the gene are shown in black. The six CG sites around the promoter are shown in more detail below the constructs. The level of expression of γ-globin RNA from each construct is shown on the right as a percentage of the expression from a fully unmethylated construct.

stranded version of the gene as a template and primed synthesis of the second strand using 5-methyl dCTP instead of dCTP in the reaction. This method creates a DNA molecule containing 5-methyl C in place of C in one strand. After isolation of colonies containing such constructs, you find they have 5-methyl C on both strands but only at CG sequences. Explain the retention of 5-methyl C in CG sequences and their loss elsewhere.

B. Do the restriction patterns of the constructs in the isolated cell lines (Figure 10–13) indicate that the CG sequences that were methylated during creation of the constructs (Figure 10–12) were maintained in the cell?

C. Does the γ-globin RNA synthesis associated with the cell lines containing the various constructs (Figure 10–12) indicate that a single critical site of methylation determines whether the gene is expressed?

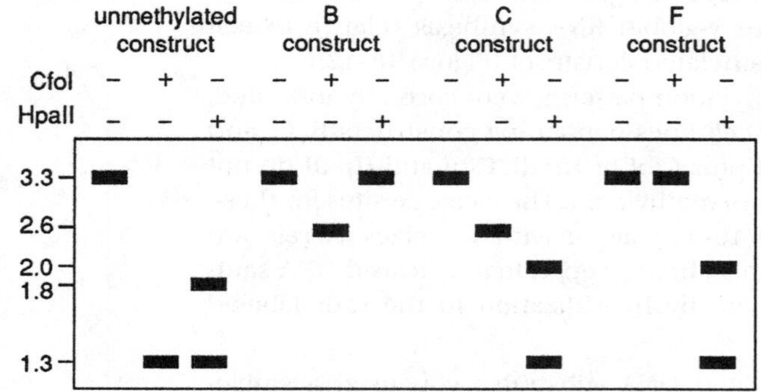

Figure 10–13 Restriction patterns from cell lines containing constructs B, C, and F (Problem 10–20). HindIII was included in all digests. Fragments less than 1 kb are not shown.

Posttranscriptional Controls (MBOC 588–599)

10–21 Fill in the blanks in the following statements.

A. The premature termination of transcription of an RNA molecule as a means for controlling gene expression is known as ____________.

B. Many genes in higher eucaryotes produce several different spliced mRNAs from a single primary transcript by means of ____________.

C. Different proteins of comparable function that are produced from mRNAs derived from a single primary RNA transcript as a result of alternative splicing are called ____________.

D. A ____________ is any DNA sequence that is transcribed as a single unit and encodes one or a set of closely related polypeptide chains or structural RNA molecules.

E. The translation of ferritin mRNA molecules is blocked by proteins that bind to their 5′ ends in the absence of iron; this is an example of ____________ control.

F. ____________ control may be mediated through special sequences in the mRNA that preferentially attract ribosomes.

G. ____________, which is common in retroviruses, allows different amounts of two or more proteins to be synthesized from a single mRNA.

H. In some instances the actual sequence of nucleotides in a primary RNA transcript is altered in a process known as ____________.

10–22 Indicate whether the following statements are true or false. If a statement is false, explain why.

__ A. In procaryotes and eucaryotes transcriptional attenuation is mediated by ribosomes that have stalled during translation of the nascent RNA chain.

__ B. Although the exon changes caused by alternative RNA splicing usually produce related proteins, there are exceptions in which two entirely different proteins are produced.

__ C. The P element of *Drosophila* transposes in germ cells but not in somatic cells because somatic cells fail to remove a particular intron from the transposase mRNA.

__ D. A change in the site of RNA transcript cleavage and poly-A addition can change the carboxyl terminus of a protein only by adding (or subtracting) amino acids.

__ E. Late in adenovirus infection the transport of host-cell RNAs from the nucleus is blocked, so that most of the RNAs that reach the cytoplasm are encoded by the adenovirus genome.

__ F. The binding of iron to the iron-response element at the 5′ end of ferritin mRNA increases the stability of the mRNA, thereby allowing increased numbers of ferritin molecules to be synthesized in response to increased levels of iron.

__ G. Eucaryotic mRNAs with unusually long 5′ leader sequences containing extra AUGs may require the binding of translation-activator molecules to a translation-enhancer sequence adjacent to the appropriate AUG for initiation.

__ H. Since all maternal mRNAs in clam eggs are translated *in vitro* if stripped of their associated proteins, regulatory molecules must account for the absence of translation of some classes of maternal mRNAs in the egg.

__ I. Transferrin receptor mRNA stability and ferritin mRNA translatability are mediated by the same iron-sensitive RNA-binding protein; in both cases binding of the protein to the mRNA increases the level of the encoded protein.

__ J. In the RNA transcripts that code for proteins in the mitochondria of trypanosomes, one or more U nucleotides are either added or removed from selected regions of a transcript, thereby altering the meaning of the message.

__ K. Many of the RNA-catalyzed reactions in present-day cells may represent molecular fossils—descendants of the complex network of RNA-mediated reactions that are presumed to have dominated cellular metabolism in the beginning.

10–23 The segmentation of eucaryotic genes into exons and introns presents an opportunity for the production of multiple gene products from a single gene by alternative RNA processing. Developmental programs often use differential splicing or differential polyadenylation to produce tissue-specific variants from a single transcription unit.

The gene encoding the small peptide hormone calcitonin is one such differentially utilized gene. The calcitonin gene contains six exons. In thyroid cells an mRNA that encodes calcitonin is produced; it contains exons 1, 2, 3, and 4 and uses a polyadenylation site at the end of exon 4. In neuronal cells no calcitonin is produced from this gene. Instead, calcitonin gene-related peptide (CGRP) is produced; its mRNA consists of exons 1, 2, 3, 5, and 6. The gene and its tissue-specific pattern of processing are diagrammed in Figure 10–14. In both cell types transcription begins in the same place and extends beyond exon 6.

The mechanism of differential processing of the calcitonin/CGRP transcript is not understood. Because different poly-A sites and different splice sites are utilized in the two processing pathways, the tissue-specific factors that regulate calcitonin and CGRP expression could be involved either in polyadenylation or in splicing. There are two popular models. One is that thyroid cells produce calcitonin because they contain a specific factor that recognizes the poly-A site in exon 4 with high efficiency and causes cleavage of the precursor RNA before splicing of exon 3 to exon 5 can occur. Neuronal cells lack this factor with the result that splicing of exon 3 to exon 5 predominates, leading to CGRP mRNA production. A second model is that splice-site selection determines which RNA is produced. Thyroid cells produce calcitonin because they splice exon 3 to exon 4; neuronal cells produce CGRP because they splice exon 3 to exon 5. Presumably, one or both cell types produce a factor that favors one splice over the other.

To test these hypotheses, the splicing and polyadenylation signals at the ends of exon 4 were altered by mutation (Figure 10–14). The altered genes were transfected into a lymphocyte cell line, which produces only calcitonin from the wild-type gene. The mutant lacking the exon-4 polyadenylation site produced no mRNA at all; the mutant lacking the exon-4 splice site produced only CGRP mRNA.

A. Does the lymphocyte cell line contain the splicing and polyadenylation factors necessary to produce both calcitonin and CGRP mRNAs?
B. If differential processing results from polyadenylation-site selection, which mutant would you expect to produce CGRP mRNA when transfected into the lymphocyte cell line?
C. If differential processing results from splice-site selection, which mutant would you expect to produce CGRP mRNA when transfected into the lymphocyte cell line?
D. Which model for differential processing best explains the ability of the lymphocyte cell line to produce calcitonin mRNA but not CGRP mRNA?

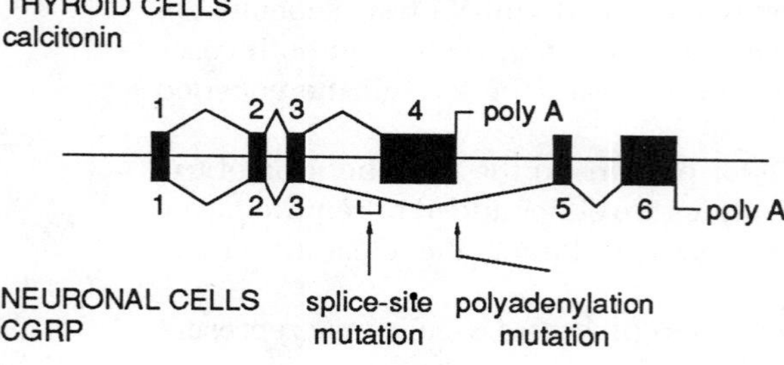

Figure 10–14 Structure and tissue-specific splicing of the gene encoding calcitonin and CGRP (Problem 10–23). Black boxes indicate exons. The splicing/polyadenylation choices used to produce calcitonin are diagrammed above the line; those used to produce CGRP, below the line. Arrows mark the positions of the splice-site and polyadenylation mutations.

Table 10–4 Synthesis of Ferritin in the Rat After Various Treatments (Problem 10–24)

Injection	Actinomycin D	Fraction	Total Synthesis	Ferritin Synthesis
Saline	absent	polysomes	750,000	700
		supernatant	255,000	1400
Iron	absent	polysomes	500,000	900
		supernatant	400,000	500
Saline	present	polysomes	800,000	800
		supernatant	600,000	3000
Iron	present	polysomes	780,000	1380
		supernatant	550,000	700

Numbers show radioactivity (cpm) incorporated into total proteins or into ferritin.

10–24 Ferritin is the protein that stores iron in many tissues. The synthesis of ferritin increases up to twofold in the presence of iron. You wish to define the molecular mechanism for this induction of ferritin synthesis. In particular, you wish to know whether regulation is transcriptional or posttranscriptional.

You carry out a series of experiments in which rats are given an injection of iron (as a ferric salt solution) or an injection of saline with or without simultaneous administration of actinomycin D (which is a powerful inhibitor of RNA synthesis). Three hours later the rats are sacrificed, their livers are homogenized, and polysomal and supernatant fractions are prepared. RNA is then extracted from each fraction and translated in a cell-free system in the presence of radioactive amino acids. You measure total protein synthesis by incorporation of label into protein, and you measure the synthesis of ferritin by precipitation using ferritin-specific antibodies (Table 10–4).

A. For each sample calculate the percentage of total protein synthesis that is due to synthesis of ferritin. Given that 85% of the bulk mRNA is bound to ribosomes in the polysomal fraction and 15% is free (in the supernatant fraction), determine the percentage of total ferritin mRNA in the polysomal and supernatant fractions under each condition of treatment. (Assume that the percentages of polysomal and supernatant mRNA are not changed by treatment with actinomycin D.)

B. How do your results distinguish between transcriptional and posttranscriptional control of ferritin synthesis by iron?

C. How would you account for the twofold increase in ferritin synthesis in the presence of iron?

10–25 A very active cell-free protein synthesis system can be prepared from reticulocytes, which are immature red blood cells that have already lost their nucleus but still contain ribosomes. A reticulocyte lysate can translate each globin mRNA many times provided heme is added. Heme serves two functions: it is required for assembly into hemoglobin, and, surprisingly, it is required to maintain a high rate of protein synthesis. If heme is omitted, protein synthesis stops after a brief lag (Figure 10–15).

The first clue to the molecular basis for the effect of heme on globin synthesis came from a simple experiment. A reticulocyte lysate was incubated for several hours in the absence of heme. When 5 μl of this preincubated lysate were then added to 100 μl of a fresh lysate in the presence of heme, protein synthesis was rapidly inhibited (Figure 10–15). When further characterized, the inhibitor (termed heme-controlled repressor or HCR) was shown to be a protein with a molecular weight of

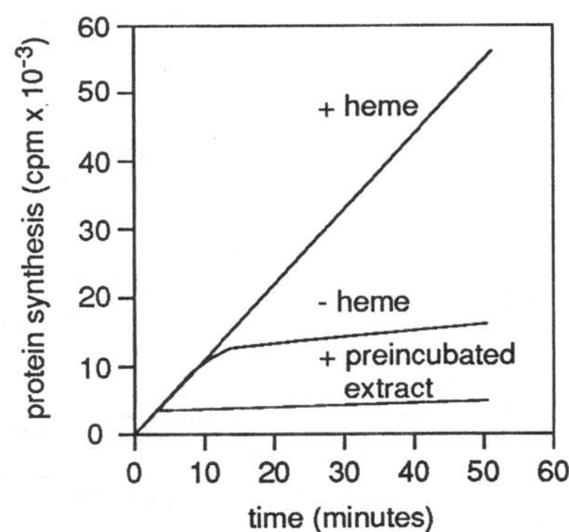

Figure 10–15 Protein synthesis in a reticulocyte lysate (Problem 10–25).

180,000. Pure preparations of HCR at a concentration of 1 μg/ml completely inhibit protein synthesis in a fresh, heme-supplemented lysate.

A. Calculate the ratio of HCR molecules to ribosomes and globin mRNA at the concentration of HCR that inhibits protein synthesis. Reticulocyte lysates contain 1 mg/ml ribosomes (molecular weight, 4 million), and the average polysome contains 4 ribosomes per globin mRNA.

B. Do the results of this calculation favor a catalytic or a stoichiometric mechanism for HCR inhibition of protein synthesis in a reticulocyte lysate?

***10–26** The level of tubulin gene expression is established in cells by an unusual regulatory pathway in which the intracellular concentration of free tubulin dimers (composed of one α-tubulin and one β-tubulin subunit) regulates the rate of new tubulin synthesis. The initial evidence for such an autoregulatory pathway came from studies with drugs that cause assembly or disassembly of all cellular tubulin. For example, when cells are treated with colchicine, which causes microtubule depolymerization into tubulin subunits, there is a tenfold repression of tubulin synthesis. This autoregulation of tubulin synthesis by tubulin dimers occurs not at the level of transcription but, rather, at the level of tubulin mRNA stability. The first 12 nucleotides of the coding portion of the mRNA were found to contain the site responsible for this autoregulatory control.

Since the critical segment of the mRNA involves a coding region, it is not clear whether the regulation of mRNA stability results from an interaction of free tubulin dimers with the RNA or with the nascent protein. Either interaction might plausibly trigger a nuclease that would destroy the mRNA.

These two possibilities were tested by mutagenizing the regulatory region on a cloned version of the gene. The mutant genes were then transfected into cells and the stability of their mRNAs was assayed when the intracellular concentration of free tubulin dimers was increased. The results from a dozen mutants that affect a short region of the mRNA are shown in Figure 10–16.

Does the regulation of tubulin mRNA stability result from an interaction with the RNA or from an interaction with the encoded protein? Explain the reasoning behind your answer.

```
   M  R  E  I    regulation
--ATGAGGGAAATC--     +
-----T----------     –
-----C----------     +
------C---------     –
-------A--------     +
--------T-------     –
---------G------     –
----------G-----     +
-----TA---------     –
-----C-C--------     +
-----G--A-------     –
-----G---T------     –
-----C----G-----     +
```

Figure 10–16 Effects of mutations on the regulation of tubulin mRNA stability (Problem 10–26). The wild-type sequence for the first twelve nucleotides of the coding portion of the gene is shown at the top, and the first 4 encoded amino acids beginning with methionine (M) are indicated above the codons. The nucleotide changes in the twelve mutants are shown below; only the altered nucleotides are indicated. Regulation of mRNA stability is shown on the right: (+) indicates wild-type response to changes in intracellular tubulin concentration and (–) indicates no response to changes.

10–27 The *c-fos* gene is the cellular homolog of the oncogene carried by the FBJ murine osteosarcoma virus. Its function is unknown. Activation of *c-fos* is one of the earliest transcriptional responses to growth factors: the *c-fos* transcription rate in mouse cells increases markedly within 5 minutes, reaches a maximum by 10 to 15 minutes, and abruptly decreases thereafter.

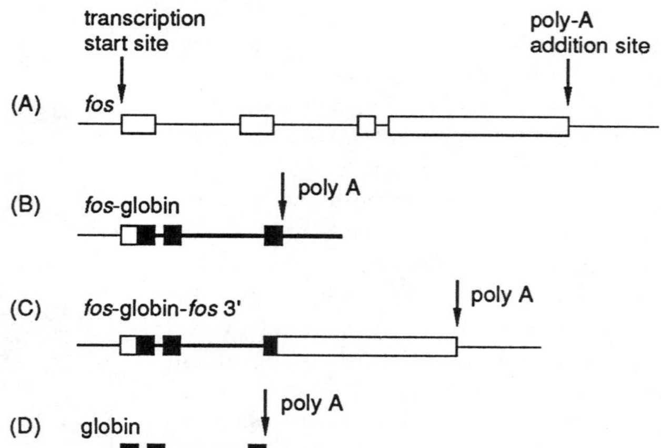

Figure 10–17 Structures of the human *c-fos* gene and the hybrid genes of *c-fos* with the human β-globin gene (Problem 10–27). Open boxes denote *c-fos* exons, black boxes denote β-globin exons. The junctions between *fos* and globin sequences in the hybrid genes are located in exons.

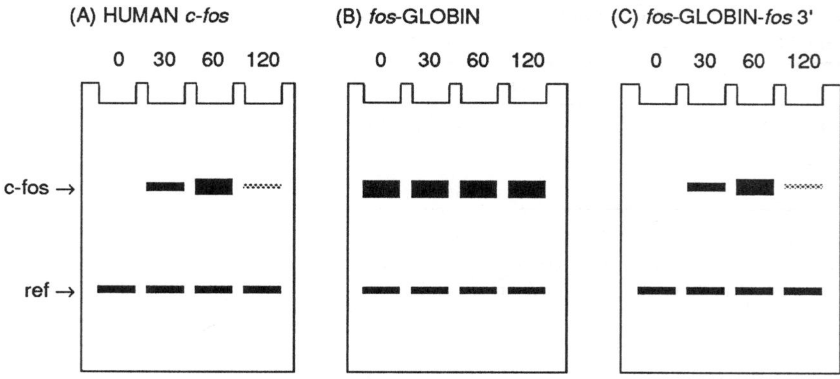

Figure 10–18 Responses of *c-fos* and hybrid genes to addition of serum (Problem 10–27). The upper band in each gel is the transcript containing *c-fos* sequences. The lower band is a reference transcript (to control for recoveries of RNA) from a gene that does not respond to serum addition.

To study the mechanism of transient induction of the human *c-fos* gene, you clone a DNA fragment that contains the complete transcription unit starting 750 nucleotides upstream of the transcription start site and ending 1.5 kb downstream of the poly-A addition site (Figure 10–17A). When you transfect this cloned segment into mouse cells (so you can distinguish the human *c-fos* mRNA from the endogenous cell product) and stimulate cell growth one day later by adding serum (a rich source of growth factors), you observe the same sort of transient induction, although the timescale is slightly longer than for the mouse gene (Figure 10–18A).

You show by analyzing a series of deletion mutants that an enhancerlike element (SRE, serum response element) 300 nucleotides upstream of the transcription start site is necessary for increased transcription in response to serum. You also investigate the stability of the *c-fos* mRNA by creating various hybrid genes containing portions of the human β-globin gene, which encodes a very stable mRNA. The structures of the globin gene and two of the hybrid genes are shown in Figure 10–17B, C, and D. When the hybrid genes are transfected into mouse cells in low serum, they respond to serum added 24 hours later as indicated in Figure 10–18B and C.

A. Which portion of the *c-fos* gene confers instability on *c-fos* mRNA?
B. The *fos*-globin hybrid gene carries all the normal *c-fos* regulatory elements, including the SRE, and yet the mRNA is present at time zero (24 hours after transfection but before serum addition) and does not increase appreciably after serum addition. Can you account for this behavior in terms of mRNA stability?

***10–28** Two closely related forms of apolipoprotein B (apo-B) are found in blood as constituents of the plasma lipoproteins. In humans, apo-B100 is synthesized in the liver and is necessary for the assembly of very low density lipoproteins (VLDL) and for the transport of endogenously synthesized triglycerides. Apo-B48 is synthesized by the intestine and is essential for chylomicron formation and for absorption and transport of dietary cholesterol and triglycerides. Several studies indicate that apo-B48 represents the amino-terminal half of apo-B100. What is the relationship between these two gene products? Are they produced from different genes, or are they produced from the same gene by tissue-specific processing of the RNA or tissue-specific cleavage of the protein?

Using recombinant DNA techniques, cDNA copies of the mRNA in human liver and human intestinal cells were cloned. Characterization of several clones from each tissue revealed a single difference: cDNAs from intestinal cells had a T, as part of a stop codon, at a point where the cDNAs from liver cells had a C, as part of a glutamine codon (Figure 10–19). To test for these presumptive differences in the mRNA more directly and to search for corresponding differences in the genome, the PCR (poly-

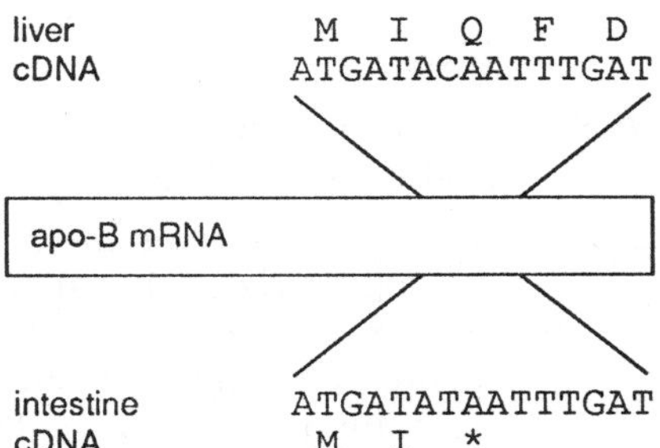

Figure 10–19 The location of the sequence differences in cDNA clones from apo-B RNA isolated from liver and intestine (Problem 10–28). The encoded amino-acid sequences indicated are above the cDNA sequences.

Table 10–5 Hybridization of Specific Oligonucleotides to the Amplified Segments from Liver and Intestine RNA and DNA (Problem 10–28)

	RNA		DNA	
	Liver	**Intestine**	**Liver**	**Intestine**
oligo-Q	+	–	+	+
oligo-STOP	–	+	–	–

The oligonucleotide complementary to the sequence derived from liver cDNA is oligo-Q: the oligonucleotide complementary to the intestinal cDNA sequence is oligo-STOP. Hybridizations were carried out under very stringent conditions so that a single nucleotide mismatch was sufficient to prevent hybridization.

merase chain reaction) technique was used to amplify the region that contains the alteration. RNA and DNA were isolated from intestinal cells and from liver cells and then subjected to PCR amplification using oligonucleotides that flank the region of interest. The resulting amplified DNA segments from each of the four samples were tested for the alteration directly by hybridization to oligonucleotides containing either the liver cDNA sequence (oligo-Q) or the intestinal cDNA sequence (oligo-STOP). The results are shown in Table 10–5.

How do these results distinguish among the possibilites for the tissue-specific production of apo-B100 in liver cells and apo-B48 in intestinal cells? Are the two forms of apo-B produced by transcriptional control from two different genes, by a processing control of the RNA transcript from a single gene, or by differential cleavage of the protein product from a single gene?

The Organization and Evolution of the Nuclear Genome (MBOC 599–609)

10–29 Fill in the blanks in the following statements.

A. Tandem repeats of simple sequence are called ____________ because the first DNAs of this type to be discovered had an unusual ratio of nucleotides that made it possible to separate them from the bulk of the cell's DNA as a minor component.

B. Some ____________ move from place to place within chromosomes directly as DNA, while many others move via an RNA intermediate.

C. The nearly simultaneous transposition of several types of transposable elements, called ____________, can produce cataclysmic changes in the genome.

D. Two transposable DNA sequences seem to have overrun the human genome: the longer ____________, which accounts for about 4% of our DNA, and the shorter ____________, which accounts for about 5% of our DNA.

10–30 Indicate whether the following statements are true or false. If a statement is false, explain why.

__ A. In any given species the functions of most genes have probably already been optimized with respect to variation by point mutation.

__ B. Tandemly repeated functional genes tend to remain the same due to unequal crossing over and gene conversion; however, the sequences of the nonfunctional spacer DNA between such genes tend to drift apart rapidly.

__ C. The separation of duplicated genes with distinct functions probably helps to stabilize them by protecting them from the homogenizing processes that act on closely linked genes of similar DNA sequence.

__ D. Long introns between exons provide an increased opportunity for recombination to duplicate exons or link exons from different genes.

__ E. The absence of introns in procaryotic genes indicates that introns were added to the eucaryotic line some time after the evolutionary separation of procaryotes and eucaryotes.

— F. Satellite DNA sequences are generally not transcribed and are most often located in the heterochromatin associated with the centromeric regions of chromosomes.

— G. Although transposable elements are common in the genomes of higher eucaryotes, they move so rarely that they contribute very little to the variability of a species.

— H. The organization of higher eucaryotic genomes—long noncoding segments and short coding segments—and the regulation of transcription from great distances mean that movements of transposable elements will usually affect gene expression rather than disrupt coding sequences.

— I. By simultaneously changing several properties of an organism, transposition bursts increase the probability that two new traits that are useful in combination will appear in a single individual in a population.

— J. Since *Alu* sequences are transcribed by RNA polymerase II, their continued movement in the genome depends on their insertion in the vicinity of a polymerase II promoter.

10–31 The slow change in frequency of neutral mutations in the gene pool of a species ensures that there will often be several slightly different forms of an individual gene represented in the population as a whole. Some mutations alter or eliminate the function of the encoded product; consequently, they can cause genetic disease. Other mutations, usually outside of critical coding regions, create restriction-site differences that lead to restriction-fragment-length polymorphisms (RFLPs). RFLPs can be used to follow the inheritance of specific chromosomal regions. Under certain circumstances, RFLPs that are near a defective gene can be used to determine whether the deleterious gene is present in an unborn child.

A concerned couple has come to you for genetic counseling. Their second child died shortly after birth from an inherited genetic disease, and the mother is pregnant again. The deceased child was the second individual in the family lineage to be affected: a brother of the paternal grandmother of the child was the other. The couple wish to know whether their unborn child has this genetic disease. You have studied the genetics of this autosomal recessive disease and are the recognized world's expert. The chromosomal region, in which the disease gene is located, has several restriction-site polymorphisms within the population as a whole, as indicated in Figure 10–20A. The restriction-site polymorphisms in the population are indicated with a +/− designation.

Figure 10–20 Restriction map (A) of the chromosomal region carrying the disease gene and restriction patterns (B) from various family members (Problem 10–31). The polymorphic sites are labeled A, B, and C. Numbers represent kb. In the family tree circles represent females, squares represent males, and the triangle indicates the unborn child.

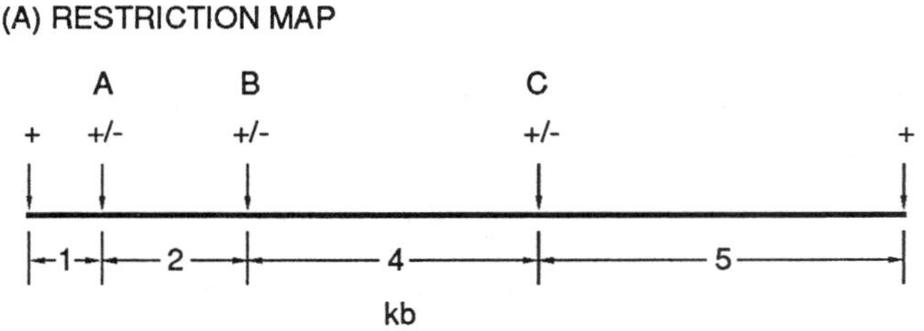

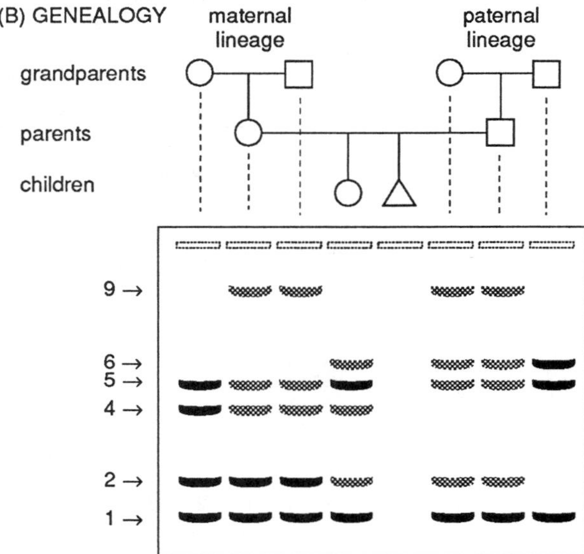

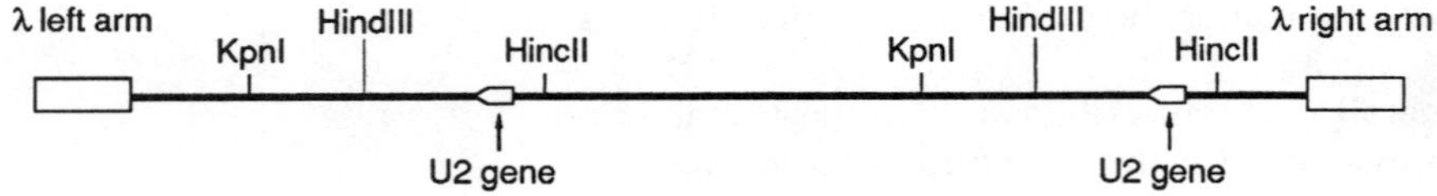

Figure 10–21 Restriction map of a bacteriophage lambda clone carrying two U2 genes (Problem 10–32).

You isolate DNA samples from both parents, both sets of grandparents, and the unaffected child and characterize them by restriction mapping, as shown in Figure 10–20B. You are now ready to test the fetus. What restriction pattern will indicate to you that the fetus is likely to have inherited the disease?

***10–32** You are interested in the genes that encode the human U2 small nuclear RNA (U2 snRNA), which is present at thousands of copies per nucleus and plays an important role in mRNA processing. Using radioactive U2 snRNA, you have isolated a bacteriophage lambda clone that carries two copies of the U2 gene, which are located 6 kb apart. The restriction map of this clone is shown in Figure 10–21. When you cut human genomic DNA to completion with HindIII, HincII (H2), or KpnI (K) and analyze the restriction digest by blot hybridization against the U2 gene, you detect a single intense band at 6 kb (Figure 10–22, lanes 9 to 11). If you cut genomic DNA with BglII (B), EcoRI (R), or XbaI (X), which do not cut the cloned genes (Figure 10–21), you also detect a single, intense band, but of a size greater than 50 kb (Figure 10–22, lanes 1 to 3). If you incubate the genomic DNA with HindIII and remove samples at various times, you see a ladder of bands (lanes 4 to 9). If you cut 2 ng of the cloned DNA with KpnI and run it alongside 10 μg of the genomic KpnI digest, two bands are visible—each of equal intensity to the the 6-kb band from the genomic digest (compare lanes 11 and 12).

A. Explain how the restriction digests define the organization of the U2 genes in the human genome.
B. Why are two bands visible in the digest of the cloned DNA (lane 12), whereas only one is visible in the digest of genomic DNA (lane 11)?
C. Given that 2 ng of cloned DNA produces a band of equal intensity to that from 10 μg of genomic DNA (lanes 11 and 12), calculate how many copies of the U2 gene there are in the human genome. (The bacteriophage lambda clone is 43 kb, and the human genome is 3 million kb.)

***10–33** Color vision in humans is mediated by three different visual pigments that absorb light in the red, green, and blue part of the visible spectrum. Loss of any one of these pigments causes color blindness. Surprisingly, about 8% of all males have X-linked color vision defects that involve the

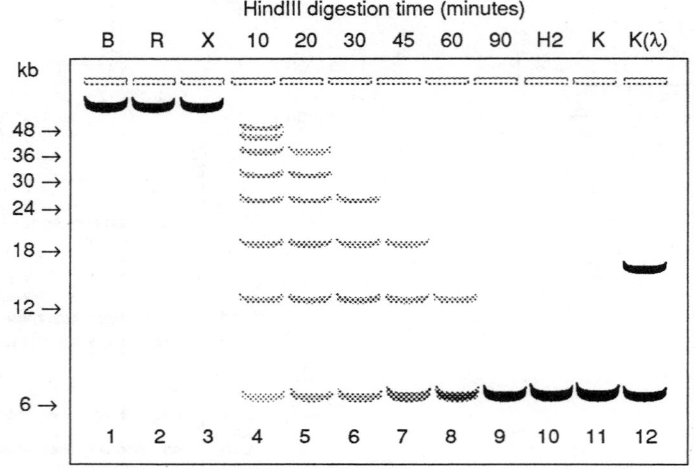

Figure 10–22 Autoradiograph of various restriction digests of human genomic DNA probed with a radiolabeled U2 gene (Problem 10–32). Numbers under HindIII indicate time of digestion in minutes. B is BglII; R is EcoRI; X is XbaI; H2 is HincII; K is KpnI. K(λ) indicates cloned DNA that was digested with KpnI.

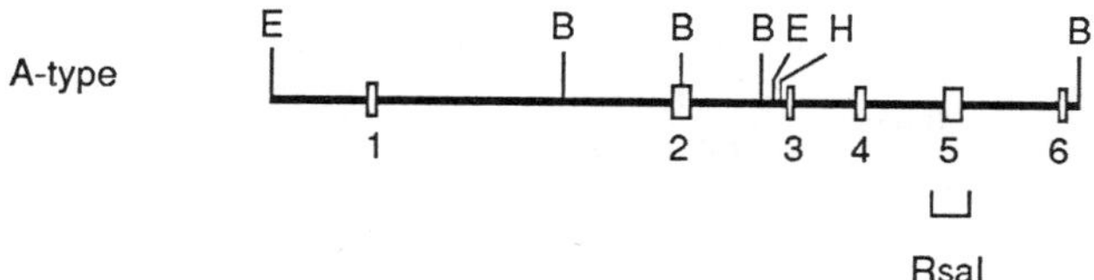

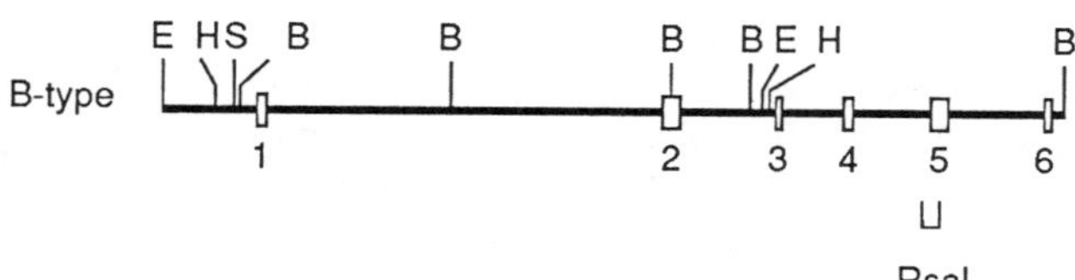

Figure 10–23 Restriction maps of A-type and B-type visual pigment genes (Problem 10–33). Exons are shown as small open boxes. RFLPs generated by RsaI digestion are indicated below the genes. E is EcoRI, B is BamHI, H is HindIII, and S is SalI.

red or green pigments. Blue color blindness, which is autosomal, is extremely rare.

The human genes for the visual pigments were found by searching for homologues of a cloned bovine rhodopsin gene, which encodes the visual pigment that mediates black and white vision in retinal rod cells. Four types of genes were identified: the rhodopsin gene and three others—one autosomal and two X-linked—that encode proteins that are structurally very similar to rhodopsin. The two genes on the X chromosome, which presumably encode the red and green pigments, are 98% identical throughout most of their length, in both exons and introns. Restriction maps of the two genes (A-type and B-type) are shown in Figure 10–23. The genes can be distinguished by restriction-fragment-length polymorphisms (RFLPs), one of which (generated by digestion with RsaI) is shown below the genes in Figure 10–23. To test whether these genes encode the red and green pigments, several normal, red-blind, and green-blind males were screened using a hybridization probe specific for the RsaI RFLP (Figure 10–24).

The surprising variability in the apparent number of A-type genes was investigated by digesting the DNA from selected individuals with NotI (which cleaves at very rare sites), separating the long restriction fragments by pulse-field gel electrophoresis, and hybridizing with a probe that recognizes both genes (Figure 10–25).

A. Which gene encodes the red visual pigment, and which encodes the green visual pigment?
B. Genetic studies indicate that the genes encoding the red and green visual pigments are close together on the X chromosome. How do the above experiments prove that these genes are physically linked?
C. A probe that is specific for unique sequences just upstream from the 5′ end of the B-type gene hybridizes to a 32-kb restriction fragment generated by cutting with SfiI. One end of this SfiI fragment is generated by cleavage *within* the gene and the other by cleavage outside the gene. This SfiI fragment is also cleaved by NotI, which was used in the analysis

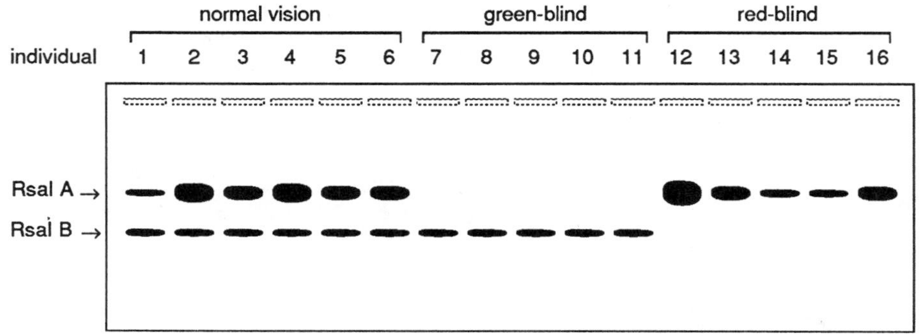

Figure 10–24 RsaI RFLPs in normal, green-blind, and red-blind males (Problem 10–33). The RFLP specific for the A-type gene is indicated as RsaI A; the RFLP for the B-type gene is RsaI B. Individual subjects are identified with a number.

shown in Figure 10–25. From this information decide which gene is at the 5′ end of the cluster and which gene is at the 3′ end. (The 5′ end of the cluster is defined by convention as the end nearer the 5′ end of the first gene.)

D. What is the basis for the variability in the number of A-type genes in males with normal color vision? How might your explanation for variability in gene number in normal males account for the high frequency of color blindness?

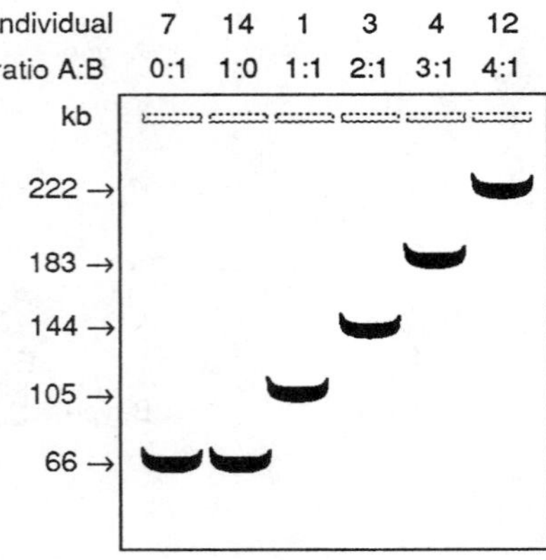

Figure 10–25 NotI digests of DNA from selected normal and color-blind individuals (Problem 10–33). Numbers for individuals correspond to the numbers in Figure 10–24. The ratio of A-type to B-type is estimated from the intensity of hybridization in Figure 10–24. The sizes of the NotI fragments are indicated in kb.

10–34 Almost two centuries ago Thomas Young advanced the hypothesis that humans perceive color by three independent light-sensitive mechanisms. These mechanisms are now known to be embodied in three classes of cone photoreceptor cells in the retina. Each class contains a different visual pigment—red, blue, or green—that determines the spectral properties of all the cones of that class. Two sorts of pigment abnormalities can lead to color blindness. Individuals who lack one of the visual pigments are missing one class of cones; they are called dichromats. Individuals that make a visual pigment with an anomolous absorption spectrum have all three classes of cones but one of them is abnormal; they are called anomalous trichromats.

You have analyzed the structure of the genes for red and green pigments in 25 males with red-green color deficiencies. Examples of gene structures for red-blind (G^+R^-) and green-blind (G^-R^+) dichromats and red-anomalous (G^+R') and green-anomalous ($G'R^+$) trichromats are shown in Figure 10–26 along with three different structures for normal (G^+R^+) males (trichromats).

A. For each of the color-deficient males show how recombination between two normal (trichromat) gene arrays could give rise to the observed abnormal gene structure. (The green-blind dichromat—G^-R^+—is more difficult than the others.)

B. How do you think each of the four hybrid genes in the color-deficient males will be expressed? Will they be expressed like red genes or like green genes?

C. Based on the genetic structures in Figure 10–26, offer an explanation for each color deficiency.

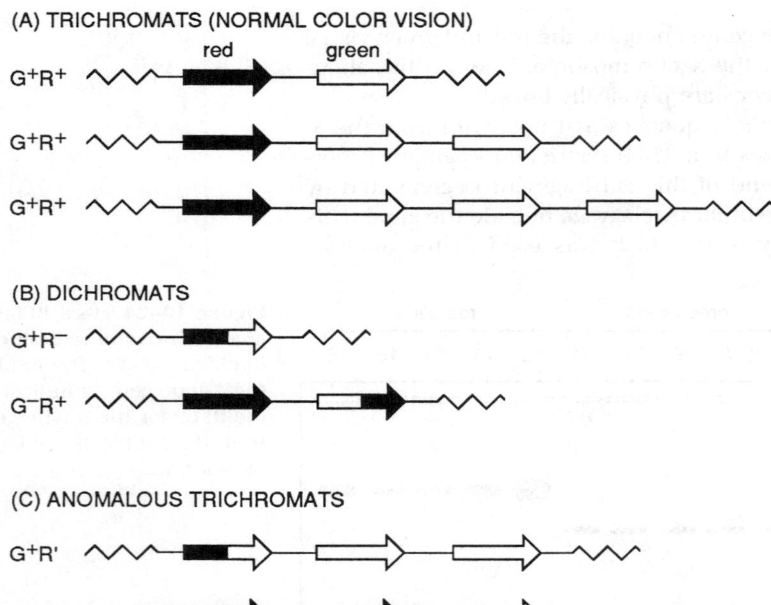

Figure 10–26 Genetic structures for (A) normal trichromats, (B) color-blind dichromats, and (C) color-anomalous trichromats (Problem 10–34). Genes (or parts of genes) for red pigment are shown as black arrows; genes (or parts of genes) for green pigments are shown as white arrows. The base of an arrow represents the 5′ end of a gene; the tip represents the 3′ end. Thin lines indicate homologous intergenic regions; wavy lines indicate single-copy flanking chromosomal sequences.

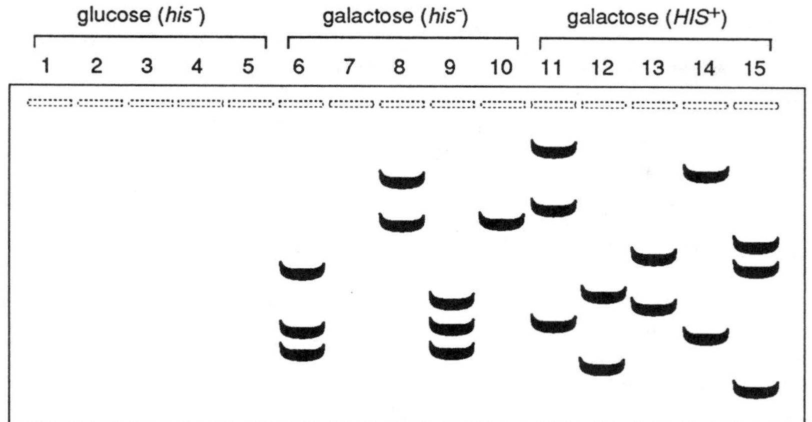

Figure 10–27 Analysis of cells that harbor a plasmid carrying a modified Ty element (Problem 10–35). Cells were initially grown on glucose or galactose as a carbon source. *his*$^-$ cells were grown in the presence of histidine; *HIS*$^+$ cells were grown in its absence. Bands indicate restriction fragments that hybridize to the marker DNA originally present in the Ty element carried by the plasmid.

***10–35** The Ty elements of the yeast *Saccharomyces cerevisiae* move to new locations in the genome by transposition through an RNA intermediate. Normally, the Ty-encoded reverse transcriptase is expressed at such a low level that transposition is very rare. To study the transposition process, you engineer a cloned version of the Ty element so that the gene for reverse transcriptase is linked to the galactose control elements. You also "mark" the element with a segment of bacterial DNA so that you can detect it specifically and thus distinguish it from other Ty elements in the genome. As a target gene to detect transposition, you use a defective histidine gene whose expression is dependent on the insertion of a Ty element near its 5′ end. You show that yeast cells carrying a plasmid with your modified Ty element generate *HIS*$^+$ colonies at a frequency of 5×10^{-8} when grown on glucose. When the same cells are grown on galactose, however, the frequency of *HIS*$^+$ colonies is 10^{-6}: an increase of twentyfold.

You notice that cultures of cells with the Ty-bearing plasmid grow normally on glucose but very slowly on galactose. To investigate this phenomenon, you isolate individual colonies that arise under three different conditions: *his*$^-$ colonies grown in the presence of glucose, *his*$^-$ colonies grown in the presence of galactose, and *HIS*$^+$ colonies grown in the presence of galactose. You "cure" each colony (eliminate the plasmid by growth under special conditions), isolate DNA from each culture, and analyze it by gel electrophoresis and blot hybridization using the bacterial marker DNA as a probe. Your results are shown in Figure 10–27.

A. Why does transposition occur so much more frequently in cells grown on galactose than it does in cells grown on glucose?
B. As shown in Figure 10–27, cells grown on galactose in the presence of histidine (*his*$^-$) have about the same number of marked Ty elements in their chromosomes as cells that were grown in the absence of histidine (*HIS*$^+$). If transposition is independent of histidine selection, why is the frequency of Ty-induced *HIS*$^+$ colonies so low (10^{-6})?
C. Why do you think it is that cells with the Ty-bearing plasmid grow so slowly on galactose?

10–36 *Alu* sequences are present at six sites in the introns of the human serum-albumin and α-fetoprotein genes. (These genes are evolutionary relatives that are located side by side in mammalian genomes.) The same pair of genes in the rat contains no *Alu* sequences. The lineages of rat and humans diverged more than 85 million years ago at the time of the mammalian radiation. Does the presence of *Alu* sequences in the human genes and their absence in the corresponding rat genes mean that *Alu* sequences invaded the human genes only recently, or does it mean that the *Alu* sequences have been removed in some way from the rat genes?

```
       ← Alu repeat (300 nucleotides) →
     TTAAATAGGCCGGG----------AAAAAAAAAAAAATTAAATA
    TGTGTGGGGATCAGG----------AAAAAAAAAAAAATCTGTGGG
    TCTTCTTAGGCTGGG----------GAAAAAAAAAAAATCTTCTTA
ATAATAGTATCTGTCGGCTGGG----------AGAAAAAAAAAAAATAAATAGTATCTGTC
  GGATGTTGTGGGGCCGGG----------AAAAAAAAAAAAAGGATGTTGTGG
  AGAACTAAAAGGGCTAGG----------AAAAAAGAGAAGAAGAACCGAAAG
```

Figure 10–28 Nucleotide sequences of the six Alu inserts in the human albumin-gene family (Problem 10–36). Dashed lines indicate nucleotides in the internal part of the *Alu* sequences.

To examine this question you have sequenced all six of the *Alu* sequences in the human albumin-gene family. The sequences around the ends of the inserted *Alu* elements are shown in Figure 10–28.

A. Mark the left and right boundaries of the inserted *Alu* sequences and underline the nucleotides in the flanking chromosomal DNA that have been altered by mutation.
B. The rate of nucleotide substitution in introns has been measured at about 3×10^{-3} mutations per million years at each site. Assuming the same rate of substitution into the intron sequences that flank these *Alu* sequences, calculate how long ago the *Alu* sequences inserted into these genes. (Lump all the *Alu* sequences together to make this calculation; that is, treat them as if they inserted at about the same time.)
C. Why are these particular flanking sequences used in the calculation? Why were larger segments of the intron not included? Why were the mutations in the *Alu* sequences themselves not used?
D. Did these *Alu* sequences invade the human genes recently (after the time of the mammalian radiation), or have they been removed from the rat genes?

The Cytoskeleton

11

Muscle Contraction (MBOC 613–629)

11–1 Fill in the blanks in the following statements.

A. The __________ is a complex network of protein filaments that enables eucaryotic cells to adopt a variety of shapes and to carry out coordinated and directed movements.

B. About two-thirds of the dry mass of muscle fibers is made up of cylindrical __________, which are usually 1 to 2 μm in diameter and as long as the muscle cell itself.

C. The striated appearance of muscle cells comes from regular repeating units called __________, each of which contains a series of light and dark bands.

D. The most abundant of all the cytoskeletal proteins is __________, which is found both as globular subunits and as 8-nm wide filaments.

E. The thick filaments in myofibrils are composed mainly of the protein __________.

F. Many cytoskeletal proteins contain two α-helices wrapped around each other to form a __________.

G. Actin filaments have structurally distinct ends called the __________ (or pointed end) and the __________ (or barbed end).

H. The two major accessory proteins involved in Ca^{2+} regulation in vertebrate skeletal muscle are __________ and __________.

I. The most "primitive" muscle, which is found in regions of the body where slow and sustained contractions are needed, has no striations and is called __________.

J. The eventual separation of two daughter cells during cell division depends on the activity of a beltlike bundle of actin filaments and myosin molecules beneath the plasma membrane known as the __________.

K. The temporary contractile bundles of actin filaments and myosin, which are prominent components of fibroblast cells in culture, are called __________.

11–2 Indicate whether the following statements are true or false. If a statement is false, explain why.

__ A. Bacteria do not have a cytoskeleton.

__ B. Muscle contraction is caused by the sliding of thick filaments past thin filaments, with no change in the length of either filament.

__ C. Actin polymerization requires ATP, but not the energy of ATP hydrolysis.

__ D. Each myosin molecule consists of four polypeptide chains: two heavy chains and two light chains.

___ E. In the absence of actin, myosin cannot hydrolyze ATP to ADP and P_i.

___ F. Muscle contraction occurs when cytosolic Ca^{2+} levels rise due to the opening of Ca^{2+} channels in the sarcoplasmic reticulum.

___ G. A muscle contraction terminates when a membrane-bound Ca^{2+}-dependent ATPase lowers the ATP level.

___ H. Troponin I inhibits the interaction of myosin and actin, whereas troponin C in the presence of Ca^{2+} relieves the inhibition, permitting myosin to bind to actin.

___ I. Unlike striated muscle, smooth muscle contraction is triggered by the Ca^{2+}-dependent phosphorylation of one of the myosin light chains.

___ J. Epinephrine relaxes smooth muscle by causing the phosphorylation of myosin light chain kinase.

___ K. Stress fibers are like tiny myofibrils that connect focal contacts in the plasma membrane to one another or to the networks of intermediate filaments inside the cell.

___ L. White muscles are specialized for aerobic contraction; red muscles are specialized for anaerobic contraction.

11–3 Two electron micrographs of striated muscle in longitudinal section are shown in Figure 11–1. The sarcomeres in these micrographs are in two different stages of contraction.

Figure 11–1 Two electron micrographs of striated muscle seen in longitudinal section (Problem 11–3). The micrographs have been photographed at different exposures. (Courtesy of Hugh Huxley.)

A. Using the micrograph in Figure 11–1A identify the location of the following:

1. Dark band
2. Light band
3. Z disc
4. Myosin filaments
5. Actin filaments (show plus and minus ends)
6. α-Actinin
7. Myomesin
8. Titin

B. Locate the same features on the micrograph in Figure 11–1B. Be careful!

11–4 Protein assembly principles are nowhere better illustrated than in muscle and the cytoskeleton. If a protein has a binding site that is complementary to a region of its own surface, it will assemble spontaneously into an aggregate. Depending on the geometric relationship of the complementary sites, the resulting structure can be a ring (with the simplest ring being a dimer) or a helix. These simple assemblies can interact to form more complex ones, using the same principle of complementary binding. Aggregates built in this way possess geometric symmetry as a necessary consequence. Biological symmetry is relatively straightforward, but many people find it abstract and somewhat daunting. Nevertheless, the underlying principles are enormously powerful conceptual tools for analyzing biological structure.

Consider, for example, a myosin thick filament, which is a bipolar helical structure constructed from a single type of subunit (the rodlike myosin molecule). The hexagonal packing of actin and myosin filaments in muscle indicates that the myosin heads are arrayed around the helix so that they can point to the vertices of the hexagon for optimal interactions with actin filaments. A helix with six myosin molecules (Figure 11–2A) per turn would satisfy this requirement, as suggested by the schematic diagram in Figure 11–2B, which shows one half of a bipolar thick filament. The actual structure of a myosin filament is more complex with three chains of myosin molecules coiled around one another like strands of a rope. The diagram in Figure 11–2, however, is easier to think about and illustrates the important features of the true structure.

How well does this simple picture account for the appearance of a myosin thick filament?

A. The bipolar appearance of myosin thick filaments with a bare zone in the middle arises because two myosin helices are joined end to end (top end to top end as drawn in Figure 11–2B). Can two myosin helices of the type illustrated in Figure 11–2 actually fit together in this manner? Would the two ends dovetail nicely or not?

B. How long would the bare zone be in the joined helices? Assume the bare zone extends from the first myosin head on one helix to the first myosin head on the oppositely oriented helix.

C. How would you explain the tapering that can be seen at the two ends of a myosin thick filament? (The tapering can be seen clearly in the micrograph shown in MBOC Figure 11–12.)

D. Myosin thick filaments from striated muscle tend to be quite uniform in overall length with the bare zone located at the exact middle of the filament. Is there any feature of the helix in Figure 11–2 that could explain this uniformity of filament length?

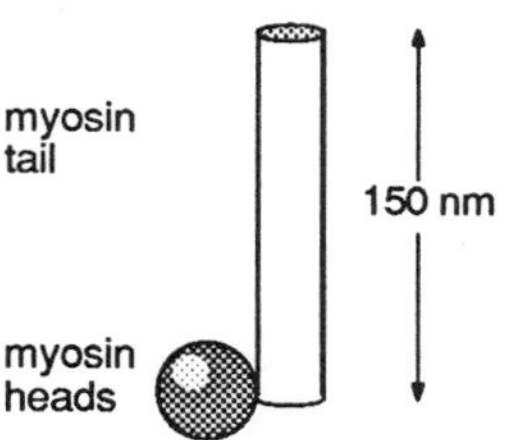

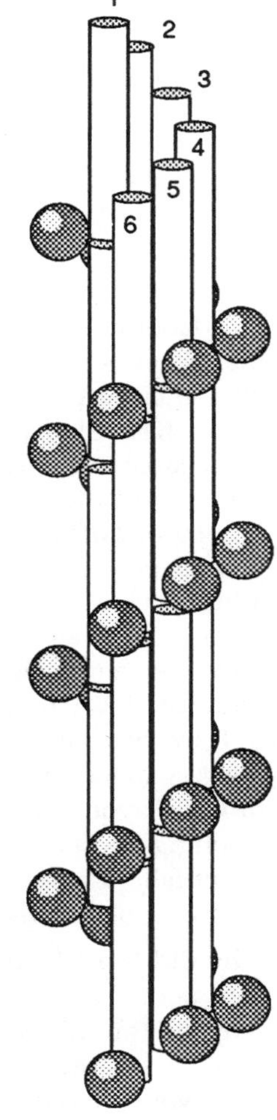

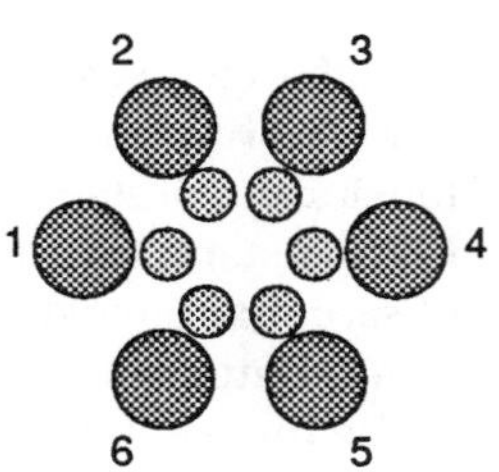

Figure 11–2 Schematic illustration of (A) a myosin molecule and (B) a helix of myosin molecules (Problem 11–4). The two myosin heads are shown as one protrusion for simplicity. The six myosin molecules that form the first helical turn are numbered.

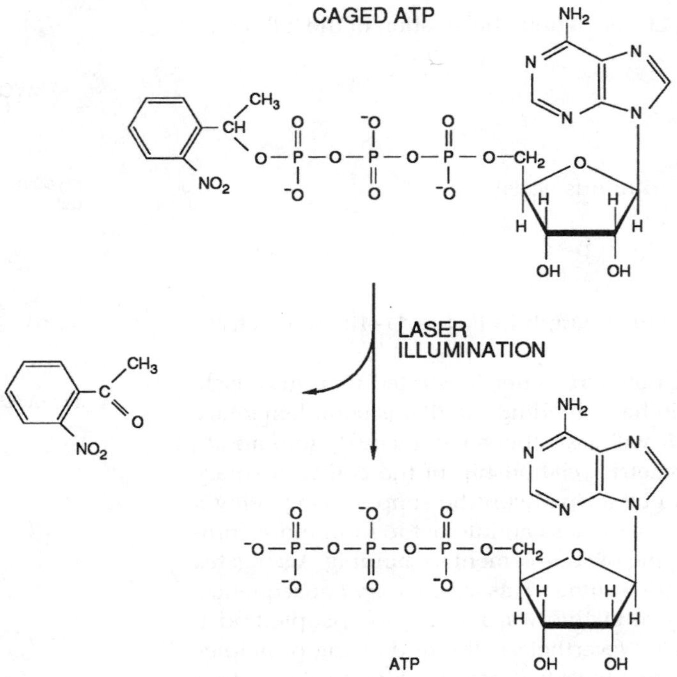

Figure 11–3 "Caged ATP" (Problem 11–5).

***11–5** As a laboratory exercise, you and your classmates are carrying out experiments on isolated muscle fibers using a new compound, called "caged ATP" (Figure 11–3). Since caged ATP does not bind to muscle components, it can be added to a muscle fiber without stimulating activity. Then, at some later time it can be split by laser illumination to release ATP instantly throughout the muscle fiber.

To begin the experiment, you treat an isolated, striated muscle fiber with glycerol to make it permeable to nucleotides. You then suspend it in a buffer containing ATP in an apparatus that allows you to measure any tension generated by fiber contraction. As illustrated in Figure 11–4, you measure the tension generated after several experimental manipulations: removal of ATP by dilution, addition of caged ATP, and activation of caged ATP by laser light. You are somewhat embarrassed because your results are very different from everyone else's. In checking over your experimental protocol, you realize that you forgot to add Ca^{2+} to your buffers. The teaching assistant in charge of your section tells you that your experiment is actually a good control for the class but you will have to answer the following questions to get full credit.

A. Why did the ATP in the suspension buffer not cause the muscle fiber to contract?

B. Why did the subsequent removal of ATP generate tension? Why did tension develop so gradually? (If our muscles normally took a full minute to contract, we would all move very slowly.)

C. Why did laser illumination of a fiber containing caged ATP lead to relaxation?

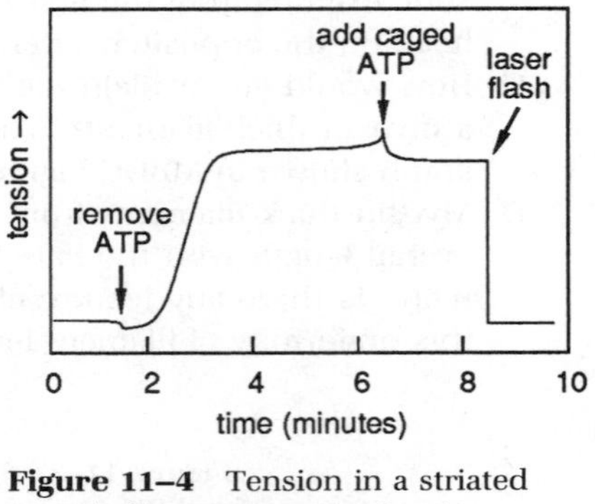

Figure 11–4 Tension in a striated muscle fiber as a result of various experimental manipulations (Problem 11–5).

***11–6** The change in sarcomere length during muscle contraction was one of the key observations that suggested a sliding filament model. The degree of tension generated at different sarcomere lengths also changes in a way that is consistent with the model. Detailed measurements of the relationship of sarcomere length to the tension generated during isometric contraction in a striated muscle are shown in Figure 11–5. In this muscle the length of the myosin filament is 1.6 μm and the lengths of the actin thin filaments that project from the Z discs are 1.0 μm.

*Problems with an asterisk (*) are answered in the Instructor's Manual.

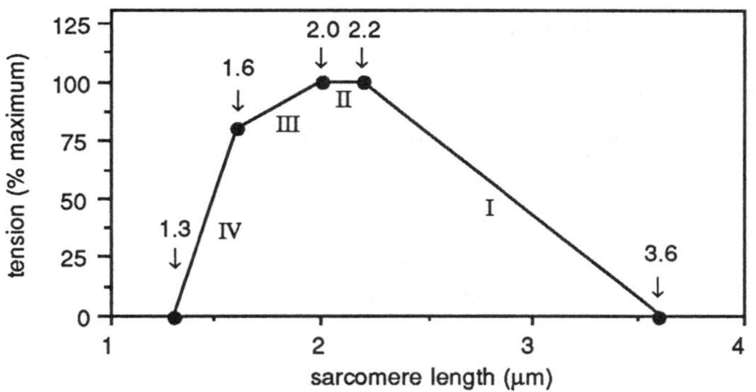

Figure 11–5 Tension as a function of sarcomere length during isometric contraction (Problem 11–6).

Based on your understanding of the sliding filament model and the structure of a sarcomere, present a molecular explanation for the relationship of tension to sarcomere length in the segments marked I, II, III, and IV in the curve in Figure 11–5.

11–7 Living systems continually transform chemical free energy into motion. Muscle contraction, ciliary movement, cytoplasmic streaming, cell division, and active transport are examples of the ability of cells to transduce chemical free energy into mechanical work. In all these instances a protein motor harnesses the free energy released in a chemical reaction to drive an attached molecule (the ligand) in a particular direction. The analysis of free-energy transduction in favorable biological systems suggests that a set of general principles governs the process in cells.

1. A cycle of reactions is used to convert chemical free energy into mechanical work.
2. At some point in the cycle a ligand binds very tightly to the protein motor.
3. At some point in the cycle the motor undergoes a major conformational change that changes the physical position of the ligand.
4. At some point in the cycle the binding constant of the ligand markedly decreases, allowing the ligand to detach from the motor.

These principles are illustrated by the two examples of cycles for free-energy transduction shown in Figure 11–6: (1) the sliding of actin and myosin filaments against each other and (2) the active transport of Ca^{2+} from inside the cell, where its concentration is low, to the cell exterior, where its concentration is high. An examination of these cycles underscores the principles of free-energy transduction.

A. What is the source of chemical free energy that powers these cycles, and what is the mechanical work that each cycle accomplishes?
B. What is the ligand that is bound tightly and then released in each of the cycles? Indicate the points in each cycle where the ligand is bound tightly.
C. Identify the conformational changes in the protein motor that constitute the "power stroke" and "return stroke" of each of the cycles.

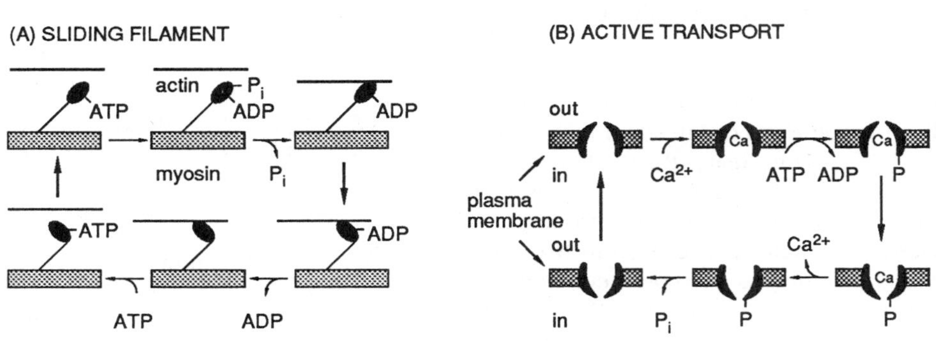

Figure 11–6 Transduction of chemical free energy into mechanical work (Problem 11–7). (A) Sliding of actin filaments relative to myosin filaments. (B) Active transport of Ca^{2+} from the inside to the outside of the cell. In both cycles arrows are drawn in only one direction to emphasize their normal operation. The phosphorylation and dephosphorylation steps in the active transport cycle are catalyzed by enzymes that are not shown in the diagram.

Actin Filaments and the Cell Cortex (MBOC 629–644)

11–8 Fill in the blanks in the following statements.

A. The dense network of actin filaments and associated proteins that lies just beneath the plasma membrane of the cell constitutes the ____________.

B. The most abundant actin cross-linking protein in many cells is ________, a long flexible molecule composed of two identical polypeptide chains.

C. The best characterized protein with the property of fluidizing actin gels in the presence of Ca^{2+} is ____________, which severs actin chains and caps the plus end.

D. Plant cells, because of their large size and stiff cell walls, require extensive ____________ to ensure effective mixing of their cytoplasm.

E. The fingerlike extensions that are found on the surface of many animal cells are called ____________.

F. The specialized cortex at the apex of intestinal epithelial cells is known as the ____________; it contains a dense network of spectrin molecules that overlies a layer of intermediate filaments.

G. Cells are anchored to the substrate at specialized regions called ____________, which are points of attachment of stress fibers to the plasma membrane.

H. The continual transfer of actin monomers from one end of a thin filament to the other is a process called ____________.

I. Cells in culture often extend thin, stiff protrusions, called ____________, which are about 0.1 μm wide and 5 to 10 μm long.

J. The leading edge of crawling cells and growth cones periodically extends thin sheetlike processes known as ____________.

11–9 Indicate whether the following statements are true or false. If a statement is false, explain why.

__ A. Gels made from actin and a cross-linking protein such as filamin resist sudden change, but they deform readily when a slow steady pressure is applied.

__ B. Myosin is required for contraction and streaming in nonmuscle cells.

__ C. Cytoplasmic streaming in *Nitella* is probably mediated by a layer of polarized microtubules that lies just below a static monolayer of chloroplasts.

__ D. In mature red blood cells actin filaments are attached directly to the plasma membrane.

__ E. The actin filaments in the cores of microvilli are held rigidly together by actin-bundling proteins that include fimbrin and fascin.

__ F. The so-called critical concentration of actin is the concentration of actin required to bring about the nucleation step that precedes polymerization.

__ G. Treadmilling of actin filaments is driven by the energy obtained from ATP hydrolysis.

__ H. The extension of the acrosomal process in some invertebrate sperm is caused by the rapid polymerization of stored actin monomers.

__ I. Actin assembly is controlled by the regulation of nucleation sites for actin filament growth at the plasma membrane.

__ J. Cytochalasin inhibits the separation of chromosomes at mitosis, suggesting that actin is involved in this process.

***11–10** ATP plays two roles in the contraction of the terminal web, which controls the movement of the microvilli on the surface of intestinal cells. These two functions of ATP have been differentiated using the ATP analogues, ATP-γ-S and inosine triphosphate (ITP), which differ from ATP as indicated by the arrows in Figure 11–7. Intestinal membranes with microvilli and their associated terminal webs were isolated and used in two types of experiments. In one the intestinal membranes were preincubated with or without ATP-γ-S in the presence of Ca^{2+}, and then ATP, ITP, or

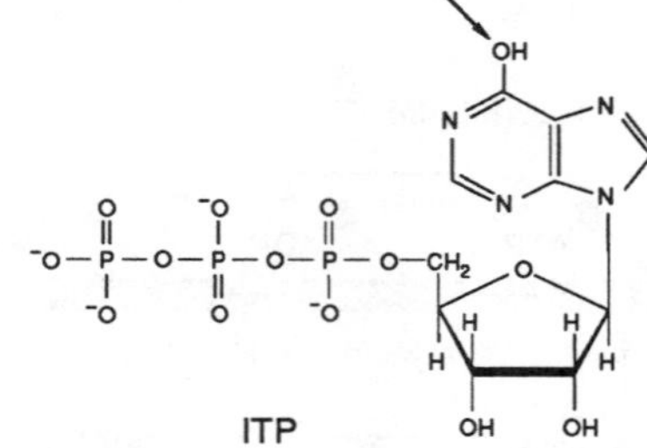

Figure 11–7 ATP and two ATP analogues, ATP-γ-S and ITP (Problem 11–10).

Table 11–1 Use of ATP Analogues to Study Contraction of the Terminal Web in Intestinal Membranes (Problem 11–10)

Experiment	Preincubation	Incubation	Contraction
1	no analogue	ATP	yes
2	no analogue	ITP	no
3	no analogue	ATP-γ-S	no
4	ATP-γ-S	ATP	yes
5	ATP-γ-S	ITP	yes
6	ATP-γ-S	ATP-γ-S	no

ATP-γ-S was added and contraction of the terminal web was assayed (Table 11–1). In the second type of experiment, intestinal membranes were incubated with labeled ATP analogues, and the resulting phosphorylated proteins were analyzed: the light chain of myosin was shown to be phosphorylated in the presence of ATP-γ-^{32}P and ATP-γ-^{35}S, but it was not phosphorylated in the presence of ITP-γ-^{32}P.

A. What two roles does ATP hydrolysis play in the contraction of the terminal web? For which role can ATP-γ-S substitute? For which role can ITP substitute?

B. Both functions of ATP depend on the hydrolysis of the terminal (γ) phosphodiester bond. Why do you think it is that the ATP analogues behave differently in the two types of experiment?

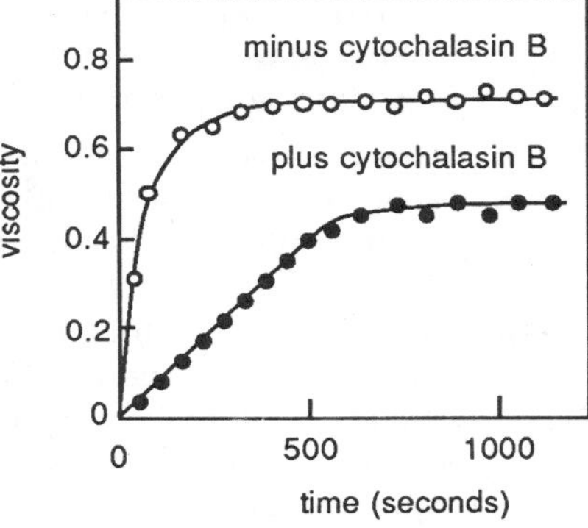

Figure 11–8 Increase in the viscosity of actin solutions in the presence and absence of cytochalasin B (Problem 11–11).

11–11 Cytochalasin B strongly inhibits certain forms of cell motility, such as cytokinesis and the ruffling of growth cones, and it dramatically decreases the viscosity of gels formed with mixtures of actin and a wide variety of actin-binding proteins. These observations suggest that cytochalasin B interferes with the assembly of actin filaments; however, it does not bind to actin monomers. How then does cytochalasin B interfere with motility?

Consider the following experiment. Short lengths of actin filaments were decorated with myosin heads and then monomeric actin was added to the decorated filaments in the presence or absence of cytochalasin B. Assembly of actin filaments was measured by assaying the viscosity of the solution (Figure 11–8) and also by examining samples in an electron microscope (Figure 11–9).

A. What does the electron microscope reveal about the way actin filaments normally grow?

B. Suggest a plausible mechanism to explain how cytochalasin B inhibits actin filament assembly. Account for both the viscosity measurements and the appearance of the filaments in the electron micrographs.

C. The normal growth characteristics of an actin filament and the actin-binding properties of cytochalasin B argue that actin monomers undergo a conformational change upon addition to an actin filament. How so?

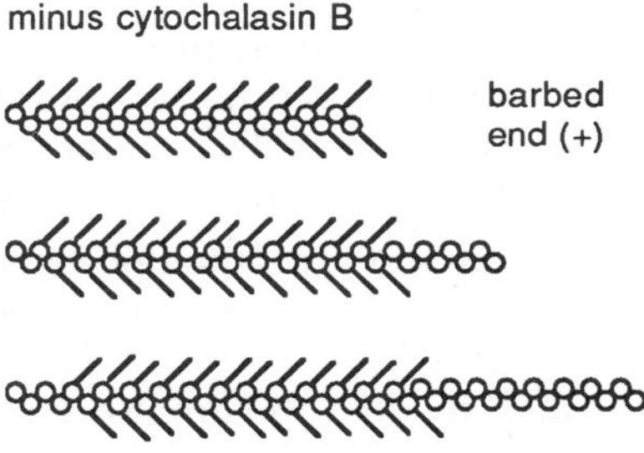

Figure 11–9 Appearance of typical actin filaments formed in the presence and absence of cytochalasin B (Problem 11–11). The decorated actin filaments present before addition of actin monomers are shown at the top. Filaments present after increasing times of incubation in the presence of actin monomers are shown below.

11–12 Your ultimate goal is to understand human consciousness—however, your advisor wants you to understand some basic facts about actin assembly first. He tells you that ATP binds to actin monomers and is required for assembly but that ATP hydrolysis is not necessary for polymerization, since ADP can, under certain circumstances, substitute for the ATP requirement. However, ADP filaments are much less stable than ATP filaments, thus supporting your secret suspicion that the free energy of ATP hydrolysis really is used to drive actin assembly.

Your advisor suggests that you make careful measurements of the quantitative relationship between the number of ATP molecules hydrolyzed and the number of actin monomers linked into polymer. The experiments are straightforward. To measure ATP hydrolysis, you add ATP-γ-^{32}P to a solution of polymerizing actin, take samples at short intervals, and determine how much radioactive phosphate has been produced. To measure polymerization, you follow (in a spectrophotometer) the increase in light scattering that is caused by formation of the actin filaments. Your results are shown in Figure 11–10. Your light-scattering measurements indicate that 20 μmoles of actin monomers were polymerized. Since the number of polymerized actin monomers matches exactly the number of ATP molecules hydrolyzed, you conclude that one ATP is hydrolyzed as each new monomer is added to an actin filament.

When you show your advisor the data and tell him your conclusions, he smiles and very gently tells you to look more closely at the graph. He says your data prove that actin can polymerize without ATP hydrolysis.

A. What does your advisor see in the data that you have overlooked?

B. What do your data imply about the distribution of ATP and ADP in polymerizing actin filaments?

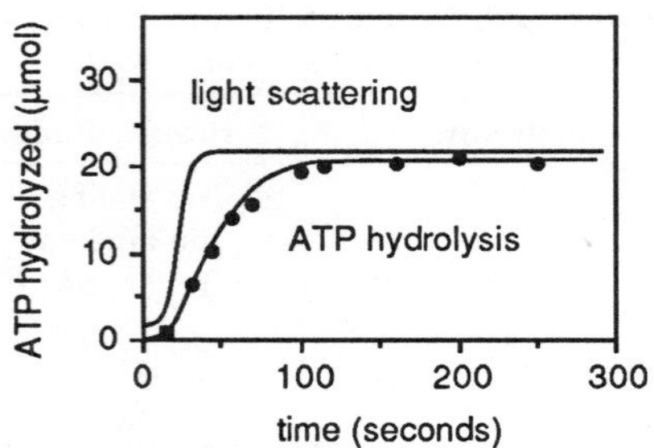

Figure 11–10 The kinetics of actin polymerization and ATP hydrolysis (Problem 11–12).

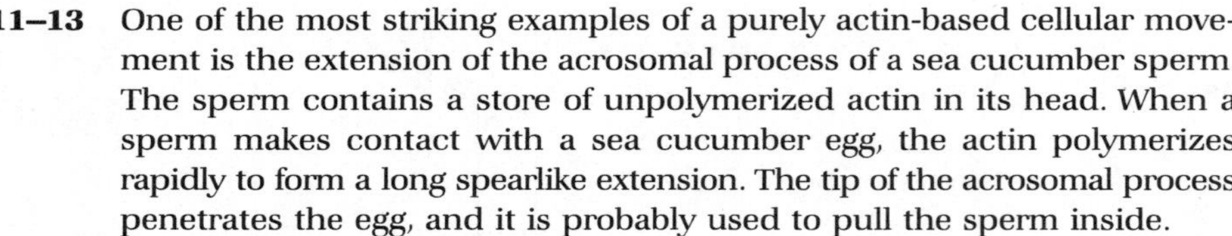

***11–13** One of the most striking examples of a purely actin-based cellular movement is the extension of the acrosomal process of a sea cucumber sperm. The sperm contains a store of unpolymerized actin in its head. When a sperm makes contact with a sea cucumber egg, the actin polymerizes rapidly to form a long spearlike extension. The tip of the acrosomal process penetrates the egg, and it is probably used to pull the sperm inside.

Are actin monomers added to the base or to the tip of the acrosomal bundle of actin filaments during extension of the process? If the supply of monomers to the site of assembly depends on diffusion, it should be possible to distinguish between these alternatives by measuring the length of the acrosomal process with increasing time. If actin monomers are added to the base of the process, which is inside the head, the rate of growth should be linear with time because the distance between the site of assembly and the pool of monomers does not change with time. On the other hand, if the subunits are added to the tip, the rate of growth should decline progressively as the acrosomal process gets longer because the monomers must diffuse all the way down the shaft of the process. In this case the rate of extension should be proportional to the square root of time. Plots of the length of the acrosomal process versus time and the square root of time are shown in Figure 11–11.

A. Are the ascending portions of the plots in Figure 11–11 more consistent with addition of actin monomers to the base or to the tip of the acrosomal process?

B. Why does the process grow so slowly at the beginning and at the end of the acrosomal reaction?

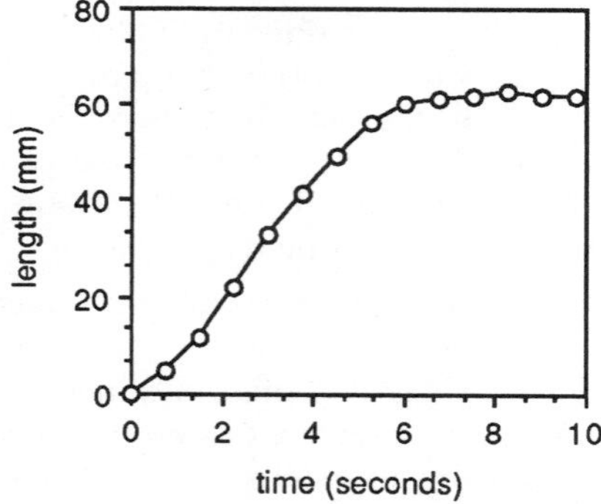

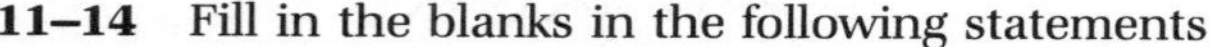

Ciliary Movement (MBOC 644–652)

11–14 Fill in the blanks in the following statements.

A. ______________ are hairlike cellular appendages that are constructed from microtubules and move like tiny whips.

B. Sperm "swim" by means of ______________, which are long, thin processes that propagate quasi-sinusoidal waves.

C. The core of a cilium is a complex structure called an ______________, which is composed entirely of microtubules and their associated proteins.

D. Microtubules are formed from molecules of ______________.

E. The protein complex that is responsible for the sliding of outer microtubule doublets against one another to produce ciliary bending is called ______________.

F. Basal bodies contain ______________, which are small cylindrical organelles with nine groups of three fused microtubules.

G. The ______________, which is also known as the cell center, organizes the array of cytoplasmic microtubules during interphase.

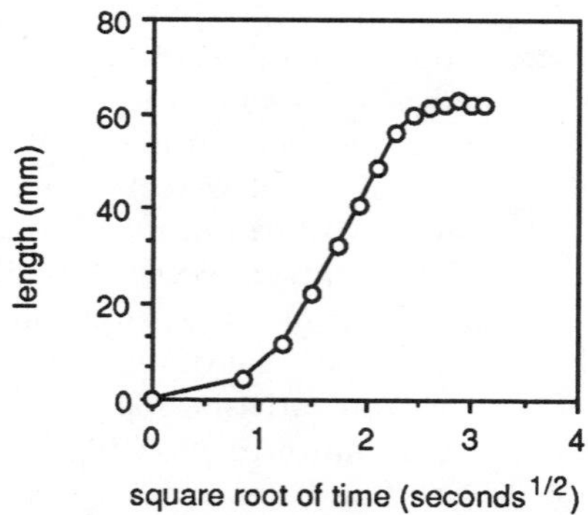

Figure 11–11 Plots of the length of the acrosome versus time and the square root of time (Problem 11–13).

11–15 Indicate whether the following statements are true or false. If a statement is false, explain why.

___ A. Eucaryotic cilia and flagella contain an outer ring of nine doublet microtubules surrounding two single microtubules.

___ B. Microtubules are composed almost entirely of multiple subunits of two slightly different polypeptide chains.

___ C. Ciliary movement is catalyzed by myosin, which forms sets of arms that join neighboring doublets in the outer ring.

___ D. The bending forces that lead to ciliary motion are generated by the sliding between the central pair of microtubules and the outer ring of doublet microtubules.

___ E. When the nexin links in isolated axonemes are severed by mild protease treatment, the outer doublets telescope out of the axoneme if low levels of ATP are added.

___ F. The organized beating of cilia is controlled by fluxes of Ca^{2+} across the ciliary membrane.

___ G. Mutant flagella lacking the central pair of microtubules cannot beat, but movement can be restored by additional mutations that affect the outer dynein arms.

___ H. Kartagener's syndrome, which is caused by immotile flagella, includes a complex set of abnormalities that affect *Chlamydomonas.*

___ I. Although centrioles lack the central pair of microtubules, they appear to serve as nucleating structures for axoneme growth.

___ J. Centrosomes usually contain centrioles.

___ K. Centrioles normally do not arise *de novo*, but they can be induced to form in certain cells under special circumstances.

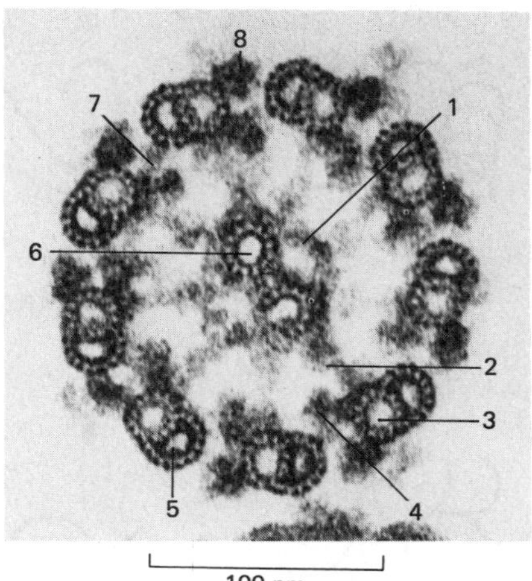

Figure 11–12 Electron micrograph of a cross-section through a flagellum of *Chlamydomonas reinhardtii* (Problem 11–16). (Courtesy of Lewis Tilney.)

***11–16** An electron micrograph of a cross-section through a flagellum is shown in Figure 11–12.

A. Assign the following components to the indicated positions on the figure.

A tubule	Inner sheath
B tubule	Nexin
Outer dynein arm	Radial spoke
Inner dynein arm	Single microtubule

B. Which of the above structures are composed of tubulin?

C. Which, if any, of the structures are continuous with components of the basal body?

11–17 On ciliated cells the beating of individual cilia is usually coordinated so that the cilia move in the same direction, thereby imparting unidirectional motion to the cell (or to the surrounding fluid). In principle, the coordinated, unidirectional beating of adjacent cilia could be determined by some feature of their structure or, alternatively, by some cellular control mechanism that is independent of ciliary structure.

An electron micrograph of a cross-section through the cortex of the ciliated protozoan, *Tetrahymena*, is shown in Figure 11–13. The plane of section grazes the surface of the cell, showing in successive sections how the "9 + 2" arrangement of microtubules in the axoneme leads into the

Figure 11–13 Electron micrograph of a cross-section through the cortex of a ciliated protozoan, *Tetrahymena* (Problem 11–17). (Courtesy of Keith Roberts.)

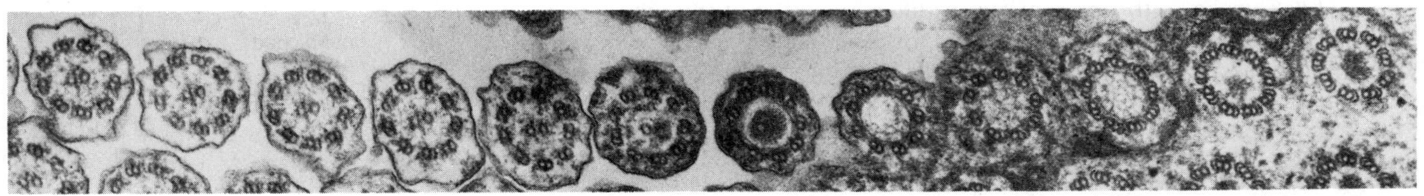

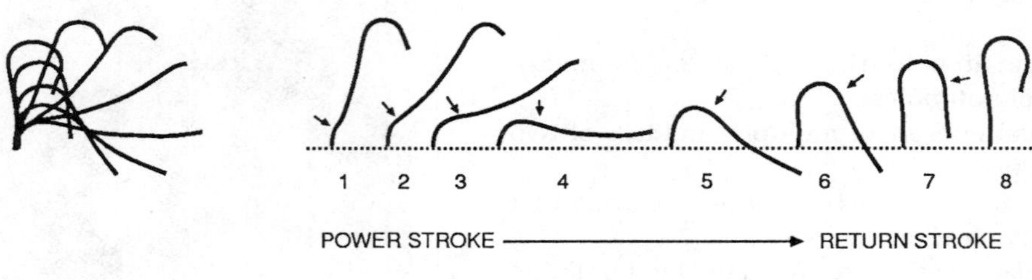

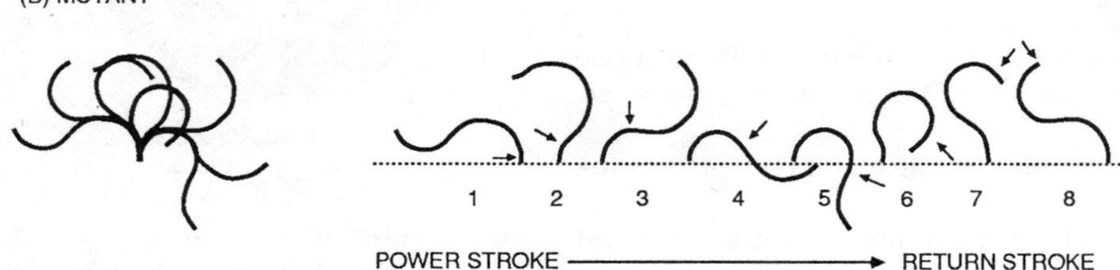

Figure 11–14 Beat cycles for wild-type (A) and mutant (B) flagella from *Chlamydomonas* (Problem 11–18). The beating flagella at left were photographed with stroboscopic illumination under a microscope. Individual frames from these pictures represent flagella at successive stages in the beat cycle. Arrows show the leading edge of a bent segment of flagellum as it progresses from the bottom of the flagellum to the tip during the beat cycle.

nine triplet microtubules of the basal body. Are there any clues in the micrograph that allow you to decide whether axoneme structure or cellular control is the basis for the *unidirectional* beating of adjacent cilia? Explain your reasoning.

***11–18** When analyzed in detail, the rhythmic beating of a cilium is revealed as a series of precisely repeated movements. In *Chlamydomonas* the flagellar beat cycle is straightforward (Figure 11–14A). The beat cycle begins with a power stroke, which is initiated by a bend at the base of the flagellum (arrow at base of flagellum 1 in Figure 11–14A). The power stroke ends when the bent segment of flagellum extends roughly through half the circumference of a circle (flagellum 5 in Figure 11–14A). The return stroke is formed by the movement of the semicircular segment of the flagellum outward toward the tip, which is accomplished by further bending at the leading edge of the semicircle and relaxation at the trailing edge (flagella 6 to 8 in Figure 11–14A). Any complete molecular mechanism for axoneme function must be able to account for these gross movements of the flagellum.

A. How much sliding of microtubule doublets against one another is required to account for the observed bending of the flagellum into a semicircle? Calculate how much farther the doublet on the inside of the semicircle protrudes beyond the doublet on the outside of the semicircle at the tip of the flagellum (Figure 11–15A).

B. The elastic nexin molecules that link adjacent outer doublets must stretch to accommodate the bending of a flagellum into a semicircle. If the length of an unstretched nexin molecule at the base of a flagellum is 30 nm, what is the length of a stretched nexin molecule at the tip of a flagellum (Figure 11–15B)?

C. *Chlamydomonas* mutants that are missing radial spokes have paralyzed flagella. The paralysis can be overcome by mutations in a second gene (called *sup*$_{pf}$, for *supressor* of *paralyzed flagella*), which encodes a component of the outer dynein arm. Although the flagella now move, their beat pattern is aberrant (Figure 11–14B). At the gross level, how does the beat stroke of the mutant strain differ from that of the wild type? What does this gross difference suggest for the function mediated by the radial spokes in *Chlamydomonas*?

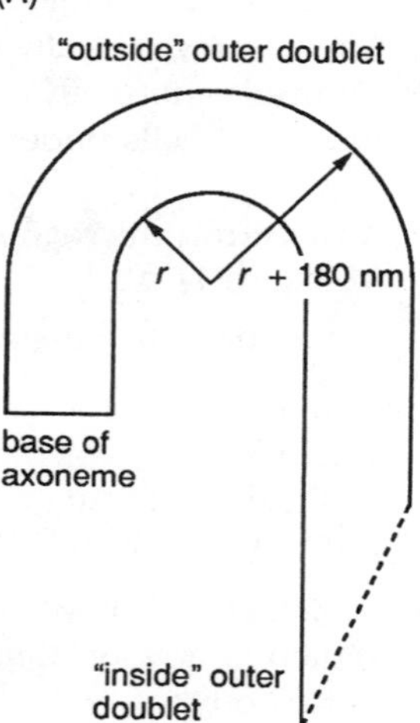

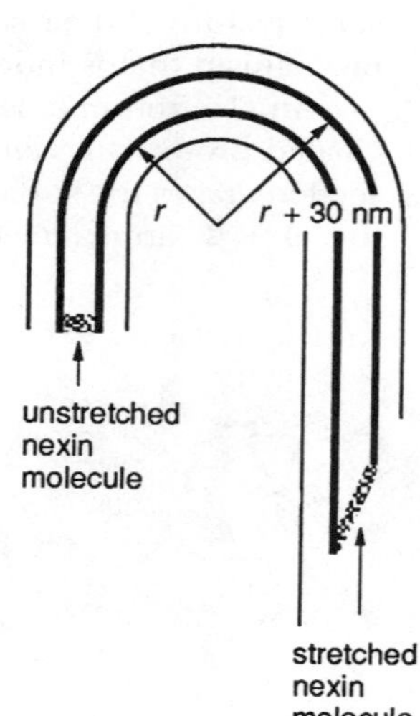

Figure 11–15 Flagella bent into half circles (Problem 11–18). (A) Representation showing the "inside" and "outside" doublets, which are 180 nm apart. (B) Representation showing adjacent doublets, which are 30 nm apart, and the nexin molecules that link them.

11–19 The sliding microtubule mechanism for ciliary bending is undoubtedly correct. The consequences of sliding are straightforward when a pair of outer doublets is considered in isolation. It is confusing, however, to think about sliding in the circular array of outer doublets in the axoneme. The dynein arms are arranged so that, when activated, they push their neighboring outer doublet outward toward the tip of the cilium. In a circular array if all the dynein arms were equally active, there could be no significant relative motion. (The situation is equivalent to a circle of strongmen, each trying to lift his neighbor off the ground; if they all succeeded, the group would levitate.)

Devise a pattern of dynein activity (consistent with axoneme structure and the directional pushing of dynein) that can account for bending of the axoneme in one direction. How would this pattern change for bending in the opposite direction?

11–20 The structure of the ciliary axoneme, which is composed of more than 200 different proteins, is exceedingly complex. *Chlamydomonas reinhardtii,* which bears two flagella, is an extremely useful organism for analyzing axoneme structure: physiological and microsopic observation are straightforward, but even more important is the ease of genetic and biochemical analysis. It is a simple matter to isolate mutants with paralyzed flagella because they cannot move. These mutants can then be assigned to specific genes by genetic crosses, which are routine with *Chlamydomonas.* Finally, wild-type and mutant flagella can be detached readily (for example, by pH shock) and recovered in highly purified fractions for easy biochemical analysis.

Many of the mutants with paralyzed flagella are missing one or another of the major substructures of the axoneme, such as the radial spokes, the outer dynein arms, the inner dynein arms, or one or both central microtubules. In most cases loss of the axonemal substructure is caused by a mutation that affects a single gene, and yet biochemical analysis shows that the defective axoneme is missing multiple proteins. Consider, for example, the mutant *pf*14 (*p*aralyzed *f*lagella): electron micrographs of its flagella show a complete absence of radial spokes (Figure 11–16A), and two-dimensional electrophoretic analysis shows that it lacks 17 different proteins (Figure 11–16B).

A single-gene defect that results in multiple protein deficiencies could have two underlying explanations: (1) the defect is in a regulatory gene

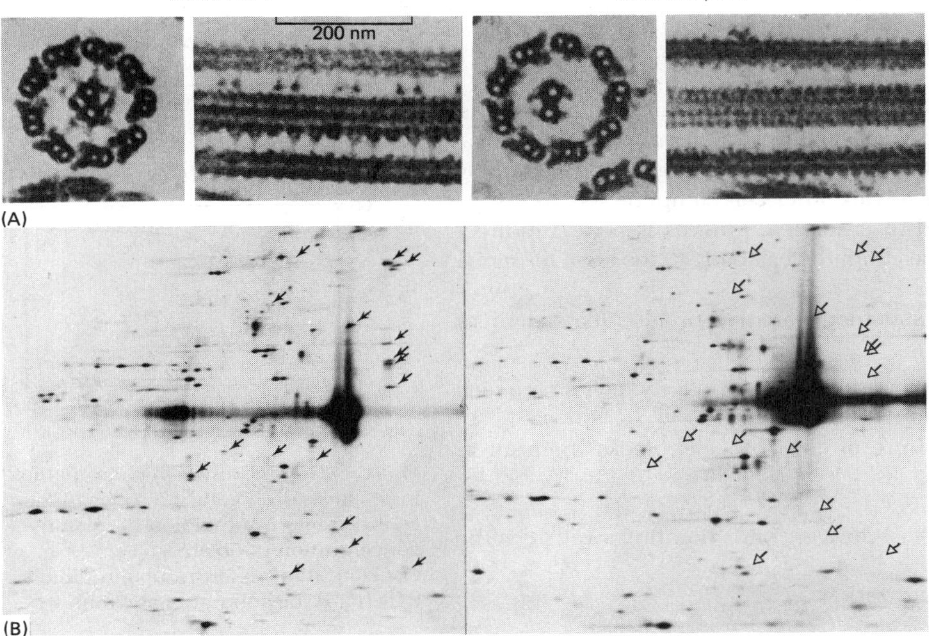

Figure 11–16 Comparison of flagella from wild-type *Chlamydomonas* with those from the mutant, *pf*14 (Problem 11–20). (A) Electron micrographs showing flagella in transverse and longitudinal sections. Notice the absence of radial spokes in *pf*14. (B) Analysis of flagella by two-dimensional gel electrophoresis. The first dimension (horizontal) is separation by isoelectric focusing with the more acidic proteins on the right; the second dimension is separation by molecular weight using SDS-gel electrophoresis. Arrows indicate the positions of proteins that are present in wild type but missing in *pf*14. The highly exposed areas correspond to α– and β-tubulin, which far outnumber the other axonemal proteins. (From G. Piperno, B. Huang, Z. Ramanis, and D. Luck, *J. Cell Biol.* 88:73–79, 1981. Reprinted by permission of the Rockefeller University Press.)

that controls the synthesis of the missing proteins or (2) the defect is in a gene whose product must be present in the structure before the other proteins can be added. Two approaches have been used to evaluate these possibilities.

A. The first method takes advantage of a feature of the regular mating cycle of *Chlamydomonas*. In the mating reaction, biflagellate gametes fuse efficiently to give a population of temporary dikaryons with four flagella. In a mating of *pf*14 with wild-type gametes, the paralyzed flagella recover function after fusion, indicating that the defective structures can be repaired without completely rebuilding them. (In normal cells there is a pool of flagellar components sufficient to rebuild an entire flagellum in the absence of protein synthesis.) To distinguish between the possible explanations for flagellar defects, investigators labeled mutant cells by growth in $^{35}SO_4$ and then fused the labeled gametes to nonradioactive wild-type gametes in the presence of an inhibitor of protein synthesis. After recovery of function, the flagella were isolated and the radioactive proteins were analyzed by two-dimensional gel electrophoresis followed by autoradiography.

   Predict the expected electrophoretic pattern of *radioactive* proteins from the dikaryon if the affected gene controlled the synthesis of the missing proteins. How would it differ from the electrophoretic pattern that would be expected if the affected gene product participated in assembly?

B. The second approach was to expose *pf*14 to a mutagen to generate revertants that regained flagellar function not because the original defect has been corrected, but because a second alteration within the gene compensates for the first one. (Depending on the gene, such intragenic revertants can be very common.) The proteins from several such revertants were compared to those in the wild type by two-dimensional gel electrophoresis.

   How might this method distinguish between the two possible explanations for the defect in *pf*14?

Cytoplasmic Microtubules (MBOC 652–661)

11–21 Fill in the blanks in the following statements.

A. The drug __________ binds tightly to tubulin and prevents its polymerization.
B. The minus ends of microtubules are buried in the __________ where the aster originates.
C. Microtubules in cells display a property known as __________; that is, individual microtubules either grow steadily or suddenly depolymerize.
D. __________ serve both to stabilize microtubules against disassembly and to mediate their interactions with other cell components.
E. A large protein complex called __________ moves vesicles unidirectionally along axonal microtubules from the cell body to the axon terminus.

11–22 Indicate whether the following statements are true or false. If a statement is false, explain why.

___ A. Microtubules are responsible for regulating cell polarity, cell shape, cell movement, and the plane of cell division.
___ B. Addition of colchicine to a culture of growing cells blocks them all in mitosis within a few minutes.
___ C. Taxol stabilizes microtubules.
___ D. Microtubules always have their fast-growing ends pointing away from the spindle pole.
___ E. Tubulin requires GTP for polymerization.

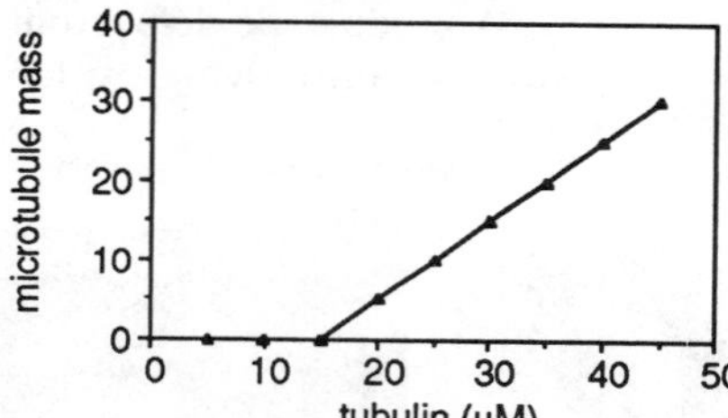

(B) PLUS CENTROSOMES

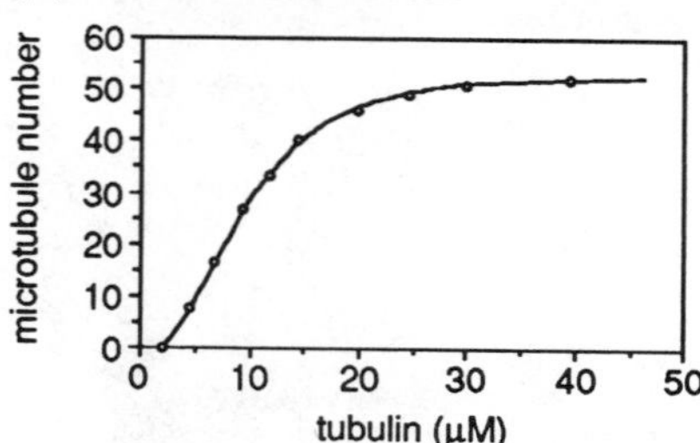

Figure 11–17 Growth of microtubules in the absence (A) and presence (B) of centrosomes as a function of tubulin concentration (Problem 11–23). Concentrations refer to tubulin dimers, which are the subunit of assembly.

— F. All microtubules, even those in cilia and flagella, show dynamic instability.
— G. Both detyrosination and acetylation mark the conversion of microtubules into more permanent forms that remain intact even when cells are treated with colchicine.
— H. Posttranslational modifications to tubulin occur only when tubulin dimers are in the unpolymerized state.
— I. In order to support the bidirectional movement of vesicles and organelles, microtubules run in both directions in nerve axons.
— J. Purified kinesin moves vesicles in only one direction along microtubules.

11–23 The function of microtubules is thought to depend on their specific spatial organization within the cell. How are specific spatial arrangements created, and what determines the formation and disappearance of individual microtubules?

To address these questions, investigators have studied the *in vitro* assembly of tubulin into microtubules. In solutions of tubulin below 15 μM no microtubules are formed, but when the concentration is raised above 15 μM, microtubules form readily (Figure 11–17A). If centrosomes are added to the solution of tubulin, microtubules begin to form at less than 5 μM (Figure 11–17B). (Different assays were used in the two experiments—total weight of microtubules in Figure 11–17A and number of microtubules per centrosome in Figure 11–17B—but the lowering of the critical concentration for microtubule assembly in the presence of centrosomes is independent of the method of assay.)

A. Why do you think that the concentration at which microtubules begin to form (the critical concentration) is different in the two experiments?
B. Why do you think that the plot in Figure 11–17A increases linearly with increasing tubulin concentration above 15 μM, whereas the plot in Figure 11–17B reaches a plateau at about 25 μM?
C. The concentration of tubulin dimers (the subunits for assembly) in a typical cell is 1 mg/ml and the molecular weight of a tubulin dimer is 110,000. What is the molar concentration of tubulin in cells? How does the cellular concentration compare with the critical concentrations in the two experiments in Figure 11–17? What are the implications for assembly of microtubules in cells?

***11–24** In addition to centrosomes, flagellar axonemes and kinetochores also can serve as nucleation sites for microtubule assembly. Do these structures nucleate microtubule growth by binding to the plus end or to the minus end of the nascent microtubule? The following experiment was designed to determine which end of a microtubule is attached to centrosomes and kinetochores. Flagellar axonemes were included as a control since their plus and minus ends can be distinguished. Centrosomes and kinetochores (and flagellar axonemes) were incubated briefly in unlabeled tubulin to nucleate microtubule growth. A high concentration of biotin-labeled tubulin was then added and the incubation was continued for 10 minutes. At that point the preparations were fixed and the biotin-labeled segments were visualized by adding fluorescein-labeled antibodies specific for biotin. The lengths of the biotin-labeled segments were measured and plotted as shown in Figure 11–18.

A. Which end of a newly assembled microtubule is attached to the plus end of the flagellar axoneme?
B. Which end of a microtubule assembled on a flagellar axoneme grows faster?
C. Which end of an assembled microtubule is attached to a centrosome? To a kinetochore? Explain your reasoning.

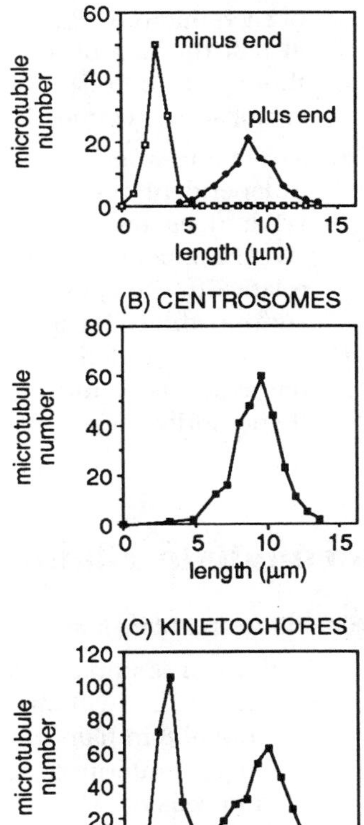

Figure 11–18 Length distributions of microtubules attached to (A) axonemes, (B) centrosomes, and (C) kinetochores (Problem 11–24).

11–25 The complex kinetics of microtubule assembly make it hard to predict the behavior of individual microtubules. Some microtubules in a popu-

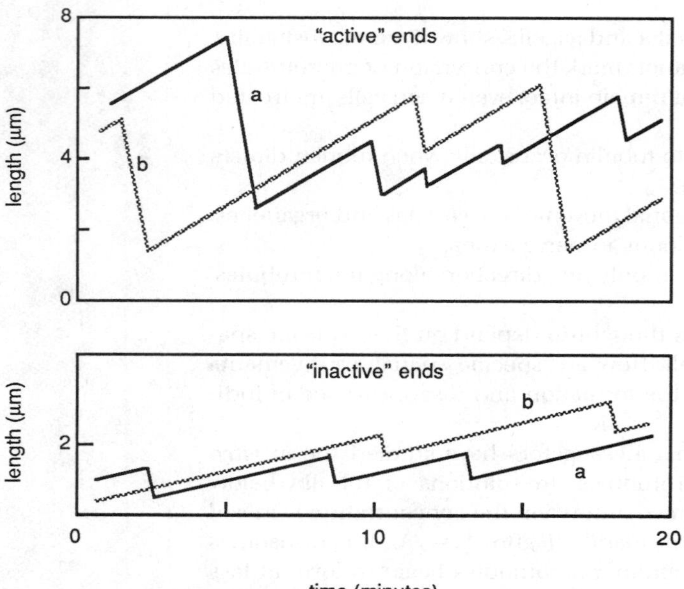

Figure 11–19 Changes in length at the ends of individual microtubules (Problem 11–25). Results from the individual microtubules are indicated with a and b.

lation can grow, even as the majority shrink to nothing. One simple hypothesis to explain this behavior is that growing ends are protected from disassembly by a GTP cap and that faster growing ends have a longer GTP cap. Recent advances in video techniques now allow real-time observations of individual microtubules. Typical observations on the changes in length with time are shown for two microtubules in Figure 11–19. Measurements of their rates of growth and shrinkage show that one end of each microtubule (the "active" end) grows three times faster and shrinks at half the rate of the other end (the "inactive" end). The active end is thought to correspond to the plus end, but these experiments do not establish the connection.

A. Are changes in length at the two ends of a microtubule dependent or independent of one another? How can you tell?
B. What does the simple GTP-cap hypothesis predict about the rate of switching between growing and shrinking states at the fast growing end relative to the slow growing end? Does the outcome of this experiment support the GTP-cap hypothesis?
C. These observations were made with pure tubulin. How do you think the observations would change if you added centrosomes to the reaction? If you added microtubule-associated proteins (MAPs) to the reaction?

Intermediate Filaments (MBOC 661–667)

11–26 Fill in the blanks in the following statements.

A. The most complex class of intermediate filament proteins are the ____________, with at least 19 distinct forms in human epithelia and an additional 8 in hair and nails.
B. The type II intermediate filament protein ____________ is widely distributed in cells of mesenchymal origin, such as fibroblasts, endothelial cells, and white blood cells.
C. The type II intermediate filament protein ____________ is found in both smooth and striated muscle cells.
D. Glial filaments in astrocytes and some Schwann cells are composed of ____________.
E. Type III intermediate filament proteins assemble into ____________, which are the major cytoskeletal elements in nerve axons and dendrites.

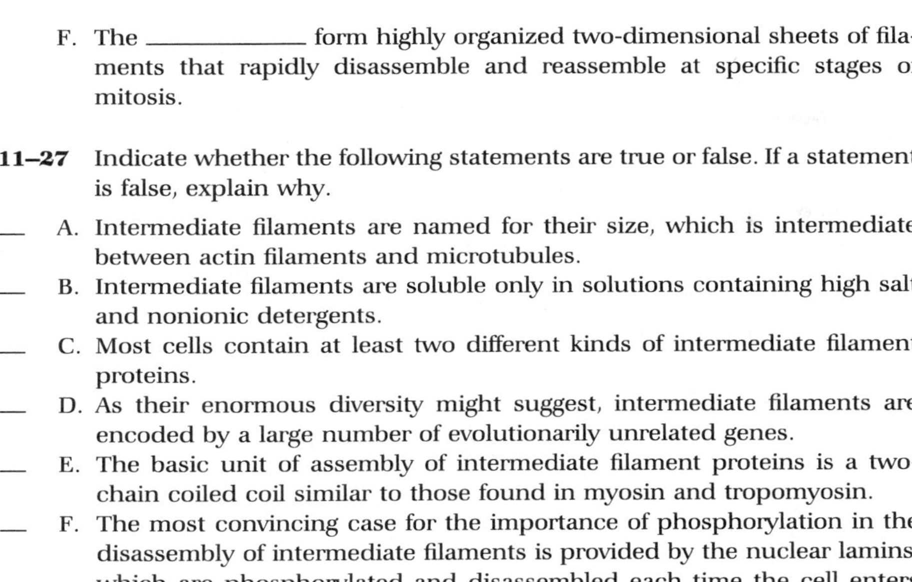

F. The ____________ form highly organized two-dimensional sheets of filaments that rapidly disassemble and reassemble at specific stages of mitosis.

11–27 Indicate whether the following statements are true or false. If a statement is false, explain why.

__ A. Intermediate filaments are named for their size, which is intermediate between actin filaments and microtubules.

__ B. Intermediate filaments are soluble only in solutions containing high salt and nonionic detergents.

__ C. Most cells contain at least two different kinds of intermediate filament proteins.

__ D. As their enormous diversity might suggest, intermediate filaments are encoded by a large number of evolutionarily unrelated genes.

__ E. The basic unit of assembly of intermediate filament proteins is a two-chain coiled coil similar to those found in myosin and tropomyosin.

__ F. The most convincing case for the importance of phosphorylation in the disassembly of intermediate filaments is provided by the nuclear lamins, which are phosphorylated and disassembled each time the cell enters mitosis.

__ G. Cytoplasmic intermediate filaments are thought to be essential for cell survival.

__ H. The "fingerprint" provided by a cell's intermediate filament composition can be very useful for tracing the origins of tumors.

11–28 You have just deduced the amino acid sequence of nuclear lamin C from the nucleotide sequence of a cDNA clone. Based on ultrastructural evidence and nucleotide sequence homology, it appears that the nuclear lamins belong to the intermediate filament family. If nuclear lamin C is a member of the intermediate filament family, it should show regions of the coiled-coil heptad repeat motif, AbcDefg, where A and D are hydrophobic amino acids and b, c, e, f, and g can be almost any amino acid. Your sequence is shown in Figure 11–20 with potential coiled-coil regions in bold. Examine the segment marked coil 1A. Does it conform to the heptad repeat? (The mnemonic "FAMILY VW" will help you recognize hydrophobic amino acids.)

coil 1A

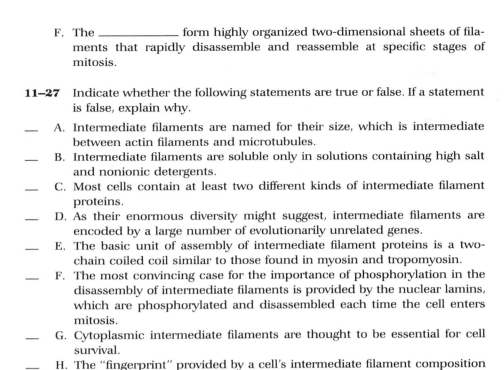

METPSQRRATRSGAQASSTPLSPTRITRLQEKED**LQELNDRLAVYIDRVRSLETENA**

coil 1B

GLRLRITESEEVVSREVSGIKAA**YEAELGDARKTLDSVAKERARLQLELSKVREEFK**

ELKARNTKKEGDLIAAQARLKDLEALLNSKEAALSTALSEKRTLEGELHDLRGQVAK

LEAALGEAKKQLQDEMLRRVDAENRLQTMKEELDFQKNIYSEELRETKRRHETRLVE

coil 2

IDNGKQREFESRLAD**ALQQLRAQHEDQVEQYKKELEKTYSAKLDNARQSAERNSNLV**

GAAHEELQQSRIRIDSLSAQLSQLQKQLAAKEAKLRDLEDSLARERDTSRRLLAEKE

REMAEMRARMQQQLDEYQQLLDIKLALDMQIHAYRKLLEGEEERLRLSPSPTSQRSR

GRASSHSSQTQGGGSVTKKRKLESTESRSSPSQHARTSGRVAVEEVDEEGKFVRLRN

KSNEDQSMGNWQIKRQNGDDPLLTYRFPPKFTLKAGQVVTIWAAGAGATHSPPTDLV

WKAQNTWGCGNSLRTALINSTGEEVAMRKLVRSVTVVEDDEDEDGDDLLHHHHVSGS

RR

Figure 11–20 The amino acid sequence of nuclear lamin C (Problem 11–28).

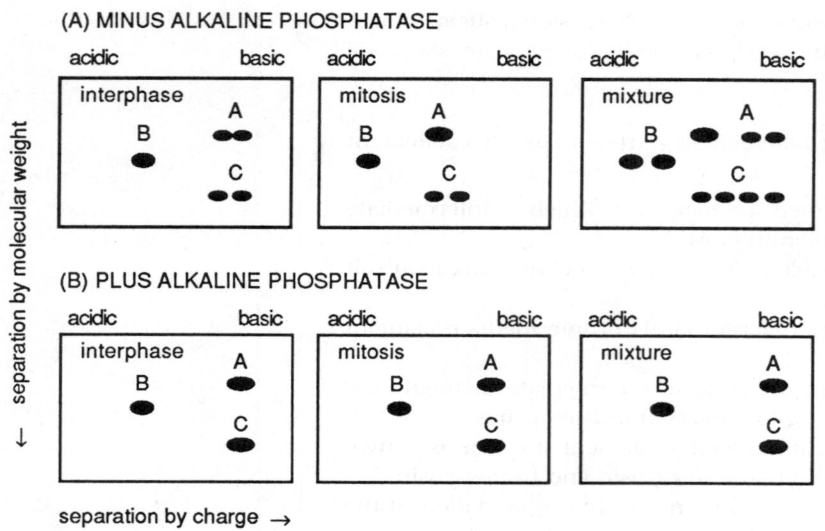

Figure 11–21 Two-dimensional separation of nuclear lamins from cells in interphase and mitosis (Problem 11–29). (A) No treatment with alkaline phosphatase. (B) Treatment with alkaline phosphatase. Letters identify the positions of lamins A, B, and C. The purified lamins from interphase and mitotic cells were added together to create the mixture. Acidic proteins are more negatively charged; basic proteins are more positively charged.

***11–29** The nuclear envelope is strengthened by a fibrous meshwork of lamins (the nuclear lamina), which supports the membrane on the nuclear side. When cells enter mitosis, the nuclear envelope breaks down and the nuclear lamina disassembles. Assembly and disassembly of the nuclear lamina may be controlled by reversible phosphorylation of lamins A, B, and C, since the lamins from cells that are in mitosis carry significantly more phosphate than do the lamins from cells that are in interphase.

To investigate the role of phosphorylation, you label cells with ^{35}S-methionine and then purify lamins A, B, and C from mitotic cells and from interphase cells. You then analyze each of the purified lamins and a mixture of the lamins from mitotic and interphase cells by two-dimensional gel electrophoresis (Figure 11–21A). You also treat identical samples with alkaline phosphatase, which removes phosphates from proteins, and analyze them in the same way (Figure 11–21B).

A. Why does treatment with alkaline phosphatase reduce the number of lamin spots to three regardless of the number seen in the absence of phosphatase treatment?
B. How many phosphate groups are attached to lamins A, B, and C during interphase? How many are attached during mitosis? How can you tell?
C. Why was ^{35}S-methionine rather than ^{32}P-phosphate used to label lamins in experiments designed to measure phosphorylation differences? How would the autoradiograms have differed if ^{32}P-phosphate had been used instead?
D. Do you think that these results prove that lamin disassembly during mitosis is caused by their reversible phosphorylation?

Organization of the Cytoskeleton (MBOC 667–677)

11–30 Fill in the blanks in the following statements.

A. Effective movement of a crawling animal cell requires that its plasma membrane is relatively quiescent everywhere except at its ________, where lamellipodia and microspikes periodically project outward.
B. When two moving cells collide, the encounter usually causes an immediate paralysis of the cells, a phenomenon known as ________.
C. The specialized epithelial cells found in the cochlea and vestibule of the inner ear are called ________.

11–31 Indicate whether the following statements are true or false. If a statement is false, explain why.

— A. Most, if not all, of the enzymes in the cytosol are attached to the cytoskeleton.
— B. The polarized movement of cells is organized by microtubules in some cells and by actin filaments in others.
— C. The outgrowth of neurites is inhibited by colchicine but not by cytochalasin.
— D. Myosin is required for cell division but not for movement in slime molds.
— E. Membrane recycling occurs almost exclusively at the leading edge of a moving cell.

Figure 11–22 Tubulin-decorated microtubules in a cross-section through a nerve axon (Problem 11–32). The hooks represent the tubulin decoration.

***11–32** In addition to conducting impulses in both directions, nerve axons carry vesicles to and from the cell body. The vesicles appear to move along microtubule tracks. Do outbound vesicles move along microtubules that are oriented in one direction and incoming vesicles move along microtubules that are oriented in the opposite direction? Or are microtubules all oriented in the same direction with different protein "motors" providing the directionality of vesicle movement?

To distinguish between these possibilities, you prepare a cross-section through a nerve axon and decorate the microtubules with tubulin hooks. The decorated microtubules are illustrated in Figure 11–22. Do all the microtubules run in the same direction or not? How can you tell?

11–33 Phosphorylation seems to control the intracellular movement of particles in the melanophore cells of the African fish, *Tilapianossambica*. Melanophore cells, which are on the surface of the fish, allow it to change color. These cells contain small granules of black pigment that can be dispersed throughout the cell (making the cell darker) or aggregated in a small spot in the middle of the cell (making it appear lighter) (Figure 11–23). Changes from one state to the other occur in a matter of minutes in response to hormonal stimulation. The pigment granules run along microtubule tracks.

Melanophores can be made permeable to small molecules by washing them gently in a low concentration of detergent. Pigment aggregates when ATP is added to the treated cells, but when cyclic AMP is also included, the pigment disperses. Melanophores can be made to undergo repeated cycles of pigment dispersion and aggregation by adding and removing cyclic AMP. Cyclic AMP often affects cellular processes by stimulating the activity of a cyclic AMP-dependent protein kinase. Could a similar system be responsible for melanophore pigment mobility?

To test this hypothesis, various agents known to affect phosphorylation and dephosphorylation were tested for their effects on pigment dispersal and aggregation. The results are summarized below:

1. Addition of a protein kinase inhibitor inhibits the cyclic AMP-induced dispersion.
2. Sodium vanadate, a potent inhibitor of protein phosphatases, inhibits aggregation but does not affect dispersal.
3. Addition of ATP-γ-S without any ATP or cyclic AMP causes a slow dispersion (see Figure 11–7 for structure of ATP-γ-S). ATP-γ-S can serve as a substrate for many protein kinases, but it usually does not serve as a source of energy for systems that depend on the free energy of ATP hydrolysis (see Problem 11–8).
4. Pigment that has been dispersed with ATP-γ-S reaggregates extremely slowly when new buffer containing ATP is added, in contrast to pigment that has been dispersed with ATP and cyclic AMP.
5. When ATP-γ-^{32}P is added in the presence of cyclic AMP, a protein of molecular weight 57,000 is labeled; when cyclic AMP is removed, the protein loses its label.

A. Draw a plausible molecular pathway that describes the control of pigment dispersal and aggregation.
B. Do pigment aggregation, pigment dispersal, or both require the free energy of ATP hydrolysis?

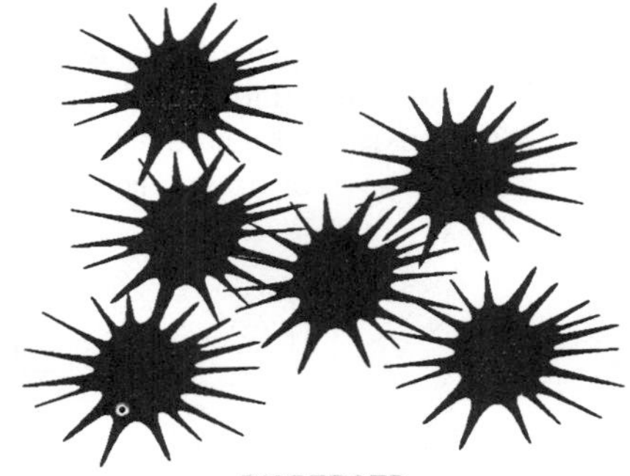

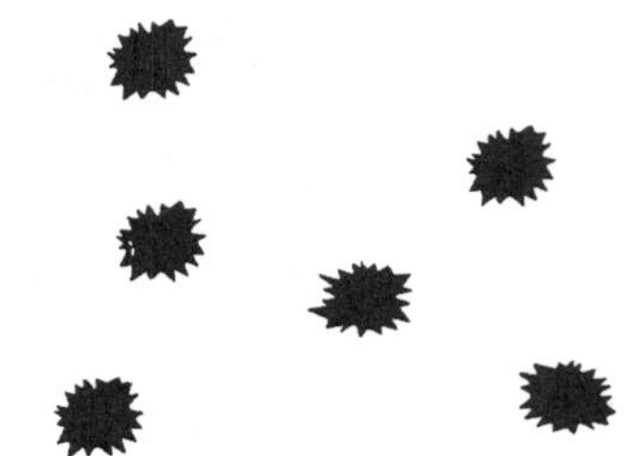

Figure 11–23 Dispersed and aggregated pigment granules in melanophore cells (Problem 11–33).

11–34 It should be a simple matter to discover how nerve cells grow. By adding radioactive amino acids to a nerve cell body and following their incorporation into proteins, it has been demonstrated that proteins move out of the cell body and down the axons. In the experiment shown in Figure 11–24, ^{3}H-leucine was injected adjacent to the nerve that controls the guinea pig tongue, and the animal was sacrificed nine days later. The nerve was dissected and cut into 2-mm lengths, which were then analyzed by SDS polyacrylamide gel electrophoresis. Broadly speaking, there are three distinct groups of protein. A heterogeneous group of glycoproteins travels rapidly in vesicles that have long since disappeared from the section of nerve shown in Figure 11–24. Actin and various soluble enzymes move faster (about 3 mm per day) than do the neurofilament proteins (about 1 mm per day). Tubulin, however, seems to belong to both classes.

On the basis of these data, it has been proposed that newly synthesized neurofilaments and microtubules are assembled in the cell body and move down the axon as a coherent structure that remains intact until it reaches the tip of the axon, where it is destroyed or recycled.

However, your own observations of nerve growth in culture (the tips progress at about 40 μm per hour) have made you skeptical of this conventional account of axonal growth. It looks to you as if the growing tip can choose where it goes—not as if it is being pushed from behind. To discover where microtubule assembly occurs, you apply (using a micropipet) a microtubule inhibitor (colchicine) either to the tip or to the body of an axon. When colchicine is applied to a growth cone, it stops growing, while its untreated sister axons continue unaffected. By contrast, no inhibition of nerve growth takes place when colchicine is applied to the cell body. Since the plus ends of microtubules are at the nerve tip, you conclude that the evidence from the labeling experiments is somehow misleading and that nerve growth in fact occurs at the tip. Your paper is published, but it provokes a lively correspondence.

A. How does the rate of nerve growth as measured under the microscope compare with the rate of movement of proteins down the axon as measured in the guinea pig?
B. If you were a proponent of assembly in the cell body, how might you explain away the colchicine result?
C. As a supporter of assembly at the tip of the axon, how would you explain the labeling result in Figure 11–24?
D. If you could label nerve cells by injecting biotin-tagged tubulin, how would you expect the labeled segment of microtubules to move according to the two views of nerve growth?

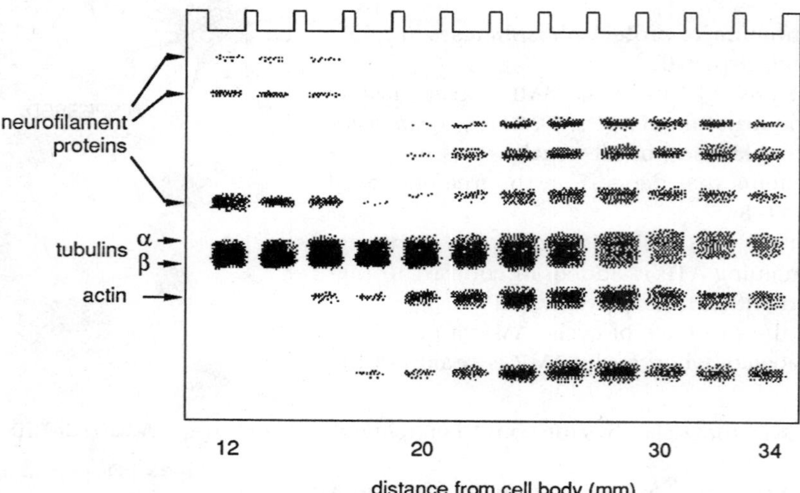

Figure 11–24 SDS gel analysis of the movement of labeled proteins down an axon (Problem 11–34).

Cell Signaling

12

Three Strategies of Chemical Signaling: Endocrine, Paracrine, and Synaptic (MBOC 682–690)

12–1 Fill in the blanks in the following statements.

A. Specialized endocrine cells secrete ____________, which are molecules that travel through the bloodstream to influence target cells throughout the body.

B. Chemical mediators that act only on cells in the immediate environment in which they are released participate in the process known as ____________.

C. Signaling between cells in the nervous system is mediated by __________, which are secreted at specialized junctions called chemical synapses.

D. The endocrine system in vertebrates is physically and functionally linked to the nervous system by a specific region of the brain called the ____________.

E. The ____________ comprise an important family of local chemical mediators that are derived from 20-carbon fatty acids.

12–2 Indicate whether the following statements are true or false. If a statement is false, explain why.

__ A. Endocrine signaling is relatively slow because it depends on diffusion and blood flow.

__ B. The specificity of endocrine signaling depends on responsive cells possessing receptors that bind the hormone tightly by means of multiple weak chemical bonds.

__ C. The concentration of a neurotransmitter at a neuromuscular junction may be as much as 5000 times higher than the effective concentration of a hormone in the bloodstream.

__ D. Hormones are rapidly removed from the bloodstream by hydrolytic enzymes.

__ E. The specificity of signaling molecules is such that they always function in the same signaling mode: endocrine, paracrine, or synaptic.

__ F. If the same signaling molecule has different effects on different target tissues, the receptors are usually different.

__ G. One reason that responses mediated by peptide hormones such as insulin are slow is that the peptide must first be synthesized in the endocrine cell of origin.

__ H. Water-soluble hormones interact with cell-surface receptors, whereas lipid-soluble hormones usually bind to intracellular receptors.

__ I. Mast cells secrete histamine, which mediates the inflammatory response; they also secrete two tetrapeptides to attract eosinophils, which produce antihistamines to terminate the response.

12–3 To make antibodies against the acetylcholine receptor from electric eel electric organ, you inject the purified receptor into mice. You note an interesting correlation: mice with high levels of antibodies against the receptor appear weak and sluggish; those with low levels are lively. You suspect that the antibodies against the eel acetylcholine receptors are cross-reacting with the mouse acetylcholine receptors, causing many of the receptors to be destroyed. Since a reduction in the number of acetylcholine receptors is also the basis for the human autoimmune disease, myasthenia gravis, you wonder whether an injection of the drug neostigmine might give a temporary restoration of strength, as it does for myasthenic patients. Sure enough, when you inject your mice with neostigmine, they immediately stand up and become very lively. Propose an explanation for how neostigmine might restore temporary function to a neuromuscular synapse with a reduced number of acetylcholine receptors.

***12–4** Succinylcholine, which is an acetylcholine analogue, is used by surgeons as a muscle relaxant. Care must be taken in its use because some individuals recover abnormally slowly from this paralysis, with life-threatening consequences. Such individuals are deficient in an enzyme called pseudocholinesterase, which is normally present in the blood.

If succinylcholine is an analogue of acetylcholine, why do you think it causes muscles to relax and not contract as acetylcholine does?

***12–5** Radioimmunoassay (RIA) is a powerful tool for quantifying virtually any substance of biological interest because it is sensitive, accurate, and fast. RIA technology arose from studies on adult onset diabetes, which demonstrated the existence of antibodies with high affinity for insulin and developed methods to distinguish free insulin from antibody-bound insulin.

How can high-affinity antibodies and separation techniques be exploited to measure low concentrations of insulin? When a small amount of anti-insulin antiserum is mixed with an equally small amount of very highly radioactive insulin, some binds and some remains free according to the equilibrium.

$$\text{Insulin} + \text{Antibody} \leftrightarrows \text{Insulin-Antibody Complex}$$

$$K = k\,\frac{[\text{Insulin-Antibody Complex}]}{[\text{Insulin}]\,[\text{Antibody}]}$$

When increasing amounts of unlabeled insulin are added to a fixed amount of labeled insulin and antiserum, the ratio of bound to free radioactive insulin decreases as expected from the equilibrium expression (Figure 12–1). If the concentration of the unlabeled insulin is known, then the resulting curve serves as a calibration against which other unknown samples can be compared.

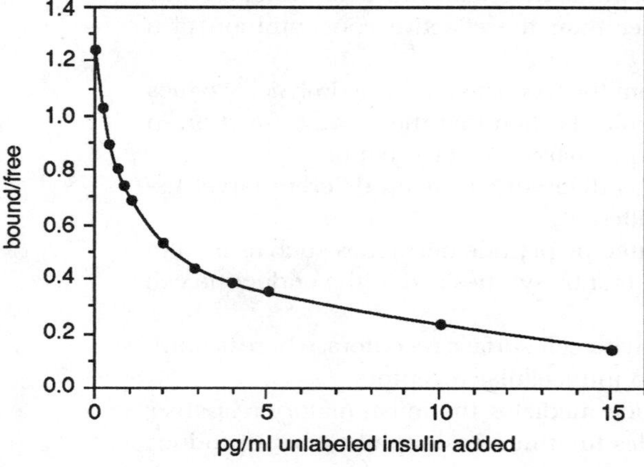

Figure 12–1 Calibration curve for radioimmunoassay of insulin (Problem 12–5).

*Problems with an asterisk (*) are answered in the Instructor's Manual.

You have three samples of insulin whose concentrations are unknown. When mixed with the same amount of radioactive insulin and anti-insulin antibody used in Figure 12–1 the three samples gave the following ratios of bound to free insulin:

Sample 1	0.67
Sample 2	0.31
Sample 3	0.46

A. What is the concentration of insulin in each of these unknown samples?
B. What portion of the standard curve is the most accurate, and why?
C. If the antibodies were raised against pig insulin, which is similar but not identical to human insulin, would the assay still be valid for measuring human insulin concentrations?

12–6 The optimal sensitivity of radioimmunoassay occurs when the concentrations of the unknown and the radioactive tracer are equal. Thus the sensitivity of radioimmunoassay is limited by the specific activity of the radioactive ligand. The more highly radioactive the ligand, the smaller the amount needed per assay and, therefore, the smaller amount of unknown that can be detected.

You wish to measure an unknown sample of insulin (molecular weight, 11,466) using an insulin tracer labeled with radioactive iodine, which has a half-life of 7 days. Assume that you can attach one atom of radioactive iodine per molecule of insulin, that iodine does not interfere with antibody binding, that each radioactive disintegration has a 50% probability of being detected as a "count," and that the limit of detection in the radioimmunoassay requires a total of at least 1000 counts per minute (cpm) distributed between the bound and free fractions.

A. Given these parameters, calculate how many picograms of radioactive insulin will be required for an assay.
B. At optimal sensitivity, how many picograms of unlabeled insulin will you be able to detect?

12–7 The thyroid hormone, thyroxine, is composed of two linked, iodinated tyrosine residues (Figure 12–2). It is stored in the thyroid gland in a structure called a follicle, as part of a much larger protein called thyroglobulin. The follicle consists of a cellular epithelium surrounding an extracellular space or lumen. When the thyroid is stimulated by TSH (thyroid-stimulating hormone), thyroxine is digested out of thyroglobulin by proteases and released into the bloodstream.

The actual pathway for thyroxine release was difficult to identify. When the thyroid is stimulated by TSH, "colloid droplets" appear in the cytoplasm of the follicle cells. The similarity of the material in these droplets to the material in the lumen of the follicle sparked an intense debate: Do the droplets represent material on the way out of the cell to the lumen (to replenish the supply), or do they represent lumenal material engulfed by the cell (to generate thyroxine)? This question has been resolved by a series of experimental observations.

1. If the colloid in the lumen is prelabeled with ^{131}I and the follicles are then stimulated with TSH under conditions that block further incorporation of iodine, the intracellular droplets are labeled.
2. Intracellular droplets form about 4 minutes after exposure to TSH and are seen first in the apical cell processes, which abut the lumen of the follicle, then in the apical region of the cell, and finally in the basal region.
3. Thyroglobulin in the lumen of the follicle carries mannose 6-phosphate, which normally targets proteins for delivery to lysosomes.

Given these observations, propose a pathway for thyroxine production and release from follicle cells.

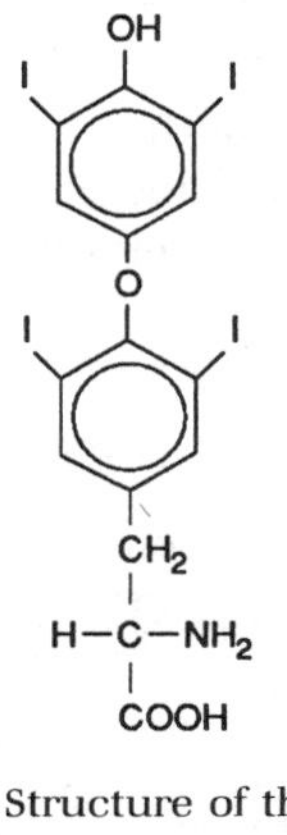

OH
I I
O
I I
CH_2
H–C–NH_2
COOH

Figure 12–2 Structure of thyroxine (Problem 12–7).

Signaling Mediated by Intracellular Receptors: Mechanisms of Steroid Hormone Action

(MBOC 690–693)

12–8 Fill in the blanks in the following statements.

A. A small number of ____________, all of which are synthesized from cholesterol, regulate developmental and physiological processes in organisms from fungi to man.

B. The binding of a steroid hormone causes its receptor to undergo a conformational change (a process called ____________) that increases its affinity for DNA and enables it to bind to specific genes in the nucleus and regulate their transcription.

C. The molting hormone in *Drosophila* is called ____________.

D. The syndrome in which genetically male mammals with defective testosterone receptors develop the secondary sexual characteristics of females is called ____________.

12–9 Indicate whether the following statements are true or false. If a statement is false, explain why.

__ A. All steroid hormones isolated so far are DNA-binding proteins.

__ B. The response to steroid hormones often takes place in two steps, only the first of which (the primary response) is directly caused by the binding of the receptor-hormone complex to DNA.

__ C. Steroid receptors have separate domains for ligand binding and for DNA recognition and gene activation.

__ D. The receptor for estradiol, cortisol, and progesterone is encoded by a single gene.

__ E. All cells that respond to a particular steroid hormone contain the same receptor; their responses, however, can vary because other proteins in addition to the activated steroid receptor may be required to turn on particular genes.

12–10 You are studying the expression of genes linked to a segment of the Moloney murine sarcoma virus, which is regulated by glucocorticoids. You made a series of constructs with the viral segment in both orientations, upstream and downstream of a reporter gene (chloramphenicol acetyl transferase, *CAT*). You then transfected the constructs into two cell lines derived from different tissues and measured CAT activity in the presence and absence of a glucocorticoid (dexamethasone). The orientation and location of the viral segment made relatively little difference in the expression of the reporter gene, which is the expected result if the viral segment carries an enhancer of transcription. Results from the *CAT* gene alone and a construct with the viral segment in one orientation are shown in Figure 12–3. You are puzzled by the results with cell line 1 because the viral segment increased CAT expression twentyfold in the absence of dexamethasone.

A. Do both cell lines contain glucocorticoid receptors? How can you tell?

B. How does cell line 1 differ from cell line 2? Propose an explanation for the difference.

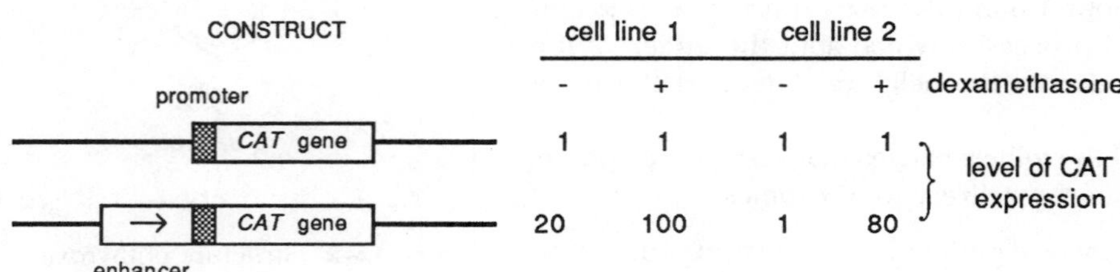

Figure 12–3 Results of transfecting two different constructs into two different cell lines (Problem 12–10). Presence (+) and absence (−) of the hormone (dexamethasone) is indicated. Numbers indicate expression of the *CAT* gene product; in all cases, the values are expressed relative to a construct without the viral segment.

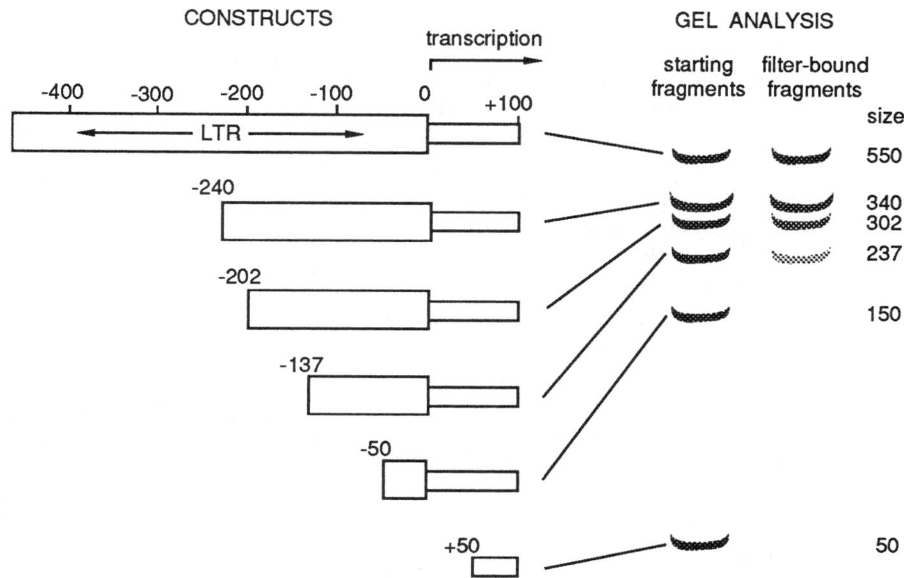

Figure 12–4 Schematic diagram of the LTR deletions and the electrophoretic patterns of the starting and bound mixtures of DNA fragments (Problem 12–11). Nucleotides are numbered relative to the start site for transcription, which is at +1. Negative numbers are in front of the start site, and positive numbers are after it. The electrophoretic pattern is an autoradiograph of the agarose gel.

C. Based on your explanation, predict the outcome of an experiment in which a variety of shorter pieces of the viral segment are placed in front of the *CAT* gene and tested for CAT activity in the two cell lines.

***12–11** Glucocorticoids induce transcription of mouse mammary tumor virus (MMTV) genes. Using hybrid constructs containing the MMTV long terminal repeat (LTR) linked to an easily assayable gene, you have shown that the LTR contains regulatory elements that respond to glucocorticoids. To map the glucocorticoid response elements within the LTR, you generate a series of deletions that remove different extents of the LTR (Figure 12–4) and then measure the binding of the DNA segments to glucocorticoid receptors. To measure binding, you cut each of the mutant DNAs into fragments, purify the fragments containing LTR sequences, and label the ends with ^{32}P. You then incubate a mixture of the labeled fragments with the purified glucocorticoid receptor. You assess binding by passing the incubation mixture through a nitrocellulose filter, which binds protein (and any attached DNA) but not free DNA. You display the DNA segments that were bound to the receptor by agarose gel electrophoresis. The electrophoretic patterns of the starting mixture of segments and the bound segments are shown in Figure 12–4.

A. Where in the LTR are the glucocorticoid response elements located?

B. A list of eleven MMTV sequences (several from the LTR) that are bound by the glucocorticoid receptor are shown in Figure 12–5. Can you find the consensus sequence to which the receptor binds?

```
 1.   CCAAGGAGGGGACAGTGGCTGGACTAATAG
 2.   GGACTAATAGAACATTATTCTCCAAAAACT
 3.   TCGTTTTAAGAACAGTTTGTAACCAAAAAC
 4.   AGGATGTGAGACAAGTGGTTTCCTGACTTG
 5.   AGGAAAATAGAACACTCAGAGCTCAGATCA
 6.   CAGAGCTCAGATCAGAACCTTTGATACCAA
 7.   CATGATTCAGCACAAAAAGAGCGTGTGCCA
 8.   CTGTTATTAGGACATCGTCCTTTCCAGGAC
 9.   CCTAGTGTAGATCAGTCAGATCAGATTAAA
10.   GATCAGTCAGATCAGATTAAAAGCAAAAAG
11.   TTCCAAATAGATCCTTTTTGCTTTTAATCT
```

Figure 12–5 DNA sequences that are bound by the glucocorticoid receptor (Problem 12–11).

12–12 *Drosophila* larvae molt in response to an increase in the concentration of the steroid hormone ecdysone. The polytene chromosomes of the *Drosophila* salivary glands are an excellent experimental system in which to study the pattern of gene activity initiated by the hormone because active genes enlarge into puffs that are visible in the light microscope. Furthermore, the size of a puff is proportional to the rate at which it is being transcribed. Prior to addition of ecdysone, a few puffs—termed intermolt puffs—are already active. Upon exposure of dissected salivary glands to ecdysone, these intermolt puffs regress, and two additional sets of puffs appear. One set of puffs (early puffs) arises within a few minutes after addition of ecdysone; the other set (late puffs) arises within 4 to 10 hours. The concentration of ecdysone does not change during this time period. The pattern of puff appearance and disappearance is illustrated for a typical puff in each category in Figure 12–6A.

Two critical experiments help to define the relationships between the different classes of puff. In the first, cycloheximide, which blocks protein synthesis, is added at the same time as ecdysone. As illustrated in Figure 12–6B, under these conditions the early puffs do not regress and the late puffs are not induced. In the second experiment, ecdysone is washed out after a 2-hour exposure. As illustrated in Figure 12–6C, this treatment causes an immediate regression of the early puffs and a *premature induction* of the late puffs.

A. Why do you think the early puffs do not regress and the late puffs are not induced in the presence of cycloheximide? Why do you think the intermolt puffs are unaffected?

B. Why do you think the early puffs regress immediately when ecdysone is removed? Why do you think the late puffs arise prematurely under these conditions?

C. Outline a model for ecdysone-mediated regulation of the puffing pattern.

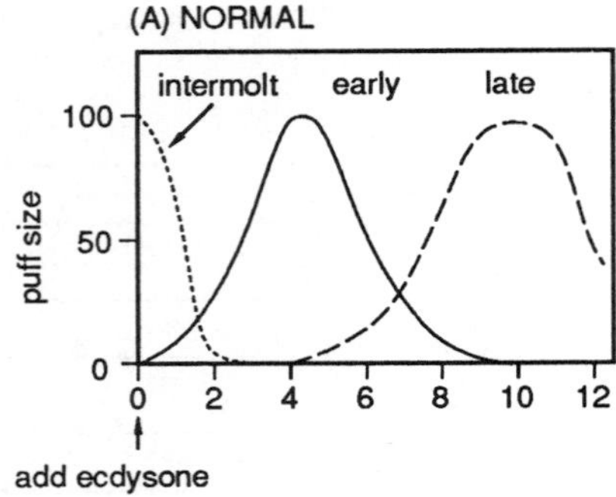

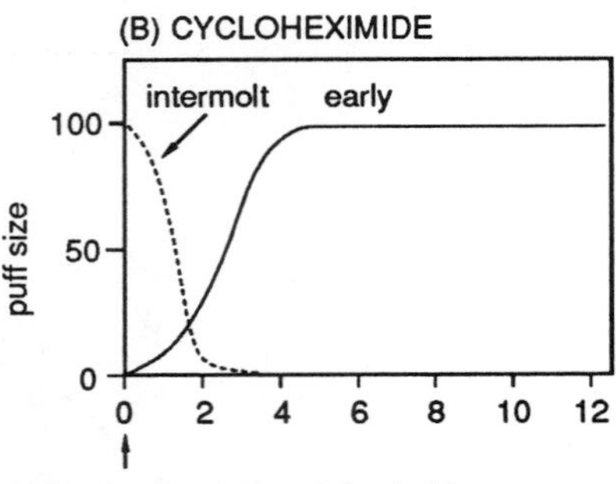

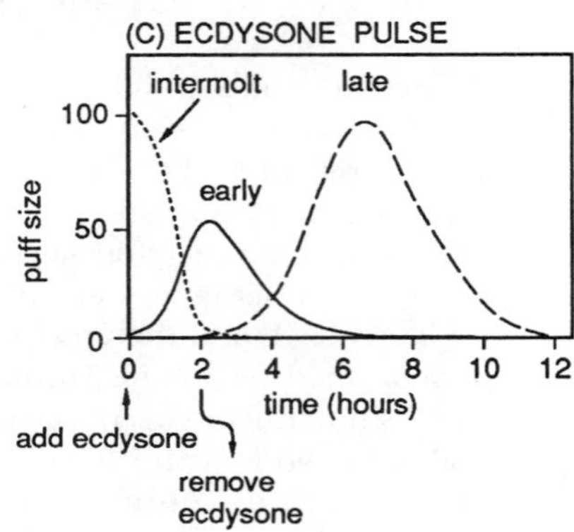

Figure 12–6 Patterns of puffing in salivary gland chromosomes (Problem 12–12). (A) Normal puffing pattern. (B) Puffing pattern in the presence of cycloheximide. (C) Puffing pattern after removal of ecdysone.

Mechanisms of Transduction by Cell-Surface Receptor Proteins (MBOC 693–708)

12–13 Fill in the blanks in the following statements.

A. ______________ receptors are cell-surface proteins that are mainly involved in rapid synaptic signaling between electrically excitable cells.

B. ______________ receptors, when activated by their ligand, function directly as enzymes.

C. ______________ receptors indirectly activate or inactivate a separate plasma-membrane-bound enzyme or ion channel.

D. Many extracellular signals act by altering the intracellular levels of ______________, of which cyclic AMP and Ca^{2+} ions are two of the most important examples.

E. Cyclic AMP is synthesized from ATP by the plasma-membrane-bound enzyme ______________, and it is destroyed by the enzyme ______________.

F. Receptors modulate the activity of the enzymes involved in synthesis and breakdown of cyclic AMP indirectly through GTP-binding regulatory proteins known as ______________.

G. Transfer of ADP-ribose from NAD^+ to a G_s protein, which is catalyzed by ______________, activates adenylate cyclase indefinitely.

H. α_2-adrenergic receptors are functionally coupled to adenylate cyclase by an ______________, which contains the same β and γ subunits as a G_s protein but a different α subunit.

I. Many cells contain a specialized compartment for Ca^{2+} storage and release (the ______________) that is distinct from the endoplasmic reticulum and homologous with the sarcoplasmic reticulum of muscle cells.

J. Certain extracellular signaling molecules stimulate incorporation of radioactive phosphate into ____________, which is a minor phospholipid in cell membranes.

K. ____________ is a small water-soluble molecule that releases Ca^{2+} from its intracellular storage compartment.

L. The Ca^{2+}-dependent enzyme activated by diacylglycerol is called ____________.

M. The ____________ encoded by viral oncogenes differ from their normal counterparts by one or two amino acid substitutions that impair their GTPase function.

N. Many catalytic receptors are single-pass transmembrane proteins with ____________ activity.

12–14 Indicate whether the following statements are true or false. If a statement is false, explain why.

___ A. Cell-surface receptors often carry their ligands into the cell by receptor-mediated endocytosis, but this process is not the basis of their signaling activity.

___ B. Catalytic receptors, which act directly as enzymes, usually function as tyrosine-specific protein kinases.

___ C. The enzyme glycogen phosphorylase is a protein kinase that is stimulated by cyclic AMP.

___ D. The synthesis of cyclic AMP in response to hormone stimulation requires GTP as well as ATP.

___ E. When G_s proteins bind GTP, they dissociate into α and $\beta\gamma$ subunits.

___ F. Replacement of GDP by GTP on G proteins is catalyzed by a ligand-activated receptor.

___ G. Adenylate cyclase remains activated until the G_s protein hydrolyzes its bound GTP to GDP and dissociates.

___ H. Activation of adenylate cyclase by nonhydrolyzable GTP analogues requires that a suitable hormone be present, whereas activation by cholera toxin does not.

___ I. Alterations to intracellular Ca^{2+} levels can be mediated by activation of phospholipase C, which transiently permeabilizes the plasma membrane to Ca^{2+} ions by hydrolyzing membrane phospholipids.

___ J. Inositol trisphosphate acts by direct stimulation of protein kinase C.

___ K. The highest levels of protein kinase C are found in the brain, where it probably modulates the activity of ion channels by reversible phosphorylation.

___ L. Phorbol esters stimulate protein kinase C directly.

___ M. The G protein transducin, which is found in vertebrate eyes, stimulates cyclic GMP phosphodiesterase, thereby reducing cyclic GMP levels in response to light.

___ N. The *sis* oncogene encodes a functionally active version of the platelet-derived growth factor receptor.

12–15 You wish to measure the number of β-adrenergic receptors on the membranes of frog erythrocytes. These receptors normally bind epinephrine and stimulate adenyl cyclase activity; however, you have chosen to use a competitive inhibitor of epinephrine (alprenolol), which binds to the receptors 500 times more tightly. Your basic experimental protocol is to mix labeled alprenolol with erythrocyte membranes, leave them for 10 minutes at 37°C, pellet the membranes by centrifugation, and measure the radioactivity in the pellet. You perform the experiment in two ways. First, you measure the binding of increasing amounts of ^{3}H-alprenolol to a fixed amount of erythrocyte membranes in order to determine total binding. Second, you repeat the experiment in the presence of a vast excess of unlabeled alprenolol to measure nonspecific binding. Your results are shown in Figure 12–7.

A. Sketch in the curve for specific binding of alprenolol to β-adrenergic receptors. Has alprenolol binding to the receptors reached saturation?

B. Assuming that one molecule of alprenolol binds per receptor, calculate the number of β-adrenergic receptors on the membrane of a frog erythrocyte. The specific activity of the labeled alprenolol is 1×10^{13} cpm/mmol, and there are 8×10^{8} frog erythrocytes per milligram of membrane protein.

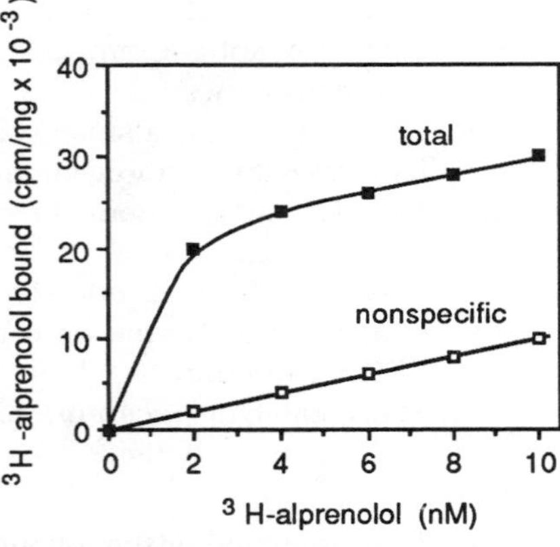

Figure 12–7 Binding of ^{3}H-alprenolol to frog erythrocyte membranes (Problem 12–15).

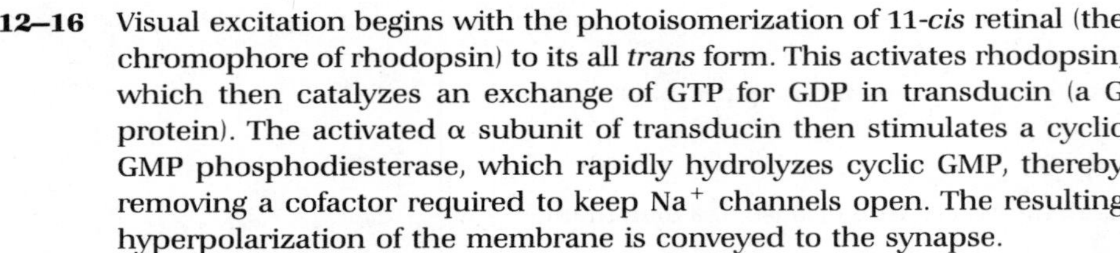

***12–16** Visual excitation begins with the photoisomerization of 11-*cis* retinal (the chromophore of rhodopsin) to its all *trans* form. This activates rhodopsin, which then catalyzes an exchange of GTP for GDP in transducin (a G protein). The activated α subunit of transducin then stimulates a cyclic GMP phosphodiesterase, which rapidly hydrolyzes cyclic GMP, thereby removing a cofactor required to keep Na^+ channels open. The resulting hyperpolarization of the membrane is conveyed to the synapse.

It is estimated that one activated rhodopsin leads to hydrolysis of 5×10^{5} cyclic GMP molecules per second. One stage in this enormous signal amplification is achieved by cyclic GMP phosphodiesterase, which hydrolyzes 1000 molecules of cyclic GMP per second. The additional factor of 500 could arise because one activated rhodopsin activates 500 transducins, or because one activated transducin activates 500 cyclic GMP phosphodiesterases, or through a combination of both effects. One experiment to address this question measured the amount of GppNp (a nonhydrolyzable analogue of GTP) that is bound by transducin in the presence of different amounts of activated rhodopsin. As indicated in Figure 12–8, 5.5 mmol of GppNp were bound per mole of total rhodopsin when 0.0011% of the rhodopsin was activated.

A. Assuming each transducin molecule binds one molecule of GppNp, calculate the number of transducin molecules that are activated by each activated rhodopsin molecule. Which mechanism of amplification does this measurement support?

B. Binding studies have shown that transducin-GDP has a high affinity for activated rhodopsin and that transducin-GTP has a low affinity; conversely, transducin-GTP has a high affinity and transducin-GDP has a low affinity for cyclic GMP phosphodiesterase. Are these affinities consistent with the mechanism of amplification you deduced from the above experiment? How so?

12–17 Acetylcholine acts on muscarinic receptors in the heart to open K^+ channels, thereby slowing the heart rate. Treatment of heart cells with pertussis toxin blocks this physiological response, suggesting that a G protein is responsible for coupling receptor stimulation to channel activation.

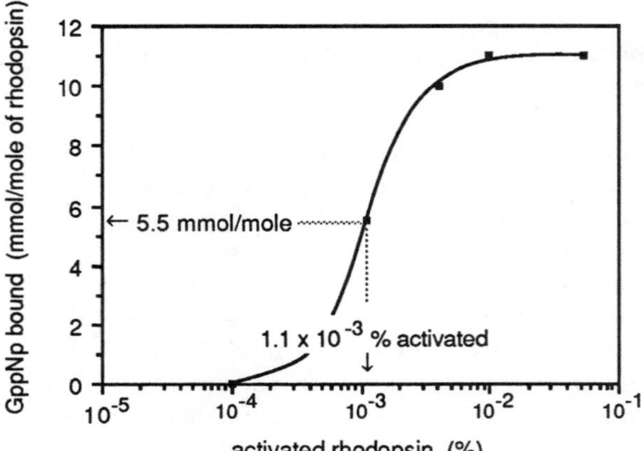

Figure 12–8 Binding of GppNp to rod cell membranes as a function of the fraction of activated rhodopsin (Problem 12–16). Background binding of GppNp to rod cell membranes in the dark has been subtracted from the values shown.

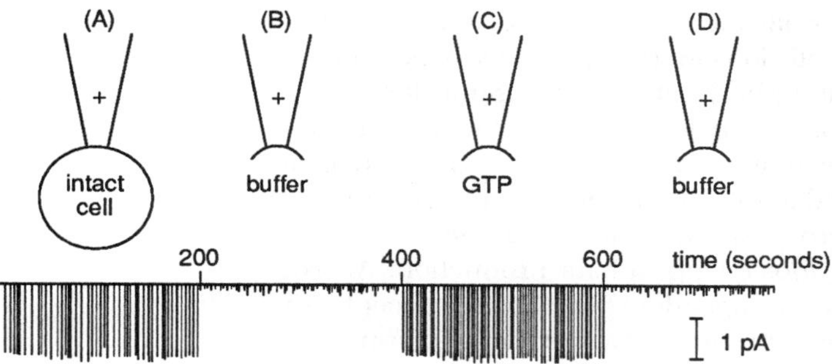

Figure 12–9 Experimental setup and typical results of patch-clamp analysis of K^+ channel activation by acetylcholine (Problem 12–17). The buffer is a buffered salts solution that does not contain nucleotides or Ca^{2+}. In all these experiments, acetylcholine is present inside the pipette, as indicated by the +. The current through the membrane is measured in picoamps (pA). In (C) the GTP is added to the buffer.

This process can be studied directly using the inside-out membrane patch-clamp technique. In this technique a patch of membrane is pulled from a cell with a pipette. The external surface of the membrane is in contact with the solution in the bore of the pipette, and the cytoplasmic surface faces outward and can be exposed readily to a variety of solutions (Figure 12–9). Receptors, G proteins, and K^+ channels remain associated with the membrane patch.

The status of the K^+ channel can be assessed by measuring the current through the membrane. A typical experiment is illustrated in Figure 12–9. When acetylcholine is added to a pipette (indicated by +) with a whole cell attached, K^+ channels open as indicated by the flow of current (Figure 12–9A). Under similar circumstances with a patch of membrane inserted into a buffered salts solution, no current flows (Figure 12–9B). When GTP is added to the buffer, however, current resumes (Figure 12–9C). Subsequent removal of GTP stops the current (Figure 12–9D). The results of several similar experiments to test the effects of different combinations of components are summarized in Table 12–1.

A. As shown in Table 12–1, line 4, addition of GppNp (a nonhydrolyzable analogue of GTP) caused the K^+ channel to open in the absence of acetylcholine. The flow of current, however, rose very slowly and reached its maximum only after a minute (compare with the immediate rise in Figure 12–9A and C). How do you think GppNp caused the channels to open in the absence of acetylcholine?
B. Why do you think it is that $G_{\beta\gamma}$ activated the channel when the complete G protein did not? Is the active subcomponent of the G protein in this system the same as the subcomponent that activates adenyl cyclase in other cells?
C. Do these experiments suggest that the K^+ channel is likely to be activated by an intracellular messenger?
D. To the extent these experiments allow, draw a scheme for the activation of K^+ channels in heart cells in response to acetylcholine.

Table 12–1 Responses of K^+ Channel to Various Experimental Manipulations (Problem 12–17)

	Acetylcholine	Small Molecules Added to Buffer	Purified G-Protein Components Added to Buffer	K^+ Channel
1.	+	none	none	closed
2.	+	GTP	none	open
3.	–	GTP	none	closed
4.	–	GppNp	none	open
5.	–	none	G protein	closed
6.	–	none	G_α	closed
7.	–	none	$G_{\beta\gamma}$	open
8.	–	none	boiled G protein	closed

***12–18** In a cell line derived from normal rat thyroid, stimulation of the α_1-adrenergic receptor increases both inositol phosphate formation and release of arachidonic acid. Inositol phosphate elevates intracellular Ca^{2+}, which mediates thyroxine efflux, whereas arachidonic acid serves as a source of prostaglandin E_2, which stimulates DNA synthesis. How is arachidonic acid release connected to the adrenergic receptor? Arachidonic acid could arise by diacylglycerol-lipase-mediated cleavage from the diacylglycerol that accompanies inositol phosphate production. Alternatively, it could arise through an independent effect of the receptor on phospholipase A_2, which can directly release arachidonic acid from intact phosphoglycerides. Consider the following experimental observations:

1. Addition of norepinephrine to cell cultures stimulates production of both inositol phosphate and arachidonic acid.
2. If the adrenergic receptors are made unresponsive to norepinephrine by treatment with phorbol esters (which presumably act through protein kinase C to cause phosphorylation, hence inactivation, of the receptor), addition of norepinephrine causes no increase in either inositol phosphate or arachidonic acid.
3. When cells are made permeable to GTP-γ-S (a nonhydrolyzable analogue of GTP), production of both inositol phosphate and arachidonic acid is increased.
4. If cells are treated with neomycin (which blocks the action of phospholipase C), subsequent treatment with GTP-γ-S stimulates arachidonic acid production but causes no increase in inositol phosphate.
5. If cells are treated with pertussis toxin, subsequent treatment with GTP-γ-S stimulates production of inositol phosphate but causes no increase in arachidonic acid.

A. Which of the two proposed mechanisms for arachidonic acid production in these cells do the observations support?
B. Describe a molecular pathway for activation of arachidonic acid production that is consistent with the experimental results.

The Mode of Action of Cyclic AMP and Calcium Ions (MBOC 708–717)

12–19 Fill in the blanks in the following statements.

A. Cyclic AMP exerts its effects in animal cells mainly by activating an enzyme called ____________.
B. The multipurpose intracellular Ca^{2+} receptor that mediates most Ca^{2+}-regulated processes is ____________.
C. One of the most important of the targets regulated by intracellular Ca^{2+}-calmodulin complexes is a family of enzymes called ____________, which phosphorylate proteins on serine or threonine residues.
D. The enzyme ____________ catalyzes the formation of cyclic GMP from GTP.

12–20 Indicate whether the following statements are true or false. If a statement is false, explain why.

___ A. Elevated cyclic AMP levels in muscle cells promote glycogen synthesis and inhibit glycogen breakdown.
___ B. In some cells an increase in cyclic AMP turns on specific genes as a result of phosphorylation of a DNA-binding protein.
___ C. Cyclic AMP activates cyclic AMP-dependent protein kinase by binding to

its regulatory subunits, thereby releasing the catalytic subunits as an active dimer.

___ D. The effects of A-kinase-mediated phosphorylation of key enzymes is reversed by the action of phosphorylases, which remove attached phosphate groups from proteins.

___ E. Calmodulin is an integral part of the enzyme phosphorylase kinase.

___ F. Cyclic nucleotides regulate ion channels in sensory organs such as the eye and the nose by direct binding rather than by influencing reversible phosphorylation of target proteins.

___ G. Cells possess efficient mechanisms for degrading cyclic AMP and sequestering Ca^{2+}, not only to terminate their responses to these effectors, but also to permit rapid increases in their concentrations in response to an incoming signal.

___ H. The calmodulin-dependent protein kinase is a Ca^{2+}-triggered switch in brain cells that may contribute to memory: a single burst of Ca^{2+} can turn it on permanently, since one of the targets it activates by phosphorylation is itself.

12–21 Does cyclic AMP work exclusively through A-kinase or do cyclic AMP-binding proteins have other critical roles, for example, as DNA-binding proteins as in bacteria? You are working with a hamster cell line that makes genetic analysis of this question possible. Because of chromosomal rearrangements, this cell line possesses only one functional copy of many genes, making isolation of recessive mutations much easier than in a fully diploid line. In addition, high intracellular levels of cyclic AMP stop their growth. By stimulating adenyl cyclase with cholera toxin and cyclic AMP phosphodiesterase with theophylline, cyclic AMP can be artificially elevated. Under these conditions only cells that are resistant to the effects of cyclic AMP can grow.

In this way you isolate several resistant colonies that grow under the selective conditions and assay them for A-kinase activity: they are all defective. About 10% of the resistant lines are completely missing A-kinase activity. The remainder possess A-kinase activity, but a very high level of cyclic AMP is required for activation. To characterize the resistant lines further, you fuse them with the parental cells and test the hybrids for resistance to cholera toxin. Hybrids between parental cells and A-kinase negative cells are sensitive to cholera toxin, which indicates that these mutations are recessive. By contrast, hybrids between parental cells and resistant cells with altered A-kinase responsiveness are resistant to cholera toxin, which indicates that these mutations are dominant.

A. Is A-kinase an essential enzyme in these hamster cells?

B. A-kinase is a tetramer consisting of two catalytic (protein kinase) and two regulatory (cyclic AMP-binding) subunits. Propose an explanation for why the mutations in some cyclic AMP-resistant cell lines are recessive and why others are dominant.

C. Do these experiments support the notion that all cyclic AMP effects in hamster cells are mediated by A-kinase?

***12–22** Unlike myosin from skeletal muscle, smooth muscle myosin interacts with actin only when its light chains are phosphorylated. Phosphorylation is controlled by variations in the intracellular concentration of Ca^{2+}, which is mediated through calmodulin. You have purified myosin light-chain kinase from a smooth muscle, but the kinase activity is the same in the presence or absence of Ca^{2+}-calmodulin. A colleague suggests that you add protease inhibitors to ensure that the kinase remains intact through the purification. Under these conditions the kinase in the extract shows no activity unless Ca^{2+}-calmodulin is present.

You partially purify the kinase by gel filtration and ion-exchange chromatography and then pass it over a calmodulin-affinity column in the

Table 12–2 Activities of Myosin Light-Chain Kinase Purified in the Presence and Absence of Protease Inhibitors (Problem 12–22)

Purification Scheme	Additions to Assay Mix	Relative Activity
Minus inhibitors	none	50
Minus inhibitors	Ca^{2+}	50
Minus inhibitors	calmodulin	50
Minus inhibitors	Ca^{2+}-calmodulin	50
Plus inhibitors	none	1
Plus inhibitors	Ca^{2+}	1
Plus inhibitors	calmodulin	1
Plus inhibitors	Ca^{2+}-calmodulin	100

presence of Ca^{2+}. To your delight, all the kinase activity sticks to the column and then elutes quantitatively when the column is washed with the calcium chelator, EGTA. As shown in Table 12–2, the purified kinase now behaves as expected; it shows an absolute dependence on Ca^{2+}-calmodulin. Buoyed by this result, you attempt to rescue a sample of the original purified enzyme by passing it directly over the calmodulin-affinity column. To your surprise, the kinase passes straight through the column, whether or not Ca^{2+} is present.

A. What is your explanation for why the original purified enzyme was active independent of Ca^{2+}-calmodulin and was not retained on the calmodulin-affinity column?
B. Outline the sequence of molecular events that leads to contraction of smooth muscles. Begin with the entry of Ca^{2+} into the cytoplasm.
C. Do you think it is possible to use calmodulin-affinity chromatography as the first step in purification of myosin light-chain kinase?

12–23 The primary role of platelets is to control blood clotting. When they encounter the exposed basement membrane (collagen fibers) of a damaged blood vessel or a newly forming fibrin clot, they change their shape from round to spiky and stick to the damaged area. At the same time they begin to secrete serotonin and ATP, which accelerate similar changes in newly arriving platelets, leading to the rapid formation of a clot. The platelet response is regulated by protein phosphorylation. Significantly, platelets contain high levels of two protein kinases: protein kinase C, which initiates serotonin release, and myosin light-chain kinase, which mediates the change in shape.

When platelets are stimulated with thrombin, the light chain of myosin and an unknown protein of 40,000 daltons are phosphorylated. When platelets are treated with a calcium ionophore, only the myosin light chain is phosphorylated; when they are treated with diacylglycerol, only the 40 kd protein is phosphorylated. Experiments using combinations of calcium ionophore and diacylglycerol show that the extent of phosphorylation of the 40 kd protein depends only on the concentration of diacylglycerol (Figure 12–10A); however, serotonin release depends on diacylglycerol and the calcium ionophore (Figure 12–10B).

A. Based on these experimental observations, describe the normal sequence of molecular events that leads to phosphorylation of the myosin light chain and the 40 kd protein. Indicate how the calcium ionophore and diacylglycerol treatments interact with the normal sequence of events.
B. Why do you think serotonin release requires both calcium ionophore and diacylglycerol?

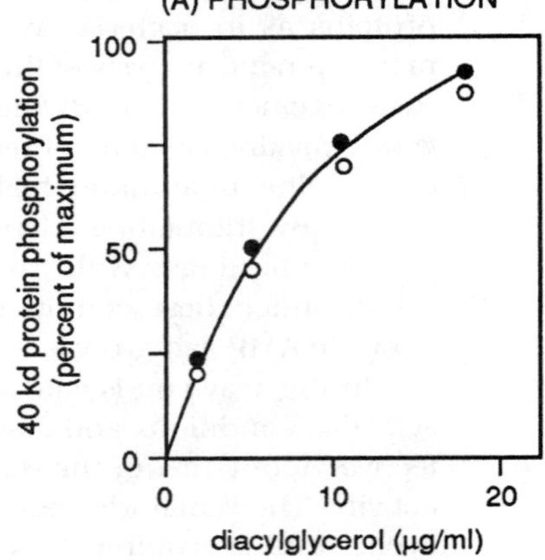

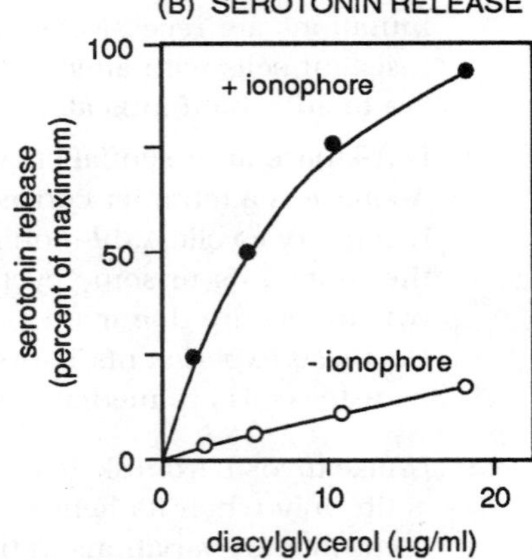

Figure 12–10 Effects of combined treatments of platelets with calcium ionophore and diacylglycerol (A) on phosphorylation of the 40 kd protein and (B) on serotonin release (Problem 12–23). Filled circles indicate experiments in which calcium ionophore was included; open circles indicate its absence.

12–24 Sea urchin eggs provide a useful assay system for components that influence internal Ca^{2+} levels. Normally, sperm binding triggers an increase in intracellular Ca^{2+}, which in turn causes exocytosis of thousands of

Table 12–3 Activation of Sea Urchin Eggs (Problem 12–24)

Injected Inositides	Addition to Medium	Activation of Egg
1. (1,4,5)$InsP_3$	none	no
2. (1,4,5)$InsP_3$	Ca^{2+}	yes
3. (1,4,5)$InsP_3$	Ca^{2+} and EGTA	no
4. (2,4,5)$InsP_3$	Ca^{2+}	no
5. (1,3,4)$InsP_3$	Ca^{2+}	no
6. (1,3,4,5)$InsP_4$	Ca^{2+}	no
7. (2,4,5)$InsP_3$ and (1,3,4,5)$InsP_4$	Ca^{2+}	yes
8. (2,4,5)$InsP_3$ and (1,3,4)$InsP_3$	Ca^{2+}	no
9. (2,4,5)$InsP_3$ and (w,x,y,z)$InsP_4$	Ca^{2+}	no

The random mixture of $InsP_4$s is indicated by (w,x,y,z)$InsP_4$.

small vesicles containing precursors for formation of the fertilization membrane. Since this membrane is easy to see by light microscopy, its formation provides a simple all-or-none test for egg activation. The normal requirement for sperm can be bypassed by incubating eggs with a calcium ionophore, provided there is Ca^{2+} in the medium.

When inositol phosphates were shown to mobilize internal Ca^{2+} stores, you immediately tested them on sea urchin eggs. Sure enough, when you injected 10^{-17} mole of (1,4,5)$InsP_3$, the fertilization membrane formed. However, this activation depended on the presence of external calcium, since inclusion of EGTA (a calcium chelator) in the medium blocked activation. A dependence on external calcium surprised you, since (1,4,5)$InsP_3$ does not open calcium channels in the plasma membrane. Other inositol trisphosphates, (2,4,5)$InsP_3$ and (1,3,4)$InsP_3$, which are known to mobilize internal calcium stores in other cells, did not activate eggs upon injection. An inositol tetrakisphosphate, (1,3,4,5)$InsP_4$, also failed to activate eggs upon injection. However, when you injected a combination of two "inactive" inositol phosphates, (2,4,5)$InsP_3$ and (1,3,4,5)$InsP_4$, eggs were activated completely. Combinations of (2,4,5)$InsP_3$ with (1,3,4)$InsP_3$ were inactive, as were combinations of (2,4,5)$InsP_3$ with a random mixture of $InsP_4$s, which did not include (1,3,4,5)$InsP_4$.

You are puzzled by these results, which are summarized in Table 12–3. You show them to some of your colleagues and seek their advice. One of them has just heard a seminar at which the isolation of an inositol kinase that specifically phosphorylates inositol (and its derivatives) at the 3 position was described. This piece of information makes everything much clearer; you can now answer the questions you posed to your colleagues.

A. Why do you think that the combination of (2,4,5)$InsP_3$ and (1,3,4,5)$InsP_4$ activates eggs, whereas neither alone is effective?

B. Why do you think that (1,4,5)$InsP_3$ activates eggs alone? Why do you think that the combination of (2,4,5)$InsP_3$ and (1,3,4)$InsP_3$ is ineffective?

***12–25** A particularly graphic illustration of the kind of subtle, yet important, role of cyclic AMP in the whole organism comes from studies of the fruit fly, *Drosophila melanogaster*. In search of the gene for cyclic AMP phosphodiesterase, one laboratory measured enzyme levels in flies with chromosomal duplications or deletions and found consistent alterations in flies with mutations involving bands 3D3 and 3D4 on the X chromosome. Duplications in this region have about 1.5 times the normal activity; deletions have about half the normal activity. Deletions in this region caused partial female sterility.

An independent laboratory in the same institution was led to the same chromosomal region through work on behavioral mutants of fruit flies. The researchers had developed a learning test in which flies were presented with two metallic grids, one of which was electrified. If the electrified grid was painted with a strong-smelling chemical, normal flies quickly learned to avoid it even when it was no longer electrified. The mutant flies, on the other hand, never learned to avoid the smelly grid; they were aptly called *dunce* mutants. The *dunce* mutation was mapped genetically to bands 3D3 and 3D4. Flies that had been selected for this kind of stupidity were also partially female sterile.

Is the learning defect really due to lack of cyclic AMP phosphodiesterase or are the responsible genes simply closely linked? Further experiments showed that the level of cyclic AMP in *dunce* flies was 1.6 times higher than in normal flies. Furthermore, sucrose gradient analysis of homogenates of *dunce* and normal flies revealed two cyclic AMP phosphodiesterase activities, one of which was missing in *dunce* flies (Figure 12–11).

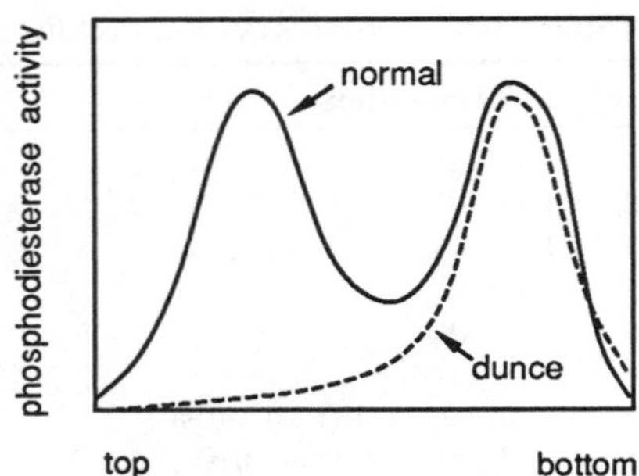

Figure 12–11 Sucrose gradient analysis of cyclic AMP phosphodiesterase activity in homogenates of normal and *dunce* flies (Problem 12–25).

A. Why do *dunce* flies have higher levels of cyclic AMP than normal flies?
B. Explain why homozygous (both chromosomes affected) duplications of the nonmutant *dunce* gene cause cyclic AMP phosphodiesterase levels to be elevated 1.5-fold and why homozygous deletions of the gene reduce enzyme activity to half the normal value?
C. What would you predict would be the effect of caffeine, a phosphodiesterase inhibitor, on the learning performance of normal flies?
D. Does the experimental evidence prove that the *dunce* gene is the structural gene for cyclic AMP phosphodiesterase? If not, how else might these results arise?

Target Cell Adaptation (MBOC 718–724)

12–26 Fill in the blanks in the following statements.

A. Cells reversibly adjust their sensitivity to a stimulus by a process of ____________.
B. Receptor-mediated endocytosis of ligands is often associated with a decrease in the total number of cell-surface receptors as a result of enhanced receptor degradation, a mechanism known as ____________.
C. When receptors are internalized in the presence of ligand but are not degraded, cells become less responsive to added ligand; this process is called ____________.
D. In bacteria the presence of attractants and repellents in the environment is transmitted across the membrane by four types of ____________.

12–27 Indicate whether the following statements are true or false. If a statement is false, explain why.

__ A. Most receptors, when they are endocytosed, deliver their ligands to lysosomes for degradation but are themselves repeatedly retrieved and recycled.

__ B. Prolonged exposure of a cell to a stimulus usually results in loss of sensitivity to that stimulus.

__ C. Prolonged exposure of fibroblasts to prostaglandin PGE_1 desensitizes them to other agents that act via G_s proteins; this process is known as homologous desensitization because a common protein is involved.

__ D. Drug addicts need higher doses of morphine for pain relief than normal people because they lose functional G_i proteins—not because of receptor down regulation.

__ E. Owing to an inherent handedness in the construction of their flagella, *E. coli* and *S. typhimurium* swim in straight lines when their flagella rotate anticlockwise, but they tumble more or less randomly when their flagella rotate clockwise.

__ F. If the concentration of an attractant remains constant, bacteria continue swimming in a straight line.

— G. When chemotaxis receptors are activated by a bound ligand, they can be methylated, which deactivates them and leads to an increased frequency of tumbling.

12–28 After prolonged exposure to hormones that bind to β-adrenergic receptors, cells become refractory and cease responding. To examine this desensitization phenomenon, you use a newly developed reagent, CGP-12177, which is a hydrophilic molecule that specifically binds to β-adrenergic receptors. In contrast to the binding of dihydroalprenolol, which is hydrophobic, CGP-12177 binding exactly parallels the decrease in hormone-dependent adenylate cyclase activity observed in extracts from cells treated with isoproterenol for increasing times (Figure 12–12). To understand the difference in receptor binding by these two molecules, you lyse untreated cells and isoproterenol treated (desensitized) cells, fractionate them by centrifugation through sucrose-density gradients, and measure binding by dihydroalprenolol and CGP-12177 (Figure 12–13). In addition to ligand binding, you also measure 5′-nucleotidase activity, which is a marker enzyme for the plasma membrane.

A. Give an explanation for the differences in binding by dihydroalprenolol and CGP-12177.

B. What do you think might be the basis for isoproterenol-induced desensitization in these cells?

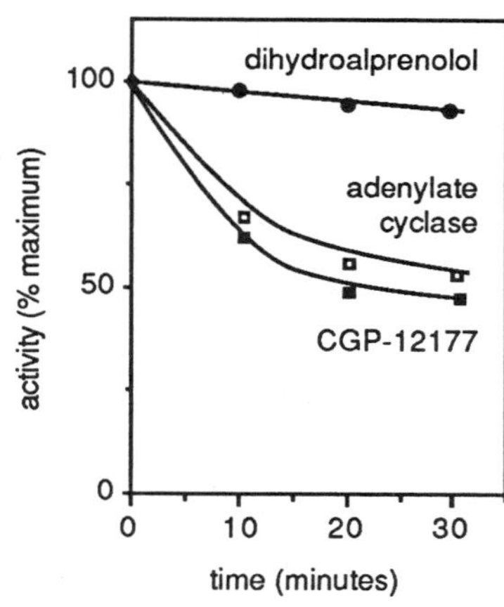

Figure 12–12 Adenylate cyclase activity, ^{3}H-CGP-12177 binding, and ^{3}H-dihydroalprenolol binding at various times after treatment with isoproterenol (Problem 12–28). All activities are expressed as a percentage of the values at time zero.

***12–29** Desensitization is a general phenomenon that results in reduced responsiveness of a cell to a hormone (or other agent) after prolonged exposure. If the response is diminished only to the desensitizing hormone (or other agents that work through the same receptor), the phenomenon is called homologous desensitization. By contrast, if the response is diminished not only to the desensitizing hormone, but also to other agents that work through different receptors, the phenomenon is called heterologous desensitization.

The β-adrenergic receptor is susceptible to homologous and heterologous desensitization, with phosphorylation of the receptor common to both modes. You have isolated two different protein kinases that you suspect are involved in desensitization of the β-adrenergic receptor. Under appropriate conditions each of the kinases will phosphorylate purified β-adrenergic receptors that have been reconstituted into phospholipid vesicles. One of the kinases appears to be A-kinase, since it requires cyclic AMP for activity; the other kinase (which you term X-kinase because it is unknown) is independent of cyclic AMP, cyclic GMP, Ca^{2+}/calmodulin, and Ca^{2+}/diacylglycerol. You measure the ability of each of these kinases to phosphorylate the β-adrenergic receptor in the presence and absence of isoproterenol (which stimulates the receptor). Your results are shown in Figure 12–14.

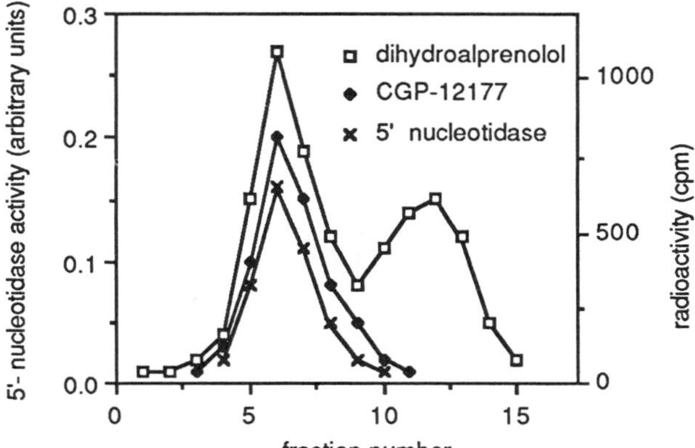

Figure 12–13 Ligand binding in sucrose-gradient fractions from untreated and isoproterenol-treated cells (Problem 12–28).

A. Which of these kinases do you think is responsible for homologous desensitization of the β-adrenergic receptor and which is responsible for heterologous desensitization? Give the reasoning for your answer.

B. Suggest three ways that phosphorylation of the β-adrenergic receptor might lead to desensitization.

12–30 The nicotinic acetylcholine receptor is a neurotransmitter-dependent ion channel, which is composed of four types of subunit. Phosphorylation of the receptor by A-kinase attaches one phosphate to the γ subunit and one phosphate to the δ subunit. Fully phosphorylated receptors are desensitized much more rapidly than unmodified receptors. To study this process in detail, you phosphorylate two preparations of receptor to different extents (0.8 mole phosphate/mole receptor and 1.2 mole phosphate/mole receptor) and measure desensitization over several seconds (Figure 12–15). Both preparations behave as if they contain a mixture of receptors: one form that is rapidly desensitized (the initial steep portion of the curves) and another form that is desensitized at the same rate as the untreated receptor.

A. Assuming that the γ and δ subunits are independently phosphorylated at equal rates, calculate the percentage of receptors that carry zero, one, and two phosphates per receptor at the two extents of phosphorylation.

B. Do these data suggest that desensitization requires one phosphate or two phosphates per receptor? If you decide that desensitization requires only one phosphate, indicate whether the phosphate has to be on one specific subunit or can be on either of the subunits.

***12–31** Four types of chemotaxis receptors have been identified in *E. coli.* These receptors mediate chemotactic responses to two different amino acids, to sugars, and to dipeptides. As part of a practical demonstration in bacterial chemotaxis, your instructor has given you a wild-type strain with all four receptors intact and four mutant strains with one or more of the receptors missing. Your assignment is to identify which receptor mediates the response to which attractant. The experimental assay is very simple. You fill a capillary pipette with a solution of the attractant, dip it into a buffered solution containing bacteria, remove it after 5 minutes, and count the number of bacteria in the capillary. Your results are shown in Table 12–4. Identify each attractant and its appropriate receptor.

12–32 To clarify the relationship between the structure of a chemotaxis receptor and the functions of stimulus recognition, signal transduction, and adaptation, you have cloned the gene for the aspartate receptor from *Salmonella typhimurium.* Inadvertently, you also cloned a mutant form of the gene that is missing the C-terminal 35 amino acids. By introducing the wild type and truncated forms of the gene back into a mutant of *Salmonella* that is missing the normal gene for the aspartate receptor, you can test for functional differences between the two cloned genes. To your surprise, even though the truncated receptor still contains the peptide sequences that are the targets for methylation, it is not methylated in cells. The binding of aspartate by the wild type and truncated receptors, however, is identical to the normal cellular receptor. The cloned receptors are about 15 times more abundant than normal.

To test for signal transduction by the cloned receptors and to assess their adaptive properties, you expose bacteria containing the receptors to a sudden change in the concentration of aspartate. Wild-type bacteria in the absence of an attractant change their direction of rotation (tumble) every few seconds. Upon exposure to an attractant, however, the changes in direction of rotation are suppressed, which leads to a period of smooth swimming. If the concentration of attractant remains constant (even if high), wild-type bacteria quickly adapt and begin again to tumble every few seconds. To observe these behavioral changes experimentally, you

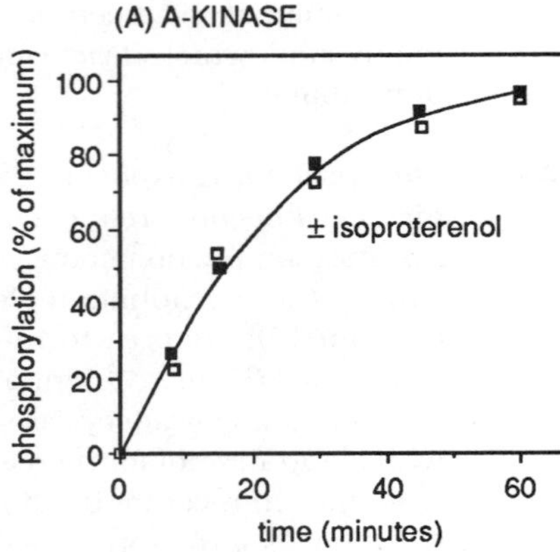

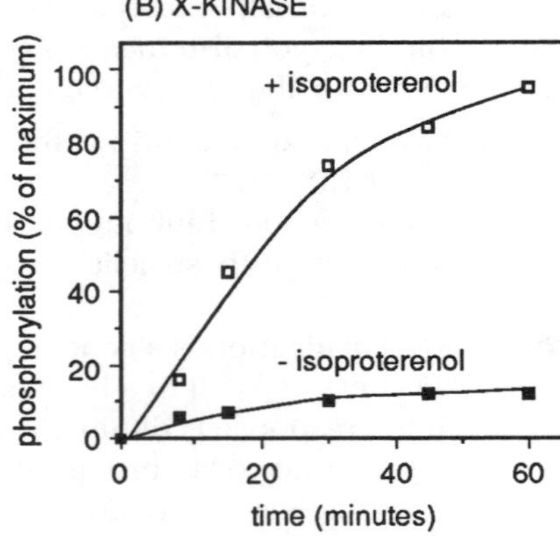

Figure 12–14 Time course of phosphorylation of the β-adrenergic receptor by A-kinase (A) and X-kinase (B) in the presence and absence of isoproterenol (Problem 12–29).

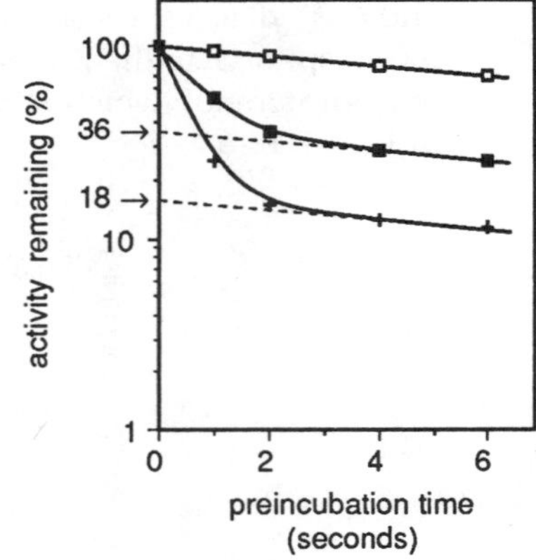

Figure 12–15 Desensitization rates of untreated acetylcholine receptor and two preparations of phosphorylated receptor (Problem 12–30). Arrows indicate the fractions of the phosphorylated preparations that behaved like the untreated receptor.

Table 12–4 Chemotaxis in Wild-Type and Mutant Strains of *E. coli* (Problem 12–31)

		Number of Cells (1000s) in Capillary				
Strain	**Intact Receptors**	**Serine**	**Aspartate**	**Ribose**	**Prolylglycine**	**None**
1	Tap, Tar, Trg, Tsr	59	105	95	6.6	0.5
2	Tap, Tar, Trg	0.7	84	77	13	0.8
3	Trg, Tsr	34	0.7	59	0.6	0.6
4	Tap, Trg, Tsr	55	0.6	65	4.1	0.5
5	Tar, Trg, Tsr	70	59	85	0.9	0.8

tether bacteria by their flagella to coverslips so that you can observe their direction of rotation. You then expose them to aspartate and count the number of bacteria that do not reverse their direction of rotation in 1-minute intervals after addition of aspartate. The results for wild-type cells and for cells containing the cloned aspartate receptors are shown in Figure 12–16.

A. Is signal transduction by the two cloned receptors normal?
B. Are the adaptive properties of the cloned receptors normal?
C. Suggest molecular explanations for why the cloned normal receptor and the cloned truncated receptor, when introduced into bacteria, respond differently from the normal receptor in wild-type cells (Figure 12–16).

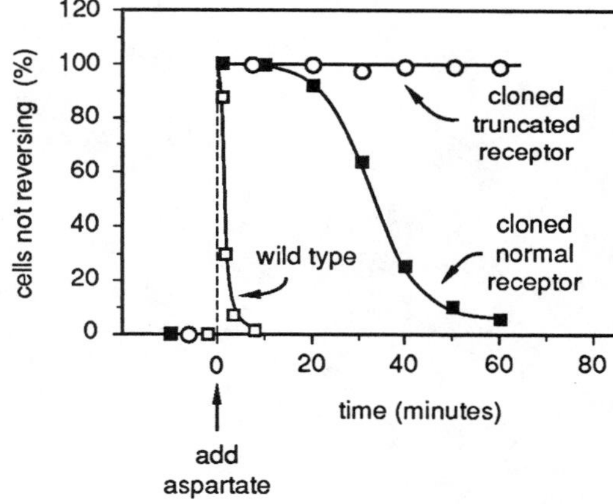

Figure 12–16 Behavior of wild-type cells and cells containing the cloned receptors (Problem 12–32).

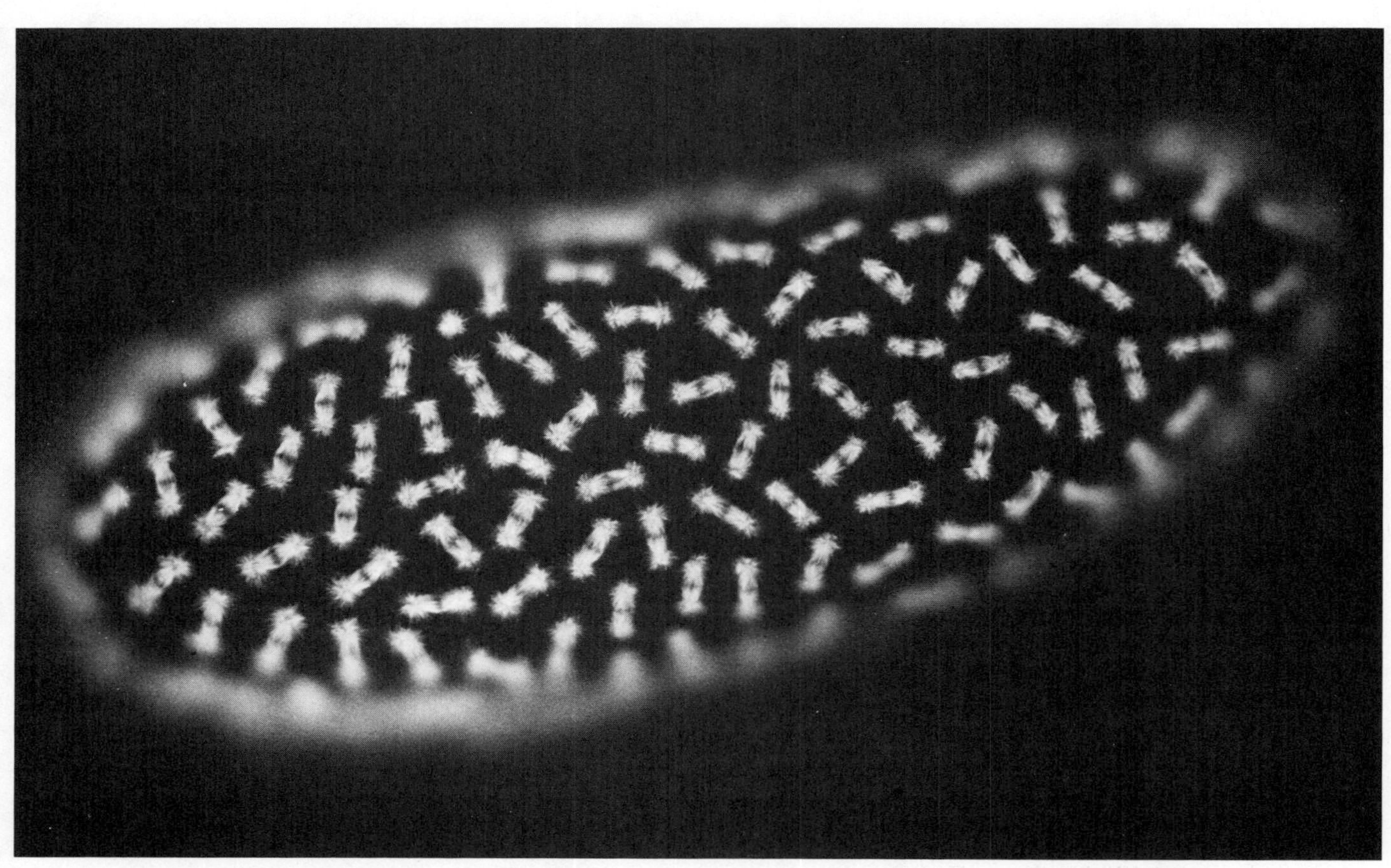

An early *Drosophila* embryo stained with an anti-tubulin antibody reveals hundreds of mitotic spindles, thanks to the perfect synchrony of division at this stage. (Courtesy of Bruce Alberts.)

Cell Growth and Division

13

The Steps of the Cell Cycle and Their Causal Connections (MBOC 728–738)

13–1 Fill in the blanks in the following statements.

A. The contents of the nucleus condense to form visible chromosomes at ____________.

B. In the process of ____________ a cell splits into two daughter cells.

C. The easily visible events of mitosis and cytokinesis together occupy only a brief period of the cell cycle known as the ____________.

D. The period that elapses between one mitosis and the next is known as ____________.

E. The period of the cell cycle devoted to DNA synthesis is known as the ____________.

F. Because cells in mitosis round up and adhere weakly to the culture dish, a synchronized population can be gathered by gently agitating the cells and collecting them in a process known as ____________.

G. M-phase cytoplasm contains a factor called ____________ that is capable of driving a nucleus at any phase of the cell cycle into mitosis.

H. Cleaving eggs from clams, frogs, and sea urchins contain a protein known as ____________, whose concentration rises steadily from zero and then halfway through M phase suddenly drops back to zero again.

13–2 Indicate whether the following statements are true or false. If a statement is false, explain why.

__ A. During cell division the duplication of most of a cell's constituents need not be controlled exactly.

__ B. Cell-cycle times vary from one cell type to another, with most of the variability occurring in the G_1 phase.

__ C. It is not possible to measure the cycle times of cells in the tissues of an animal.

__ D. Synchronous populations of cells can be prepared by centrifugation.

__ E. In the G_1 phase cells undergo a critical transition called Start, which is an internal change that marks the onset of DNA synthesis.

__ F. The rates of synthesis of many proteins are altered at specific stages of the cell cycle.

__ G. When an S-phase cell is fused with an early G_1-phase cell, the G_1-phase nucleus immediately begins DNA synthesis.

__ H. When a G_2-phase cell is fused with an S-phase cell, DNA synthesis is inhibited in the S-phase nucleus. This inhibition is known as the DNA re-replication block.

__ I. When mitotic cells are fused with cells that are in any other phase of the cell cycle, all the nuclei in the common cytoplasm enter mitosis.

— J. In normal cells every step of the cell cycle is dependent on the proper completion of the previous step.

— K. Neither RNA nor protein synthesis is necessary for cells to enter mitosis.

— L. *Xenopus* oocytes can be made to mature in at least three different ways: by exposure to progesterone, by microinjection of MPF protein, or by microinjection of cyclin mRNA.

***13–3** The frequency of cells undergoing mitosis (the mitotic index) is a convenient way to estimate the length of the cell cycle. You and a friend have decided to measure the cell cycle in the liver of the adult mouse by measuring the mitotic index. Accordingly, you have prepared liver slices and stained them to make cells in mitosis easy to recognize. After 3 days of counting, you have found only 3 mitoses in 25,000 cells. Assuming that M phase lasts 1 hour, calculate the length of the cell cycle in the liver of an adult mouse.

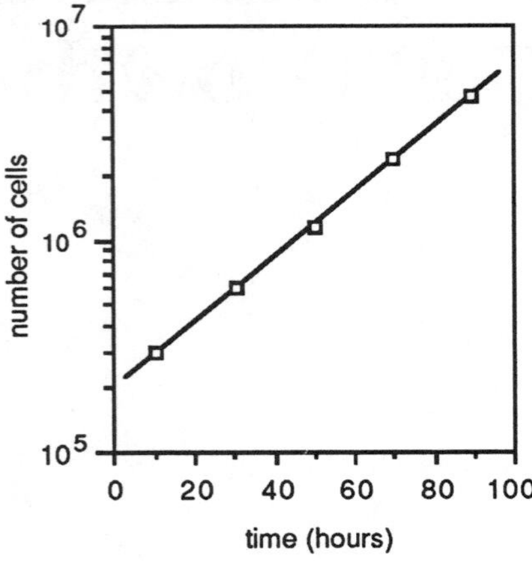

Figure 13–1 Increase in the number of mouse L cells with time (Problem 13–4).

13–4 The overall length of the cell cycle and the portions allotted to G_1, S, G_2, and M can be determined by using rather straightforward microscopic and autoradiographic analyses. Consider, for example, the following set of experiments that were used to define the cell cycle in mouse L cells.

A. The overall length of the cell cycle was measured from the growth rate of a population of exponentially growing cells. The growth rate was determined by counting the number of cells in samples of culture fluid at various times (Figure 13–1). What is the overall length of the cell cycle in mouse L cells?

B. With the exception of mitosis, which is clearly visible in the light microscope and lasts about 1 hour, the phases of the cell cycle require careful experimental analysis to define them. ^{3}H-thymidine was added to an asynchronously growing population of cells (randomly distributed throughout the cell cycle); at various times thereafter cells were stained and prepared for autoradiography. Cells that incorporated ^{3}H-thymidine exposed the photographic emulsion and were covered by silver grains. In Figure 13–2A the fraction of *mitotic cells* that are labeled is plotted as a function of time after addition of ^{3}H-thymidine. In Figure 13–2B the average number of silver grains above *mitotic cells* is plotted as a function of time after addition of ^{3}H-thymidine. From this and other information in the problem, deduce the duration of the G_1, S, and G_2 phases of the cell cycle in mouse L cells and give your reasoning.

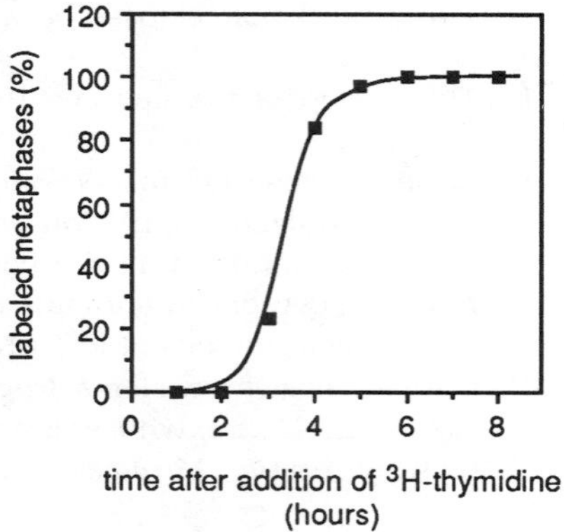

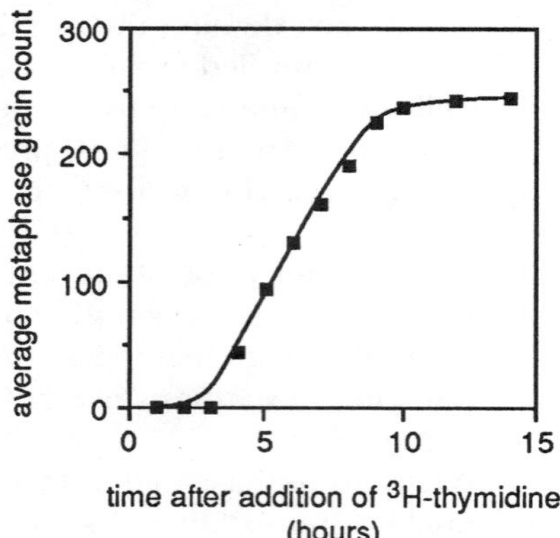

Figure 13–2 Labeled mitotic cells as a function of time after addition of ^{3}H-thymidine (Problem 13–4). (A) Fraction of labeled mitotic cells. (B) Average number of silver grains above labeled mitotic cells.

***13–5** For many experiments it is desirable to have a population of cells that are traversing the cell cycle synchronously. One of the first, and still often used, methods for synchronizing cells is the so-called double thymidine block. If high concentrations of thymidine are added to the culture fluid, cells stop DNA synthesis. The excess thymidine blocks the enzyme ribonucleotide reductase, which is responsible for converting ribonucleotides into deoxyribonucleotides. When this enzyme is inhibited, the supply of deoxyribonucleotides falls and DNA synthesis stops. When the excess thymidine is removed by changing the medium, the supply of deoxyribonucleotides rises and DNA synthesis resumes normally.

For a cell line with a 22-hour cell cycle divided so that M = 1 hour, G_1 = 10 hours, S = 7 hours, and G_2 = 4 hours, a typical protocol for synchronization by a double thymidine block would be as follows:

1. At 0 hours (t = 0 hours) add excess thymidine.
2. After 18 hours (t = 18 hours) remove excess thymidine.
3. After an additional 10 hours (t = 28 hours) add excess thymidine.
4. After an additional 16 hours (t = 44 hours) remove excess thymidine.

A. At what point in the cell cycle is the cell population when the second thymidine block is removed?

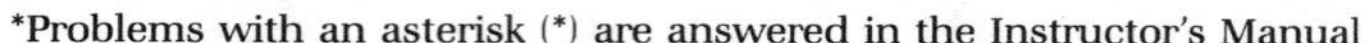
*Problems with an asterisk (*) are answered in the Instructor's Manual.

Table 13–1 Correlation Between Length of S Phase and DNA Content (Problem 13–6)

Organism	DNA Content of Nucleus (pg)	Length of S Phase (hours)
Lizard	3.2	15
Frog	15	26
Newt	45	41

B. Explain how the times of addition and removal of excess thymidine synchronize the cell population.

13–6 What determines the length of S phase? One possibility is that its length depends on how much DNA the nucleus contains. As a test, you measure the length of S phase in dividing cells of a lizard, a frog, and a newt, each one of which has a different amount of DNA. As shown in Table 13–1, the length of S phase does increase with increasing DNA content.

Even though these organisms are similar in that they are all cold-blooded, they are different species. You recall that it is possible to obtain haploid embryos of frogs and repeat your measurements with haploid and diploid frog cells. Haploid frog cells have the same length S phase as diploid frog cells. Further research in the literature show that in plants, tetraploid strains of beans and oats have the same length S phase as their diploid cousins.

Propose an explanation to reconcile these apparently contradictory results. Why is it that the length of S phase increases with increasing DNA content in different species but remains constant with increasing DNA content in the same species?

13–7 Frog oocytes mature into eggs when incubated with progesterone. This maturation is characterized by disappearance of the nucleus (termed germinal vesicle breakdown) and formation of a meiotic spindle. The requirement for progesterone can be bypassed by microinjecting 50 nl of egg cytoplasm directly into a fresh oocyte (1000 nl), which then matures normally (Figure 13–3). The control experiment of microinjecting cytoplasm from untreated oocytes into other oocytes causes no maturation, as expected. The activity in the egg cytoplasm that is responsible for maturation is called MPF (maturation—or M-phase—promoting factor), and it is thought to be a protein complex.

Progesterone-induced maturation requires protein synthesis, as indicated by its sensitivity to cycloheximide; however, MPF-induced maturation does not. By placing progesterone-stimulated oocytes into cycloheximide at different times after stimulation, it can be shown that maturation becomes cycloheximide independent (no longer inhibited by cycloheximide) a few hours before the oocytes become eggs. In addition, the time at which the oocytes become cycloheximide independent corresponds to the appearance of MPF activity.

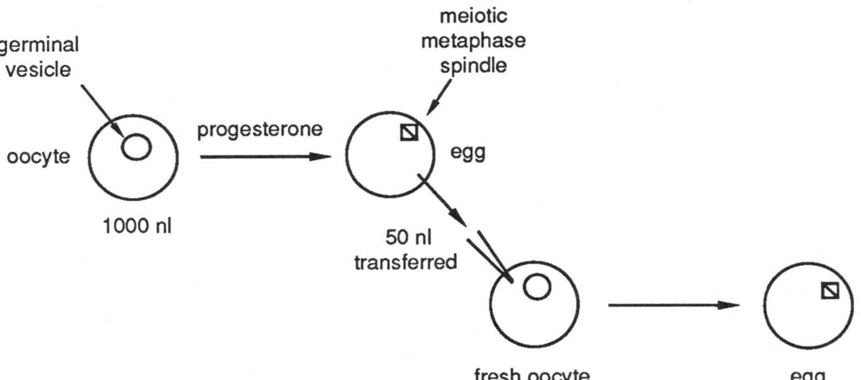

Figure 13–3 Progesterone- and MPF-induced maturation of oocytes (Problem 13–7).

Is synthesis of MPF itself the cycloheximide-sensitive event? To test this possibility, you transfer MPF serially from egg to oocyte to test whether its activity diminishes with dilution. You first microinject 50 nl of cytoplasm from an activated egg into an immature oocyte; when the oocyte matures into an egg, you transfer 50 nl of its cytoplasm into another immature oocyte; and so on. Surprisingly, you find that you can continue this process for at least 10 transfers, even if the recipient oocytes are bathed in cycloheximide! Moreover, the apparent MPF activity in the last egg is equal to that in the first egg.

A. What dilution factor is achieved by 10 serial transfers of 50 nl into 1000 nl? Do you consider it likely that a molecule might have an undiminished biological effect over this concentration range?
B. How can MPF activity, which is due to a protein, be absent from immature oocytes yet appear in activated eggs, even when protein synthesis has been blocked by cycloheximide?
C. Propose a means by which MPF might maintain its activity through repeated serial transfers.
D. Propose a role for the cycloheximide-sensitive factor that is required for the appearance of MPF activity in a progesterone-stimulated oocyte.

Yeasts as a Model System (MBOC 738–743)

13–8 Fill in the blanks in the following statements.

A. The organism *Saccharomyces cerevisiae* is a ____________.
B. The organism *Schizosaccharomyces pombe* is a ____________.
C. Temperature-sensitive mutants do not grow at the ____________ temperature, but they do grow at the ____________ temperature.
D. Yeast ____________ mutants become blocked, or misbehave, in a specific part of the cell cycle.
E. There is a critical point in the yeast cell cycle called ____________ that marks the moment of commitment to complete a cell-division cycle.

13–9 Indicate whether the following statements are true or false. If a statement is false, explain why.

___ A. Yeasts are important for studies of the cell cycle primarily because they can be grown in the large amounts necessary for biochemical analysis.
___ B. Food and sex are the most important regulators of the yeast cell-division cycle.
___ C. If DNA synthesis is inhibited in yeast, cytokinesis is inhibited; mutants that fail to go through cytokinesis, however, will proceed through multiple rounds of DNA synthesis.
___ D. For a given cell type the volume of the cell is roughly proportional to the amount of DNA it contains.
___ E. The homologous proteins encoded by *CDC28* (in *S. cerevisiae*) and $CDC2^{+}$ (in *S. pombe*) are protein kinases.
___ F. Starving yeasts rapidly pass Start and return to the cell cycle when placed in rich medium.

13–10 Mutations that block the progress of cells through the cell cycle are important for defining the regulation and control of the cell cycle. A large number of such mutants have been isolated in yeasts. A common first step in characterizing cell-division-cycle (*cdc*) mutants is to define the phase of the cell cycle at which the mutational block stops the cell's progress. Temperature-sensitive *cdc* mutants are particularly useful because they grow normally at one temperature (the permissive temperature) but express a mutant phenotype when grown at a higher temperature (the restrictive temperature). One method for characterizing temperature-sensitive *cdc* mutants uses the drug hydroxyurea, which blocks

DNA synthesis by inhibiting ribonucleotide reductase (which provides deoxyribonucleotide precursors). Hydroxyurea blockade of DNA synthesis can be reversed simply by changing the incubation medium. Consider the following results with the hypothetical *cdc* mutants 101 and 102.

You incubate a culture of a yeast *cdc*101 mutant at its restrictive temperature (37°C) for 2 hours (the approximate length of the cell cycle in yeasts) so that its mutant phenotype is expressed. Then you transfer it to medium containing hydroxyurea at the permissive temperature (20°C). None of the cells divide.

You now reverse the order of treatment. You incubate *cdc*101 at 20°C for 2 hours in medium containing hydroxyurea and then transfer it to medium without hydroxyurea at 37°C. The cells undergo one round of division.

You repeat these two experiments with the *cdc*102 mutant. The cells do not divide in either case.

A. In what phase of the cell cycle is *cdc*101 blocked at the restrictive temperature? Explain the results of the reciprocal temperature-shift experiments.

B. In what phase of the cell cycle is *cdc*102 blocked at the restrictive temperature? Explain the results of the reciprocal temperature-shift experiments.

13–11 You have isolated a temperature-sensitive mutant of a budding yeast. It grows well at 25°C but at 35°C all the cells develop a large bud and then stop growing. The characteristic morphology of the cells at the time they stop growing is known as the landmark morphology.

It is very difficult to synchronize the growth of this yeast, but you would like to know as exactly as possible at what point in the cell cycle the temperature-sensitive gene product must function in order for the cell to complete the cycle. The critical point in the cycle at which a gene product functions is its execution point, in the terminology of the field. A clever friend, who has a good microscope with a heated stage and a time-lapse video recorder, suggests that you take pictures of a field of cells as they experience the temperature increase and follow the behavior of individual cells as they stop growing. Since the cells do not move much, it is relatively simple to study individual cell behavior. To make sense of what you see, you arrange a circle of photos of cells at the start of the experiment in order of the size of their daughter buds. You then find the corresponding photos of those same cells 6 hours later, when growth has completely stopped. The results with your mutant are shown in Figure 13–4.

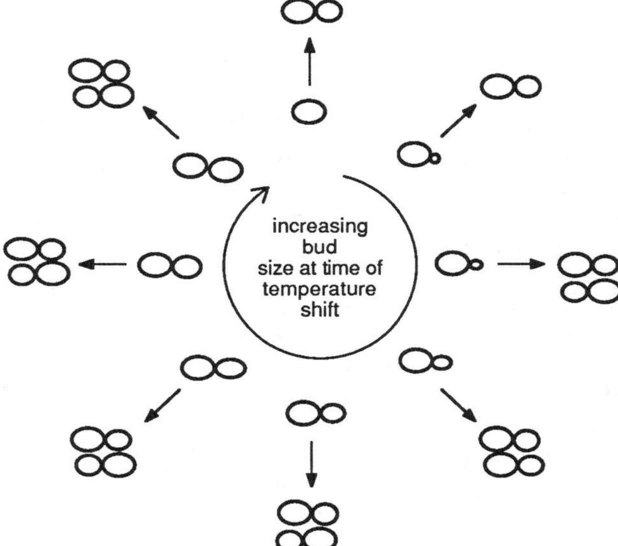

Figure 13–4 Time-lapse photography of a temperature-sensitive mutant of yeast (Problem 13–11). Cells on the inner circle are arranged in order of their bud sizes, which corresponds to their position in the cell cycle. After 6 hours at 35°C, they have given rise to the cells shown on the outer circle. No further growth or division occurs.

A. Indicate on the diagram in Figure 13–4 where the execution point for your mutant lies.
B. Does the execution point correspond to the time at which the cell cycle is arrested in your mutant? How can you tell?

Cell-Division Controls in Multicellular Organisms

(MBOC 743–752)

13–12 Fill in the blanks in the following statements.

A. There is a point of no return late in the G_1 phase of the cell cycle of higher eucaryotic cells called the ____________, where cells pause when environmental conditions limit their progress through the cycle.
B. Proteins in serum that directly and specifically stimulate cell division are called ____________.
C. The principal factor in serum that enables fibroblasts in tissue culture to divide is ____________.
D. When normal cells are cultured in suspension, unattached to any solid surface, they almost never divide, a phenomenon known as ____________ of cell division.
E. Cells that are deprived of their licenses to divide are unable to pass the restriction point and become arrested in a ____________.
F. Fibroblasts taken from a normal human fetus will go through about 50 cell divisions and then stop dividing and die, a phenomenon called ____________.

13–13 Indicate whether the following statements are true or false. If a statement is false, explain why.

__ A. The time it takes a cell to pass from the beginning of S phase to the completion of mitosis is more or less constant.
__ B. When starved of an essential nutrient, cells of higher eucaryotes arrest in the G_1 phase of the cell cycle at a point that corresponds to Start in yeasts.
__ C. If cells in a tissue divided synchronously, it might prove a mechanical disaster because they would round up and lose contact with one another each time they passed through mitosis.
__ D. Serum supports the growth of fibroblasts whereas plasma does not because plasma contains blood-clotting factors that inhibit cell growth.
__ E. Nontransformed cells will grow and divide only if they are well spread out by firm attachments to their substrate; transformed cells are able to grow rounded up in suspension culture.
__ F. The control of cell division is apparently coupled to the organization of the cytoskeleton.
__ G. Loss of growth control in cancer cells is almost always associated with a significant increase in cell adhesiveness.
__ H. Cells in G_1 phase grow; cells in G_0 do not.
__ I. Cells from mouse embryos grow better in a defined medium with a cocktail of specific growth factors than they do in complete serum, indicating that serum contains growth inhibitors as well as growth stimulators.
__ J. People with Werner's syndrome age prematurely.

13–14 You have been led by a bizarre accident to a productive line of experimentation. You lost one of your contact lenses while transferring a line of tissue culture cells; a few days later you found the lens on the bottom of a Petri dish. Interestingly, the cells attached to the lens were rounded up and very sparse, whereas those on the rest of the dish were flat and nearly confluent. Ah ha! you thought, perhaps this observation can be used to investigate the relationship between cell shape and growth control. As someone once said, "Chance favors the prepared mind."

The manufacturer graciously sends you a supply of the plastic—poly(HEMA)—from which your soft contact lenses were made. When an alcoholic mixture of poly(HEMA) is pipetted into a plastic culture dish, a thin, hard, sterile film of optically clear polymer remains bound to the plastic surface after the alcohol evaporates. Serial dilutions of the alcohol-polymer solution, introduced into each dish at a constant volume, result in decreasing thicknesses of the polymer film. The thinner the film, the more strongly cells adhere to the dish. Moreover, there is a gradual change in cell shape from round to flat with decreasing thickness of the film. Using the height of the cells as an indicator of cell shape (no mean technical feat), you demonstrate that there is a smooth relationship between cell shape and growth potential: the flatter the cells, the better they incorporate ^{3}H-thymidine.

Now for the big question: Is density-dependent inhibition of cell growth mediated by changes in cell shape? You grow cells to different densities (different degrees of confluency) on normal plastic dishes and measure the height of the cells and their ability to incorporate ^{3}H-thymidine. As shown in Table 13–2, the more confluent the cells, the greater their height and the lower their incorporation of ^{3}H-thymidine. Is the decrease in growth due to the increase in cell crowding or to the change in cell shape? To answer this question, you distribute cells at a low density on plates with poly(HEMA) films, such that the height of the cells in the sparse cultures matches the height of cells in the various confluent cultures. Your measurements of ^{3}H-thymidine incorporation in these sparse cultures are shown in Table 13–2.

Based on the results in Table 13–2, would you conclude that density-dependent inhibition of cell growth correlates completely, partially, or not at all with changes in cell shape? Explain your reasoning.

***13–15** Vertebrate cells pause in the G_1 phase of the cell cycle until growth conditions are appropriate for their entry into S phase with subsequent cell division. Some of the growth-factor requirements for the passage of fibroblasts through G_1 have been defined using mouse 3T3 cells, which are a fibroblastlike cell line. In the absence of serum these cells do not enter S phase. If serum is added to a culture of such arrested cells, they progress through G_1 and begin to enter S phase 12 hours later. The serum requirement can be met by supplying three growth factors: PDGF, EGF, and Somatomedin C. When these growth factors are mixed with appropriate nutrients and added to quiescent cells, the cells begin to enter S phase 12 hours later. If any one of the growth factors is left out, the cells do not enter S phase.

Do all three growth factors have to be present at the same time? Is their stimulation of cells independent of one another? Or do they stimulate cells in an ordered sequence? To address these questions, you pretreat cells with the growth factors in a defined order and then add complete medium (containing serum and nutrients) in the presence of ^{3}H-thymidine. At various times thereafter you fix cells and subject them

Table 13–2 Incorporation of ^{3}H-Thymidine by Cells Grown on Normal Dishes and on Poly(HEMA)–treated Dishes (Problem 13–14)

Type of Dish	Cell Density (cells/dish)	Confluency	Cell Height (μm)	^{3}H Incorporation (cpm/dish)
Normal	60,000	subconfluent	6	15,200
Normal	200,000	confluent	15	11,000
Normal	500,000	confluent	22	3,500
Poly(HEMA)	30,000	sparse	6	7,500
Poly(HEMA)	30,000	sparse	15	1,500
Poly(HEMA)	30,000	sparse	22	210

Table 13–3 Effect of Growth-Factor Pretreatment of 3T3 Cells on the Timing of Entry into S Phase (Problem 13–15)

Experiment	Order of Addition 1	2	3	4	Entry into S Phase
1	EGF	PDGF	SomC	medium	12 hours
2	EGF	SomC	PDGF	medium	12 hours
3	PDGF	EGF	SomC	medium	1 hour
4	PDGF	SomC	EGF	medium	6 hours
5	SomC	EGF	PDGF	medium	12 hours
6	SomC	PDGF	EGF	medium	6 hours

Cells were treated for 6 hours with the indicated growth factors in the order listed. They were thoroughly washed to remove one growth factor before the next one was added. After the regimen of growth-factor pretreatment, complete medium with ^{3}H-thymidine was added and the time before labeled nuclei appeared was determined.

to autoradiography. You define the time of appearance of the first labeled nuclei as the time of entry into S phase. The results of these experiments are given in Table 13–3.

Do the cells require these growth factors simultaneously, independently, or in an ordered sequence? Explain your answer.

13–16 The molecular details of how peptide growth factors accomplish their effects are still unclear, but individual steps in the process are yielding to experimental investigation. For example, EGF stimulates the proliferation of many types of epithelial cells by first binding to EGF receptors on their surface. The role of the EGF receptor in propagating the proliferation signal is now being clarified by study of the receptor itself. The mouse fibroblast A-431 cell line, which fortuitously carries enormously increased numbers of EGF receptors, makes characterization of the receptor much easier. Consider the following set of experiments.

1. Plasma membrane preparations from A-431 cells contain many proteins as shown on the SDS gel in Figure 13–5A. However, when ^{125}I-EGF is added to such a preparation in the presence of a protein cross-linking agent, two proteins become labeled (Figure 13–5B, lane 1). When excess unlabeled EGF is included in the incubation mixture, the labeled band at 170 kd disappears (Figure 13–5B, lane 2).
2. If the membrane preparation is incubated with γ-^{32}P-ATP, several proteins, including the 170 kd protein, become phosphorylated. This reaction is significantly stimulated by including EGF in the incubation mixture.

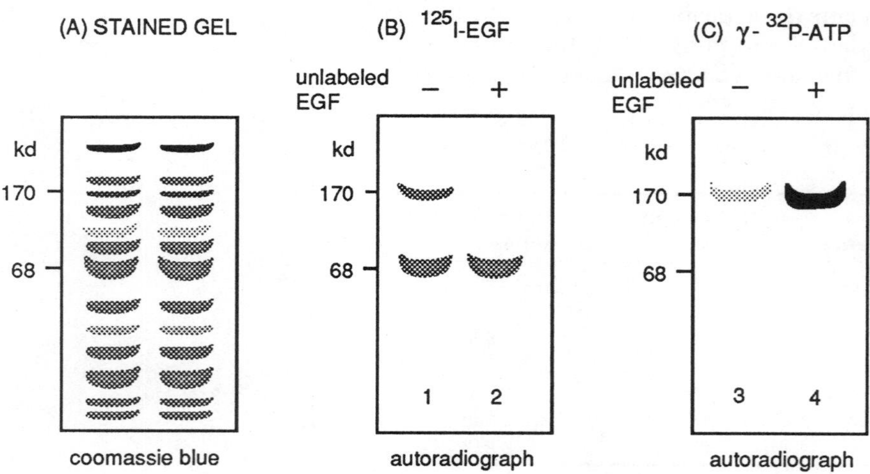

Figure 13–5 Analysis of the EGF receptor (Problem 13–16). (A) SDS gel of a membrane preparation from A-431 cells. (B) SDS gel of a membrane preparation from A-431 cells incubated with ^{125}I-EGF and a protein cross-linking agent in the presence and absence of excess unlabeled EGF. (C) SDS gel of antibody-precipitated EGF receptor incubated with γ-^{32}P-ATP in the presence and absence of EGF.

3. When antibodies specific for the 170 kd protein are used to precipitate the protein and the incubation with γ-^{32}P-ATP is repeated with the precipitate, the 170 kd protein is phosphorylated in an EGF-stimulated reaction (Figure 13–5C, lanes 3 and 4).
4. If the antibody-precipitated protein is first run on the SDS gel and then renatured in the gel, subsequent incubation with γ-^{32}P-ATP in the presence and absence of EGF yields the same pattern shown in Figure 13–5C.

A. Which of these experiments demonstrates most clearly that the 170 kd protein is the EGF receptor?
B. Is the EGF receptor a substrate for an EGF-stimulated protein kinase? How do you know?
C. Which experiments show that the EGF receptor is a protein kinase?
D. Is it clear whether the EGF receptor is a substrate for its own protein kinase activity?

***13–17** It has been suggested that normal cells are limited to about 50 cell divisions to restrict the maximum size of tumors, thus affording some protection against cancer. Assuming that 10^8 cells weigh 1 gram, calculate the weight of a tumor that originated from 50 doublings of a single cancerous cell.

Genes for the Social Control of Cell Division

(MBOC 752–761)

13–18 Fill in the blanks in the following statements.

A. Malignant tumors invade and colonize other tissues of the body to generate secondary tumors known as ____________.
B. Certain types of tumors are caused by infectious ____________.
C. Cells that evade the social controls of cell division and outgrow normal cells are said to be ____________.
D. Rous sarcoma virus belongs to the class of viruses known as ____________.
E. Certain genes called ____________, when introduced into normal cells, can transform them into tumor cells.
F. The transforming gene of Rous sarcoma virus is called the ____________.
G. The normal cellular counterparts of oncogenes are called ____________.

13–19 Indicate whether the following statements are true or false. If a statement is false, explain why.

__ A. Transformed cells show a complex set of characteristics, which can be classified under three headings: plasma-membrane-related abnormalities, adherence abnormalities, and growth and division abnormalities.
__ B. Cell transformation can be caused by a single gene.
__ C. Temperature-sensitive mutants of the v-*src* gene from Rous sarcoma virus have been used to show that the transforming gene acts like a switch at a specific point in the cell cycle and is not required to maintain transformation at other times.
__ D. The cell transformation assay for oncogenes only detects dominant oncogenes.
__ E. Recessive mutations in social control genes may be a more common cause of cancer than dominant mutations.
__ F. Virtually all viral oncogenes correspond either to a natural growth factor or a natural growth-factor receptor.
__ G. The tyrosine protein kinase activity of the v-*src* gene from Rous sarcoma virus is thought to be essential for cell transformation.

Table 13–4 Transformation-associated Properties of Uninfected Cells and Cells Infected with Wild-Type or Mutant RSV (Problem 13–20)

Transformation Parameters	Uninfected Cells	Wild-Type Infected Cells	Mutant Infected Cells
Growth in soft agar	–	+ + +	–
Surface fibronectin	+ + +	–	+ + +
Plasminogen activator	–	+ + +	–
Adhesion plaques	+ + +	–	+ + +
Glucose uptake	+	+ + +	+
Saturation density (cells/plate)	2×10^6	1×10^7	3×10^6

— H. The v-*src* gene product is attached to the plasma membrane by a short hydrophobic stretch of amino acids at its N terminus.

— I. The connection between cell proliferation and cell adhesion is not understood.

— J. Normal cells proliferate only when they are firmly attached to the substratum, but the proliferation of transformed cells is markedly inhibited when they are artificially forced to attach to the substratum.

— K. The similar body and organ sizes of newts with differing ploidy suggests that control of cell division to regulate bodily dimensions may depend on measurements of distances rather that simple counting of cell numbers or division cycles.

13–20 Rous sarcoma virus (RSV) carries an oncogene called v-*src*, which encodes a 60 kd protein called $p60^{src}$. This protein is thought to cause transformation of cells by virtue of its activity as a tyrosine protein kinase. $p60^{src}$ is attached to the cytoplasmic surface of the plasma membrane through its N-terminal linkage to myristic acid (a 14-carbon fatty acid). You have isolated a mutant of RSV, in which $p60^{src}$ does not become myristylated due to an alteration at its N terminus. To determine the importance of myristylation on transformation, you infect cells with the mutant and wild-type viruses and compare the properties of the infected and uninfected cells. As shown in Table 13–4, the cells infected with the mutant virus show almost none of the classical symptoms of transformation.

Analysis of the mutant-infected cells shows that they contain high levels of $p60^{src}$, but it is free in the cytoplasm rather than membrane bound. Nevertheless, the overall levels of tyrosine kinase activity in mutant-infected and wild-type-infected cells are the same; both are elevated 100-fold over the activity in uninfected cells.

You are surprised and puzzled by this result. How can transformation be due to tyrosine kinase activity if mutant and wild-type viruses have the same level of activity, yet differ in their ability to transform cells? One possibility is that a key target for phosphorylation remains unphosphorylated by the mutant $p60^{src}$. Accordingly, you analyze the known targets of $p60^{src}$ phosphorylation in infected cells. As summarized in Table 13–5, there are relatively small differences between wild-type- and mutant-infected cells. Even the slightly lower levels of phosphorylation of p36, p81, and lactate dehydrogenase in mutant-infected cells are probably unimportant differences: other strains of RSV, which transform cells very well, phosphorylate these particular proteins to an even lesser extent.

A. Do these experimental results rule out the possibility that $p60^{src}$ causes transformation through its tyrosine kinase activity? Explain your answer.

B. It is clear that myristylation of $p60^{src}$ and its subsequent attachment to membrane is critical for transformation. Propose two ways in which membrane association might be important for transformation by $p60^{src}$.

***13–21** Retinoblastoma is an extremely rare cancer of the nerve cells in the eye. The disease mainly affects children up to the age of five years because it

Table 13–5 Phosphorylation of Proteins in Uninfected Cells and Cells Infected with Wild-Type or Mutant RSV (Problem 13–20)

Phosphorylated Protein	Uninfected Cells	Wild-Type Infected Cells	Mutant-Infected Cells
Vinculin	4	100	800
p36	<1	100	35
p81	<1	100	30
Enolase	<1	100	100
Lactate dehydrogenase	<1	100	55
p50	<1	100	100

All values are expressed as a percentage of the degree of phosphorylation in wild-type-infected cells.

can only occur while the nerve cells are still dividing. In some cases tumors occur in only one eye, but in other cases tumors develop in both eyes. The bilateral cases all show a familial history of the disease; most of the cases affecting only one eye arise in families with no previous history of the disease.

An informative difference between unilateral and bilateral cases becomes apparent when the fraction of still undiagnosed cases is plotted against the age at which diagnosis is made (Figure 13–6). The regular decrease with time shown by the bilateral cases suggests that a single chance event is sufficient to trigger onset of bilateral retinoblastoma. By contrast, the presence of a "shoulder" on the unilateral curve suggests that multiple events in one neuron are required to trigger unilateral retinoblastoma. (A shoulder arises because the events accumulate over time. For example, if two events are required, most affected cells at early times will have suffered only a single event and will not generate a tumor. With time the probability increases that a second event will occur in an already affected cell and, therefore, cause a tumor.)

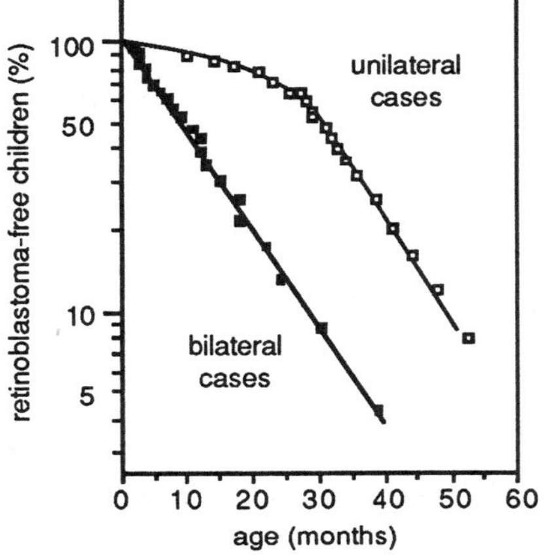

Figure 13–6 Time of onset of unilateral and bilateral cases of retinoblastoma (Problem 13–21). A population of children who ultimately developed retinoblastoma are represented in this graph. The fraction of the population that is still retinoblastoma free is plotted against the time after birth.

A possible explanation for these observations is that tumors develop when both copies of the critical gene (the retinoblastoma, *Rb*, gene) are lost or mutated. In the inherited (bilateral) form of the disease, a child receives a defective *Rb* gene from one parent: tumors develop in an eye when the other copy of the gene in any nerve cell in the eye is lost through somatic mutation. In fact, the loss of a copy of the gene is frequent enough that tumors usually occur in both eyes. If a person starts with two good copies of the *Rb* gene, tumors arise in an eye only if both copies are lost *in the same cell*. Since such double loss is very rare, it is usually confined to one eye.

To test this hypothesis, you use a cDNA clone of the *Rb* gene to probe the structure of the gene in cells from normal individuals and from patients with unilateral or bilateral retinoblastoma. As illustrated in Figure 13–7, normal individuals have four restriction fragments that hybridize to the cDNA probe (which means each of these restriction fragments contains at least one exon). Fibroblasts (nontumor cells) from the two patients also show the same four fragments, although three of the fragments from the child with bilateral retinoblastoma are present in only half the normal amount. Tumor cells from the two patients are missing some of the restriction fragments.

A. Explain why fibroblasts and tumor cells from the same patient show different band patterns.
B. What are the structures of the *Rb* genes in the fibroblasts from the two patients? In the tumor cells from the two patients?
C. Are these results consistent with the hypothesis that retinoblastoma is due to the loss of the *Rb* gene?
D. Suggest a plausible explanation for how the loss of the *Rb* gene product might cause retinoblastoma.

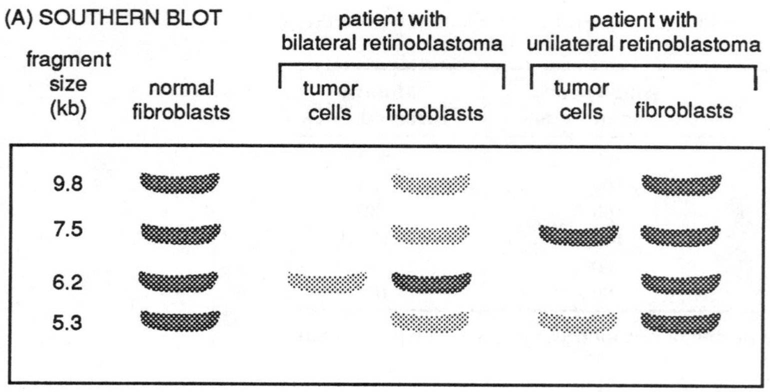

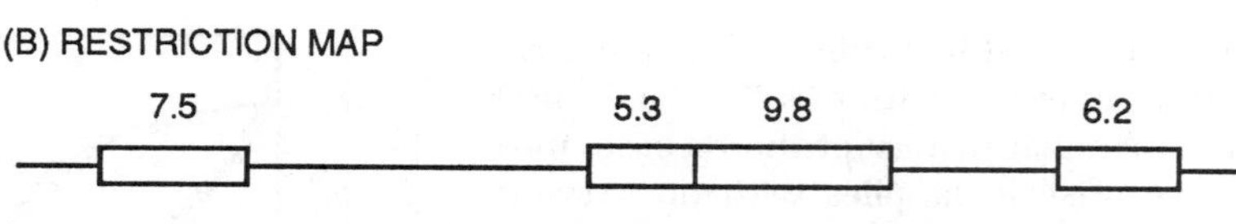

Figure 13–7 Patterns of blot hybridization of restriction fragments from the retinoblastoma gene (Problem 13–21). (A) Hybridization patterns (Southern blot) for normal individuals and for patients with unilateral and bilateral retinoblastoma. Lighter shading of some bands indicates half the normal number of copies. (B) The order of the restriction fragments. Fragments that contain exons (shown as rectangles) hybridize to the cDNA clone that was used as a probe in these experiments.

13–22 The formation of tumors is a multistep process that may involve the successive activation of several oncogenes. This notion is supported by the discovery that certain pairs of oncogenes, of which *ras* and *myc* are among the best-studied examples, transform cultured cells more efficiently than either alone. Similar experiments with pairs of oncogenes have now been carried out in transgenic mice. In one experiment the *ras* oncogene was placed under the control of the MMTV (mouse mammary tumor virus) promoter and incorporated into the germ lines of several transgenic mice. In a second experiment the *myc* oncogene under control of the same MMTV promoter was incoporated into the germ lines of several transgenic animals. In a third experiment mice containing the individual oncogenes were mated to produce mice with both oncogenes.

All three kinds of mice developed tumors at a higher frequency than normal animals. Female mice were most rapidly affected because the MMTV promoter, which is responsive to steroid hormones, turns on the transferred oncogenes in response to the hormonal changes at puberty. In Figure 13–8 the rate of appearance of tumors is plotted as the percent of tumor-free females as a function of time after puberty.

A. Assume that the lines drawn through the data points are an accurate representation of the data. How many events in addition to expression of the oncogenes are required to generate a tumor in each of the three kinds of mice? (You may wish to reread Problem 13–21.)

B. Is activation of the cellular *ras* proto-oncogene the event required to trigger tumor formation in mice that are already expressing the MMTV-regulated *myc* oncogene (or vice versa)?

C. Why do you think the rate of tumor production is so high in the mice containing both oncogenes?

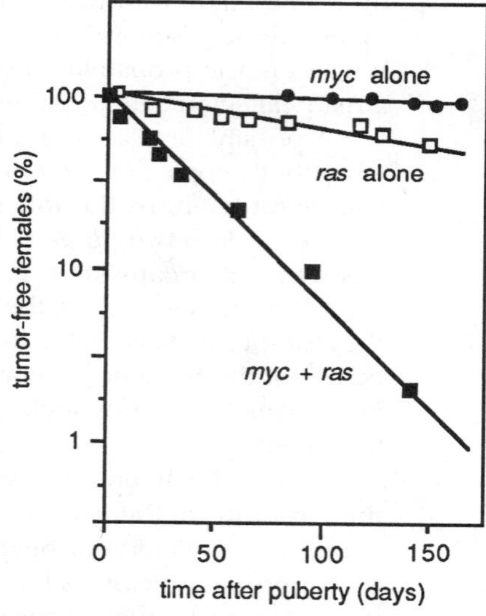

Figure 13–8 Fraction of tumor-free female mice as a function of time after puberty (Problem 13–22).

The Mechanics of Cell Division (MBOC 762–787)

13–23 Fill in the blanks in the following statements.

A. Mitosis is marked by the reorganization of the cytoskeleton into a bipolar ____________ composed of microtubules and their associated proteins.

B. The principal microtubule organizing center in most animal cells is the ____________, a cloud of amorphous pericentriolar material containing a pair of centrioles.

C. The first stage in mitosis is called ____________.

D. Replicated chromosomes bind to the mitotic spindle via structures called ____________.

E. Sister chromatids are joined near their ____________, which consist of a specific DNA sequence required for chromosome segregation.

F. The breakdown of the nuclear envelope in mitosis signals the end of prophase and marks the beginning of ____________.

G. In mitosis, ____________ begins abruptly with the synchronous splitting of each chromosome into its sister chromatids.

H. The poleward movement of chromosomes and concomitant shortening of kinetochore mictotubules is known as ____________; the separation of the poles themselves accompanied by elongation of the polar microtubules is known as ____________.

I. The final stage of mitosis is called ____________.

J. During ____________, the cytoplasm divides by a process called cleavage.

K. The first visible sign of cleavage in animal cells is a puckering and ____________ of the plasma membrane during anaphase.

L. Cleavage depends on the contraction of a bundle of actin filaments, known as the ____________, which underlies the cytoplasmic face of the plasma membrane.

M. The two daughter cells of a mitotic division remain tethered by a structure called the ____________, which is composed of the remains of the polar microtubules embedded in a dense matrix.

N. In plants, the new cross-wall formed between two daughter cells after division is known as the ____________.

O. The residual polar microtubules in plant cells that have almost completed division form an open cylindrical structure called the ____________, which guides vesicles containing cell wall precursors to deposit their contents at the newly forming cell wall.

13–24 Indicate whether the following statements are true or false. If a statement is false, explain why.

__ A. M phase is turned on by protein phosphorylation and terminated by protein dephosphorylation.

__ B. Chromosomes play no active part in mitosis.

__ C. Mitosis is a remarkably uniform process that is found in essentially every living cell.

__ D. In yeasts, two sister chromosomes make the error of going to the same pole (leaving the other daughter cell without a copy of the chromosome) about once in every 100,000 cell divisions.

__ E. In contrast to the highly dynamic interphase array of microtubules, the microtubules that are nucleated from the mitotic spindle poles are much more stable.

__ F. Unlike yeasts, which have very small centromeres, mammalian centromeric DNA encodes the proteins of the kinetochore, which accounts for their much greater length.

__ G. The microtubules that run from chromosomes to the spindle poles are unusually stable because they are capped at the plus end by the kinetochore and at the minus end by the centrosome.

__ H. Chromosomes are aligned on the metaphase plate mainly by the tension generated by the kinetochore microtubules.

__ I. Several lines of evidence suggest that mitotic chromosomes separate into their sister chromatids at the beginning of anaphase as a result of increased cytosolic Ca^{2+}.

__ J. Addition of taxol or D_2O to cells in anaphase blocks the movement of chromosomes toward the poles, but not the separation of the poles.

__ K. Unlike anaphase A, anaphase B is inhibited by agents that interfere with actin and myosin, suggesting that anaphase B depends on an actin-based motility system.

__ L. Cell-free extracts of *Xenopus* eggs can assemble nuclei around DNA from any source, provided that it contains a eucaryotic centromeric sequence.

— M. The plane of cell division at cytokinesis is determined by the position of the metaphase plate during mitosis, which somehow aligns the actin filaments that constitute the contractile ring.

— N. The mechanism of cytokinesis in plant cells is fundamentally different from animal cells: in plants a new cell wall is constructed inside the mother cell to divide it into the two daughter cells.

— O. No special mechanisms exist to ensure the inheritance of mitochondria during mitosis.

— P. In many unicellular organisms mitosis occurs without breakdown of the nuclear envelope.

13–25 DNA sequences involved in centromere function have been isolated from many yeast chromosomes. These centromeric sequences confer two chromosomelike properties on autonomously replicating circular plasmids in yeasts: (1) they lower the number of copies per cell to one or two, and (2) they promote correct segregation at mitosis, one plasmid to each daughter cell.

What would happen if two such sequences were present on the same DNA molecule? In higher eucaryotes, rare chromosomes containing two centromeres at different locations are highly unstable: they are literally torn apart at anaphase when the chromosomes separate. Yeast chromosomes are too small, however, to analyze microscopically. So other means (in this case cloning and restriction mapping) must be used to answer the question.

You construct a plasmid with two centromeric sequences as shown in Figure 13–9. Growth of this plasmid in bacteria requires the bacterial origin of replication (*ori*) and a selectable marker (*amp*^{R}); its growth in yeasts requires the yeast origin of replication (ARS1) and a selectable marker (*TRP1*). You prepare a stock of this plasmid by growing it in *E. coli.* This plasmid transforms yeast with about the same efficiency as a plasmid that contains a single centromeric sequence. However, the individual colonies selected after transformation with the dicentric plasmid vary considerably in size, unlike the uniform colonies arising from transformation with a monocentric plasmid. You find that the larger colonies all contain plasmids with a single centromeric sequence, whereas the smaller colonies contain plasmids that have lost both centromeric sequences. In no case did you recover a plasmid that still contained the original two centromeric sequences. By contrast, colonies transformed with the monocentric plasmid invariably contained intact plasmids.

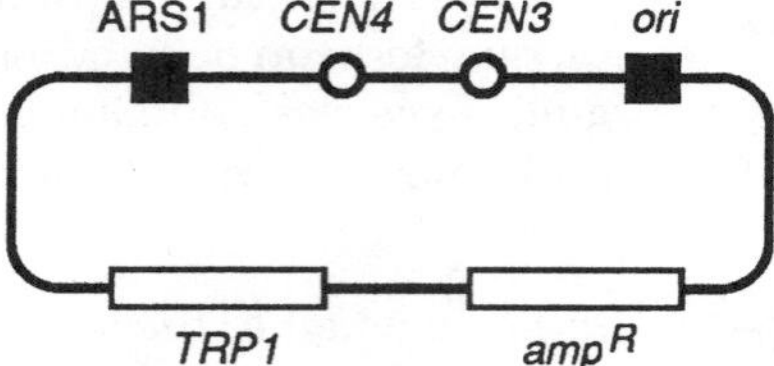

Figure 13–9 Structure of a dicentric plasmid (Problem 13–25). *CEN3* and *CEN4* refer to centromeric sequences from yeast chromosomes 3 and 4, respectively.

A. Considering their extreme instability in yeasts, why are dicentric plasmids stable in bacteria?

B. Why do you think that the dicentric plasmid is unstable in yeasts?

C. Suggest a mechanism for deletion of one of the centromeric sequences from a dicentric plasmid grown in yeast. Can this mechanism account for loss of both centromeric sequences from some of the plasmids?

***13–26** Circular yeast plasmids that contain an origin of replication but no centromere are distributed among individual cells in a peculiar way. In cultures grown under conditions that require a plasmid-encoded product, only 5% to 25% of the cells harbor the plasmids. However, in these plasmid-bearing cells the plasmid copy numbers range from 20 to 50 copies per cell. To investigate the apparent paradox of a high average copy number but only a small fraction of plasmid-bearing cells, you perform a pedigree analysis to determine the pattern of plasmid segregation during mitosis. You use a yeast strain that requires histidine for growth and a plasmid that carries the histidine gene missing from the host cell. The strain carrying the plasmid grows well under selective conditions, that is, when histidine is absent from the medium. By micromanipulation you separate mother and daughter cells for five divisions under selective conditions and then score for those cells that can form a colony. In Figure 13–10

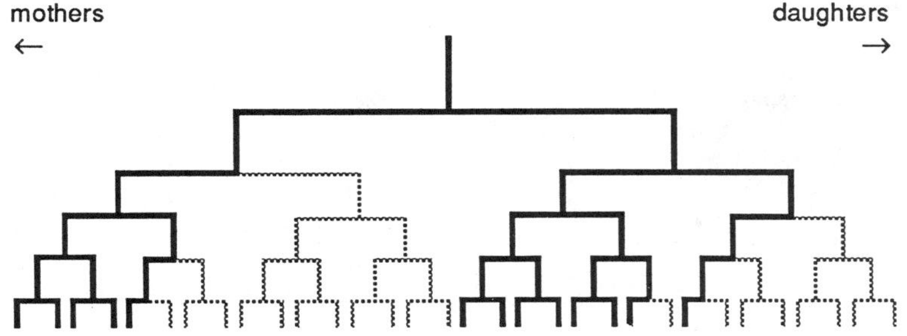

Figure 13–10 A pedigree analysis showing the inheritance of a plasmid that contains an origin of replication and a selectable histidine marker (Problem 13–26). The heavy lines show cells containing the plasmid, and the dotted lines show cells lacking the plasmid. At each division mother cells are shown to the left and daughter cells are shown to the right.

cells that formed colonies are indicated with thick lines and cells that failed to form colonies are shown with dotted lines.

A. From the pedigree analysis, it is apparent that cells that lack the plasmid can grow for several divisions in selective medium. How can this be?
B. Does this plasmid segregate equally to mother and daughter cells?
C. Assuming that plasmids in yeast cells replicate only once per cell cycle as the chromosomes do, how can there be 20 to 50 molecules of the plasmid per plasmid-bearing cell?
D. When grown under selective conditions, cells containing plasmids with one centromere (1–2 plasmids per cell) form large colonies, whereas cells containing plasmids with no centromere (20–50 plasmids per cell) form small colonies (see Problem 13–25). Does the pedigree analysis help to explain the difference?

13–27 One of the least well-understood aspects of the cell cycle is the reproduction of the spindle poles. As illustrated in Figure 13–11, the centrosome normally splits at the beginning of mitosis to form the two spindle poles, which orchestrate chromosome segregation. During the next interphase, the centriole pair within the centrosome is duplicated so that the centrosome can split at the next mitosis. The cycles of centrosome duplication and splitting normally keep step with cell division so that all cells have the capacity to produce bipolar spindles. However, it is possible to throw the two cycles out of phase as indicated by experiments first performed in the late 1950s.

If a fertilized sea urchin egg at the metaphase stage of the first mitotic division is exposed to mercaptoethanol, the mitotic spindle disassembles

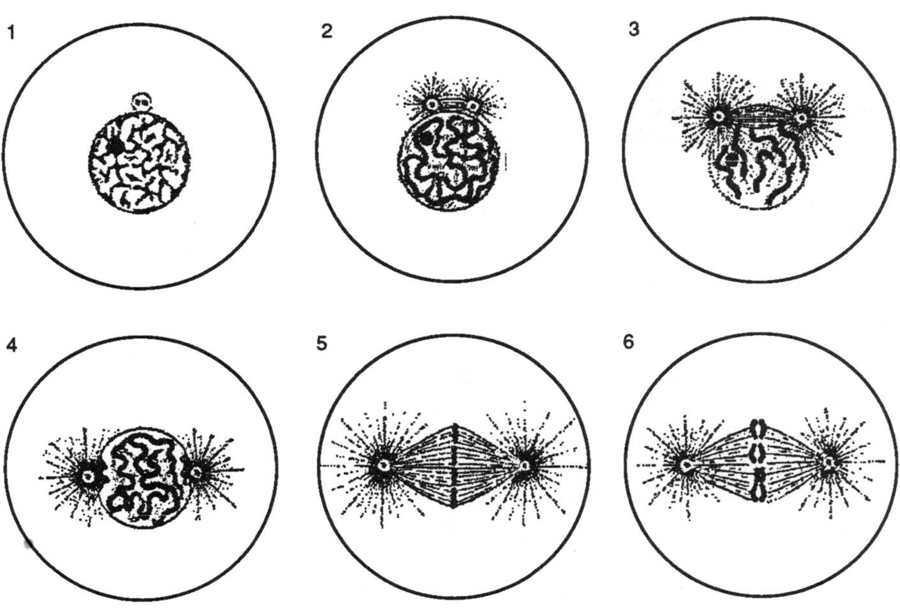

Figure 13–11 Normal process of centrosome splitting during mitosis to form a bipolar spindle (Problem 13–27). (Adapted from E.B. Wilson, The Cell in Development and Inheritance, 1st ed., 1896. Figures 19 and 20. New York and London: Johnson Reprint Corporation, 1966.)

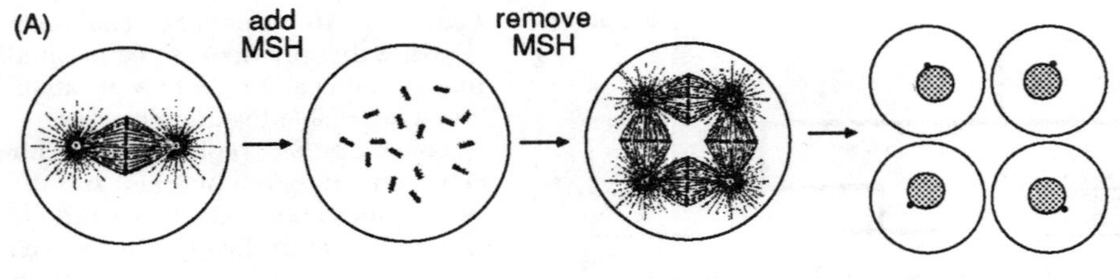

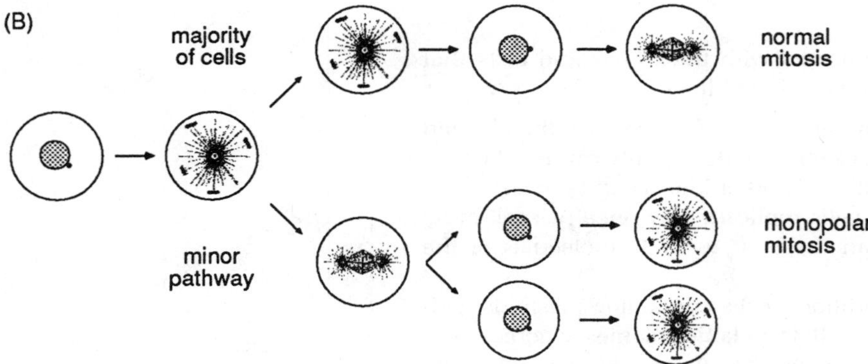

Figure 13–12 Abnormal spindles and cell divisions induced by mercaptoethanol (MSH) treatment (Problem 13–27). (A) Formation of tetrapolar spindles upon treatment of fertilized sea urchin eggs with mercaptoethanol followed by four-way division. (B) Major and minor pathways for spindle formation and cell division among the daughter cells from a four-way division.

(Figure 13–12A). (It is not known how mercaptoethanol has its effect, but the effect is reversible.) While the eggs are kept in mercaptoethanol, the nucleus does not re-form, no DNA synthesis occurs, and the chromosomes stay condensed. When the mercaptoethanol is washed out, the spindle re-forms and cell division takes place. However, although some eggs re-form a bipolar spindle and divide normally, the majority of eggs form a tetrapolar spindle and divide into four daughter cells (Figure 13–12A). No matter how long the eggs are arrested in mercaptoethanol, they never divide into more than four cells.

The daughter cells from a four-way division re-form the nucleus and traverse the next cell cycle; however, at mitosis they form a monopolar spindle. In a majority of cases these cells stay in mitosis a little longer than usual, then decondense their chromosomes, disassemble the spindle, and re-form a nucleus (Figure 13–12B). At the next mitosis these cells form a normal bipolar spindle and divide normally (Figure 13–12B). More rarely, the cells with monopolar spindles stay in mitosis much longer, the monopole splits to form a bipolar spindle, and the cell divides normally (Figure 13–12B). However, the daughter cells from such a division once again form a monopolar spindle at the next mitosis (Figure 13–12B).

Describe patterns of centriole duplication and splitting that can account for the observations shown in Figure 13–12.

***13–28** The microtubules that link centrosomes to kinetochores guide or pull chromosomes to the poles during mitosis. How are microtubules arrayed to carry out this process? What manner of connection allows relative movement of spindles and chromosomes? After many clever experiments, the picture is still not clear.

Nevertheless, some aspects of the connections between centrosomes and chromosomes have been clarified by experiment. Consider the following observation. Centrosomes were used to initiate microtubule growth, and then chromosomes were added. The chromosomes bound to the free ends of the microtubules, as illustrated in Figure 13–13. The complexes were then diluted to very low tubulin concentration and examined again (Figure 13–13). As is evident, only the connecting microtubules were stable to dilution.

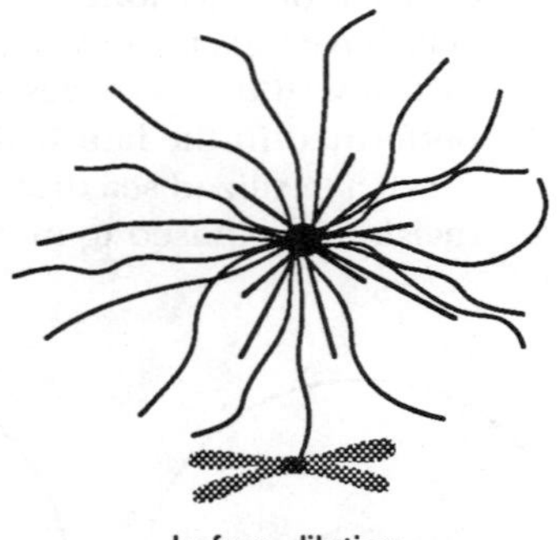

Figure 13–13 Arrangements of centrosomes, chromosomes, and microtubules before and after dilution to low tubulin concentration (Problem 13–28).

A. Why do you think that the connecting microtubules are stable?
B. Explain the disappearance of the nonconnecting microtubules after dilution. Do they detach from the centrosome, depolymerize from an end, or disintegrate along their length at random?
C. How would a time course after dilution help to distinguish among these possible mechanisms of disappearance?

***13–29** When cells divide after mitosis, their surface area increases—a natural consequence of dividing a constant volume into two compartments. The increase in surface requires an increase in the amount of plasma membrane. One can estimate the increase in plasma membrane by making certain assumptions about the geometry of cell division. Assuming that the parent cell and the two progeny cells are spherical, one can apply the familiar equations for the volume and surface area of a sphere.

$$\text{Volume} = 4/3\pi r^3$$
$$\text{Area} = 4\pi r^2$$

A. Assuming that the progeny cells are equal in size, calculate the increase in plasma membrane that accompanies cell division. (Although this problem can be solved algebraically, you may find it easier to substitute real numbers. For example, let the volume of the parent cell equal 1.) Do you think that the magnitude of this increase is likely to cause any problem for the cell? Explain your answer.
B. During early development many fertilized eggs undergo several rounds of cell division without any overall increase in total volume. For example *Xenopus* eggs undergo 12 rounds of division before growth commences and the total cell volume increases. Assuming once again that all cells are spherical and equal in size, calculate the increase in plasma membrane that accompanies development of the early embryo: in going from one large cell (the egg) to 4096 small cells (12 divisions).

13–30 Cytokinesis—the actual process of cell division—has attracted theorists for well over 100 years. Indeed, it has been said that all possible explanations of cytokinesis have been proposed; the problem is to decide which one is correct. Consider the following three hypotheses about cytokinesis:

1. *Chromosome signaling:* When chromosomes split at anaphase, they emit a signal to the nearby cell surface to initiate furrowing.
2. *Polar relaxation:* Asters relax the tension in the nearest region of the cell surface (the polar region), allowing the region of the membrane farthest from the poles (the equatorial plane) to contract and initiate furrowing.
3. *Aster stimulation:* The asters stimulate contraction in the region of the cell surface where oppositely oriented spindle fibers overlap (that is, the equatorial region), thereby initiating furrowing.

These hypotheses have been tested in a number of ways. One particularly informative experiment involved pressing a glass ball onto the center of a dividing sand dollar egg so as to deform it into a torus (donut shape). As illustrated in Figure 13–14, at the first division the egg divided into a single sausage-shaped cell; at the second division it divided into four cells.

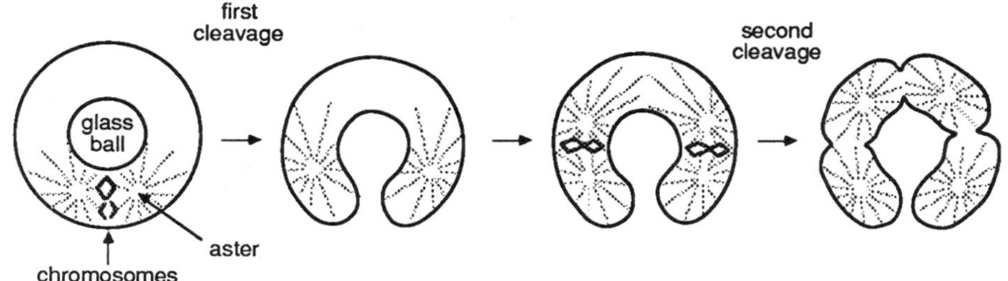

Figure 13–14 First and second divisions in a torus-shaped sand dollar egg (Problem 13–30).

A. What does the chromosome-signaling hypothesis predict for the result of this experiment? Do the predictions match the experimental observations?
B. What does the polar-relaxation hypothesis predict for the experimental outcome? Do the predictions match the experimental observations?
C. What does the aster-stimulation hypothesis predict? Do the predictions match the experimental observations?

Cell Adhesion, Cell Junctions, and the Extracellular Matrix

14

Cell Junctions (MBOC 792–802)

14–1 Fill in the blanks in the following statements.

A. A sheet of cells is called an ____________.

B. Specialized junctions between cells can be classified into three general groups: ____________ junctions make molecule-tight seals between cells; ____________ junctions mechanically connect cells and their cytoskeletons to each other or to the extracellular matrix; and ____________ junctions mediate the passage of small molecules from cell to cell.

C. The calcium-dependent junctions that seal epithelia so molecules cannot leak from one side of the sheet to the other are known as ____________ junctions.

D. Epithelial cells in the gut have one set of carrier proteins on their ____________ surface, which faces the lumen of the gut, and a second set of carrier proteins on their ____________ surface, which faces away from the gut.

E. ____________ junctions connect the actin filaments of neighboring cells; they are composed of transmembrane linker proteins, which hold the cells together, and intracellular attachment proteins, which connect the actin filaments to the linker proteins.

F. Epithelial cells are connected by a beltlike structure called the ____________, which is thought to mediate the folding of cell sheets into tubes during morphogenesis in animals.

G. The calcium-dependent linker glycoproteins mediating cell adhesion in epithelia are members of a family of adhesion molecules called ____________.

H. ____________ is a major component of the complex of intracellular attachment proteins that mediates actin attachments to transmembrane linker glycoproteins.

I. Fibroblasts in culture adhere to the substratum at specialized regions of the plasma membrane called ____________, which link actin filaments to the extracellular matrix.

J. ____________ are buttonlike points of intercellular contact, that serve as anchoring sites for intermediate filaments and help hold adjacent cells together.

K. The basal surface of an epithelial cell is joined to the basal lamina at ____________, which link intermediate filaments to the extracellular matrix.

L. The most common type of communicating junction between cells is the ____________; it allows substances with molecular weights under 1000 to pass freely between cells.

M. The protein structures that connect adjacent cell interiors by continuous aqueous channels are called ____________.

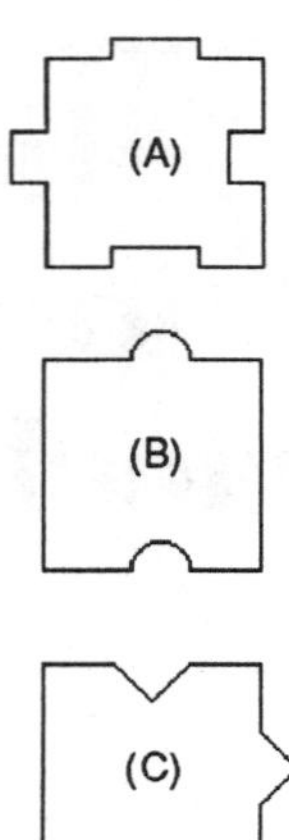

Figure 14–1 Three monomeric membrane proteins (Problem 14–3).

14–2 Indicate whether the following statements are true or false. If a statement is false, explain why.

__ A. Tight junctions get their name from their property of holding cells together so tightly that they cannot be separated by mechanical forces.

__ B. Directional pumping of nutrients across epithelia would be impossible if the proteins on the apical and basolateral surfaces were the same.

__ C. Epithelial cell sheets differ markedly in the permeability of their tight junctions; for example, bladder epithelium is much more leaky to ions than is the intestinal epithelium.

__ D. When Ca^{2+} ions are removed from the medium bathing an epithelium, the cells stop sticking to one another because their tight junctions are disrupted.

__ E. Gap junctions connect the cytoskeletal elements of one cell to a neighboring cell or to the extracellular matrix.

__ F. A desmosome bears the same relationship to a hemidesmosome that an adhesion belt does to a focal contact.

__ G. The permeability of gap junctions is regulated by the extracellular Ca^{2+} and pH.

14–3 Examine the three protein monomers in Figure 14–1. From the arrangement of complementary binding domains, which are indicated by similarly shaped protrusions and invaginations, decide which monomer might assemble into a strand of a tight junction, which monomer might assemble into a desmosome, and which monomer could not assemble into either.

***14–4** Two structures for tight junctions have been proposed. In one ingenious model, which is based on observations from freeze-fracture electron microscopy, each sealing strand in a tight junction results from a membrane fusion that forms cylinders of lipid at the points of fusion (Figure 14–2A). The other model proposes that each strand of a tight junction is formed by a chain of transmembrane proteins whose extracellular domains bind to one another to seal the epithelial sheet (Figure 14–2B).

As you compare these lipid and protein models for tight junctions, you realize that they might be distinguishable on the basis of lipid diffusion between the apical and basolateral surfaces. Both models predict that lipids in the cytoplasmic leaflet will be able to diffuse freely between the apical and the basolateral surfaces. However, the models suggest different fates for lipids in the external leaflet. In the lipid model, lipids in the outer leaflet will be confined to either the apical surface or the basolateral surface, since the cylinder of lipids interrupts the external leaflet, preventing diffusion through it. By contrast, in the protein model the apical and basolateral

*Problems with an asterisk (*) are answered in the Instructor's Manual.

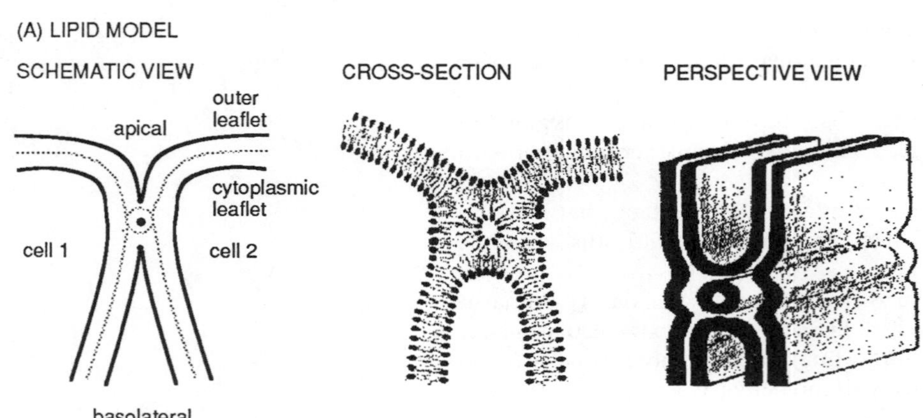

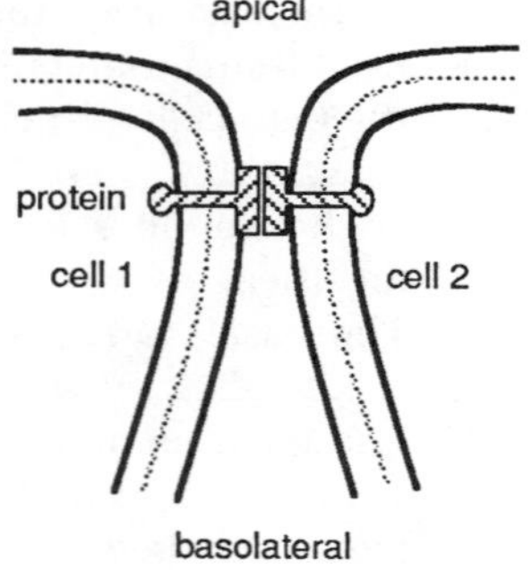

Figure 14–2 Models for tight-junction structure (Problem 14–4). (A) Two views, perspective and molecular, of the cylinder of lipids that is proposed to form a tight-junction according to the lipid model. (B) Schematic representations of the lipid and protein models for tight-junction structure.

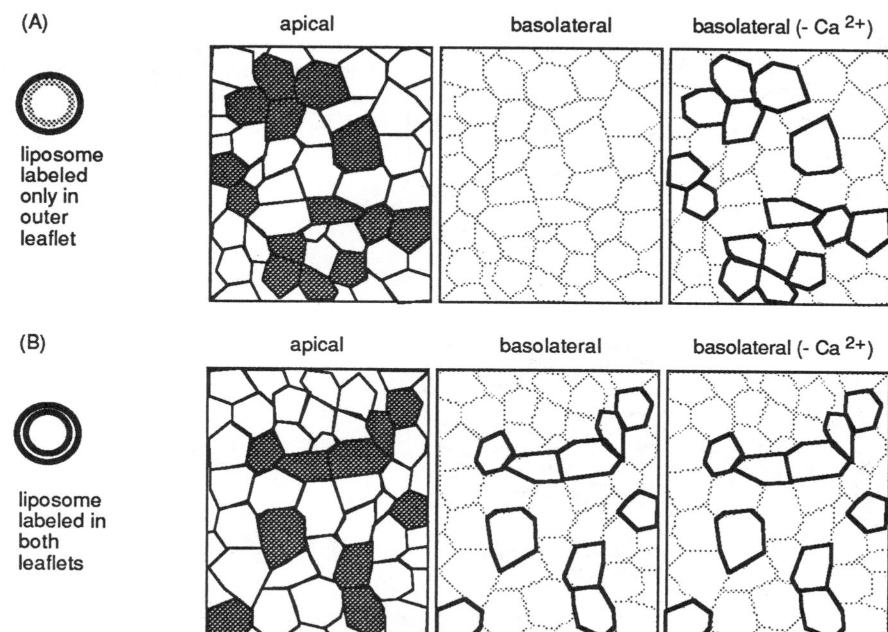

Figure 14–3 Experimental test of the lipid and protein models for tight-junction structure (Problem 14–4). (A) Liposomes labeled in outer leaflet. (B) Liposomes labeled in both leaflets. Only about half the cells in the epithelium in each experiment were infected with virus. Only infected cells are competent to fuse with the labeled liposomes under the conditions of the experimental protocol.

surfaces appear to be connected by a continuous external leaflet, suggesting that lipids in the external leaflet should be able to diffuse freely between the two surfaces.

You have exactly the experimental tools to resolve this issue! You have been working with a line of dog kidney cells that forms an exceptionally tight epithelium with well-defined apical and basolateral surfaces. In addition, after infection with influenza virus, the cells express a fusogenic protein only on their apical surface. This feature allows you to fuse liposomes specifically to the apical surface of infected cells very efficiently by brief exposure to low pH, which activates the fusogenic protein. Thus, you can add fluorescently labeled lipids to the apical surface and detect their migration to the basolateral surface using fluorescence microscopy.

For the experiment you prepare two sets of labeled liposomes: one with a fluorescent lipid only in the outer leaflet, the other with the fluorescent lipid equally distributed between the inner and outer leaflets. You fuse these two sets of liposomes to epithelia in which about half the cells were infected with virus. By adjusting the focal plane of the microscope, you examine the apical and basolateral surfaces for fluorescence. As a control, you remove Ca^{2+} from the medium—a treatment that disrupts tight junctions—and reexamine the basolateral surface. The results are shown in Figure 14–3.

You are delighted! These results show clearly that lipids in the external leaflet are confined to the apical surface, whereas lipids in the cytoplasmic leaflet diffuse freely between the apical and basolateral surfaces. Triumphantly, you show these results to your advisor as proof that the lipid model for tight-junction structure is correct. He examines your results carefully, shakes his head knowingly, gives you that penetrating look of his, and tells you that, although the experiments are exquisitely well done, you have drawn exactly the wrong conclusion. These results prove that the lipid model is incorrect.

What has your advisor seen in the data that you have overlooked? How do your results disprove the lipid model? If the protein model is correct, why do you think it is that the fluorescent lipids are confined to the apical surface?

14–5 Most of the current carried by small ions across an epithelium must pass through the gaps between cells because the cellular membranes are ex-

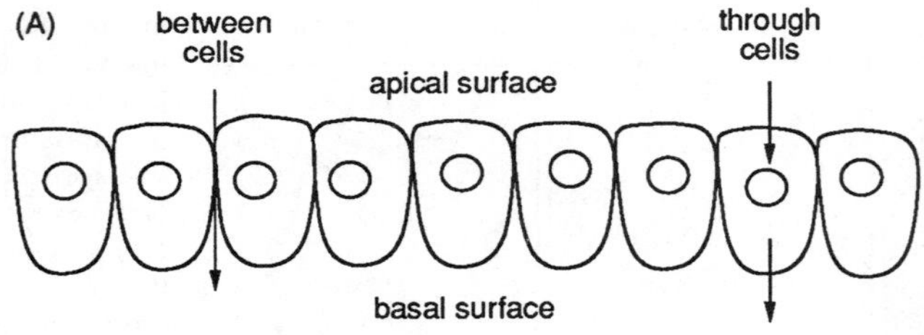

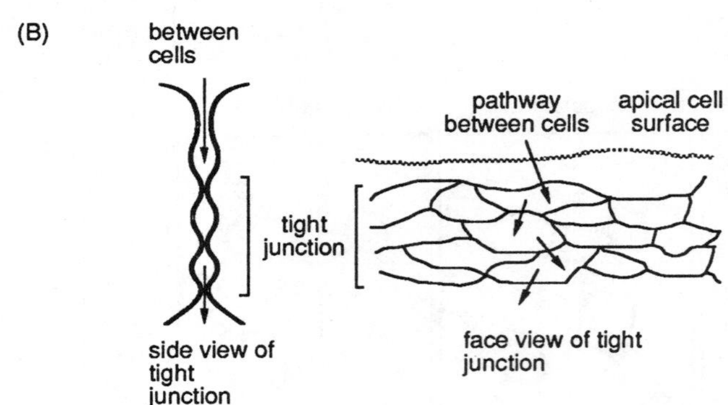

Figure 14–4 Side view of an epithelium (A) and two views of the tight junctions (B) that link cells in an epithelium (Problem 14–5).

cellent electrical insulators. Thus, the electrical resistance of an epithelium depends on the properties of the tight junctions that seal them (Figure 14–4).

You and your advisor some time ago observed that there is a rough correlation between the electrical resistance of an epithelium and the number of sealing strands in the tight junction. You can imagine two ways that resistance might depend on the number of sealing strands. If each sealing strand provided a given resistance, then the overall resistance of a tight junction would be linearly related to the number of sealing strands (like electrical resistors in series). On the other hand, suppose each sealing strand could exist in two states: a closed, high-resistance state and an open, low-resistance state. The resistance of the tight junction would then be related to the probability that all strands in a given pathway through the junction would be open at the same time. In that case the overall resistance would be logarithmically related to the number of sealing strands.

To put the data on a quantitative basis so that you can distinguish between these two possibilities, you measure the resistance of four different epithelia from a rabbit: the very leaky proximal tubule of the kidney, the less leaky gall bladder, the tight distal tubule of the kidney, and the very tight bladder epithelium. In addition, you prepare freeze-fracture electron micrographs, from which you determine the average number of sealing strands in the tight junctions that surround each cell in these epithelia. The results are shown in Table 14–1. Which of the two proposed interpretations of the correlation between electrical resistance of the epithelium and the number of sealing strands in a tight junction is supported by your measurements?

Table 14–1 Correlation Between Electrical Resistance and the Number of Strands in the Tight Junctions from Various Epithelia (Problem 14–5)

Epithelium	**Mean Number of Strands in Tight Junction**	**Specific Resistance of Tight Junction**
Rabbit proximal tubule	1.2	1.2×10^4
Rabbit gall bladder	3.3	5.6×10^4
Rabbit distal tubule	5.3	6.2×10^5
Rabbit urinary bladder	8.0	5.6×10^6

*14–6 When properly maintained in culture, mouse heart cells beat regularly with a characteristic frequency that can be increased by addition of cyclic AMP or by inhibitors of cyclic AMP hydrolysis. Addition of norepinephrine increases the beat frequency by raising the intracellular cyclic AMP level.

Rat ovary cells in culture respond to follicle stimulating hormone (FSH) by increasing the synthesis of a protease activator called tissue-plasminogen activator (TPA). This response is also mediated by an increase in intracellular cyclic AMP levels.

FSH has no effect on the beating of heart cells, and norepinephrine has no effect on synthesis of TPA by ovary cells. However, when the two cell types are mixed together and co-cultured, addition of FSH or norepinephrine increases both the beat frequency of the heart cells and TPA synthesis in the ovary cells. Adding an enzyme to the medium that hydrolyzes cyclic AMP to 5′ AMP has no effect on the collaboration.

Suggest an explanation for these results. How might you test your hypothesis?

14–7 Fertilized mouse eggs divide very slowly at first. They reach two cells after about 24 hours and eight cells by 48 hours. At the eight-cell stage they undergo a process known as compaction, as illustrated in Figure 14–5. Although the mechanism is not clear, the cells appear to adhere to one another more strongly; consequently, they change from being a clump of loosely associated cells to a tightly sealed ball. You wish to know what kinds of intercellular junctions are present before and after this change in adhesion.

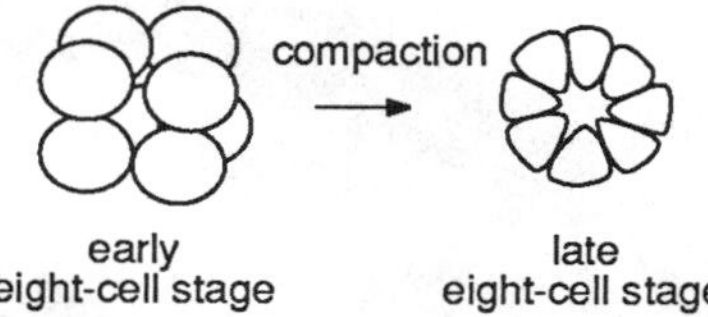

Figure 14–5 Compaction of the eight-cell mouse embryo (Problem 14–7).

To study this question, you use very fine glass micropipettes, which allow you to measure electrical events and at the same time to microinject either the enzyme, horseradish peroxidase (HRP), 40,000 daltons, or the fluorescent dye, fluorescein, 330 daltons. Fluorescein glows bright yellow under UV illumination, while HRP can be detected by fixing the cells and incubating them with appropriate substrates.

You inject embryos at various stages of development with the two marker substances. At both the two-cell and eight-cell stages, different results are obtained, depending on whether the injections are made immediately after cell division or later (Figure 14–6); some of this difference can be attributed to the cytoplasmic bridges that linger for a while before cytokinesis is truly completed.

A. Why do both HRP and fluorescein enter neighboring cells early, but not late, at the two-cell stage?

B. Why does fluorescein enter all cells in the compacted eight-cell embryo, whereas HRP is confined to the injected cell?

C. In which of the four stages of development diagrammed in Figure 14–6 would you detect electrical coupling if you injected current from the HRP injection electrode and recorded voltage changes in the fluorescein electrode?

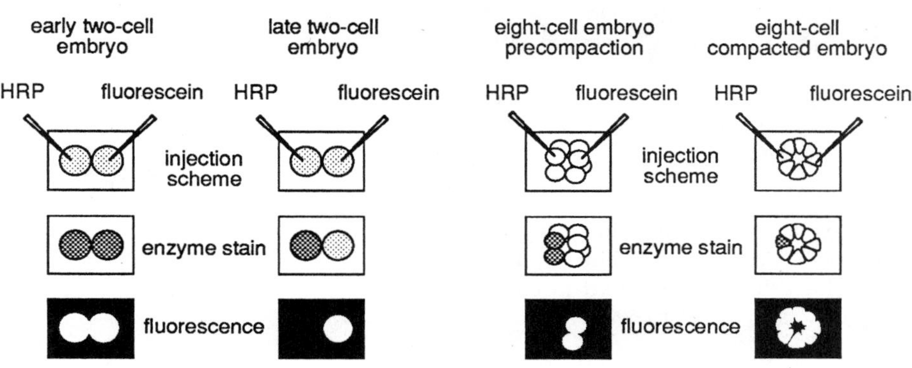

Figure 14–6 Microinjection of HRP and fluorescein in two-cell and eight-cell mouse embryos (Problem 14–7).

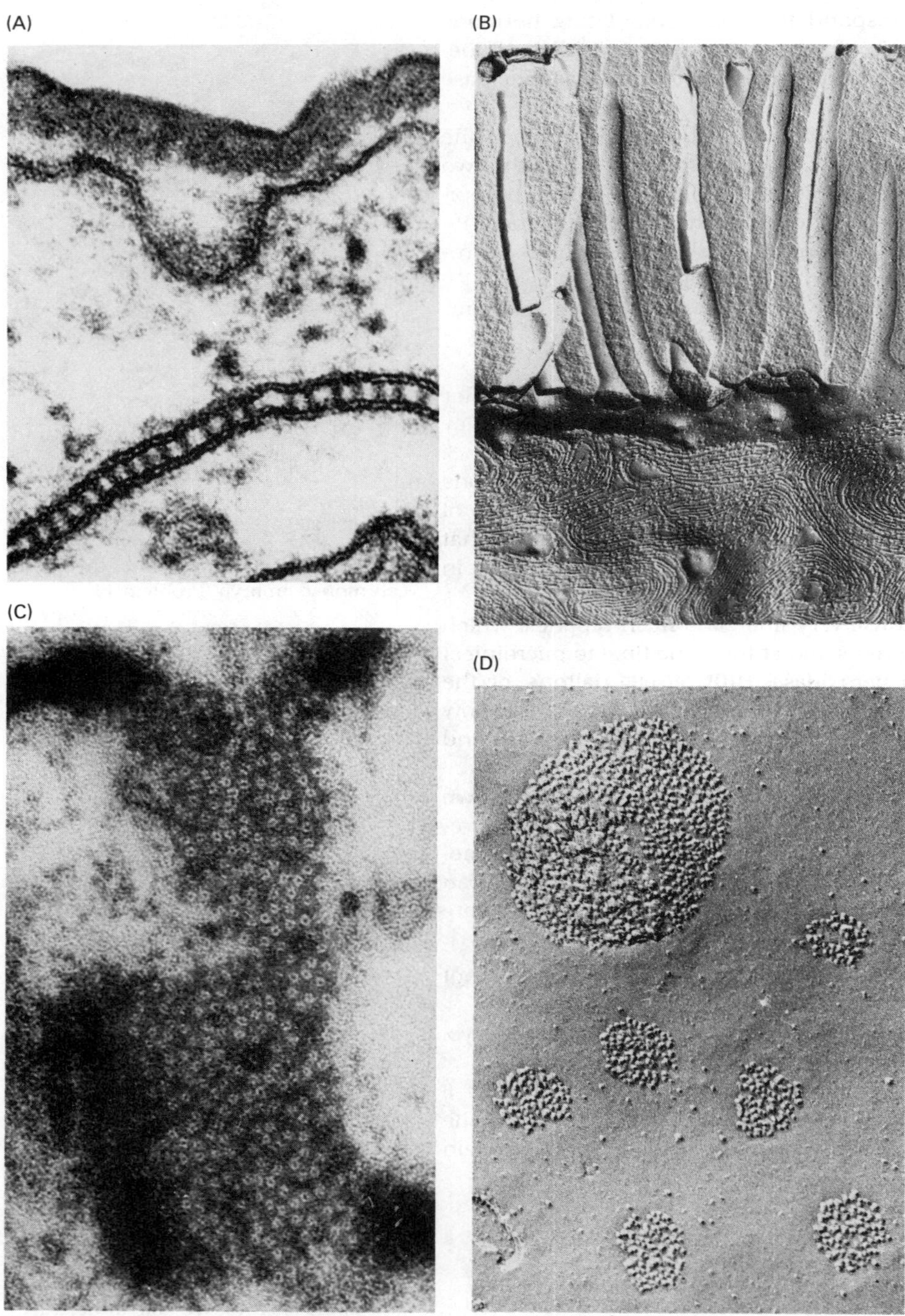

Figure 14–7 Electron micrographs of a variety of cell junctions (Problem 14–8). (Courtesy of Dr. Nancy Lane.)

14–8 You are studying cell junctions in insects, and the first electron micrographs just came back from the photolab. Unfortunately, the labels were lost. Can you deduce the type of junction that is illustrated in each micrograph?

The Extracellular Matrix (MBOC 802–824)

14–9 Fill in the blanks in the following statements.

A. The network of interacting protein and polysaccharide molecules in contact with the outside surface of most cells in multicellular organisms is called the ____________.

B. Skin and bone are composed mainly of ____________, a term that is often used to describe the extracellular matrix plus the cells found in it.

C. ____________ are long, unbranched polysaccharide chains composed of repeating disaccharide units that always contain an amino sugar.

D. ____________ is an abundant polysaccharide of the extracellular matrix of developing animals; its large size, lack of sulfation, and simple repeating disaccharide structure distinguish it from other glycosaminoglycans.

E. ____________ are synthesized much like glycoproteins; however, the polysaccharide chains are attached to serine residues, and the molecular weight of the carbohydrate can exceed that of the core protein by a factor of 10 to 20.

F. The ____________ are the most abundant proteins in mammals; their distinguishing feature is a triple-stranded helix rich in glycine and proline.

G. The main component of elastic fibers is ____________, which is a highly hydrophobic, nonglycosylated protein that contains little hydroxyproline and no hydroxylysine.

H. The best characterized of the extracellular adhesive glycoproteins is ____________, which helps cells adhere to their substratum by binding both to cell-surface receptors and to various other components of the extracellular matrix.

I. The continuous thin layer of specialized extracellular matrix that underlies all epithelia cell sheets and tubes and surrounds individual muscle cells and fat cells is called the ____________.

J. ____________, which is a glycoprotein composed of three polypeptides arranged in the shape of a cross, binds to type IV collagen, heparan sulfate, and cell surfaces.

14–10 Indicate whether the following statements are true or false. If a statement is false, explain why.

___ A. The extracellular matrix is a relatively inert scaffolding that stabilizes the structure of tissues.

___ B. The main chemical difference between glycoproteins and proteoglycans lies in the structure of their carbohydrate side chains: glycoproteins contain short, highly branched oligosaccharides, whereas proteoglycans contain much longer, unbranched polysaccharide side chains.

___ C. Proteoglycans in the basal lamina of the kidney glomerulus play a critical role in regulating the passage of macromolecules from the blood into the urine.

___ D. Breakdown and resynthesis of collagen must be important in maintaining the extracellular matrix; otherwise, vitamin C deficiency in adults would not cause scurvy, which is characterized by a progressive weakening of connective tissue due to inadequate hydroxylation of collagen.

___ E. During maturation of the fibrillar collagens, three peptide bonds in each monomeric polypeptide must be broken.

___ F. When actin microfilaments in fibroblasts are disaggregated with the drug cytochalasin, the cells lose contact with the fibronectin fibrils in the substratum, thereby proving a direct attachment between fibronectin and actin.

___ G. Although most types of collagen assemble into fibrils, type IV collagen assembles into a sheetlike network that forms the core of all basal lamina.

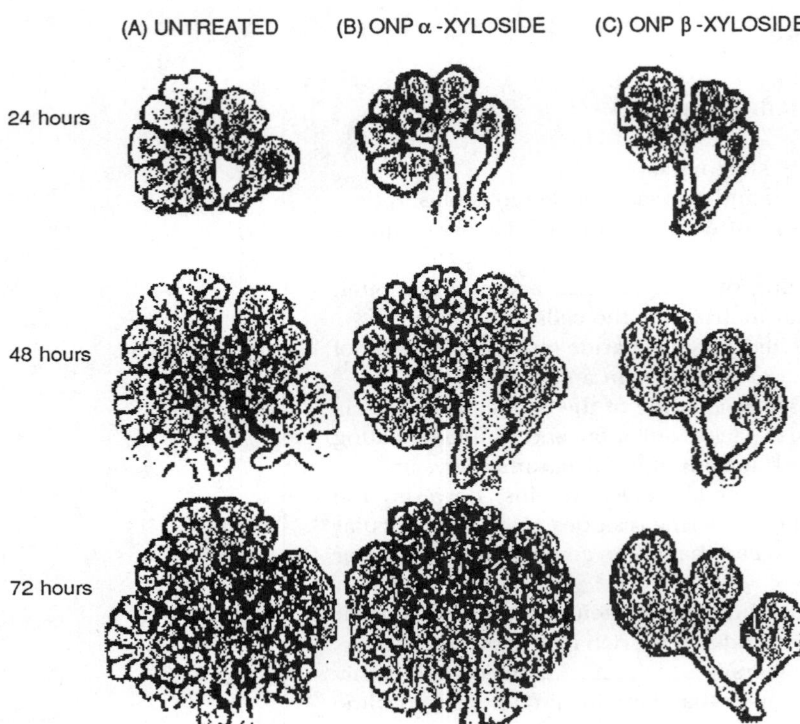

Figure 14–8 Development of mouse salivary glands in culture (Problem 14–11).

— H. The elasticity of elastin derives from its high content of alpha helices, which act as molecular springs.

— I. Cells never bind directly to molecules in the extracellular matrix; instead, they bind indirectly through extracellular adaptor glycoproteins.

14–11 Embryonic mouse salivary glands are composed of an epithelium that undergoes a series of repetitive branching and folding events to form the ducts and lobes that make up the mature gland. Salivary glands in culture undergo much the same development as they would in the animal, typically forming 7 to 10 times more lobes after 3 days than were present at the end of day 1 (Figure 14–8). The process of lobe development is known as branching morphogenesis.

The basal lamina is critical for branching morphogenesis. For example, inhibitors of collagen synthesis like the proline analogue, azetidine-2-carboxylic acid, inhibit branching. One of the other major constituents of the basal lamina is proteoglycan. What would happen if its synthesis was blocked? Glycosaminoglycans are built one sugar at a time on the core protein, starting with the unusual sugar β-D-xylose, which is linked to a serine residue in the polypeptide backbone (Figure 14–9). The xyloside analogue, *o*-nitrophenyl-β-D-xyloside (ONP-β-D-xyloside, Figure 14–9), acts as a competitor of glycosaminoglycan addition to proteins in the Golgi. When this analogue is added to growing salivary glands, the glands grow but do not form lobes or branches (Figure 14–8). Treatment with ONP-α-D-xyloside has no effect on gland development (Figure 14–8). This shows that the effect is specific for the naturally occurring isomer and that the inhibition is not due to nonspecific toxicity.

To determine how ONP-β-D-xyloside affects proteoglycan synthesis, the incorporation of $^{35}SO_4$ into newly made glycosaminoglycans was measured under a variety of conditions, as shown in Table 14–2. All the $^{35}SO_4$ was incorporated into glycosaminoglycans, as judged by its sensitivity to hyaluronidase digestion.

A. Why does cycloheximide inhibit $^{35}SO_4$ incorporation in the absence of ONP-β-D-xyloside but not in its presence?

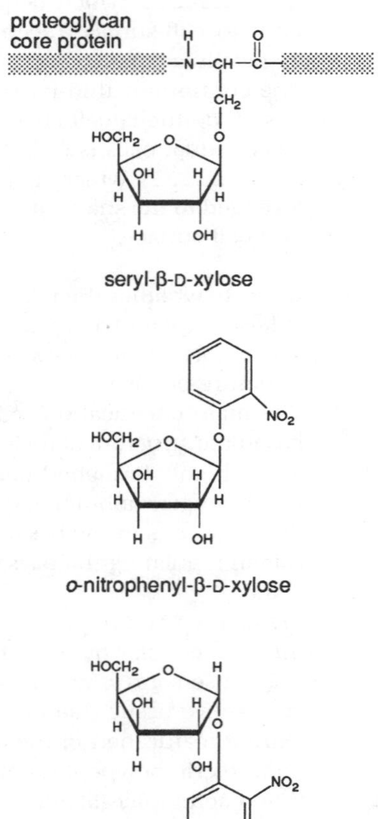

Figure 14–9 Structures of the protein-xylose linkage, ONP-β-D-xyloside, and ONP-α-D-xyloside (Problem 14–11).

Table 14–2 Effects of Xylosides on Glycosaminoglycan Synthesis (Incorporation of $^{35}SO_4$) in Salivary Glands in Culture (Problem 14–11)

Cell Treatment	Counts in Tissue	Counts in Medium	Total Counts
Control	1000	300	1300
ONP-α-D-xyloside	1000	300	1300
ONP-β-D-xyloside	200	3000	3200
Cycloheximide	ND*	ND	200
Cycloheximide + ONP-α-D-xyloside	ND	ND	200
Cycloheximide + ONP-β-D-xyloside	ND	ND	3000

ND stands for not determined.

B. Why are such large amounts of $^{35}SO_4$-labeled material found in the medium when ONP-β-D-xyloside is present?

C. Why does ONP-β-D-xyloside, but not ONP-α-D-xyloside, cause such profound changes in $^{35}SO_4$ incorporation?

D. How might ONP-β-D-xyloside suppress branching morphogenesis of salivary glands in tissue culture?

***14–12** Defects in collagen genes are responsible for several inherited diseases. For example, osteogenesis imperfecta, a disease characterized by brittle bones, can result from a defect in the gene encoding the type I α1 collagen chain. Similarly, Ehlers-Danlos syndrome, which can lead to sudden death due to ruptured internal organs or blood vessels, can result from a defect in the type III α1 collagen gene.

In both diseases the medical problems arise because the defective gene in some way compromises the function of collagen fibrils. For example, homozygous deletions of the type I α1 gene eliminates α1(I) collagen entirely, thereby preventing formation of any type I collagen fibrils. Such homozygous mutations are usually lethal in early development. The more common situation is for an individual to be heterozygous for the mutant gene, having one normal gene and one defective gene. Here the consequences are less severe.

A. Calculate the fraction of type I collagen molecules, $[\alpha1(I)]_2\alpha2(I)$, that will be normal in an individual who is heterozygous for a deletion of the entire α1(I) gene. Repeat the calculation for an individual who is heterozygous for a point mutation in the α1(I) gene.

B. Calculate the fraction of type III collagen molecules, $[\alpha1(III)]_3$, that will be normal in an individual who is heterozygous for a deletion of the entire α1(III) gene. Repeat the calculation for an individual who is heterozygous for a point mutation in the α1(III) gene.

C. Which kind of collagen gene defect—deletion or point mutation—is more likely to be dominant (that is, cause the heterozygote to display a mutant phenotype)?

14–13 The formation of a mature collagen molecule is a complex process. Procollagen is formed first from three collagen chains, which have extensions at the N and C termini. Once the chains have been properly wound together, the terminal propeptides are removed. A principal function of the terminal propeptides may be to align the chains correctly to facilitate their assembly.

Two forms of type III collagen molecules have been used to study collagen assembly: (1) the mature type III collagen molecule and (2) a precursor with the N-terminal propeptides still attached, type III pN-collagen (Figure 14–10). In both types of collagen molecule the individual chains are held together by disulfide bonds. These bonds hold the chains in register, even after they have been completely unwound, so that they reassemble collagen molecules correctly (Figure 14–10).

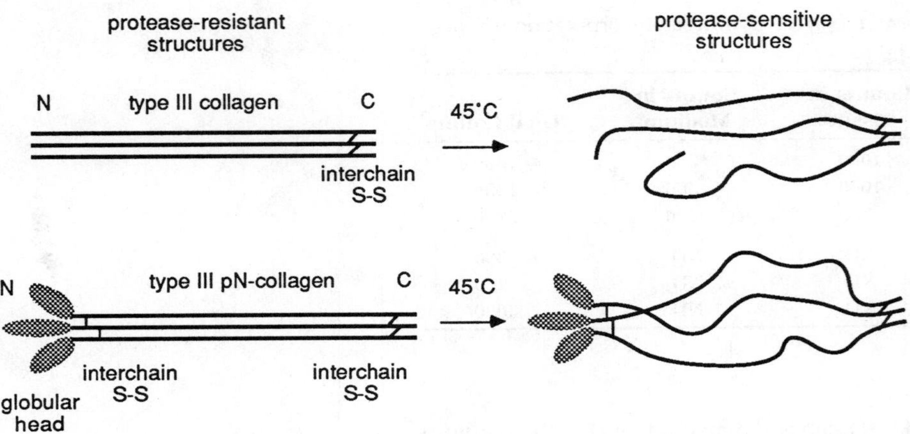

Figure 14–10 Native and denatured forms of type III collagen and type III pN-collagen (Problem 14–13).

Reassembly of these two collagen molecules was studied after denaturation at 45°C under conditions that leave the disulfide bonds intact. The temperature was then reduced to 25°C to allow reassembly, and samples were removed at intervals up to 60 minutes. Each sample was immediately digested with trypsin, which rapidly cleaves denatured chains but does not attack the collagen helix. When the samples were analyzed by SDS-gel electrophoresis in the presence of 2-mercaptoethanol, which breaks disulfide bonds, both collagens yielded identical patterns (Figure 14–11). Significantly, if the disulfide bonds were left intact during SDS-gel electrophoresis, all bands were replaced by bands with three times the molecular weight.

A. Why did all the resistant peptides increase threefold in molecular weight when the disulfide bonds were left intact?
B. Which set of disulfide bonds in type III pN-collagen (N-terminal or C-terminal) is responsible for the increase in molecular weight of its resistant peptides?
C. Does reassembly of these collagen molecules begin at a specific site or at random sites? If they reassemble from a specific site, deduce its location.
D. Does reassembly follow a zipperlike or an all-or-none mechanism? How do these results distinguish between these mechanisms?

***14–14** Fibronectin is a large glycoprotein component of the extracellular matrix. It contains several binding domains along its length, one of which binds to fibronectin receptors on cell surfaces.

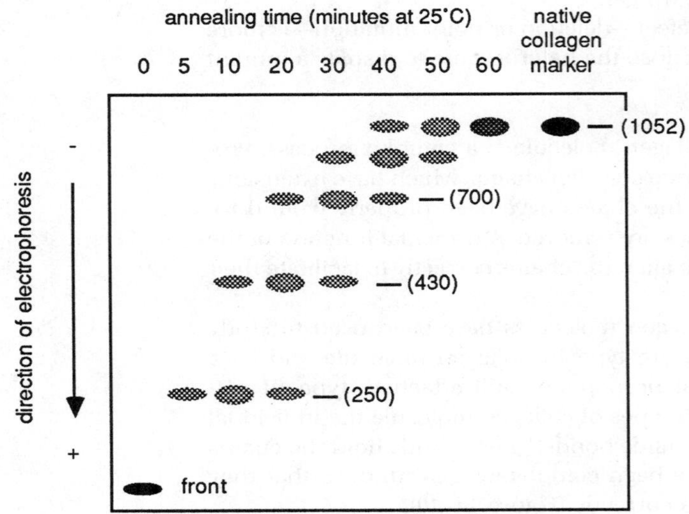

Figure 14–11 Results of reassembly analysis of type III collagen and type III pN-collagen (Problem 14–13). After various times of reannealing at 25°C, samples were digested with trypsin and subjected to electrophoresis. Shaded areas indicate the positions of the trypsin-resistant peptides. Numbers in parentheses indicate the approximate number of amino acids in the trypsin-resistant peptides.

Table 14–3 Fibronectin-related Peptides Tested for Their Ability to Promote Cell Sticking (Problem 14–14)

Peptide	Sequence	Concentration Required for 50% Cell Attachment (nmol/ml)
Fibronectin		0.10
Peptide 1	YAVTGRGDSPASSKPISINYRTEIDKPSQM(C)*	0.25
Peptide 2	VTGRGDSPASSKPI(C)	1.6
Peptide 3	SINYRTEIDKPSQM(C)	>100
Peptide 4	VTGRGDSPA(C)	2.5
Peptide 5	SPASSKPIS(C)	>100
Peptide 6	VTGRGD(C)	10
Peptide 7	GRGDS(C)	3.0
Peptide 8	RGDSPA(C)	6.0
Peptide 9	RVDSPA(C)	>100

*The (C) at the C terminus indicates the cysteine linkage to the carrier protein.

Fibronectin can stick cells to surfaces to which they would otherwise not bind, forming the basis of a simple assay for the part of the molecule recognized by the fibronectin receptor. Fibronectin is coated on the surface of plastic dishes. A suspension of cells is then added and left to incubate for 30 minutes. Finally, the dishes are washed, and the number of cells that stick are counted. Without fibronectin, no cells stick; with it, 80–90% of the cells stick. Other proteins, such as serum albumin, will stick to the plastic, but they do not promote cell sticking.

Very small fragments of fibronectin will work in this assay, although they have to be chemically attached to larger molecules such as albumin in order for them to adhere to the plastic dishes. By making fragments of fibronectin, it was possible to identify the cell-binding domain as a 108-amino-acid segment about three-quarters of the way from the N terminus.

Synthetic peptides corresponding to different portions of the 108-amino-acid segment were then tested in the cell-binding assay to localize the active region precisely. Two kinds of experiment were conducted. In the first, peptides were attached covalently to protein-coated plastic via a cysteine residue and tested for their ability to promote cell sticking. The results are shown in Table 14–3.

In the second experiment, plastic dishes were coated with native fibronectin, and cells were incubated in the dishes for 30 minutes in the presence of the synthetic peptides indicated in Table 14–4. The dishes were washed and the number of stuck cells was counted.

A. The two experiments use different assays to detect the cell-binding segment of fibronectin. Does the sticking of cells to the dishes mean the same thing in both assays? Explain the difference between the assays.

B. From the results in the tables, deduce what amino acid sequence in fibronectin is recognized by cells.

C. How might you make use of these results to design a method for isolating the fibronectin receptor?

Table 14–4 Fibronectin-related Peptides Tested for Their Ability to Block Cell Sticking (Problem 14–14)

Peptide	Percent of Input Cells Sticking
GRGDSPC	2.0
GRGDAPC	1.9
GKGDSPC	48
GRADSPC	49
GRGESPC	44
None	47

14–15 One way to obtain mutations in mice is to infect embryos with retroviruses, which integrate randomly into the genome. If they integrate into a cell that becomes part of the germ line, they can be passed on to future generations. Using this method, you have isolated a particularly interesting strain in which the retrovirus appears to have integrated in a gene that is crucial for early embryonic development (Figure 14–12A). The crucial nature of the gene was revealed when you mated a brother and sister, each heterozygous for the retroviral insert, and analyzed DNA from 12-day embryos. Using a probe that lies just outside the site of integration, you find three distinct patterns of hybridization (Figure 14–12B):

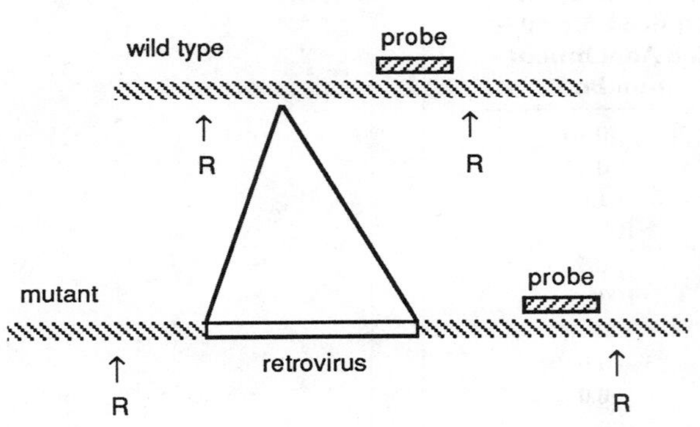

(B) GEL ANALYSIS

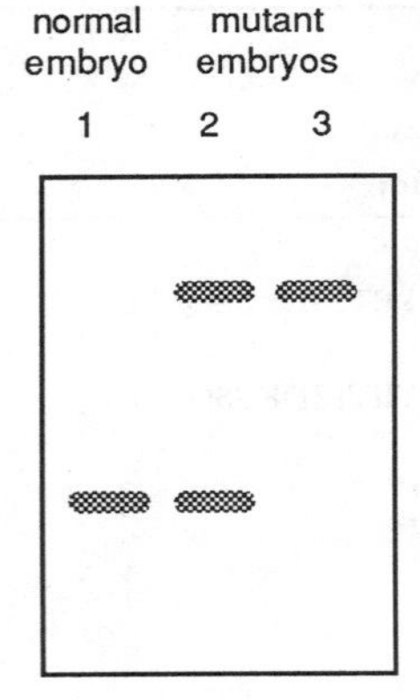

Figure 14–12 Analysis of DNA from embryos from a brother-sister mating (Problem 14–15). The schematic diagram (A) illustrates the relationship between the normal gene and the gene with the retroviral insert. The autoradiogram (B) was obtained by digesting the DNA with a restriction enzyme, R, which does not cut the retrovirus, and running the fragments on a gel. The DNA was then transferred to a nitrocellulose filter, hybridized to a radioactive probe that corresponds to cellular sequences just outside the site of integration, and subjected to autoradiography.

pattern 1 is homozygous for the normal gene; pattern 2 is heterozygous; and pattern 3 is homozygous for the mutant gene.

Although a quarter of the 12-day embryos show pattern 3, you have never observed this pattern in a live birth. You find that around day 14 these embryos die, apparently from massive hemorrhaging from large blood vessels. In all other respects the major tissues and cell types appear normal. This result suggests that the mutation, when homozygous, causes a stage-specific developmental defect.

Upon further study, you find that the mRNA corresponding to the affected gene is made only by fibroblasts, myoblasts, and chondrocytes. In addition, this mRNA is readily detectable at day 12 and then increases markedly as development proceeds. The levels of expression, the cell types involved, and the burst blood vessels lead you to suspect that the affected gene may encode collagen or some other component of the extracellular matrix. Accordingly, you borrow several collagen-gene clones from other researchers and use them to analyze the mRNA present in 12-day-old normal and homozygous, mutant embryos, as shown in Figure 14–13.

A. What gene did the retrovirus integration interrupt? Given the apparent sensitivity of blood vessels in the mutant embryos, does the identity of the affected gene surprise you?
B. In matings between heterozygous brothers and sisters, what fraction of 12-day embryos do you expect to display patterns 1, 2, and 3 in Figure 14–12? What fraction of newborn mice will display these patterns?
C. If you are familiar with recombinant DNA techniques, try this question. One distinct advantage of using retroviral insertions is that the gene it disrupts can be readily cloned using the retrovirus DNA sequences as a "tag." Outline briefly how a retrovirus might be used in this way to clone the normal, unaffected gene.

your gene — collagen genes α1(I), α2(I)
RNA — c m | c m | c m
6.5 –
5.2 –

Figure 14–13 Analysis of mRNA from control (c) and mutant (m) embryos (Problem 14–15). RNA was isolated from normal mouse embryos and from homozygous mutant embryos, separated by electrophoresis on a gel, and probed with radiolabeled DNA from your gene and from the collagen clones. Numbers indicate the sizes of the mRNAs in kb. Two bands of hybridizing RNA are seen in several lanes; it is common for single genes in eucaryotic cells to produce multiple species of mRNA.

Cell-Cell Recognition and Adhesion (MBOC 824–834)

14–16 Fill in the blanks in the following statements.

A. *Dictyostelium discoideum* is a well-known example of the class of organisms known as ____________.
B. The process by which a cell senses a molecule in the external environment and moves along a concentration gradient of the molecule is termed ____________.
C. ____________, which is a lectin, is secreted by starving *Dictyostelium* cells to help amoebae move toward aggregation centers, much as fibronectin promotes cell migration in vertebrates.

D. During the first 8 hours of starvation, *Dictyostelium* amoebae adhere by a Ca^{2+}-dependent mechanism involving ____________; after 8 hours they adhere by a Ca^{2+}-independent mechanism involving ____________.

E. If cells adhere to one another using one kind of molecule, the cell adhesion is said to occur by ____________ binding; if cells adhere to one another through interactions between different kinds of molecules, the cell adhesion is said to occur by ____________ binding.

F. ____________ and ____________ are plasma membrane glycoproteins that mediate adhesion between nerve cells and between liver cells, respectively.

G. Antibodies against ____________, which is also called L-CAM or uvomorulin, prevent the compaction of cleavage-stage mouse embryos.

14–17 Indicate whether the following statements are true or false. If a statement is false, explain why.

__ A. "Were the various types of cells to lose their stickiness for one another and for the supporting extracellular matrix, our bodies would at once disintegrate and flow off into the ground in a mixed stream of cells." Warren Lewis, 1922. (Quoted by J.P. Trinkaus, Cells into Organs, 2nd ed., Englewood Cliffs, N.J.: Prentice Hall, Inc., 1984.)

__ B. Tissues form from specialized cells either by growth and division of founder cells whose progeny stay together or by the guided migration of cells that only stop moving when they recognize specific target sites.

__ C. The sorting out of cell types that occurs when dissociated cells from two different organs are mixed mimics similar sorting-out processes that occur during the development of most tissues.

__ D. Antibodies against E-cadherin block both epithelial cell adhesion and compaction of blastomeres in the early mouse embryo.

__ E. One of the difficulties in studying cell-adhesion mechanisms is that almost any antibody directed against cell-surface components will block cell adhesion.

__ F. The cell-surface receptors responsible for binding cells to each other and to the extracellular matrix have much lower affinity for their ligands than do most hormone receptors.

__ G. Migrating embryonic cells do not form junctional contacts.

__ H. Cell-adhesion molecules are dispersed over the surface of a cell until the cell makes contact with another cell, whereupon they concentrate at particular sites.

***14–18** Not all slime molds use cyclic AMP to signal aggregation. You have just discovered such a species living in a compost heap in your garden. It is indifferent to cyclic AMP, yet still shows strong aggregation when starved. Since the usual chemical signal is ineffective, you wonder whether something other than chemical signaling might be used.

To investigate the nature of the signal, you repeat some of the classic work that was done with *Dictyostelium*. You find that the amoebae will aggregate if placed on a glass coverslip underwater, provided that simple salts are present. The center of the aggregation pattern can be removed with a pipette and placed in a field of fresh amoebae, which immediately start streaming toward it. Thus, the center is emitting some sort of attractive signal.

You now prepare four experiments using an existing center of aggregation as the source of the signal and previously unexposed amoebae as the target cells. The arrangements of aggregation centers and test amoebae at the beginning and end of the experiments are shown in Figure 14–14.

Do these results show that your species of slime mold aggregates by chemical signaling? How so?

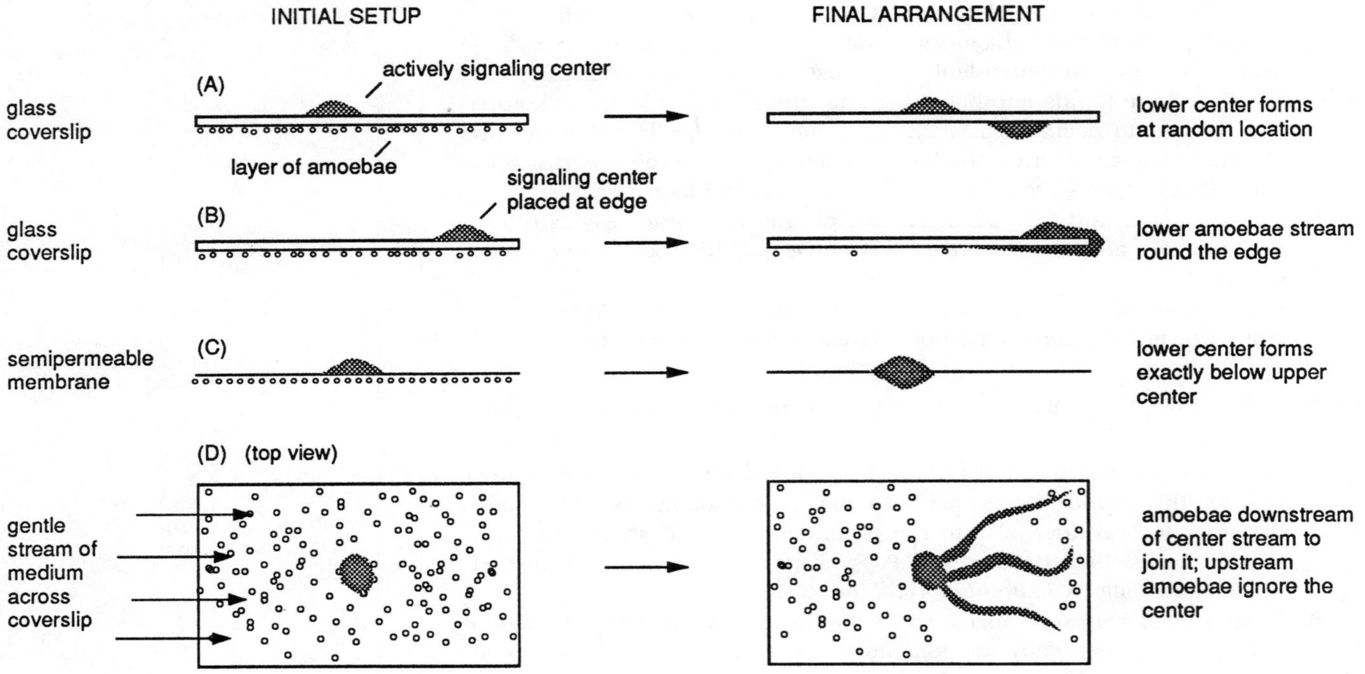

Figure 14–14 Four experiments to study the nature of the attractive signal generated by aggregation centers (Problem 14–18).

14–19 The attachment of bacteriophage T4 to *E. coli* K is an instructive model for cell-cell adhesion. It illustrates the value of multiple weak interactions, which allow relative motion until fixed connections are made. During infection, T4 first attaches to the surface of *E. coli* by the tips of its six tail fibers. It then wanders around the surface until it finds an appropriate place for attachment of its baseplate. When the baseplate is securely fastened, the tail sheath contracts, injecting the phage DNA into the bacterium (Figure 14–15). The initial tail-fiber-cell-surface interaction is critical for infection: phages that lack tail fibers are totally noninfectious.

Analysis of T4 attachment is greatly simplified by the ease with which resistant bacteria and defective viruses can be obtained. Bacterial mutants resistant to T4 infection fall into two classes: one lacks a major outer membrane protein called ompC (*o*uter *m*embrane *p*rotein C); the other contains alterations in the long polysaccharide chain normally associated with bacterial lipopolysaccharide (LPS, a lipid with a long polysaccharide chain attached to its head group). The infectivity of T4 on wild-type and mutant cells is indicated in Table 14–5. These results suggest that each T4 tail fiber has two binding sites: one for LPS and one for ompC. Electron micrographs showing the interaction between isolated tail fibers and LPS suggest that individual associations are not very strong, since only about 50% of the fibers are seen bound to LPS.

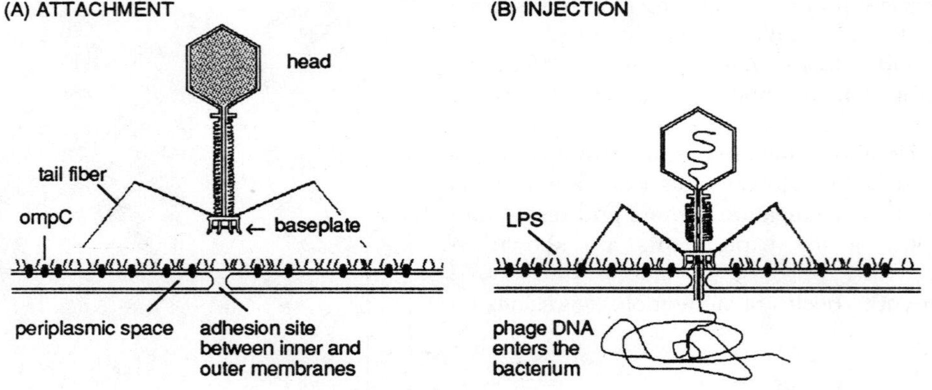

Figure 14–15 T4 attachment (A) and injection (B) of its DNA into a bacterium (Problem 14–19).

A. Assume that at any instant each of the six tail fibers has a 0.5 probability of being bound to LPS and the same probability of being bound to ompC. With this assumption, the fraction of the phage population on the bacterial surface that will have none of its six tail fibers attached in a given instant is $(0.5)^{12}$ (which is the probability of a given binding site being unbound, 0.5, raised to number of binding sites, two on each of six tail fibers.) In light of these considerations, what fraction of the phage population will be attached at any one instant by at least one tail fiber? (The attached fraction is equal to one minus the unattached fraction.) Suppose that the bacteria were missing ompC. What fraction of the phage population would now be attached by at least one tail fiber at any one instant?

B. Surprisingly, the above comparison of wild-type and *ompC*$^-$ bacteria suggests only a very small difference in the attached fraction of the phage population at any one instant. However, as shown in Table 14–4, phage infectivities on these two strains differ by a factor of 1000. Can you suggest an explanation that might resolve this apparent paradox?

Table 14–5 Infectivity of Phage T4 on Various Bacterial Mutants (Problem 14–19)

Bacterial Strain	Phage T4 Infectivity Relative to Nonmutant Bacteria
ompC$^+$LPS$^+$	1
ompC$^-$LPS$^+$	10^{-3}
ompC$^+$LPS$^-$	10^{-3}
ompC$^-$LPS$^-$	10^{-7}

14–20 Platelets are very small blood cells that lack a nucleus. They play a vital part in the repair of damaged blood vessels (Figure 14–16). When underlying collagen fibrils are exposed by damage to the endothelial layer of blood vessels, they bind a plasma protein called von Willebrand's factor (vWF). A receptor on the surface of the platelet binds to vWF after it attaches to collagen fibrils. Receptor binding triggers the development of a mutual platelet cohesiveness, which is accompanied by a rapid change of shape from smooth and flat to round and spiny and by secretion of chemoattractants for cells involved in the repair of tissue damage.

Platelet aggregation could involve one kind of cell-surface adhesion molecule interacting directly with itself (Figure 14–17A) or interacting through a bridge molecule (Figure 14–17B). It could also involve two kinds

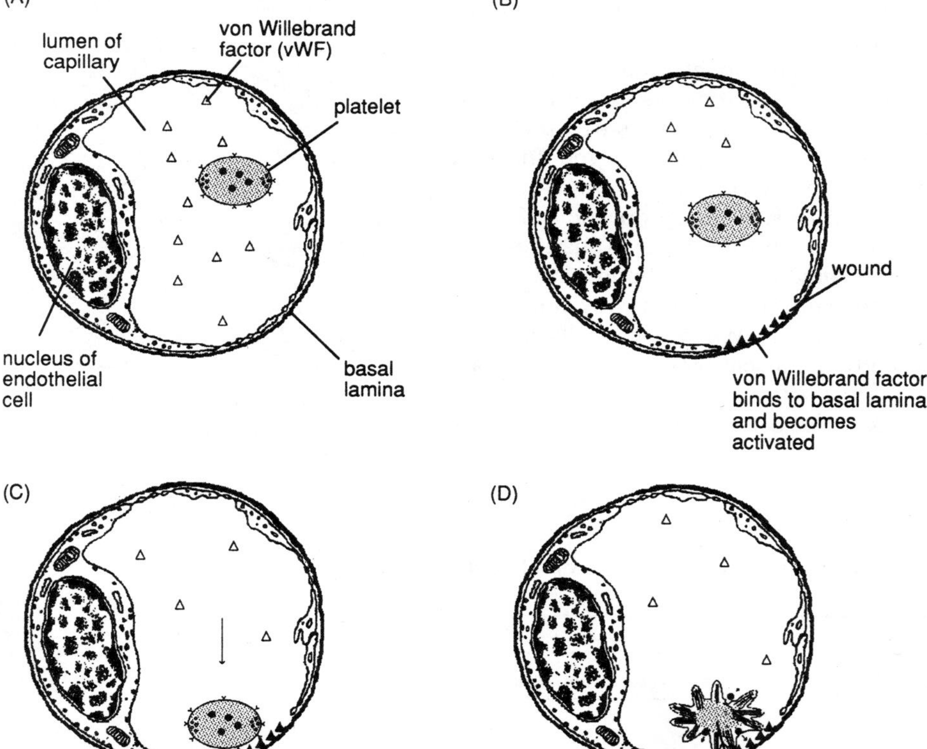

Figure 14–16 Role of platelets in repair of damage to the blood vessel epithelium (Problem 14–20). (A) Normal epithelium of blood vessel. (B) Damaged epithelium with bound vWF. (C) Platelet binding to vWF. (D) Change in platelet shape with release of chemoattractants.

of adhesion molecules interacting directly (Figure 14–17C) or through a bridge molecule (Figure 14–17D). The following facts about platelet aggregation allow you to decide which one of these four types of binding mechanisms is used by platelets.

1. The aggregation of platelets requires fibrinogen and platelets that carry receptors for fibrinogen on their surface. (Fibrinogen is a serum protein involved in blood clotting.)
2. Patients with platelets that lack a fibrinogen receptor have a serious blood-clotting disorder called Glanzman's syndrome.
3. Platelet aggregation can be blocked by either one of two peptides, which correspond to two different regions of the fibrinogen molecule.
4. An excess of either peptide blocks only about 50% of fibrinogen binding.

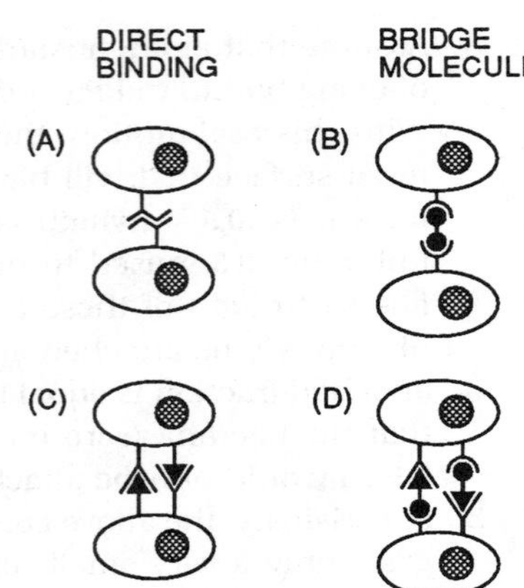

Figure 14–17 Four different types of cell-cell interaction involving identical cells (Problem 14–20).

A. Which one of the four binding mechanisms shown in Figure 14–17 does platelet aggregation resemble most closely? Explain how each of the experimental observations is accounted for by the mechanism you select.

B. Cells from patients with Glanzman's syndrome do not aggregate with themselves when activated by tissue damage. On the basis of the binding mechanism you chose, predict whether Glanzman's cells will co-aggregate with normal cells.

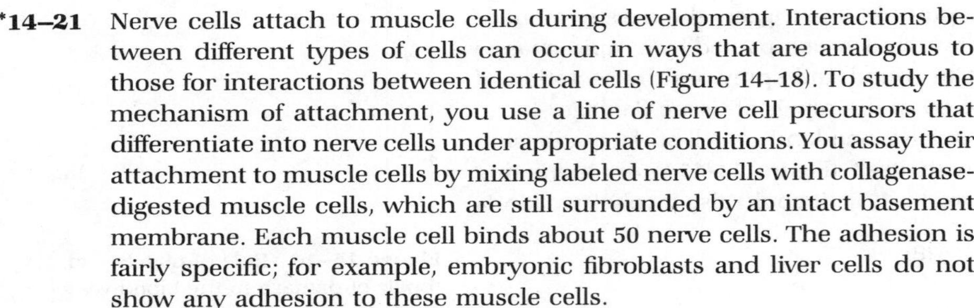

***14–21** Nerve cells attach to muscle cells during development. Interactions between different types of cells can occur in ways that are analogous to those for interactions between identical cells (Figure 14–18). To study the mechanism of attachment, you use a line of nerve cell precursors that differentiate into nerve cells under appropriate conditions. You assay their attachment to muscle cells by mixing labeled nerve cells with collagenase-digested muscle cells, which are still surrounded by an intact basement membrane. Each muscle cell binds about 50 nerve cells. The adhesion is fairly specific; for example, embryonic fibroblasts and liver cells do not show any adhesion to these muscle cells.

To define the interacting cell-surface components, you treat the nerve and muscle cells with neuraminidase, which removes *N*-acetyl neuraminic acid (sialic acid) from sugar polymers, and pronase, which cleaves proteins. The results are shown in Table 14–6. In addition, you find that sialic acid alone among all sugars tested inhibits nerve cell binding when added to the assay. Mucin, which contains a large proportion of sialic acid, is even more effective than the monomeric sugar. Nonsialic-acid-rich polymers such as heparin, hyaluronic acid, and chondroitin sulfate have no effect. When the muscle cells are preincubated with mucin and then washed, they no longer bind nerve cells. When nerve cells are pretreated with mucin and then tested for muscle binding, however, they still adhere perfectly.

Describe the interaction between nerve cells and muscle cells as completely as these data allow.

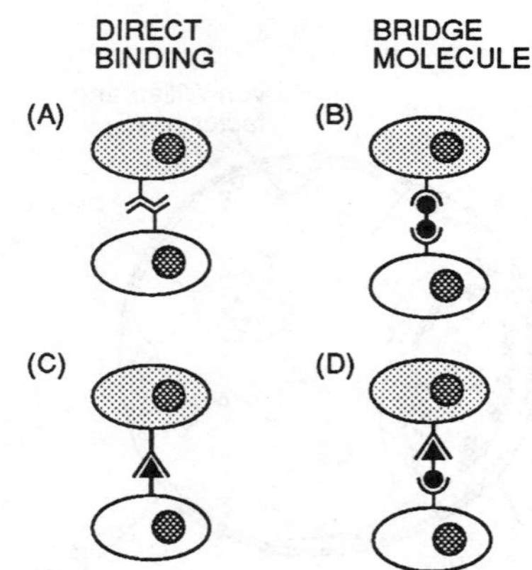

Figure 14–18 Four different types of interaction involving nonidentical cells (Problem 14–21).

Table 14–6 Effects of Enzyme Treatments on Adhesion of Nerve Cells to Muscle Cells (Problem 14–21)

	Treatment		Result
Experiment	**Nerve Cells**	**Muscle Cells**	**Nerve Cells/Muscle Cells**
1	None	none	58
2	Neuraminidase	none	4
3	None	neuraminidase	56
4	Neuraminidase	neuraminidase	2
5	Pronase	none	55
6	None	pronase	5

Table 14–7 Effects of Treatments on Aggregation of Type 5 and Type 21 Yeast Cells (Problem 14–22)

Experiment	Treatment: Type 5	Treatment: Type 21	Aggregation
1	None	none	+
2	Trypsin	none	+
3	None	trypsin	−
4	2-mercaptoethanol	none	−
5	None	2-mercaptoethanol	+

14–22 Another example of interactions between nonidentical cells occurs in yeasts. The yeast *Hansenula wingei* has two haploid mating types called 5 and 21. Cells of one mating type do not aggregate with themselves; however, when the two mating types are mixed together, they do aggregate. The aggregation assists mating, although it is not essential. To determine the nature of the binding, you treat the two mating types with trypsin, which cleaves proteins, and 2-mercaptoethanol, which reduces disulfide bonds. The results are summarized in Table 14–7.

In other experiments, you have purified a factor from type 5 cells by treating them with an enzyme that cleaves polysaccharides. This factor when added to type 21 cells promotes their aggregation. In the presence of 2-mercaptoethanol the factor dissociates into high and low molecular weight components, which are individually inactive in promoting aggregation of type 21 cells. When these components are recombined under oxidizing conditions, which allow reformation of disulfide bonds, they are once again active in promoting aggregation of type 21 cells.

Describe the interaction between mating types 5 and 21.

Answers

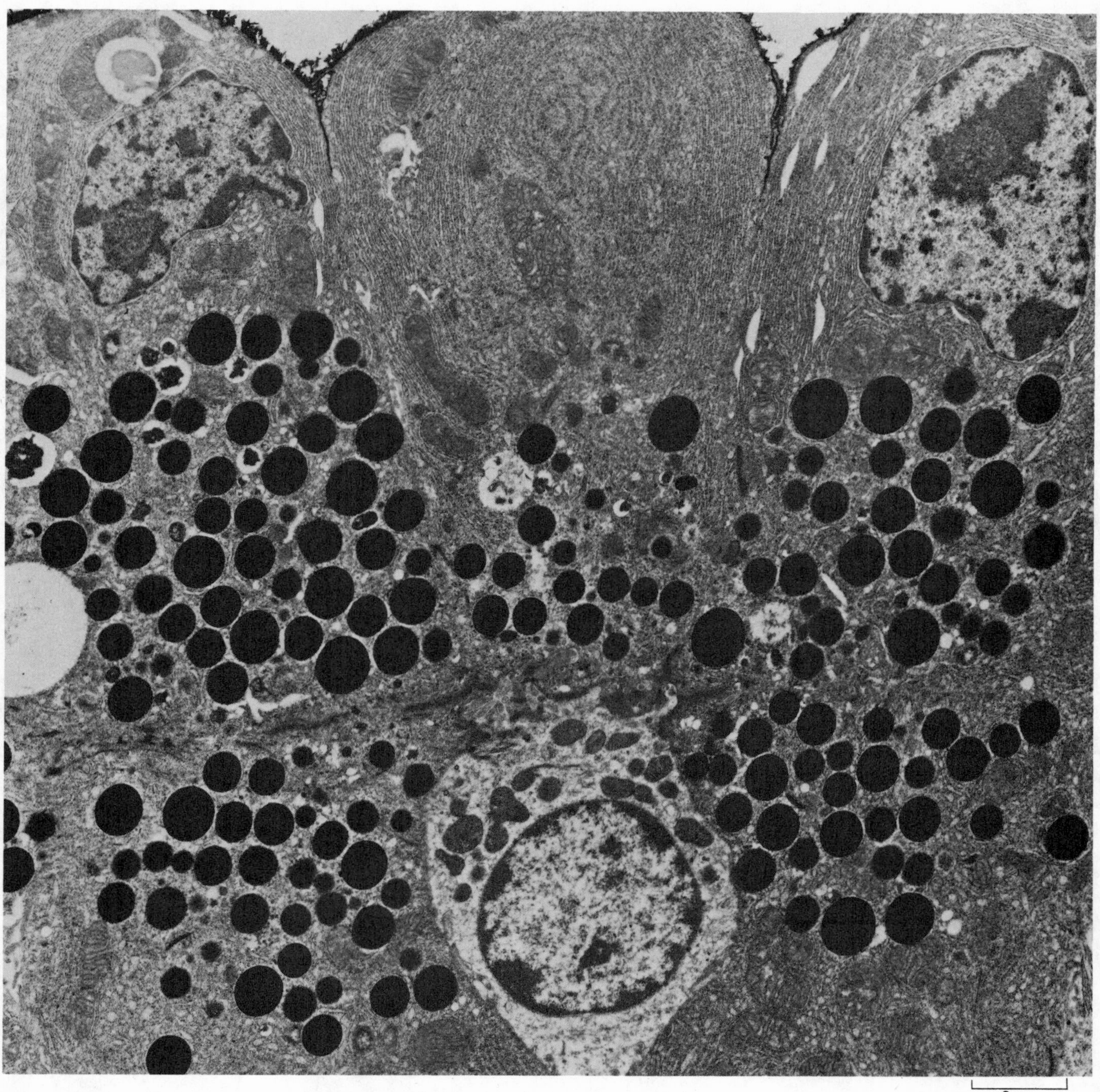

Transmission electron micrograph of pancreas from a starved guinea pig. Fixed with glutaraldehyde and osmium tetroxide, stained with uranyl acetate and lead citrate. (Courtesy of Dr. Brij Gupta.)

Basic Genetic Mechanisms

5

RNA and Protein Synthesis

5–1

A. RNA polymerase, DNA transcription
B. promoter, termination signal
C. anticodon, codon
D. aminoacyl-tRNA synthetases, aminoacyl-tRNA
E. degenerate
F. ribosome, peptidyl-tRNA binding site, aminoacyl-tRNA binding site
G. peptidyl transferase, rRNA
H. release factors, stop
I. initiator tRNA, start, methionine

5–2

A. False. Binding to the promoter orients RNA polymerase and the choice of template strand because the RNA chain, which is synthesized in the 5′-to-3′ direction, must be antiparallel to the template strand.
B. True
C. True
D. False. Modified nucleotides are produced by covalent modification of the standard nucleotides after RNA synthesis.
E. False. A single-base change would alter $tRNA^{Tyr}$ to recognize two serine codons, UCU/C, (due to Wobble pairing). In a cell-free system competition between the modified $tRNA^{Tyr}$ and the normal $tRNA^{Ser}$ would probably produce a protein with a mixture of serine and tyrosine at positions specified by UCU and UCC. However, at the positions in the protein specified by the other four serine codons, there would be serine alone.
F. True
G. False. Wobble base-pairing occurs between the third position of the codon and the first position in the anticodon.
H. True
I. False. Protein synthesis consumes much more total energy than transcription because hundreds to thousands of protein molecules are made from each mRNA.
J. False. AUG also encodes methionine in the interior of the mRNA; the selection of one AUG as the initiation site depends on other features of the mRNA nucleotide sequence.
K. True
L. True

5–3

A. $^{5'}$GUAGCCUACCCAUAGG$^{3'}$
B. If translation begins at the 5′ end of the RNA, the synthesized protein would be valine-alanine-tyrosine-proline (VAYP).

Only after a peptide bond has been formed between alanine and tyrosine will $tRNA^{Ala}$ leave the ribosome. Thus, the next tRNA that will bind to the ribosome after $tRNA^{Ala}$ has left is $tRNA^{Pro}$.

When the amino group of alanine forms a peptide bond, the ester bond between valine and $tRNA^{Val}$ is broken, $tRNA^{Val}$ is expelled from the ribosome, and $tRNA^{Ala}$ moves from the A-site to the P-site.

C. This short mRNA encodes three different peptides, since there are three different reading frames. In the second reading frame, the first codon is the stop codon UAG; however, the subsequent codons can be translated.

5′-GUAGCCUACCCAUAGG-3′

Frame 1 V A Y P *
Frame 2 * P T H R
Frame 3 S L P I

The other possible mRNA from this DNA would read

5′-CCUAUGGGUAGGCUAC-3′

Frame 1 P M G R L
Frame 2 L W V G Y
Frame 3 Y G *

Thus, the sequence of the peptides would be completely different. Be very careful to keep the polarity of the strands correct; it is very easy to fall into the trap of thinking that the complementary sequence of the first mRNA is $^{5'}$CAUCGGAUGGGUAUCC$^{3'}$, which is incorrect because the strands of DNA run in opposite directions.

D. Since there is no AUG or even GUG (which is sometimes used as start signal for translation in *E. coli*), this sequence cannot come from the beginning of the coding region of a gene. It could be from the end of a gene, if the first or second reading frames were used, or from the middle of a gene, if the third reading frame were used. More information is required to distinguish between these possibilities.

***5–4**

5–5

A. The sequence data for the *Tetrahymena* protein is unusual because it indicates that UAG and UAA, which are stop codons in other organisms, specify glutamine (Q) in *Tetrahymena*.

B. The very minor protein from the pure TMV mRNA is produced by reading through the normal stop codon. Although the mechanism of such a rare event is difficult to know, it is thought to represent the frequency with which the reticulocyte translation system mistakenly inserts an amino acid at the site of the stop codon instead of terminating properly. It is a little surprising that a second termination codon is not encountered for 506 codons.

C. Given that *Tetrahymena* uses UAG and UAA as codons for glutamine, the increase in the proportion of the readthrough TMV protein is most likely due to the presence of $tRNA^{Gln}$ species with anticodons complementary to the normal TMV stop codon, which is UAG. The addition of *Tetrahymena* RNA causes a small shift in the proportions because it contains some charged $tRNA^{Gln}$. The cytoplasm causes a larger shift because it also contains the appropriate aminoacyl tRNA synthetase. (The additional shift with the cytoplasm suggests that the tRNA synthetases in the reticulocyte lysate cannot recharge the special *Tetrahymena* tRNA.) These results suggest that at least two components from *Tetrahymena*—a special tRNA and its cognate tRNA synthetase—must be added to a reticulocyte lysate to allow *Tetrahymena* mRNA to be translated efficiently. These components compete effectively with the reticulocyte release factors, allowing the *Tetrahymena* mRNAs to be read.

D. Although slight variations in the genetic code were discovered several years ago in mitochondrial genomes, they were not so surprising as the *Tetrahymena* changes. After all, mitochondrial genomes are small and encode relatively few proteins, so it is less difficult to imagine how changes might occur. However, the *Tetrahymena* genome encodes thousands of proteins. It is much more surprising that it managed to survive the presumptive transition from the standard code to its present-day code.

References: Horowitz, S.; Gorovsky, M.A. An unusual genetic code in nuclear genes of *Tetrahymena*. *Proc. Natl. Acad. Sci. USA* 82:2452–2455, 1985.

*Problems with an asterisk (*) are answered in the Instructor's Manual.

Andreasen, P.H.; Dreisig, H.; Kristiansen, K. Unusual ciliate-specific codons in *Tetrahymena* mRNAs are translated correctly in a rabbit reticulocyte lysate supplemented with a subcellular fraction from *Tetrahymena. Biochem. J.* 244:331–335, 1987.

5–6

A. The data in Figure 5–2 indicate that the N terminus of the protein is synthesized first. The linear gradient of radioactivity from the start of the chain—the N terminus—to the finish is exactly what you would expect according to the model shown in Figure 5–46A and B. Here, all the ribosomes carry the lysine at position 8, but the ribosome at the 5′ end of the mRNA has not yet reached the lysine at position 16, so there is less radioactivity in it, and so on down the line. Almost none of the ribosomes [actually (147 − 144)/147 or just over 2%] will carry the lysine at position 144.

B. The slopes of the lines for the α and β chains are very similar, indicating that roughly equal *numbers* of each chain are being synthesized. However, there is not enough information to decide whether the numbers of α- and β-globin mRNA molecules are equal. You would need to know how many ribosomes there were on each mRNA—the average polyribosome size for α- and β-globin mRNA—to deduce the relative abundance of the two mRNAs from this kind of data. Actually, there is about twice as much α-globin mRNA as β-globin mRNA, but the α-globin mRNA is less efficient; that is, fewer ribosomes initiate synthesis on α-globin mRNA per unit time than on β-globin mRNA. These factors cancel out to give a fairly balanced production of the two chains.

C. The graph hits zero right at the end of the coding region, which indicates that chains are released from ribosomes as soon as they encounter the stop codon—or at least they do so without a measurable pause on this time scale.

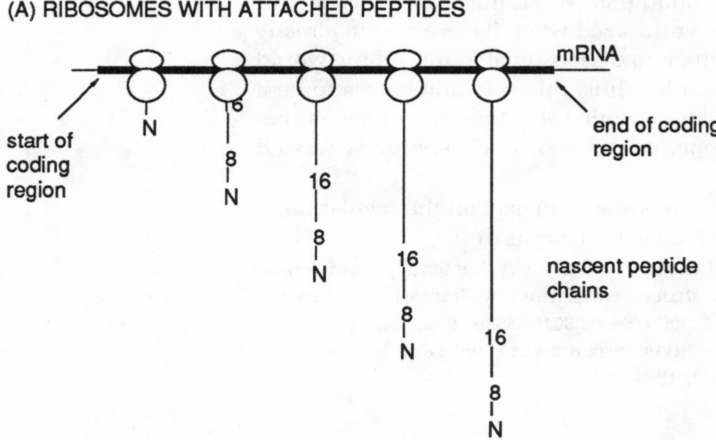

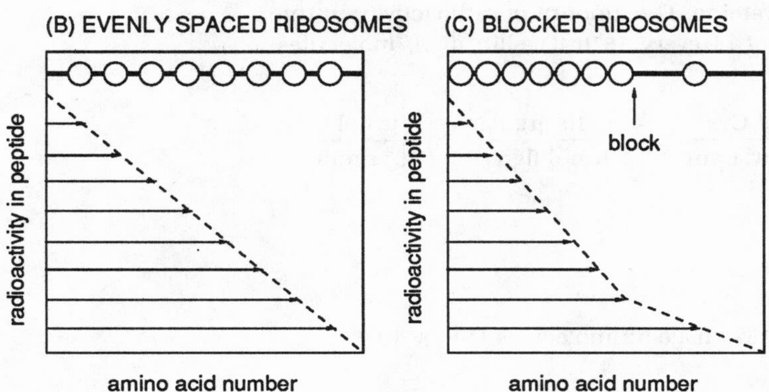

Figure 5–46 Relationship of ribosome position to peptide length and labeling pattern (Answer 5–6). (A) Lengths of peptides associated with ribosomes at various positions along β-globin mRNA. Numbers refer to positions of the first two lysine residues. (B) Pattern of peptide labeling for evenly spaced ribosomes. (C) Pattern of peptide labeling for ribosomes whose movement is inhibited at a point midway down the mRNA. Peptides associated with each ribosome are shown on the graph as arrows. Arrowheads correspond to the C terminus of the polypeptide and are aligned immediately below the ribosome on which they are synthesized. Dashed lines at tips of arrows show the expected patterns of peptide labeling.

D. If there were a significant roadblock to ribosome movement, the data would resemble that in Figure 5–3A. A roadblock would result in more densely packed ribosomes in front of the block and less densely packed ribosomes beyond the block. The consequences of inhibited ribosome movement are illustrated schematically in Figure 5–46C.

***5–7**

5–8

A. The DNA sequence GGG TAT CTT *TGA* CTA CGA CGC should not encode the protein sequence of RF2, since UGA is a termination codon. It appears that this sequence must break the usual rules of the triplet code, with a leucyl tRNA decoding the italicized quadruplet.

GGG TAT *CTTT* GAC TAC GAC GCC

In essence, the ribosome must shift its frame of reading in the middle of the gene!

Frameshift mutations were originally isolated by Benzer in his work on the r_{II} genes of bacteriophage T4 and exploited by Crick in the discovery of the triplet code. Later, mutant tRNA molecules that could read four bases at a time were isolated by clever genetic selection and shown to suppress certain frameshift mutations. It comes as a great surprise, however, to find occasional *natural* examples of frameshift suppression. The first example was found in bacteriophage T7 gene 10. Since then, several retroviruses and retroposons have been found to use frameshift suppression of termination codons as a way of making minor gene products. The mechanism of suppression in these cases is not clear and is the subject of ongoing research.

B. The occurrence of an inframe suppressible UGA codon (which is recognized uniquely by RF2) in the sequence of RF2 immediately suggests a novel form of gene control. Although the mechanism of frameshifting is undefined, there is very likely a competition between frameshifting and termination at the UGA codon. When the level of RF2 in the cell is high, termination should occur more frequently at the UGA codon than when the level of RF2 is low. Thus, very little new RF2 would be synthesized when its levels were already adequate, but if the levels fell, the chances of ribosomal frameshifting would increase and more RF2 would be made. Thus, this situation seems to be a very cleverly appropriate autoregulation. Notice also that the frameshift occurs near the beginning of the gene, so not too much energy is wasted making a useless polypeptide.

Although this is a very attractive hypothesis to explain the regulation of RF2 synthesis, there is no direct evidence for or against it.

References: Craigen, W.J.; Cook, R.G.; Tate, W.P.; Caskey, C.T. Bacterial peptide chain release factors: conserved primary structure and possible frameshift regulation of release factor 2. *Proc. Natl. Acad. Sci. USA* 82:3616–3620, 1985.

Jacks, T.; Varmus, H. Expression of the Rous sarcoma virus *pol* gene by ribosomal frameshifting. *Science* 230:1237–1242, 1985.

5–9

A. Since the bacteria were labeled for one generation, which represents a doubling in mass, 4 μg of the 8 μg of flagellin isolated from the gel were synthesized in the presence of ^{35}S cysteine. The amount of radioactivity in the sample indicates that about 1 out of every 1670 flagellin (flgn) molecules contains a cysteine.

$$\frac{\text{Cys}}{\text{flgn}} = \frac{300\ \text{cpm Cys}}{4\ \mu\text{g flgn}} \times \frac{\text{pmol Cys}}{5 \times 10^3\ \text{cpm}} \times \frac{4 \times 10^4\ \mu\text{g flgn}}{\mu\text{mol flgn}} \times \frac{\mu\text{mol}}{10^6\ \text{pmol}}$$

$$= \frac{6 \times 10^{-2}\ \text{pmol Cys}}{100\ \text{pmol flgn}}$$

$$\frac{\text{Cys}}{\text{flgn}} = 6 \text{ x } 10^{-4}$$

which is equal to 1 cysteine per 1670 flagellin molecules ($1/6 \times 10^{-4}$).

B. The normal codons for cysteine are UGU and UGC. Thus, the error in anticodon-codon interaction is a mistake at the first position of the codon (third position of the anticodon). The experiment described, and other experiments too, suggest that ribosomes tend to mistake U for C and C for U in the first two positions of the codon, and C and U for A in the first position.

C. Assuming that all six arginine codons are equally likely, then there should be six sensitive (CGC and CGU) arginine codons ($2/6 \times 18$) in a flagellin molecule. Therefore, the actual error frequency per codon-at-risk is

$$\text{error frequency} = \frac{\text{1 cysteine}}{\text{1670 flagellin molecules}} \times \frac{\text{flagellin molecule}}{\text{6 sensitive codons}}$$

$$\text{error frequency} = 10^{-4}$$

D. If the probability of making a mistake at each codon is 10^{-4}, the probability of not making a mistake at each codon is $(1 - 10^{-4})$. The probability of not making a mistake at n codons is then $(1 - 10^{-4})^n$. Thus, the percentage of correctly synthesized molecules 100 amino acids in length is $(1 - 10^{-4})^{100}$, or 99%. For a protein 1000 amino acids long, 90% are correct. For a molecule 10,000 amino acids long, only 37% are correct. Given these sorts of estimates, it is perhaps not unexpected that proteins more than 3000 amino acids long are rare.

Reference: Edelman, P.; Gallant, J. Mistranslation in *E. coli*. *Cell* 10:131–137, 1977.

***5–10 Reference:** Safer, B.; Kemper, W.; Jagus, R. Identification of a 48S preinitiation complex in reticulocyte lysate. *J. Biol. Chem.* 253:3384–3386, 1978.

DNA Repair Mechanisms

5–11

A. DNA repair, mutation
B. fibrinopeptides
C. depurination, deamination
D. DNA repair nucleases, DNA polymerase, DNA ligase
E. AP endonuclease
F. DNA glycosylase
G. bulky lesion
H. SOS response

5–12

A. True
B. True
C. False. The nucleotide sequences of histone H4 genes from different species vary considerably; however, the nucleotide changes are confined for the most part to third positions in codons so that they encode the same amino acid sequence.
D. True
E. False. Repair depends on the two copies of genetic information contained in the two strands of the DNA double helix.
F. True
G. True
H. False. The principal function of the SOS response is to relax the fidelity of DNA synthesis so that replication can proceed past a block. Since a cell will die if replication remains blocked, the benefit is survival; the cost is mutation.
I. True. Deamination of A, G, or C (T does not carry an amino group) leads to formation of a base that is unnatural in DNA. For example, C is deaminated to U—which may be why DNA uses T instead of U. A deamination problem does arise in eucaryotic cells in which many CG dinucleotides

are methylated at the 5 position of the C ring. Deamination of 5-methyl C gives a T.

5–13

A. The extreme UV sensitivity of *uvrArecA* double mutants relative to pairs of *uvr* mutants suggests that there are two separate pathways for dealing with UV damage. The *uvr* gene products are involved in one pathway, whereas the *recA* gene product is involved in a different pathway. As a rule of thumb, if a combination of defective genes produces no more mutant a phenotype than the individual defective genes, the gene products are likely to act in the same biochemical pathway.

The *uvr* gene products form the uvrABC endonuclease, which specifically removes a 12-nucleotide-long oligonucleotide that encompasses a pyrimidine dimer. The recA protein is involved in two pathways for handling UV damage: the SOS response and recombinational repair. The *uvr* and *recA* pathways are not entirely independent since expression of the *uvr* genes is substantially increased as a part of the SOS response.

B. A lethal hit in the *uvrArecA* strain corresponds to about one pyrimidine dimer. The number of pyrimidine dimers per lethal hit can be calculated as follows: Since *E. coli* is 50% GC, all four bases are equally represented in the genome. If they are arranged randomly (which they are not, but this assumption is a reasonable approximation), then of the 16 possible dinucleotide pairs in DNA, one-quarter are pyrimidine pairs; hence, *E. coli* contains 10^6 possible UV targets. Given that a dose of 400 J/m^2 converts 1% of the pyrimidine (pyr) pairs into pyrimidine dimers, the number of pyrimidine dimers per lethal hit in *E. coli* is

$$\frac{\text{pyr dimers}}{\text{lethal hit}} = \frac{10^6 \text{ pyr pairs}}{E.\ coli} \times \frac{0.04 \text{ J/m}^2}{\text{lethal hit}} \times \frac{1 \text{ pyr dimer}}{100 \text{ pyr pairs}} \times \frac{1}{400 \text{ Jm}^2}$$

$$\frac{\text{pyr dimers}}{\text{lethal hit}} = 1$$

***5–14**

***5–15**

5–16

A. The even distribution of frameshift mutations indicates that UV damage is distributed throughout the gene, since a frameshift mutation anywhere in the gene would be detected by the gene-fusion assay (which is independent of repressor function). Since UV damage is evenly distributed, the nonrandom distribution of missense mutations in the *lacI* gene presumably reflects the functional importance of the ends of the lacI protein. Most mutations in the ends yield a nonfunctional protein; this enables one to detect them as mutants. However, the middle of the gene, being less critical for function, can accommodate some alterations and still produce a functional protein. These "silent" mutations would not be detected in an assay that depends on loss of function.

B. The common deletion of one nucleotide in response to UV damage is thought to occur as a mistake during error-prone DNA synthesis opposite a pyrimidine dimer. Presumably, in response to the abnormal spacing of bases caused by the pyrimidine dimer, error-prone synthesis inserts a single nucleotide rather than two. The frameshift hotspots presumably are hotspots because they contain runs of T's and therefore multiple possibilities for dimer formation.

Reference: Miller, J.H. Mutagenic specificity of ultraviolet light. *J. Mol. Biol.* 182:45–65, 1985.

5–17 The variable in these experiments is light. For a given UV dose, the brighter the light, the less the observed killing. Thus, visible light can reverse the effects of UV irradiation. Direct reversal of UV damage is common in microorganisms and is called enzymatic photoreactivation. Although the mechanistic details are unclear, the energy of visible light in some way is harnessed to split apart pyrimidine dimers, thereby reversing the damage.

The account here is not so much different than the original discovery of photoreactivation by Albert Kelner in the 1940s. While investigating the effects of postirradiation temperature on UV survival, Kelner was plagued by another variable. In his own words:

> Careful consideration was made of variable factors which might have accounted for such tremendous variation. We were using a glass-fronted water bath placed on a table near a window, in which were suspended transparent bottles containing the irradiated spores. The fact that some of the bottles were more directly exposed to light than others suggested that light might be a factor. . . . Experiments showed that exposure of UV-irradiated suspensions to light resulted in an increase in survival rate or a recovery of 100,000- to 400,000-fold. Controls kept in the dark . . . showed no recovery at all.

Reference: Friedberg, E.C. DNA Repair. New York: W.H. Freeman, 1984.

***5–18** **Reference:** Teo, I.; Sedgwick, B.; Kilpatrick, M.W.; McCarthy, T.V.; Lindahl, T. The intracellular signal for induction of resistance to alkylating agents in *E. coli*. *Cell* 45:315–324, 1986.

5–19

A. As shown in Figure 5–13, untreated bacteria and bacteria adapted to low levels of MNNG differ only in the amount of O^6-methylguanine. The absence of O^6-methylguanine in adapted bacteria correlates with the low level of mutation, suggesting that O^6-methylguanine is the mutagenic lesion. O^6-methylguanine is thought to be mutagenic because it can mispair with T during replication.

B. The kinetics of removal of the methyl group from O^6-methylguanine are peculiar because the amount removed does not increase with time as one might expect for a typical enzyme. In addition, the amount of O^6-methylguanine that is demethylated is directly proportional to the amount of purified protein added to the reaction. One possible explanation for such behavior is that the enzyme is very unstable; however, the identical endpoints at 5°C and 37°C argue against this explanation.

C. A calculation of the number of mutagenic bases that are demethylated per enzyme molecule indicates that each enzyme molecule removes only one methyl group. This calculation shows that the protein is used stoichiometrically instead of catalytically, which explains the peculiar kinetics.

For example, 2.5 ng of protein removes 0.13 pmol (0.5 × 0.26 pmol) of methyl groups from DNA. Thus, the number of enzyme molecules is

$$\text{enzyme molecules} = 2.5 \text{ ng} \times \frac{\text{nmol}}{19{,}000 \text{ ng}} \times \frac{6.0 \times 10^{14} \text{ molecules}}{\text{nmol}}$$
$$= 7.9 \times 10^{10} \text{ molecules}$$

and the number of methyl groups is

$$\text{methyl groups} = 0.13 \text{ pmol} \times \frac{6 \times 10^{11} \text{ methyl groups}}{\text{pmol}}$$
$$= 7.8 \times 10^{10} \text{ methyl groups}$$

It turns out that methyl groups are transferred to one particular cysteine residue in the protein. Once methylated, the protein is dead and ultimately is degraded. Because the methyltransferase inactivates itself during the reaction, it is not an enzyme in the usual sense. (An enzyme is a catalyst, which by definititon is not consumed during the reaction.) Note that repair of O^6-methylguanine is similar to enzymatic photoreactivation (Problem 5–17) in that both proceed by direct reversal of DNA damage.

Reference: Lindahl, T.; Demple, B.; Robins, P. Suicide inactivation of the *E. coli*. O^6-methylguanine-DNA methyltransferase. *EMBO J.* 1:1359–1363, 1982.

DNA Replication Mechanisms

5–20

A. DNA polymerase
B. DNA replication fork
C. Okazaki fragments
D. DNA ligase
E. leading strand, lagging strand
F. primer strand
G. exonuclease
H. RNA primase
I. DNA helicase
J. helix destabilizing proteins (single-stranded DNA-binding proteins)
K. mismatch proofreading (mismatch repair)
L. replication origins
M. DNA topoisomerases

5–21

A. True. (If the replication fork moves forward at 500 nucleotide pairs per second, the DNA ahead of it must rotate at $500/10.5 = 48$ revolutions per second, or 2880 revolutions per minute.)
B. True
C. False. The sequence of nucleotides in the progeny strand is quite different from that in the parental strand, even though the two strands are related by complementary base-pairing.
D. True
E. False. All DNA synthesis occurs in the 5′-to-3′ direction. DNA on the lagging strand is made in pieces that are joined together later so that the lagging strand lengthens in the 3′-to-5′ direction.
F. True
G. False. In the absence of the 3′-to-5′ proofreading exonuclease activity, DNA synthesis will be much more error prone.
H. False. Single-strand binding proteins keep DNA strands apart by binding to the phosphate backbone; they leave the bases exposed so that they can serve as template for DNA synthesis.
I. False. The methylation-dependent repair system relies on methyl groups in the parent strand and their absence in the progeny strand in order to distinguish the two strands.
J. True
K. True
L. True

5–22

A. The indicated phosphate (P) is at the 5′ end of the fragment to which it is attached.
B. The gap will be filled in by continuous DNA repair synthesis, starting at the indicated OH on the bottom strand and proceeding in the 5′-to-3′ direction (leftward) until it reaches the phosphate on the adjacent fragment.
C. In the absence of DNA ligase, the two pieces on the bottom strand will remain unlinked even after the gap is filled in.

***5–23** **Reference:** Inman, R.B.; Schnos, M. Structure of branch points in replicating DNA: presence of single-stranded connections in lambda DNA branch points. *J. Mol. Biol.* 56:319–325, 1971.

5–24

A. The different labels used for the T and C nucleotides make it easy to measure their respective losses from the polymer. The radioactive disintegrations from the energetic ^{32}P and from the rather weak ^{3}H can be distinguished using a liquid scintillation counter. (The measurement could have been done using a single isotope and chromatographic separation of the released nucleotides, but the procedure is more time-consuming.)

B. Because the nuclease activity of DNA polymerase I is an exonuclease (that is, it removes nucleotides from the ends of strands), the T nucleotides cannot be released until all the C nucleotides have been removed, hence the lag.

C. When dTTP is added to the reaction, polymerization will begin just as soon as a proper AT nucleotide pair is found. Polymerization cannot occur from a mismatched AC pair. Since the rate of polymerization exceeds the rate of exonuclease by two or three orders of magnitude, the labeled T residues will be buried quickly and will be unavailable to the exonuclease.

D. The results will not be affected by the presence of dCTP. Since the template is poly (dA), C nucleotides cannot be incorporated. If they are incorporated by mistake, the mismatched C will not serve as a primer for polymerization.

Reference: Brutlag, D.; Kornberg, A. Enzymatic synthesis of deoxyribonucleic acid. 36. A proofreading function for the 3′ to 5′ exonuclease activity in deoxyribonucleic acid polymerases. *J. Biol. Chem.* 247:241–248, 1972.

***5–25** **Reference:** Cha, T.A.; Alberts, B.M. Studies of the DNA helicase-RNA primase unit from bacteriophage T4. A trinucleotide sequence on the DNA template starts RNA primer synthesis. *J. Biol. Chem.* 261:7001–7010, 1986.

5–26

A. ATP hydrolysis is required for unwinding because energy is needed to melt DNA. Strand separation is energetically unfavorable because stacking interactions between the planar base pairs are largely lost upon strand separation. In addition, the H bonds that link the bases present a kinetic barrier to strand separation.

B. Since dnaB melts off only the 3′ half-fragment of substrate 3, it must bind to the long single strand and move along it in the 5′-to-3′ direction until it reaches the double-stranded region formed by the 3′ half-fragment, at which point it unwinds the fragment. The 5′-to-3′ movement of dnaB suggests that it unwinds the parental duplex at the replication fork by moving along the lagging strand.

If dnaB moves in the 5′-to-3′ direction, why does it not melt the 5′ half-fragment off of substrate 3 by binding to the short 5′ tail? Pat yourself on the back if you wondered about this. In real experiments a small amount of the 5′ half-fragment is melted off. Melting due to the short 5′ tail is presumed to be inefficient because of the difference in target size: dnaB is much more likely to bind to the long single strand rather than the short one.

C. If SSB is added first, it inhibits dnaB-mediated unwinding because it coats the single-stranded DNA, preventing dnaB from binding. By contrast, if SSB is added after dnaB has bound, it stimulates unwinding by preventing the unwound DNA from reannealing.

Reference: LeBowitz, J.H.; McMacken, R. The *Escherichia coli* dnaB replication protein is a DNA helicase. *J. Biol. Chem.* 261:4738–4748, 1986.

5–27 As always, you come through with flying colors. Although you were initially bewildered by the variety of structures, you quickly realized that H forms were just like the bubbles except that cleavage occurred within the bubble instead of outside it. Next you realized that by reordering the molecules according to increasing size of the bubble (and flipping some structures end-for-end), you could present a convincing visual case for bidirectional replication away from a unique origin of replication (Figure 5–47). Finally, you remind your lab mates that this experiment does not define the location of the origin, since it could be clockwise or counterclockwise from the restriction site at which the circle was cleaved. You are planning to repeat the experiment using a different restriction enzyme. Your adviser is pleased.

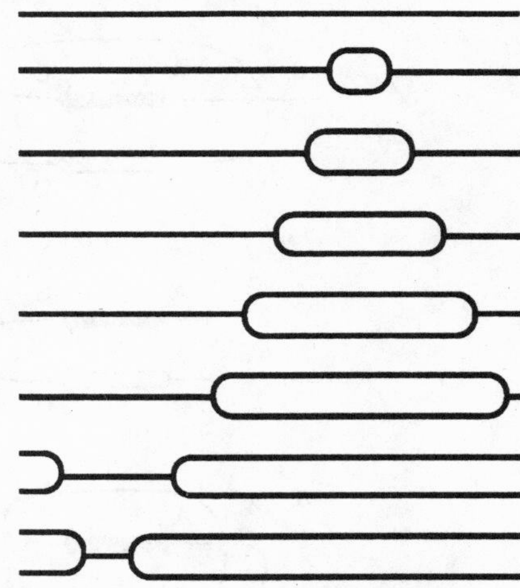

Figure 5–47 Bidirectional replication from a unique origin (Answer 5–27).

***5–28**

Genetic Recombination Mechanisms

5–29

A. general recombination
B. heteroduplex joint (staggered joint)
C. DNA renaturation (hybridization), helix nucleation
D. recA protein
E. branch migration (directed branch migration)
F. cross-strand exchange, Holliday junction
G. gene conversion
H. site-specific

5–30

A. True
B. True
C. False. This statement would be true for the recBCD protein. The recA protein is required for the pairing of homologous duplexes.
D. True
E. True
F. False. Crossing and noncrossing pairs of strands can be interconverted by rotational movements that do not require strand breakage.
G. False. Gene conversion has nothing to do with sex change; it refers to the unequal recovery of parental alleles in the progeny.
H. True
I. True

5–31 The recombination substrates and products are shown in Figure 5–48. The first rule for deducing the recombination products is to align the homologous segments, that is, to draw the arrows one above the other so that

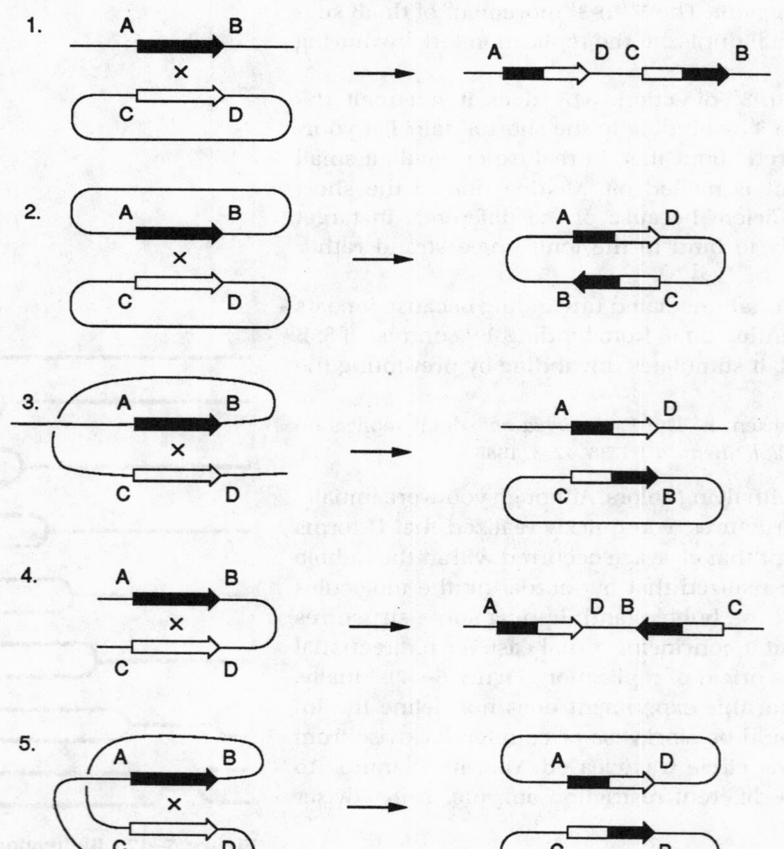

Figure 5–48 Alignment and crossover in various recombination substrates (Answer 5–31).

they are pointing in the same direction. Alignment requires a twisting of substrates 3, 4, and 5. Alignment is necessary in order to form a Holliday junction, as would become apparent if real sequences were used instead of arrows.

Substrates 3 and 4 illustrate a useful rule. Recombination between direct repeats in a chromosome (as in substrate 3) deletes one copy of the repeat and the intervening DNA. Recombination between inverted repeats in a chromosome (as in substrate 4) simply inverts the DNA between the repeats.

***5–32** **Reference:** Ponticelli, A.S.; Schultz, D.W.; Taylor, A.F.; Smith, G.R. Chi-dependent DNA strand cleavage by recBCD enzyme. *Cell* 41:145–151, 1985.

5–33

A. If binding saturates at a 1:12 weight ratio of nucleotides to SSB protein, then the ratio of nucleotides to SSB molecules is 8.8.

$$\frac{\text{nucleotides}}{\text{SSB molecule}} = \frac{1 \text{ d nucleotide}}{12 \text{ d SSB}} \times \frac{35{,}000 \text{ d SSB}}{\text{SSB molecule}} \times \frac{1 \text{ nucleotide}}{330 \text{ d nucleotide}}$$
$$= 8.8 \text{ nucleotides/SSB molecule}$$

B. If there are 10 nucleotides per 3.4 nm of single-stranded DNA, then 8.8 nucleotides would stretch about 3 nm. (If the single-stranded DNA were fully extended, it would stretch about twice as far.) The 12-nm length of an SSB molecule suggests that at saturation SSB proteins are very likely to be in contact with one another and probably overlap considerably.

C. The absence of significant binding at a low concentration of SSB protein, but nearly quantitative binding at a tenfold higher concentration, suggests that binding of SSB protein to DNA is cooperative. In essence, cooperative binding means that once one monomer has bound, additional monomers can bind more readily. If the monomers actually overlap with one another when they are bound, as suggested by the calculation in part B, cooperativity is easy to understand, for it suggests that each monomer has two binding sites—one for DNA and one for other monomers. Under these conditions binding of the first monomer to DNA will be weaker than the binding of subsequent monomers. That is because the first monomer can bind to the DNA only through its DNA binding site, whereas the second monomer can bind adjacent to an already bound monomer and, thereby, make use of both of its binding sites. Mathematically, this type of interaction leads to a steep dependence of binding on concentration.

Reference: Alberts, B.M.; Frey, L. T4 bacteriophage gene 32: a structural protein in the replication and recombination of DNA. *Nature* 227:1313–1318, 1970.

***5–34** **Reference:** Cox, M.; Lehman, I.R. The polarity of the recA protein-mediated branch migration. *Proc. Natl. Acad. Sci. USA* 78:6023–6027, 1981.

5–35 Formation of a Holliday junction between the two parental duplexes along with its resolution and subsequent replication are shown in Figure 5–49. Note that the lower duplex was rotated to put the 3′ strand on top so that the crossover strands (in this case the 3′ strands) could be represented more simply. The crossover strands must be corresponding strands (both 3′ or both 5′); they cannot be complementary strands (one 3′ and one 5′). Do you understand why?

Resolution of the Holliday junction by breaking the 3′ strands is easy to see; however, resolution by breaking the 5′ strands is more difficult. One way to visualize the resolution is to isomerize the structure so that the 5′ strands become the crossover strands, as shown in MBOC Figure 5–63. Another way to see the relationship between the Holliday junction and the products is as follows: In the Holliday structure with the broken 5′ strands, cover the lower duplex segment to the left of the crossover and the upper duplex segment to the right of the crossover. What remains visible is the

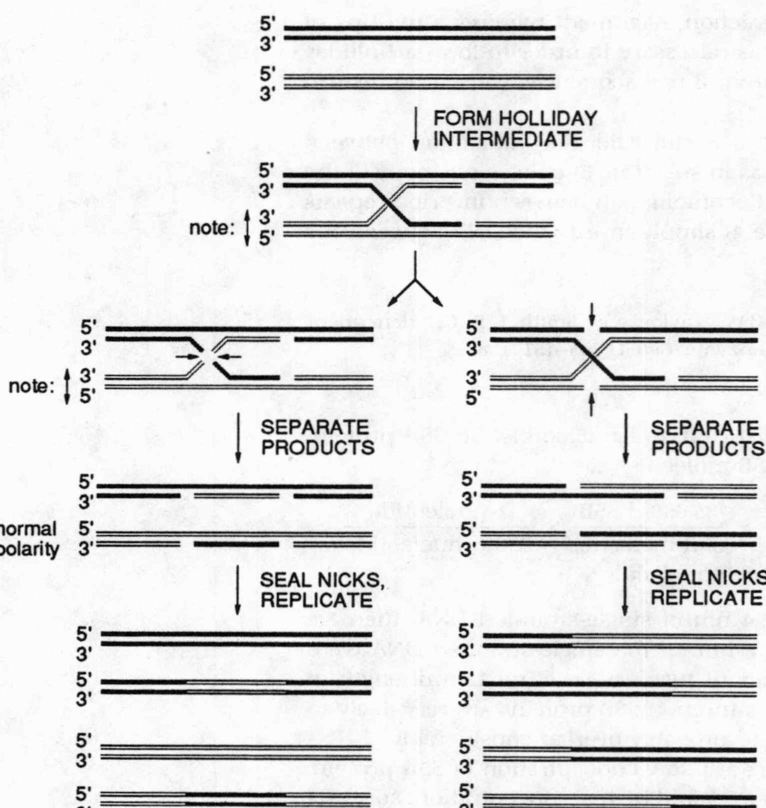

Figure 5–49 Formation and resolution of a Holliday intermediate followed by replication (Answer 5–35).

upper of the two product duplexes; it can be converted to the upper product by rotating the bottom duplex segment to put the 5′ strand on top.

Replication of the initial products of the recombination event resolves the heteroduplex segments and gives a truer picture of the recombinants as they would be detected in an actual experiment. Notice that if all four strand breaks are on the same strand (the 3′ strand in this case), the final result is insertion of a short segment of information from one duplex into the other (left-hand pathway). If two breaks are in 5′ strands and two breaks are in 3′ strands, the recombination products will be duplexes that have crossed over (right-hand pathway).

***5–36** **Reference:** Potter, H.; Dressler, D. On the mechanism of genetic recombination: electron microscopic observation of recombination intermediates. *Proc. Natl. Acad. Sci. USA* 73:3000–3004, 1976.

Viruses, Plasmids, and Transposable Genetic Elements

5–37

A. bacteriophage
B. lyse
C. capsid
D. enveloped
E. RNA-dependent RNA polymerase, replicase
F. positive-strand, negative-strand
G. lysogenic, provirus
H. lysogenic bacteriophages
I. nonpermissive
J. neoplastic transformation

K. reverse transcriptase, retroviruses
L. transposable elements, transposases
M. retrotransposon
N. plasmids
O. viroids
P. transduction

5–38

A. False. When T4 DNA enters a cell, it is completely dependent on host RNA polymerase to express its "early" genes. Later it modifies the host RNA polymerase so that it recognizes other viral promoters, leading to the coordinated expression of the T4 genome.
B. False. Although the host replication machinery provides the majority of the enzymatic apparatus, even small viruses make special proteins needed for initiation of DNA synthesis. If they did not, they would be subject to the strict rules of chromosome replication, which permit only one round of replication per cell generation, and multiple rounds of virus replication would be impossible.
C. False. It is true that the RNA genomes of negative-strand viruses do not serve directly as mRNA, but their complements do; thus, they contain genes.
D. True
E. True
F. True
G. False. Many viruses that reproduce by budding do not cause cancer; it is also possible to have cells transformed by oncogenic viruses that produce no virus particles at all.
H. False. The growth of some RNA viruses is inhibited by actinomycin D. Retroviruses, for example, are inhibited by actinomycin D because they are first converted to DNA by reverse transcriptase and then are transcribed in the usual manner, which is sensitive to actinomycin D. If the statement had been "If the growth of the virus is not inhibited by actinomycin D, it must be an RNA virus," it would have been true.
I. False. Transposable elements integrate nearly randomly and genes often are destroyed or altered by the integration event.
J. True
K. False. Overlapping genes are thought to have evolved in response to selective pressure for optimal use of small genomes that were limited by capsid size.
L. True

5–39

A. The phage suspension was diluted 1000-fold (0.1 ml/100 ml) upon mixing with the bacterial culture; therefore the initial phage titer was 10^7 phage/ml (10^{10} phage/ml $\times$ 1/1000).
B. The phage titer after 5 minutes was about tenfold lower that it was initially. This initial decrease in titer occurs because phages adsorb to the bacteria and inject their DNA. Since infectivity depends on an intact phage, the titer decreases. The low titer at 5 minutes represents phages that have not yet adsorbed to bacteria.

   Historically, this initial loss of titer (which was termed the eclipse phase of infection) was puzzling because it implied that the parental phages must be destroyed before new phages could be built. It is difficult now to appreciate the puzzle, but remember at that time the principal model for biological growth was cell division, where destruction of the parent would absolutely prevent formation of progeny.
C. The phage titer rises more slowly in the control samples because many phages (90% of the total between 20 and 40 minutes) are trapped inside the chloroform-killed bacteria. Incubation with lysozyme breaks open the bacteria, releasing the trapped phages. The titer of the control samples ultimately reaches that of the lysozyme-treated samples because the bacteria break open (lyse) naturally at the end of the infection. Lysis is con-

trolled by phages so that a maximum number of phages can be made before the host is destroyed.

D. The initial mixture contains equal numbers of bacteria and phages (10^7/ml), so there are enough phages to infect every bacterium. Since there are 10^7 bacteria/ml initially and 10^9 phage/ml at the end, there are 100 phages per bacterium.

The actual calculation of phages per *infected* bacterium is not quite so straightforward in this example. It is described briefly here so that you will be aware of an important fact: a one-to-one mixture of bacteria and phages does not mean that every bacterium will be infected by one phage. Most bacteria will be infected by one phage, but some will be infected by two or more phages, and some will not be infected at all. The fraction of bacteria in any particular class can be calculated from the Poisson distribution. From the Poisson distribution, the fraction of bacteria infected with zero phage is

$$P_0 = e^{-x}$$

where P_0 is the probability of not being infected and x is the ratio of phages to bacteria. At $x = 1$, $P_0 = 0.37$. Thus, only 63% of the bacteria will be infected. As a result, the number of phages per *infected* bacterium is 160.

The principle illustrated by this example arises in a number of different guises throughout biology. See, for example, Problem 5–13, in which delivery of one lethal UV "hit" per bacterium allowed 37% of the population to survive.

***5–40**

5–41

A. The spot test described here is a classic version of a complementation test, which allows one to decide whether two mutants are defective in the same gene or in different genes. If a pair of mutants is defective in the same gene, they cannot help each other during infection (since they are both missing the same gene product) and, therefore, grow no better in a mixed infection than they do individually. By contrast, if a pair of mutants is defective in different genes, they can help one another: between them they have at least one functional copy of every gene and therefore can grow as a mixture of mutants.

The results of the spot test with the r_{II} mutants indicate that they fall into two complementation groups. Mutants 2, 5, and 8 are defective in one gene, and mutants 1, 3, 4, 6, and 7 are defective in a second gene. Classical experiments showed in much the same way that there are two r_{II} genes—r_{IIA} and r_{IIB}.

B. As suggested by the description in part A, if you repeated the spot test using *E. coli* K infected with mutant 3, you would see the same pattern as the spot test using *E. coli* K infected with mutant 1, which is defective in the same gene.

C. The small fraction of wild-type T4 in the mixture of mutant 1 and mutant 5 arises by genetic recombination. Viral genomes growing in the same cell will occasionally recombine. If a recombination event occurs between the mutations, a wild-type genome can be produced, as illustrated in Figure 5–50. Since the frequency of recombination is roughly proportional to the separation of the mutations, careful measurements of the fraction of wild type in genetic crosses between mutants can be used (and were) to determine the order and spacing of mutations along the chromosome.

Reference: Crick, F.H.; Brenner, S. The absolute sign of certain phase-shift mutants in bacteriophage T4. *J. Mol. Biol.* 26:361–363, 1967.

***5–42**

5–43 These results indicate that a circular DNA with tandem LTRs is the most likely precursor to the integrated form of the retroviral genome. The key result is provided by the genome with two internal LTRs. The pattern of hybridization can be understood by reference to Figure 5–51. The circular

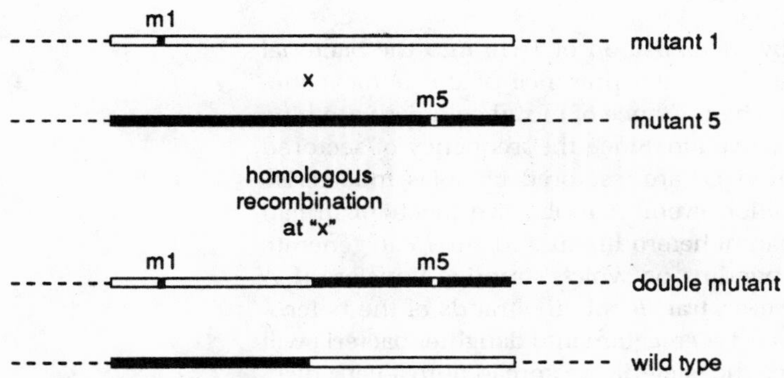

Figure 5–50 Recombination between two mutants to generate a wild-type genome (Answer 5–41).

form with two sets of tandem LTRs can integrate in either of two ways, as shown. Since the *population* of cells contains both kinds of integrants, digestion with either restriction enzyme yields two fragments of 0.8 kb and 8 kb.

A circular DNA with one LTR cannot be the precursor to integration because, by analogy with Figure 5–51, integration of circular forms with one LTR should also yield two fragments (0.4 kb and 8 kb) upon digestion with each restriction digestion.

Recent experiments using different retroviruses have shown convincingly that the linear form is the precursor to integration. The basis for these different conclusions is not yet known; it may simply reflect differences between the retroviruses.

References: Panganiban, A.T.; Temin, H.M. Circles with two tandem LTRs are precursors to integrated retrovirus DNA. *Cell* 36:673–679, 1984.

Brown, P.O.; Bowerman, B.; Varmus, H.E.; Bishop, J.M. Correct integration of retroviral DNA *in vitro*. *Cell* 49:347–356, 1987.

Fujiwara, T.; Mizuuchi, K. Retroviral integration: structure of an integration intermediate. *Cell* 54:497–504, 1988.

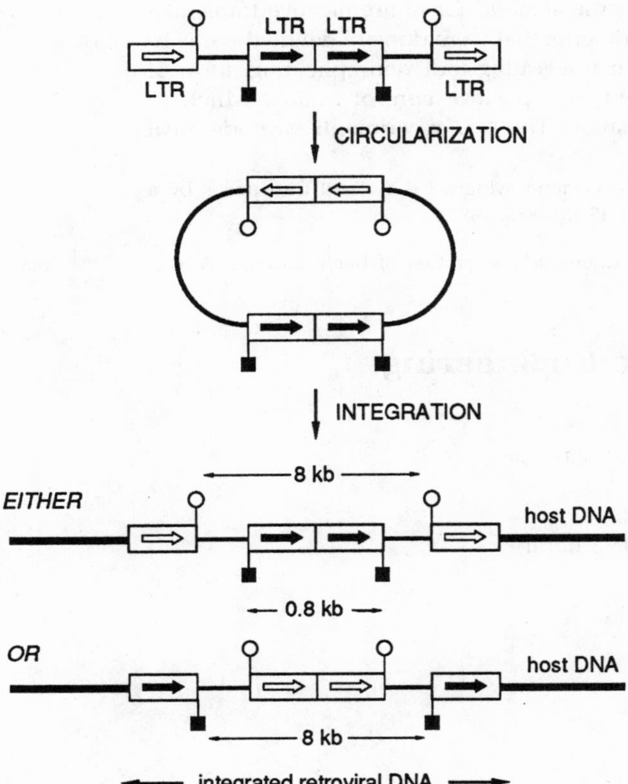

Figure 5–51 Integration of a retroviral genome with two sets of tandem LTRs (Answer 5–43).

5–44

A. All colonies must have arisen by transposition of Tn10 into the bacterial genome, because survival depends on the presence of the tetracycline-resistance gene carried by Tn10. The presence of mixed colonies with blue and white sectors is the key observation. Since the frequency of sectored colonies is high but transposition is rare, sectored colonies must arise commonly in a single transposition event. A replicative mechanism can transfer only one strand of the parent heteroduplex and, thus, can generate only white or blue colonies, depending on which strand is transferred. A nonreplicative mechanism, however, transfers both strands of the heteroduplex, which upon replication and segregation into daughter bacteria will produce a sectored colony. (Once the bacteria are spread onto a Petri dish, all the descendants of the original infected cell are confined to the immediate vicinity and, thus, grow together to form the colony. If two different daughters are produced at the first division, their descendants will grow together to produce a single colony with sectors containing the two different kinds of bacteria.) The pure blue and pure white colonies arise from transposition events that involve the homoduplexes. The proportions of blue, white, and sectored colonies are as expected from the equal mixture of heteroduplexes (which give rise to the sectored colonies) and homoduplexes (which give rise to the pure colonies).

B. Each heteroduplex contains a mismatched region of DNA corresponding to the position of the mutation in the *lacZ* gene. If these heteroduplexes were introduced into bacteria that could repair such mismatches, then the frequency of sectored colonies would decrease. In essence, each repair event would convert a heteroduplex into a homoduplex. If the mismatch repair is unbiased, the frequencies of blue colonies and white colonies would each increase equally.

C. If you used an integrating form of the phage genome, then the surviving colonies would have resulted from site-specific recombination, which is much more frequent than transposition. Site-specific recombination integrates both strands of the phage genome (as described in MBOC, pp. 246–248) (see especially Figure 5–67 on p. 248). Thus, the proportion of blue, white, and sectored colonies would be the same as for nonreplicative transposition. Indeed, in the actual experiments that were done to define the mechanism of Tn10 transposition, an integrating (but nonreplicating) form of bacteriophage lambda was used as a positive control against which to compare the results of transposition. The two experiments gave identical results.

Reference: Bender, J.; Kleckner, N. Genetic evidence that Tn10 transposes by a nonreplicative mechanism. *Cell* 45:801–815, 1986.

***5–45** **Reference:** Sanger, F.; et al. The nucleotide sequence of bacteriophage ϕX174. *J. Mol. Biol.* 125:225–246, 1978.

DNA Cloning and Genetic Engineering

5–46

A. restriction nucleases, restriction fragments
B. cloning vectors
C. clone
D. genomic DNA clone, genomic DNA library
E. cDNA library
F. subtractive hybridization
G. chromosome walking
H. hybrid selection
I. expression
J. fusion protein
K. transgenic
L. PCR (polymerase chain reaction)

5–47

A. True. (For example, the SmaI restriction nuclease cuts the sequence GGGCCC—and its complement on the other strand—right in the middle to generate restriction fragments with flush or blunt ends.)

B. True

C. True

D. False. Introns in genomic clones of eucaryotic genes make it nearly impossible to deduce the amino acid sequence of the encoded proteins. Since introns are removed during synthesis of mRNA, amino acid sequences can be reliably deduced from cDNA clones.

E. False. The antibody must be directed against the protein encoded by the desired mRNA.

F. True

G. False. A eucaryotic genomic clone is likely to contain introns, which will prevent correct expression of the protein in bacteria.

H. False. Transgenic animals are generated by incorporating DNA into the chromosomes of germ line cells so that the foreign DNA is present in future generations of the organism.

5–48

A. The 5′ and 3′ ends of the cut molecules are indicated in Figure 5–52. It is standard practice to represent DNA sequences so that the 5′ end of the top strand is on the left.

B. As indicated in Figure 5–52, the BamHI ends can be filled in by DNA polymerase, but the PstI ends cannot. These different fates follow from the requirements of DNA polymerase: a primer with a 3′-OH to which dNTPs can be added and a template strand to specify correct addition. These requirements are met by the BamHI ends but not by the PstI ends, which have recessed 5′ ends that cannot serve as primers and, thus, cannot be filled in.

NOTE: A standard technique in recombinant DNA technology is to use T4 DNA polymerase to blunt both types of ends. It will blunt BamHI ends

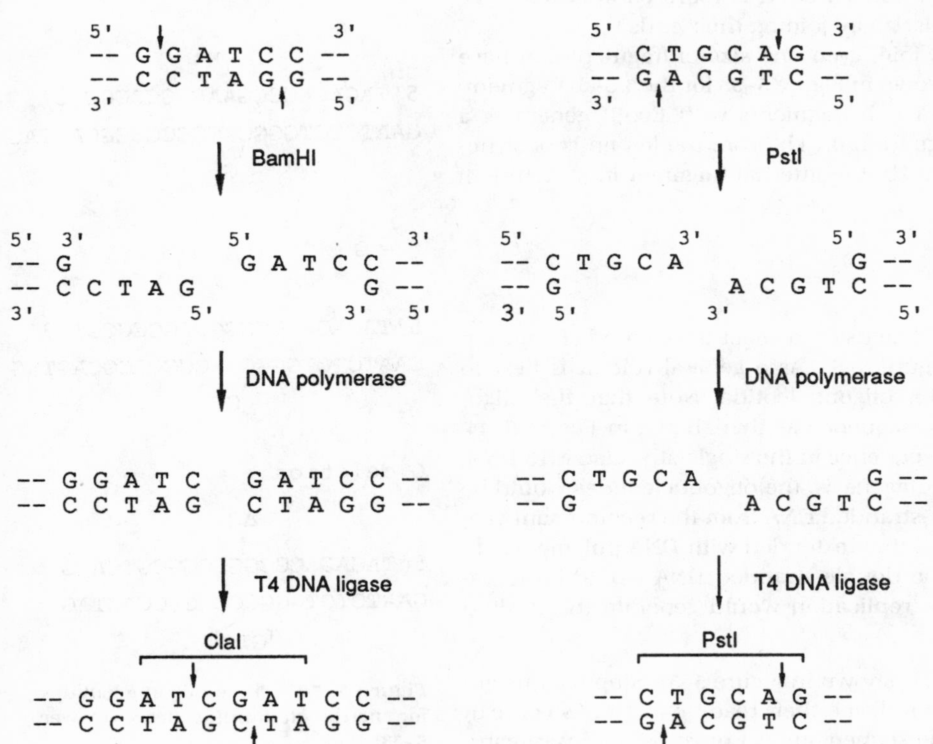

Figure 5–52 Cleavage, modification, and joining of DNA containing a BamHI site or a PstI site (Answer 5–48).

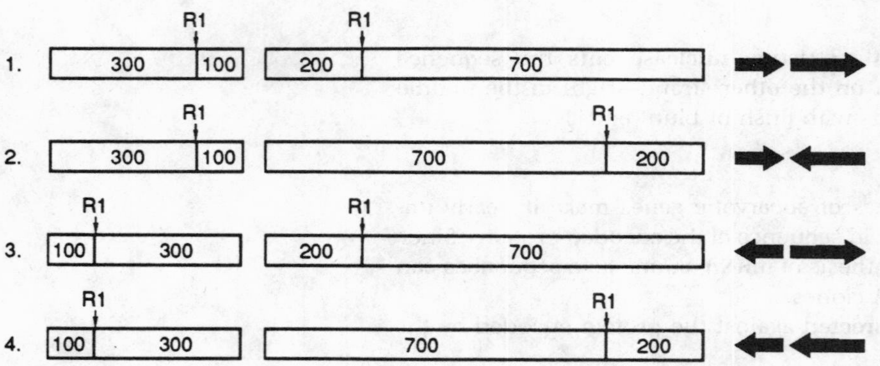

Figure 5–53 Various arrangements of 0.4-kb and 0.9-kb BamHI fragments to form a 1.3-kb fragment (Answer 5–50).

by filling them in, as indicated in Figure 5–52. However, it will also blunt PstI ends by virtue of an associated 3′-to-5′ exonuclease activity, which removes the 3′ extension, leaving a blunt end.

C. As indicated in Figure 5–52, the blunted BamHI ends and the unmodified PstI ends can both be joined by T4 DNA ligase.

D. Joining of the treated ends regenerates the PstI site but not the BamHI site. Joining of the filled-in BamHI ends generates two new restriction sites, as indicated in Figure 5–52. Cleavage, filling in the ends, and rejoining often generates new restriction sites that sometimes are useful for further manipulation of the DNA.

***5–49**

5–50

A. The complexity of the original ligation pattern arises because any two BamHI ends can join together. Thus, the 0.4-kb fragments can join together to generate a set of fragments with sizes 0.8 kb, 1.2 kb, 1.6 kb, 2.0 kb, etc. Similarly, the 0.9-kb fragments will produce a set of fragments with sizes 1.8 kb, 2.7 kb, 3.6 kb, and so forth. Finally, combinations of the two fragments generate a third set of fragments with sizes 1.3 kb, 1.7 kb, 2.1 kb, 2.2 kb, and so forth. (The actual pattern often is more complicated still, since these fragments can circularize by joining their ends.)

B. Since any two BamHI ends can join, even one size of fragment can have several different structures, as shown in Figure 5–53 for the 1.3-kb fragment. Digestion of the population of 1.3-kb fragments with EcoRI generates a variety of fragments, which range from 0.1 kb (from the left ends of structures 3 and 4, Figure 5–53) to 1.0 kb (the internal fragment in structure 4, Figure 5–53).

***5–51**

***5–52**

5–53 Three oligonucleotides that could be used to effect the desired changes in the protein are illustrated in Figure 5–54. As a general rule, it is best to center the mismatch within the oligonucleotide. Note that the oligonucleotides have the same basic sequence as that shown in Figure 5–44, which is the complement of the sequence in the single-stranded M13 DNA. To carry out the site-directed mutagenesis, the oligonucleotides would be hybridized to the circular, single-stranded DNA from the recombinant vector (as shown in Figure 5–54) and then extended with DNA polymerase to complete the second strand. The double-stranded DNA would be transfected into bacterial cells where replication would generate the desired mutant.

5–54 The sequence of the cloned DNA is shown in Figure 5–55. Stop codons are underlined and labeled 2 or 3 to indicate their reading frame. As you can appreciate from this exercise, the sequencing gel must be read very care-

```
Q → K

              K
5'TAGAGACCCGAAGGGCGGCG 3'
GAATCTCTGGGC TCCCGCCGCAGTAG
             \ /
              G

Q → G

              G
5'TAGAGACCCGGGGGGCGGCGT 3'
GAATCTCTGGGC  CCCGCCGCAGTAG
             \ /
              GT

Q deletion

              ΔQ
5'TAGAGACCCGGGCGGCGTCA 3'
GAATCTCTGGGCCCGCCGCAGTAG
             GTC
```

Figure 5–54 Three oligonucleotides for site-directed mutagenesis (Answer 5–53).

```
 Y  K  L  D  N  Q  F  E  L  V  F  V  V  G  F  Q  K  I  L  T
GTATAAACTGGACAACCAGTTCGAGCTGGTGTTCGTGGTCGGTTTCAGAAGATCCTAAC
    3                                                   2

 L  T  Y  V  D  K  L  I  D  D  V  H  R  L  F  R  D  K  Y
GCTGACGTACGTAGACAAGTTGATAGATGATGTGCATCGGCTGTTTCGAGACAAGTAC
   2        2        2  2   3
```

Figure 5–55 Nucleotide and amino acid sequence of a cloned gene (Answer 5–54). Stop codons are underlined. Amino acids are encoded in reading frame 1.

fully; omission of a single nucleotide would have disastrous consequences for determining the open reading frame. To minimize this problem, it is best to determine the sequence of both strands of DNA. Since the two strands are complementary, any mistakes will be readily apparent.

The Plasma Membrane

The Lipid Bilayer

6–1

A. lipid bilayer
B. phospholipids, cholesterol, glycolipids
C. amphipathic
D. polar, hydrophobic hydrocarbon (fatty acid)
E. micelles, bilayer sheets
F. liposomes, black. (The black membranes are so called because destructive interference between the reflected light from the two surfaces makes them appear black. Soap bubbles show interference colors that depend on the thickness of the film.)
G. spin label
H. phase transition
I. glycolipids
J. galactocerebroside, myelin
K. gangliosides, G_{M1}

6–2

A. True
B. False. Lipid bilayers are thermodynamically stable structures. Energy is required to make the various lipids in the first place, but no energy is needed to maintain the bilayer arrangement in the membrane.
C. True
D. False. The length of the fatty acid side chains and the number of *cis*-double bonds they contain are also important determinants of membrane fluidity.
E. True
F. False. Mutant cells that cannot synthesize cholesterol require its presence in the culture medium. Their membranes rapidly break down in the *absence* of cholesterol.
G. False. Although the choline head group is indeed positively charged, it is linked to the rest of the lipid via a phosphodiester bond, and the phosphate carries a negative charge at physiological pH. Hence, phosphatidylcholine does not carry a *net* charge.
H. True
I. True. (Glycolipids are synthesized in the lumen of the Golgi apparatus and cannot flip-flop across the bilayer. The enzymes that add carbohydrates to lipids are not found free in the cytoplasm.)

6–3 Each microvillus approximates a cylinder 0.1 μm in diameter and 1.0 μm in height. The ratio of the area of the sides of a cylinder, which represent new membrane (new surface area), to the top of a cylinder (which is equivalent to the plasma membrane that would have been present anyway had the microvillus not been extruded) gives the increase in surface area due to an individual microvillus. The area of the sides of a cylinder ($2\pi rh$, where r is the radius and h is the height) is 0.31 μm^2; the area of the top of the cylinder (πr^2) is 0.0079 μm^2. Thus, the increase in surface area for one microvillus is 0.31 μm^2/0.0079 μm^2 or 40. However, this value overestimates the increase for the entire plasma membrane, since the microvilli occupy only a portion of the surface. An estimate of the fraction of plasma membrane occupied by microvilli can be obtained from the cross-section in Figure 6–1. A conservative estimate is that about half the plasma membrane is covered by microvilli. Thus, microvilli increase the surface area in contact with the lumen of the gut by approximately 40/2 or twentyfold.

***6–4**

6–5

A. Only phosphatidylserine and phosphatidylethanolamine have primary amino groups, which can react with SITS. Since these phospholipids are labeled only when the red cells are made permeable (ghosts), they presumably reside in the inner monolayer. This conclusion is supported by the results from experiments with sea snake venom, which degrades phosphatidylserine and phosphatidylethanolamine only in ghosts. These results, taken together, indicate that the phosphatidylserine and phosphatidylethanolamine are localized almost exclusively in the inner monolayer of red cell membranes.

Phospholipase degradation of phosphatidylcholine and sphingomyelin in intact cells indicates that they are present in the outer monolayer. This conclusion depends on the red cell remaining intact during the treatment. In the case of sea snake venom, the absence of degradation of phosphatidylserine and phosphatidylethanolamine in intact cells provides an internal control. In the case of sphingomyelinase, there is no internal control, but the absence of lysis shows that the membrane is intact.

The *summary* of results in Table 6–2 does not exclude the possibility that phosphatidylcholine and sphingomyelin are also located in the inner monolayer. However, the quantitation of sphingomyelin degradation by sphingomyelinase (provided in the body of the problem) indicates that sphingomyelin is localized almost entirely in the outer monolayer of the membrane. No such data are provided for phosphatidylcholine; thus, it is incorrect to conclude from the data given that phosphatidylcholine is located exclusively in the outer monolayer. However, other experiments not reported here do suggest that phosphatidylcholine is found almost entirely in the outer monolayer.

B. You chose red cells for these experiments because they contain no internal membranes. If the same experiments were performed on cells with internal membranes, it would have been impossible to measure directly the phospholipid composition of the inner monolayer, since phospholipids from the inner monolayer would have been hopelessly confused with those from internal membranes.

References: Bretscher, M. Asymmetrical lipid bilayer structure for biological membranes. *Nature New Biol.* 236:11–12, 1972.

Deenen, L.L.M.; DeGier, J. Lipids of the red cell membrane. In The Red Blood Cell (D. MacN. Surgenor, ed.), pp. 147–211. New York: Academic Press, 1974.

***6–6** **Reference:** Rousselet, A.; Guthmann, C.; Matricon, J.; Bienvenue, A.; Devaux, P.F. Study of the transverse diffusion of spin labeled phospholipids in biological membranes: I. Human red blood cells. *Biochim. Biophys. Acta* 426:357–371, 1976.

6–7

A. One can estimate the half-time for flip-flop in these experiments by extending the curve in Figure 6–4 to the point at which 50% of the ESR signal is lost. For cells labeled in the inner monolayer, these data suggest a half-time for flip-flop of about 7 hours. For cells labeled in the outer monolayer, the half-time of flip-flop is much longer but cannot be estimated reliably. These data indicate that the rate of flip-flop of phospholipids between the two monolayers of the plasma membrane in red cells is extremely low. Similar experiments using synthetic bilayers have given even longer times; in fact, in the best experiments, when great care was taken not to allow oxidation or other damage to the lipids, the rate of flip-flop was immeasurably low (less than once per month).

*Problems with an asterisk (*) are answered in the Instructor's Manual.

B. Phospholipid 2 was used to label the inner monolayer and phospholipid 1 was used to label the outer monolayer. As shown by the experiments in Figure 6–3B, phospholipid 2 in the inner monolayer is not reduced by the cytoplasm of red cells; when it is present in the outer monolayer, it can be reduced by ascorbate. Thus, phospholipid 2 is appropriate for measuring the rate of flip-flop from the inner to the outer monolayer. As shown by the experiments in Figure 6–3A, phospholipid 1 in the inner monolayer is reduced by red cell cytoplasm, but, it is stable in the outer monolayer in the absence of ascorbate. Thus, phospholipid 1 is appropriate for measuring the rate of flip-flop from the outer to the inner monolayer.

C. One can make intact red cells with spin-labeled phospholipids exclusively in the inner monolayer by introducing phospholipid 2 into the membrane and then incubating the red cells for 1 hour in the presence of ascorbate. Ascorbate reduces the lipids in the outer monolayer, leaving red cells that are labeled only in the inner monolayer. Similarly, one can make intact red cells with spin-labeled phospholipids exclusively in the outer monolayer by introducing phospholipid 1 into the membrane and then incubating the red cells for 15 minutes in the absence of ascorbate. In this case the spin-labeled lipids in the inner monolayer are reduced by agents in the cytoplasm, leaving red cells that are labeled only in the outer monolayer.

Reference: Rousselet, A.; Guthmann, C.; Matricon, J.; Bienvenue, A.; Devaux, P.F. Study of the transverse diffusion of spin labeled phospholipids in biological membranes: I. Human red blood cells *Biochim. Biophys. Acta* 426:357–371, 1976.

Membrane Proteins

6–8

A. transmembrane
B. peripheral membrane, integral membrane
C. detergents
D. denatured
E. vectorial labeling
F. spectrin
G. band 3 protein
H. freeze-fracture, P face, E face
I. bacteriorhodopsin
J. photosynthetic reaction center
K. rotational, lateral, flip-flop
L. heterocaryons
M. fluorescence recovery after photobleaching (FRAP)

6–9

A. True
B. False. This statement was once thought to be an accurate description of biological membranes, but it is now clear that many membrane proteins are inserted directly into the bilayer itself.
C. False. Such proteins are more likely to have their transmembrane segments arranged as α helices. An α-helical structure would allow all of the hydrogen-bonding moieties along the peptide backbone to be satisfied, whereas a β-sheet structure would leave about half the hydrogen-bonding moieties unsatisfied (see MBOC Figures 3–25 and 3–26).
D. True
E. False. Human red blood cells contain no internal membranes; at an early stage in their development they extrude their nuclei.
F. True
G. True
H. True
I. True
J. False. The apical and basolateral surfaces of epithelial cells, which are separated by intercellular tight junctions, have different lipid compositions.

6–10 Thus far, arrangements A, B, D, E, F, and I have been found in biological membranes. Arrangement C, which has carbohydrate on the cytoplasmic side of the membrane, does not seem to exist. Arrangements G and H, which show proteins completely buried or with only their tips embedded in the membrane, have not been found and are thought to be unlikely to occur on theoretical grounds.

***6–11**

6–12

A. The elimination of sialic acid staining after sialidase treatment indicates that carbohydrate is exposed on the external surface. Because the carbohydrate is attached to glycophorin, it follows that glycophorin is also exposed on the external surface. This conclusion is supported by the results with pronase digestion, which eliminates PAS staining, presumably by clipping the peptide backbone. The results with pronase digestion indicate that band 3 is exposed to the external surface as well. In this case the appearance of the new protein band at about 70,000 daltons allows you to estimate that approximately 30,000 daltons of band 3 are exposed on the external surface. In neither digestion were the two spectrin bands affected, suggesting that spectrin is not exposed on the external surface.

B. One direct experimental approach to testing your colleague's objection is to break open the red cell ghosts before digesting them with pronase. If spectrin is resistant to pronase, its mobility on SDS polyacrylamide gels should be unaltered. However, if spectrin is located on the cytoplasmic surface, its mobility should be altered dramatically. These control experiments have been done; they show that spectrin is sensitive to pronase.

Another approach is to make inside-out ghosts and see if it is possible to dissociate spectrin from the membrane by treatments that do not actually disrupt the membrane. This approach also has been successful, confirming that spectrin is on the cytoplasmic side and is not embedded in the membrane.

C. To determine which of the red cell proteins span the membrane using this basic experimental approach, it is necessary to prepare inside-out vesicles. Such vesicles can be readily prepared from red cell ghosts by disrupting them and allowing them to reseal under defined ionic conditions. When inside-out vesicles are treated with pronase, the mobilities of band 3 and glycophorin are altered. These results, along with the results above, indicate that band 3 and glycophorin are exposed on both surfaces of the red cell membrane and, therefore, must be transmembrane proteins.

Reference: Bennett, V.; Stenbuck, P.J. The membrane attachment protein for spectrin is associated with band 3 in human erythrocyte membranes. *Nature* 280:468–473, 1979.

Bennett, V.; Stenbuck, P.J. Association between ankyrin and the cytoplasmic domain of band 3 isolated from the human erythrocyte membrane. *J. Biol. Chem.* 255:6424–6432, 1980.

***6–13**

6–14 The presence of both proteins in the pellet, as in mixtures 3, 4, and 6 in Table 6–4, indicates an interaction between the proteins. The results with pairwise mixtures suggest that the four proteins are arranged as shown below:

band 3—ankyrin—spectrin—actin

An artist's conception of how these molecules are linked together to form the supporting meshwork on the cytoplasmic surface of red cells is shown in MBOC Figure 6–26. In reality, the interaction between actin and spectrin is too weak to be detected by this method, unless a third protein, band 4.1, is added.

***6–15** **Reference:** Bretscher, M.S. Endocytosis: relation to capping and cell locomotion. *Science* 224:681–686, 1984.

Membrane Carbohydrate

6–16

A. glycoproteins, glycolipids, proteoglycans
B. *N*-linked, *O*-linked
C. lectins
D. cell coat, glycocalyx

6–17

A. True
B. True
C. False. Just the reverse is true.
D. True
E. False. The carbohydrate on internal membranes is directed away from the cytoplasm.
F. False. Although carbohydrate is attached mainly to integral membrane proteins, the glycocalyx can also contain adsorbed glycoproteins and proteoglycans.

***6–18**

6–19

A. Cytochalasin B inhibits glucose transport competitively, suggesting that it binds at or near the site of D-glucose binding. If an excess of D-glucose is present, the binding site on the transporter will be occupied by D-glucose, preventing cytochalasin from binding and thereby interfering with cross-linking. On the other hand, L-glucose does not interfere with cross-linking, because it does not bind to the transporter and protect it from the binding of cytochalasin.
B. Since treatment of the native glucose transporter with an enzyme that removes oligosaccharide side chains sharpens the electrophoretic band, the fuzziness must be due to heterogeneity of the carbohydrate moieties attached to the protein. Whether this heterogeneity represents variable occupancy of potential *O*- and *N*-linked oligosaccharide addition sites on the protein or is due to actual variability in the length or sequence of the oligosaccharide side chains is not known. This degree of heterogeneity is unusual; most glycoproteins form much sharper bands on SDS polyacrylamide gels. Although there are about 350,000 molecules of this protein in each red cell (about the same as glycophorin and band 3), it went unnoticed for many years. In addition, there was considerable controversy about the molecular identity of the glucose transporter, with estimates of its molecular weight going as high as 200,000. All because it was a fuzzy band.

Reference: Allard, W.J.; Lienhard, G.E. Monoclonal antibodies to the glucose transporter from human erythrocytes: identification of the transporter as a Mr = 55,000 protein. *J. Biol. Chem.* 260:8668–8675, 1985.

Membrane Transport of Small Molecules

6–20

A. membrane transport
B. carrier, channel
C. passive (facilitated diffusion), active
D. electrochemical
E. symport
F. anion, antiport
G. Na^+–K^+ pump (NA^+–K^+ ATPase)
H. sarcoplasmic reticulum
I. Na^+-H^+, amiloride
J. microvilli
K. group translocation

L. porins, periplasmic substrate–binding
M. channel, ion channels
N. voltage changes, mechanical stimulation, ligand binding, ionic changes
O. membrane potential (resting potential), K^+ leak
P. action potential
Q. patch-clamp
R. tetrodotoxin, saxitoxin, voltage-gated
S. chemical synapses, neurotransmitter
T. acetylcholine, acetylcholine receptors
U. ionophores, mobile-ion, channel, K^+, Ca^{2+}

6–21

A. False. Lipid bilayers are impermeable to ions, but the plasma membrane contains specific ion channels and carriers that make it very permeable to particular ions under certain circumstances.
B. True
C. False. For carrier proteins to work like revolving doors would require that they flip–flop across the bilayer—which they do not.
D. True
E. True
F. False. The phosphorylation and dephosphorylation cycle of the Ca^{2+} pump, like that of the Na^+-K^+ pump, is part of its mechanism of action; ATP hydrolysis provides the energy to transfer the ions against a steep electrochemical gradient. The release of Ca^{2+} from the sarcoplasmic reticulum occurs via a channel other than the Ca^{2+} pump, whose identity and gating mechanism are still uncertain.
G. False. There is no direct connection between the light-activated proton pump (which indeed pumps protons out of the bacterium in sunlight) and the synthesis or hydrolysis of ATP. However, the bacteria do contain a separate membrane protein that can act as an ATP synthetase when protons pass through it in an inward direction.
H. True
I. True
J. False. Although the Na^+-K^+ pump is electrogenic and makes a small (20%) direct contribution to the membrane potential because of the unequal stoichiometry of the exchange, the K^+ leak channel, which endows the membrane with a selective permeability to K^+, is responsible for the major portion of the membrane potential. (The Na^+-K^+ pump does make an important though indirect contribution to the membrane potential by maintaining the K^+ gradient across the membrane.)
K. True
L. True
M. True

***6–22**

6–23

A. If the entire free-energy change due to ATP hydrolysis ($\Delta G = -12$ kcal/mole) could be used to drive transport, then the maximum concentration gradient that could be achieved by ATP hydrolysis would have a free-energy change of +12 kcal/mole.

$$\Delta G_{in} = -2.3\ RT \log_{10} \frac{C_o}{C_i} + zFV$$

Rearranging the equation gives

$$\log_{10} \frac{C_o}{C_i} = \frac{-\Delta G_{in} + zFV}{2.3\ RT}$$

For an uncharged solute, the electrical term (zFV) drops to 0. Thus,

$$\log_{10} \frac{C_o}{C_i} = \frac{-\Delta G_{in}}{2.3\ RT}$$

Substituting for ΔG_{in}, R, and T gives

$$\log_{10} \frac{C_o}{C_i} = \frac{-12 \text{ kcal/mole}}{2.3 \times 1.98 \times 10^{-3} \text{ kcal/°K mole} \times 310\text{°K}}$$

$$\log_{10} \frac{C_o}{C_i} = -8.50$$

$$\log_{10} \frac{C_i}{C_o} = 8.50$$

$$\frac{C_i}{C_o} = 3.2 \times 10^8$$

Thus, for an uncharged solute a transport system that couples hydrolysis of 1 ATP to transport of 1 solute molecule could, in principle, drive a concentration difference across the membrane of more than eight orders of magnitude. Amazing!

B. If the entire free-energy change due to ATP hydrolysis ($\Delta G = -12$ kcal/mole) could be used to drive transport of Ca^{2+} out of the cell, then the maximum concentration gradient would yield a free-energy change of +12 kcal/mole.

$$\Delta G_{out} = 2.3\ RT \log_{10} \frac{C_o}{C_i} - zFV$$

Rearranging the equation gives

$$\log_{10} \frac{C_o}{C_i} = \frac{\Delta G_{out} + zFV}{2.3\ RT}$$

Since Ca^{+2} is charged, the electrical term must be included. Substituting for ΔG_{out}, R, T, z, F, and V, gives

$$\log_{10} \frac{C_o}{C_i} = \frac{12 \text{ kcal/mole} + (2 \times 23 \text{ kcal/V mole} \times -0.06 \text{ V})}{2.3 \times 1.98 \times 10^{-3} \text{ kcal/°K mole} \times 310\text{°K}}$$

$$\log_{10} \frac{C_o}{C_i} = 6.54$$

$$\frac{C_o}{C_i} = 3.5 \times 10^6$$

Thus a transport system that couples hydrolysis of 1 ATP to transport of 1 Ca^{2+} ion on the outside of the cell could, in principle, drive a concentration difference across the membrane of more than six orders of magnitude. Note, by comparison with uncharged solute, that pumping against the membrane potential reduces the theoretical limit by two orders of magnitude. The difference in Ca^{2+} concentration across a typical mammalian plasma membrane is more than four orders of magnitude, but well within the theoretical limit.

C. The free-energy change for transporting Na^+ out of the cell is

$$\Delta G_{out} = 2.3\ RT \log_{10} \frac{C_o}{C_i} - zFV$$

Substituting (with $2.3\ RT = 1.41$ kcal/mole),

$$\Delta G_{out} = \left(1.41 \frac{\text{kcal}}{\text{mole}} \times \log_{10} \frac{145 \text{ mM}}{10 \text{ mM}}\right) - \left(1 \times \frac{23 \text{ kcal}}{\text{V mole}} \times -0.06 \text{ V}\right)$$

$$\Delta G_{out} = 3.0 \text{ kcal/mole } Na^+$$

$$\Delta G_{out} = 9.0 \text{ kcal/3 mole } Na^+$$

The free-energy change for transporting K^+ into the cell is

$$\Delta G_{in} = -2.3\ RT \log_{10} \frac{C_o}{C_i} + zFV$$

Substituting (with 2.3 RT = 1.41 kcal/mole)

$$\Delta G_{\text{in}} = -\left(1.41\ \frac{\text{kcal}}{\text{mole}} \times \log_{10} \frac{5\ \text{mM}}{140\ \text{mM}}\right) + \left(1 \times \frac{23\ \text{kcal}}{\text{V mole}} \times -0.06\ \text{V}\right)$$

$$\Delta G_{\text{in}} = 0.66\ \text{kcal/mole K}^+$$

$$\Delta G_{\text{in}} = 1.3\ \text{kcal/2 mole K}^+$$

The overall free-energy change for the Na^+-K^+ pump is

$$\Delta G = \Delta G_{\text{out}} + \Delta G_{\text{in}}$$

$$\Delta G = 9.0\ \text{kcal/3 mole Na}^+ + 1.3\ \text{kcal/2 mole K}^+$$

$$\Delta G = 10.3\ \text{kcal/ (3 mole Na}^+ \text{ and 2 mole K}^+)$$

D. Since the hydrolysis of ATP provides 12 kcal/mole and the pump requires 10.3 kcal to transport 3 Na^+ out and 2 K^+ in, the efficiency of the Na^+-K^+ pump is

$$\text{eff} = \frac{10.3}{12.0}$$

$$= 86\%$$

Even with this remarkable efficiency the Na^+-K^+ pump typically accounts for a third of a mammalian cell's energy requirements and thus, presumably, a corresponding fraction of a mammal's total caloric intake.

6–24

A. The expected membrane potential due to differences in K^+ concentration across the resting membrane is

$$V = 58\ \text{mV} \times \log_{10} \frac{C_o}{C_i}$$

$$V = 58\ \text{mV} \times \log_{10} \frac{9\ \text{mM}}{344\ \text{mM}}$$

$$V = -92\ \text{mV}$$

For Na^+, the equivalent calculation gives a value of +48 mV.

The assumption that the membrane potential is due solely to K^+ leads to a value near that of the resting potential. The assumption that the membrane potential is due solely to Na^+ leads to a value near that of the action potential.

These assumptions approximate the resting potential and action potential because K^+ *is* primarily responsible for the resting potential and Na^+ *is* responsible for the action potential. A resting membrane is 100-fold more permeable to K^+ than it is to Na^+ because of the presence of K^+ leak channels. The leak channel allows K^+ to leave the cell until the membrane potential rises sufficiently to oppose the K^+ concentration gradient. The theoretical maximum gradient (based on calculations like those above) is lowered somewhat by the entrance of Na^+, which carries positive charge into the cell (compensating for the positive charges on the exiting K^+). Were it not for the Na^+-K^+ pump, which continually removes Na^+, the resting membrane potential would be dissipated completely.

The action potential is due to a different channel, a voltage-gated Na^+ channel. These channels open when the membrane is stimulated, allowing Na^+ ions to enter the cell. The magnitude of the resulting membrane potential is limited by the difference in the Na^+ concentrations across the membrane. The influx of Na^+ reverses the membrane potential locally, which opens adjacent Na^+ channels and ultimately causes an action potential to propagate away from the site of original stimulation.

B. The substitution of choline chloride for sodium chloride eliminates the action potential, as expected, since the action potential is due to specific Na^+ channels. As illustrated in the calculation above, the difference in concentrations of Na^+ across a membrane determine the magnitude of the action potential that results from Na^+ influx. Thus, if the Na^+ concentration outside the cell were reduced to half the normal value, the calculated membrane potential would be reduced to half the value calculated above. Measurements of the action potential for various mixtures of choline chloride and sodium chloride match these expectations.

Reference: Hille, B. Ionic Channels of Excitable Membranes, pp. 23–57. Sunderland, Mass.: Sinauer Associates, 1984.

***6–25** **Reference:** Hille, B. Ionic Channels of Excitable Membranes, pp. 1–19. Sunderland, Mass.: Sinauer Associates, 1984.

6–26

A. The resting potential in normal seawater is

$$V = 58 \text{ mV} \times \log_{10} \frac{9 \text{ mM}}{344 \text{ mM}} = -92 \text{ mV}$$

whereas the resting potential in seawater that is 60 mM KCl is

$$V = 58 \text{ mV} \times \log_{10} \frac{60 \text{ mM}}{344 \text{ mM}} = -44 \text{ mV}$$

Thus, the magnitude of the resting potential decreases by a factor of about 2.

B. The lack of activation in the absence of calcium suggests that activation requires an influx of Ca^{2+} into the cell from the extracellular fluid. The change in membrane potential in response to increased KCl opens a voltage-gated Ca^{2+} channel in the plasma membrane. The influx of calcium then initiates the other intracellular changes.

C. As you might expect from the answer to part B, addition of A23187 activates intracellular changes in the egg in regular seawater but not in calcium-free seawater.

Not all eggs are like clam eggs, although many can be activated by some manipulation of their ionic environment. Thus, the sperm does more than just provide DNA. In case you were wondering, eggs activated by ionic changes rather than by sperm do not develop into embryos, although they often go through some abortive cell division cycles.

***6–27** **Reference:** Hille, B. Ionic Channels of Excitable Membranes, pp. 205–209. Sunderland, Mass.: Sinauer Associates, 1984.

Membrane Transport of Macromolecules and Particles: Exocytosis and Endocytosis

6–28

A. exocytosis
B. endocytosis
C. histamine, mast
D. pinocytosis, phagocytosis
E. lysosomes, endosomes
F. coated pits
G. clathrin, triskelion
H. receptor-mediated endocytosis, fluid-phase endocytosis
I. low-density lipoproteins
J. endosomal, peripheral endosomes, perinuclear (internal) endosomes
K. transferrin
L. epidermal growth factor
M. down regulation
N. transcytosis
O. membrane flow, capping
P. macrophages, neutrophils

Q. phagocytosis, phagosomes, phagolysosomes
R. membrane fusion, fusogenic

6–29

A. True
B. False. The difference between the triggered and constitutive pathways of secretion lies in the conditional block to exocytosis of vesicles on the triggered pathway; vesicles on the constitutive pathway exocytose without hindrance.
C. True
D. True
E. True
F. True
G. False. Sorting occurs in the acidic environment of endosomes, not lysosomes.
H. False. Acidification of endosomes is driven by an ATP-dependent H^+ pump, called the vacuolar H^+ ATPase.
I. False. Transferrin carries iron into cells. Ferritin binds iron and stores it in the cytosol.
J. False. Transferrin receptors escape destruction by avoiding the lysosomal compartment altogether; they continually recycle from endosomes back to the surface to pick up more iron.
K. True
L. True
M. True
N. True
O. True

6–30

A. Vesicles on the endocytic pathway will be labeled with colloidal gold; vesicles on the exocytic pathway will be labeled with ferritin.
B. Clathrin-coated vesicles are enzymatically uncoated within a few seconds after they pinch off from the plasma membrane, so some will be caught with their coats off while others will still have their coats on.

6–31

A. At 0°C endocytosis is blocked; therefore, the labeled transferrin receptors are trapped on the cell surface and are accessible to trypsin treatment. The majority of the receptor in intact cells is not sensitive to trypsin because it is inside the cell (presumably in endosomes) and, therefore, is not accessible to the trypsin. When cells are incubated at 37°C the labeled receptors are endocytosed and cycle through the endosomal compartment of the cell, thereby becoming inaccessible to trypsin.
B. Both trypsin treatment and antibody binding indicate that 30% of the total transferrin receptor is on the cell surface. When the transferrin receptors are allowed to recycle by incubation at 37°C, 30% is accessible to trypsin treatment of intact cells; therefore, 30% is on the surface. Similarly, antibody binds to 30% of the total receptor in the absence of detergent (0.54%/1.76% = 30%). Since recycling of transferrin receptors is very fast (see Problem 6–32), this distribution between the surface and internal compartments is the equilibrium distribution for transferrin receptors.

Reference: Bleil, J.D.; Bretscher, M.S. Transferrin receptor and its recycling in HeLa cells. *EMBO J.* 1:351–355, 1982.

***6–32** **Reference:** Bleil, J.D.; Bretscher, M.S. Transferrin receptor and its recycling in HeLa cells. *EMBO J.* 1:351–355, 1982.

6–33

A. Binding of LDL by normal cells and JD's cells reaches a plateau because there are a limited number of LDL receptors per cell and they become saturated at high levels of LDL. The slope of the binding curve gives a measure of the binding affinity and the plateau gives a measure of the total number of binding sites (about 20,000 to 50,000, though you could not calculate this from the data shown here). JD has slightly fewer receptors on his cells, but they have an affinity similar to the normal cells.

Cells from patient FH bind essentially no LDL even at saturating external LDL levels. Either these cells completely lack the LDL receptor or the receptor is defective, so that its affinity for LDL is drastically reduced. It could also be that the cells do contain receptors, but for some reason they fail to appear on the surface of the cell.

B. Neither of the hypercholesterolemic patients' cells take up any LDL. Lack of entry is readily explained for patient FH because no LDL bound to the cells: no receptor, no uptake. This result indicates that the receptor is crucial for LDL-contained cholesterol to enter cells. Since LDL is not taken up by JD's cells, his LDL receptors must also be defective, but in a different way than FH's LDL receptors. JD's cells bind LDL with the same affinity as normal and almost to the same level. Although his receptors are normal as far as LDL binding is concerned, the bound LDL does not get in. Thus, mere possession of a receptor on the cell surface is no guarantee of entry.

C. LDL must enter cells in order for the contained cholesterol esters to be released and hydrolyzed to cholesterol, which causes inhibition of cholesterol synthesis. In a normal person, LDL enters the cells and inhibits cholesterol synthesis in the normal way. In the affected patients, LDL does not enter the cells and, therefore, does not inhibit cholesterol synthesis.

D. If the defects in the hypercholesterolemic patients are due to defects in their LDL receptors, then free cholesterol should inhibit cholesterol synthesis in their cells as well as in normal cells. Free cholesterol does inhibit cholesterol synthesis in all these cells, strongly supporting the idea that the defects in the patients are due solely to problems with their LDL receptors.

Reference: Brown, M.S.; Goldstein, J.L. Receptor-mediated endocytosis: insights from the lipoprotein receptor system. *Proc. Natl. Acad. Sci. USA* 76:3330–3337, 1979.

***6–34** **Reference:** Brown, M.S.; Goldstein, J.L. Receptor-mediated endocytosis: insights from the lipoprotein receptor system. *Proc. Natl. Acad. Sci. USA* 76:3330–3337, 1979.

6–35

A. HRP does not bind to a specific cellular receptor and is taken up only by fluid-phase endocytosis. Since endocytosis is a continuous (constitutive) process, HRP gets taken up steadily and its uptake does not saturate. By contrast, EGF binds to a specific EGF receptor and is internalized by receptor-mediated endocytosis. The limit to the amount of EGF that gets taken up is set by the number of EGF receptors on the cells; when the receptors are saturated, no further increase in uptake occurs (except at enormously higher concentrations, where fluid-phase endocytosis becomes significant).

B. At saturation there are 4 pmol of EGF bound per 10^6 cells. This binding represents

$$\text{EGF bound} = \frac{4 \times 10^{-12}\ \text{mole EGF}}{10^6\ \text{cells}} \times \frac{6 \times 10^{23}\ \text{molecules}}{\text{mole}}$$
$$= 2.4 \times 10^6\ \text{EGF molecules/cell}$$

This number of receptors is about 10 times more than a typical cell would have. The cell line used for these studies was selected for its high EGF receptor content, which may in part account for its cancerous nature.

C. An endocytic vesicle 20 nm (2×10^{-6} cm) in radius contains 3.3×10^{-17} ml of fluid.

$$\begin{aligned} \text{vesicle vol} &= \tfrac{4}{3}\pi r^3 \\ &= \tfrac{4}{3} \times 3.14 \times (2 \times 10^{-6}\ \text{cm})^3 \\ &= 3.3 \times 10^{-17}\ \text{cm}^3 \\ &= 3.3 \times 10^{-17}\ \text{ml/vesicle} \end{aligned}$$

The solution contains 1.5×10^{16} molecules/ml of HRP.

$$\text{HRP} = \frac{1 \text{ mg HRP}}{\text{ml}} \times \frac{\text{mmol}}{40{,}000 \text{ mg}} \times \frac{6.0 \times 10^{20} \text{ molecules}}{\text{mmol}}$$
$$= 1.5 \times 10^{16} \text{ molecules/ml}$$

Hence each vesicle contains 0.5 molecule of HRP.

$$\text{HRP} = \frac{1.5 \times 10^{16} \text{ molecules}}{\text{ml}} \times \frac{3.3 \times 10^{-17} \text{ ml}}{\text{vesicle}}$$
$$= 0.5 \text{ molecule/vesicle}$$

Since only half the vesicles contain HRP when the concentration is 1 mg/ml, it is not surprising that very few vesicles stained positively at a fiftyfold lower concentration of HRP.

D. These calculations, as alluded to by the authors, make the point that by having tight-binding specific receptors on the cell surface, cells can take up molecules from their surroundings at a much higher rate than they could simply by taking in fluid. Fishing provides an analogy. You could fish by taking random net-fulls from a stream, and occasionally you might catch a fish. But if you put bait where you cast your net, you increase your chances of success enormously. Each time a molecule of EGF hits a receptor, it sticks and subsequently makes its way to a coated pit to be internalized. If the EGF were simply trapped like HRP, its rate of uptake would be infinitesimal at the usual *in vivo* concentrations.

Reference: Haigler, H.T.; McKanna, J.A.; Cohen, S. Rapid stimulation of pinocytosis in human A-431 carcinoma cells by epidermal growth factor. *J. Cell Biol.* 83:82–90, 1979.

Energy Conversion: Mitochondria and Chloroplasts

The Mitochondrion

7–1

A. matrix space, intermembrane space
B. outer
C. respiratory chain (electron-transport chain), inner
D. cristae
E. triacylglycerols (triglycerides)
F. glycogen
G. citric acid cycle (tricarboxylic acid cycle or Krebs cycle)
H. oxidative phosphorylation
I. electrochemical proton gradient
J. proton-motive
K. ATP synthetase

7–2

A. False. The intermembrane space is chemically equivalent to the cytosol with respect to small molecules because the outer mitochondrial membrane contains many copies of a transport protein that forms large aqueous channels. However, the composition of the matrix space is much more specialized because the inner mitochondrial membrane contains transport proteins that only allow passage of a restricted set of small molecules.
B. True
C. False. Animal cells store fuel in the form of fats (from fatty acids) and glycogen (from glucose).
D. True
E. False. During electron transport protons are pumped out of the mitochondrial matrix into the intermembrane space.
F. True
G. True
H. False. ATP synthetase is oriented in the inner membrane so that ATP is synthesized in the matrix space. It is transported out of the matrix by the ADP-ATP antiporter.
I. False. Favored reactions have a negative ΔG; that is, they proceed with a *decrease* in free energy.
J. True

***7–3**

7–4

A. The complete oxidation of citrate to CO_2 and H_2O occurs according to the balanced chemical reaction shown below.

$$C_6H_8O_7 + 4.5O_2 \rightarrow 6CO_2 + 4H_2O$$

Thus each molecule of citrate would require 4.5 molecules of oxygen for its complete oxidation.

The results in Table 7–1 were surprising to Krebs and others at the time because much more oxygen is consumed (40 mmol) than could be accounted for by oxidation of citrate itself. Only 13.5 mmol of oxygen would

*Problems with an asterisk (*) are answered in the Instructor's Manual.

be required to oxidize 3 mmol of citrate completely (3 × 4.5). This calculation shows that citrate is acting catalytically in the oxidation of carbohydrates (which in these experiments were endogenous in the minced pigeon breasts). Although others were aware of the catalytic nature of other intermediates, Krebs was the first person to complete the circle of chemical reactions that constitute the citric acid cycle.

Krebs's experimental rationale is clearly laid out in the paper: "Since citric acid reacts catalytically in the tissue, it is probable that it is removed by a primary reaction but regenerated by a subsequent reaction. In the balance sheet no citrate disappears and no intermediate products accumulate. The first object of the study of intermediates is therefore to find conditions under which citrate disappears in the balance sheet."

B. The consumption of oxygen is low in the presence of the metabolic poisons because citrate is prevented from acting catalytically. The balanced equations for the conversion of citrate to α-ketoglutarate and succinate show that the amount of oxygen consumed is approximately what is expected.

For citrate conversion to α-ketoglutarate, half a molecule of oxygen is consumed.

$$C_6H_8O_7 + 0.5O_2 \rightarrow C_5H_6O_5 + CO_2 + H_2O$$

For citrate conversion to succinate, one molecule of oxygen is consumed.

$$C_6H_8O_7 + O_2 \rightarrow C_4H_6O_4 + 2CO_2 + H_2O$$

Thus the observed stoichiometry of oxygen consumption matches the expectations.

C. The absence of oxygen is crucial for demonstrating an accumulation of citrate from an intermediate in the cycle. In the presence of oxygen, citrate acts catalytically—is consumed and then regenerated—so that it does not accumulate no matter what intermediate is added. In the absence of oxygen, however, the conversion of citrate to α-ketoglutarate is blocked, since that conversion requires oxygen. Under these conditions citrate will accumulate if an appropriate intermediate is present. Of all the intermediates, only conversion of oxaloacetate to citrate does not require oxygen. The immediate precursor of oxaloacetate is malate. Since the conversion of malate to citrate requires oxygen, all other intermediates also must require oxygen to be converted to citrate. (The requirement for oxygen is indirect and is mediated through the cofactors, NAD^+ and FAD; they accept electrons from the substrates and transfer them to the electron-transport chain and ultimately to oxygen.)

This reasoning might lead you to expect a quantitative conversion of oxaloacetate to citrate. However, in Krebs's experiments 300 μmol of oxaloacetate were added but only 13 μmol of citrate accumulated. What Krebs did not know was that citrate is generated by addition of acetyl CoA (undiscovered at the time) to oxaloacetate. The generation of acetyl CoA from its immediate precursor, pyruvate, is dependent on oxygen.

D. *E. coli* and yeast do indeed use the citric acid cycle. Krebs got this point wrong because he did not realize (nor did anyone for a long time) that citrate cannot get into these cells. Therefore, when he added citrate to intact *E. coli* and yeast, he found no stimulation of oxygen consumption. Passage of citrate across a membrane requires a membrane transport system, which is present in mitochondria but is not present in yeast and *E. coli*.

Reference: Krebs, H.A.; Johnson, W.A. The role of citric acid in intermediate metabolism in animal tissues. *Enzymologia* 4:148–156, 1937.

7–5

A. When the concentrations of the reactants and products are all 1 M, the reaction is at standard conditions and ΔG equals ΔG^o, which is −7.3 kcal/mole.

$$\Delta G = \Delta G^o + 2.3\,RT \log_{10} \frac{[ADP][P_i]}{[ATP]}$$

$$= -7.3 \text{ kcal/mole} + 2.3\ (0.00198 \text{ kcal/°K mole})(310°\text{K}) \log_{10} \frac{1 \times 1}{1}$$

Since the $\log_{10}$ of 1 is 0,

$$\Delta G = -7.3 \text{ kcal/mole}$$

When the concentrations of the reactants and products are all 1 mM, ΔG equals -11.5 kcal/mole.

$$\Delta G = -7.3 \text{ kcal/mole} + (1.4 \text{ kcal/mole}) \log_{10} \frac{10^{-3} \times 10^{-3}}{10^{-3}}$$

$$= -7.3 \text{ kcal/mole} + (1.4 \text{ kcal/mole})(-3)$$

$$= -7.3 \text{ kcal/mole} - 4.2 \text{ kcal/mole}$$

$$\Delta G = -11.5 \text{ kcal/mole}$$

B. At the given concentrations of ATP, ADP, and P_i, the ΔG for ATP hydrolysis is -11.1 kcal/mole.

$$\Delta G = -7.3 \text{ kcal/mole} + (1.4 \text{ kcal/mole}) \log_{10} \frac{(0.001)(0.010)}{(0.005)}$$

$$= -7.3 \text{ kcal/mole} + (1.4 \text{ kcal/mole})(-2.7)$$

$$= -7.3 \text{ kcal/mole} - 3.8 \text{ kcal/mole}$$

$$\Delta G = -11.1 \text{ kcal/mole}$$

C. At equilibrium ΔG is 0. At equilibrium there is no longer any tendency for a reaction to proceed. If $[P_i]$ is 10 mM at equilibrium, then the ratio of [ATP] to [ADP] will be 6.1×10^{-8}.

$$0 = -7.3 \text{ kcal/mole} + (1.4 \text{ kcal/mole}) \log_{10} \frac{[\text{ADP}] \times (0.01)}{[\text{ATP}]}$$

$$7.3 \text{ kcal/mole} = (1.4 \text{ kcal/mole})(\log_{10} 0.01 + \log_{10} [\text{ADP}]/[\text{ATP}])$$

$$= (-2)(1.4 \text{ kcal/mole}) + (1.4 \text{ kcal/mole}) \log_{10} [\text{ADP}]/[\text{ATP}]$$

$$\log_{10} [\text{ADP}]/[\text{ATP}] = \frac{10.1 \text{ kcal/mole}}{1.4 \text{ kcal/mole}}$$

$$= 7.2$$

$$\log_{10} [\text{ATP}]/[\text{ADP}] = -7.2$$

$$[\text{ATP}]/[\text{ADP}] = 6.1 \times 10^{-8}$$

D. At a constant $[P_i]$, every tenfold change in the ratio of [ATP] to [ADP] will alter ΔG by 1.4 kcal/mole. As shown below, a tenfold increase in [ATP]/[ADP] will decrease ΔG by 1.4 kcal/mole.

$$\Delta G = \Delta G^o + 1.4 \text{ kcal/mole} \log_{10} \frac{[\text{ADP}][P_i]}{[\text{ATP}]}$$

$$= \Delta G^o + 1.4 \text{ kcal/mole} \log_{10} [P_i] + 1.4 \text{ kcal/mole} \log_{10} \frac{[\text{ADP}]}{[\text{ATP}]}$$

A tenfold increase in [ATP]/[ADP], which is equal to a tenfold decrease in [ADP]/[ATP], causes the $\log_{10}$ of the ratio in the expression above to decrease by -1. Thus each tenfold increase in the ratio causes 1.4 kcal/mole to be subtracted from the right-hand side, thereby decreasing ΔG by 1.4 kcal/mole. A 100-fold increase in the ratio of [ATP]/[ADP] decreases ΔG by 2.8 kcal/mole; a 1000-fold increase in the ratio decreases ΔG by 4.2 kcal/mole.

***7–6**

7–7

A. The ΔG^o for conversion of 3-phosphoglycerate (3PG) to pyruvate (PYR) and phosphate is the sum of ΔG^o values for the individual steps in the reaction.

$$\Delta G^o_{3PG \rightarrow PYR} = \Delta G^o_{3PG \rightarrow PEP} + \Delta G^o_{PEP \rightarrow PYR}$$

$$= 0.4 \text{ kcal/mole} + (-14.8 \text{ kcal/mole})$$

$$\Delta G^o_{3PG \rightarrow PYR} = -14.4 \text{ kcal/mole}$$

B. The ΔG^o for conversion of 3-phosphoglycerate to pyruvate and phosphate is independent of the pathway for the conversion. Thus, the ΔG^o is -14.4 kcal/mole.

The ΔG^o value for conversion of glycerate to pyruvate is obtained by subtracting ΔG^o for 3-phosphoglycerate to glycerate (GLY) from the overall ΔG^o.

$$\begin{aligned} \Delta G^o{}_{GLY\rightarrow PYR} &= \Delta G^o{}_{3PG\rightarrow PYR} - \Delta G^o{}_{3PG\rightarrow GLY} \\ &= -14.4 \text{ kcal/mole} - (-3.3 \text{ kcal/mole}) \\ \Delta G^o{}_{GLY\rightarrow PYR} &= -11.1 \text{ kcal/mole} \end{aligned}$$

C. The analysis above indicates that a very large standard free-energy change occurs between glycerate and pyruvate. Removal of water ($\Delta G^o = -0.5$ kcal/mole) does not account for very much of this free-energy change. Thus it appears that the conversion of enolpyruvate to pyruvate is accompanied by a large standard free-energy change of around -10.6 kcal/mole. This reasoning suggests that the majority of the standard free-energy change associated with conversion of phosphoenolpyruvate to pyruvate (-10.6 kcal/mole out of -14.8 kcal/mole) comes from the conversion of enolpyruvate to pyruvate and not from the hydrolysis of the phosphate bond.

In fact, the standard free-energy change for phosphoenolpyruvate to pyruvate (-14.8 kcal/mole) is close to the sum of the enolpyruvate to pyruvate step (about -11 kcal/mole) and a normal standard free-energy change for hydrolysis of a simple phosphate ester bond (about -3.0 kcal/mole). Thus, the phosphate bond in phosphoenolpyruvate is a high-energy bond because its hydrolysis is linked to the very favorable conversion of enolpyruvate to pyruvate.

D. The ΔG^o for the linked conversion of phosphoenolpyruvate to pyruvate and of ADP to ATP is -7.5 kcal/mole. The ΔG^o for the linked reaction can be obtained by adding together the ΔG^o values for the individual reactions. The individual reactions are

$$\begin{array}{lll} & \text{phosphoenolpyruvate} \rightarrow \text{pyruvate} + P_i & \Delta G^o = -14.8 \text{ kcal/mole} \\ & \text{ADP} + P_i \rightarrow \text{ATP} & \Delta G^o = 7.3 \text{ kcal/mole} \\ \hline \text{NET:} & \text{PEP} + \text{ADP} \rightarrow \text{PYR} + \text{ATP} & \end{array}$$

$$\begin{aligned} \Delta G^o{}_{PEP+ADP\rightarrow PYR+ATP} &= \Delta G^o{}_{PEP\rightarrow PYR} + \Delta G^o{}_{ADP\rightarrow ATP} \\ &= -14.8 \text{ kcal/mole} + 7.3 \text{ kcal/mole} \\ \Delta G^o{}_{PEP+ADP\rightarrow PYR+ATP} &= -7.5 \text{ kcal/mole} \end{aligned}$$

Reference: Lipmann, F. Metabolic generation and utilization of phosphate bond energy. *Adv. Enzymol.* 1:99–162, 1941.

***7–8** **References:** Nicholls, D.G. Bioenergetics, pp. 159–164. London: Academic Press, 1982. Tzagoloff, A. Mitochondria, pp. 212–213. New York: Plenum Press, 1982.

The Respiratory Chain and ATP Synthetase

7–9

A. ATP synthetase
B. cytochromes
C. iron-sulfur center
D. quinone
E. respiratory enzyme complexes
F. NADH dehydrogenase complex
G. b-c_1 complex
H. cytochrome oxidase complex
I. conjugate redox pairs
J. redox potential (oxidation-reduction potential)
K. respiratory control

7–10

A. True

B. True

C. False. ATP synthetase is a reversible enzyme complex. Its direction of action depends on the balance between the steepness of the electrochemical proton gradient and the local ΔG for ATP hydrolysis.

D. True. (Because submitochondrial particles are inside-out, protons are pumped into the vesicle causing the medium to become more basic.)

E. False. Although most proteins in the respiratory chain use iron atoms as electron carriers, one uses a flavin molecule and two use copper atoms as electron carriers.

F. True

G. False. The three respiratory enzyme complexes appear to exist as independent entities in the plane of the inner membrane and the ordered transfers of electrons is due entirely to the specificity of the functional interactions between the components of the chain.

H. True

I. True

J. False. Lipophilic weak acids act as uncoupling agents that dissipate the proton-motive force and stop ATP synthesis; however, they increase the flow of electrons through the respiratory chain by eliminating the respiratory control imposed by the electrochemical proton gradient.

K. True

L. True

M. True

7–11

A. This experiment distinguishes very nicely between mechanisms involving a one phosphate transfer and those involving two phosphate transfers. Since each phosphate transfer results in inversion of the configuration around the phosphate atom, a one-transfer mechanism results in inversion and a two-transfer mechanism results in retention (inversion followed by inversion gives retention). As illustrated in Figure 7–25, direct attack of water on ATP to generate ADP and phosphate is a one-step mechanism and therefore produces inversion of configuration. Hydrolysis of ATP via an intermediate phosphorylated substance is a two-step mechanism and therefore the configuration is retained (Figure 7–25). (Note that the result does not, however, distinguish between a one-step mechanism and a mechanism involving three—or any odd number of—phosphate transfers.)

B. Inversion of configuration during the hydrolysis of ATP by ATP synthetase indicates that the hydrolysis reaction does not occur through a two-transfer mechanism and therefore argues against the involvement of a single phosphorylated intermediate. Thus, hydrolysis of ATP by ATP synthetase probably involves the direct attack of H_2O on ATP. If hydrolysis of ATP by ATP synthetase is the reverse of the synthetic reaction (as it is thought to be), then synthesis of ATP from ADP and phosphate also occurs directly and not through a phosphorylated intermediate. (A mechanism involving three phosphate transfers is consistent with this analysis, but it is thought to be much less likely.)

Reference: Webb, M.R.; Grubmeyer, C.; Penefsky, H.S.; Trentham, D.R. The stereochemical course of phosphoric residue transfer catalyzed by beef heart mitochondrial ATPase. *J. Biol. Chem.* 255:11637–11639, 1980.

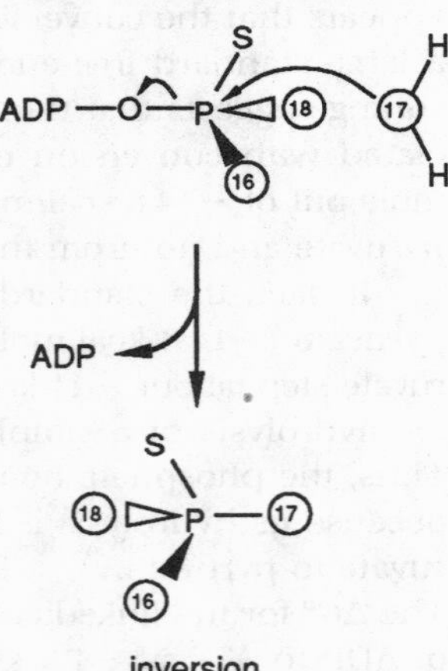

Figure 7–25 Stereochemical consequences of ATP hydrolysis by one-step (A) and two-step (B) mechanisms (Answer 7–11).

7–12

A. Oxygen accepts electrons from the electron-transport chain and is reduced to H_2O. Therefore, in the presence of oxygen the cytochromes would be drained of their electrons, that is, oxidized. Since the absorption bands do not show up in the presence of oxygen, the oxidized forms must not absorb light. The reduced forms of the cytochromes absorb light and are responsible for the characteristic absorption patterns. In the absence of oxygen the cytochromes pick up electrons from substrates (become reduced) but cannot get rid of them by transfer to oxygen. In the presence of oxygen, the electrons are transferred efficiently, leaving the cytochromes in their electron-deficient or oxidized state.

B. Keilin's observations indicate that the order of electron flow through the cytochromes is

$$\begin{matrix}\text{reduced} \\ \text{substrates}\end{matrix} \rightarrow \text{cytochrome } b \rightarrow \text{cytochrome } c \rightarrow \text{cytochrome } a \rightarrow O_2$$

This order can be deduced from Keilin's results. Since the bands become visible in the absence of oxygen, they represent the reduced (electron-rich) forms of the cytochromes. When oxygen is added, they are all converted to the oxidized (electron-poor) form. When cyanide is added, all the cytochromes are reduced, indicating that cyanide blocks the flow of electrons from the cytochromes to oxygen; that is, all the cytochromes are "upstream" of oxygen (in the sense of electron flow).

When urethane is added, cytochrome *b* remains reduced but cytochromes *a* and *c* become oxidized. Thus, urethane interrupts the flow of electrons from cytochrome *b* to cytochromes *a* and *c*, indicating that cytochrome *b* is "upstream" of cytochromes *a* and *c*.

These results indicate that either cytochrome *a* or *c* transfers electrons to oxygen. The inability of oxygen to oxidize a preparation of cytochrome *c* suggests, by elimination, that cytochrome *a* is responsible for transfer of electrons to oxygen. This ordering of cytochromes *a* and *c* is weak since it is based on a negative result (which could have other interpretations). Keilin himself confirmed this order by observing subtle spectral shifts in the cytochrome *a* band in the presence of cyanide under reducing conditions; he named the active component cytochrome a_3. We now know that cytochrome *a* is a large complex with several redox centers, one of which reacts with molecular oxygen.

C. The rapid oxidation of glucose to CO_2 prevents the disappearance of the absorption bands by providing a source of reduced substrates (ultimately NADH and $FADH_2$) that transfer electrons into the electron transport chain faster than oxygen can remove them. Under these conditions the cytochromes remain reduced (electron rich) and therefore continue to absorb light.

Reference: Keilin, D. The History of Cell Respiration and Cytochrome. Cambridge, U.K.: Cambridge University Press, 1966.

***7–13** **References:** Smith, H.T.; Ahmed, A.J.; Millet, F. Electrostatic interaction of cytochrome *c* with cytochrome c_1 and cytochrome oxidase. *J. Biol. Chem.* 256:4984–4990, 1981.

Capaldi, R.A.; Darley-Usmar, V.; Fuller, S.; Millet, F. Structural and functional features of the interaction of cytochrome *c* with complex III and cytochrome *c* oxidase. *FEBS Letters* 138:1–7, 1982.

7–14

A. The rate of oxygen consumption is determined by the rate of electron transport down the respiratory chain. Electron transport generates an electrochemical proton gradient, which opposes the flow of electrons. In the complete absence of a way to dissipate the gradient, the flow of electrons ultimately would stop when the electron pressure balances the opposing electrochemical proton gradient. In the experiment in Figure 7–9, the electrochemical proton gradient is dissipated at a slow background rate, which accounts for the slow background rate of oxygen consumption. Addition of ADP and its subsequent conversion to ATP allows protons to flow back into the mitochondria, dramatically reducing the electrochemical proton gradient and permitting the rapid transport of electrons to oxygen. The increased rate of electron transport produces an increased rate of oxygen consumption. When all the ADP is converted to ATP, proton flow again slows to the background rate, and the increased electrochemical proton gradient once again reduces the flow of electrons.

B. The slow background rate of oxygen consumption by mitochondria in the absence of added ADP indicates that electrons continue to flow down the electron-transport chain to oxygen in the absence of ATP synthesis. Such a flow can continue only if the electrochemical proton gradient is slowly being dissipated. If the mitochondrial inner membrane was completely impermeable to protons, the rate of oxygen consumption would drop to zero when proton pumping due to electron transport was balanced by the back pressure of the electrochemical proton gradient. Thus, the protons must be crossing the membrane in the absence of ATP synthesis.

Several processes other than ATP synthesis from added ADP might account for the slow passage of protons across the membrane and the slow background rate of oxygen consumption. (1) The mitochondrial inner membrane is not completely impermeable to protons, which can slowly cross the membrane even in the absence of ATP synthesis. (2) The internal mitochondrial supply of ATP may be hydrolyzed to ADP and then reconverted to ATP using the proton-motive force. (3) If some mitochondria in the preparation are damaged so that their inner membranes are not intact, they will transport electrons to oxygen continuously because there will be no electrochemical proton gradient to oppose electron flow.

C. Since each pair of electrons that flows down the respiratory chain from NADH to oxygen reduces one oxygen atom, the $P/2e^-$ ratio is equivalent to the P/O ratio. The P/O ratio, as calculated below, is between 2.5 and 2.8 molecules of ATP per O atom. Uncertainty in the P/O ($P/2e^-$ ratio) arises from the uncertainty in how much oxygen is consumed during conversion of 500 nmol ADP to ATP. If oxygen consumption is calculated as the difference between the dashed lines in Figure 7–9, which is 100 nmol O_2, then the P/O ratio is 500 nmol ATP/ 200 nmol O, which is 2.5. On the other hand, if oxygen consumption is calculated as the difference between the dotted lines in Figure 7–9, which is 90 nmol O_2, then the P/O ratio is 500 nmol ATP/ 180 nmol O, which is 2.8. The latter calculation makes the implicit assumption that the background rate of oxygen consumption continues during the conversion of ADP to ATP, which is a perfectly reasonable assumption. It turns out, however, that the natural slow flow of protons across intact inner membranes is quite sensitive to the size of the electrochemical proton gradient. The slight decline in the proton-motive force during ATP synthesis may reduce the leakage to nearly zero, in which case the larger value for oxygen consumption may be the more valid one (giving a P/O ratio of 2.5).

D. Several processes in these kinds of experiment, in addition to ATP synthesis, are driven by the electrochemical proton gradient. The uptake of substrate (β-hydroxybutyrate) into mitochondria may require symport with protons. The import of phosphate into mitochondria also requires symport with a proton. Finally, the exchange of internal ATP for external ADP is driven by the membrane potential, which is one component of the electrochemical proton gradient. Given that several processes are driven by the electrochemical proton gradient, it is not surprising that the P/O ratio is not an integer. Before the chemiosmotic theory, when chemical coupling hypotheses were fashionable, integral values were expected and values of 2.5 or 2.8 were assumed to "really" mean 3.

Reference: Nicholls, D.G. Bioenergetics. London: Academic Press, 1982.

***7–15** **Reference:** Nicholls, D. G. Bioenergetics, pp. 86, 110. London: Academic Press, 1982.

***7–16** **Reference:** Blaut, M.; Gottschalk, G. Evidence for a chemiosmotic mechanism of ATP synthesis in methanogenic bacteria. *Trends Biochem. Sci.* 10:486–489, 1985.

7–17

A. Each of the observations with ionophores is consistent with the idea that the movement of protons down the electrochemical proton gradient powers the flagella, as explained below for each observation.

1. During oxidation of glucose, bacteria pump protons out of the cell, establishing an electrochemical proton gradient, which is the sum of a proton gradient and a membrane potential. Addition of FCCP makes the membranes permeable to protons, thereby collapsing both the proton gra-

dient and the membrane potential. In the absence of an electrochemical proton gradient to drive protons across the membrane, the flagellar motor cannot function.

2. In a medium containing K^+, valinomycin collapses the membrane potential specifically by allowing an influx of K^+ to balance the efflux of protons. Under these circumstances it is entirely the proton gradient (which is larger than usual because it is not opposed by the membrane potential) that drives the proton flux through the flagellar motor. The ability of bacteria to swim normally in the presence of the proton gradient alone is strong evidence that the flagellar motor is proton-powered.

3. In the absence of glucose (or any other substrate) for oxidation, there is no electrochemical proton gradient. In the presence of external K^+, valinomycin facilitates a flow of K^+ into the cell; this results in a membrane potential that is positive inside. Although there are protons available in the medium (from H_2O), this membrane potential is in the wrong orientation to drive the protons into the cell. As a result, the bacteria remain motionless.

4. In the absence of glucose, there is no electrochemical proton gradient. In the absence of external K^+ (that is when Na^+ is in the medium), addition of valinomycin allows internal K^+ to move out of the cell (down its concentration gradient), creating a membrane potential that is positive outside. This membrane potential can drive protons into the cell for a while. Each proton that enters the cell lessens the membrane potential until the membrane potential is dissipated, at which point the cells stop swimming.

B. At first glance it seems peculiar that normal bacteria can swim in the absence of oxygen. In the absence of oxygen, there is no electron flow down the electron-transport chain and, therefore, no transport-linked proton translocation across the membrane. What then is the source of protons to power the motor under anaerobic conditions? The mutant strain provides the essential clue. In the absence of the ATP synthetase, bacteria cannot swim, which suggests that the ATP synthetase in some way generates the proton gradient. In normal bacteria in the absence of oxygen, ATP that is generated anaerobically is used to drive the ATP synthetase in *reverse,* causing protons to flow out of the cell. The resulting electrochemical proton gradient drives the protons back through the flagellar motor, allowing the bacteria to swim. The mutant bacteria cannot swim in the absence of glucose because they have no ATP synthetase and, therefore, cannot create an electrochemical gradient in the absence of electron flow.

Reference: Manson, M.D.; Tedesco, P.; Berg, H.C.; Harold, F.M.; van der Drift, C. A protonmotive force drives bacteria flagella. *Proc. Natl. Acad. Sci. USA* 74:3060–3064, 1977.

Chloroplasts and Photosynthesis

7–18

A. stroma
B. thylakoids
C. photosynthetic electron-transfer (light), carbon-fixation (dark)
D. ribulose bisphosphate carboxylase
E. carbon-fixation (Calvin-Benson)
F. sucrose
G. starch
H. C_4, C_3
I. chlorophyll
J. antenna complex, photochemical reaction center
K. noncyclic photophosphorylation
L. Z scheme
M. cyclic photophosphorylation

7–19

A. True
B. False. The formation of O_2 requires light energy directly, whereas the fixation of CO_2 requires light energy only indirectly.
C. True
D. True
E. True
F. True
G. False. When an electron in a chlorophyll molecule is excited, it transfers its energy—not the electron—from one chlorophyll molecule to another by resonance energy transfer.
H. True
I. True
J. False. Each electron that is transferred from H_2O to $NADP^+$ requires two photons, one for each photosystem. Therefore, the reduction of $NADP^+$ to NADPH, which uses two electrons, requires four photons.
K. False. Cyclic photophosphorylation generates only ATP (not NADPH), and the balance between cyclic and noncyclic photophosphorylation is regulated by NADPH (not ATP).
L. True
M. True

7–20 The corn plant (C_4) eventually will kill the geranium (C_3). Because both plants fix CO_2, the concentration in the chamber falls. At low CO_2 concentration, the corn plant has a distinct advantage since the enzyme responsible for its initial carbon fixation has a high affinity for CO_2. By contrast, the geranium depends on ribulose bisphosphate carboxylase, which has a lower affinity for CO_2; furthermore, at low CO_2 concentrations O_2 competes with CO_2 for addition to ribulose 1,5-bisphosphate, ultimately liberating CO_2 in the process known as photorespiration. Not only does the geranium give up CO_2 in an abortive attempt at photosynthesis, it continues to respire (using its mitochondria), thereby providing even more CO_2 for the corn plant. The corn plant continues to fix CO_2 until the geranium wastes away and dies.

Reference: Becker, W.M. The World of the Cell, p. 282. Menlo Park, Calif.: Benjamin-Cummings, 1986.

***7–21**

7–22

A. Starch formation requires light in the cactus and in C_4 plants (as well as C_3 plants). The synthesis of starch requires ATP and NADPH. These compounds are present in cells in only small amounts; they are not stored. During starch synthesis ATP and NADPH must continuously be regenerated in order for synthesis to continue. Regeneration of ATP and NADPH requires the photosynthetic electron-transfer reactions. Energy in sunlight energizes electrons in chlorophyll. Some electrons are passed to $NADP^+$ to generate NADPH; others are transferred along an electron-transport chain, generating an electrochemical proton gradient, which is coupled to ATP production.
B. CO_2 fixation in the cactus is outlined in Figure 7–26. Reactions shown with thick lines occur during the night; reactions shown with thin lines occur during the day. The carbon-fixation reactions in the cactus are essentially the same as those in C_4 plants. The key difference in the metabolic *pathways* of CO_2 fixation is that the cactus uses starch in the CO_2 pumping cycle. However, the common reactions of the pumping cycle are distributed differently in both space and time in C_4 plants and the cactus. In C_4 plants the reactions involve several cell types but occur all at the same time. By contrast, in the cactus they all occur in the same cell but at different times.
C. Starch is not required for CO_2 pumping in C_4 plants because the compounds that constitute the pump are used catalytically. In principle, a few molecules of phosphoenolpyruvate (PEP) could pump an unlimited amount

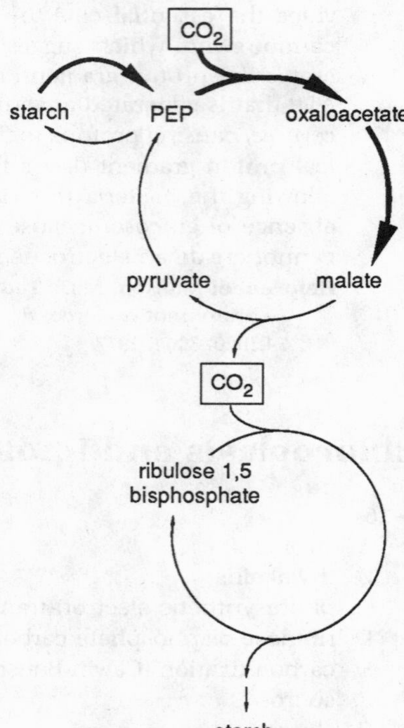

Figure 7–26 CO_2 fixation in the cactus (Answer 7–22). Night reactions are shown as thick lines; day reactions are shown as thin lines. Only the carbon pathways are indicated: the cofactor requirements are not shown.

of CO_2, because PEP is regenerated at the end of each pumping cycle. By contrast, the reactions in the cactus are stoichiometric: each CO_2 molecule that is stored as malate requires one molecule of PEP. Starch in the cactus is used as the source of PEP molecules (via glycolysis): the number of CO_2 molecules that can be fixed is limited by the amount of starch.

D. The principal advantage of this method of CO_2 fixation is that the cactus can seal itself off (close its stomata) during the heat of the day, thereby preventing water loss. Yet it can still provide a rich supply of CO_2 (from stored malate) for sugar synthesis during the day, when the production of ATP and NADPH are maximal due to photosynthetic electron-transfer reactions. At night, when there is less risk of water loss, it can open its stomata and fix CO_2.

Reference: Foyer, C.H. Photosynthesis, pp. 176–195. New York: Wiley, 1984.

***7–23** **Reference:** Curtis, H. Biology, 4th ed., p. 216. New York: Worth, 1983.

7–24 The burst of oxygen production when the illumination is switched to 650 nm suggests that this wavelength stimulates photosystem II, which accepts electrons directly from water and generates oxygen. Similarly, the dip in oxygen production when the illumination is switched to 700 nm suggests that this wavelength stimulates photosystem I, which accepts electrons from the electron-transport chain and, thus, is farther removed from the reactions that generate oxygen. This interpretation is supported by the more detailed analysis of the chromatic transients below.

The chromatic transients result because the two photosystems are out of balance with one another. Each separate wavelength preferentially (but not absolutely) stimulates one of the two photosystems. Thus, when photosystem I is stimulated (by 700-nm light), it pumps electrons out of the electron-transport chain that links the two photosystems, leaving them in a relatively oxidized state, primed to accept electrons from photosystem II. When the light is switched to 650 nm (which stimulates photosystem II), there is an initial rush of electrons (from H_2O) into the cytochrome chain that causes a burst of O_2 evolution. However, the flow of electrons through the cyctochromes is quickly limited by the electrons' ability to be transferred to photosystem I, which is suboptimally stimulated, and O_2 evolution slows.

When the light is switched back to 700 nm, the electron pressure from photosystem II (which is now suboptimally stimulated) is insufficient to push electrons into the relatively reduced (electron-rich) cytochromes. As a result, O_2 evolution is depressed transiently while electrons are bled off from the cytochromes. Once the cytochromes have been partially drained of their electrons, they can accept new electrons from photosystem II, thereby reestablishing the normal level of oxygen production.

References: Emerson, R. *Ann. Rev. Plant Physiol.* 9:1–24, 1958.

Lawlor, D.W. Photosynthesis: Metabolism, Control, and Physiology. New York: Wiley, 1987.

***7–25** **Reference:** Duysens, L.N.M.; Amesz, J.; Kamp, B.M. Two photochemical systems in photosynthesis. *Nature* 190:510–511, 1961.

7–26

A. These results support a gear-wheel connection between the abstraction of electrons from water and their activation in photosystem II reaction centers. The periodicity of O_2 evolution in response to flashes rules out the possibility that four photons must be delivered simultaneously to the reaction center. If four photons were needed simultaneously, then each flash should yield an equal burst of O_2.

The periodicity also argues against cooperation among four reaction centers to produce a molecule of O_2. At saturating light intensities, most of the reaction centers should be stimulated during each flash; if they could cooperate, they would generate O_2 at each flash. Furthermore, the results of the DCMU experiment definitely eliminate the possibility of cooperation. If four reaction centers were required to cooperate, one might expect a fourth-power dependence on the concentration of active centers. However, a thirtyfold reduction in active centers (DCMU inhibited 97% of the active centers) gave only a thirtyfold reduction in O_2 evolution (peaks of oxygen production were 3% of those in the absence of DCMU) instead of the enormous reduction (30^4) expected from a fourth-power dependence.

A periodicity in O_2 evolution is exactly what one would expect from a gear-wheel link between extraction of multiple electrons from water and photon excitation of single electrons in photosystem II reaction centers. Furthermore, each gear wheel must service a single reaction center. If one gear wheel could interact with four reaction centers, for example, then it could donate its four electrons from water during each flash, which would allow it to evolve O_2 during each flash, eliminating the periodicity.

B. The four-flash periodicity in the evolution of O_2 argues strongly that the gear wheel picks up four electrons at a time from two water molecules and passes them on to the photosystem II reaction center one at a time. The timing of the appearance of the first burst of O_2 says something about the dark-adapted state of the gear wheel, namely, that it holds three electrons. The first three flashes transfer those electrons. The gear wheel can then pick up four new electrons from water (in a reaction that depends on light), generating a molecule of oxygen in the process. (Actually, about a quarter of the gear wheels carry four electrons in the dark-adapted state, which is why there is significant oxygen evolution on the fourth flash.)

C. The periodicity is gradually damped out with increasing flash number because the multiple photosystems fall out of phase with one another. During a single flash most of the photosystem reaction centers capture one photon; however, some capture two photons, and some capture no photons. Those reaction centers that capture zero or two photons are out of step with the majority. After several flashes the number of out-of-step reaction centers increases sufficiently to obscure any periodicity. The period of dark adaptation at the beginning of the experiment is required to bring the majority of the reaction centers to the same state so that periodicity can be observed at all.

Reference: Forbush, B.; Kok, B.; McGloin, M. Cooperation of charges in photosynthetic oxygen evolution II. Damping of flash yield, oscillation and deactivation. *Photochem. Photobiol.* 14:307–321, 1971.

***7–27** **Reference:** Jagendorf, A.T.; Uribe, E. ATP formation caused by acid-base transition of spinach chloroplasts. *Proc. Natl. Acad. Sci. USA* 55:170–177, 1966.

7–28

A. The balanced equation for reduction of O_2 by Fe^{2+} is

$$4Fe^{2+} + O_2 + 4H^+ \rightarrow 4Fe^{3+} + 2H_2O$$

The two half-cell reactions are

$$4H^+ + O_2 + 4e^- \rightarrow 2H_2O \qquad E_o = 0.82\ V$$
$$Fe^{3+} + e^- \rightarrow Fe^{2+} \qquad E_o = 0.77\ V$$

In the balanced reaction Fe^{2+} is donating electrons, therefore

$$\Delta E_o = 0.82\ V - 0.77\ V$$
$$\Delta E_o = 0.05\ V$$

If the reaction occurs under standard conditions, $\Delta E = \Delta E_o$.

Using the relationship betwen ΔE and ΔG,

$$\Delta G = -nF\,\Delta E$$
$$= -\ 4 \times 23\ \text{kcal/V mole} \times 0.05\ V$$
$$\Delta G = -\ 4.6\ \text{kcal/mole}$$

or as it is sometimes stated,

$$\Delta G = -\ 1.15\ \text{kcal/mole for each electron}$$

Thus the flow of electrons from Fe^{2+} to O_2 is thermodynamically favorable; the free-energy change for each electron, however, is fairly small. Fortunately, *T. ferrooxidans* does not depend on this redox reaction as a source of energy but rather as a way of detoxifying entering protons and as a source of electrons for reducing $NADP^+$.

B. The balanced reaction for reduction of $NADP^+ + H^+$ by Fe^{2+} is

$$NADP^+ + H^+ + 2Fe^{2+} \rightarrow NADPH + 2Fe^{3+}$$

The two half-cell reactions are

$$NADP^+ + H^+ + 2e^- \rightarrow NADPH \qquad E_o = -0.32\text{ V}$$
$$Fe^{3+} + e^- \rightarrow Fe^{2+} \qquad E_o = 0.77\text{ V}$$

In the balanced reaction Fe^{2+} is donating electrons, therefore

$$\Delta E_o = -0.32\text{ V} - 0.77\text{ V}$$
$$\Delta E_o = -1.09\text{ V}$$

Under nonstandard conditions

$$\Delta E = \Delta E_o - \frac{2.3\ RT}{nF} \log_{10} \frac{[\text{NADPH}]\,[Fe^{2+}]^2}{[\text{NADP}^+]\,[Fe^{3+}]^2}$$

Since the concentrations of Fe^{2+} and Fe^{3+} are equal they cancel out, and

$$\Delta E = -1.09\text{ V} - \frac{2.3}{2} \times \frac{1.98 \text{ x } 10^{-3}\text{ kcal}}{°\text{K mole}} \times 310°\text{K} \times \frac{\text{V mole}}{23\text{ kcal}} \log_{10} \frac{10}{1}$$
$$= -1.09\text{ V} - 0.03\text{ V}$$
$$\Delta E = -1.12\text{ V}$$

Under standard conditions $\Delta E = \Delta E_o$, and

$$\Delta G = -nF\,\Delta E$$
$$= -2 \times 23\text{ kcal/V mole} \times (-1.09\text{ V})$$
$$\Delta G = 50.1\text{ kcal/mole (or 25 kcal/mole for each electron)}$$

Under nonstandard conditions

$$\Delta G = -2 \times 23\text{ kcal/V mole} \times (-1.12\text{ V})$$
$$\Delta G = 51.5\text{ kcal/mole (or 26 kcal/mole for each electron)}$$

These calculations make it very clear that reduction of $NADP^+$ by Fe^{2+} is extremely unfavorable.

C. In the absence of a membrane potential, the free-energy change available from inward proton transport is

$$\Delta G = 2.3\ RT \log_{10} \frac{[H^+]_{in}}{[H^+]_{out}}$$
$$= 2.3 \times \frac{1.98 \times 10^{-3}\text{ kcal}}{°\text{K mole}} \times 310°\text{K} \log_{10} \frac{10^{-6.5}}{10^{-2.0}}$$
$$= 2.3 \times \frac{1.98 \times 10^{-3}\text{ kcal}}{°\text{K mole}} \times 310°\text{K} \log_{10} 10^{-4.5}$$
$$\Delta G = -6.4\text{ kcal/mole}$$

If the ΔG for ATP synthesis is 11 kcal/mole, it would take at least two moles of protons (2×-6.4 kcal/mole $= -12.8$ kcal/mole), to drive ATP synthesis. Thus, each molecule of ATP would require that two protons be transported into the cell.

The energy of transport would have to be coupled to the synthesis of ATP, but thermodynamic calculations give no clue to the actual mechanism of coupling. The protons could enter singly or together, depending on the mechanism. If they entered one at a time, the energy from the first proton would have to be stored in such a way that the energy of the second proton could be added to it. If the ATP synthetase in *T. ferrooxidans* works as it does in other cells (that is, without a high-energy intermediate), then both protons would have to enter at the same time.

D. If under standard conditions 50.1 kcal/mole are needed to reduce $NADP^+$, then a minimum of 8 moles of protons would have to be transported

(8 × −6.4 kcal/mole = −51.2 kcal/mole) to drive the electrons from Fe^{2+} to $NADP^+$.

Once again the thermodynamic calculations give no clue as to the actual mechanism by which electrons from Fe^{2+} are used to reduce $NADP^+$. The transport of protons could be coupled to the reverse flow of electrons in any number of ways. In principle, the transport of eight protons could be linked directly to the transfer of a pair of electrons from $2Fe^{2+}$ to $NADH^+$. Or, the electrons could be activated independently in a mechanism requiring the participation of four protons per electron. However, it seems more likely that the electrons are activated in increments, by being pushed from carrier to carrier up an electron-transport chain—much like the reverse of normal electron transport in mitochondria.

E. The fixation of each mole of CO_2 into glyceraldehyde 3-phosphate requires 3 moles of ATP and 2 moles of NADPH. The synthesis of these molecules requires transport of 22 moles of protons (3 × $2H^+$ for ATP + 2 × $8H^+$ for NADPH). Therefore, 22 moles of Fe^{2+} must be oxidized to neutralize the transported protons. In addition, 2 moles of Fe^{2+} are required to provide electrons for each mole of NADPH. Thus, a total of 26 moles of Fe^{2+} must be oxidized for each mole of CO_2 fixed into glyceraldehyde 3-phosphate.

T. ferrooxidans, therefore, produces enormous quantities of Fe^{3+} during its normal growth. Were it not for the presence of other convenient reductants in the slag heaps, all the iron would be oxidized and the bacteria would stop growing.

Reference: Ingledew, J.W. *Thiobacillus ferrooxidans:* the bioenergetics of an acidophilic chemolithotroph. *Biochim. Biophys. Acta* 683:89–117, 1982.

The Evolution of the Electron-Transport Chains

7–29

A. fermentation

7–30

A. True
B. True
C. True
D. True
E. True
F. True

The Genomes of Mitochondria and Chloroplasts

7–31

A. non-Mendelian inheritance (cytoplasmic inheritance)
B. mitotic segregation
C. maternal (uniparental)
D. cytoplasmic petite
E. urea cycle
F. endosymbiont hypothesis

7–32

A. False. Energy-converting organelles divide throughout interphase, out of phase with the division of the cell or with each other. Similarly, replication is not limited to S phase but occurs throughout the cell cycle. However, the process is regulated so that the total number of organelle DNA molecules doubles in every cell cycle.
B. True

C. False. Protein synthesis in both chloroplasts and mitochondria is much more like that in bacteria than that in the cytoplasm. It is true that the machinery in chloroplasts resembles bacterial machinery more closely than mitochondria, but both are clearly bacteriumlike.

D. True

E. False. The mitochondrial genetic code differs slightly from the nuclear code, but it also varies slightly from species to species.

F. True

G. True

H. False. The presence of introns in organelle genes is surprising precisely because corresponding introns have not been found in related bacterial genomes.

I. True

J. False. Variegated leaves are caused by the mitotic segregation of normal and defective chloroplasts.

K. True

L. True

M. False. Mitochondria from different tissues of the same organism often show characteristic tissue-specific differences in their content of nuclear proteins.

N. True

O. True

P. True

7–33

A. The results in Figure 7–20 are exactly what you would expect if mitochondrial DNA were replicated at random times throughout the cell cycle. Regardless of length of the chase, a constant fraction of the labeled DNA is triggered to replicate. Even the fraction of the DNA that is shifted (about 10%) is what you expect, since the labeling time with BrdU (2 hours) is about 10% of the cell cycle (20 hours).

If replication of mitochondrial DNA were confined to a specific part of the cell cycle, then the DNA that was labeled with ^{3}H-thymidine in the first pulse would not be replicated a second time until the critical phase of the cell cycle came around again. As a result, very little of the labeled DNA should be shifted in density until that time. The critical time in the cell cycle would show up in this experiment as a high fraction of labeled DNA that was density shifted at a particular chase time.

B. It is true that the cell population is asynchronous, but asynchrony has no bearing on the interpretation of the experiment. If the mitochondrial DNA is replicating at random times, then the synchrony of the cell population is irrelevant. Your colleague's concern is directed at the possibility that an asynchronous cell population might obscure your ability to detect a timed replication of mitochondrial DNA. Your elegant experimental design, however, nicely gets around that potential objection. If mitochondria replicated at a specific time during the cell cycle, only those cells in that portion of the cycle would be labeled by the brief pulse of ^{3}H-thymidine. Since in the remainder of the experiment you follow only the radioactive mitochondrial DNA molecules, the brief labeling period has, in essence, synchronized the cell population—you are blind to what happens in any cells that were outside the critical labeling period.

C. Your analysis of nuclear DNA should show a peak of density shifting between 15 and 20 hours, with very little shifting of radioactive DNA at shorter chase periods (Figure 7–27). Since nuclear DNA replicates in a specific phase of the cell cycle, only those cells in that portion of the cell cycle will be labeled with the pulse of ^{3}H-thymidine. The nuclear DNA in the labeled cells will not replicate again until they pass through the entire cell cycle and arrive once again in S phase. If the cells were radioactively labeled at the end of S phase initially, they will come into S phase after an additional 15 hours or so—at which point their density can be shifted by exposure

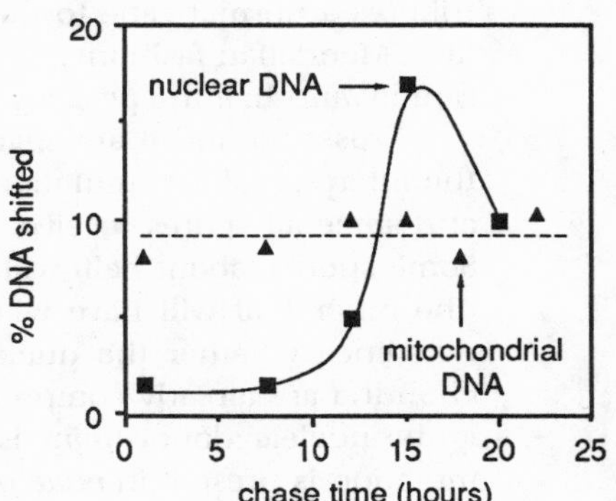

Figure 7–27 Peak of density-shifted nuclear DNA (Answer 7–33).

to BrdU. If they were at the beginning of S phase when they were labeled, they will not enter S phase again for nearly 20 hours. A peak of density shifting of labeled nuclear DNA is indeed observed between 15 and 20 hours. The density-shifted DNA shows up as a peak and not a plateau because at times longer than 20 hours the labeled DNA passes out of S phase and once again becomes refractory to density shifting.

D. If mitochondrial DNA molecules were replicated at all times during the cell cycle, but individual molecules had to wait one cell cycle between replication events, there would be a peak of density shifting at 18 to 20 hours. Those molecules that were replicated during the pulse of ^{3}H-thymidine would be labeled. If these molecules had to wait one cell cycle to be replicated again, then they would not be subject to density shifting until one full cell cycle had passed. Thus, the mitochondrial DNA molecules labeled initially would not be density shifted until approximately 18 to 20 hours of chase. (The experimental results would resemble those for nuclear DNA replication, since nuclear DNA also has to wait one full cycle; however, the timing would be slightly different because mitochondrial DNA replicates in 2 hours whereas nuclear DNA takes 5 hours.)

Reference: Bogenhagen, D.; and Clayton, D.A. Mouse L cell mitochondrial DNA molecules are selected randomly for replication throughout the cell cycle. *Cell* 11:719–727, 1977.

***7–34** **References:** Montoya, J.; Ojala, D.; Attardi, G. Distinctive features of the 5′-terminal sequences of the human mitochondrial mRNAs. *Nature* 290:465–470, 1981.

Ojala, D.; Montoya, J.; Attardi, G. tRNA punctuation model of RNA processing in human mitochondria. *Nature* 290:470–474, 1981.

***7–35** **Reference:** Stern, D.B.; Palmer, J.D. Extensive and widespread homologies between mitochondrial DNA and chloroplast DNA in plants. *Proc. Natl. Acad. Sci. USA* 81:1946–1950, 1984.

7–36 The abnormal patterns of cytochrome absorption suggest that both *poky* and *puny* affect mitochondrial function. The genetic analysis is consistent with a cytoplasmic mode of inheritance for *poky*, but a nuclear mode of inheritance for *puny*.

Crosses 7, 8, and 9 in Table 7–4 are control crosses, which show that wild type always yields fast-growing progeny and the mutants always yield slow-growing progeny.

Crosses 1 and 2 show the cytoplasmic mode of inheritance of *poky*. When *poky* was present in the protoperithecial parent (cytoplasmic donor), all the spores grew slowly (cross 1); when it was in the fertilizing parent, the spores grew rapidly (cross 2). This result is expected if the cytoplasmic donor determines the type of mitochondria present in the spores. In cross 1 *poky* was the cytoplasmic donor and the spores grew slowly. In cross 2 wild type was the cytoplasmic donor and the spores grew rapidly.

Crosses 3 and 4 show the nuclear mode of inheritance of *puny*. In both crosses *puny* contributes a mutant gene to the fusion and wild type contributes a normal gene to the fusion. These genes are divided up equally (in a Mendelian fashion) among the spores so that half the progeny grow rapidly and half the progeny grow slowly.

Crosses 5 and 6 are slightly more complicated because they involve the interplay of two mutations. In cross 5 *poky* is the cytoplasmic donor, and since all spores receive "*poky*" mitochondria, all spores grow slowly. Some spores (about half) will also carry the *puny* mutation in their nuclei (the other half will have wild-type nuclei—from *poky*), but it makes no difference whether the nuclei are normal or mutant because the mitochondria are already compromised by the *poky* mutation. In cross 6 *poky* is the nuclear donor (*puny* is the cytoplasmic donor); therefore the *poky* mutation is present in *none* of the spores. Once again, half the spores will carry the *puny* mutation and half will be wild type; however, in the absence of "*poky*" mitochondria, the nuclear phenotypes are expressed. Thus, half the spores will grow rapidly and half will grow slowly.

It was this sort of distortion from the expected Mendelian behavior of genes that led ultimately to the realization that mitochondria (and later chloroplasts) carried genetic material.

References: Mitchell, M.B.; Mitchell, H.K. A case of "maternal" inheritance in *Neurospora crassa. Proc. Natl. Acad. Sci. USA* 38:442–449, 1952.

Mitchell, M.B.; Mitchell, H.K.; Tissieres, A. Mendelian and non-Mendelian factors affecting the cytochrome system in *Neurospora crassa. Proc. Natl. Acad. Sci. USA* 39:605–613, 1953.

7–37

A. The deletions that suppress the *pet494* mutation do not affect the coding portion of the mRNA. Therefore, they do not alter the *coxIII* gene product and cannot affect its stability. By contrast, the replacement of the normal 5′ untranslated region with one from any of several other genes is perfectly consistent with an alteration in translation. These results suggest that the normal *PET494* gene product promotes translation of coxIII from the wild-type mitochondrial mRNA.

B. The rearrangements of the 5′ end of the *coxIII* gene result in deletion of essential mitochondrial genes, which normally would produce a cytoplasmic petite strain of yeast. Yet these strains have all the usual mRNAs and grow perfectly well. These observations suggest that the deleted DNA must be present somewhere else in the mitochondria. It turns out that the *pet494* suppressor strains contain both wild-type and deleted mitochondrial genomes. Although it is not uncommon for mitochondria to contain more than one DNA molecule, the mixture of DNAs is quite unusual. This so-called heteroplasmic state is normally quite unstable, and the individual mitochondrial genomes segregate rapidly. However, by demanding that the cells grow on glycerol, it is possible to maintain the heteroplasmic state indefinitely. In the presence of the nuclear *pet494* mutation, both mitochondrial genomes are required for growth on glycerol: the deleted genome provides translatable coxIII mRNA and the wild-type genome provides all other essential gene products.

Reference: Fox, T.D. Nuclear gene products required for translation of specific mitochondrially coded mRNAs in yeast. *Trends in Genetics* 2:97–100, 1986.

***7–38** **Reference:** Whatley, J.M.; John, P.; Whatley, F.R. From extracellular to intracellular: the establishment of mitochondria and chloroplasts. *Proc. R. Soc. Lond. B.* 204:165–187, 1979.

Intracellular Sorting and the Maintenance of Cellular Compartments

The Compartmentalization of Higher Cells

8–1

A. lumen
B. secretory vesicles
C. regulated, constitutive
D. signal peptide
E. signal patches

8–2

A. True
B. False. The membranes of intracellular compartments are selectively permeable (not impermeable). Selective permeability is conferred by transport proteins that help to establish the unique chemical identity of each compartment.
C. True
D. False. The lumen of the ER is topologically equivalent to the outside of the cell, but the interior of the nucleus is topologically equivalent to the cytosol.
E. False. Proteins destined for mitochondria, chloroplasts, the nucleus, or peroxisomes are exported from the cytosol; they never enter the ER.
F. True
G. True
H. True
I. False. Signal peptides are used to direct proteins into the ER, mitochondria, chloroplasts, and the nucleus. Signal patches may be used for other sorting steps, including the recognition of certain proteins for sorting into lysosomes.
J. True
K. False. The information required to construct a membrane-bounded organelle, such as the ER or Golgi, does not reside exclusively in the DNA that specifies the organelle proteins. Epigenetic information in the form of at least one distinct protein in the organelle membrane is also required. The epigenetic information is passed from parent cell to progeny cell in the form of the organelle itself.

8–3

A. If the equivalent of one plasma membrane transits the ER every 24 hours and individual membrane proteins remain in the ER for 30 minutes (0.5 hr), then at any one time 0.021 (0.5 hr/24 hr) plasma membrane equivalents are present in the ER. Since the area of the ER membrane is 20 times greater than the area of the plasma membrane, the fraction of plasma membrane proteins in the ER is 0.021/20 = 0.001. Thus, the ratio of plasma membrane proteins to other membrane proteins in the ER is 1 to 1000. Out of every 1000 proteins in the ER membrane only 1 is in transit to the plasma membrane.
B. In a cell that is dividing once per day the equivalent of one Golgi apparatus also must transit the ER every 24 hours. Thus, if the membrane of the Golgi apparatus is three times the area of the plasma membrane, three times as many Golgi apparatus membrane proteins will be present in the ER. Therefore, the ratio of Golgi apparatus membrane proteins to other membrane proteins in the ER is 3 to 1000.

C. If the areas of the membranes of all the rest of the compartments are equal to the area of the plasma membrane, then the ratio of membrane proteins bound for these compartments to the membrane proteins in the ER is 1 to 1000. Summing the contributions from all compartments, the ratio of membrane proteins, in transit, to proteins that are permanent residents of the ER membrane is 5 to 1000. Thus, 99.5% of the membrane proteins in the ER are permanent residents.

The Cytosolic Compartment

8–4

A. cytoskeleton
B. ubiquitin-dependent, ubiquitin
C. heat-shock (stress-response)

8–5

A. False. The cytoskeleton plays a much less specific role. Most of the specificity of vesicular traffic resides in the receptor systems located on the cytoplasmic surface of the vesicles themselves.
B. True
C. True
D. False. Regulatory proteins tend to be short-lived so that their concentrations can be quickly changed by changing their rate of synthesis.
E. False. Ubiquitin is the small protein whose attachment to a target protein marks it for degradation by a separate ATP-dependent protease.
F. False. The sequence of the gene yields the amino acid sequence of the protein as synthesized. However, the N-terminal amino acid and a few others are often removed after synthesis. Thus, the functional form of a cytosolic protein often does not have the exact amino acid sequence predicted from the sequence of the corresponding gene.

8–6

A. Although the first codon of β-galactosidase could have been changed by recombinant DNA techniques, it would no longer have served as a start site for translation. All proteins, bacterial and eucaryotic, are initially translated with methionine at their N terminus. In many cases methionine is removed (and occasionally additional amino acids as well), leaving a new N terminus. However, the rules for N-terminal modification are not understood at present. Thus, it is tricky to generate a protein with any desired N terminus.

The procedure described here was arrived at by chance! The investigators were originally interested in whether ubiquitin at the N terminus would cause a protein to be degraded. This question led them to generate the fusion gene. In bacteria, which do not have a ubiquitin-dependent protease, the fusion protein was made as they anticipated; however, in yeast the same plasmid produced only β-galactosidase, suggesting that the ubiquitin was removed. To try to prevent this cleavage, they altered the codons at the junction (using recombinant DNA techniques). The ubiquitin was still removed, but now the resulting β-galactosidases differed remarkably in stability. The focus of their study quickly changed, leading to insights into the role of the N terminus in determining the stability of proteins.

B. The half-lives of the different β-galactosidases can be estimated from the graph in Figure 8–2B by finding the time at which half the β-galactosidase remains. The three β-galactosidases have quite different half-lives: R-β-galactosidase has a half-life of about 2 minutes; I-β-galactosidase has a half-life of about 30 minutes; and M-β-galactosidase has a half-life that is too long to be measured in this experiment (it was estimated to be greater than 20 hours). These three β-galactosidases define the three stability classes that were observed in these experiments.

Reference: Bachmair, A.; Finley, D.; Varshavsky, A. *In vivo* half-life of a protein is a function of its amino-terminal residue. *Science* 234:179–186, 1986.

***8–7** **Reference:** Bachmair, A.; Finley, D.; Varshavsky, A. *In vivo* half-life of a protein is a function of its amino-terminal residue. *Science* 234:179–186, 1986.

8–8

A. Although ODCase is being made at the same rate in normal and mutant cells, it is losing activity at a much slower rate (50-fold) in the mutant cells. Since each ODCase molecule remains in its active state for so much longer, ODCase activity accumulates to a much higher level. The activity of any cellular enzyme depends on the balance between its rate of synthesis (or activation) and its rate of destruction (or inactivation). The relative rates of gain and loss define the steady-state level of enzymatic activity.

B. Your experiment measured ODCase activity and, therefore, does not distinguish between destruction of the protein and reversible inactivation of the enzyme. To resolve these possibilities, you need an assay that measures the level of ODCase protein. For example, ODCase protein levels could be assayed by precipitation with antibodies specific for ODCase followed by electrophoretic separation and staining as described for β-galactosidase in problem 8–6. When ODCase protein was assayed, it was found that the protein levels declined at the same rate as the enzymatic activity, indicating that the ODCase protein is very unstable in normal cells.

C. Since other proteins in the mutant cell line have unaltered half-lives, the change in ODCase half-life must be specific for ODCase. Given the apparent importance of the N-terminal amino acid in determining the protein stability, the change in ODCase half-life could be due to a change in the amino acid at its mature N terminus. (Such a change might not have shown up in your preliminary characterization of ODCase structure and enzymatic properties.) Alternatively, there could be some specific "tagging" system that normally marks ODCase for destruction. In that case, the mutant cell line would likely be missing some component of the tagging system.

Reference: Pritchard, M.L.; Pegg, A.E.; Jefferson, L.S. Ornithine decarboxylase from hepatoma cells and a variant cell line in which the enzyme is more stable. *J. Biol. Chem.* 257:5892–5899, 1982.

The Transport of Proteins and RNA Molecules into and out of the Nucleus

8–9

A. nuclear envelope
B. inner nuclear, outer nuclear
C. nuclear pores, nuclear pore complex
D. nuclear import

8–10

A. True
B. False. The lipid bilayer of the inner and outer nuclear membranes are continuous with one another around the margin of each nuclear pore.
C. True
D. False. It seems likely that nuclear export, like nuclear import, also requires special recognition systems and a source of energy.
E. True

8–11

A. The portion of nucleoplasmin responsible for localization in the nucleus must reside in the tail. The nucleoplasmin head does not localize to the nucleus when injected into the cytoplasm, and it is the only injected fragment that is missing the tail.

B. These experiments suggest that the nucleoplasmin tail carries a nuclear import signal and that accumulation in the nucleus is not the result of passive diffusion. The observations involving complete nucleoplasmin or fragments that retain the tail do not distinguish between the two models;

*Problems with an asterisk (*) are answered in the Instructor's Manual.

they say only that the tail carries the important part of nucleoplasmin—be it an import signal or a binding site. The key observations that argue against passive diffusion are the results with the nucleoplasmin head. Its lack of accumulation in the nucleus after injection into the cytoplasm could be rationalized (according to passive diffusion) on the basis of a missing binding site for some nuclear component. If the head is missing a binding site, however, it should not be retained after injection into the nucleus. Its retention in the nucleus suggests that the head is too large to pass through the nuclear pore. Since more massive forms of nucleoplasmin do pass through nuclear pores, passive diffusion of nucleoplasmin appears to be ruled out.

Reference: Dingwall, C.; Sharnick, S.V.; Laskey, R.A. A polypeptide domain that specifies migration of nucleoplasmin into the nucleus. *Cell* 30:449–458, 1982.

***8–12** **Reference:** Barnes, G; Rine, J. (1985) Regulated expression of endonuclease EcoRI in *Saccharomyces cerevisiae*: nuclear entry and biological consequences. *Proc. Natl. Acad. Sci. USA.* 82:1354–1358, 1985.

8–13

A. The critical flaw in your original protocol is that the killer protein, which was made at the high temperature but denied access to the nucleus in the translocation mutants, will still be present when the cells are shifted to low temperature. When nuclear translocation resumes at the low temperature, the killer protein will be imported and the mutant cells will die. Your original protocol ensured that no new killer protein would be made (by shifting to low temperature in the presence of glucose) but did not take into account the killer protein that had been made in the presence of galactose before the temperature shift.

B. You need to modify your experimental protocol so that the previously made killer protein is rendered inactive before nuclear import is allowed to resume. There are many possible ways to accomplish this. For example, you might try leaving the cells at high temperature in the presence of glucose (so there is no new synthesis) for increasing periods of time to allow the previously made killer protein to be inactivated by normal degradation processes. You might also try to increase its rate of degradation by engineering its N terminus so that it carries a destabilizing amino acid (see problem 8–6). Such a modification could turn the killer protein into a very short-acting molecule, which would disappear very rapidly in the absence of new synthesis. Alternatively, you might try a temperature-sensitive mutant of EcoRI that is active at the high temperature and inactive at the low temperature. Such a *cold-sensitive* protein would be active when nuclear transport was blocked in the import mutant and inactive when nuclear transport resumed.

C. There are several types of mutants that would be expected to survive the selection protocol without affecting the nuclear-transport machinery. For example, mutants that cannot transport galactose into the cell would be unable to turn on the hybrid gene and thus would survive the shift to high temperature in the presence of galactose. Other mutants in which EcoRI was not expressed from the hybrid gene would also survive the selection scheme. These mutants might include mutations in the promoter (which would prevent expression of the hybrid gene), mutations in the EcoRI portion of the hybrid gene (which would render EcoRI inactive), and mutations in the nuclear import signal in the hybrid gene (which would prevent import of EcoRI into the nucleus).

Genetic selection schemes are rarely specific for the precise mutant you are seeking. In some cases, other classes can be predicted and screened out by an additional step. However, the real beauty of genetic selection schemes, the aspect that makes them like treasure hunts, is that they often give classes of mutants that you did not foresee. Sometimes these classes turn out to be trivial and uninteresting; however, they can also be extremely interesting and informative, leading you to insights that you did not anticipate.

The Transport of Proteins into Mitochondria and Chloroplasts

8–14

A. matrix space, inner membrane, intermembrane space, outer membrane
B. thylakoid membrane, thylakoid space
C. mitochondrial precursor
D. contact sites
E. thylakoid

8–15

A. False. Mitochondrially encoded proteins are located mostly in the inner mitochondrial membrane; however, the proteins encoded by chloroplasts are located mostly in the thylakoid membrane.
B. False. Mitochondrial signal peptides are amphipathic helices with positively charged amino acids on one side and uncharged hydrophobic amino acids on the other side.
C. True
D. True
E. True
F. True
G. False. The pores in the outer mitochondrial membrane allow free passage of molecules less than 10,000 daltons. Since most proteins are larger than that, the outer membrane does form a permeability barrier to most proteins.
H. False. Mitochondria use the electrochemical proton gradient to help drive protein import. In chloroplasts, however, the electrochemical proton gradient is across the thylakoid membrane and, therefore, cannot aid import across the outer and inner membranes.

8–16 Normally, translation is much faster than mitochondrial import, so that proteins completely clear the ribosome before interacting with the mitochondrial membrane. By blocking protein synthesis with cycloheximide, you have made the rate of translation artificially slower than the rate of import. Since the signal peptide for protein import into mitochondria resides at the N terminus, some of the partially synthesized mitochondrial proteins, which are still attached to ribosomes, will be able to interact with the mitochondrial membrane. The attempted import of even one such protein will attach the ribosome and the mRNA (and all other ribosomes translating the same mRNA molecule) to the mitochondrial membrane.

Reference: Kellems, R.E.; Allison, V.F.; Butow, R.A. Cytoplasmic type 80S ribosomes associated with yeast mitochondria. IV. Attachment of ribosomes to the outer membrane of isolated mitochondria. *J. Cell Biol.* 65:1–14, 1975.

***8–17**

8–18

A. Import of all four proteins into chloroplasts in your experiments is very efficient, as indicated by the small fraction of precursor (Figure 8–8B, upper band lane 2) that remains after incubation with the chloroplasts. This small fraction of precursor is still outside the chloroplast in all cases because it is digested by added protease (Figure 8–8B, lane 3).
B. Ferredoxin is localized to its normal compartment in your experiments, as indicated by its abundance in the stromal fraction (Figure 8–8B, FDFD lane 5) and its absence from the other fractions. Plastocyanin is also localized to its normal compartment—the thylakoid lumen, since the great majority is associated with thylakoids (Figure 8–8B, PCPC lane 6, lower band) in such a way that it cannot be digested with an added protease (Figure 8–8B, PCPC lane 7).
C. The hybrid proteins are imported into chloroplast compartments that are consistent with their N-terminal sequences. This result is most clear for FDPC, which is localized exclusively in the stromal fraction (Figure 8–8B, FDPC lane 5) just like ferredoxin. By contrast, only a very small fraction of PCFD makes it into the lumen of the thylakoid (Figure 8–8B, PCFD lane 6,

lower band). Some seems to be bound to the thylakoid membrane, since it is digested when treated with a protease (Figure 8–8B, compare upper bands, lanes 6 and 7); however, the majority is found in the stromal fraction (Figure 8–8B, lane 5).

There are several reasons why import of PCFD to the thylakoid lumen may be so inefficient. (1) It may be difficult for the ferredoxin domain to cross the thylakoid membrane. However, it does manage to cross the outer and inner membranes and its overall charge is roughly the same as plastocyanin, which does cross the thylakoid membrane. (2) Ferredoxin normally picks up an iron-sulfur center at some point in its maturation. Thus, it is possible that it picks up the iron-sulfur center in the stroma and for that reason cannot cross the thylakoid membrane. (3) Ferredoxin normally functions in association with other proteins in the stroma. It may be that the ferredoxin domain in PCFD associates with these proteins and is, therefore, held in the stroma. These kinds of concerns often complicate otherwise straightforward mixing and matching experiments designed to elucidate protein import signals.

D. The multiple bands in your experiments are the key to understanding protein import into chloroplasts. The highest band for all proteins is the precursor—that is, the primary translation product, since it is present in the *in vitro* translation mixture in the absence of chloroplasts (Figure 8–8B, lane 1). The lower bands have had some portion of the protein removed. Although you anticipated that the protein would be removed from the N terminus (which is why you set up the experiment as you did), your results confirm that the signal peptides are located at the N terminus. The two-band pattern is associated with the N-terminal segment from ferredoxin (Figure 8–8B, FD and FDPC lane 2), whereas the three-band pattern is associated with the N-terminal segment from plastocyanin (Figure 8–8B, PC and PCFD, lane 2).

The two-band pattern associated with the ferredoxin signal peptide suggests that one cleavage event accompanies the import of ferredoxin to the stroma. The lower band corresponds to the functional form of ferredoxin in the stroma (Figure 8–8B, compare FD lanes 2 and 5). The three-band pattern associated with the plastocyanin signal peptide suggests that two cleavage events are involved in the import of plastocyanin to the thylakoid lumen. The lowest band corresponds to the functional form of plastocyanin in the thylakoid (Figure 8–8B, compare PC lanes 2 and 7). The intermediate band is probably an intermediate in import, suggesting that the signal peptide has two components that are removed sequentially. The N-terminal component of the signal peptide directs the protein into the stroma, and the C-terminal component directs the protein into the thylakoid lumen.

E. A model that summarizes the role of the signal peptides in the import of ferredoxin and plastocyanin into their proper chloroplast compartments

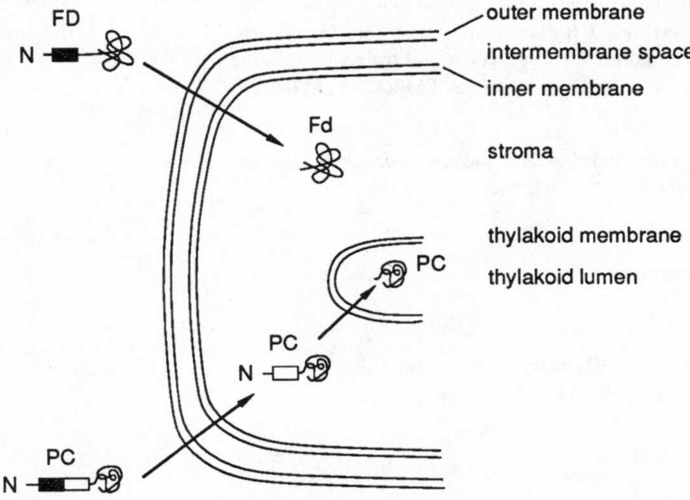

Figure 8–21 A schematic model illustrating the role of signal peptides in directing ferredoxin and plastocyanin to their appropriate chloroplast compartments (Answer 8–18).

is illustrated in Figure 8–21. For each protein the signal peptide is shown as a box at the N terminus of the protein. The shaded portion of the box corresponds to that portion of the signal peptide that is needed for import across the outer and inner chloroplast membranes. This signal peptide is removed as the proteins cross the membranes and enter the stroma. The unshaded segment of the box associated with plastocyanin is needed for import across the thylakoid membrane. It is removed during import into the thylakoid lumen.

Reference: Smeekens, S.; Bauerle, C.; Hageman, J.; Keegstra, K.; Weisbeek, P. The role of the transit peptide in the routing of precursors toward different chloroplast compartments. *Cell* 46:365–375, 1986.

Peroxisomes

8–19

A. peroxisomes

B. glyoxylate cycle, glyoxysomes

8–20

A. False. With rare exceptions, such as prythrocytes, all mammalian cells contain peroxisomes, but only a few cell types contain large peroxisomes.

B. True

C. False. New peroxisomes arise from preexisting ones by organelle growth and fission. All the membrane proteins and lipids of peroxisomes are imported from the cytosol.

8–21

A. The hybridization results in Figure 8–9 indicate that mRNAs for PGK genes 1 and 3 are expressed in humans and that mRNAs for PGK genes 1 and 2 are expressed in tsetse flies.

B. The glycosomal form of PGK is expressed only in trypanosomes from humans. Since the oligonucleotide probe for PGK gene 3 hybridizes to an mRNA that is expressed uniquely in trypanosomes from humans, PGK gene 3 probably encodes the glycosomal form of PGK.

C. The results in Figure 8–9 suggest that the low level of cytosolic PGK activity in trypanosomes from humans is probably not due to inaccurate sorting into glycosomes. PGK gene 1 is expressed at low levels in trypanosomes from both humans and tsetse flies. Since all the PGK activity in trypanosomes from tsetse flies is present in the cytosol, PGK gene 1 must encode a cytosolic form of PGK. Therefore, since PGK gene 1 is expressed in trypanosomes from humans, it is probably responsible for the low level of cytosolic PGK activity in trypanosomes from humans. Thus, there is no indication that import into glycosomes in trypanosomes from humans is inaccurate.

Reference: Osinga, K.A.; Swinkels, B.W.; Gibson, W.C.; Borst, P.; Veeneman, G.H.; Van Boom, J.H.; Michels, P.A.M.; Opperdoes, F.R. Topogenesis of microbody enzymes: sequence comparison of the genes for the glycosomal (microbody) and cytosolic phosphoglycerate kinases of *Trypanosoma brucei*. *EMBO J.* 4:3811–3817, 1985.

***8–22** **Reference:** Borst, P. How proteins get into microbodies (peroxisomes, glyoxysomes, glycosomes). *Biochim. Biophys. Acta* 866:179–203, 1986.

The Endoplasmic Reticulum

8–23

A. endoplasmic reticulum (ER), ER lumen (ER cisternal space)

B. membrane-bound ribosomes, rough endoplasmic reticulum

C. transitional elements

D. sarcoplasmic reticulum

E. microsomes

F. signal hypothesis
G. signal recognition particle (SRP), SRP receptor
H. signal peptidase
I. start-transfer peptide, stop-transfer peptide
J. binding protein (BiP)
K. protein disulfide isomerase
L. glycoproteins
M. glycosylation, dolichol

8–24

A. True
B. True
C. False. The cytochrome P450 enzymes do not cleave drugs and metabolites into small pieces. Instead, they detoxify molecules by catalyzing the addition of hydroxyl groups. These groups serve as sites for addition of water-soluble molecules (such as sulfate or glucuronic acid). Ultimately, the target molecule is rendered soluble enough so that it can be excreted in the urine.
D. False. Rough microsomes are more dense than smooth microsomes because the attached ribosomes contain large amounts of RNA.
E. True
F. True
G. False. The binding of the signal recognition particle to the signal peptide causes translation to be arrested. Translational arrest is lifted when the ribosomes carrying SRP bind to the SRP receptor, which is exposed on the cytosolic surface of the rough ER.
H. False. The import of proteins into the ER requires ATP hydrolysis but not ongoing protein synthesis.
I. True
J. True
K. True
L. False. The ER lumen does not contain reducing agents (they are in the cytosol) and, therefore, S-S bonds can form in the ER.
M. True
N. False. Proteins that are linked to glycosylated phosphatidylinositol molecules are attached to the external surface of the plasma membrane. The attachment reaction occurs in the lumen of the ER, which is topologically equivalent to the outside of the cell.
O. True
P. False. Transport vesicles carry new phospholipids to the plasma membrane, Golgi, and lysosomes. However, new phospholipids are transferred to mitochondria and peroxisomes by phospholipid exchange proteins.

8–25

A. In the absence of microsomes a unique protein is synthesized (Figure 8–10, lane 1). This protein is accessible to protease digestion whether or not detergent is present (Figure 8–10, lanes 2 and 3), indicating that the protein is not protected by a membrane bilayer. Finally, treatment of the protein with endoglycosidase H does not alter its mobility (Figure 8–10, lane 4), indicating that the protein carries no *N*-linked sugars of the type added in the ER.
B. By the three criteria outlined in the problem (protease protection, *N*-linked sugars, and cleaved signal peptide), this protein is translocated across the microsomal membrane. (1) The protein is fully sensitive to protease in the presence of detergent (Figure 8–10, lane 7), but it is only partially sensitive to protease in the absence of detergent (Figure 8–10, lane 6). Thus, the protein is partially protected from protease in the presence of microsomes. (2) The rate of migration of the protein increases after treatment with endoglycosidase H (Figure 8–10, compare lanes 5 and 8), indicating that sugars are attached to the protein when it is translated in the presence of microsomes. (3) When the sugars are removed, the protein migrates faster than the precursor protein (Figure 8–10, compare lanes 1 and 8), indicating that a portion of the protein—presumably the signal peptide—is removed

from the precursor when the protein is translated in the presence of microsomes.

C. The partial sensitivity of the protein to protease treatment (Figure 8–10, lane 6) indicates that a portion of the protein remains on the outside of the microsomes. In combination with the results indicating cleavage of the signal peptide and addition of *N*-linked sugars, this result shows that the protein spans the membrane. Thus the protein is inserted only part way through the membrane and is presumably anchored in the membrane by a stop-transfer segment.

***8–26** **Reference:** Perara, E.; Rothman, R.E.; Lingappa, V.R. Uncoupling translocation from translation: implications for transport of proteins across membranes. *Science* 232:348–352, 1986.

8–27 The predicted arrangement of the proteins in the membrane of the ER is illustrated in Figure 8–22. These arrangements agree with the rules for co-translational insertion of proteins into membranes. In every case, the start-transfer peptides correspond to the odd-numbered membrane-spanning segments and the stop-transfer peptides correspond to the even-numbered membrane-spanning segments. All start-transfer peptides have their N-terminal ends pointing toward the cytoplasm and their C-terminal ends pointing toward the lumen. All stop-transfer peptides have their N-terminal ends pointing toward the lumen and their C-terminal ends pointing toward the cytoplasm. The leader peptides (the first membrane-spanning segments) have been removed from proteins (A) and (B).

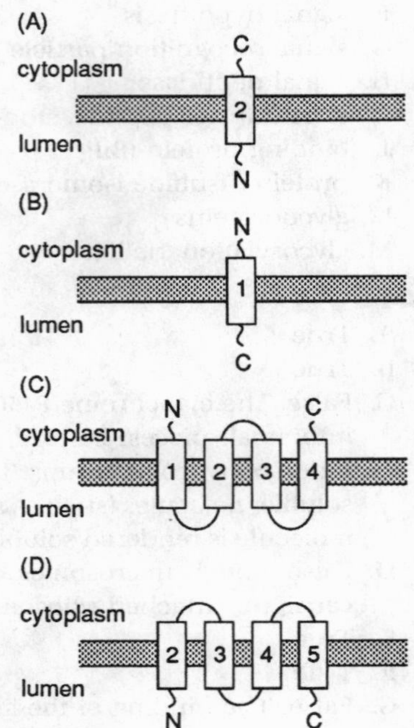

Figure 8–22 The arrangement of proteins across the membrane of the ER (Answer 8–27). The numbered boxes correspond to the membrane-spanning segments shown in Figure 8–13.

***8–28** **Reference:** Manoil, C; Beckwith, J. A genetic approach to analyzing membrane protein topology. *Science* 233:1403–1408, 1986.

8–29

A. Experiment 1 tests whether the acceptor membranes (red cell ghosts) are in excess. Since the PC transfer protein catalyzes an *exchange* reaction, there is a simple theoretical limit to how much transfer can occur at equilibrium. If the amount of donor and acceptor membranes were equal, for example, the limit of possible transfer would be 50%. Doubling the amount of acceptor membrane would raise the limit to 67% (a 2 to 1 ratio of donor to acceptor); tripling the acceptor membranes would raise the limit to 75% (a 3 to 1 ratio); and so on. Since adding more acceptor membranes made no difference, the red cell membranes must be in excess. Thus the 70% limit is not an equilibrium point for the exchange.

Experiment 2 rules out the possibility that the enzyme is inactivated during the reaction, since addition of fresh transfer protein causes no further exchange.

Experiment 3 eliminates the possibility that the starting labeled material was impure (that is, untransferable by the PC transfer protein, which is specific for PC) or was somehow altered during the course of the incubation.

B. One simple explanation for the 70% limit is that the PC transfer protein transfers PC only from the outer monolayer of the vesicle bilayer. The area of the outside face of the donor vesicles is about 2.5 times the area of the inner face. The area of the surface of a sphere is $4/3\ \pi r^2$. Thus the ratio of the areas of the outer and inner faces of the donor vesicle is the ratio of squares of their radii, which is $10.5^2/(10.5–4.0)^2$ or 2.5. Since the outer surface is 2.5 times the inner surface, 71% (2.5/3.5) of the lipid is in the outer monolayer. Thus, 70% transfer is about the expected limit if the transfer protein can only exchange PC from the outer leaflet and PC does not flip-flop.

C. If the transfer protein exchanges PC only between outer leaflets, the label in the acceptor red cell membranes will all be in the outer leaflet and, therefore, all available for transfer. This result supports the idea that the PC transfer protein only transfers PC between outer monolayers.

Reference: Rothman, J.E.; Dawidowicz, E.A. Asymmetric exchange of vesicle phospholipids catalyzed by the phosphatidylcholine exchange protein. Measurement of inside-outside transitions. *Biochemistry* 14:2809–2816, 1975.

The Golgi Apparatus

8–30

A. Golgi apparatus (Golgi complex)
B. *cis* face, *trans* face
C. *N*-linked oligosaccharides
D. high-mannose, complex
E. *O*-linked glycosylation
F. *cis, medial, trans*
G. *trans* Golgi network
H. coated vesicles

8–31

A. True
B. True
C. False. The function of *N*-linked oligosaccharides is unknown, but they evidently do not aid in transport through the ER and Golgi. Drugs that block glycosylation generally do not interfere with transport through the ER and Golgi.
D. True
E. True
F. True

8–32

A. The radioactive label (GlcNAc) is added in the *medial* compartment, and the lectin precipitation depends on the presence of galactose, which is added in the *trans* compartment. Therefore, this experiment is following the movement of material between the *medial* and the *trans* compartments of the Golgi apparatus.
B. If proteins moved through the Golgi apparatus by progression of the cisternae, then a protein that entered the Golgi in a mutant cell should remain with that stack and mature as the newly formed cisterna moves through the stack. Thus, the cisternal progression model predicts that none of the labeled G protein (which was labeled in the *medial* compartment of the Golgi apparatus in the mutant cell) should have galactose attached to it (which could only have been added in the Golgi apparatus from the wild-type cell). For this model the fusion of the infected mutant cells to uninfected wild-type cells (Table 8–2, line 1) should be the same as the fusion of infected mutant cells to uninfected mutant cells (Table 8–2, line 2).

   By contrast, if material moved through the Golgi apparatus by vesicle transport, there is the possibility that proteins might move between separated Golgi stacks inside transport vesicles. However, the frequency of movement of vesicles between different Golgi stacks is not addressed by the vesicle transport model. The vesicle transport model predicts only that some labeled G protein may acquire galactose in this way. For this model the fusion of infected mutant cells to uninfected wild-type cells (Table 8–2, line 1) should be more than for fusion of infected mutant cells to uninfected mutant cells (Table 8–2, line 2) but less than for fusion of infected wild-type cells to uninfected wild-type cells (Table 8–2, line 3).
C. The results in Table 8–2 support the vesicle transport model, since nearly half the labeled G protein acquired galactose. The extent of galactose addition is surprising because it suggests that once a vesicle leaves a cisterna, it has roughly an equal chance of fusing with a cisterna in the same or different Golgi stack. A number of other control experiments showed that the morphology of the Golgi stacks was unaltered by the fusion procedure, that the mutant and wild-type Golgi stacks remained distinct from one another, and that G protein did move into the wild-type Golgi stack.

Reference: Rothman, J.E.; Miller, R.L.; Urbani, L.J. Intercompartmental transport in the Golgi complex is a dissociative process: facile transfer of membrane protein between two Golgi populations. *J. Cell Biol.* 99:260–271, 1984.

***8–33**

8–34

A. The altered G proteins with "membrane-spanning" segments that are 12, 8, or 0 amino acids long do not make it to the plasma membrane (Table 8–4). The presence of oligosaccharides indicates that each of these proteins is inserted into the ER membrane, which is expected since the signal peptide was not altered. The presence of the small C-terminal domain on the proteins with segments 12 and 8 amino acids long indicates that these proteins are anchored in the membrane much like the normal G protein. By contrast, the complete protease resistance of the G protein with a zero amino acid transmembrane segment indicates that it passed all the way through the ER membrane into the lumen. Thus, the G proteins with segments 12 and 8 amino acids long are in an internal membrane, but the G protein that is missing the membrane-spanning segment is in an internal lumen.

The partial endo H resistance of the G protein with a membrane-spanning segment of 12 amino acids suggests that some fraction of this G protein makes it as far as the *medial* compartment of the Golgi, which is where the sugar modification occurs that renders the oligosaccharide endo H resistant. The remainder of this protein is either in the membrane of the ER or the *cis* compartment of the Golgi. The endo H sensitivity of the G proteins with 8 and 0 amino acid segments indicates that they do not make it past the *cis* compartment of the Golgi and may not make it out of the ER.

B. For the VSV G protein, the minimum length of the membrane-spanning segment appears to be 8 amino acid residues or less, since G proteins with modified membrane-spanning segments only 8 amino acids long are anchored in the membrane much like the normal G protein. This result is surprising since 8 amino acids arranged in an α helix are not thought to be long enough to span the membrane. There are several possibilities: the short membrane-spanning segments may be arranged as extended chains rather than as α-helices; the membrane may be less than 3 nm thick at the point where these segments penetrate the membrane; and adjacent portions of the G protein, including at least one basic amino acid (K or R) may be pulled into the membrane.

C. The minimum length of a membrane-spanning segment that is consistent with proper sorting of the G protein is 13 or 14 amino acids, since G proteins with segments 14 amino acids long are sorted to the plasma membrane like normal G proteins and G proteins with segments 12 amino acids long are not (Table 8–4). It is curious that shorter membrane-spanning segments anchor the protein in the membrane perfectly well but interfere with sorting. Two of several possibilities are (1) the folding of the cytoplasmic or the luminal domain is altered, thereby destroying the sorting signal and (2) the altered arrangement of amino acids in or near the membrane-spanning segment causes the protein to bind to a permanent resident of the ER or of the *cis* compartment of the Golgi.

Reference: Adams, G.A.; Rose, J.K. Structural requirements of a membrane-spanning domain for protein anchoring and cell surface transport. *Cell* 41:1007–1015, 1985.

Transport of Proteins from the Golgi Apparatus to Lysosomes

8–35

A. lysosomes
B. acid hydrolases
C. endolysosome (endolysosomal compartment)
D. autophagy, autophagosome
E. phagosome, phagolysosome
F. I-cell disease

8–36

A. False. The proton pump in lysosomes pumps protons into the lysosome to maintain a low pH.
B. True
C. True
D. False. Materials taken up by endocytosis follow a pathway that leads from coated pits to endosomes to lysosomes.
E. True
F. False. Addition of a weak base causes M6P receptors to accumulate in endolysosomes. M6P receptors, which bind lysosomal enzymes quite well at neutral pH, normally release bound enzymes at the lower pH of the endolysosome and are then recycled to the Golgi. When the pH of the endolysosome is raised, M6P receptors cannot release their bound enzymes, and because they cannot be recycled, they become trapped in the endolysosome.
G. True
H. True
I. True

8–37

A. The corrective factors are the lysosomal enzymes themselves. The enzyme missing in Hunter's syndrome is supplied by Hurler's cells and vice versa (that is, the enzyme missing in Hurler's syndrome is supplied by Hunter's cells). These enzymes are present in the medium because of a certain degree of inefficiency in sorting. Since they carry mannose 6-phosphate, which normally should direct them to lysosomes, they presumably escaped capture by the lysosomal pathway and were secreted. They are taken into cells and delivered to lysosomes by a scavenger pathway, which operates due to a small number of mannose 6-phosphate receptors on the cell surface. The degradative enzymes, bound to receptors, are taken up through coated pits into endosomes and are eventually delivered to lysosomes. Since lysosomes are the normal site of action for these degradative enzymes, the defect is corrected.
B. Protease treatment destroys the lysosomal enzymes themselves. Periodate treatment and alkaline phosphatase treatment both remove the mannose 6-phosphate signal that is required for binding to the receptor, thus preventing the enzymes (which are still active) from entering the cell.
C. Such a scheme is unlikely to work for defects in cytosolic enzymes. External proteins normally do not cross membranes; thus even when they are taken into cells, they remain in the lumen of a membrane-bound compartment. In addition, foreign proteins are usually delivered to lysosomes and degraded.

Reference: Kaplan, A.; Achord, D.T.; Sly, W.S. Phosphohexosyl components of a lysosomal enzyme are recognized by pinocytosis receptors on human fibroblasts. *Proc. Natl. Acad. Sci. USA* 74:2026–2030, 1977.

***8–38**

Transport from the Golgi Apparatus to Secretory Vesicles and to the Cell Surface

8–39

A. constitutive, regulated (triggered)
B. secretory vesicles (secretory granules)
C. apical, basolateral
D. capsid, envelope

8–40

A. False. Secretory vesicles bud from the *trans* Golgi network.
B. True

C. False. Special sorting signals are required for proteins destined for lysosomes and secretory vesicles. However, the flow of material to the plasma membrane may involve an unselected "bulk-flow" pathway that does not require a sorting signal.
D. False. Apical and basolateral proteins might have different sorting signals to direct them to the appropriate domain. However, it is also possible that only one pathway requires a sorting signal and the other pathway operates by default.
E. True
F. True

8–41 The slow step in the constitutive secretion of transferrin relative to albumin occurs in the ER. The slow step in the constitutive secretion of albumin occurs in the Golgi. From Figure 8–20 it is clear that most of the transferrin in the cell is in the ER and most of the albumin is in the Golgi. The steady-state distribution of proteins along the constitutive pathway tells you where the proteins spend the majority of their time. As with any pathway, an accumulation occurs at the slow step. Therefore, the location of the majority of material corresponds to the slow step.

The constitutive secretion of transferrin is slow relative to albumin because it is delayed in the ER. This result appears to be general: if the constitutive secretion of a protein is slow, the protein is delayed for some reason in the ER.

References: Lodish, H.F.; Kong, N.; Snider, M.; Strous, G.J.A.M. Hepatoma secretory proteins migrate from rough endoplasmic reticulum to Golgi at characteristic rates. *Nature* 304:80–83, 1983.

Fries, E.; Gustafsson, L.; Peterson, P.A. Four secretory proteins synthesized by hepatocytes are transported from the endoplasmic reticulum to Golgi complex at different rates. *EMBO J.* 3:147–152, 1984.

***8–42** **References:** Kondor-Koch, C.; Bravo, R.; Fuller, S.D.; Cutler, D.; Garoff, H. Protein secretion in the polarized epithelial cell line MDCK. *Cell* 43:297–306, 1985.

Gottlieb, T.A.; Beaudry, G.; Rizzolo, L.; Colman, A.; Rindler, M.J.; Adesnik, M.; Sabatini, D.D. Secretion of endogenous and exogenous proteins from polarized MDCK monolayers. *Proc. Natl. Acad. Sci. USA* 83:2100–2104, 1986.

Vesicular Transport and the Maintenance of Compartmental Identity

8–43
A. clathrin
B. non-clathrin

8–44
A. True
B. True

8–45 Your experiments show that non-clathrin-coated vesicles transport G protein without concentrating their contents. The concentration of G protein in the cisternal space was actually slightly higher than in the vesicles and vesicle buds, as measured in two different ways. If the vesicles were transporting G protein in a selective way (like clathrin-coated vesicles), the concentration of G protein in the vesicles should have been substantially higher than in the Golgi cisternae.

Reference: Orci, L.; Glick, B.S.; Rothman, J.E. A new type of coated vesicular carrier that appears not to contain clathrin: its possible role in protein transport within the Golgi stack. *Cell* 46:171–184, 1986.

The Cell Nucleus

Chromosomal DNA and Chromosomal Proteins

9–1

A. chromosome, genome
B. DNA replication origins, centromere, telomeres
C. gene
D. exons, introns
E. gene regulatory proteins
F. gel retardation assay
G. zinc fingers
H. helix-turn-helix
I. cooperative binding
J. B-form, A-form, Z-form
K. nucleosome
L. histones, nonhistone chromosomal, chromatin
M. nucleosomal, H1
N. nuclease-hypersensitive sites
O. 30-nm chromatin

9–2

A. True
B. False. Chromosomes are not replicated precisely and do lose nucleotides from the ends each time that they are replicated. The telomere solves this end-replication problem by confining the loss of nucleotides to the telomere itself. A special enzyme periodically extends the simple repeating sequence that constitutes the telomere, thereby *compensating* for the inevitable loss of nucleotides associated with replication of the linear chromosome.
C. True
D. False. Although it is true that introns are usually larger than exons, exons always outnumber introns by one in every gene.
E. True
F. True
G. True
H. False. Although the carefully studied examples of DNA-binding proteins follow this pattern, it is unlikely that such useful structural motifs would be segregated between bacteria and eucaryotes. In fact, amino acid sequence homologies suggest that the helix-turn-helix motif is present in some eucaryotic DNA-binding proteins.
I. True
J. False. If two proteins bind to partially overlapping DNA sequences, the binding of one will block binding by the other. Since the binding of one excludes binding by the other, their binding will be competitive instead of cooperative.
K. True
L. False. Special sequences allow DNA to be bent in the absence of interaction with proteins. However, inside cells, proteins such as histones can bend most DNA sequences into a tight coil, for example, as in the formation of nucleosomes.
M. True
N. True

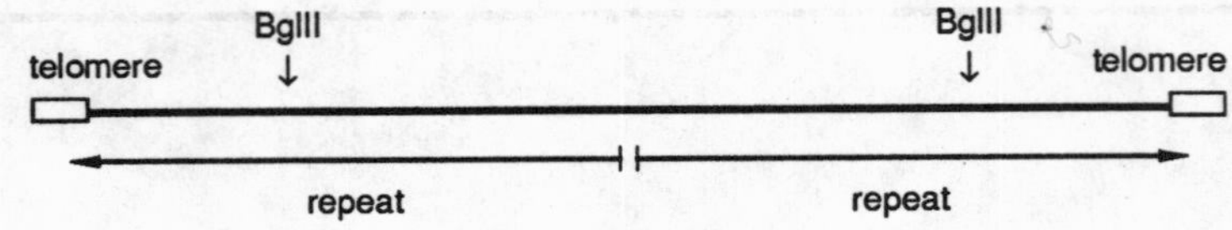

Figure 9–32 Palindromic structure of the ribosomal minichromosome from *Tetrahymena* (Answer 9–3).

O. True
P. False. Nuclease-hypersensitive sites are not found in the short stretches of linker DNA between nucleosomes but rather in long stretches of nucleosome-free DNA.
Q. True
R. False. Electron micrographs of spread chromatin generally show a regular pattern of nucleosome beads throughout both its transcribed and untranscribed regions.

9–3 The lengths of the restriction fragments do not sum to 21 kb and the electrophoretic patterns change with denaturation and reannealing because the ribosomal minichromosome is an inverted dimer or palindrome (Figure 9–32). That is to say, the sequences on the left half of the minichromosome are repeated in the opposite orientation on the right half. Thus, a restriction enzyme cuts each arm (that is, each repeated segment) at sites that are the same distance from the ends, thereby generating one central fragment and two identical copies of each terminal fragment. For BglII digestion the central fragment is 13.4 kb and the two terminal fragments are each 3.8 kb. The fragments on the gel did not add up to 21 kb because the terminal fragment should have been counted twice: 2 times 3.8 kb plus 13.4 kb does sum to 21 kb.

Denaturing and reannealing the minichromosome or its digestion products alters the electrophoretic pattern because the left and right halves of the single strands derived from the central fragment are complementary and, therefore, can reanneal internally. Because the two complementary halves are part of the same molecule, they reanneal internally very much faster than they do with other molecules. Self-reannealing reduces the apparent size of the fragment by a factor of 2. Thus, the uncut minichromosome, when denatured and reannealed, is reduced in size from 21 kb to 10.5 kb. Similarly, the 13.4-kb central BglII fragment is reduced to 6.7 kb. Of course, the single strands from the terminal fragments are not self-complementary and so can reanneal only with other complementary single strands to re-form their usual double-stranded structure.

Most unexpectedly, the ribosomal genes of *Tetrahymena* exist in a micronuclear chromosome as one half of the inverted repeat that makes up the macronuclear minichromosome. Since the micronucleus generates a new macronucleus after conjugation, the ribosomal genes must be cleaved out of the chromosome in a way that specifically generates an inverted dimer. You might try to imagine how this could be accomplished before looking up the speculation by scientists involved in some of these studies (Yao, M-C.; Zhu, S-G.; Yao, C-H. *Mol. Cell. Biol.* 5:1260, 1985).

Reference: Karrer, K.M.; Gall, J.G. The macronuclear ribosomal DNA of *Tetrahymena pyriformis* is a palindrome. *J. Mol. Biol.* 104:421–453, 1976.

***9–4** **Reference:** Szostak, J.W.; Blackburn, E.H. Cloning yeast telomeres on linear plasmid vectors. *Cell* 29:245–255, 1982.

9–5

A. The number of repeats in the terminal fragment must be quite variable, as indicated by the broad band that results from cleavage by AluI near the end of the minichromosome (observation 6). If the number of repeats were the

*Problems with an asterisk (*) are answered in the Instructor's Manual.

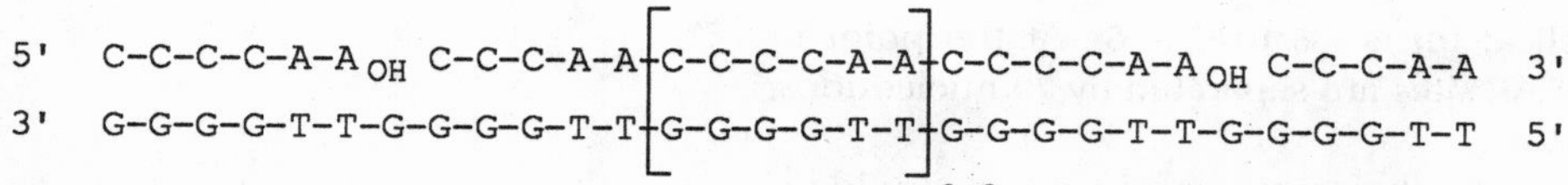

Figure 9–33 A portion of the terminal repeated sequence of the ribosomal minichromosome, showing positions of the specific one-nucleotide gaps (Answer 9–5).

same for every molecule, the band containing the terminal fragment would be sharp instead of broad. The difference between the leading and trailing edges of the band, which is about 160 nucleotide pairs, corresponds to about 27 repeats, which represents the variability in the number of repeats per telomere.

It is more difficult to estimate the average number of repeats per telomere from these data because the location of the AluI cleavage site relative to the beginning of the repeats is not known. However, if AluI cut exactly at the start of the repeats, then the number of repeats would vary between 60 (360/6) and 87 (520/6). It is thought that there are about 70 repeats per telomere.

B. The CCCCAA repeats are at the 5′ ends of the individual strands of the minichromosome. Since DNA synthesis that begins in the tandemly repeated DNA moves progressively toward the center of the minichromosome (observation 7), the repeats must be at the 5′ ends. If the repeats were at the 3′ ends, DNA synthesis would proceed toward the ends of the minichromosome.

C. The single-strand interruptions in the CCCCAA repeats are, for the most part, single nucleotide gaps. Since denaturation releases single-stranded fragments (observation 4), there must be breaks in the phosphodiester backbone. These discontinuities presumably have a 3′-OH since they serve as sites for DNA synthesis (observations 1, 3, and 7); however, they cannot be simple breaks with a 5′-PO_4 and a 3′-OH, since treatment with DNA ligase does not reduce incorporation by DNA polymerase (observation 2). The nature of the single-strand interruptions is revealed by replacing free 5′ phosphates with labeled phosphates and then breaking all bonds to purine nucleotides, which yields predominantly the labeled fragment CCC (observation 5). This result indicates that most of the discontinuities are single-nucleotide gaps, where the first C (5′ C) of the repeat is missing. (If the 3′ C were missing —CCC_AA—, then the label at the 5′ phosphate would have been added to an A and the CCC fragment would not have been labeled.) The gap is unlikely to be longer than one nucleotide because DNA polymerase can incorporate labeled C in the absence of other nucleotides (observation 1). (If the gap were two nucleotides long, for example, then the first nucleotide incorporated by DNA polymerase would have to be an A.)

D. Since denaturation of the telomere releases single-stranded fragments corresponding to 2, 3, and 4 CCCCAA repeats (observation 4), the single-strand interruptions must be present on average about once every two to four repeats.

E. These data suggest that the structure of the telomere on the ribosomal minichromosome is as shown in Figure 9–33. This model encompasses all the information in the experimental observations.

Reference: Blackburn, E.H.; Gall, J.G. A tandemly repeated sequence at the termini of the extrachromosomal ribosomal RNA genes in *Tetrahymena*. *J. Mol. Biol.* 120:33–53, 1978.

***9–6** **References:** Konkel, D.A.; Maizel, J.V.; Leder, P. The evolution and sequence comparison of two recently diverged mouse chromosomal β-globin genes. *Cell* 18:865–873, 1979.

Staden, R. An interactive graphics program for comparing and aligning nucleic acid and amino acid sequences. *Nucleic Acids Res.* 10:2951–2961, 1982.

9–7

A. At the point of minimum relative migration, the CAP sites are separated by 85 nucleotides (Figure 9–6C). At 10.6 nucleotides per turn, this number of nucleotides corresponds to 8 helical turns (85/10.6 = 8). At the point of maximum relative migration, the CAP sites are separated by 79 nucleotides, which corresponds to 7.5 helical turns.

B. The two CAP sites must be bent exactly the same way since they are identical. Therefore, they will both have the same groove of the helix facing the inside of the bend at the center of bending. In order for the DNA to bend into the *cis* configuration, the two centers of bending must be on the same side of the helix. The major grooves (or minor grooves) are on the same side of the helix at integral numbers of helical turns. Thus, it is expected that the point of minimum relative migration (the *cis* configuration) will occur after an integral number of helical turns. Similarly, the point of maximum relative migration (the *trans* configuration) will occur when the centers of bending are on opposite sides of the helix, that is, at half integral numbers of helical turns.

C. At the point of minimum migration of the construct with one CAP site and one $(A_5N_5)_4$ site, the centers of bending are separated by 101 nucleotides (Figure 9–6D). At 10.6 nucleotides per helical turn, the centers of bending are separated by 9.5 helical turns (101/10.6 = 9.5).

D. Since the point of minimum relative migration (the *cis* configuration) occurs at a half integral number of turns, the two centers of bending cannot have the same groove of the helix facing the inside of the bend. As discussed in part B, if the same groove of the helix faced the inside of the bend, the centers of bending in the *cis* configuration would be separated by an integral number of turns. Therefore, the two centers of bending must have opposite grooves facing the inside of the bend. Because the $(A_5N_5)_4$ site is known to bend with the major groove facing the inside of the bend (as was stated in the problem), the CAP-binding site must be bent so that the minor groove faces the inside of the bend at the center of bending.

References: Zinkel, S.S.; Crothers, D.M. DNA bend direction by phase sensitive detection. *Nature* 328:178–181, 1987.

Gartenberg, M.R.; Crothers, D.M. DNA sequence determinants of CAP-induced bending and protein binding affinity. *Nature* 333:824–829, 1988.

***9–8** **Reference:** Prunell, A.; Kornberg, R.D.; Lutter, L.; Klug, A.; Levitt, M.; Crick, F.H. Periodicity of deoxyribonuclease I digestion of chromatin. *Science* 204:855–858, 1979.

***9–9**

9–10

A. Micrococcal nuclease generates fragments whose lengths vary depending on the spacing of the internucleosomal cleavages that define the ends of the fragments (Figure 9–34). Since micrococcal nuclease does not cleave at precise sites within the linker DNA, there is some variability in the lengths of fragments produced by cleavage even between the same two pairs of nucleosomes. Furthermore, similar-size fragments can be produced by cleavage between several different pairs of internucleosomal sites. These

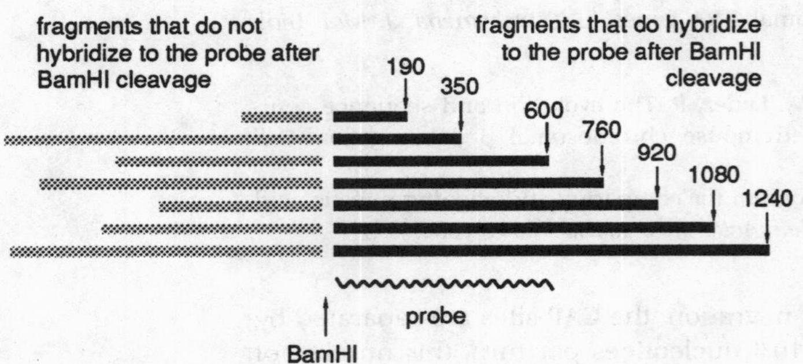

Figure 9–34 Diagram relating indirect end labeling to the fragment lengths observed in Figure 9–9 (Answer 9–10). Sites of micrococcal-nuclease cleavage are indicated by the downward pointing arrows. The small gap in the micrococcal-nuclease fragments shows the position of BamHI cleavage. Numbers refer to the lengths of the fragments that hybridize to the probe; they correspond to the lengths shown in Figure 9–9.

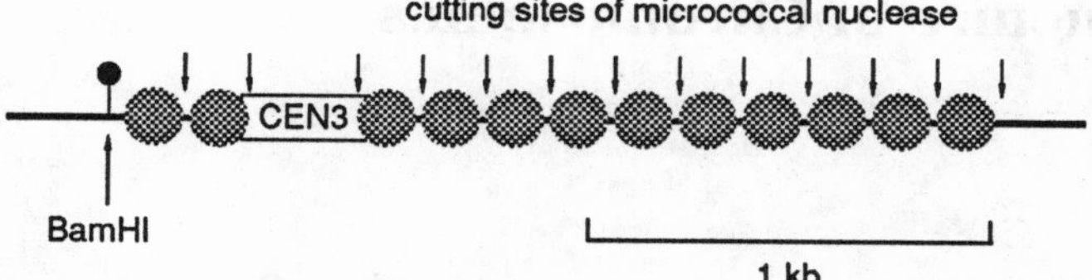

Figure 9–35 Positions of micrococcal-nuclease-cleavage sites and arrangement of nucleosomes around the centromere (Answer 9–10). Nucleosomes are shown as balls.

sorts of variability obscure the fine-structure details of the ordering of adjacent nucleosomes.

Digestion with BamHI sharpens the pattern of bands because it precisely defines one end of each DNA fragment. As shown in Figure 9–34, only the fragments to the right of the BamHI-cleavage site hybridize to the radioactive probe. The resulting pattern is easy to interpret because the length of each fragment gives the distance from the nuclease-cleavage site to the BamHI site directly. In the absence of BamHI cleavage the bands are defined by micrococcal-nuclease cleavage at both ends. Such a pattern does not allow one to deduce the exact sites of nuclease cleavage relative to the probe, since nuclease cleavage at several pairs of sites can yield the same-size fragment. The method for mapping nuclease-cut sites that is illustrated in this problem is called indirect end labeling because a defined end (the BamHI-cleavage site) is labeled indirectly through hybridization to a radiolabeled probe.

B. The sizes of the bands indicate the distances between the nuclease-cut sites and the BamHI cleavage site (Figure 9–34). Since micrococcal nuclease cleaves between nucleosomes, the cut sites define the positions of the nucleosomes relative to the BamHI site (Figure 9–35). With the exception of the region around the centromere the cut sites are spaced at 160-nucleotide intervals, suggesting that the nucleosomes occupy about 160 nucleotides of DNA. However, the cut sites on either side of the centromere are 250 nucleotides apart, suggesting that some special (nonnucleosomal) structure covers the centromere. It is thought that centromere-specific proteins bind to and protect the centromere from nuclease digestion. The cleavage sites on either side of the centromere indicate that there is unprotected DNA (analogous to the linker DNA between nucleosomes) between the centromere and the adjacent nucleosomes on either side.

C. The naked DNA control is important because all DNA sequences are not equally susceptible to micrococcal-nuclease cleavage. It is essential to know the susceptibility of the specific DNA sequence under investigation. Otherwise, one can be fooled into thinking that a specific band results from the binding of a protein adjacent to the cleavage site, when it actually derives from the cleavage specificity of the nuclease. Indeed, the centromere itself is a preferred site of cleavage (although that was left out of the naked DNA digestion shown in Figure 9–9); the absence of cutting at this sensitive site in chromatin is all the more evidence that it is specifically protected.

D. Your results answer this question very elegantly. The band patterns from the three plasmids are the key result. If the nucleosomes were ordered simply because they were lined up next to the special structure at the centromere, then it should not make any difference what DNA sequence was present beyond the centromere. Your results with plasmids 2 and 3, however, show clearly that the ordered arrangement disappears at the point where the bacterial sequences (plasmid 2) or the noncentromeric yeast sequences (plasmid 3) begin. This result argues strongly that the regular ordering of nucleosomes around the centromere is due to some feature of the sequence of the neighboring DNA itself.

Reference: Bloom, K.S.; Carbon, J. Yeast centromere DNA is in a unique and highly ordered structure in chromosomes and small circular minichromosomes. *Cell* 29:305–317, 1982.

The Complex Global Structure of Chromosomes

9–11

A. looped domains
B. chromatids (chromosomes)
C. karyotype
D. lampbrush chromosomes
E. polytene chromosomes
F. chromosome puffs
G. active
H. heterochromatin

9–12

A. True
B. True
C. True
D. False. Most of the DNA in lampbrush chromosomes is in the chromomeres, not in the loops.
E. False. Side-by-side adherence of chromatin strands gives rise to polytene chromosomes.
F. True
G. False. Classical genetic studies suggested that each band probably corresponded to a gene; however, more recent molecular data indicate that there are three times as many distinct mRNAs as bands. Thus, the "one band, one gene" hypothesis seems unlikely.
H. True
I. True
J. False. Although transcriptionally inactive chromatin is condensed into a relatively nuclease-resistant form, only about 10% to 20% of it is packed into the highly condensed conformation known as heterochromatin.

9–13 The uniform pattern of labeling observed with the smaller chromatin loops is the expected pattern. At first, it might seem that, if transcription proceeds from one end of a loop to the other, the labeling pattern should also progress from one end to the other as it does for the large loop in Figure 9–10. However, since transcription occurs throughout a chromatin loop (by multiple RNA polymerases) as illustrated in Figure 9–11, then ^{3}H-uridine should also be incorporated throughout the length of the loop as each polymerase molecule adds a uridine nucleotide to the growing RNA chain (Figure 9–36). With increasing time more label will be incorporated; thus the intensity of labeling over the entire loop is expected to increase.

What then is the explanation for the labeling pattern observed in the large chromatin loops? The answer is not yet known. Because the loops do not label until after a day, it is thought that these loops may not be transcribed at all. Instead, they may be storage sites for RNA that is synthesized elsewhere—with an entry site into the loop at one end.

Reference: Callan, H.G. The nature of lampbrush chromosomes. *Int. Rev. Cytol.* 15:1–34, 1963.

Gall, J.G. Personal communication.

***9–14** **Reference:** Spierer, A.; Spierer, P. Similar levels of polyteny in bands and interbands of *Drosophila* giant chromosomes. *Nature* 307:176–178, 1984.

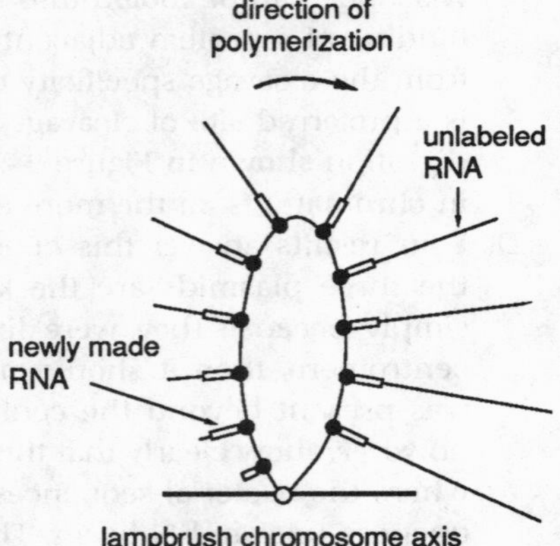

Figure 9–36 Uniform incorporation of radioactive uridine into a chromatin loop (Answer 9–13). Newly synthesized RNA is indicated by open rectangles adjacent to RNA polymerase molecules, which are represented by filled circles.

9–15

A. DNase I preferentially digests active chromatin. Red cells express globin and treatment of red cell nuclei with DNase I reduces the ability of the DNA to protect globin cDNA. Thus, the chromatin from which globin RNA is transcribed is preferentially degraded by DNase I. By contrast, fibroblasts do not express globin, and treatment of fibroblast nuclei with DNase I does not reduce the ability of the DNA to protect globin cDNA. Thus, in fibroblasts the globin genes are no more sensitive than the bulk of the chromatin.

B. DNase I digestion of red cell nuclei preferentially degrades regions of active chromatin. A comparison of the extents of protection of ^{3}H-labeled red cell DNA by total DNA (95%) and by DNase-I-digested DNA (78%) suggests that about 17% (95%–78%) of red cell DNA is sensitive to DNase I—and by that criterion, in active chromatin.

C. Trypsin treatment of nucleosome monomers affects a specific population of monomers—namely, those monomers that were present in active chromatin. This conclusion comes from a comparison of trypsin-treated monomers with DNase-I-treated red cell DNA. Digestion of trypsin-treated nucleosome monomers with micrococcal nuclease yields DNA that protects globin cDNA and red cell DNA (25% and 83%, respectively) to the same extents as DNase-I-treated red cell DNA (25% and 78%, respectively) as shown in Table 9–1.

(If a random population of nucleosomes were affected, all the DNA sequences present in the untreated nucleosomes would still be present in the trypsin-treated nucleosomes. If that were the case, both the untreated and treated monomers would behave identically in their capacity to protect globin cDNA and total red cell DNA.)

D. Since the DNA in individual nucleosome monomers shows the same sensitivity to DNase I as chromatin in nuclei, the property of active chromatin that distinguishes it from bulk chromatin must be present in individual nucleosomes. This viewpoint is supported further by the observation that trypsin treatment of nucleosome monomers renders those from active chromatin sensitive to micrococcal nuclease. Individual monomers from regions of active chromatin must be physically distinct from other nucleosome monomers.

Reference: Weintraub, H.; Groudine, M. Chromosomal subunits in active genes have an altered conformation. *Science* 193:848–856, 1976.

Chromosome Replication

9–16

A. S phase
B. replication forks, replication origins
C. replication units
D. T-antigen
E. re-replication block

9–17

A. False. Replication forks in eucaryotic cells travel at about one-tenth the rate they do in bacteria. This slower rate may reflect the difficulty of replicating DNA packaged into chromatin.
B. True
C. True
D. False. Unlike most proteins, which are made continuously throughout interphase, histones are synthesized mainly in the S phase, during which the level of histone mRNA increases about fifty-fold as a result of both increased transcription and decreased mRNA degradation.
E. True
F. True
G. False. The active X chromosome is replicated throughout the S phase, whereas the inactive X chromosome, which is completely condensed into heterochromatin, is replicated late in S phase.
H. True
I. True
J. False. In such fusion experiments G_1-phase nuclei, not G_2-phase nuclei, are stimulated to synthesize DNA. Replication origins in G_2-phase nuclei have a block to DNA re-replication, which was acquired as they passed through S phase.

*9–18 **Reference:** Huberman, J.A.; Riggs, A.D. On the mechanism of DNA replication in mammalian chromosomes. *J. Mol. Biol.* 32:327–341, 1968.

9–19

A. Hybridization at the 4.5-kb position is due to plasmid molecules that were not replicating at the time DNA was isolated. The intensity of this spot indicates that the majority of plasmid molecules were not replicating. The low frequency of replicating plasmid molecules, even during S phase, has been one of the contributing factors in the difficulty of proving that an ARS is an origin.

B. The results in Figure 9–16 indicate that ARS1 behaves as an origin of replication. The gel pattern with BglII-digested DNA looks like the pattern due to replicating molecules with two branches (Figure 9–15C). The gel pattern with PvuI-digested DNA looks like the pattern due to replication intermediates with asymmetrically located replication bubbles (Figure 9–15D). (The very short tail on the spot at 9 kb in Figure 9–16B indicates that the replication bubbles are only slightly asymmetrically situated in the replicating molecules.) These gel patterns are exactly what would be expected if replication began at ARS1. As shown in Figure 9–37, cleavage with BglII, which cuts at ARS1, would generate molecules with two branches; cleavage with PvuI, which cuts almost half way around the circle from ARS1, generates molecules with slightly asymmetrically located replication bubbles.

C. The discontinuity in the arc of hybridization to PvuI-cut plasmids (Figure 9–16B) results from the difference in migration of bubble forms and branched forms. Molecules that have just begun replicating will be converted to bubble forms by PvuI cleavage, whereas molecules in which replication has proceeded beyond the PvuI site will be converted to branched forms. Thus, a replicating molecule that is cleaved either has a bubble or it is branched—there is no intermediate. Since the two forms migrate differently, there is a gap in the electrophoretic pattern.

Reference: Brewer, B.J.; Fangman, W.L. The localization of replication origins on ARS plasmids in *S. cerevisiae*. *Cell* 51:463–471, 1987.

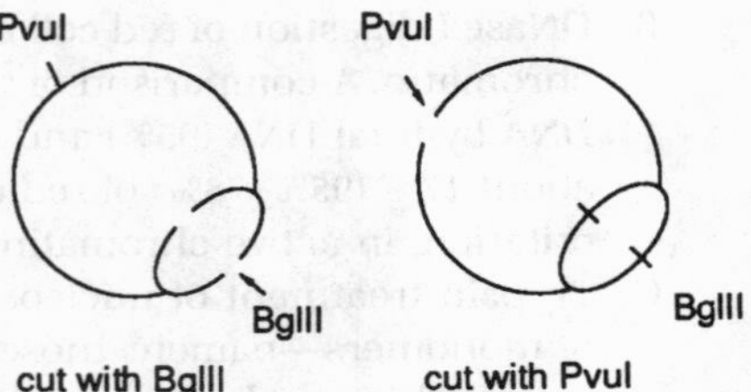

Figure 9–37 Conversion of replicating plasmid molecules into linear forms with two branches by BglII or linear forms with slightly asymmetrically located replication bubbles by PvuI (Answer 9–19).

9–20

A. In addition to its site-specific DNA binding, T-antigen possesses an ATP-dependent helicase activity. A helicase activity is necessary for unwinding DNA (see MBOC Chapter 5). The presence of T-antigen at the forks is also consistent with its activity as a helicase.

The ability of T-antigen to bind specifically to SV40 origins of replication and unwind them is a natural first step in DNA replication. These activities expose single-stranded regions so that primases and DNA polymerases can gain access to the DNA. However, T-antigen probably also guides the entry of one or more of these components: antibodies to T-antigen immunoprecipitate a DNA polymerase-primase complex, and T-antigen stimulates replication at SV40 origins only in certain cell types. Both these observations suggest that initiation depends on specific interactions between T-antigen and one or more components of the actual replication machinery.

B. To demonstrate that the unwound regions are at the origin, you can digest the DNA with a restriction enzyme that cuts at a defined location relative to the origin. (Since the two ends of a linear molecule cannot be distinguished in the electron microscope, at least two different restriction digestions are required to position unwound regions unambiguously.) If unwinding does not occur at the origin, the unwound region will not include the origin (Figure 9–38A). If unwinding occurs at the origin, the unwound region will include the origin. If unwinding occurs in one direction, one end of the unwound region will coincide with the origin (Figure 9–38B). If unwinding occurs in both directions (at the same rate), the center of the unwound region will coincide with the origin (Figure 9–38C). The actual experimental results indicate that unwinding occurs in both directions at approximately the same rate.

(A) UNWINDING DOES NOT START AT ORIGIN

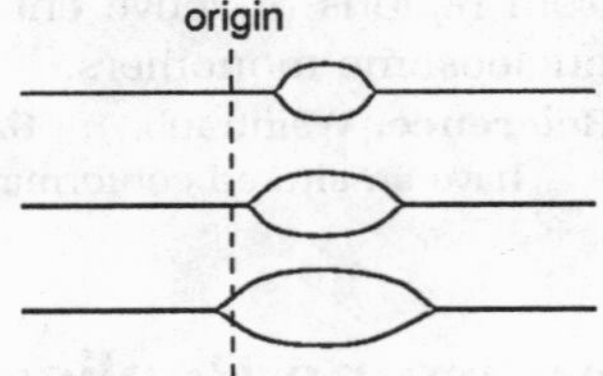

(B) UNIDIRECTIONAL UNWINDING

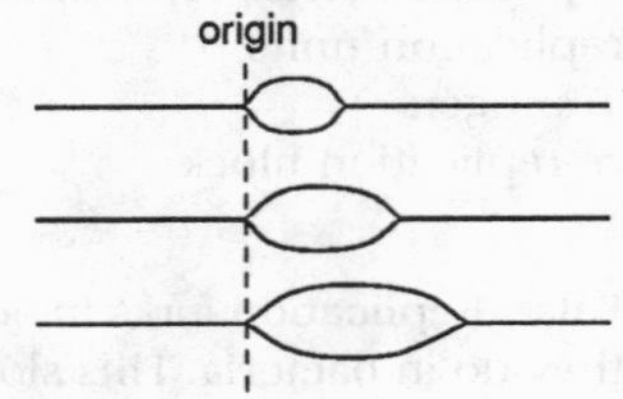

(C) BIDIRECTIONAL UNWINDING

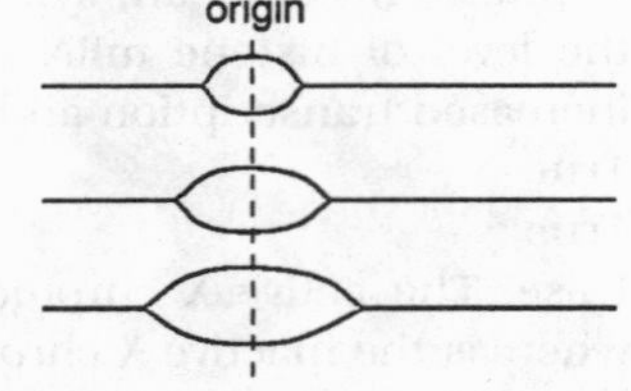

Figure 9–38 The use of restriction digestion to position the site of unwinding by T antigen relative to the SV40 origin of replication (Answer 9–20). The ends of the linear molecule were generated by digestion with a restriction enzyme.

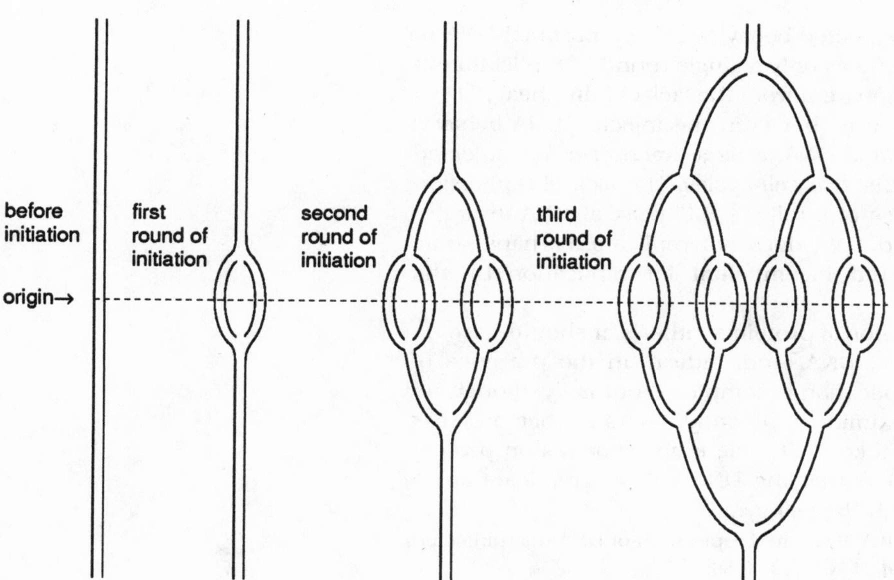

Figure 9–39 Multiple initiation events at a chromosomal SV40 origin of replication (Answer 9–20).

C. Topoisomerase I is required for unwinding closed circular DNA molecules in order to relieve overwinding strain in the duplex part of the molecule. In a covalently closed circle the removal of duplex winding in one segment causes the rest of the duplex to become overwound, which is energetically unfavorable. The transient nicking-closing activity of topoisomerase I allows this winding tension to be relieved.

D. If T-antigen initiated replication multiple times from an SV40 origin integrated in a chromosome, a complex multistranded structure would be produced. Three rounds of initiation at a chromosomal origin are illustrated in Figure 9–39.

Apparently, a chromosomal SV40 origin in the presence of T-antigen replicates in a manner similar to that shown in Figure 9–40. This process is termed "onion-skin" replication because the resulting structure has a layered appearance reminiscent of an onion.

Reference: Dodson, M.; Dean, F.B.; Bullock, P.; Echols, H.; Hurwitz, J. Unwinding of duplex DNA from the SV40 origin of replication by T-antigen. *Science* 238:964–967, 1987.

***9–21** **Reference:** Orr-Weaver, T.L.; Spradling, A.C. *Drosophila* chorion gene amplification requires an upstream region regulating s18 transcription. *Mol. Cell. Biol.* 6:4624–4633, 1986.

9–22

A. The three density peaks represent, from light to heavy, unreplicated DNA, once replicated DNA, and twice replicated DNA (Figure 9–40). The injected DNA is labeled with ^3H but is otherwise normal DNA, which is "light." Each newly synthesized strand incorporates ^{32}P label and BrdU, which increases its density. Thus, after one round of replication, the DNA will be intermediate in density, containing one "light" ^3H-labeled strand and one "heavy" ^{32}P-labeled strand. After the second round of replication, the hybrid DNA will give rise to one hybrid density duplex and to one duplex that contains two ^{32}P-labeled "heavy" strands. The fully "heavy" duplex will appear at the densest position in the gradient. Since the fully "light" DNA is unreplicated, it will contain no ^{32}P label; since the fully "heavy" DNA contains two new strands, it will contain no ^3H label.

The formation of discrete peaks in this experiment makes an important point: most of the observed labeling is due to replication and not to repair synthesis. If the incorporation of label were due to repair synthesis, which is patchy, the label would be smeared through the gradient rather than concentrated in discrete peaks.

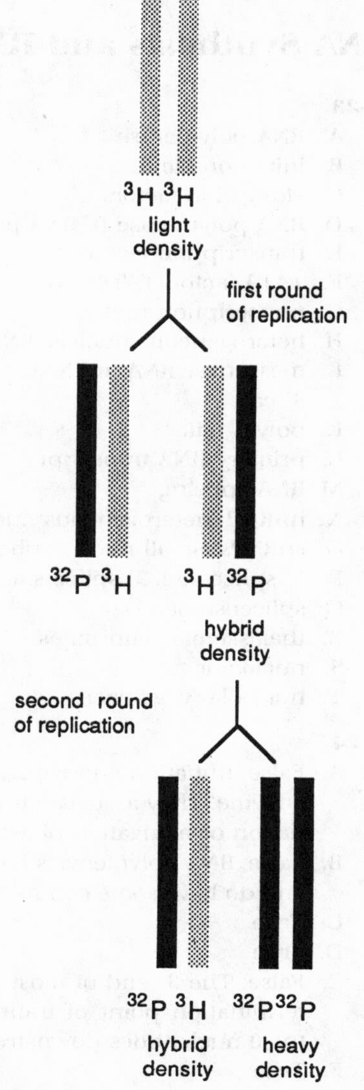

Figure 9–40 Schematic representation of strand labeling (Answer 9–22).

B. The injected DNA mimics the expected behavior of chromosomal DNA in one very important way: it undergoes only a single round of replication in one cell cycle. This behavior is apparent from the lack of fully "heavy" DNA after one cell cycle. In another way, however, the injected DNA behaves very differently from chromosomal DNA: a large fraction of the injected DNA does not replicate even after two cell cycles. The lack of replication is apparent from the persistence of a fully "light" peak of DNA. It is not clear why some of the injected DNA does not replicate. Perhaps some of the eggs have been rendered incompetent for replication by the experimental protocol.

C. Since cycloheximide is an inhibitor of protein synthesis, it should have no direct effect on the synthesis of DNA. And, indeed, in the presence of cycloheximide one round of replication is completed normally, though no more occur thereafter. Cycloheximide apparently blocks further progress through the cell cycle because a key cell-cycle event depends on protein synthesis. The important point is that the DNA will not replicate again unless the cells progress through the cell cycle.

Reference: Harland, R.M.; Laskey, R.A. Regulated replication of DNA microinjected into eggs of *Xenopus laevis*. *Cell* 21:761–771, 1980.

RNA Synthesis and RNA Processing

9–23

A. RNA polymerase
B. initiation factor
C. elongation factors
D. RNA polymerase II, RNA polymerase I, RNA polymerase III
E. transcription factors
F. TATA factor, TATA box
G. transcription unit
H. heterogeneous nuclear RNA (hnRNA)
I. messenger RNA (mRNA)
J. 5′ cap
K. poly-A tail
L. primary RNA transcript
M. RNA splicing
N. hnRNP (heterogeneous nuclear ribonucleoprotein)
O. snRNPs (small nuclear ribonucleoproteins)
P. 5′ splice site, 3′ splice site
Q. spliceosome
R. thalassemia syndromes
S. nucleolus
T. nucleolar organizer

9–24

A. False. Initiation and elongation factors are not permanent subunits of the enzyme. They associate transiently with the enzyme during either the initiation or elongation phase of RNA synthesis.
B. False. RNA polymerases I, II, and III are structurally similar to one another and do have some common subunits, although other subunits are unique.
C. True
D. True
E. False. The 3′ end of most polymerase II transcripts is defined not by the termination point of transcription but by cleavage of the RNA chain 10 to 30 nucleotides downstream of the sequence AAUAAA.
F. True
G. True
H. False. Both hnRNP particles and snRNPs are composed of multiple poly-

peptide chains complexed with RNA. However, hnRNP particles contain mRNA, which is very unstable.

I. False. Although intron sequences are mostly dispensable, they must be removed precisely because an error of even one nucleotide would shift the reading frame in the resulting mRNA molecule and make nonsense of its message.

J. True

K. True

L. False. 28S rRNA, 18S rRNA, and 5.8S rRNA are transcribed as part of one large 45S precursor RNA, which then is cleaved to give one copy each of the three rRNA products. The derivation of these three rRNAs from the same primary transcript ensures that they will be made in equal quantities.

M. False. Ribosomal RNAs are packaged with ribosomal proteins in the nucleolus.

N. True

O. True

P. False. Interphase chromosomes tend to occupy discrete domains in interphase nuclei and are not thought to be extensively intertwined with other chromosomes.

9–25

A. The 400-nucleotide transcript is absent from lane 4 (Figure 9–20) because GTP was included in the reaction mixture. GTP allows transcription to proceed beyond the C-minus sequence, thereby generating transcripts longer than 400 nucleotides. In the absence of GTP (lane 2) transcription cannot proceed beyond the C-minus sequence. In the presence of GTP and RNase T1 (lanes 6 and 8) the longer transcripts are cleaved at the first G to yield the 400-nucleotide transcript.

B. One of the difficulties in assaying promoter function *in vitro* is the high background of nonspecific initiation of transcription. It is this background that is so evident in lane 3. Its source is not altogether clear, but transcription may start at sequences in the rest of the plasmid that bear a weak resemblance to true RNA polymerase II promoters.

C. A 400-nucleotide transcript is present in lane 5 because cleavage with RNase T1 liberates it from any randomly initiated transcript that has traversed the C-minus sequence. It is actually a few nucleotides longer than the specifically initiated transcript since its 5′ end is defined by the first G that precedes the C-minus sequence.

The 400-nucleotide transcript is absent from lane 7 because 3′O-methyl GTP will terminate most transcripts that are initiated in front of the C-minus sequence. The combination of 3′O-methyl GTP and RNase T1 eliminates virtually all the background synthesis from the control plasmid.

D. You should have no difficulty assaying specific transcription in crude extracts (that is, in the presence of GTP). As shown in Figure 9–20 (lanes 7 and 8), specific transcription can be assayed in the presence of G nucleotides if 3′O-methyl GTP and RNase T1 are included (to inhibit background transcription and to cleave any random transcripts into small pieces).

Reference: Sawadogo, M.; Roeder, R.G. Factors involved in specific transcription by human RNA polymerase II: analysis by a rapid and quantitative *in vitro* assay. *Proc. Natl. Acad. Sci. USA* 82:4394–4398, 1985.

***9–26** **Reference:** Sawadogo, M.; Roeder, R.G. Factors involved in specific transcription by human RNA polymerase II: analysis by a rapid and quantitative *in vitro* assay. *Proc. Natl. Acad. Sci. USA* 82:4394–4398, 1985.

***9–27** **Reference:** Workman, J.L.; Roeder, R.G. Binding of transcription factor TFIID to the major late promoter during *in vitro* nucleosome assembly potentiates subsequent initiation by RNA polymerase II. *Cell* 51:613–622, 1987.

9–28

A. Since RNA polymerase is blocked by pyrimidine dimers, the sensitivity of transcription of a gene will depend on the distance between the promoter and the probe. It is a simple function of the size of the target for UV damage. If the polymerase must go twice as far to make a transcript, the chances of encountering a block to transcription are twice as great.

B. Transcription through the VSG gene is seven times more sensitive to UV irradiation than transcription through the ribosomal transcription unit at the site of rRNA probe 4, which is about 7 kb from its promoter. Thus, the beginning of the VSG gene is located about 50 kb (7 x 7) away from its promoter. This calculation assumes that the DNA between the VSG promoter and the VSG gene has about the same sensitivity to UV light as the DNA in the ribosomal RNA transcription unit.

C. If the nearby gene is 20% less sensitive to UV irradiation than the VSG gene, it is inactivated at 80% the rate of the VSG gene. Therefore, its promoter is 40 kb away (0.80 x 50 kb). Given that the nearby gene is 10 kb in front of the VSG gene, its promoter must map very near the promoter for the VSG gene. Thus, it is likely that the two genes are transcribed from the same promoter.

Reference: Johnson, P.J.; Kooter, J.M.; Borst, P. Inactivation of transcription by UV irradiation of *T. brucei* provides evidence for a multicistronic transcription unit including a VSG gene. *Cell* 51:273–281, 1987.

***9–29** **Reference:** Berget, S.M.; Berk, A.J.; Harrison, T.; Sharp, P.A. Spliced segments at the 5′ termini of adenovirus-2 late mRNA: a role for heterogeneous nuclear RNA in mammalian cells. *Cold Spring Harbor Symp. Quant. Biol.* 42:523–529, 1977.

9–30

A. The 5′ ends of the RNA molecules were labeled. Only labeled fragments show up in the autoradiograph (Figure 9–25). Thus, if the shortest fragments (those that run at the bottom of the gel) are from the 5′ end, the 5′ end must have been labeled.

B. The bands corresponding to the A's in the AAUAAA signal sequence are missing from the ladder of bands in polyadenylated and cleaved RNA (Figure 9–24, lanes 3 and 4) because modification of any one of those A's interferes with cleavage and polyadenylation. Thus, RNA molecules that carry a single modification in the signal sequence are not recognized by the components of the extract and, as a result, do not show up in the population of molecules that carry poly-A tails (lane 3) or in the population of molecules that are cleaved (lane 4).

C. The band at the arrow in Figure 9–25 is absent in the polyadenylated RNA but present in the cleaved RNA because modification of this A does not prevent cleavage, but it does prevent polyadenylation. Thus, RNA molecules with this A modified are present in the cleaved molecules (lane 4) but not present in the polyadenylated molecules (lane 3).

D. The analysis of the missing bands in parts B and C above indicates that the AAUAAA signal sequence is important for the cleavage of precursor RNAs and that the AAUAAA sequence and the single A are required for polyadenylation.

E. If the other end—the 3′ end—of the RNA molecules were labeled, it would have been possible to determine whether any of the A's or G's on the 3′ side of the cleavage site were important for polyadenylation. These experiments have been done; they show that no single modification 3′ of the polyadenylation site prevents polyadenylation.

Reference: Conway, L.; Wickens, M. Analysis of mRNA 3′-end formation by modification interference: the only modifications which prevent processing lie in AAUAAA and the poly (A) site. *EMBO J.* 6:4177–4184, 1987.

9–31

A. Your idea was to try to cleave the RNA component of the snRNP that you suspected was interacting with the conserved sequence at the 3′ end of the histone precursor. If the snRNP was interacting by hybridizing to the precursor RNA, then an oligonucleotide that matches the sequence in the precursor RNA should be able to hybridize to the snRNA. Formation of a

```
         3' GTGTCGATGAAACCA 5' human
               ||||||////
5' m3G-NNGUGUUACAGCUCUUUUAGAAUUUGUCUAGU 3' human U7 snRNA
               ||||||||||
         3' TTGTCGAGAAAGGC 5' mouse
               |||||||||
         3' TGGTCGAGAGAAAGAAA 5' consensus
```

Figure 9–41 Pairing between the three oligonucleotides and the human U7 snRNA (Answer 9–31).

DNA-RNA hybrid would render the snRNA sensitive to cleavage by added RNase H. Cleavage of the snRNA in this critical region of interaction should render the extract incapable of processing the precursor. This result was the one you observed for the mouse and consensus oligonucleotides.

B. The inability of the human oligonucleotide to block processing was not anticipated, since you were using a human extract. However, an examination of the hybrids that can be formed between the various oligonucleotides and the U7 snRNA reveal that the mouse and consensus oligonucleotides can hybridize perfectly for a 10-nucleotide and a 9-nucleotide stretch, respectively (Figure 9–41). By contrast, hybridization to the human oligonucleotide is split by an unmatched nucleotide into two segments of 6 and 4 nucleotides (Figure 9–41). The stability of pairing of two separate segments is not as great as for a continuous pairing segment. Hence, the human oligonucleotide does not pair with sufficient stability to render the U7 snRNA sensitive to RNase H cleavage.

Reference: Mowry, K.L.; Steitz, J.A. Identification of human U7 snRNP as one of several factors involved in the 3′-end maturation of histone premessenger RNAs. *Science* 238:1682–1687, 1987.

***9–32**

***9–33** **Reference:** Krause, M.; Hirsh, D. A trans-spliced leader sequence on actin mRNA in *C. elegans*. *Cell* 49:753–761, 1987.

9–34

A. If the splicing machinery binds to one splice site and scans across the intron to find its complementary splice site, it must use the first appropriate splice site it encounters. (Not using the first appropriate splice site is equivalent to skipping an exon.) The expected products from intron scanning in your two minigenes are shown in Figure 9–42. If the splicing machinery binds to a 5′ splice site and scans toward a 3′ splice site, minigene 1 should generate one product (Figure 9–42A) and minigene 2 should generate two products (Figure 9–42B). By contrast, if the splicing machinery binds to a 3′ splice site and scans toward a 5′ splice site, minigene 1 should generate two products (Figure 9–42A) and minigene 2 should generate one product (Figure 9–41B).

B. The results of your experiment do not match the expectations for either direction of intron scanning. Therefore, selection of splice sites by a mechanism involving unidirectional scanning through introns in either a 5′-to-3′ or in a 3′-to-5′ direction seems unlikely. The mechanism by which cells avoid exon skipping has not yet been defined.

Reference: Kuhne, T.; Wieringa, B.; Reiser, J.; Weissmann, C. Evidence against a scanning model for RNA splicing. *EMBO J.* 2:727-733, 1983.

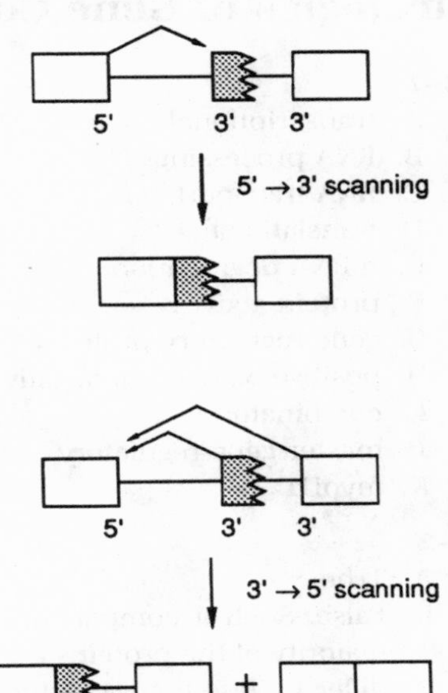

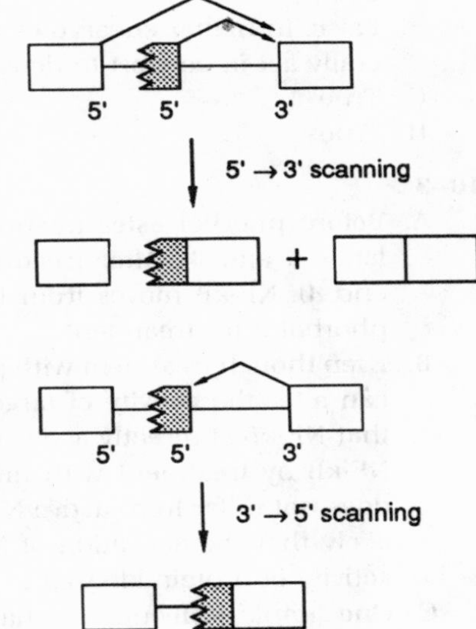

Figure 9–42 Expected products for minigene 1 (A) and minigene 2 (B) for 5′ to 3′ scanning and 3′ to 5′ scanning (Answer 9–34). Open boxes indicate complete exons, hatched boxes represent partial exons.

Control of Gene Expression

10

Strategies of Gene Control

10–1

A. transcriptional
B. RNA processing
C. RNA transport
D. translational
E. mRNA degradation
F. protein activity
G. gene regulatory proteins
H. positive regulation, negative regulation
I. combinatorial
J. master gene regulatory
K. myoD1

10–2

A. True
B. False. Such a comparison reveals remarkably few differences. The great majority of the proteins are synthesized in different cell types at rates that differ by less than a factor of five; only a few percent of the proteins are present in very different amounts in different tissues.
C. True
D. False. Some gene regulatory proteins inhibit transcription of the adjacent gene when they bind to their recognition sequence.
E. True
F. False. In higher eucaryotes whole clusters of gene activator proteins generally act in concert to determine whether a gene is to be transcribed.
G. True
H. True

10–3

A. Before phorbol ester treatment NF-κB is in the cytoplasm (Figure 10–1, lanes 5 and 6). After treatment NF-κB is found in the nucleus (lanes 3 and 4). NF-κB moves from the cytoplasm to the nucleus in response to phorbol ester treatment.
B. Even though treatment with phorbol ester activates protein kinase C, which can alter the activity of target proteins by phosphorylation, it is unlikely that NF-κB is directly activated by phosphorylation. The ability to activate NF-κB by treatment with mild denaturants suggests that inactive NF-κB does not differ from active NF-κB by covalent modification. It seems more likely that the activation of NF-κB is at least one step removed from the activity of protein kinase C.
C. One simple molecular mechanism to account for NF-κB activation by phorbol ester treatment of pre-B cells assumes that NF-κB is inactive because it is complexed with an inhibitor. Inactivation of NF-κB by a bound inhibitor is consistent with the activation of NF-κB by mild denaturants, which could exert their effect by causing the dissociation of the inhibitory subunit. The inhibitor could function by masking the enhancer-binding site of NF-κB and perhaps the nuclear localization signal as well. According to this model, treatment with phorbol ester would activate NF-κB by causing

dissociation of the inhibitor. Since the usual effect of phorbol ester treatment is to activate protein kinase C, dissociation of the inhibitor might occur as a consequence of direct phosphorylation of the inhibitor or as a more indirect consequence of the phosphorylation of some other protein.

Reference: Baeuerle, P.A.; Baltimore, D. Activation of DNA-binding activity in an apparently cytoplasmic precursor of the NF-κB transcription factor. *Cell* 53:211–217, 1988.

***10–4** **Reference:** Schleif, R.F. *Genetics and Molecular Biology*, Chap. 13. Reading, MA: Addison Wesley, 1986.

10–5

A. Probes 2 and 3 are useful because they are specific for mRNAs that are not present in untreated 10T½ cells. You are searching for an mRNA that is present in both kinds of myoblast but is not present in 10T½ cells. The reason for hybridizing the radioactive myoblast cDNA probes with RNA from 10T½ cells is to remove from the probe all the sequences that correspond to mRNAs that are common between the 10T½ cells and the myoblasts. This subtractive-hybridization procedure makes the probe more specific; it eliminates from analysis a large class of cDNA clones that you do not think will contain the gene of interest.

B. The A class of clones includes cDNAs corresponding to RNAs that are common to 10T½ cells and to induced and normal myoblasts. In this class are all the normal housekeeping genes present in all cells. This is the class of clones that subtractive hybridization was meant to eliminate. Since probes 2 and 3 hybridized to only 1% of the cDNA clones identified by probe 1, these housekeeping RNAs must represent the vast majority of the mRNA species in cells.

The B class of clones includes cDNAs corresponding to RNAs that are induced by 5-aza C treatment but are not present in normal myoblasts or in the 10T½ cells. Since 5-aza C causes widespread demethylation, it is not surprising that it activates some genes that are not normally expressed in myoblasts.

The C class of clones includes cDNAs corresponding to RNAs that are present in normal myoblasts but are not present in 5-aza-C-induced myoblasts. If the induced myoblasts were identical to the normal myoblasts, this class of clones should not exist. It would be natural to suspect some deficiency in the induced myoblasts; however, the problem seems to lie with the normal myoblasts. The normal myoblasts contain a small fraction of fully differentiated myotubes, whereas the induced myoblasts do not. Thus the RNA isolated from the normal myoblast cell population includes RNA from more differentiated cell types. When analyzed, the C class of clones are found to encode muscle-specific gene products, such as troponin I, and myosin heavy and light chains.

The D class of clones includes cDNAs that correspond to myoblast-specific RNAs. It is among these clones that you expect to find the regulatory gene that controls myoblast differentiation.

The actual gene that seems to control myoblast differentiation (*myoD1*) was found among this class of clones. It was selected out of this class after further tests that were based on the assumptions that (1) the regulatory gene should not be expressed at all in 10T½ cells, (2) its expression should reach a maximum in myoblasts, (3) its expression should decline in myotubes, and (4) it should not be expressed in variants of 10T½ cells that do not differentiate after treatment with 5-aza C. The final test was that the cloned cDNA, when introduced into 10T½ cells in an expressed form, should induce the cells to differentiate into myoblasts—which it does!

Reference: Davis, R.L.; Weintraub, H.; Lassar, A.B. Expression of a single transfected cDNA converts fibroblasts to myoblasts. *Cell* 51:987–1000, 1987.

*Problems with an asterisk (*) are answered in the Instructor's Manual.

Controlling the Start of Transcription

10–6

A. promoter
B. lactose repressor
C. gene repressor, negative regulation
D. positive regulation, gene activator
E. catabolite activator
F. sigma factor
G. TATA factor (transcription factor IID—TFIID), transcription complex
H. upstream promoter element
I. enhancer element (enhancer)

10–7

A. False. Allolactose binds to the lactose repressor. When allolactose reaches a high enough concentration, it binds to the repressor and induces an allosteric conformational change that causes the repressor to loosen its hold on the DNA so that transcription can proceed.
B. True
C. True
D. False. "Action at a distance" is less prevalent in procaryotes than in eucaryotes, but it is not uncommon. For example, the phosphorylated form of the ntrC protein can stimulate transcription even when its binding sites are moved more than 1000 nucleotide pairs away from the promoter.
E. False. Sigma factors do interact with specific DNA sequences but only when the factors are part of RNA polymerase. Similarly, activator proteins interact with RNA polymerase but only when they are bound to their specific DNA recognition sequences.
F. True
G. True
H. False. Only a few enhancers function in almost any cell type. Most function well only in a restricted range of cell types.
I. True
J. False. Eucaryotic gene regulatory proteins are activated by a variety of mechanisms—including protein synthesis, protein phosphorylation, and regulatory subunits—in addition to the binding of small molecules.
K. True

10–8

A. The rapid bacterial growth at the beginning of the experiment results from the metabolism of glucose, and the slower growth at the end results from metabolism of lactose. The bacteria stopped growing in the middle of the experiment because they ran out of glucose but did not yet possess the enzymes necessary for lactose metabolism. Before they could utilize the lactose in the medium, they had to induce the *lac* operon. The delay in growth represents the time required for the induction.
B. Induction of the *lac* operon requires that two conditions be met: lactose must be present and glucose must be absent. During the first part of the experiment, glucose and lactose are both present; therefore, the conditions for induction are not met. Only when glucose is exhausted are the requirements for induction satisfied.

   The requirements for induction are mediated by CAP and the lactose repressor (Figure 10–29). For the operon to be on, CAP must be bound and the lactose repressor must not be bound. The presence of lactose in the medium increases the intracellular concentration of allolactose, which binds to the lactose repressor, thereby lowering its affinity for its binding site and causing its release from the DNA. Removal of the lactose repressor satisfies one condition for induction. The second condition is tied to the concentration of glucose. When the concentration of glucose falls, the intracellular level of cAMP rises. cAMP binds to CAP and alters its conformation so that it can bind to its binding site. When CAP is in place (and the lactose

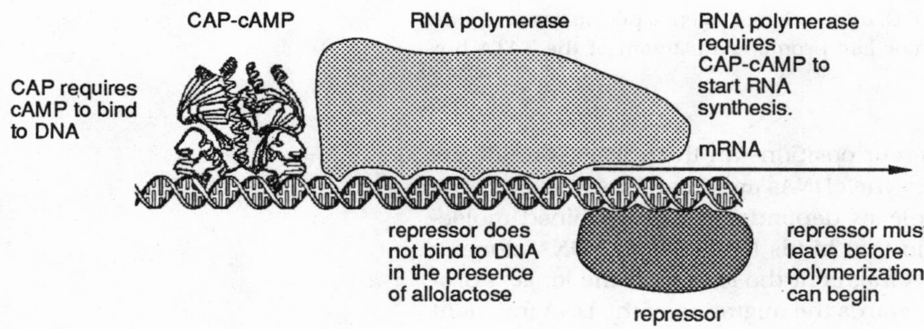
CAP-cAMP
RNA polymerase
RNA polymerase requires CAP-cAMP to start RNA synthesis.
CAP requires cAMP to bind to DNA
mRNA
repressor does not bind to DNA in the presence of allolactose
repressor must leave before polymerization can begin
repressor

Figure 10–29 Induction of the *lac* operon (Answer 10–8). The proteins and DNA are drawn approximately to scale. The three-dimensional structure of CAP is known, but the structures of RNA polymerase and repressor have not yet been determined.

repressor is absent), RNA polymerase can bind to the promoter and initiate transcription.

Reference: Monod, J. The phenomenon of enzymatic adaptation. *Growth Symposium* XI:223–289, 1947. [Reprinted in *Selected Papers in Molecular Biology by Jacques Monod* (A. Lwoff, A. Ullmann, eds.), pp. 68–134. New York: Academic Press, 1947].

***10–9** **Reference:** Ninfa, A.J.; Reitzer, L.J.; Magasanik, B. Initiation of transcription at the bacterial *glnAp2* promoter by purified *E. coli* components is facilitated by enhancers. *Cell* 50:1039–1046, 1987.

10–10 Neither the propagation of an altered DNA structure nor the oligomerization of a protein from the repression site would be expected to be sensitive to small changes in the spacing between the repression site and the start site of transcription. Nor is there any obvious reason in those mechanisms why some insertions and deletions would prevent repression, while other interspersed insertions and deletions would maintain repression.

The third mechanism—formation of a loop in the DNA—is consistent with the observations. Repression of the *galK* gene occurs when integral numbers of helical turns (multiples of 10.5 nucleotides, which is the number of nucleotide pairs per helical turn) are added to or deleted from the DNA. By contrast, when half integral numbers of turns are involved, repression is prevented. This is exactly the behavior expected if DNA must bend into a tight loop to allow araC at site 2 to interact with another protein near the transcription start site. As shown in Figure 10–30, nonintegral turns would place the araC protein on the wrong face of the DNA, which would require that the DNA twist half a turn to allow proper positioning of the proteins. Although twisting a DNA helix by half a turn may not seem difficult, it actually requires about 4 kcal/mole for a DNA 200 nucleotides in length. The binding energy available from typical protein-DNA interactions is only about 10–15 kcal/mole. Since a substantial fraction of the binding energy would be required to twist the DNA, it is not unreasonable to expect that twisting the DNA could alter a delicately balanced interaction required for repression.

Other experiments suggest that araC at site 2 may interact with araC at site 1 to form the DNA loop. In the absence of arabinose, the *araBAD* genes are fully repressed, presumably by interference of the DNA loop with the binding of RNA polymerase. If araC binding site 2 is deleted (or if the araC protein is absent because of mutation), the DNA loop cannot form and the binding of RNA polymerase is not prevented, thereby leading to a 10-fold elevation in transcription of the *araBAD* cluster of genes. When arabinose is present (and glucose is absent), the araC protein undergoes a conformational change that prevents formation of the DNA loop and also facilitates the binding of RNA polymerase or aids its conversion to an open complex, thereby increasing transcription 1000-fold.

Reference: Dunn, T.M.; Hahn, S.; Ogden, S.; Schleif, R.F. An operator at −280 base pairs that is required for repression of *araBAD* operon promoter: addition of DNA helical turns between the operator and promoter cyclically hinders repression. *Proc. Natl. Acad. Sci. USA* 81:5017–5020, 1984.

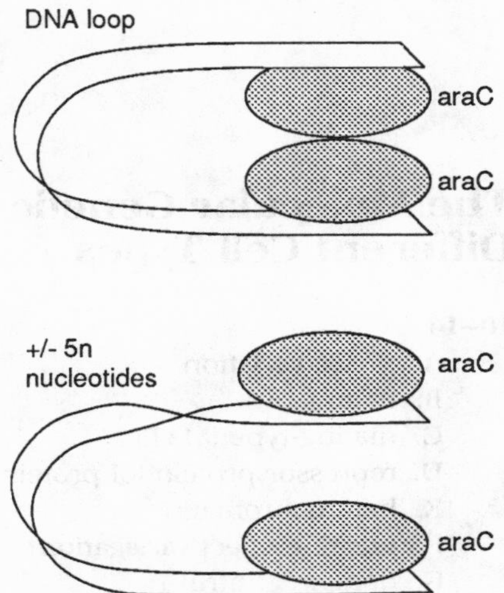
DNA loop
araC
araC
+/- 5n nucleotides
araC
araC

Figure 10–30 Diagram showing consequences of introducing a half integral number of turns into a DNA loop formed by interaction between two proteins (Answer 10–10).

*10–11 **Reference:** Sawadogo, M.; Roeder, R.G. Interaction of a gene-specific transcription factor with the adenovirus major late promoter upstream of the TATA box region. *Cell* 43:165–175, 1985.

10–12

A. The retarded bands run at different positions on the polyacrylamide gel because the proteins encoded by the cDNAs are different sizes. Since the migration of protein-DNA complexes depends on the combined molecular weight, the shortest protein that binds (encoded by cDNA clone 2) retards the migration of the DNA fragment the least, and the longest protein (encoded by cDNA clone 4) retards the migration of the DNA fragment the most.

B. Since cDNA clones 2, 3, and 4 cause gel retardation, they must encode the binding domain for the enhancer. The weak binding by the protein encoded by cDNA clone 2 suggests that it may be missing some portion of the mRNA sequence that is essential for encoding normal binding. The absence of binding by the protein encoded by cDNA clone 1 indicates that it does not encode the complete binding domain. Thus an essential portion of the binding domain must map between the 5′ ends of cDNA clones 1 and 2. These experiments do not define how far the binding domain extends in the 3′ direction. The 3′ end of the binding domain could be defined more precisely using a set of deletions that removed different extents of the 3′ end of the gene, while leaving the 5′ end intact.

C. The presence of three distinct retarded bands in the mixture of cDNA clones 3 and 4 indicates that the encoded proteins interact with one another. The presence of one new band suggests that the transcription factor normally binds to the enhancer as a dimer. The new band arises because one molecule from cDNA clone 3 interacts with one molecule from cDNA clone 4, thereby forming a dimer with a molecular weight intermediate between those of the homogeneous dimers. The intermediate molecular weight gives rise to an intermediate gel retardation.

Reference: Treisman, R. Identification and purification of a polypeptide that binds to the c-fos serum response element. *EMBO J.* 6:2711–2717, 1987.

Norman, C.; Runswick, M.; Pollock, R.; Treisman, R. Isolation and properties of cDNA clones encoding SRF, a transcription factor that binds to the *c-fos* serum response element. *Cell,* in press, 1988.

*10–13 **Reference:** Godowski, P.J.; Rusconi, S.; Miesfeld, R.; Yamamoto, K.R. Glucocorticoid receptor mutants that are constitutive activators of transcriptional enhancement. *Nature* 325:365–368, 1987.

The Molecular Genetic Mechanisms That Create Different Cell Types

10–14

A. phase variation
B. mating
C. mating-type (*MAT*)
D. repressor protein (cI protein), cro protein
E. heterochromatin
F. position effect variegation
G. domain control
H. DNA gyrase
I. 5-methylcytosine (5-methyl C)
J. CG islands, housekeeping
K. tissue-specific

10–15

A. False. Phase variation in *Salmonella* occurs by gene inversion but in *N. gonorrhoeae* it occurs by gene conversion.

B. False. Even though the original resident gene at the MAT locus is discarded during mating-type switching, the process is reversible because information for both the α-type and **a**-type genes are maintained elsewhere as silent genes.

C. False. The silent genes contain all the regulatory sites they need for transcription. They are not expressed because an adjacent DNA sequence some distance downstream somehow blocks their transcription.

D. True

E. True

F. False. Constitutive heterochromatin is condensed in all cells; facultative heterochromatin is condensed only in some cell types.

G. True

H. False. Diffusible gene regulatory proteins cannot explain the heritability of heterochromatic forms of chromosome inactivation, since identical DNA sequences on the active and inactive chromosomes are regulated differently in the same cell nucleus.

I. True

J. True

K. False. Topological effects generated by unwinding DNA at one specific site can be felt throughout an entire looped domain, but not throughout the chromosome. The same constraints that make a looped domain topologically active also insulate it from the topological effects of neighboring looped domains.

L. True

M. True

N. False. The preservation of CG islands in the promoters of housekeeping genes is thought to occur because sequence-specific DNA-binding proteins protect them from methylation in germ cells.

***10–16** **Reference:** Zieg, J.; Silverman, M.; Hilmen, M.; Simon, M. Recombinational switch for gene expression. *Science* 196:170–172, 1977.

10–17

A. In the presence of $\mathbf{a}_1$, α_2 exists in two forms with different binding specificities. Your second set of experiments supports this interpretation and rules out the possibility that α_2 is present in a single form that can bind to both **a**-specific and haploid-specific regulatory sequences. Addition of excess unlabeled **a**-specific DNA eliminates binding to the radioactive **a**-specific fragments, but not to the radioactive haploid-specific fragments. Similarly, addition of excess unlabeled haploid-specific DNA eliminates binding to the radioactive haploid-specific fragments. If a single form of α_2 were able to bind to both regulatory sequences, either unlabeled site in excess would have eliminated binding to both kinds of radioactive fragments.

Your third experiment shows that the ratio of binding activities for **a**-specific and haploid-specific sequences varies depending on the amount of $\mathbf{a}_1$ protein. If the α_2 repressor in a diploid cell were shifted entirely into a form that could bind both sites, the ratio should be independent of the amount of $\mathbf{a}_1$ protein.

B. Your experiments are most easily explained if $\mathbf{a}_1$ acts stoichiometrically to alter the binding specificity of the α_2 repressor, presumably by binding to it. In the fragment binding experiments shown in Figure 10–10, when $\mathbf{a}_1$ is low, the binding to haploid-specific fragments is low; when $\mathbf{a}_1$ is high, the binding to haploid-specific fragments is high. The simplest explanation for the effects of the defective α_2 repressor is that it binds to $\mathbf{a}_1$ protein, thereby reducing the availability of the $\mathbf{a}_1$ protein for binding to the normal α_2 repressor.

Note that neither of these experiments rules out the possibility that $\mathbf{a}_1$ protein acts catalytically on the α_2 repressor. However, a catalytic mechanism for $\mathbf{a}_1$ protein would require special assumptions to account for the experimental observations. For these reasons it is considered most likely that the form of the repressor that binds to haploid-specific sequences will be found to contain both the $\mathbf{a}_1$ protein and the α_2 repressor.

Reference: Goutte, C.; Johnson, A.D. $\mathbf{a}_1$ protein alters the DNA-binding specificity of α_2 repressor. *Cell* 52:875–882, 1988.

10–18 A regulatory scheme that accounts for the behavior of the mutants is shown in Figure 10–31. F-specific genes are ON unless they are repressed by the product of the *M1* gene. M-specific genes are ON unless they are repressed by the product of the *F2* gene. Sporulation-specific genes are OFF unless they are activated by the combined products of the *M2* and *F1* genes, which are present only in diploid cells.

At first, such a collection of mutants and phenotypes may seem impossible to decipher. However, most models of gene expression were first developed from just such genetic data. (Only later were the predicted molecular interactions tested by biochemical experiments and elaborated in full detail.) In the genetic data in Table 10–2, there are three principal clues that allow the regulatory scheme to be deduced. In mating-type M cells, an $M1^-$ mutation allows expression of both M-specific and F-specific genes, suggesting that the product of the *M1* gene may be a repressor of the F-specific genes. In mating type F cells, an $F2^-$ mutation allows expression of both F-specific and M-specifc genes, suggesting that the product of the *F2* gene may be a repressor of M-specific genes. Finally, although $M2^-$ and $F1^-$ mutations seem to have no effect in haploid cells, either mutation in diploid cells prevents expression of sporulation-specific genes, suggesting that they may function in combination as an activator of sporulation-specific genes. These three clues suggest three regulatory interactions; these provide a consistent interpretation of the entire data set. Further genetic and biochemical tests would be necessary before the regulatory scheme in Figure 10–31 could be considered proven.

10–19

A. The methylation status of the 5S RNA gene does not affect its transcriptional activity, as indicated by the equal intensities of the maxigene RNA bands and the 5S RNA bands in the mixtures of templates that were not treated with restriction enzymes (the lanes marked "none" in Figure 10–11B).

B. The pattern of transcription after cleavage is exactly as you expected. Transcription from the fully methylated 5S RNA maxigene is specifically

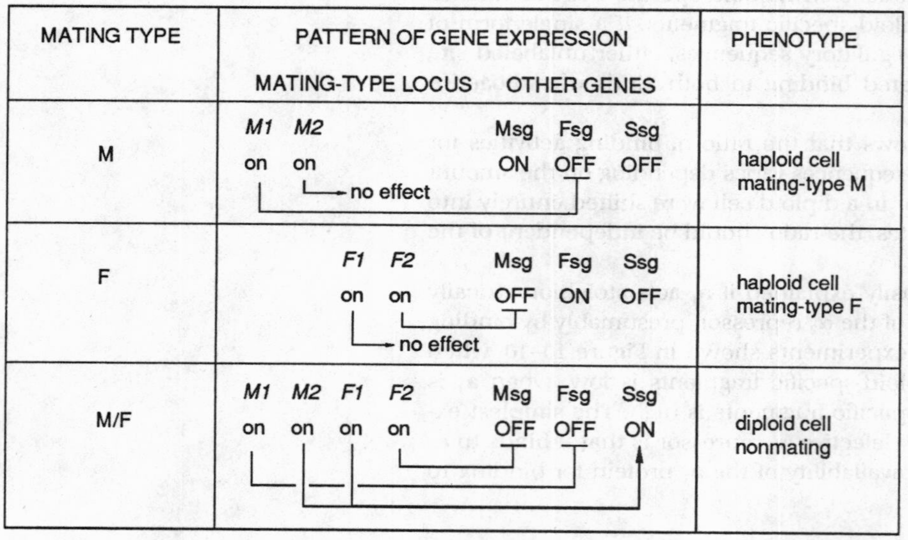

MATING TYPE	PATTERN OF GENE EXPRESSION: MATING-TYPE LOCUS	PATTERN OF GENE EXPRESSION: OTHER GENES	PHENOTYPE
M	*M1* on, *M2* on (*M2* → no effect)	Msg ON, Fsg OFF, Ssg OFF	haploid cell mating-type M
F	*F1* on, *F2* on (*F1* → no effect)	Msg OFF, Fsg ON, Ssg OFF	haploid cell mating-type F
M/F	*M1* on, *M2* on, *F1* on, *F2* on	Msg OFF, Fsg OFF, Ssg ON	diploid cell nonmating

Figure 10–31 Regulation of gene expression by mating-type genes in a new strain of yeast (Answer 10–18).

abolished after cleavage with DpnI, which cleaves only fully methylated restriction sites. Cleavage with MboI specifically abolishes transcription from unmethylated 5S RNA genes. And cleavage with Sau3A, which is insensitive to the methylation status of the restriction site, abolishes transcription from all 5S RNA genes.

C. The pattern of transcription after replication and cleavage indicates that transcription complexes do not remain associated with the 5S RNA maxigene during replication. If the replicated molecules retained an active transcription complex, transcriptional activity would have been evident after DpnI digestion, which does not cleave the replicated molecules. The activity that remains after MboI cleavage derives from fully methylated DNA molecules, which were not replicated. If transcriptional complexes were not erased by replication, there would have been activity after DpnI cleavage.

D. If only 50% of the molecules had been assembled into active transcription complexes, the pattern would have been unchanged (except for a reduction in the intensity of the bands). You could no longer conclude, however, that replication eliminated the transcription complexes. If only 50% of the molecules were assembled into complexes and only 50% were replicated, then a skeptic (that is, a good scientist) would raise the possibility that the assembly into transcription complexes inhibits replication so that only the unassembled molecules were replicated. Thus, the experiment would fail to test what it was designed to test. The point of the objection is clearer if you imagine that 10% of the molecules were assembled into transcription complexes and 10% were replicated. For your conclusion to be valid, it is essential to prove that molecules with transcriptional complexes were replicated. Although there might be ways to test specifically for replication of transcriptional complexes, the easiest way is to show that the fraction of molecules that are replicated is significantly greater than the fraction of molecules that are not assembled into transcription complexes.

Reference: Wolffe, A.P.; Brown, D.D. DNA replication *in vitro* erases a *Xenopus* 5S RNA gene transcription complex. *Cell* 47:217–227, 1986.

***10–20** **Reference:** Murray, E.J.; Grosveld, F. Site-specific demethylation in the promoter of human γ-globin does not alleviate methylation mediated suppression. *EMBO J.* 6:2329–2335, 1987.

Posttranscriptional Controls

10–21

A. transcriptional attenuation
B. alternative RNA splicing
C. protein isoforms
D. gene
E. negative translational
F. positive translational
G. translational frameshifting
H. RNA editing

10–22

A. False. In procaryotes transcriptional attenuation is mediated by stalled ribosomes. In eucaryotes, however, there are no functional ribosomes in the nucleus. Thus, in eucaryotes it seems more likely that a regulatory molecule that binds to a specific RNA sequence is responsible for attenuation of transcription.

B. True

C. True

D. False. RNA splicing can create mRNAs that cause the original carboxyl terminus of a protein to be removed entirely and to be replaced with a new one.

E. True

F. False. Iron binds to a regulatory protein, not to the iron-response element of ferritin mRNA. In the absence of iron the regulatory protein binds to the iron-response element and prevents translation of the mRNA. In the presence of iron the regulatory protein binds to the iron and releases the ferritin mRNA, which is then translated. This mechanism allows increased numbers of ferritin molecules to be made in response to increased levels of iron.

G. True

H. True

I. False. The stability of transferrin receptor mRNA and the translatability of ferritin mRNA are regulated by the same iron-sensitive RNA-binding protein. The consequences of binding, however, are different for the two mRNAs. Binding to the iron-response element at the 5′ end of ferritin mRNA blocks translation and decreases the level of ferritin. On the other hand, binding to the iron-response element at the 3′ end of transferrin receptor mRNA stabilizes the mRNA, allowing more transferrin receptor to be made.

J. True

K. True

10–23

A. Because calcitonin mRNA is produced when the cells are transfected with the wild-type gene, and CGRP mRNA is produced when they are transfected with the exon-4 splice-site mutant, the lymphocytes must contain all the processing factors necessary to generate both mRNAs.

B. If selection of a polyadenylation site was the critical choice in the expression of calcitonin mRNA in the lymphocyte cell line, then the mutant that was missing the exon-4 polyadenylation site would be expected to produce CGRP mRNA. If the splicing of exon 3 to exon 5 (to produce CGRP mRNA) is precluded by use of the polyadenylation site in exon 4, then removal of the site should permit CGRP mRNA production.

By contrast, the mutant lacking the exon-4 splice site might still be expected to be preferentially polyadenylated at exon 4, which would prevent production of CGRP mRNA. (As explained in part D, although CGRP mRNA is not made in the exon-4 splice-site mutant, the aberrant RNA that is generated does not match this simple expectation.)

C. If selection of the exon-4 splice site was the critical choice in the expression of calcitonin mRNA in the lymphocyte cell line, then the mutant that was missing the exon 4 splice site would be expected to produce CGRP mRNA. If the splicing of exon 3 to exon 4 is favored in lymphocytes, then removal of the exon-4 splice site should permit the exon-5 splice site to be used, thus generating CGRP mRNA.

By contrast, the mutant lacking the exon-4 polyadenylation site might still be expected to splice exon 3 to exon 4 preferentially, which might be expected to lead to an aberrant RNA containing the fourth intron along with exons 5 and 6. (As explained in part D, although an aberrant RNA is made, it is not the one expected by this simple reasoning.)

D. The predictions of the splice-site-selection model best match the results from the two mutants. As explained in parts B and C, the splice-site-selection model correctly predicts that CGRP mRNA will be made by the mutant lacking the exon-4 splice site. The polyadenylation-site-selection model, by contrast, predicts incorrectly that CGRP mRNA will be made by the mutant that is missing the exon-4 polyadenylation site. Thus, these results favor splice-site selection as the critical choice that explains the ability of the lymphocyte cell line to produce calcitonin mRNA instead of CGRP mRNA.

However, neither of these simple models predicts the structure of the aberrant RNA that is produced when the exon-4 polyadenylation mutant is transfected into the lymphocyte cell line. The aberrant RNA retains both the third and the fourth introns even though the 5′ splice site in exon 3 and the 3′ splice sites in exons 4 and 5 are both present. Neither simple model for differential processing predicts this result. For this reason, differential processing of the calcitonin/CGRP transcript is thought to be a somewhat more complex version of the splice-site-selection model, whose details are not yet understood.

Reference: Leff, S.E.; Evans, R.M.; Rosenfeld, M.G. Splice commitment dictates neuron-specific alternative RNA processing in calcitonin/CGRP gene expression. *Cell* 48:517–524, 1987.

10–24

A. The percentage of total protein synthesis that is due to synthesis of ferritin for each sample is equal to ferritin synthesis divided by the total protein synthesis. For the first sample, this value is 700/750,000 = 0.093. All other values are listed in Table 10–6.

To obtain the distribution of ferritin mRNA in the polysomal and supernatant fractions, the ferritin synthesis in each sample must be adjusted to take into account the distribution of bulk mRNA in the polysomal and supernatant fractions. To do this, it is necessary to multiply the percentage of ferritin synthesis in the polysomal fraction by 0.85 and to multiply the percentage of ferritin synthesis in the supernatant fraction by 0.15. These values are listed in Table 10–6 under the column labeled "adjusted ferritin." The percentage of total ferritin mRNA in the polysomal fraction from a particular treatment is equal to the "adjusted ferritin" divided by the total "adjusted ferritin." For the first sample this value is 0.079/0.161 = 49%. The rest of the values are listed in the last column in Table 10–6.

B. Two features of the data show clearly that iron does not control ferritin synthesis by regulating the rate of transcription. First, injection of iron does not increase the amount of ferritin mRNA. As shown under the "adjusted ferritin" column, the total amount of ferritin mRNA present after saline injection or iron injection is nearly the same. Second, the RNA synthesis inhibitor actinomycin D has no effect on the amount of total ferritin mRNA. If the increased synthesis of ferritin induced by iron were due to an increase in the amount of ferritin mRNA, the increase in ferritin mRNA should have been detectable and it should have been blocked by actinomycin D.

C. The major effect of iron is to alter the distribution of ferritin mRNA between the polysomal and supernatant fractions. In the absence of iron about 50% of the ferritin mRNA is not bound to polysome. When iron is present, about 90% of the ferritin mRNA is in the polysome fraction. Thus, the fraction of ferritin mRNA on polysomes increases by nearly a factor of two in the presence of iron. This shift from free mRNA to polysomal

Table 10–6 Synthesis of Ferritin in the Rat After Various Treatments (Answer 10–24)

Injection	Actinomycin D	Fraction	Total Synthesis	Ferritin Synthesis	Percent Ferritin	Adjusted Ferritin	Distribution of Ferritin
Saline	absent	polysomes	750,000	700	0.093	0.079	49%
		supernatant	255,000	1400	0.549	0.082	51%
						0.161	
Iron	absent	polysomes	500,000	900	0.180	0.153	89%
		supernatant	400,000	500	0.125	0.019	11%
						0.172	
Saline	present	polysomes	800,000	800	0.100	0.085	53%
		supernatant	600,000	3000	0.500	0.075	47%
						0.160	
Iron	present	polysomes	780,000	1380	0.177	0.150	89%
		supernatant	550,000	700	0.127	0.019	11%
						0.169	

mRNA accounts nicely for the twofold increase in ferritin synthesis in the presence of iron, since only mRNAs that are in polysomes are translated into protein.

The molecular mechanism by which ferritin mRNA is kept from binding to ribosomes and entering the polysomal fraction is not yet known. Ferritin genes from a rat, human, chicken, and frog have a highly conserved 28 nucleotide sequence (the iron-response element) in their 5′ untranslated regions that is essential for regulation by iron. It appears that an iron-sensitive regulatory protein binds to these regions of ferritin mRNAs and prevents ribosome binding. In the presence of iron the ferritin mRNAs are released and bound by ribosomes with a consequent increase in ferritin synthesis. The protein no longer binds to ferritin mRNA, thereby permitting its translation.

References: Zahringer, J.; Baliga, B.S.; Munro, H.N. Novel mechanism for translational control in regulation of ferritin synthesis by iron. *Proc. Natl. Acad. Sci. USA* 73:857–861, 1976.

Liebold, E.A.; Munro, H.N. Cytoplasmic protein binds *in vitro* to a highly conserved sequence in the 5′ untranslated region of ferritin heavy- and light-subunit mRNAs. *Proc. Natl. Acad. Sci. USA* 85:2171–2175, 1988.

10–25

A. The concentration of ribosomes in a reticulocyte lysate is 2.5×10^{-7} M, and the concentration of HCR that completely blocks protein synthesis is 5.6×10^{-9} M.

$$[\text{ribosomes}] = \frac{1\text{ mg}}{\text{ml}} \times \frac{1000\text{ ml}}{\text{L}} \times \frac{\text{mole}}{4 \times 10^6\text{ g}} \times \frac{\text{g}}{10^3\text{ mg}}$$

$$[\text{ribosomes}] = 2.5 \times 10^{-7}\text{ M}$$

$$[\text{HCR}] = \frac{1\ \mu\text{g}}{\text{ml}} \times \frac{1000\text{ ml}}{\text{L}} \times \frac{\text{mole}}{180{,}000\text{ g}} \times \frac{\text{g}}{10^6\ \mu\text{g}}$$

$$[\text{HCR}] = 5.6 \times 10^{-9}\text{ M}$$

Thus, when protein synthesis is completely blocked, the ratio of HCR molecules to ribosomes is 1 to 45 ($2.5 \times 10^{-7}/5.6 \times 10^{-9} = 45$). Since there are an average of 4 ribosomes per globin mRNA, the ratio of HCR molecules to globin mRNA molecules is about 1 to 10.

B. The ratios of HCR molecules to ribosomes and to globin mRNA indicate that HCR is unlikely to inhibit protein synthesis by a stoichiometric interaction with either of these components. These ratios, however, do not rule out the possibility that HCR stoichiometrically inactivates some other factor that is essential for protein synthesis, and that is present at a concentration tenfold below that of globin mRNA.

It is now known that HCR is a protein kinase that inactivates protein synthesis by a catalytic mechanism. HCR phosphorylates the initiation factor eIF-2.

Reference: Farrell, P.J.; Balkow, K.; Hunt, T.; Jackson, R.J.; Trachsel, H. Phosphorylation of initiation factor eIF-2 and the control of reticulocyte protein synthesis. *Cell* 11:187–200, 1977.

***10–26** **References:** Gay, D.A.; Yen, T.J.; Lau, J.T.Y.; Cleveland, D.W. Sequences that confer β-tubulin autoregulation through modulated mRNA stability reside within exon 1 of a β-tubulin mRNA. *Cell* 50:671–679, 1987.

Yen, T.J.; Machlin, P.S.; Cleveland, D.W. Autoregulated instability of β-tubulin mRNAs by recognition of the nascent amino terminus of β-tubulin. *Nature* 334:580–585, 1988.

10–27

A. The mRNA from the *fos*-globin-*fos* hybrid gene, which includes the 3′ end of the *c-fos* gene, has the same stability characteristics as the mRNA from the normal *c-fos* gene (Figure 10–18A and C). By contrast, the *fos*-globin hybrid gene, which includes the same 5′ *fos* sequences as the *fos*-globin-*fos* gene (but is missing the 3′ *fos* sequences) is very stable (Figure 10–18B). Thus, the 3′ end of the human *c-fos* gene confers instability on the *c-fos* mRNA. The instability element almost certainly must be included in the mRNA to make it unstable. Therefore, the element is presumably located in the 3′ exon of the *c-fos* gene, rather than in the 3′ flanking sequences.

B. Although not obvious at first, the behavior of the mRNA from the *fos*-globin hybrid gene can be accounted for in terms of mRNA stability. If the *fos*-globin mRNA is very stable—like normal globin mRNA—then a low rate of transcription in the absence of serum is sufficient to allow the mRNA to accumulate to high levels in the 24-hour period before serum was added and the first measurement was made. If the *fos*-globin mRNA is already present at high levels, then the transient burst of transcription that follows serum addition will not appreciably increase the total amount of the *fos*-globin mRNA. Thus, the enhanced stability of the mRNA from the *fos*-globin hybrid gene can account for both the high initial levels and the lack of induction observed with the *fos*-globin hybrid gene.

These results emphasize the need for instability if a system must respond rapidly to change. This requirement has many familiar analogues in every-day life. For example, if images on a TV screen persisted for more than a fraction of a second, moving objects would be trailed by their ghosts. In a similar way, echoing acoustics blur the perception of both speech and music. Biological signaling pathways have built in mechanisms to return the system to the starting state: old signals are continually "erased" so that they do not blur the perception of new signals.

Reference: Treisman, R. Transient accumulation of *c-fos* RNA following serum stimulation requires a conserved 5′ element and *c-fos* 3′ sequences. *Cell* 42:889–902, 1985.

Wilson, T.; Treisman, R. Removal of poly(A) and consequent degradation of c-*fos* mRNA facilitated by 3′ AU-rich sequences. *Nature* 336:396–399, 1988.

***10–28** **Reference:** Powell, L.M.; et al. A novel form of tissue-specific RNA processing produces apolipoprotein-B48 in intestine. *Cell* 50:831–840, 1987.

The Organization and Evolution of the Nuclear Genome

10–29

A. satellite DNAs
B. transposable elements
C. transposition bursts
D. L1 transposable element, *Alu* sequences

10–30

A. True
B. False. The sequences of tandemly repeated genes and their spacer DNAs are both homogenized by unequal crossing over and gene conversion.
C. True
D. True
E. False. Split genes are thought to be the ancient condition. Bacteria are thought to have lost their introns—after most of their proteins had evolved—in response to strong selective pressure to reproduce at the maximum rate permitted by the level of nutrients in the environment.
F. True
G. False. Although most transposable elements do move rarely, so many elements are present that their movement has a major effect on species variability. For example, more than half the spontaneous mutations in *Drosophila* are due to insertion of a transposable element in or near the mutant gene.
H. True
I. True
J. False. *Alu* sequences are transcribed by RNA polymerase III. Since polymerase III promoters are internal to the transcript, an *Alu* sequence carries the information necessary for its own transcription wherever it goes.

10–31 The restriction pattern that indicates the fetus has inherited the genetic disease will have bands at 1, 2, and 9 kb.

Most of the difficulty in sorting out these restriction patterns arises because each individual is diploid and, therefore, carries two copies of the genetic locus. It is easiest to begin to define the patterns of single chromosomes by identifying individuals who are homozygous for one pattern. Homozygous individuals can be identified in two ways: they have patterns composed of equal intensity bands and the sum of the lengths of the bands is 12 kb (the size of the region being analyzed—Figure 10–20). By those criteria the maternal grandmother and the paternal grandfather are homozygous. By necessity they must have contributed a chromosome with their characteristic patterns to their progeny. Therefore, the mother must have one chromosome with a pattern identical to her mother's, and the father must have one chromosome with a pattern identical to his father's. Knowledge of one chromosome makes it simpler to deduce the pattern of cutting on the other chromosome.

Within the family tree you have analyzed, there are three different patterns of cutting: Pattern I is + at sites A, B, and C, which leads to bands at 1, 2, 4, and 5 kb; Pattern II is + at sites A and C, but − at site B, which leads to bands at 1, 5, and 6 kb; and Pattern III is + at sites A and B, but − at site C, which leads to bands at 1, 2, and 9 kb. Since Pattern I is homozygous in the maternal grandmother and Pattern II is homozygous in the paternal grandfather, neither of these patterns is likely to be associated with the genetic disease. The father is heterozygous for Paterns I and III, whereas the mother is heterozygous for Patterns II and III. The unaffected child is heterozygous for Patterns I and II. Only the homozygous Pattern III is not represented among living members of the family. Also, Pattern III is present in the DNA of the paternal grandmother, whose brother was affected by the disease. Collectively, these observations indicate that Pattern III (bands at 1, 2, and 9 kb) is most likely the one associated with the genetic disease.

***10–32** **Reference:** van Arsdell, S.W.; Weiner, A.M. Human genes for U2 small nuclear RNA are tandemly repeated. *Mol. Cell. Biol.* 4:492–499, 1984.

***10–33** **Reference:** Nathans, J.; Thomas, D.; Hogness, D.S. Molecular genetics of human color vision: the genes encoding blue, green, and red pigments. *Science* 232:193–202, 1986.

Nathans, J.; Piantanida, T.P.; Eddy, R.L.; Shows, T.B.; Hogness, D.S. Molecular genetics of inherited variation in human color vision. *Science* 232:203–210, 1986.

Vollrath, D.; Nathans, J.; Davis, R.W. Tandem array of human visual pigment genes at Xq28. *Science* 240:1669–1671, 1988.

10–34

A. Recombination events that could have given rise to the abnormal gene structures associated with dichromats and anomalous trichromats are illustrated in Figure 10–32. These recombination events are not unique; most could have arisen by equivalent events between different chromosome arrays. Nevertheless, they serve to illustrate the principles of unequal crossing over.

(Because the genes are sex-linked, recombination between different chromosome arrays would require that the event occur in the female. Recombination between identical arrays could also occur between sister chromatids in the male. Either event would have to occur in the germ line in order to be transmitted to the next generation.)

The recombination event necessary to generate the green-blind dichromat (G^-R^+) deserves special comment. This event may have resulted from two unequal crossing-over events, or it may have been the product of a gene conversion event. Either event (and the two are indistinguishable in terms of the final product) results in the replacement of a segment of one DNA molecule by a homologous segment from another DNA molecule.

(A) SINGLE CROSSOVER

G^+R^-

+

$G'R^+$

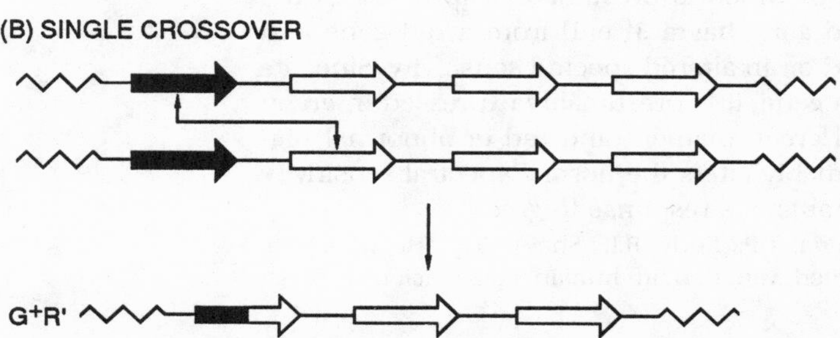

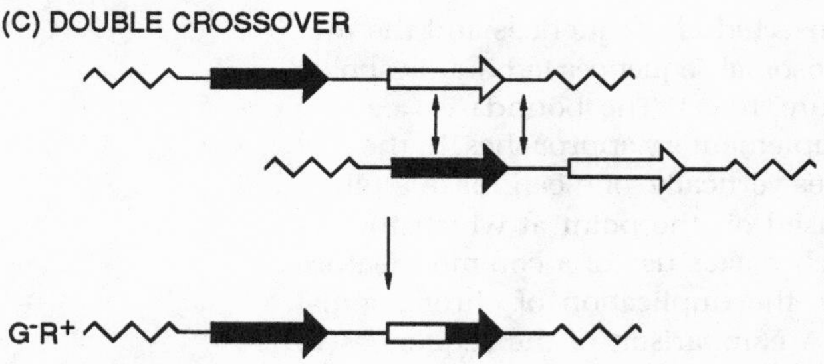

Figure 10–32 Unequal recombination events to generate gene structures of dichromats and anomalous trichromats (Answer 10–34).

B. Control elements for transcriptional regulation of gene expression are usually located around the 5′ ends of genes. Thus, if expression of these genes is controlled at the level of initiation of transcription—as is likely to be the case—you might reasonably expect that the hybrid genes (like the normal genes) would be expressed according to the sequences at their 5′ ends. Consequently, the hybrid genes in the red-blind dichromat (G^+R^-) and the red-anomalous trichromat (G^+R') are probably expressed like red genes because their 5′ ends are derived from red genes. Similarly, the hybrid genes in the green-blind dichromat (G^-R^+) and in the green-anomalous trichromat ($G'R^+$) are probably expressed like green genes because their 5′ ends are derived from green genes.

C. The single gene present in the red-blind dichromat (G^+R^-) must have the spectral sensitivity of a green gene, even though it contains only a portion of the green gene. (Results from many other color-deficient males support the idea that the 3′ half of the pigment gene encodes the domain of the visual pigment that is responsible for the absorption properties of the pigment.) If the single hybrid gene encodes a "green" pigment, then this male would be expected to be red-blind. Interestingly, it may be that the "green" pigment is expressed in cells that would normally become red cones since the hybrid gene has the 5′ end characteristic of a red pigment gene. Cells that would normally become green cones may have no pigment at all since there is no gene with a 5′ end characteristic of a green pigment gene.

The two genes present in the green-blind dichromat (G^-R^+) probably behave like red genes since the 3′ half of the hybrid gene is derived from a red pigment gene. Since the 5′ end of the hybrid gene is from a green gene, the hybrid "red" pigment is likely to be expressed in cells that would normally become green cones. Thus, the normal red cones presumably express red pigment, and the normal green cones may express the hybrid "red" pigment.

The red-anomalous trichromat (G^+R') has two normal green genes that are presumably expressed normally in green cones. The hybrid gene, which is presumably expressed in red cones, must encode a pigment with altered spectral sensitivity in order to account for the anomalous color vision in the red-anomalous trichromat.

The green-anomalous trichromat ($G'R^+$) has one normal red gene and one normal green gene, each of which is presumably expressed in the appropriate cones. The hybrid gene has a 3′ end from a red gene and thus presumably has either red or an altered spectral sensitivity. Since its 5′ end is derived from a green gene, it is presumably expressed in green cones. The mixture of normal green pigment and red or abnormal pigment in the same cone presumably alters the normal spectral sensitivity of the cone, resulting in an anomalous response to green.

References: Nathans, J.; Piantanida, T.P.; Eddy, R.L.; Shows, T.B.; Hogness, D.S. Molecular genetics of inherited variation in human color vision. *Science* 232:203–210, 1986.

***10–35** **Reference:** Boeke, J.D.; Garfinkel, D.J.; Styles, C.A.; Fink, G.R. Ty elements transpose through an RNA intermediate. *Cell* 40:491–500, 1985.

10–36

A. The left and right boundaries of the inserted *Alu* sequences and the mutational changes in the flanking chromosomal sequences (arbitrarily shown on the 5′ side) are indicated in Figure 10–33. The boundaries can be located unambiguously using two complementary approaches. In the first approach, by comparing the sequences vertically, one can make a tentative assignment of the boundaries based on the point at which the sequences diverge. The second approach makes use of a common feature of the *Alu* insertion process, namely, the duplication of chromosomal sequences at the target of insertion. A comparison of the sequences to the left and right of each *Alu* sequence shows that they are tandemly duplicated—one end of each duplication is precisely at the tentative boundary assigned on the basis of the vertical comparison.

The mutations in the flanking sequences can be located easily by comparing the repeated sequences that were generated when each *Alu* sequence inserted into the chromosome.

B. As indicated in Figure 10–33, there are five nucleotide changes in the 120 nucleotides of duplicated DNA that flank the *Alu* sequences. Using the estimate of 3×10^{-3} substitutions per site per million years, the *Alu* sequences inserted into the human albumin-family genes about 14 million years ago.

$$\text{years after insertion} = \frac{10^6 \text{ years} \times 1 \text{ site}}{3 \times 10^{-3} \text{ mutations}} \times \frac{5 \text{ mutations}}{120 \text{ sites}}$$
$$= 14 \times 10^6 \text{ years}$$

C. These particular flanking sequences are critical for the calculation because they were generated by the *Alu* sequences when they inserted into the human albumin-family genes. Thus, the sequences that constitute the target-site duplications mark the time of *Alu* insertion.

Additional intron sequences would not help in the calculation because mutations outside the target-site duplication are unrelated to the time of *Alu*-sequence insertion. The mutations in the *Alu* sequences themselves are also not useful for estimating the time of insertion. Some of the

```
              ← Alu repeat (300 nucleotides) →
       TTAAATA|GGCCGGG--------AAAAAAAAAAAAA|TTAAATA
      TGTGTGGG|GATCAGG--------AAAAAAAAAAAAA|TCTGTGGG
      TCTTCTTA|GGCTGGG--------GAAAAAAAAAAAA|TCTTCTTA
ATAATAGTATCTGTC|GGCTGGG--------AGAAAAAAAAAAA|TAAATAGTATCTGTC
    GGATGTTGTGG|GGCCGGG--------AAAAAAAAAAAAA|GGATGTTGTGG
    AGAACTAAAAG|GGCTAGG--------AAAAAAGAGAAGA|AGAACCGAAAG
```

Figure 10–33 Boundaries of *Alu* inserts and mutational alterations in the flanking target-site duplication (Answer 10–36). Boundaries are indicated by vertical lines; mutational changes are indicated by underlining.

observed mutations in the *Alu* sequences very likely were generated while they sat in the genome at another location—prior to the time at which a copy inserted into the human albumin-gene family.

D. The calculation in part B indicates that these *Alu* sequences invaded the human albumin-gene family about 14 million years ago, that is, well after the mammalian radiation and the separation of the lineages leading to rats and humans.

Reference: Ruffner, D.E.; Sprung, C.N.; Minghetti, P.P.; Gibbs, P.E.M.; Dugaiczyk, A. Invasion of the human albumin-α-fetoprotein gene family by *Alu*, *Kpn*, and two novel repetitive DNA elements. *Mol. Biol. Evol.* 4:1–9, 1987.

The Cytoskeleton

11

Muscle Contraction

11–1

A. cytoskeleton
B. myofibrils
C. sarcomeres
D. actin
E. myosin
F. coiled coil
G. plus end, minus end
H. tropomyosin, troponin
I. smooth muscle
J. contractile ring
K. stress fibers

11–2

A. True
B. True
C. True
D. False. Myosin has two heavy chains and two *pairs* of light chains, making a total of six subunits altogether.
E. False. Myosin binds and hydrolyzes one molecule of ATP very rapidly in the absence of actin; however, it cannot release the hydrolysis products in the absence of actin and is, therefore, a very poor ATPase on its own.
F. True
G. False. A muscle contraction terminates because Ca^{2+} is rapidly pumped out of the cytosol, a task that is carried out by an ATP-driven pump. ATP levels do not change substantially during a contraction.
H. True
I. True
J. True
K. True
L. False. White muscle cells are specialized for anaerobic contraction (they derive ATP from glycolysis, which is anaerobic), and red muscle cells are specialized for aerobic contraction (they derive ATP from oxidative phosphorylation in mitochondria, which is aerobic). Red muscle cells derive much of their color from extensive stores of myoglobin, which binds oxygen and buffers the cells against transient oxygen deprivation.

11–3

A. The locations of the striated muscle components in the electron micrograph are illustrated schematically in Figure 11–25A. α-actinin is a component of the Z disc; titin links the myosin filaments to the Z disc; and myomesin links adjacent myosin filaments together into a hexagonal array along the midline of the sarcomere.
B. The micrograph in Figure 11–1B shows a hypercontracted muscle. Thus the light band has entirely disappeared, and a new band, caused by the overlap of actin filaments, has appeared in the middle of the sarcomere. The schematic relationship of the two electron micrographs in Figure 11–1 is shown in Figure 11–25B.

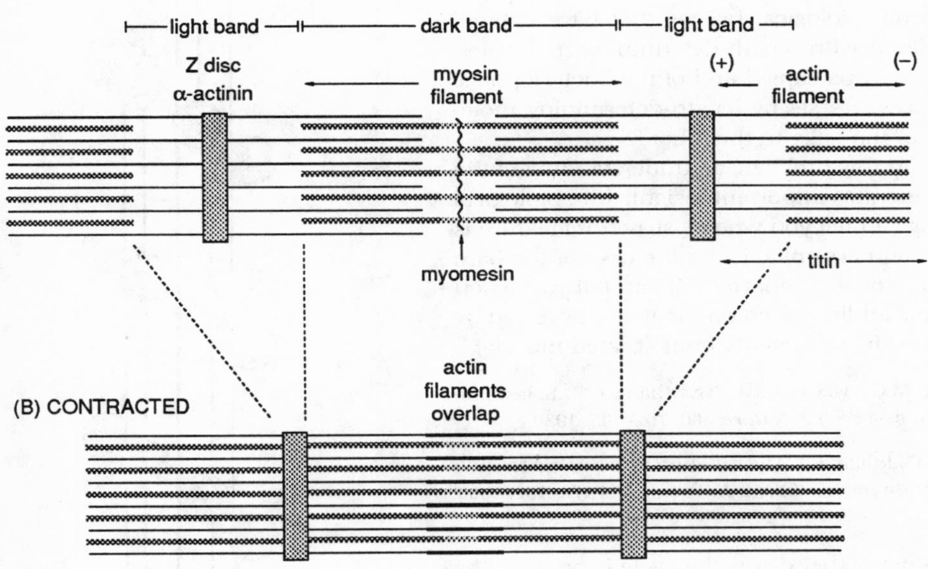

Figure 11–25 Schematic diagrams of electron micrographs in Figure 11–1 (Answer 11–3). (A) Normal muscle. (B) Contracted muscle.

11–4

A. Two helices of myosin molecules would dovetail perfectly (Figure 11–26). Using the numbering scheme in Figure 11–2, the individual myosin molecules at the ends of each helix would abut end to end as follows: 1 with 6′, 2 with 5′, 3 with 4′, 4 with 3′, 5 with 2′, and 6 with 1′ (where the numbers with primes indicate a second copy of the helix).

If you tried to match the two ends in your imagination, you undoubtedly discovered what a difficult mental feat this is. However, it can be readily demonstrated with a concrete object. For example, arrange six pencils around a central one and secure the bundle with a rubber band. Recess successive pencils equally around the cylinder to produce helically staggered ends. Two identical bundles will fit together perfectly. To become familiar with the geometric principles of protein assembly, one must play with real objects; the ability to visualize will improve accordingly.

B. The bare zone is determined by the distance between the first myosin heads on the oppositely oriented helices (Figure 11–26). The closest heads (using the numbering in Figure 11–2) would be the ones on myosins 1 and 1′. Their separation would be equal to the length of the myosin rod (150 nm) plus one-sixth that amount (25 nm) due to the helical stagger (myosin 1′ abuts myosin 6). This theoretical estimate of the length of the bare zone (175 nm) compares reasonably well with the measured length of the bare zone, which is 160 nm.

C. Tapering of the myosin thick filament at its ends is expected if the filament is a helix. Successive cross-sections through the end would show six myosin molecules, then five, then four, and so on to one: a natural thinning of material at the end (Figure 11–26). In electron micrographs the tapering is apparent over the last 100 to 150 nm of the filament, as expected according to this explanation.

D. There is nothing inherent in the structure of a helix composed of subunits such as myosin that defines (or dictates) its length. The average length of a helix is determined by the overall concentration of subunits and by the relative rates of assembly and disassembly at its ends; but even when conditions are constant, considerable variation in length will occur. The remarkable uniformity of length of myosin thick filaments from striated muscle demands something in addition to the myosin molecules themselves. Thus, there may be a length-determining molecule that is associated with myosin thick filaments. In fact, some other biological helices that have defined lengths are known to be associated with length-determining molecules. The lengths of the tobacco mosaic virus capsid and of the bacteriophage lambda tail, which are both helices, are set by length-determining molecules that stretch from one end of the helix to the other.

As we have tried to illustrate in this problem, an understanding of the principles of protein assembly generates important insights into biological structure. Such an understanding can tell you when a structural feature is a reasonable consequence of protein assembly (as in the case of the bare zone and the tapering at the tip). Equally important, it can tell you when a structural feature demands some additional component (as suggested by the uniformity of length of myosin thick filaments from striated muscle).

***11–5** **Reference:** Goldman, Y.E.; Hibberd, M.G.; McCray, J.A.; Trentham, D.R. Relaxation of muscle fibers by photolysis of caged ATP. *Nature* 300: 701–705, 1980.

***11–6** **Reference:** Gordon, A.M.; Huxley, A.F.; Julian, F.J. The variation in isometric tension with sarcomere length in vertebrate muscle fibres. *J. Physiol.* 184:170–192, 1966.

11–7

A. In each cycle the chemical free energy that drives the cycle is provided by hydrolysis of ATP. Although ATP hydrolysis is a common source of chemical free energy, it is not the only one. For example, sugar transport in animal cells is usually powered directly by the free energy in a Na^+ ion gradient, and movements on the ribosome during protein synthesis are powered by GTP hydrolysis.

The mechanical work accomplished during muscle contraction is the motion of actin thin filaments relative to myosin thick filaments. The mechanical work done during active transport of Ca^{2+} is the pumping of ions against their concentration gradient from the inside of the cell to the outside.

B. Actin is alternately bound tightly and then released in each cross-bridge cycle during muscle contraction; Ca^{2+} is alternately bound tightly and then released during its active transport.

In the diagram in Figure 11–6A, actin is tightly bound to myosin at each point where the two are in contact. The binding of ATP to the myosin head converts it to a weak binding form, allowing it to detach from actin and to assume a "vertical" conformation. (Although each of these steps is shown separately in the diagram, the binding of ATP is thought to initiate a conformational change, which in turn reduces the affinity of myosin for actin, thereby promoting detachment of actin and the completion of the conformational change.)

In the diagram in Figure 11–6B, Ca^{2+} is tightly bound to the transport protein when it is on the inside of the cell (upper drawing) but only weakly bound when it faces the outside of the cell (lower drawing). Although the tightness of binding is not immediately apparent in the diagramatic representation, it follows from the concept of active transport. Since the pump is transporting Ca^{2+} against its concentration gradient, the pump must have a high affinity for Ca^{2+} on the inside of the cell (so that Ca^{2+} can be bound effectively at the low intracellular concentration of Ca^{2+}) and a low affinity for Ca^{2+} on the outside of the cell (so that Ca^{2+} can be released effectively at the high external concentration of Ca^{2+}).

C. In both cycles the "power stroke" is the conformational change indicated on the right side of the cycles as drawn in Figure 11–6. The "return stroke" in each case is the conformational change indicated on the left side of the drawings in Figure 11–6.

Reference: Eisenberg, E.; Hill, T.L. Muscle contraction and free energy transduction in biological systems. *Science* 227:999–1006, 1985.

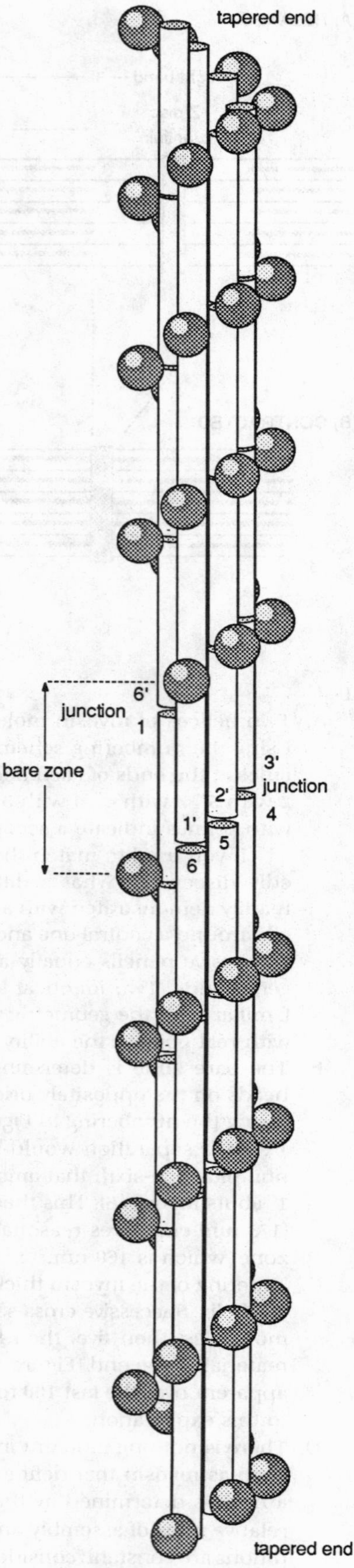

Figure 11–26 A myosin thick filament (Answer 11–4).

*Problems with an asterisk (*) are answered in the Instructor's Manual.

Actin Filaments and the Cell Cortex

11–8

A. cell cortex
B. filamin
C. gelsolin
D. cytoplasmic streaming
E. microvilli
F. terminal web
G. focal contacts (adhesion plaques)
H. treadmilling
I. microspikes
J. lamellipodia

11–9

A. True
B. True
C. False. Cytoplasmic streaming in *Nitella* probably is mediated by a polarized layer of actin filaments.
D. False. Actin in the form of very short filaments is attached to spectrin, which in turn is attached to ankyrin, which in turn is attached to band 3, which is the transmembrane protein that actually links these proteins to the plasma membrane.
E. True
F. False. The critical concentration of actin is the concentration at which, on average, actin filaments neither shrink nor grow.
G. True
H. True
I. True
J. False. Cytochalasin inhibits cytokinesis (daughter cell separation at mitosis) but has no effect at all on chromosome separation or nuclear division.

***11–10** **Reference:** Broschat, K.O.; Stidwell, P.R.; Burgess, D.R. Phosphorylation controls brush border motility by regulating myosin structure and association with the cytoskeleton. *Cell* 35:561–571, 1983.

11–11

A. The electron microscopic examination reveals that actin monomers normally add four times faster to the barbed (plus) ends of the decorated actin filaments than to the pointed (minus) ends. The different rates of assembly at the ends can be estimated by measuring the lengths (counting the subunits in Figure 11–9) of newly assembled actin at the plus and minus ends.
B. As is evident from the micrographs, cytochalasin B interferes with filament assembly by stopping actin polymerization at the plus end, which is normally the preferred end for addition of monomers. One plausible mechanism to explain this inhibition is that cytochalasin B binds to the plus end of the actin filament and physically blocks addition of new actin monomers.

This mechanism can also account for the viscosity measurements. Since growth at the minus end is unaffected, the filaments continue to grow, but much more slowly. The slower growth rate explains the slower increase in viscosity in the presence of cytochalasin B. The lower viscosity at the plateau indicates that the actin filaments are shorter in the presence of cytochalasin B. Why is it that the filaments do not ultimately grow to the same length even though their growth rate is slower? The filaments are shorter when they are growing only from the minus ends because the critical concentration for assembly at the minus end is higher than the critical concentration for assembly at the plus end. This is another way of saying that the equilibrium for assembly at the minus end is shifted more toward the free subunits than the equilibrium for assembly at the plus end. The difference in equilibrium constants means that filaments that are growing at the plus end (or both ends) will be longer than filaments growing only at the minus end.

C. An actin filament normally grows at different rates at the plus and minus ends. This observation indicates that the monomer probably undergoes a conformational change upon addition to an actin filament. If all subunits, assembled and free, were identical in conformation, the rates of growth at the two ends should be the same. Since the subunits are joined to the polymer by identical sets of interactions at the two ends, their on and off rates should be the same. Hence, the rates of growth should be the same. (See Panel 11–1 in MBOC.)

The apparent binding of cytochalasin B to the plus end of a filament, but not to an actin monomer, is also consistent with a conformational change upon actin addition. If an actin monomer exists in two conformations, it might reasonably bind cytochalasin B in one conformation but not in the other. This argument is weaker than the one above because cytochalasin B could have the same effect by binding to a site on the polymer that spans adjacent subunits (a site present only on the polymer). These two models make different predictions about how many cytochalasin B molecules should be bound per filament. Although this number is difficult to measure accurately, the estimates favor a single cytochalasin B molecule per filament.

Reference: MacLean-Fletcher, S.; Pollard, T.D. Mechanism of action of cytochalasin B on actin. *Cell* 20:329–341, 1980.

11–12

A. Although the endpoints for polymerization and ATP hydrolysis were the same, the initial rate of ATP hydrolysis was less than the initial rate of polymerization. (Compare the slopes of the two curves in Figure 11–10 at short times.) At the time when all the actin was polymerized (about 30 seconds), less than half the ATP was hydrolyzed. It is the difference in initial rates that your advisor noticed, and, as he said, it proves that actin polymerization can occur in the absence of ATP hydrolysis.

B. Since the rate of polymerization is faster than the rate of ATP hydrolysis, newly added actin subunits must still retain bound ATP. Since the bound ATP is not hydrolyzed until sometime after assembly, growing actin filaments have ATP "caps." Once an ATP-actin monomer has bound to a filament, the ATP can be hydrolyzed. One way to imagine how ATP might be hydrolyzed in the polymer but not in the monomer is illustrated in Figure 11–27. If the "top" of an actin monomer carries the binding site for ATP, whereas the "bottom" of the monomer carries the catalytic site for ATP hydrolysis, then only the polymer would be able to hydrolyze ATP. (The true arrangement of the binding and hydrolytic sites is not known.) This model predicts that eventually all the actin subunits will carry ADP with the exception of the one subunit at the end, which will carry ATP.

Reference: Carlier, M.-F.; Pantaloni, D.; Korn, E.D. Evidence for an ATP cap at the ends of actin filaments and its regulation of the F-actin steady state. *J. Biol. Chem.* 259:9983–9986, 1984.

***11–13** **Reference:** Tilney, L.G.; Inoue, S. Acrosomal reaction of *Thyone* sperm. II. The kinetics and possible mechanism of acrosomal process elongation. *J. Cell Biol.* 93:820–827, 1982.

Ciliary Movement

11–14

A. cilia
B. flagella
C. axoneme
D. tubulin

(A) ACTIN MONOMER

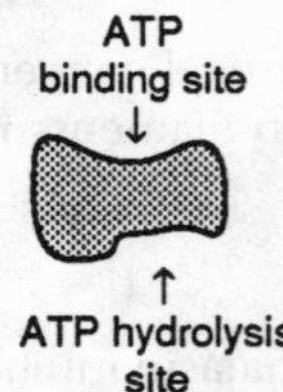

(B) ACTIN POLYMER

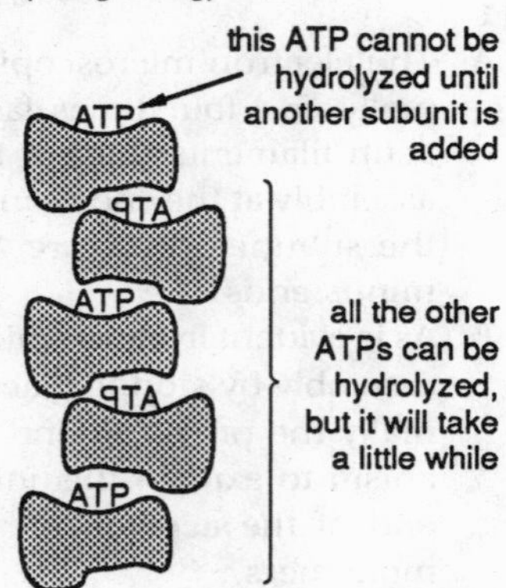

Figure 11–27 A model for actin hydrolysis in the assembled polymer (Answer 11–12). (A) Hypothetical arrangement of the ATP binding site and the ATP hydrolysis site in an actin monomer. (B) Hypothetical arrangement of binding and hydrolytic sites in an actin filament. The rotated subunits with the backward ATPs are meant to suggest the helical nature of actin filaments.

E. dynein
F. centrioles
G. centrosome

11–15

A. True
B. True
C. False. The sliding between microtubules in the axoneme is catalyzed by dynein, not by myosin. However, dynein is thought to work in very much the same way as myosin.
D. False. Sliding occurs between adjacent outer doublet microtubules; the role of the central pair is mainly regulatory.
E. True
F. False. Although it is not known what controls and coordinates the beating of cilia, Ca^{2+} fluxes are not thought to be involved since isolated axonemes continue to beat normally in the absence of the plasma membrane.
G. True
H. False. Kartagener's syndrome affects humans, not unicellular algae.
I. True
J. True
K. True

***11–16**

11–17 Adjacent cilia in the electron micrograph in Figure 11–13 are oriented identically with reference to the central pair of microtubules. The identical orientation suggests that some structural feature of the axoneme constrains the direction of bending, that is, that cilia are designed to bend in a particular way. The orientation of the central pair of microtubules correlates with the direction of bending, which is always in a plane drawn between the two central microtubules. To make this relationship clearer, imagine that the axoneme shown in cross-section in Figure 11–12 extends straight up out of the page; this axoneme could bend toward the top or bottom of the page, but not to the left or right. (In addition, in many axonemes one adjacent set of outer doublet microtubules—specifically, the pair at the bottom of Figure 11–12—are cross-linked so that they cannot slide relative to one another. This modification further confines the plane of bending to the one observed.)

If the microtubules of the central pair are aligned parallel to one another throughout the length of the cilium, then all bending in the power stroke and in the return stroke will be in one plane. However, it is not uncommon for the central pair of microtubules to be twisted around one another, in which case the direction of bending rotates around the axis of the cilium as the bend propagates up the cilium. The consequence of this arrangement is a unidirectional power stroke (which depends only on the orientation of the central pair at the base of the cilium, where bending is initiated) and a helical return stroke as the bend moves to the tip of the cilium.

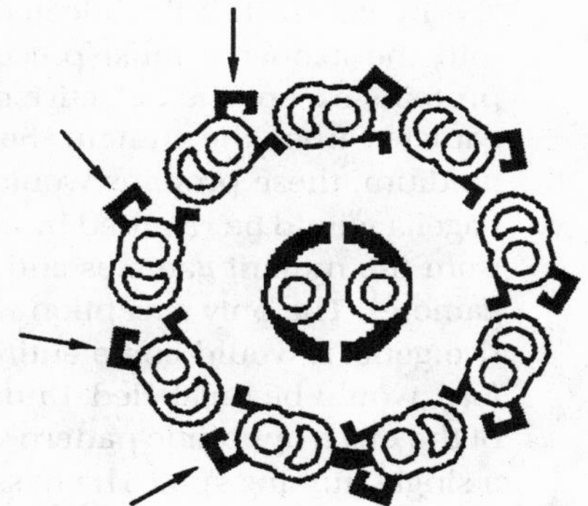

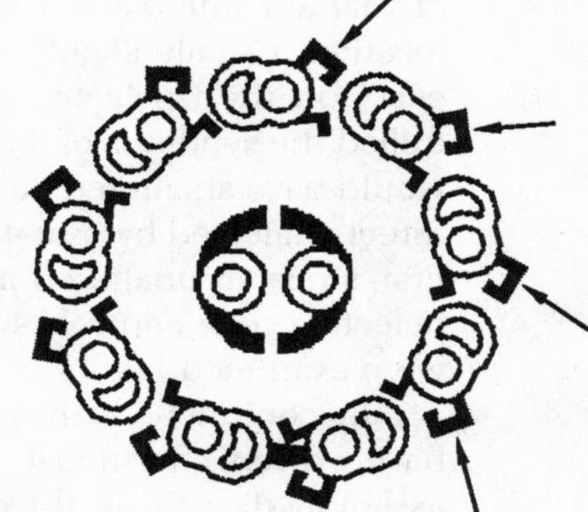

Figure 11–28 One possible pattern of dynein activity that could produce planar bending of an axoneme (Answer 11–19). (A) Upward bend. (B) Downward bend. Arrows indicate active dynein arms.

***11–18** **References:** Gibbons, I.R. Cilia and flagella of eukaryotes. *J. Cell Biol.* 91:107s-124s, 1981.

Brokaw, C.J.; Luck, D.J.L.; Huang, B. Analysis of the movement of *Chlamydomonas* flagella: the function of the radial-spoke system is revealed by comparison of wild-type and mutant flagella. *J. Cell Biol.* 92:722–732, 1982.

11–19 One pattern of dynein activity that could account for the planar bending of an axoneme is depicted in Figure 11–28. If the dynein arms on the left half of the axoneme are active (arrows in Figure 11–28A) and the ones on the right half are passive, the cilium will bend upward. This is difficult to imagine in three dimensions, but take it slowly. First, the orientation of the axonemes shown in Figure 11–28 is the standard one, that is, with the tip of the axoneme *below* the plane of the page. Second, the dynein arms push their neighbor doublets toward the *tip* of the axoneme, so the doublets are being pushed *below* the plane of the page. Third, the doublet at the *top* of the diagram in Figure 11–28A will be pushed the farthest below the page because its total displacement is the sum of incremental displacements produced by all four active dynein arms. Fourth, the doublet that moves the farthest defines the "inside" of the bend (see Figure 11–15). Therefore, since the top doublet moves the farthest, the axoneme will bend upward (toward the top of the page) when the dynein arms on the left half of the axoneme are active.

The same reasoning argues that the axoneme will bend downward (toward the bottom of the page) if the dynein arms on the right half of the axoneme are active (Figure 11–28B) and the ones on the left half are passive.

The actual pattern of dynein activity that gives rise to planar bending is not yet understood. The two central singlet microtubules are natural candidates for regulatory elements: they are surrounded by nonidentical proteins; they contact different subsets of outer doublets; and they are linked (indirectly) to the two sets of dynein arms used in the model proposed above.

11–20

A. If the affected gene controlled the synthesis of the missing proteins in the mutant flagella, then none of those proteins would be present in the gametes from the mutant. After fusion the mutant flagella would be repaired by addition of unlabeled components from the nonradioactive wild-type gametes, since all protein synthesis was inhibited. As a result, the *autoradiograph* of the electrophoretic pattern would look exactly like the mutant alone.

By contrast, if the affected gene encoded a protein whose assembly into the axoneme must precede the addition of other proteins, all the proteins except the defective one would be present in functional form in gametes from the mutant. Since the mutant was grown in radioactive medium, these proteins would be labeled. Thus, after fusion the mutant flagella would be repaired by addition of a mixture of labeled components from the mutant gametes and unlabeled components from the wild-type gametes. The only exception would be the protein encoded by the defective gene: it would come entirely from the wild-type gametes and, therefore, would be unlabeled. Under these circumstances the autoradiograph of the electrophoretic pattern would look like that from the wild type with a single missing spot. The missing spot would correspond to the product of the defective gene.

B. Analysis of second-site, intragenic revertants also can distinguish between the possibilities. If the affected gene encoded a product that is part of the assembled axoneme, then some revertants (those with an altered number of charged amino acids) should produce patterns with one spot at a new location (usually slightly left or right of the normal position, due to an effect on the isoelectric point of the protein). If the affected gene controlled the synthesis of the 17 missing proteins, then none of the revertants would have an altered pattern (since none of the component proteins are directly affected by mutation). This approach is less satisfactory than the first, since an unaltered pattern does not allow one to conclude that the defective gene controls synthesis—it may be that not enough revertants were examined.

In conjunction, these two methods for analyzing flagellar mutants have proven enormously powerful. Most mutants, *pf*14 included, affect assembly directly as judged by both assays; that is, they encode a protein that forms part of the axoneme structure. Moreover, the two methods agree on which protein is encoded by the defective gene: the unlabeled spot in dikaryon analysis corresponds to the shifted spot in revertant analysis.

Reference: Luck, D.J.L. Genetic and biochemical dissection of the eucaryotic flagellum. *J. Cell Biol.* 98:789–794, 1984.

Cytoplasmic Microtubules

11–21

A. colchicine
B. microtubule-organizing center (MTOC)
C. dynamic instability
D. microtubule-associated proteins (MAPS)
E. kinesin

11–22

A. True
B. False. Only cells that are actually in mitosis when colchicine is added are blocked in mitosis within a few minutes.
C. True
D. True
E. True
F. False. Only cytoplasmic microtubules with uncapped ends display dynamic instability.
G. True
H. False. Posttranslational modification of tubulin (acetylation and detyrosination) occurs on polymerized tubulin: the reversals of these processes occur on unpolymerized subunits.
I. False. Microtubules run in only one direction in axons. The bidirectional movement of vesicles and organelles is thought to be accomplished by two protein motors that run in opposite directions.
J. True

11–23

A. Centrosomes lower the critical concentration by providing nucleation sites for microtubule growth. Nucleation sites make it easier to start new microtubules; moreover, they protect the bound end from disassembly. Thus, once started, a microtubule is more likely to persist. In the absence of such a nucleation site, it is much more difficult to start a microtubule and both ends serve as sites for disassembly.
B. The shapes of the curves in the presence and absence of centrosomes differ because of the nature of the assays used to detect polymerization. In the absence of centrosomes (Figure 11–17A), the assay was for total polymer formed, which depends only on the concentration of added tubulin. Thus it increases indefinitely in a linear fashion as long as the concentration of tubulin is increased. In the presence of centrosomes (Figure 11–17B) the assay was for the number of microtubules per centrosome. Since each centrosome has only a limited number of nucleation sites (about 60 for the centrosomes used in this experiment), the measurement must reach a plateau at high tubulin concentrations.
C. A concentration of tubulin dimers of 1 mg/ml corresponds to 9.1 µM.

$$[\text{tubulin}] = \frac{1 \text{ mg tubulin}}{\text{ml}} \times \frac{\text{mmol tubulin}}{1.1 \times 10^5 \text{ mg tubulin}} \times \frac{1000 \text{ ml}}{\text{L}}$$

$$= 9.1 \times 10^{-3} \text{ mmol/L}$$

$$= 9.1 \times 10^{-3} \text{ mM}$$

$$[\text{tubulin}] = 9.1 \ \mu\text{M}$$

This value is below the critical concentration for microtubule assembly in the absence of centrosomes. Thus, without a nucleation site for growth, which is provided by the centrosome, a cell would have no microtubules. This simple consideration probably explains why the majority of microtubules originate from centrosomes in animal cells.

Reference: Mitchison, T.; Kirschner, M. Microtubule assembly nucleated by isolated centrosomes. *Nature* 312:232–237, 1984.

*11–24 **Reference:** Mitchison, T.; Kirschner, M.W. Properties of the kinetochore *in vitro*. I. Microtubule nucleation and tubulin binding. *J. Cell Biol.* 101:755–765, 1985.

11–25

A. The two ends of an individual microtubule appear to behave independently of one another. One end can grow while the other shrinks, and both ends can grow or shrink at the same time. Furthermore, the transitions between growth states at the two ends do not correlate with one another in any obvious way.

B. The GTP-cap hypothesis predicts that the faster growing end, which has the longer GTP cap, should be more stable than the slower growing end, which has a shorter GTP cap. Thus, according to the simple GTP-cap hypothesis, a fast growing end should persist in a growth state longer than a slow growing end; that is, a fast growing end should switch from a growth state to a shrinking state less frequently than a slow growing end. (The hypothesis says nothing about how frequently a shrinking end, which does not have a cap, will be converted into a growing end.)

The experimental results appear, if anything, to run counter to the predictions of the GTP-cap hypothesis. The growth periods at the "active" ends do not seem to be significantly longer (they actually appear somewhat shorter) than the growth periods at the "inactive" ends. Thus, these results do not support the simple GTP-cap hypothesis. In cells proteins other than tubulin may bind to GTP caps and help to stabilize fast growing ends.

C. Since centrosomes nucleate growth of microtubules by binding to the minus end, all the free ends are plus ends. As a consequence, only one type of behavior of ends ("active" or "inactive") should be observed. The "active" end is expected to correspond to the plus end (but the observations have yet to be made).

Since MAPs tend to stabilize microtubules against disassembly, they would be expected to reduce the frequency of switching between the two growth states and extend the length of time they remain in the growing state. This result is observed. In fact, the switches in the growth state are abolished and growth is smooth and continuous until the steady-state length is reached, after which the length remains constant.

Reference: Horio, T.; Hotami, H. Visualization of the dynamic instability of individual microtubules by dark-field microscopy. *Nature* 321:605–607, 1986.

Intermediate Filaments

11–26

A. keratins
B. vimentin
C. desmin
D. glial fibrillary acidic protein
E. neurofilaments
F. nuclear lamins

11–27

A. True
B. False. Intermediate filaments are very insoluble and make up the residue when cells are extracted with solutions containing high salt and nonionic detergents.
C. True
D. False. All cytoplasmic intermediate filaments are encoded by members of the same multigene family.
E. True
F. True

```
  hydrophobic
  amino acids   *  *   *****  *  *    * * * *     **
      coil 1A  DLQELNDRLAVYIDRVRSLETENAGLRLRITESEEVV
heptad repeat  -A--D---A--D---A--D---A--D---A--D---A
        match   +  +   +  +   +  +   -  +   +  -   +
```

Figure 11–29 Heptad repeat motif in the coil 1A region of lamin C (Answer 11–28). When a hydrophobic amino acid occurs at an A or D in the heptad repeat, it is assigned a +. The start of the heptad repeat was positioned to maximize matches.

G. False. Some perfectly healthy living cells, such as the glial cells that make myelin in the central nervous system, completely lack cytoplasmic intermediate filaments. Even these cells, however, have nuclear lamins.

H. True

11–28 The coil 1A segment of nuclear lamin C matches the heptad repeat at 9 of 11 positions (Figure 11–29), which is very good. The match need not be perfect to allow formation of a coiled coil. The matches to the heptad repeat in the other two marked segments (coil 1B and coil 2, Figure 11–20) are not as good, but they are still acceptable for formation of a coiled coil.

Reference: McKeon, F.D.; Kirschner, M.W.; Caput, D. Homologies in both primary and secondary structure between nuclear envelope and intermediate filament proteins. *Nature* 319:463–468, 1986.

***11–29** **Reference:** Ottaviano, Y.; Gerace, L. Phosphorylation of the nuclear lamins during interphase and mitosis. *J. Biol. Chem.* 260:624–632, 1985.

Organization of the Cytoskeleton

11–30

A. leading edge

B. contact inhibition of movement

C. hair cells

11–31

A. False. Most enzymes are very easily released from cells by treatment with mild detergents (to break open the membrane) and buffers that mimic the ionic composition of the cytoplasm. If cytosolic enzymes were attached to the cytoskeleton, they would be expected to remain with the cells under these conditions and not be released.

B. True

C. True

D. True

E. False. Although it is true that most of the returned membrane seems to be delivered to the leading edge of a moving cell, membrane internalization (the other component of membrane recycling) occurs all over the cell.

***11–32**

11–33

A. A plausible model for control of pigment aggregation and dispersal is shown in Figure 11–30. The 57 kd protein changes its phosphorylation state according to the cyclic AMP level (which is regulated through hormone receptors in the cell membrane). In its phosphorylated form the 57 kd protein promotes dispersal, whereas in its nonphosphorylated form it promotes aggregation. This protein is phosphorylated by a cyclic AMP-dependent protein kinase, and it is dephosphorylated by a protein phosphatase.

The regulatory scheme in Figure 11–30 accounts for all the observations except those with ATP-γ-S. This analogue of ATP can be used as a substrate by many protein kinases; presumably it serves as a substrate here as well. However, the slow rate of dispersal in the presence of ATP-

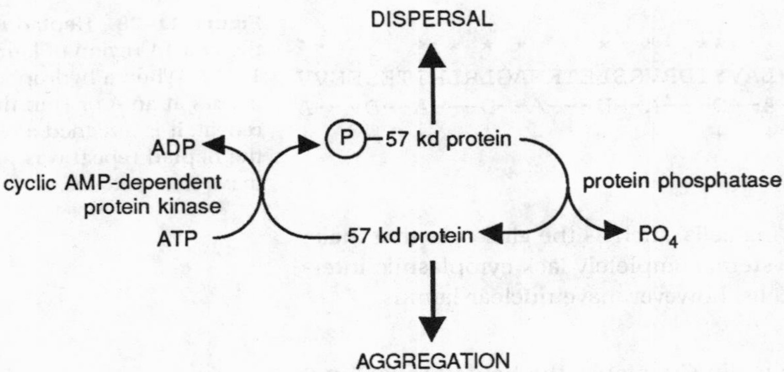

Figure 11–30 A plausible model for control of pigment aggregation and dispersal (Answer 11–33).

γ-S suggests either that the terminal thiolphosphate is transferred to the 57 kd protein more slowly or that the thiolphosphate group does not function as well on the 57 kd protein. The very slow reaggregation of pigment granules that are dispersed in the presence of ATP-γ-S suggests that the thiolphosphate group is removed very slowly from the 57 kd protein by the phosphatase.

B. Although ATP-γ-S is a reasonably good substrate for protein kinases, it is not a good substrate for enzymes, such as myosin light-chain kinase and ciliary dynein, that use its free energy of hydrolysis for movement in motile systems. Since dispersal of the pigment granules can occur in the presence of ATP-γ-S, dispersal probably does not require ATP hydrolysis. Aggregation, by contrast, requires ATP hydrolysis and, therefore, is probably an active process.

Reference: Rozdzial, M.M.; Haimo, L.T. Bidirectional pigment granule movements of melanophores are regulated by protein phosphorylation and dephosphorylation. *Cell* 47:1061–1070, 1986.

11–34

A. A growth rate of 40 μm per hour translates into a distance of about 9 mm in 9 days (40 μ/hr × 24 hr/day × 9 days), which is well within the measured rate of protein migration down the axon (about the same as neurofilament transport in Figure 11–24).

B. If you support the idea of assembly in the cell body, you might explain the inhibition of growth by colchicine added to the tip by its effect on the equilibrium between monomer and polymer. Addition of colchicine will disrupt the equilibrium at the tip and shift it in favor of disassembly. Under these conditions assembly in the cell body could be balanced by disassembly in the tip. According to this view, it is not surprising that nerves stop growing when colchicine is added to the tip or that at a higher drug concentration the axons actually retract.

You would have a great deal of difficulty explaining, however, why addition of colchicine to the cell body has no effect. If the microtubules are assembled in the cell body, colchicine applied to the cell body should stop their assembly.

C. According to the tip-growth model, the labeling experiment reveals the existence of a slowly moving supply of materials for nerve growth at the tip. Some of the tubulin moving down the axon can be used for essential repairs en route, but most would assemble at the growth cone. Nobody has yet shown precisely what form the moving tubulin takes; its insolubility in detergent-containing buffers does not prove that it is in microtubules.

D. The expected patterns of movement differ according to the two models. The cell body assembly model predicts that the distance between the body and the labeled segment will increase steadily with time, whereas the distance between the growing tip and the labeled segment will remain constant. The tip-growth model predicts that the labeled segment will move down the axon until it reaches the tip, where it will be stably incorporated into microtubules and remain thereafter at a fixed distance from the nerve cell body. It would be progressively left behind by the growing tip.

For such a fundamental issue in cell biology, it is surprising that there is no general agreement as to which of these models, if either, is correct.

References: Lasek, R.J.; Hoffman, P.N. The neuronal cytoskeleton, axonal transport and axonal growth. In Cell Motility (R. Goldman, T. Pollard, J. Rosenbaum, eds.). New York: Cold Spring Harbor Laboratory, 1976.

Bamburg, J.R.; Bray, D.; Chapman, K. Assembly of microtubules at the tip of growing axons. *Nature* 321:788–790, 1986.

Bamburg, J.R.; Bray, D.; Chapman, K. Microtubule assembly in the axon. *Nature* 323:400, 1986.

Solomon, F. Microtubule assembly in the axon. *Nature* 322:599, 1986.

Cell Signaling

12

Three Strategies of Chemical Signaling: Endocrine, Paracrine, and Synaptic

12–1

A. hormones
B. paracrine signaling
C. neurotransmitters
D. hypothalamus
E. prostaglandins

12–2

A. True
B. True
C. True
D. False. Hormones are generally removed from the bloodstream by binding to their target cells.
E. False. The same signaling molecule can act in different modes. For example, acetylcholine stimulates muscle contraction at neuromuscular junctions but dampens the contractile response of heart muscle when it is released in a paracrine mode.
F. False. The same receptor can bring about different responses according to the target cell type because of other differences in the signaling pathways or differences in the intracellular protein targets for activation or inhibition.
G. False. Insulin release, like that of other peptide hormones, occurs from stored reserves in cells and does not require new RNA or protein synthesis. Responses are slow because of the time taken for diffusion and distribution via the bloodstream.
H. True
I. True

12–3 When acetylcholine is released from the synaptic vesicles of the neurones, some of the acetylcholine finds target receptors, some diffuses away, but most is rapidly hydrolyzed to acetate and choline, which are taken up by the nerve terminal. When the density of receptors is reduced, the probability diminishes that an acetylcholine molecule will find its receptor before it is hydrolyzed. The suboptimal transmission of the signal is responsible for the muscular weakness of myasthenic patients. One way to overcome their muscular weakness is to increase the concentration of acetylcholine in response to stimulation, in order to compensate for the reduced number of receptors. There are two general ways acetylcholine levels in the synaptic cleft might be increased: more acetylcholine could be released upon stimulation, or its hydrolysis could be inhibited. The drug neostigmine inhibits the enzyme acetylcholinesterase, which is responsible for hydrolysis of acetylcholine in the synaptic cleft, and thereby increases the efficiency of signal transmission across the synapse.

(You may have guessed that neostigmine binds to the acetylcholine receptor and stimulates muscle contraction directly. However, if it did, it would cause widespread contractions, not coordinated movements.)

Reference: Rowland, L.P. Diseases of chemical transmission at the nerve-muscular synapse: myasthenia gravis. In Principles of Neural Science, 2d ed. (E.R. Kandel, J.H. Schwartz, eds.), pp. 147–185. New York: Elsevier, 1985.

***12–4**

***12–5** **Reference:** Yalow, R.S. Radioimmunoassay: a probe for the fine structure of biologic systems. *Science* 200:1236–1245, 1978.

12–6

A. Since the half-life of radioactive iodine is 7 days, two atoms of radioactive iodine will give rise to one disintegration in a week. Thus, to determine the required number of picograms of labeled insulin, it is necessary to convert 1000 counts per minute to disintegrations per week (multiply by two to get the number of radioactive iodine atoms) and then to calculate the weight of the same number of insulin molecules.

1000 counts per minute is 2.0×10^7 disintegrations (disint) per week.

$$\frac{\text{disint}}{\text{week}} = \frac{1000 \text{ counts}}{\text{min}} \times \frac{2 \text{ disint}}{\text{count}} \times \frac{60 \text{ min}}{\text{hr}} \times \frac{24 \text{ hr}}{\text{day}} \times \frac{7 \text{ days}}{\text{week}}$$
$$= 2.0 \times 10^7 \text{ disintegrations per week}$$

Thus, 1000 cpm corresponds to 4.0×10^7 atoms of radioactive iodine. The weight of this number of insulin molecules is 0.76 pg (picograms).

$$\text{insulin} = 4.0 \times 10^7 \text{ molecules} \times \frac{\text{mole}}{6 \times 10^{23} \text{ molecules}} \times \frac{11{,}466 \text{ g}}{\text{mole}} \times \frac{10^{12} \text{ pg}}{\text{g}}$$
$$= 0.76 \text{ pg}$$

B. For optimal sensitivity of the radioimmunoassay, the amounts of the tracer and unknown should be the same. Thus, given the starting assumptions, at optimum sensitivity you will be able to detect 0.76 pg of unlabeled insulin.

12–7 Finding prelabeled lumenal material in the intracellular droplets indicates that the droplets are composed of lumenal material engulfed by the follicle cells. The progression of intracellular droplets from the periphery to the interior of the cell is also more consistent with engulfment of lumenal material than with secretion. The presence of mannose 6-phosphate on lumenal thyroglobulin suggests that the engulfed material is targeted to lysosomes where thyroglobulin is degraded to produce thyroxine. The mechanism for release of thyroxine into the bloodstream is unknown. The synthesis and release of thyroxine are summarized in Figure 12–17.

Note that the presence of mannose 6-phosphate on thyroglobulin raises a very interesting cell biological problem. How does thyroglobulin manage to avoid entering the lysosome directly instead of being secreted? The answer is not known. The mannoses are phosphorylated in what appears to be the normal way. Perhaps other modifications, such as the sulfated tyrosines or high sialic acid content, mask the mannose-6-phosphate signal, permitting the protein to be secreted. Other extracellular modifications, perhaps the iodination itself, may activate the mannose-6-phosphate signal for lysosomal targeting when thyroglobulin reenters the cell.

Reference: Herzog, V.; Neumuller, W.; Holzmann, B. Thyroglobulin, the major and obligatory exportable protein of thyroid follicle cells, carries the lysosomal recognition marker mannose 6-phosphate. *EMBO J.* 6:555–560, 1987.

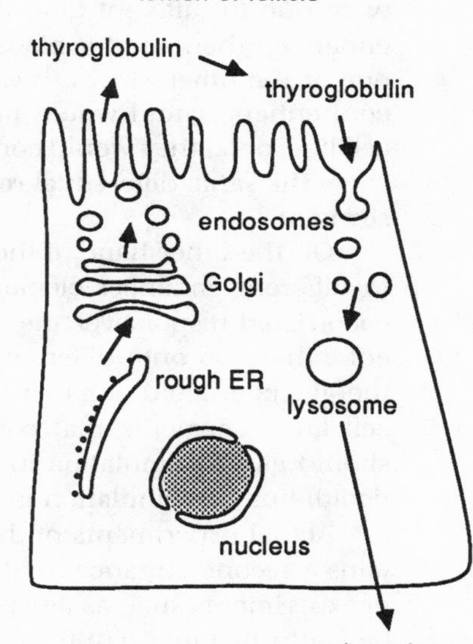

Figure 12–17 Synthesis and release of thyroxine (Answer 12–7).

Signaling Mediated by Intracellular Receptors: Mechanisms of Steroid Hormone Action

12–8

A. steroid hormones
B. receptor activation
C. ecdysone
D. testicular feminization syndrome

*Problems with an asterisk (*) are answered in the Instructor's Manual.

12–9

A. False. Steroid hormones are not DNA-binding proteins. All steroid hormone *receptors* isolated so far are DNA-binding proteins.

B. True

C. True

D. False. Cells contain separate, specific receptors for estradiol, cortisol, and progesterone. Each receptor is encoded by a different gene.

E. True.

12–10

A. Both cell lines appear to contain a glucocorticoid receptor, based on the dexamethasone-induced increases in CAT activity. When transfected with the construct carrying the glucocorticoid-responsive enhancer on the viral DNA segment, cell line 1 showed a fivefold increase and cell line 2 showed an eightyfold increase in CAT activity in the presence of dexamethasone.

B. Cell line 1 differs significantly from cell line 2 in the level of CAT activity detected in the *absence* of dexamethasone after transfection of the construct containing the glucocorticoid-responsive enhancer. There are two reasonable explanations for this difference. (1) Cell line 1 contains a mutant glucocorticoid receptor that can partially activate the glucocorticoid enhancer in the viral segment in the absence of glucocorticoid. (2) Cell line 1 contains a tissue-specific protein that recognizes and stimulates a second (nonglucocorticoid-responsive) enhancer on the viral segment.

C. These potential explanations make different predictions for the outcome of experiments in which a variety of shorter viral segments are tested for CAT activity in the two cell lines. If the difference between the cell lines were due to different glucocorticoid receptors that recognize the same enhancer, then shorter pieces of the viral segments would all behave in one or the other of two ways: (1) they would not contain the glucocorticoid enhancer and would not be activated by dexamethasone in either cell line, or (2) they would contain the glucocorticoid enhancer and would show the same differential response to dexamethasone as the intact viral segment.

On the other hand, if the difference between the cell lines were due to different enhancer elements (glucocorticoid responsive and nonglucocorticoid responsive), then it should be possible to separate the different enhancers onto different DNA segments. Segments that contain only the glucocorticoid enhancer should give identical responses in the two cell lines; segments that contain only the nonglucocorticoid enhancer should give a stimulation in cell line 1 (that is independent of glucocorticoid) but no stimulation in cell line 2.

Actual experiments of this kind indicate that the viral segment contains a second enhancer that is specifically activated in cell line 1. Results of experiments such as illustrated in this problem suggest that genes may be controlled in a tissue-specific fashion by an interplay of multiple regulatory factors. Indeed, stimulation of gene expression by steroids normally requires that the responding cell have a steroid receptor and that the chromatin structure surrounding a potentially regulatable gene be open—an effect mediated by other transcription factors.

Reference: DeFranco, D.; Yamamoto, K.R. Two different factors act separately or together to specify functionally distinct activities at a single transcriptional enhancer. *Mol. Cell. Biol.* 6:993–1001, 1986.

***12–11** **References:** Payvar, F.; DeFranco, D.; Firestone, G.L.; Edgar, B.; Wrange, O.; Okret, S.; Gustafsson, J-A.; Yamamoto, K.R. Sequence-specific binding of glucocorticoid receptor to MTV DNA at sites within and upstream of the transcribed region. *Cell* 35:381–392, 1983.

Scheidereit, C.; Geisse, S.; Westphal, H.M.; Beato, M. The glucocorticoid receptor binds to defined nucleotide sequences near the promoter of mouse mammary tumor virus. *Nature* 304:749–752, 1983.

12–12

A. The cycloheximide-induced alteration of the puffing pattern is due to its

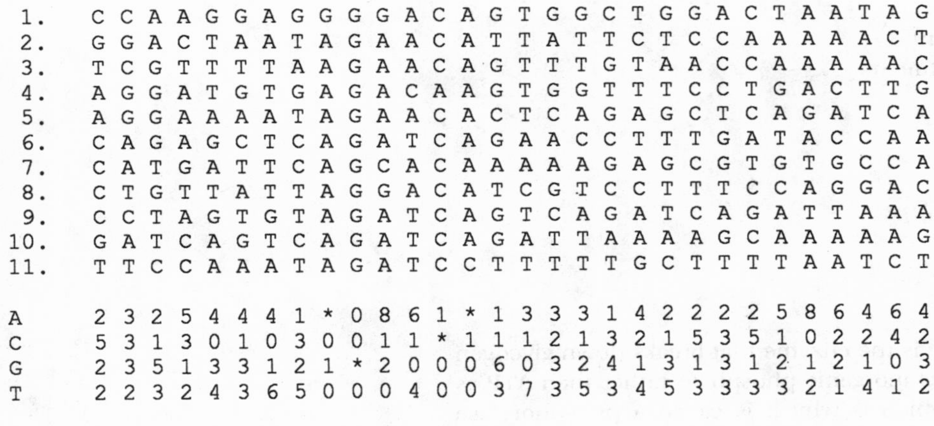

1. C C A A G G A G G G G A C A G T G G C T G G A C T A A T A G
2. G G A C T A A T A G A A C A T T A T T C T C C A A A A A C T
3. T C G T T T T A A G A A C A G T T T G T A A C C A A A A A C
4. A G G A T G T G A G A C A A G T G G T T T C C T G A C T T G
5. A G G A A A A T A G A A C A C T C A G A G C T C A G A T C A
6. C A G A G C T C A G A T C A G A A C C T T T G A T A C C A A
7. C A T G A T T C A G C A C A A A A A G A G C G T G T G C C A
8. C T G T T A T T A G G A C A T C G T C C T T T C C A G G A C
9. C C T A G T G T A G A T C A G T C A G A T C A G A T T A A A
10. G A T C A G T C A G A T C A G A T T A A A A G C A A A A A G
11. T T C C A A A T A G A T C C T T T T T G C T T T T A A T C T
A 2 3 2 5 4 4 4 1 * 0 8 6 1 * 1 3 3 3 1 4 2 2 2 2 5 8 6 4 6 4
C 5 3 1 3 0 1 0 3 0 0 1 1 * 1 1 1 2 1 3 2 1 5 3 5 1 0 2 2 4 2
G 2 3 5 1 3 3 1 2 1 * 2 0 0 0 6 0 3 2 4 1 3 1 3 1 2 1 2 1 0 3
T 2 2 3 2 4 3 6 5 0 0 0 4 0 0 3 7 3 5 3 4 5 3 3 3 3 2 1 4 1 2


```
consensus        T   A G A A C A G T                   A A   A
                 A         T                                  C
```

Figure 12–18 Schematic diagram relating ecdysone-receptor binding to the pattern of gene activity (Answer 12–12).

effect on protein synthesis. The result indicates that a newly synthesized protein is required to turn off the early puffs and to turn on the late puffs. Presumably, the protein is synthesized from one of the early puffs.

The shut off of transcription from the intermolt puffs is insensitive to cycloheximide treatment. This observation suggests that the receptor-ecdysone complex turns off these puffs directly. (The shut off presumably is mediated by a protein because ecdysone is not a large enough molecule to have such specific interactions with naked DNA.)

B. The immediate regression of the early puffs upon ecdysone removal indicates that the ecdysone-receptor complex is required continuously to keep the genes turned on.

The premature activation of the late puffs under these conditions is unexpected. If activation of the late puffs depended only on a product of the early puffs, then they should be turned on at the same time (or even delayed due to a lower level of early product). The premature activation suggests that the receptor-ecdysone complex actually functions as an inhibitor, delaying activation until the concentration of the presumptive early-puff product reaches some critical level. Removal of ecdysone allows the puffs to be induced at a lower concentration of early product.

C. These experimental observations are summarized in the schematic diagram shown in Figure 12–18. The ecdysone-receptor complex binds to regulatory regions of intermolt, early, and late puffs. Binding at intermolt puffs turns them off, binding at early puffs turns them on, and binding at late puffs keeps them off. A product from one or more early puffs binds at the regulatory regions of early and late puffs, ultimately turning off the early puffs and turning on the late puffs.

Reference: Ashburner, M.; Chihara, C.; Meltzer, P.; Richards, G. Temporal control of puffing activity in polytene chromosomes. *Cold Spring Harbor Symp. Quant. Biol.* 38:655–662, 1973.

Mechanisms of Transduction by Cell-Surface Receptor Proteins

12–13

A. channel-linked
B. catalytic
C. G-protein-linked
D. intracellular messengers (intracellular mediators)
E. adenylate cyclase, cyclic AMP phosphodiesterase
F. G proteins

G. cholera toxin
H. inhibitory G protein (G_i protein)
I. calcium-sequestering compartment
J. phosphatidylinositol (PI)
K. inositol trisphosphate ($InsP_3$)
L. protein kinase C (C-kinase)
M. ras proteins
N. tyrosine-specific protein kinase

12–14

A. True
B. True
C. False. Glycogen phosphorylase is the enzyme that breaks down glycogen to glucose 1-phosphate. It uses inorganic phosphate rather than ATP as the phosphorylating agent, which is why it is called a phosphorylase instead of a kinase.
D. True
E. True
F. True
G. True
H. True
I. False. Phospholipase C acts by releasing free inositol phosphate esters from phosphoinositides. $InsP_3$ is thought to mediate calcium entry to the cytoplasm from intracellular sources.
J. False. Protein kinase C is activated by diacylglycerol and Ca^{2+}. $InsP_3$ has no direct effect on this enzyme.
K. True
L. True
M. True
N. False. Unlike the oncogenes *erbA*, *erbB*, and *neu*, which encode altered receptors, the *sis* oncogene encodes a functionally active version of PDGF itself, not the receptor.

12–15

A. The specific binding curve is obtained by subtracting the nonspecific curve from the total. As illustated in Figure 12–19, the specific binding curve reaches a plateau above 4 nM alprenolol. Thus, the β-adrenergic receptors are saturated with alprenolol above this concentration.
B. There are 1500 β-adrenergic receptors per frog erythrocyte. Since one alprenolol binds per receptor, the number of bound alprenolol molecules is equal to the number of receptors. At saturation 20,000 cpm of alprenolol binds per mg of erythrocyte membrane (Figure 12–19). Thus, the amount of bound alprenolol is

$$\text{bound alprenolol} = \frac{20 \times 10^3 \text{ cpm}}{\text{mg}} \times \frac{\text{mmol}}{10^{13} \text{ cpm}} \times \frac{6 \times 10^{20} \text{ molecules}}{\text{mmol}} \times \frac{\text{mg}}{8 \times 10^8 \text{ erythrocyte}}$$

$$= 1500 \text{ molecules per erythrocyte}$$

Since one molecule of alprenolol binds per β-adrenergic receptor, there are 1500 β-adrenergic receptors per erythrocyte.

Reference: Lefkowitz, R.J.; Limbird, L.E.; Mukherjee, C.; Caron, M.G. The β-adrenergic receptor and adenylate cyclase. *Biochim. Biophys. Acta* 457:1–39, 1976.

***12–16** **References:** Fung, B.K-K.; Stryer, L. Photolyzed rhodopsin catalyzes the exchange of GTP for bound GDP in retinal rod outer segments. *Proc. Natl. Acad. Sci. USA* 77:2500–2504, 1980.

Fung, B.K-K.; Hurley, J.B.; Stryer, L. Flow of information in the light-triggered cyclic nucleotide cascade of vision. *Proc. Natl. Acad. Sci. USA* 78:152–156, 1981.

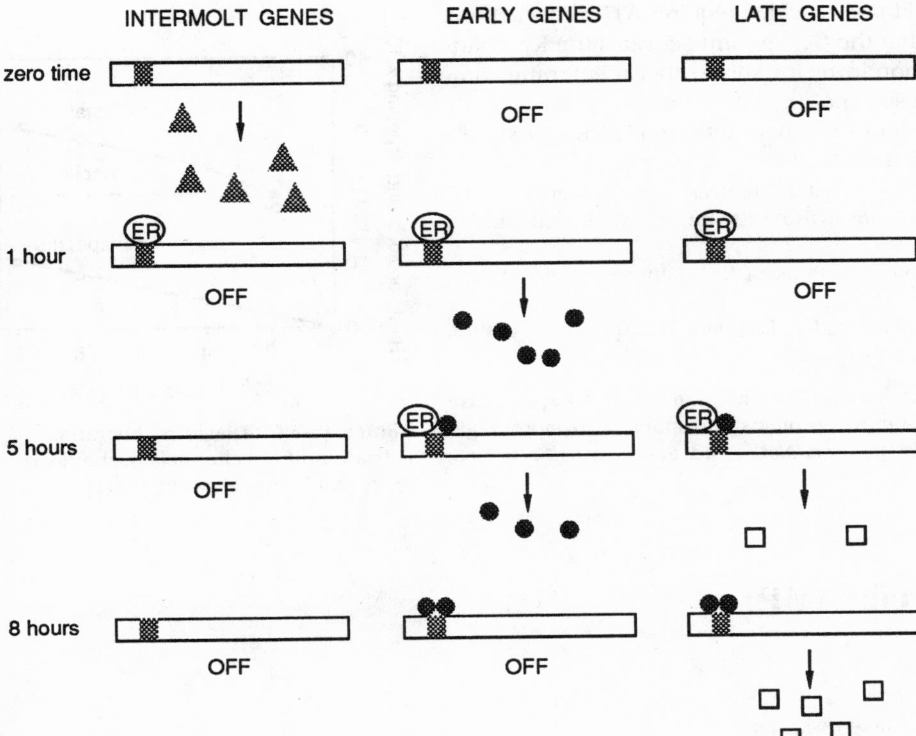

Figure 12–19 Specific binding of alprenolol to erythrocyte membranes (Answer 12–15).

12–17

A. The opening of the K^+ channel in the presence of GppNp and absence of acetylcholine may be somewhat surprising to you, since the release of GDP and the binding of GTP by G proteins normally are stimulated by an activated receptor. Even in the absence of an activated receptor, however, G proteins exchange their bound nucleotides with nucleotides in the cytoplasm. Exchange is slow, and any bound GTP is quickly hydrolyzed in the absence of an activated receptor, thereby keeping the channel closed. The K^+ channels open slowly when GppNp is present because each time a GDP is released and a GppNp is bound, the G protein is locked into an active form. Over the course of a minute, enough G protein is activated in this way to open the K^+ channels in the absence of acetylcholine.

B. The complete G protein does not activate the K^+ channels in the absence of acetylcholine presumably because, like other G proteins, the active portion is inhibited by one of the subunits. The ability of the $G_{\beta\gamma}$ subunit to open the K^+ channel in the absence of acetylcholine and GTP suggests that it is the active portion of the G protein. This conclusion is surprising because it is the G_α subunit that appears to stimulate adenyl cyclase in other cells.

As is usual (and appropriate) when a widely held scientific viewpoint is challenged, these results have sparked a lively debate whose outcome is not yet decided (see references). It is possible that the results derive from a subtle artifact because of the way the experiment was done and may not, therefore, accurately describe the regulation of the K^+ channel in the heart. The outcome will ultimately be decided by further experiments. Either the conclusions will stand or they will not. In either case our scientific understanding of cell signaling will be strengthened.

C. These experiments virtually rule out participation of an intracellular messenger in the activation of K^+ channels. Since the buffer does not contain ATP or Ca^{2+}, neither of these potential messengers can be involved in opening the K^+ channel. Nor is it likely that diglyceride or $InsP_3$ participates, at least in their normal ways. Although either of these intermediates could be produced, neither could function as it usually does. $InsP_3$ normally affects Ca^{2+} concentrations (which it cannot do here), and diglyceride normally activates protein kinase C (which requires ATP for its action). The simplest interpretation is that the $G_{\beta\gamma}$ subunit activates the K^+ channel directly, although an activation involving some other membrane component is not eliminated by these experiments.

D. A simple scheme for the G-protein mediated activation of K^+ channels by acetylcholine is shown in Figure 12–20.

References: Logothetis, D.E.; Kurachi, Y.; Galper, J.; Neer, E.J.; Clapham, D.E. The βγ subunits of GTP-binding proteins activate the muscarinic K^+ channel in heart. *Nature* 325:321–326, 1987.

Birnbaumer, L.; Brown, A.M. G protein opening of K^+ channels. *Nature* 327:21, 1987.

Logothetis, D.E.; Kurachi, Y.; Galper, J.; Neer, E.J.; Clapham, D.E. G protein opening of K^+ channels. *Nature* 327:22, 1987.

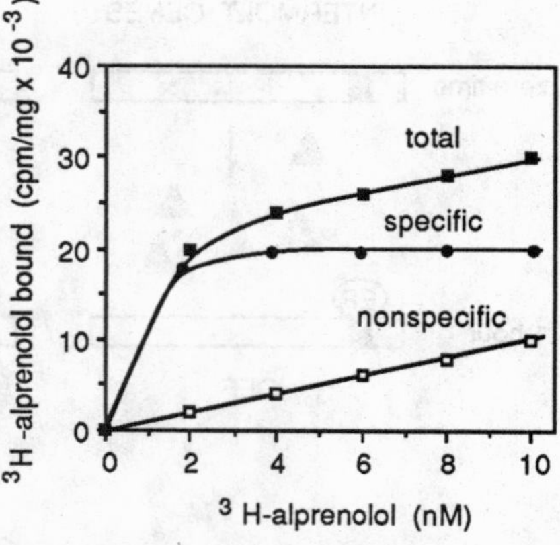

Figure 12–20 Diagram illustrating activation of K^+ channels in the heart by acetylcholine (Answer 12–17).

***12–18** **Reference:** Burch, R.M.; Luini, A.; Axelrod, J. Phospholipase A_2 and phospholipase C are activated by distinct GTP-binding proteins in response to α_1-adrenergic stimulation in FRTL5 thyroid cells. *Proc. Natl. Acad. Sci. USA* 83:7201–7205, 1986.

The Mode of Action of Cyclic AMP and Calcium Ions

12–19

A. cyclic AMP-dependent protein kinase (A-kinase)
B. calmodulin
C. calmodulin-dependent protein kinases (Ca-kinases)
D. guanylate cyclase

12–20

A. False. Elevated cyclic AMP levels in muscle cells promote glycogen breakdown and inhibit glycogen synthesis.
B. True
C. True
D. False. Enzymes that remove phosphate groups from proteins are called phosphatases. Phosphorylases cleave bonds by addition of phosphate (in analogy to hydrolases, which cleave bonds by addition of water).
E. True
F. True
G. True
H. False. All cells contain protein phosphatases that would eventually turn this kinase off.

12–21

A. If A-kinase were essential in hamster cells, it would have been impossible to isolate mutants that lack the enzyme, since they could not survive. Thus A-kinase is not essential to these hamster cells (nor is it essential in several other cell lines in which such mutants have been isolated). One should not conclude, however, that A-kinase is not essential for the organism. There are many examples of enzyme defects that have minimal consequences for cells in culture but severely affect the intact organism.
B. Mutations that eliminate the catalytic subunit would be unresponsive to high levels of cyclic AMP and therefore resistant to cyclic AMP. These mutations would be recessive, for in the presence of the wild-type catalytic subunit, cyclic AMP responsiveness would be restored. (It might seem that mutations that eliminate the regulatory subunits would be the same. However, without the regulatory subunits A-kinase would be active at all times, which is a lethal condition—excess A-kinase activity is the reason that these cells are killed by high levels of cyclic AMP. Thus, cell lines without regulatory subunits would not have been isolated in the first place.)

Dominant mutations are somewhat more difficult to explain. In general, dominance indicates an altered activity rather than complete lack of activity. Dominant mutations have been found in both the regulatory and catalytic subunits. A possible dominant mutation in the regulatory subunit is one that increases its affinity for the catalytic subunit. Such a mutation might plausibly respond only to high levels of cyclic AMP (required to displace the tightly bound regulatory subunit), and it would be dominant because the mutant subunits bind the catalytic subunits at the low cyclic AMP concentrations that would displace the normal regulatory subunits.

Dominant mutations in the catalytic subunit are more difficult to explain. One possibility is that mutant catalytic subunits bind regulatory subunits more tightly, which would explain its altered responsiveness to cyclic AMP. Its dominance might be understood if the combination of a mutant catalytic subunit with a normal catalytic subunit rendered the heterodimer mutantlike in its binding to the regulatory subunits. If this were the case, an even mixture of mutant and normal catalytic subunits would be expected to have only one-quarter the normal A-kinase activity (only one-quarter of the catalytic dimers would have two wild-type subunits).

C. These experimental results generally support the contention that all cyclic AMP effects are mediated through A-kinase, but they fall short of proving the point. Similar studies in a variety of other cell lines have also identified mutants solely in the A-kinase pathway. Furthermore, cells that completely lack A-kinase show none of the effects normally associated with cyclic AMP. Consequently, there is no convincing evidence at present in eucaryotic cells that cyclic AMP has any target other than A-kinase.

Reference: Gottesman, M.M. Genetics of cyclic-AMP-dependent protein kinases. In Molecular Cell Genetics (M.M. Gottesman, ed.), pp. 711–743. New York: Wiley, 1985.

***12–22** **Reference:** Adelstein, R.S.; Klee, C.B. Smooth muscle myosin light-chain kinase. In Calcium and Cell Function (W.Y. Cheung, ed.), Vol. 1, pp. 167–182. New York: Academic Press, 1980.

12–23

A. The activity of Ca^{2+} and that of diacylglycerol suggest that the normal sequence of events involves phospholipase C. Collagen fibers and thrombin stimulate a receptor on the surface of the platelet, which in turn activates phospholipase C, presumably through a G protein. Phospholipase C cleaves phosphatidylinositol bisphosphate to produce $InsP_3$ and diacylglycerol. $InsP_3$ mobilizes internal Ca^{2+} stores, which activates myosin light-chain kinase, resulting in the phosphorylation of the myosin light chain. This branch of the pathway can be stimulated by the calcium ionophore, A23187. Diacylglycerol activates C-kinase, which phosphorylates the 40 kd protein. This branch of the pathway can be stimulated directly by diacylglycerol. These two individual pathways interact to stimulate serotonin release. The overall pathway for platelet activation is diagrammed in Figure 12–21.

B. Secretion of serotonin seems to require both calcium and diacylglycerol, since neither alone causes any secretion (Figure 12–10B). These experiments imply that the 40 kd protein is involved, although direct proof is lacking; its role is undefined. Calcium is thought to be more directly involved in secretion and in some way enables the fusion of membranes required for exocytosis.

Reference: Nishizuka, Y. Calcium, phospholipid turnover and transmembrane signaling. *Phil. Trans. R. Soc. Lond. (Biol.)* 302:101–112, 1983.

12–24

A. The dependence of activation on external calcium and the ability of a calcium ionophore to activate eggs indicate that the key step in egg activation is the entry of calcium from outside. The requirement for a combination of inositol phosphates could be interpreted in two ways: (1) the

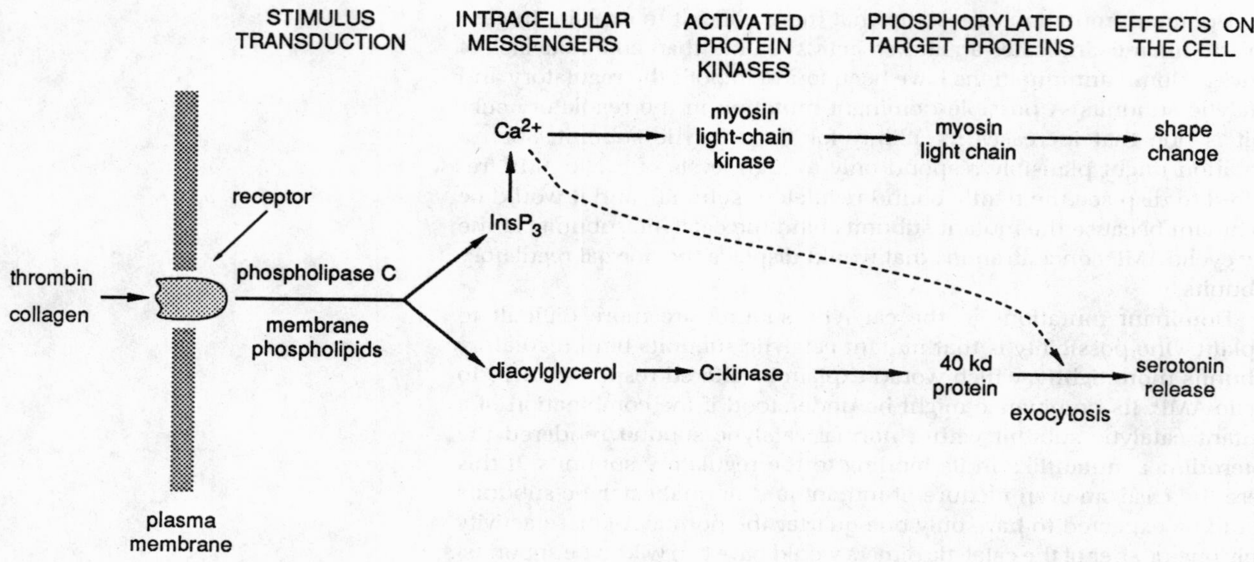

Figure 12–21 Overall pathway for platelet activation (Answer 12–23).

two inositides are required together to stimulate a critical step in the influx of calcium or (2) there are two steps in the activation process, each of which is controlled by a different inositide. The known capacity of (2,4,5)$InsP_3$ to mobilize internal calcium stores weighs slightly in favor of the second alternative. Specifically, in the first step (2,4,5)$InsP_3$ would elevate internal calcium levels somewhat by mobilizing internal stores (but not enough to activate the egg). The second step would require this level of calcium plus (1,3,4,5)$InsP_4$ in order to stimulate entry of external calcium. This two-step mechanism of activation predicts that co-injection of Ca^{2+} (at a level that does not activate by itself) and (1,3,4,5)$InsP_4$ should activate sea urchin eggs.

B. Presumably, (1,4,5)$InsP_3$ activates eggs by itself because a fraction of it can be converted to (1,3,4,5)$InsP_4$ by inositol 3 kinase. Thus, when (1,4,5)$InsP_3$ is injected, some (1,3,4,5)$InsP_4$ will be generated, allowing the two steps (or one) in the activation process to be completed. (2,4,5)$InsP_3$ and (1,3,4)$InsP_3$ are inactive because neither can be converted to (1,3,4,5)$InsP_4$ by inositol 3 kinase. Thus, although they can presumably mobilize internal calcium stores, they cannot complete the second step.

Reference: Irvine, R.F.; Moor, R.M. Microinjection of inositol 1,3,4,5-tetrakisphosphate activates sea urchin eggs by a mechanism dependent on external Ca^{2+}. *Biochem. J.* 240:917–920, 1986.

***12–25** **References:** Byers, D.; Davis, R.L.; Kiger, J.A. Defect in cyclic AMP phosphodiesterase due to the *dunce* mutation of learning in *Drosophila melanogaster*. *Nature* 289:79–81, 1981.

Chen, C.-N.; Denome, S.; Davis, R.L. Molecular analysis of cDNA clones and the corresponding genomic coding sequences of the *Drosophila* dunce$^+$ gene, the structural gene for cyclic AMP phosphodiesterase. *Proc. Natl. Acad. Sci. USA* 83:9313–9317, 1986.

Target Cell Adaptation

12–26

A. adaptation (desensitization)
B. receptor down-regulation
C. receptor sequestration
D. chemotaxis receptors

12–27

A. True
B. True

C. False. Homologous desensitization refers to desensitization to ligands that bind to a single type of receptor.
D. True
E. True
F. False. If the attractant level stays constant (no matter the level), bacteria alternate tumbling and straight swimming at fairly rapid intervals.
G. True

12–28

A. The difference in binding of CGP-12177 and dihydroalprenolol to extracts of isoproterenol-treated cells suggests that the ligand-binding sites on some receptors are not directly exposed in the lysate but instead are enclosed by membrane. Dihydroalprenolol, being hydrophobic, can cross membranes and thus bind to all receptors. By contrast, CGP-12177, which is hydrophilic, cannot cross membranes and thus can only bind to exposed receptors. These results suggest that there are two populations of vesicles in the cell lysates: one with receptors facing outward and the other with receptors facing inward. The two populations are separated on sucrose-density gradients. The presence of 5′ nucleotidase in one population but not in the other indicates that the CGP-12177-binding population represents vesicles formed from fragments of the plasma membrane.

B. The parallel between CGP-12177 binding and hormone-dependent adenylcyclase activity suggests that the two are related; that is, the receptors that bind to CGP-12177 are the same ones that can activate adenylate cyclase. This suggestion is supported by finding that CGP-12177 binding is specifically associated with vesicles formed from plasma membrane fragments. The other population of vesicles presumably represents internal vesicles formed by endocytosis, which would yield vesicles with the ligand-binding sites in the interior. These experiments suggest that isoproterenol-induced desensitization results from internalization of the receptors, making them unavailable for interaction with hormone and separating them from the proteins that couple them to adenylate cyclase.

Reference: Hertel, C.; Muller, P.; Portenier, M.; Staehelin, M. Determination of the desensitization of β-adrenergic receptors by [^{3}H]CGP-12177. *Biochem. J.* 216:669–674, 1983.

***12–29** **Reference:** Benovic, J.L.; Strasser, R.H.; Caron, M.G.; Lefkowitz, R.J. β-adrenergic receptor kinase: identification of a novel protein kinase that phosphorylates the agonist-occupied form of the receptor. *Proc. Natl. Acad. Sci. USA* 83:2797–2801, 1986.

12–30

A. If phosphorylation of the two subunits occurs independently and at equal rates, four different types of receptor will exist: nonphosphorylated receptor, receptor phosphorylated on the γ subunit, receptor phosphorylated on the δ subunit, and receptor phosphorylated on both subunits. At 0.8 mole P/mole receptor each subunit would be 40% phosphorylated and 60% nonphosphorylated. Thus the ratio of the various receptor forms would be 36% with no phosphate (0.6 × 0.6), 24% with only the γ subunit phosphorylated (0.6 × 0.4), 24% with only the δ subunit phosphorylated (0.6 × 0.4), and 16% with both subunits phosphorylated (0.4 × 0.4). At 1.2 mole P/mole receptor, the ratios would be: 16% with no phosphate, 24% with the γ subunit phosphorylated, 24% with the δ subunit phosphorylated, and 36% with both subunits phosphorylated.

B. These experiments suggest that desensitization requires only one phosphate per receptor and that phosphorylation of either the γ or the δ subunit is sufficient for desensitization. For both preparations, the fraction that behaves like the untreated receptor matches best the fraction calculated to carry no phosphate: 36% versus 36% at 0.8 mole P/mole receptor and 18% versus 16% at 1.2 mole P/mole receptor. This result suggests that phosphorylation of either subunit is sufficient to trigger desensitization. If a specific subunit were required to be phosphorylated, then the expected fractions behaving like the untreated receptor would have been 60% (24% + 36%) at 0.8 mole P/mole receptor and 40% (24% + 16%) at 1.2 mole P/mole receptor.

Reference: Huganir, R.L.; Delcour, A.H.; Greengard, P.; Hess, G.P. Phosphorylation of the nicotinic acetlycholine receptor regulates its rate of desensitization. *Nature* 321:774–776, 1986.

***12–31** **Reference:** Manson, M.D.; Blank, V.; Brade, G.; Higgins, C.F. Peptide chemotaxis in *E. coli* involves the Tap signal transducer and the dipeptide permease. *Nature* 321:253–258, 1986.

12–32

A. The two cloned receptors, normal and truncated, both carry out signal transduction like the receptors in wild-type bacteria. Upon addition of aspartate, all three kinds of bacteria immediately suppress changes in direction of rotation. Thus the presence of the attractant (aspartate) in the medium is being communicated to the flagella in all three kinds of bacteria.

B. The adaptive properties of bacteria containing the cloned receptors are very different from wild-type bacteria. Wild-type bacteria return to their normal rate of tumbling (reversal of direction of rotation) within 3 minutes. Bacteria with the cloned normal receptor return to the normal rate of tumbling only after about 50 minutes, and bacteria with the truncated receptor do not begin to tumble even after more than 3 hours. Thus bacteria with the cloned normal receptor adapt more slowly than wild-type bacteria, whereas bacteria with the cloned truncated receptor evidently do not adapt.

C. The alterations in adaptation in bacteria with the cloned receptors suggest differences in the methylation rates or extents. The inability of the truncated receptor to be methylated provides a molecular basis for the inability of bacteria containing the receptor to adapt to a high-level aspartate. The molecular basis for the difference between wild-type bacteria and bacteria with the cloned normal receptor is more subtle. The difference in time of adaptation between the two kinds of bacteria is about fifteenfold (3 minutes versus 50 minutes), which is the same as the difference in numbers of receptors per cell. (Cloned genes expressed from plasmids are often overexpressed relative to their chromosomal counterparts.) Thus a reasonable explanation is that it takes the receptor methylase 15 times longer to methylate the more abundant normal receptor.

Reference: Russo, A.F.; Koshland, D.E. Separation of signal transduction and adaptation functions of the aspartate receptor in bacterial sensing. *Science* 220:1016–1020, 1983.

Cell Growth and Division

13

The Steps of the Cell Cycle and Their Causal Connections

13–1

A. mitosis
B. cytokinesis
C. M phase
D. interphase
E. S phase
F. mitotic shake-off
G. MPF (M-phase-promoting factor)
H. cyclin

13–2

A. True. (It is of course critical that DNA be apportioned exactly between the two daughter cells.)
B. True
C. False. It is possible to measure cell-cycle times in specific cell types in complex organs either by scoring mitotic indices or by labeling the whole animal with tritiated thymidine followed by fixation, sectioning, and autoradiography of the tissue under investigation.
D. True
E. False. The G_1-phase transition known as Start is the point at which the cell becomes committed to complete the rest of the steps of the cell cycle. This commitment precedes entry into S phase and DNA synthesis.
F. False. The rates of synthesis of surprisingly few proteins are altered during different phases of the cell cycle.
G. True
H. False. Cytoplasm from G_2-phase cells does not inhibit ongoing DNA synthesis in an S-phase nucleus. The term DNA re-replication block refers to the normal absence of multiple rounds of replication during a single cell cycle. The DNA re-replication block underlies the observation that S-phase nuclei do not induce a fresh round of synthesis in G_2-phase nuclei.
I. True
J. True
K. False. Although RNA synthesis is not necessary for a cell to enter mitosis, protein synthesis is required.
L. True

***13–3**

13–4

A. The overall length of the cell cycle is equivalent to the time it takes for the entire population of cells to double in number. To find the length of the cell cycle, select any two points on the graph in Figure 13–1 between which the number of cells has doubled. The time separating those two points is the length of the cell cycle. For example, the first two data points in Figure 13–1 are at 3×10^5 cells (10 hours) and 6×10^5 cells (30 hours). Since the population of mouse L cells doubled in 20 hours (30 hours − 10 hours), the length of the cell cycle is 20 hours.

*Problems with an asterisk (*) are answered in the Instructor's Manual.

B. In outline, the length of G_2 can be derived from the data in Figure 13–2A, the length of S from the data in Figure 13–2B, and the length of G_1 from the overall length of the cell cycle minus $(M + S + G_2)$.

^3H-thymidine is incorporated only during S phase. Thus no label will be present in cells undergoing mitosis until the cells that were at the very tail end of S phase when the label was added have traversed the G_2 portion of the cell cycle. The appearance of the first labeled mitotic cells at 3 hours after ^3H-thymidine addition (Figure 13–2A) suggests that G_2 is 3 hours long. The majority of mitotic cells, however, did not become labeled until 4 hours after addition of label (and a few did not become labeled until 5 hours after addition of label). This variation suggests that there is some variability in the length of G_2: if the length of G_2 were precisely defined, 100% of mitoses would be labeled when labeling was first observed. Thus, the length of G_2 in mouse L cells is 3 to 4 hours.

The length of S phase can be deduced from the number of silver grains over labeled mitotic cells (Figure 13–2B). Cells that were at the very end of S phase when label was added will have incorporated very little ^3H-thymidine and thus will have very few silver grains, whereas cell that were at the beginning of S phase will have incorporated much more label and thus will have many more silver grains. The important realization is that cells at the beginning of S phase and cells that were in G_1 will have the same number of silver grains, since they incorporated label for the same length of time (that is, throughout S phase). Thus the beginning of S phase is the point in Figure 13–2B at which the number of silver grains per labeled cell reaches a plateau, which is about 10 hours before mitosis. Since G_2 is about 3 hours long, S phase must be about 7 hours long.

Given that M phase is 1 hour, S phase is 7 hours, G_2 is 3 to 4 hours, and the overall length of the cell cycle is 20 hours, G_1 must be 8 to 9 hours long.

Reference: Stanners, C.P.; Till, J.E. DNA synthesis in individual L-strain mouse cells. *Biochim. Biophys. Acta* 37:406–419, 1960.

***13–5** **References:** Xeros, N. Deoxyriboside control and synchronization of mitosis. *Nature* 194:682–683, 1962.

Bootsma, D.; Budke, L.; Vos, O. Studies on synchronous division of tissue culture cells initiated by excess thymidine. *Exp. Cell Res.* 33:301–309, 1964.

Rao, P.N.; Johnson, R.T. Mammalian cell fusion: I. Studies on the regulation of DNA synthesis and mitosis. *Nature* 225:159–164, 1970.

Bostock, C.J.; Prescott, D.M.; Kirkpatrick, J.B. An evaluation of the double thymidine block for synchronizing mammalian cells at the G_1-S border. *Exp. Cell Res.* 68:163–168, 1971.

13–6 The constancy of the length of S phase in haploid versus diploid and diploid versus tetraploid organisms may not be so surprising. If one assumes that particular chromosomes and regions within chromosomes have a defined order of replication, then halving or doubling the number of chromosomes would not be expected to alter the schedule. Moreover, the ratio of genes encoding the replication machinery (DNA polymerases, helicases, initiation factors, etc.) to the amount of DNA would not change. By contrast, the DNA of different organisms might well be expected to have different ratios of critical genes to DNA content, which could account for the correlation seen in Table 13–1.

Reference: Prescott, D.M. Reproduction of Eucaryotic Cells, pp. 85–86. New York: Academic Press, 1975.

13–7

A. Since each transfer accomplishes a twentyfold dilution (50 nl/1000 nl), 10 transfers yield a dilution factor of 20^{10}, which is equal to 10^{13}. It is unreasonable for a molecule to have an undiminished biological effect over this range of dilution.

B. The appearance of MPF activity in the absence of protein synthesis suggests that an inactive precursor of MPF is being activated. In principle, activation could involve one of several kinds of posttranslational modifications, such as protease cleavage or phosphorylation. It is thought that MPF is actually activated by phosphorylation.

C. In order for MPF to propagate its activated state through serial transfers, it must be able to activate itself. If it were a protease, for example, active MPF might activate its inactive precursor by cleavage, such as trypsin-mediated cleavage of trypsinogen to produce more trypsin. In the case of MPF, however, it is more likely that active MPF functions as a protein kinase that activates its inactive precursor by phosphorylation. Note that it is not necessary that MPF activate itself; for example, it could activate another protein kinase, which in turn activates the precursor to MPF. Nevertheless, the principle is the same.

D. Since there is no detectable MPF activity in an immature oocyte, MPF cannot be the source of the original activation event. Presumably, a protein synthesized in response to progesterone stimulation (therefore cycloheximide sensitive) is responsible, directly or indirectly, for the initial activation of MPF.

Reference: Wasserman, W.J.; Masui, Y. Effects of cycloheximide on a cytoplasmic factor initiating meiotic maturation in *Xenopus* oocytes. *Exp. Cell Res.* 91:381–388, 1975.

Yeasts as a Model System

13–8

A. budding yeast
B. fission yeast
C. restrictive, permissive
D. *cdc* (cell-division cycle)
E. Start

13–9

A. False. Yeasts are especially valuable for cell-cycle studies primarily because they permit a powerful genetic analysis of the problem. Yeasts provide a unique opportunity to identify, clone, and characterize genes involved in controlling the cell cycle.
B. True
C. True
D. True
E. True
F. False. It takes starving yeast cells several hours to reenter the cell cycle after refeeding.

13–10

A. The reciprocal temperature-shift experiments demonstrate that *cdc*101 is blocked at 37°C in the G_1 phase of the cell cycle. The first experiment shows that the mutational block precedes or coincides with the hydroxyurea block, or the cells would have divided when they were shifted to 20°C in the presence of hydroxyurea. The second experiment shows that the hydroxyurea block occurs after the mutational block because the cells divided once when they were shifted to 37°C in the absence of hydroxyurea. Together the two experiments indicate that the mutational block in *cdc*101 is in the G_1 phase of the cell cycle. Thus in the first experiment, at 37°C the *cdc*101 mutants accumulate in G_1; when shifted into hydroxyurea medium at 20°C, they move to S phase but are stopped there by the hydroxyurea block and thus do not divide. In the second experiment in the presence of hydroxyurea at 20°C the cells are blocked in S phase; when hydroxyurea is removed and the cells are shifted to 37°C, they progress normally through G_2 and M before they are blocked in G_1. Therefore, they undergo one round of cell division.

B. The results with *cdc*102 indicate that it is blocked at 37°C in S phase. The first experiment shows that the mutational block precedes or coincides with the hydroxyurea block, or the cells would have divided when they were shifted to 20°C. The second experiment shows that the hydroxyurea block precedes or coincides with the mutational block, or the cells would have divided when they were shifted to 37°C. Together the two experiments indicate that the mutational block and the hydroxyurea block coincide. Since hydroxyurea and the *cdc*102 mutation both affect the same phase of the cell cycle, the order of treatment makes no difference; the cells remain trapped in S phase and therefore do not divide.

Reference: Hartwell, L.H. Cell division from a genetic perspective. *J. Cell Biol.* 77:627–637, 1978.

13–11

A. The execution point for your temperature-sensitive mutant is marked on Figure 13–15. Cells that were at a point in the cell cycle before the execution point when the temperature was raised grow to the characteristic landmark morphology but do not divide. Cells that were beyond the execution point at the time when the temperature was raised divide and then stop at the landmark morphology during the next cell-division cycle.

B. The characteristic landmark morphology defines the time at which the cell stops its progress through the cell cycle, as indicated for your mutant in Figure 13–15. The landmark morphology is clearly different from the morphology at the execution point. Therefore, the execution point and the point at which growth is arrested do not correspond in your mutant.

At first glance it may seem odd that the execution point and the point of growth arrest do not coincide. An analogy may make the situation clearer. The addition of engine mounts to the chasis is an early step in the assembly of an automobile. Without engine mounts the engine cannot be added and a complete car cannot be built. However, in the absence of engine mounts assembly of other parts of the automobile can continue until a point is reached at which all further assembly depends on the engine mounts. In this case the normal execution point for engine-mount addition is early, but the arrest point for assembly is relatively late, with a characteristic landmark morphology that resembles a complete automobile (until one looks under the hood).

Reference: Hartwell, L.H. Cell division from a genetic perspective. *J. Cell Biol.* 77:627–637, 1978.

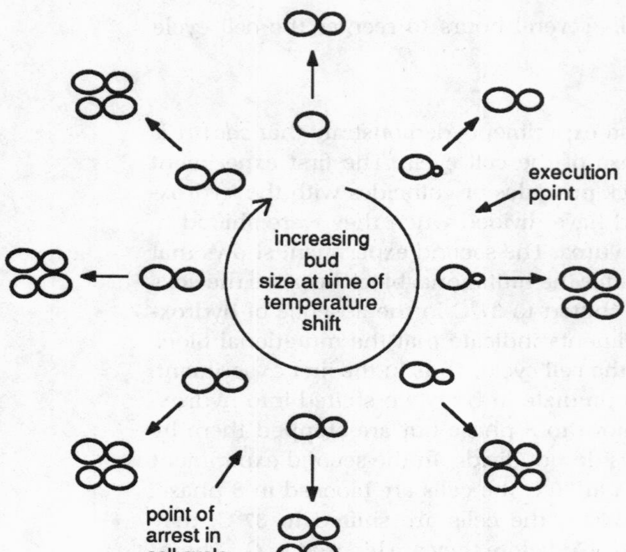

Figure 13–15 The execution point for the gene product affected by your mutant (Answer 13–11). The execution point is indicated by the arrow.

Cell-Division Controls in Multicellular Organisms

13–12

A. restriction point (R)
B. growth factors
C. PDGF (platelet-derived growth factor)
D. anchorage dependence
E. G_0 (or quiescent) state
F. cell senescence

13–13

A. True
B. True
C. True
D. False. The failure of plasma to support the growth of fibroblasts is mainly due to lack of PDGF, which platelets release into serum only when blood clots.
E. True
F. True
G. False. Cancerous cells display lower adhesiveness and less need for attachment for continued growth than do normal cells.
H. True
I. True
J. True

13–14 These results suggest that density-dependent inhibition of cell growth can be completely ascribed to changes in cell shape. This correlation becomes apparent when the ^{3}H-thymidine incorporation is expressed in a way that takes into account the difference in the number of cells per plate; for example, as cpm/1000 cells (Table 13–6). Note, however, that these data do not distinguish whether cell shape "controls" cell proliferation or whether both parameters are dependent on a third factor related in some way to the substrate. The disappearance of bundles of microfilaments, the decreased attachment points to the substratum, or the reduction in the rate of nutrient uptake are all possibilities.

Reference: Folkman, J.; Moscona, A. Role of cell shape in growth control. *Nature* 273:345–349, 1978.

***13–15** **Reference:** O'Keefe, E.J.; Pledger, W.J. A model of cell-cycle control: sequential events regulated by growth factors. *Mol. Cell. Endocrinol.* 31:167–186, 1983.

13–16

A. Experiment 1 shows that the 170 kd protein has a high-affinity binding site for EGF and therefore is most likely the EGF receptor. The control experiment of incubating the membrane preparation in the presence of excess unlabeled EGF demonstrates that EGF binding to the 170 kd protein is specific, not random.

Table 13–6 Incorporation of ^{3}H-Thymidine by Cells Grown on Normal Dishes and on Poly (HEMA)-treated Dishes (Answer 13–14)

Type of Dish	Cell Density (cells/dish)	Confluency	Cell Height (μm)	^{3}H Incorporation (cpm/1000 cells)
Normal	60,000	subconfluent	6	253
Normal	200,000	confluent	15	55
Normal	500,000	confluent	22	7
Poly(HEMA)	30,000	sparse	6	250
Poly(HEMA)	30,000	sparse	15	50
Poly(HEMA)	30,000	sparse	22	7

B. Experiments 2, 3, and 4 show that the 170 kd protein (the EGF receptor) becomes phosphorylated with radioactive phosphate in the presence of γ-^{32}P-ATP. Transfer of the phosphate from the γ position in ATP demonstrates that the EGF receptor is a substrate for a protein kinase. Since the labeling intensity of the 170 kd protein is increased in the presence of EGF, the activity of the protein kinase is stimulated by EGF.

C. Experiments 3 and 4 show that the EGF receptor can transfer phosphate from ATP to protein; thus, it is a protein kinase. Experiment 3 is less convincing than experiment 4. In experiment 3, although the antibody is specific for the EGF receptor, it is not unreasonable to question whether other proteins, perhaps including a protein kinase, might have been trapped within the antibody precipitate. In experiment 4 the EGF receptor is first separated by molecular weight from other proteins that might contaminate the antibody precipitate. Only in the unlikely event that the contaminating protein kinase was also a 170 kd protein would experiment 4 lead you astray.

D. With the caveat mentioned in part C, experiment 4 indicates convincingly that the EGF receptor is a substrate for its own protein kinase activity.

Reference: Cohen, S.; Ushiro, H.; Stocheck, C.; Chinkers, M. A native 170,000 epidermal growth factor receptor-kinase complex from shed plasma membrane vesicles. *J. Biol. Chem.* 257:1523–1531, 1982.

***13–17**

Genes for the Social Control of Cell Division

13–18

A. metastases
B. tumor viruses
C. transformed
D. retroviruses (RNA tumor viruses)
E. oncogenes
F. v-*src* gene
G. proto-oncogenes

13–19

A. True
B. True
C. False. The transformed phenotype of cells containing the v-*src* gene requires its continuous expression. If a temperature-sensitive *src* gene product is inactivated by raising the temperature, the cells very quickly behave as though they were untransformed. When the temperature is lowered, the cells return to their transformed state as soon as sufficient levels of the active *src* protein have accumulated.
D. True
E. True
F. False. There are several other kinds of oncogenes besides growth-factor-related ones.
G. True
H. False. The *src* gene product is attached to the plasma membrane by means of a fatty acid covalently bound to its N terminus.
I. True
J. True
K. True

13–20

A. The lack of significant phosphorylation differences among the known targets of p60^{src} does not rule out the possibility that p60^{src} causes transformation through it tyrosine kinase activity. The key target for transformation could be a protein that is present in very few copies per cell. Standard techniques for analyzing cellular proteins, such as two-dimensional gel electrophoresis, would not detect such rare proteins. These experimental results, however, do argue strongly that the known targets of $p60^{src}$ do not include the critical protein responsible for transformation.

B. Membrane association of $p60^{src}$ could be important for transformation for at least two different kinds of reasons. (1) The unidentified critical target for phosphorylation might be a rare membrane protein that is not phosphorylated unless $p60^{src}$ is present in the membrane. The effectiveness of the interaction between $p60^{src}$ and the putative rare membrane target would be much higher for membrane-bound $p60^{src}$ because of the differences between two-dimensional diffusion in the membrane versus three-dimesional diffusion in the cytoplasm. (2) Alternatively, transformation might depend directly on the presence of $p60^{src}$ in the membrane, and its tyrosine kinase activity might be irrelevant. For example, $p60^{src}$ could bring about transformation by interacting with G proteins or other receptors in the membrane.

Reference: Kamps, M.P.; Buss, J.E.; Sefton, B.M. Rous sarcoma virus transforming protein lacking myristic acid phosphorylates known polypeptide substrates without inducing transformation. *Cell* 45:105–112, 1986.

***13–21** **References:** Knudson, A.G. Mutation and cancer: statistical study of retinoblastoma. *Proc. Natl. Acad. Sci. USA* 68:820–823, 1971.

Fung, Y-K.T.; Murphree, A.L.; T'Ang, A.; Qian, J.; Hinrichs, S.H.; Benedict, W.F. Structural evidence for the authenticity of the human retinoblastoma gene. *Science* 236:1657–1661, 1987.

13–22

A. As discussed in Problem 13–21, the absence of a shoulder on any of the three curves suggests that in all cases only a single event is needed to trigger tumor production in mice that are already expressing one or both oncogenes.

B. Although the rate of tumor production is much higher in mice with both oncogenes, activation of the cellular *ras* proto-oncogene cannot be a required event in the production of tumors in mice that are already expressing the MMTV-regulated *myc* oncogene. Nor can activation of the cellular *myc* proto-oncogene be a required event in triggering tumor formation in mice that are already expressing the MMTV-regulated *ras* oncogene. As indicated in part A, even when mice contain both *myc* and *ras*, some additional event is required to produce a tumor. If *myc* plus *ras* were sufficient for tumor formation, then all mice would develop tumors as soon as they passed through puberty.

C. The rate of tumor production in mice with both oncogenes is much higher than expected if the effects of the individual oncogenes were additive. Thus the two oncogenes together have a synergistic effect on the rate of tumor production. However, as argued in part B, activation of both oncogenes is not sufficient to generate a tumor. Thus, the two oncogenes acting together must open up a pathway to tumor production that can be triggered by any one of several low-frequency events or that can be triggered by one very common event. The nature of the activating events is unclear for any of these transgenic mice.

Reference: Sinn, E.; Muller, W.; Pattengale, P.; Tepler, I.; Wallace, R.; Leder, P. Coexpression of MMTV/v-Ha-*ras* and MMTV/c-*myc* genes in transgenic mice: synergistic action of oncogenes *in vivo*. *Cell* 49:465–475, 1987.

The Mechanics of Cell Division

13–23

A. mitotic spindle
B. centrosome
C. prophase

D. kinetochores
E. centromere
F. prometaphase
G. anaphase
H. anaphase A, anaphase B
I. telophase
J. cytokinesis
K. furrowing
L. contractile ring
M. midbody
N. cell plate
O. phragmoplast

13–24

A. True
B. True
C. False. Procaryotes do not segregate their chromosomes by mitosis; rather, they use special membrane attachment sites to hold daughter chromosomes while the cells divide.
D. True
E. False. Most of the microtubules that assemble on centrosomes are less stable than interphase microtubules.
F. False. The DNA sequences at the centromere are binding sites for proteins in both yeasts and higher eucaryotes. In neither case do they encode mRNA or proteins.
G. True
H. True
I. True
J. True
K. False. The movements in anaphase B are due to microtubules.
L. False. No special DNA sequences are required for formation of a nucleus.
M. True
N. True
O. True
P. True

13–25

A. Dicentric plasmids are stable in bacteria because bacteria use a completely different mechanism to segregate their chromosomes. Bacterial chromosomes are attached directly to specialized regions of the cell membrane that are gradually separated by the growth of membrane between them. Fission occurs between the two attachment sites, so that each daughter receives one chromosome. Thus bacteria are indifferent to the presence of centromeric sequences on the plasmid DNA—which is fortunate for scientists who want to clone centromeric DNA.
B. Dicentric plasmids are unstable in yeasts for the same reason that dicentric chromosomes are unstable in higher eucaryotes. If the two centromeric sequences attach to opposite poles, the spindle apparatus can exert enough pull on the DNA molecule to break its phosphodiester backbone. Roughly half the time a plasmid would be expected to orient itself on the spindle so that its two centromeres are attached to opposite poles. Thus there is a very high probability that a plasmid will be broken at each cell division, hence the instability.
C. Since monocentric plasmids are very stable, it seems most likely that the mechanism for deletion of centromeric sequences from dicentric plasmids relates to the breakage they suffer during mitosis. As illustrated in Figure 13–16, a circular plasmid must suffer two breaks to permit the centromeres to separate during mitosis. This breakage naturally separates the centromeres from one another onto linear fragments of the original plasmid. If the ends of a fragment join to make a circle, the resulting

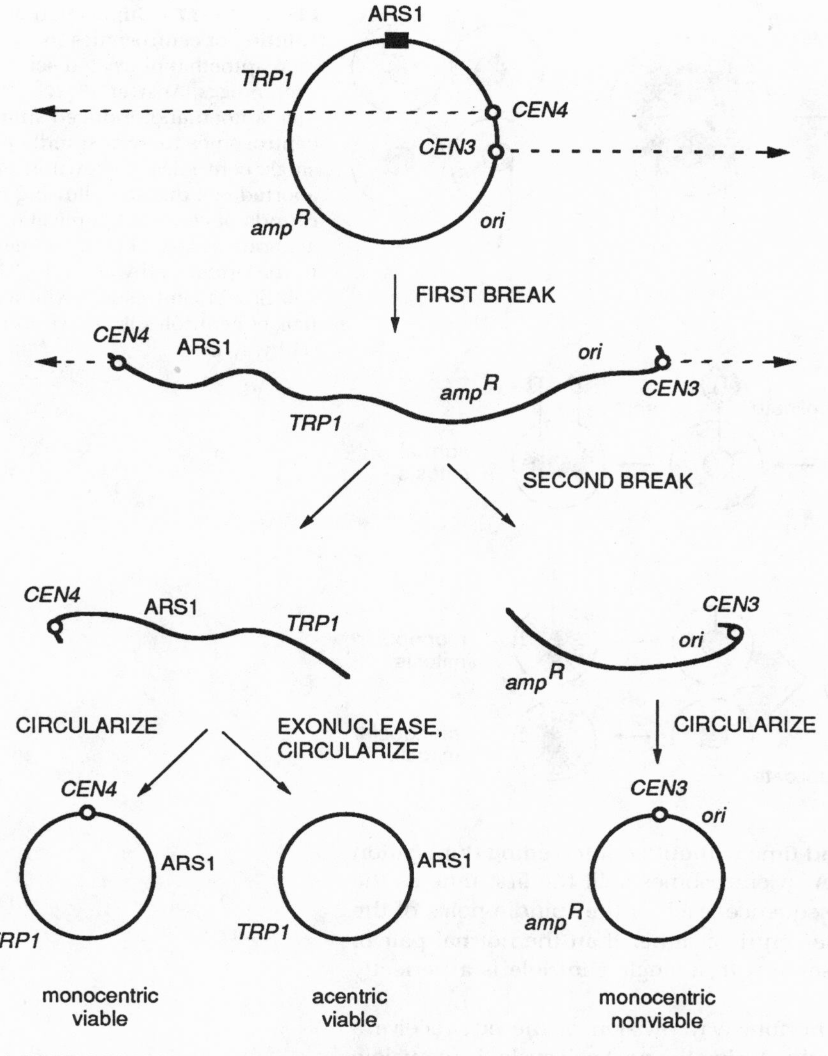

Figure 13–16 A mechanism for generating monocentric and acentric plasmids from a dicentric plasmid in yeast (Answer 13–25). Dashed arrows indicate the direction of pull toward the spindle poles. Viability refers to the ability of the plasmid to grow in yeast under selective conditions (which require *ARS1* and *TRP1*).

plasmid will contain a single centromeric sequence (Figure 13–16). However, only those fragments that contain the yeast origin of replication (*ARS1*) and the selected marker (*TRP1*) can continue to grow in future generations.

This mechanism does not readily account for the loss of both centromeric sequences; rather, it predicts that one centromeric sequence will be retained. Once the dicentric plasmid is reduced to a monocentric plasmid, it should be stable. The loss of both centromeric sequences probably involves a process other than simple breakage. One likely possibility (especially given a background knowledge of yeast that you were not provided with in the problem) is that the broken ends are digested by exonucleases, which occasionally remove the remaining centromeric sequence before the fragment circularizes (Figure 13–16).

Reference: Mann, C.; Davis, R.W. Instability of dicentric plasmids in yeast. *Proc. Natl. Acad. Sci. USA* 80:228–232, 1983.

***13–26** **Reference:** Murray, A.W.; Szostak, J.W. Pedigree analysis of plasmid segregation in yeast. *Cell* 34:961–970, 1982.

13–27 The patterns of centriole duplication and splitting that account for the mercaptoethanol-induced abnormalities in cell division are diagrammed in Figure 13–17. In essence, the treatment with mercaptoethanol allows

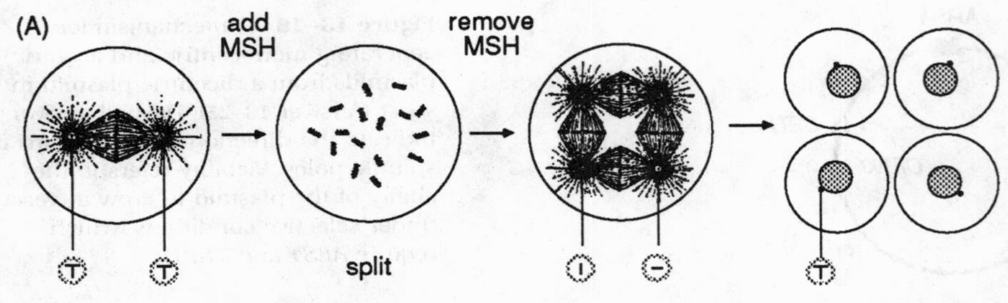

Figure 13–17 Duplication and splitting of centrosomes in mercaptoethanol-treated sea urchin eggs (Answer 13–27). The mercaptoethanol-induced splitting of centrosomes to form spindle poles with single centrioles is shown in (A). The aborted cell division allowing two rounds of centriole duplication to generate a normal centrosome is shown in the upper pathway in (B). The splitting of centrosome with a single pair of centrioles is shown in the lower pathway in (B).

the centrosome to split a second time without an intervening duplication of the centrioles (Figure 13–17A). (Centrosomes split the first time as the egg entered mitosis.) As a consequence, each of the spindle poles of the tetrapolar spindle has only one centriole rather than the normal pair of centrioles. Evidently, a centrosome with a single centriole is a perfectly adequate spindle pole.

The daughter cells from the four-way division of the egg receive a centrosome with a single centriole. During the next cell cycle the centriole is duplicated to form a normal centrosome with a centriole pair (Figure 13–17A). However, the usual form of the centrosome upon entry into mitosis has two centriole pairs instead of one. Thus the centrosome in the daughter cells looks like a single spindle pole and indeed forms a monopolar spindle (Figure 13–17B). Most commonly, cell division is aborted, and the cell traverses the cell cycle again, allowing the centrosome to be duplicated a second time so that it possesses two centriole pairs (Figure 13–17B, top). This second duplication puts the centrosome cycle back in step with the cell cycle and further cell divisions occur normally (Figure 13–17B, top). In the rarer cases in which the daugther cells form a bipolar spindle, the centrosomes split to form two centrosomes each with a single centriole (Figure 13–17B, bottom). Although the splitting allows cell division to occur, it presents the daughter cells with the same problem as the parent: a centrosome with a single centriole (Figure 13–17B, bottom). In this case the centrosome cycle remains out of step with the cell-division cycle.

Note that although the cell divisions can be restored to normal, eggs that undergo a four-way division develop abnormally because none of the cells receives a full complement of chromosomes.

References: Maizia, D.; Harris, P.J.; Bibring, T. The multiplicity of mitotic centers and the time-course of their duplication and separation. *J. Biophys. Biochem. Cytol.* 7:1–20, 1960.

Sluder, G.; Rieder, C.L. Centriole number and the reproductive capacity of spindle poles. *J. Cell Biol.* 100:887–896, 1985.

***13–28** **Reference:** Mitchison, T.J.; Kirschner, M.W. Properties of the kinetochore *in vitro*. II. Microtubule capture and ATP-dependent translocation. *J. Cell. Biol.* 101:766–777, 1985.

***13–29**

13–30

A. The chromosome-signaling hypothesis predicts that furrows will form only where chromosomes have been aligned. This prediction matches the result of the first division but not the result of the second division, where three furrows are formed instead of the expected two furrows.

B. The polar-relaxation hypothesis predicts that there should be two furrows at the first division instead of one as is observed. In the toroidal egg the spindles should relax a ring of the cell surface on either side of the equatorial plane. As a consequence, there should be two regions where the cell surface furrows: at the equatorial plane and opposite it on the other side of the torus. Note that the events of the second division match the expectations of the relaxation hypothesis.

C. The aster-stimulation hypothesis predicts that there should be a single furrow at the first cell division and three furrows at the second cell division, which matches the experimental observations. A single furrow is expected at the first division because the spindle fibers from the two poles interact only at the equatorial plane. At the second division, however, the spindle fibers interact not only at the two equatorial positions, but also at the position of the third furrow.

Reference: Rappaport, R. Establishment of the mechanism of cytokinesis in animal cells. *Int. Rev. Cytol.* 105:245–281, 1986.

Cell Adhesion, Cell Junctions, and the Extracellular Matrix

14

Cell Junctions

14–1

A. epithelium
B. occluding, anchoring, communicating
C. tight
D. apical, basolateral
E. cell-cell adherens
F. adhesion belt (*zonula adherens*)
G. cadherins
H. vinculin
I. focal contacts (adhesion plaques)
J. desmosomes
K. hemidesmosomes
L. gap junction
M. connexons

14–2

A. False. Tight junctions provide molecule-tight seals between cells.
B. True
C. False. The intestinal epithelium is 10,000 times more leaky to ions than is the bladder epithelium.
D. False. Cells adhere by calcium-independent as well as calcium-dependent junctions, and although tight junctions are disrupted by removing calcium, they play a secondary role in cell adherence. Their major role is in sealing the gaps around cells in an epithelium. The reason cells fall apart when calcium is removed from the medium is because adhesion belts depend on calcium for their integrity.
E. False. Gap junctions are communicating junctions.
F. True
G. False. The permeability of gap junctions is regulated by intracellular calcium and pH. The extracellular calcium concentration and pH are closely regulated by physiological mechanisms and do not normally change very much.

14–3 As shown in Figure 14–19, the three protein monomers have distinctly different assembly properties because of the placement of complementary binding domains on their surfaces. Monomer B can assemble into a long chain, as would be expected for one sealing strand of a tight junction. Monomer A could assemble into a large two-dimensional aggregate, as is characteristic of desmosomes. Monomer C could assemble only into a tetramer and thus would be unable (in the absence of additional binding domains) to assemble into a chain or a large aggregate.

***14–4** **Reference:** Van Meer, G.; Simons, K. The function of tight junctions in maintaining differences in lipid composition between the apical and the basolateral cell surface domains of MDCK cells. *EMBO J.* 5:1455–1464, 1986.

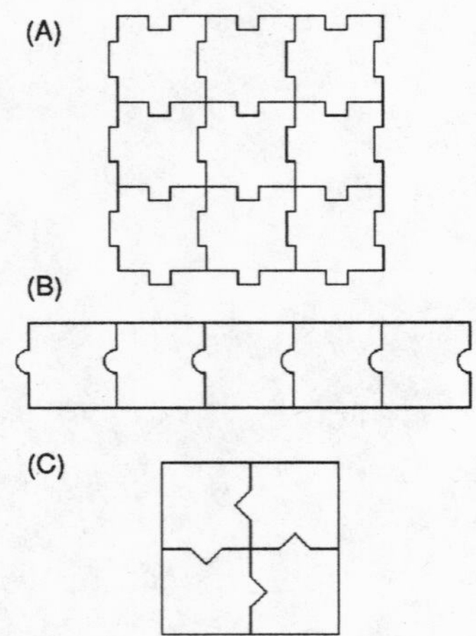

Figure 14–19 Assembly of protein monomers (Answer 14–3).

*Problems with an asterisk (*) are answered in the Instructor's Manual.

14–5 Your measurements support the two-state model of resistance of tight junctions because the resistance of an epithelium is logarithmically related to the number of sealing strands in the junction, as shown by the straight line in Figure 14–20. The line your data points define can be described by

$$R = R_{min}P^{-n}$$

where

R = specific resistance of the junction
R_{min} = minimum resistance of the junction (where there are no sealing strands in the tight junction)
P = probability that a given strand is open
n = number of strands in the tight junction

The value of P from your data is about 0.4. Thus, an individual sealing strand has a relatively high probability of being in the open state. However, if there are enough strands, the probability of their all being open at once is very low, so the overall junction is very tight.

The morphological basis for the closed and open states is unknown. There are, however, three types of protein-protein contacts in a tight junction: (1) contacts between the individual subunits to form a sealing strand in one cell, (2) contacts between individual sealing strands on the same cell to form the characteristic anastomosing network of strands, and (3) contacts between sealing strands on different cells to seal the space between the cells. If any contacts were broken, a pathway would open for the passage of small molecules across an individual sealing strand.

Reference: Claude, P. Morphological factors influencing transepithelial permeability: a model for the resistance of the zonula occludens. *J. Memb. Biol.* 39:219–232, 1978.

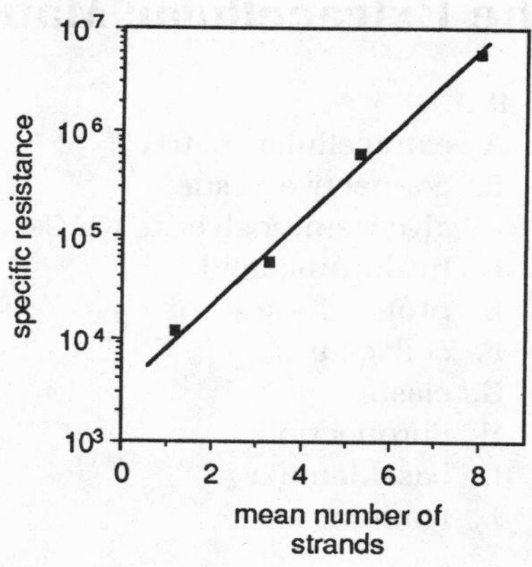

Figure 14–20 A plot of specific resistance versus the number of strands in the tight junction (Answer 14–5).

***14–6** **Reference:** Lawrence, T.S.; Beers, W.H.; Gilula, N.B. Transmission of hormonal stimulation by cell-to-cell communication. *Nature* 272:501–506, 1978.

14–7

A. HRP and fluorescein enter both cells at the early two-cell stage (but not at the late two-cell stage) because the cells are still connected by cytoplasmic bridges, which allow passage of large molecules.

B. Fluorescein enters all cells in the compacted eight-cell embryo because the cells are connected by gap junctions. Since gap junctions permit passage only of molecules less than 1000 daltons or so, HRP is confined to the cell into which it was initially injected. The different result before and after compaction indicates that formation of gap junctions is associated with compaction.

C. If you inject current from the HRP injection electrode, you would detect it in the fluorescein electrode only in the early two-cell embryo and the compacted eight-cell embryo. Only at these two stages are the adjacent cells electrically coupled. At the two-cell stage, the coupling is mediated by the cytoplasmic bridge remaining from cell division; at the eight-cell stage, the coupling is mediated by gap junctions.

Reference: Lo, C.W.; Gilula, N.B. Gap junctional communication in the preimplantation mouse embryo. *Cell* 18:399–409, 1979.

14–8 In invertebrates sheets of cells are often connected by structures known as septate junctions as well as by tight junctions. Picture A shows the characteristic appearance of septate junctions in section and picture B the regular lines of particles that are typical of these junctions when seen in freeze fracture. Septate junctions serve primarily as adhering junctions.

A. septate junction (transmission electron micrograph)
B. septate junction from an insect gut (freeze fracture)
C. gap junction (*en face* view of a heavy metal-infiltrated section)
D. gap junction (freeze fracture)

The Extracellular Matrix

14–9

A. extracellular matrix
B. connective tissue
C. glycosaminoglycans (GAGs)
D. hyaluronic acid
E. proteoglycans
F. collagens
G. elastin
H. fibronectin
I. basal lamina
J. laminin

14–10

A. False. The extracellular matrix plays an active role influencing the development, migration, proliferation, shape, and metabolism of cells that contact it.
B. True
C. True
D. True
E. True
F. False. Intracellular actin and extracellular fibronectin are linked indirectly through the fibronectin receptor. How actin is attached to the receptor and why actin disaggregation should disrupt the attachment of fibronectin to its receptor are unknown.
G. True
H. False. The elasticity of elastin fibers derives from their lack of secondary structure; elastin forms random coils. The hydrogen bonds that stabilize the alpha helix are too strong to be disrupted by the kinds of forces that deform elastin.
I. False. Cells do bind directly to molecules in the extracellular matrix via specialized glycoprotein receptor molecules in their plasma membranes. Two examples are the receptors for fibronectin and laminin. Cells also bind indirectly to the extracellular matrix via adhesive proteins.

14–11

A. Cycloheximide is an inhibitor of protein synthesis. It causes a reduction in $^{35}SO_4$ incorporation in the absence of ONP-β-D-xyloside because it blocks the synthesis of the core protein to which the polysaccharide chains—the substrate for $^{35}SO_4$ incorporation—are added. Since $^{35}SO_4$ incorporation is not sensitive to cycloheximide in the presence of ONP-β-D-xyloside, that incorporation must not depend on protein synthesis. The similarity of ONP-β-D-xyloside to the serine-xylose linkage to the protein suggests (correctly) that ONP-β-D-xylose serves as a primer for formation of polysaccharide chains. (Remember that in all cases the $^{35}SO_4$ counts were shown to be in glycosaminoglycans.)
B. In the presence of ONP-β-D-xyloside large amounts of $^{35}SO_4$-labeled material are released into the medium because they cannot be incorporated into the extracellular matrix of the tissue. An individual polysaccharide chain, even if full size, which these are not, is quite small relative to the proteoglycan to which it is normally attached.
C. ONP-β-D-xyloside serves as a primer for sugar addition, whereas ONP-α-D-xyloside does not, as indicated by its inability to block incorporation of counts into tissue or to stimulate counts in the medium (Table 14–2). Presumably, the sugar transferase responsible for adding the next sugar in the chain is specific for the β linkage between xylose and its attached group.
D. ONP-β-D-xyloside might block development of salivary glands in tissue culture in two ways. First, by competing for sugar addition to the core protein (note decrease in tissue counts in Table 14–2), it may alter the

proteoglycan content of the extracellular matrix in such a way that the salivary gland cells cannot develop. Alternatively, the increase in the concentration of free polysaccharide chains could compete for proteoglycan binding sites on the surfaces of the salivary gland cells.

Reference: Thompson, H.A.; Spooner, B.S. Inhibition of branching morphogenesis and alteration of glycosaminoglycan biosynthesis in salivary glands treated with β-D-xyloside. *Dev. Biol.* 89:417–424, 1982.

***14–12** **Reference:** Sykes, B. The molecular genetics of collagen. *Bioessays* 3:112–117, 1985.

14–13

A. The threefold increase in molecular weight when the disulfide bonds were left intact indicates that the resistant peptides in each partially reassembled collagen molecule are held together by disulfide bonds.

B. Since type III pN-collagen and type III collagen produced identical patterns after trypsin treatment, their resistant peptides almost certainly are identical. Thus, if all the resistant peptides are linked by disulfide bonds, the relevant bonds must be those at the C terminus, that is, the ones that are present in type III collagen.

C. If reassembly began at random sites, there would be a more complicated fragment pattern. More importantly, however, some of the resistant peptides would not contain the site for the disulfide bond in the C-terminal region. As a consequence, the molecular weight of those peptides would not increase because they would not contain a disulfide bond. Since all the resistant peptides do contain the disulfide bond, reassembly is not initiated at random sites. Thus reassembly seems to initiate at a specific site that must be near the position of the disulfide bonds at the C terminus.

D. The orderly progression from small to large fragments with increasing time indicates a zipperlike mechanism beginning, as argued above, from the C-terminal region (Figure 14–21). An all-or-none mechanism would not be expected to show any intermediate stages in the reassembly process.

The presence of discrete bands, which differ in size by several hundred amino acids, requires some additional explanation. If the zippering process was absolutely smooth and all trypsin-cleavage sites were equally sensi-

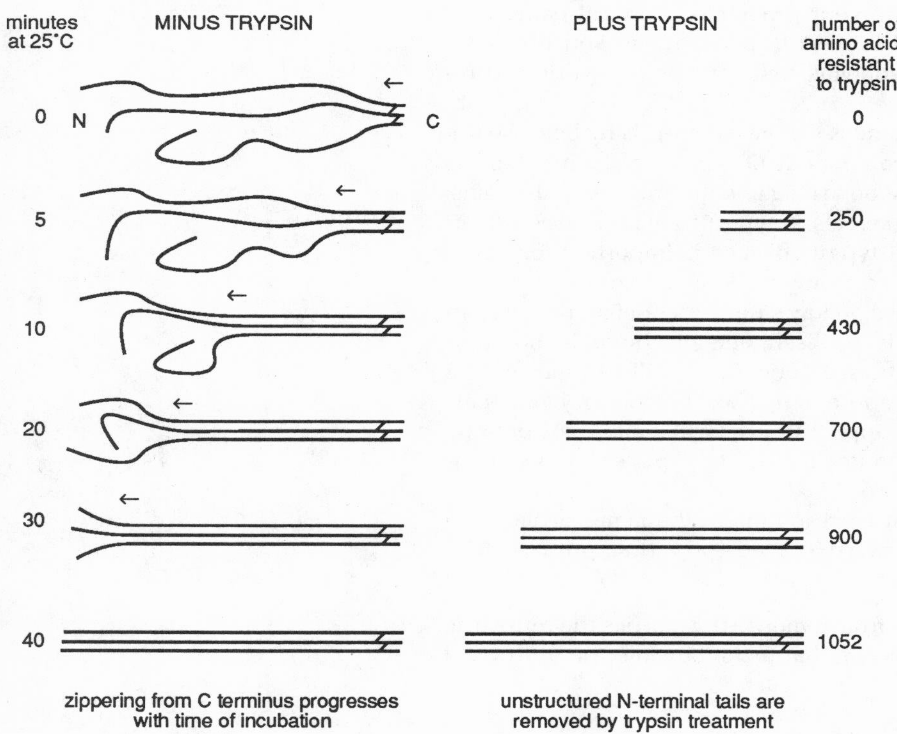

Figure 14–21 Zipperlike assembly of type III collagen molecules, initiating from the C-terminal end (Answer 14–13). Results of trypsin digestion of partially assembled molecules is indicated on the right. The trypsin-resistant peptides are the ones that are visualized after electrophoresis.

tive, then a whole series of bands would be expected, each differing from the last by an increment reflecting the spacing of the trypsin-sensitive bonds (lysines and arginines). The absence of this finely spaced ladder of bands suggests either (1) that the cleavage sites are not equally sensitive (the trypsin digestions were very brief in these experiments) or (2) that zippering is not smooth but, rather, pauses at characteristic points, representing more difficult regions to assemble.

It is important to realize that these reassembly results tell you nothing directly about the natural assembly of type III collagen. It could be argued reasonably that the disulfide bonds at the C terminus provide an artificial nucleation site for reassembly that is not present naturally. Nevertheless, these reassembly results are consistent with other *in vivo* observations. For example, point mutants of collagen typically are better assembled on the C-terminal side of the mutation than on the N-terminal side. This observation suggests that assembly is initiated toward the C terminus and progresses zipperlike toward the N terminus. A zipperlike assembly from one end also makes good theoretical sense: in such a highly repetitious molecule as collagen, random internal initiation would rarely lead to correctly aligned polypeptides.

All these considerations, taken together, form the basis for the current belief that fibrillar collagens assemble zipperlike from the C terminus and that a primary function of the C-terminal propeptide is to register the polypeptides for proper assembly.

Reference: Bachinger, H.P.; Bruckner, P.; Timpl, R.; Prockop, D.J.; Engel, J. Folding mechanism of the triple helix in type III collagen and type III pN-collagen. *Eur. J. Biochem.* 106:619–632, 1980.

***14–14** **References:** Pierschbacher, M.D.; Ruoslahti, E. Cell attachment activity of fibronectin can be duplicated by small synthetic fragments of the molecule. *Nature* 309:30–33, 1984.

Pytela, R.; Pierschbacher, M.D.; Ruoslahti, E. Identification and isolation of a 140 kd cell surface glycoprotein with properties expected of a fibronectin receptor. *Cell* 40:191–198, 1985.

Ruoslahti, E.; Pierschbacher, M.D. Arg-Gly-Asp: a versatile cell recognition signal. *Cell* 44:517–518, 1986.

14–15

A. Since the α1(I) collagen probe and your probe give identical patterns of mRNA, your gene is very likely to be the α1(I) collagen gene. You, of course, would want to confirm this by showing that your probe hydridized directly to the α1(I) probe.

The identity of the affected gene is somewhat surprising because the α1(I) collagen gene encodes a component of type I collagen, which is found primarily in skin, tendons, bones, ligaments, and internal organs. The principal collagen in blood vessels is type III collagen. (See MBOC Table 14–3, p. 810). It seems that type I collagen is important for maintaining blood vessel integrity, at least early in development.

B. Matings between heterozygotes will follow simple Mendelian patterns. In the embryos before the lethality is expresed, one-fourth will be homozygous for the unaffected gene (pattern 1), one-fourth will be homozygous for the affected gene (pattern 3), and one-half will be heterozygous (pattern 2). Since pattern 3 does not appear in live births, one-third of newborns will be homozygous for the unaffected gene (pattern 1) and two-thirds will be heterozygous (pattern 2).

C. Cloning the unaffected gene that corresponds to the gene carrying the retroviral insertion is a straightforward and very powerful approach. The general procedure is outlined below.

1. Prepare a genomic DNA library from a mouse that carries the retrovirus insert. Use a restriction enzyme that cuts outside the retrovirus sequences.

2. Using retrovirus DNA as a probe, screen the library to find clones that carry retrovirus sequences.
3. Subclone a segment of the cell DNA flanking the retrovirus sequences. (It is essential that this DNA not contain repetitive DNA sequences.) The DNA flanking the retrovirus contains the gene of interest.
4. Use the subcloned cell DNA to screen a genomic DNA library (and/or cDNA library) prepared from normal mice. These clones contain unaltered versions of the gene of interest.

References: Jaenisch, R.; Harbers, K.; Schnieke, A.; Lohler, J.; Chumakov, I.; Jahner, D.; Grotkopp, D.; Hoffmann, E. Germline integration of Moloney murine leukemia virus at the Mor13 locus leads to recessive lethal mutation and early embryonic death. *Cell* 32:209–216, 1983.

Schnieke, A.; Harbers, K.; Jaenisch, R. Embryonic lethal mutation in mice induced by retrovirus insertion into the α1(I) collagen gene. *Nature* 304:315–320, 1983.

Cell-Cell Recognition and Adhesion

14–16

A. cellular slime molds
B. chemotaxis
C. discoidin-1
D. contact site B, contact site A
E. homophilic, heterophilic
F. N-CAM, L-CAM
G. E-cadherin

14–17

A. False. Although the quote is probably true in spirit, it is incorrect in detail. Warren Lewis was a pioneer in cell biology who was trying to draw attention to the importance of the adhesive properties of cells in tissues at a time when the problem had been largely ignored by the biologists of the day. Much of our bodies, however, is connective tissue whose integrity depends on the quality of the matrix rather than of the cells that inhabit it. It is not at all easy to dissociate cells from tissues, as anyone who has eaten a tough piece of steak can testify.
B. True
C. False. The development of tissues does not normally depend on the sorting of randomly mixed cell types.
D. True
E. False. Antibodies directed against most cell-surface components do not block cell adhesion. Thus far, antibodies against cell-surface glycoproteins involved in the adhesion process are the only ones that actually inhibit adhesion.
F. True. (It is somewhat counterintuitive that cells, which stick together very tightly, are bound by weaker interactions than those between a hormone and its receptor, which form a relatively transient complex. The strength of the cell-cell binding derives from multiple weak interactions, which when summed, are very strong.)
G. True
H. True

***14–18** **Reference:** Bonner, J.T.; Savage, L.J. Evidence for the formation of cell aggregates by chemotaxis in the development of the slime mold *Dictyostelium discoideum*. *J. Exp. Zool.* 106:1–26, 1947.

14–19

A. The fraction of the phage population that will be attached by at least one tail fiber at any one instant is equal to one minus the fraction not attached by any tail fibers, which is $(0.5)^{12}$ = 0.00024 for wild-type bacteria and

$(0.5)^6 = 0.016$ for *ompC*$^-$ bacteria. Thus, at any instant 99.98% of the phage population will be attached to wild-type bacteria and 98.4% will be attached to *ompC*$^-$ bacteria.

B. The very small difference in the fraction of the phage population attached to wild-type and *ompC*$^-$ bacteria at first seems too little to account for the 1000-fold difference in infectivity. However, since T4 must wander around the surface of a bacterium to find an appropriate place to attach its baseplate, the instantaneous calculation is misleading. If, for example, T4 must stay bound to the bacterial surface for 500 "instants" during its wandering, then $(.9998)^{500} = 90\%$ will remain attached to wild-type bacteria, but only $(.984)^{500} = 0.03\%$ will remain attached to *ompC*$^-$ bacteria. This difference would be more than enough to account for the 1000-fold difference in infectivity.

By associating with the bacterial surface through multiple weak interactions, bacteriophage T4 can wander around the surface without falling off. This allows a search for relatively rare injection sites, which are at points of connection between the inner and outer membranes. Multiple weak adhesive interactions between cells presumably are important for similar reasons: they allow a cell to search its neighbors without getting stuck prematurely.

Reference: Goldberg, E. Recognition, attachment, injection. In Bacteriophage T4 (C.K. Mathews; E.M. Kutter; G. Mosig; P.B. Berget, eds.), pp. 32–39. Washington, D.C.: American Society for Microbiology, 1983.

14–20

A. These observations argue that platelets aggregate by using two different surface receptors (adhesion molecules) that are linked through fibrinogen, which serves as a bridge molecule. This is the mechanism illustrated in Figure 14–17D. Cells from patients with Glanzman's syndrome cannot aggregate with themselves because they lack one fibrinogen receptor. The finding that two different fibrinogen peptides can block platelet aggregation is consistent with the use of fibrinogen as a bridge between two different fibrinogen receptors. Furthermore, although either peptide can block aggregation by interrupting one type of cellular binding to fibrinogen, neither peptide alone can block more than 50% of fibrinogen binding—once again, consistent with each peptide binding to a different receptor.

B. Cells from patients with Glanzman's syndrome do not aggregate with themselves; however, they should be able to aggregate with normal cells (Figure 14–22). If cell binding involves two different receptors that are bridged by fibrinogen, normal cells and Glanzman's syndrome cells should be able to form one of the two kinds of interaction that are available to normal cells. If half the number of interactions is sufficient, then Glanzman's syndrome cells should co-aggregate with normal cells.

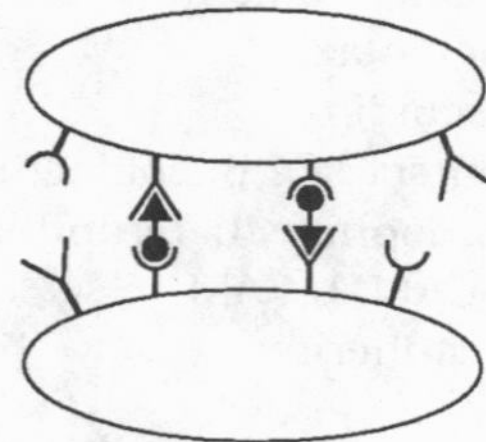

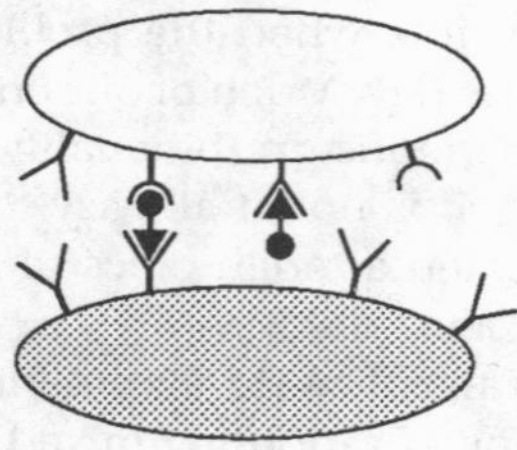

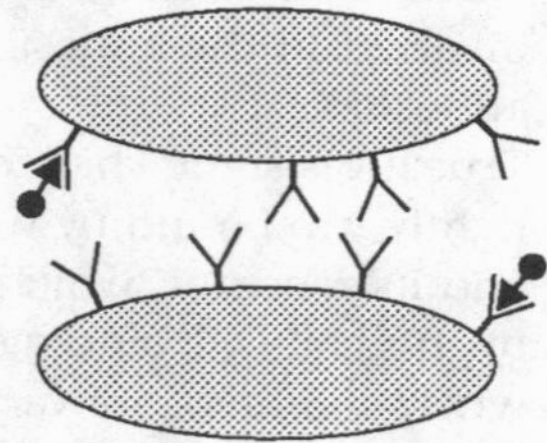

Figure 14–22 Interactions between normal platelets (A), between normal platelets and platelets from patients with Glanzman's syndrome (B), and between Glanzman's syndrome platelets (C) (Answer 14–20).

***14–21** **Reference:** Bischoff, R. Rapid adhesion of nerve cells to muscle fibers from adult rats is mediated by a sialic-acid-binding receptor. *J. Cell Biol.* 102:2273–2280, 1986.

14–22 The different sensitivities of type 5 and type 21 cells to trypsin and 2-mercaptoethanol argue that two different cell-adhesion molecules are interacting. The dissociation of the factor from type 5 cells into two components upon treatment with 2-mercaptoethanol suggests that one of these components is a bridge molecule that is attached to type 5 cells by a disulfide bond. Alternatively, it could mean that the factor from type 5 cells is a two-component cell-adhesion molecule.

Reference: Crandall, M.A.; Brock, T.D. Molecular basis of mating in the yeast *Hansenula wingei*. *Bact. Rev.* 32:139–163, 1968.

Index

A

B

C

D

E

F

G

H

I

N

O

P

R

S

T

U

V

W

X

Y

Z

Prefixes

Symbol	Name	Value
E-	exa-	10^{18}
P-	peta-	10^{15}
T-	tera-	10^{12}
G-	giga-	10^{9}
M-	mega-	10^{6}
k-	kilo-	10^{3}
h-	hecto-	10^{2}
da-	deca-	10^{1}
d-	deci-	10^{-1}
c-	centi-	10^{-2}
m-	milli-	10^{-3}
μ-	micro-	10^{-6}
n-	nano-	10^{-9}
p-	pico-	10^{-12}
f-	femto-	10^{-15}
a-	atto-	10^{-18}

Radioactive Isotopes

Isotope	Emission	Half Life	Counting[a] Efficiency	Maximum[b] Specific Activity
^{14}C	beta	5730 years	96%	62 mCi/mmol
^{3}H	beta	12.3 years	65%	29 Ci/mmol
^{35}S	beta	87.4 days	97%	1490 Ci/mmol
^{125}I	gamma, auger and conversion electrons	60.3 days	78%	2400 Ci/mmol
^{32}P	beta	14.3 days	100%	9120 Ci/mmol
^{131}I	beta and gamma	8.04 days	100%	16,100 Ci/mmol

[a] Maximum efficiency for an unquenched sample in a liquid scintillation counter. Most real samples are quenched to some extent.

[b] This value assumes one atom of radioisotope per molecule. If there are two radioactive atoms per molecule, the specific activity will be twice as great; and so on.